SILK

Penny Jordan has been writing for over 25 years. In that time, she has written over 170 books and sold over 80 million copies worldwide. She also writes under the name Annie Groves and is a mentor for new writers. *Silk* is the first in a series of novels inspired by the silk manufacturing industry in Macclesfield in Cheshire where Penny lived for 25 years with her late husband. She still lives in Cheshire today. For more information on Penny, please go to www.penny-jordan.co.uk and visit www.Author-Tracker.co.uk for exclusive updates.

PENNY JORDAN

Silk

AVON

AVON

A division of HarperCollins*Publishers*
77–85 Fulham Palace Road,
London W6 8JB

www.harpercollins.co.uk

A Paperback Original 2008

First published in Great Britain by
HarperCollins*Publishers* 2008

3

A catalogue record for this book is
available from the British Library

ISBN-13: 978-1-84756-073-5

Set in Minion by Palimpsest Book Production Limited,
Grangemouth, Stirlingshire

Printed and bound in Great Britain by
Clays Ltd, St Ives plc

Teresa Chris, my agent who gave me hope.

Maxine Hitchcock, my editor for this book.

Yvonne Holland, for her 'beyond excellent' copy editing.

Everyone at Avon and HarperCollins who made the publication of this book – which is so very special to me – possible.

My editors at Richmond, for their long years of support for Penny Jordan.

Tony who has always 'been there', to listen and research and drive me all those places I have needed to go in order to make this book possible.

For my readers – those who have read me as Penny Jordan for so many years and those who I hope will read this book and become as entranced by the fabric that is silk as I am.

Prologue

21 November 2002

Late November always had such a haunting melancholic feel about it; the best of the autumn gone, the glory of the leaves only a memory when the wind rattled the skeletal branches of the trees. Did trees have memories, Amber wondered as she looked through the window and out into the parkland of Denham Place. Did they, like her, remember the urgent joy of spring with all its budding promise? Did they still feel in the dreary grey an echo of the heavy, heady, sensual warmth that had been summer? A reminiscent smile touched her lips, thinner now than they had been when she had been in her own summer, but her smile still lifted her high cheekbones and shone in the faded beauty of her eyes. Spring and summer; they had been so long ago for her, and autumn too, patterned with its rich colours as vibrant as her beloved silk.

Winter held her now, bare and sometimes bleak but still beautiful.

There had been frost during the night, riming the grass, showing the tracks of the muntjac deer her own grandmother had installed at Denham. She had been dreaming of Blanche recently, and all those others whom she knew would be waiting for her. Time passed so slowly now and she grew impatient to be with them.

But not today.

'Are you really ninety years old today?'

The solemn question, from her youngest-but-two great-great-grandchild, made her smile and place her hand on his dark head.

'Yes,' she told him. 'I really am.'

'Harry! I'm sorry, Great-grandmother. He didn't wake you, did he?'

'No, dear. Don't worry.'

The young woman – the wife of one of Amber's great-grandsons – looked harassed and tense. Amber felt sorry for her. They didn't have an easy time of it, the young women of this modern age.

She had lived almost a whole century, a time during which there had been so many changes. Did her great-granddaughter-in-law, who complained about the demands made on her by her husband's political career, realise that when she, Amber, had been born women had not even had the vote? Did she care? Would Amber have cared in her place?

Ninety years. An eternity. Amber suspected that many of her relatives who had come here today to celebrate the event with her would think so, anyway.

Yet to her in some ways it was no longer than the length of a small sigh, a single breath in the heartbeat of time.

Life was no more than a clever game of smoke and mirrors, which now, at this stage of her life, had become so transparent for her that the past, and those with whom she had shared it, had become as accessible as a series of open doors through which she could walk freely. No longer did her memories come only as shadows in her dreams. They were as real as she was herself, sharing her joy now in what they had played a part in creating. She could hear her father's great shout of laughter and feel the bear hug of joy with which he would hold his great-great-great-grandchild.

Amber had asked for her chair to be placed where she could both see the room and look out of the window so that she could view both the past and the present.

She had always loved Denham, and the house in turn loved her. They shared secrets that were theirs alone.

As though she were there in the room, Amber could almost feel the icy disapproval of her grandmother, whose pearls were now ornamenting the slender neck of her eldest great-grandchild, Natasha, to whom Amber had given them, in part because her looks reminded her so much of Blanche. Natasha's looks might be Blanche's, but her nature was not, and with a shudder Amber prayed that her life would not turn out like Blanche's either.

So many memories: some of them of things that had brought her great joy and others that had brought her unbearable pain, but all of them precious in their own way.

The November day was bright, with that sharp sunshine that late autumn sometimes brings. The cake had been brought in and so had the champagne.

The house was older than she by two hundred years, and the room settled easily into the expectant silence – it had witnessed many celebrations, after all, some public and some very private. A small smile touched her mouth; a very private memory revived. She could almost feel the warmth of the gust of laughter of the man who had made that memory with her.

Her gaze went to the painting newly hung for the occasion. *The Silk Merchant's Daughter* had been on loan to one high-profile gallery after another for so many decades now that seeing it again was like welcoming home an old friend. But silk merchant's daughter that she was, the girl in the painting didn't look at her; she was too absorbed in the roll of silk she was coveting.

Silk. As a young woman she had thought she had known all there was to know, both about the fabric and life itself, but all she had understood had been what was on the surface. She had been ignorant then of what was beneath; of the weft and warp of the tightly woven pattern that was the fabric of human life.

In the shadows those she had loved pressed closer, their presence felt only by her.

The honour of giving the toast fell to the great-grandchild whose birthday fell on the same day as her own and who today would be seventeen.

Seventeen.

The room shimmered with the painful jolt to her heart. Some years remained burned in the memory for ever by the acid sharpness of their pain. The year that had begun with her own seventeenth birthday had been one of them. The arthritic hands she had folded in her lap beneath one of the special handmade padded silk throws that accompanied her everywhere trembled. She looked towards the window, her gaze bright with the sharp clarity of her memories.

Part One

Chapter One

Cheshire, Late November 1929

In less than an hour's time Amber was to go downstairs to her grandmother's study to receive the very special birthday gift her grandmother had promised her. Seventeen! She was almost a woman now. Grown up at last.

The fever of her anticipation had Amber dancing rather than walking across her bedroom. She knew what the 'very special gift' was, of course. How could she not?

Art school – where she would begin the training that would ultimately enable her to follow in her father's footsteps. It was all she had wanted for as long as she could remember, and now at last her dreams could start to come true. And not just *her* dreams.

There had been cards at breakfast from her grandmother and her cousin, Greg; from Jay, her grandmother's estate manager; from the household servants; from the manager of the family-owned silk mill in Macclesfield, and from Beth, her best friend at school. But, as had been the case for the past four years, there was no card from those she loved the most. Her parents.

Her emotions, mercurial today and unfamiliarly intense, turned her mood from excitement to sorrow as swiftly as the wind turned the November sky beyond the windows of her bedroom from clear autumn blue to grey.

On the desk that had been her mother's, and in which she kept her sketchbooks, there was a photograph of Amber with her parents, taken on her twelfth birthday, just three weeks before their deaths. In it, they were all smiling, her father's arm around her mother. Her mother was looking at her father with sheer adoration and he was looking back at her. Amber was standing in front of them, her mother's arm sheltering her, her father's free hand holding hers.

They had been so happy, the three of them – not wanting or needing others, their lives filled with their love for one another and for silk. Its delicate yarn had spun a web around them, like a special kind of magic that had bound them securely together, and made everything in their lives special. Amber missed them dreadfully. She could still remember how happy her parents had been on the day they died when they set out for the political rally. Her mother had kissed her lovingly and her father had seized her in one of his bear hugs, swinging her round until she was giddy with delight.

They had both been so full of life that even now there were times when she found it almost impossible to accept that they were dead.

It had been her grandmother who had coldly delivered the news of their deaths; and her cousin, Greg, who had later smuggled to her a newspaper article describing how the wooden floor of the building they were in, packed tight with those who, like them, had rallied to champion the cause of the working man and to demand better wages and conditions, had collapsed, plunging Amber's parents and twenty-six other people to their deaths.

Amber moved away from the window and back to her desk, looking down at the design on which she had been working: an interweaving of mauve and silver in the form of a Celtic knot, which would ultimately form part of a border.

Her father had been a gifted designer, a Russian émigré who had been working for a small silk manufacturer in London when he and her mother had first met and fallen in love, defying her mother's mother to be together.

Amber had always loved hearing the story of her parents' romance. She remembered sitting in bed, her mother brushing Amber's long golden hair with her antique silver brush and telling her about the day they had met.

They had both been attending a fabric fair in London, her father as a designer, and her mother as a representative of Denby Mill, the famous Macclesfield silk mill that belonged to Amber's grandmother Blanche.

Silk had been the thread that had bound them together, her mother had often said to Amber, and silk was the strongest and best of all threads, as pure and strong as love itself.

Amber's father had been in the first rank of a new wave of forward-thinking designers, and her mother had loved to tell her of the praise that had been given to his work.

It was their hope that Amber would follow in his footsteps, they had both always told her. They had passed to their daughter their passionate desire to combine silk and design to produce fabrics that were in their own right works of art. That had been their gift to her, and she was determined that hers to them would be her fulfilment of their dreams.

From the first moment she could hold a pencil, from the first moment she had been able to understand the concept of beauty and design, Amber's father had guided and taught her, just as her mother had shown her how to recognise the unique splendour that was silk.

Whilst other young children learned their dull lessons, Amber's parents taught her the history of silk, and with it the history of life, and how it bound together so many cultures and civilisations; how it stretched in the longest of journeys across deserts and seas, and how it inspired in humankind the greatest of passions, from love to greed.

The story Amber had loved best was of how the manufacture of silk had been brought out of China, firstly to Khotan, so it was said, via the silkworm eggs concealed in the headdress of a Chinese princess who had married a prince of Khotan, and then to the Byzantine Empire when the Emperor Justinian had persuaded two monks to journey to Khotan to steal the secret of sericulture. The monks had returned first with mulberry seeds and then with silkworm eggs concealed inside hollow bamboo sticks.

'See how it mirrors life,' Amber's mother had told her, the child on her knee as she let the fabric slip richly through Amber's tiny hand. 'It runs through the fingers like water, yet stretched tight it has such strength, and yet that strength is so supple that it escapes capture. The human spirit is like silk, Amber,' she had declared. 'It too cannot be captured; it too has great strength, and great beauty for those with the gift to see it. Always remember that, my darling . . .'

'Amber? Are you in there?'

The sound of her cousin Greg's voice brought her back to the present.

Greg was twenty-three years old, and a year down from Oxford, a handsome young man with broad shoulders and thick wavy fair year, confident in that way that a certain type of indulged young man from a wealthy background often was. He was his grandmother's favourite just as his father, Marcus, had been her favourite child.

Greg's father had died when Greg had been a child, killed in action in the trenches during the Great War, and his mother had died giving birth to her stillborn much-longed-for second child when the news had reached them of her husband's death, leaving Greg to be brought up by their grandmother.

Athletic and extrovert, always ready to have a joke and eager to have fun, Greg had got over the initial boredom he had felt leaving Oxford and his friends behind to return home to Macclesfield, by becoming friends with a group of young men, like himself from moneyed backgrounds, who spent their time indulging in the pleasures of racing cars, learning to fly, playing tennis and attending house parties to flirt with pretty girls. Financed by family wealth, and not required to work for a living, Greg and his set were determined not to look back over their shoulders to the terrible war that had taken so many of those born a generation before them, young men dead before they had properly lived. That was never going to happen to them, and the hectic pace of their lives was proof of their determination to make sure that it didn't. If they were haunted by the horror of what they had been spared it was never spoken of. Life was for living and that was exactly what they intended to do. The only thing they took seriously was 'having fun'.

Amber looked on Greg more as an older brother than a cousin. He was good company, and he had always been kind to her.

In addition to inheriting Denby Mill, Greg would also inherit Denham Place, its lands and the bulk of the vast fortune their grandmother had inherited, first from her father and then later from her maternal uncle, a Liverpool ship owner. Amber, meanwhile, had her own dreams. She'd make her own way.

'Happy birthday,' Greg grinned, handing her a small,

prettily wrapped box, before walking over to the fireplace with a confident swagger.

Amber had seen him drive off earlier in his new roadster and, knowing Greg as she did, she suspected that her birthday gift had probably been a spur-of-the-moment purchase, bought in Macclesfield that morning whilst he had been in the town attending a Conservative Party meeting. Greg was to become a Member of Parliament when the existing Member stepped down in six months' time, or at least that was what their grandmother said.

'Oh, Greg,' she thanked him, throwing her arms around his neck and kissing him on the cheek. 'But I can't open it yet. I've got to go and see Grandmother about my birthday surprise.'

Amber couldn't keep the excitement out of her voice. She had longed so much for this moment, talking about it, and dreaming about it even before she had left her select boarding school in the summer.

'I can hardly believe that in a few weeks' time I'll be going to London to study art. Which art school do you think Grandmother will have chosen? I do hope it's the Slade, although I'm not sure I'd be good enough. She never asked me for any of my art work to show them, but I suppose she will have asked Monsieur Lafitte at school to vouch for me. He always said that he would. Greg, I'm so excited, it's all I've ever wanted, and my parents—'

'Steady on, old girl. I don't want to spoil your fun, but I don't think you should get your hopes up too high.'

Amber frowned. 'What do you mean?'

Greg cursed himself under his breath. He wished now that he hadn't said anything. The trouble with Amber was that she just wasn't the smart sort of girl who knew what was what. If she had been then she'd have known what he

12

was trying to hint. But then, of course, if she had known he wouldn't have needed to do any hinting – or any warning.

'Dash it all, Amber,' he protested uncomfortably, 'you can't really think that Grandmother would let you go to art school. You know what she's like.'

'But she said she had a special surprise for me. Something that will change my whole life and that I'm very lucky to have.'

'I dare say she did, but it ain't art school she's talking about, Amber. I know that for a fact.'

'Then what is it?'

Greg shook his head and turned towards the door, but Amber moved faster, getting there first, closing it, leaning on it and looking determinedly at him.

'You're not leaving this room until you tell me, Greg.'

'You won't like it,' he prophesied. 'I know I wasn't keen when she told me that I've got to be an MP, but you know Grandmother, and she holds the purse strings.'

Their grandmother made no secret of her preference for her grandson, and Amber had always assumed that Greg got everything he wanted. It was a new idea to her to realise that that might not be the case, and a disturbing one, like suddenly finding that the calm waters of the estate's pretty lake concealed dangerous currents.

'But if you don't want to be a Member of Parliament then why—'

'It isn't as simple as that, Amber – nothing ever is.'

Greg sighed and sat down on one of the elegant Sheraton chairs set either side of the fireplace, the sharp sunlight cruelly picking out the faded chintz cushions.

'Come and sit down,' he told her, leaning forward to pat the seat of the chair opposite, then stretching his long legs out in front of him. 'We've got a few minutes yet before you have to go down and see Grandmother.'

13

Obediently Amber did as he asked.

'Grandmother isn't sending you to London to go to art school. She's sending you there to be finished.'

'Finished?'

'Yes, as in prepared to make your social entrance as a débutante, and find yourself a titled husband.'

It took several seconds for Amber to absorb the meaning of his words, but once she had, she shook her head in denial.

'No. She can't do that. It's impossible. I don't want . . . I won't . . .' She had left her seat without even being aware that she had moved, and was standing in front of Greg, her hands bunched into small fists. 'You're wrong, Greg. She can't mean to do that. She couldn't, anyway, since there is no one in the family who could present me.'

Amber had learned all about the arcane process of becoming a débutante, and the rules attached to it, at boarding school, where it had been impressed on her that the granddaughter of a mere mill owner, no matter how wealthy, did not have the right kind of pedigree to be accepted as a member of the exclusive club that was the aristocracy. That was fine by her. She couldn't think of a worse fate than being forced into the kind of dynastic marriage she knew would be the fate of most of the girls with whom she had been at school.

'Grandmother will always find a way to do whatever she wants to do, Amber.'

'But why would she want to?'

Greg shrugged. He felt sorry for Amber, but he had not intended to get involved in this kind of discussion. Now, though, it was too late to wish he had left well alone.

'Barrant de Vries,' he told her succinctly. 'That's why.'

'Jay's grandfather? I don't understand.'

'It's a long story, and one I've only heard pretty recently myself, but from an impeccable source.' Greg paused,

14

wondering how much he should say. Amber was naïve and trusting, and he didn't want to take unnecessary risks. Amber did not need to know the source of his information.

'When she was a young girl Grandmother set her sights on marrying Barrant de Vries and she didn't make any secret of it either.'

Amber gasped, but Greg ignored her reaction and continued hurriedly, 'Of course, the fact that the whole county knew that Barrant and his father thought she wasn't good enough or rich enough to marry into the de Vries family would be a bitter blow to Grandmother's pride. I dare say there were plenty to laugh at her behind her back for her ambitions.'

'But she must have known? I mean, everyone knows that Barrant de Vries is obscenely proud.'

'Well, yes, I don't doubt she did, but she was a great beauty, of course, and Great-grandfather was pretty well-to-do. I'd wager she convinced herself that she would land him. She was accepted socially by the county set, from what I've been told, and that must have made her think that she stood a good chance of becoming Barrant's wife.'

'The county set?' Amber queried. 'Like the Fitton Leghs and the Bromley Davenports?'

'Well, the Bromley Davenports, certainly; I'm not so sure about the Fitton Leghs, seeing as Barrant de Vries eventually married a Fitton Legh.'

'But Grandmother socialises with the Dowager Marchioness of Cholmondeley now. They are on the same charitable committees, and—'

'There is a vast difference, my dear Amber, between socialising with a person and allowing them to marry into one's family,' Greg told Amber in such a good imitation of their grandmother's voice and manner that Amber couldn't help but smile.

'One day Grandmother will hear you doing that and then you'll be in trouble.'

'You'll be the one in trouble if you go downstairs talking about art school.'

'But I still can't see what Barrant de Vries not wanting to marry Grandmother has to do with her wanting me to be presented, Greg.'

'Well, you should. She's not the kind to forget a slight or an insult, is she?'

Amber shook her head. What Greg was saying was true. Their grandmother could be ruthless when it suited her. She had certainly never forgiven Amber's own mother for marrying Amber's father against her wishes.

Amber gave a small shiver.

'Knowing what I do now, it's my belief that Grandmother only bought this estate because it's right next to the de Vrieses' lands, and to let Barrant de Vries know that she owns more land and a bigger house than he does,' Greg went on. 'She's even employing his grandson as her estate manager. It's her way of humiliating Barrant for humiliating *her*. Everyone knows that Barrant de Vries lost virtually everything after the war, including his only son – who died without producing an heir. But that's not enough for Grandmother, Amber. She wants us to get for her what she could not get for herself. Especially you. *I* cannot, after all, marry a title, but *you* can. The war has beggared any number of aristocratic families. You only have to think of how many of them are marrying off their sons to the daughters of American millionaires to know that.'

Amber did know it. After all, their neighbour, Lord Fitton Legh, had married an American heiress the previous year, and it was widely accepted that the marriage had been brokered to provide him with money and the bride with a title.

16

As though he had read her mind Greg teased her, 'You should think yourself lucky that Grandmother obviously didn't think the Fitton Legh title good enough. But then, of course she'll want one that outranks the de Vries title, you can bet on that, and that's why she'll want you to be presented at court.'

Before Amber could say anything Greg went on, 'Grandmother may have the money to buy a title for you, but it ain't that easy. What I mean is, you'll need to be mixing with the right people, and you can't do that unless you've got the right credentials, and for a girl that means a court presentation. What Grandmother wants is a granddaughter who will have a title far, far better than the one that Barrant de Vries denied her, and that she can flaunt in front of everyone who laughed at her behind her back when Barrant rejected her.'

It was almost too much for Amber to take in.

'Greg, please don't say things like that. It isn't nice,' she begged her cousin. 'I know you like to play jokes on me but—'

'Amber, I'm not joking.'

'Has Grandmother told you that this is the case?'

'No.'

'So you're just guessing, Greg. I'm sure you're wrong. For one thing—'

'I'm not wrong, Amber. If you must have the truth I happened to be outside her study when she was talking to Jay Fulshawe about it. Something to do with making a payment to some Lady somebody or other to bring you out.'

'*Jay* knows?' It seemed like a double betrayal. She liked Jay, and had even felt sorry for him, obliged to work so very hard for her grandmother, whilst Greg, who had been at Eton with him, enjoyed a life of leisure.

Amber had to sit down, she was trembling so much. It couldn't be true. It *mustn't* be true.

'I don't want a titled husband. I don't want to get married yet and when I do—'

'It's what Grandmother wants that counts. Not what we want.'

Greg wasn't joking now. In fact he looked more serious than Amber could ever remember seeing him before.

'There's no doubt about that,' he warned her. 'She always gets what she wants.' He looked at her and smiled wryly. 'Remember the way she got this house and the estate. Lord Talbot's trustees didn't really want to sell Denham Place to her, but in the end they had no choice, not with the death duties the estate had to pay after Lord Talbot died without an heir.'

Greg's mention of Denham Place momentarily diverted Amber. She loved the beautiful Vanbrugh-designed house, with its classical lines and its famously elegant row of rooms on the first floor. Not that Denham would ever be hers.

'Denham *is* beautiful, Greg,' she told her cousin dreamily. 'It's supposed to be among Vanbrugh's own favourites, even though it's one of the smallest houses he designed.'

Greg shrugged. He wasn't in the least bit interested in architecture or design.

The clock struck three. 'Grandmother will be waiting for you.'

And Greg had an appointment to keep, although the truth of the matter was that he was not so sure that he really wanted to keep it. What had begun as exciting had recently started to become burdensome. Greg didn't particularly care for intense emotions, and he certainly did not like tearful scenes, but the devil of it was that he was now in a situation from which he was finding it damnably difficult to extricate himself.

Given half a chance he would have leaped at the opportunity to go to London, with its private supper clubs and the louche living available to those of privilege. Drinking, gambling, flirting with pretty women who knew the rules of the game – these were far more to his taste than dull meetings with members of the local Conservative Party committee.

Maybe his grandmother could be persuaded that, as a loving older cousin, he would dutifully pay the occasional visit to London to keep a protective eye on Amber.

Chapter Two

Blanche Pickford surveyed her granddaughter critically. At seventeen Amber was showing the promise of great beauty. She was only of medium height, but she was slender and fine-boned, with an elegant neck and porcelain skin. Her face, once it lost the last roundness of girlhood, would be perfectly heart-shaped, with her eyes widely spaced and thickly lashed.

Blanche had not been pleased when her daughter – no doubt influenced by her husband – had announced that her child was to be named Amber, which Blanche had thought far too exotic. It was a tradition of the family that its daughters were given names that reflected the colours of silks. But there was no denying the fact that the girl's eyes were indeed the honey-gold colour of that precious resin.

Amber's straight nose and the curve of her lips, like her blonde curls, almost exactly mirrored Blanche's own looks at Amber's age, but as yet there was no sign in her granddaughter of the smouldering sensuality that she herself had possessed at seventeen – nor any sense of the power of such a gift. By temperament Amber was kind and gentle; *weak*, where she had always been so very strong, thought Blanche critically. There was no fire to her, no passion, but that didn't matter. It wasn't passion or sensuality on which the kind of marriage she wanted for her granddaughter was brokered. Quite the opposite.

And at least the girl *had* looks, unlike her mother. Blanche had been furiously angry when she had realised how plain her daughter was going to be, so very much Henry Pickford's daughter, with her attachment to the mill, and her leanings towards the labour movement and equality for the workers. However, that anger had been nothing to the fury she had felt when the plain twenty-five-year-old Blanche had assumed would remain a spinster had defied her to marry a Russian émigré, using her small inheritance from her father to do so. Not that that had lasted very long. And, of course, ultimately, just as she had known she would, her daughter had had to come begging to her.

Yes, all in all she was not entirely displeased with the raw material she had to work with. The girl's looks would certainly count in her favour, but it was Blanche's money that would bring into the family the title that Blanche craved.

'Sit down, Amber,' Blanche instructed her granddaughter. 'We've got something important to discuss.'

Amber could never remember seeing her grandmother wearing anything made from silk. Instead she favoured clothes from the French designer Chanel, and today she was wearing one of her signature jersey gowns, the bodice cleverly draped to fasten on the hip with a large brooch studded with crystals, which caught the light with every movement of her body.

Slender, and with an upright bearing, her grandmother had the figure for such clothes. Amber had inherited her slenderness, although her shape was concealed by the school-girlish lines of her own woollen pinafore worn over a plain cotton blouse. Beneath that blouse Amber's heart was beating

21

anxiously. Surely what Greg had told her couldn't possibly be true?

She looked at her grandmother, waiting apprehensively. As always Blanche was wearing her pearls, three long strands of them, their lustre possessing far more warmth than the woman herself.

'I promised you that since this is your seventeenth birthday you are to have a very special gift. This gift concerns your future, Amber. You are a most fortunate young woman, and I hope you realise that. As my grandchild you will have opportunities and benefits beyond the reach of many young women of your age and station, and whilst you are enjoying them I want you to remember just why you have been given them and what your responsibility is to them and to me. Now,' Blanche permitted herself a slight smile, 'in January you will be travelling to London to prepare for your presentation at court. I have made arrangements—'

So it was true. Greg had been right. Amber felt sick with despair.

'No,' she protested frantically. 'No, I don't want to be presented. I want to go to art school.'

Blanche looked aghast. The girl's parents had done more damage with their irritating and worthless talk of art and design than she had realised. The Russian was to blame for that. He may have filled his daughter's head with his own folly, but Blanche had no intention of allowing such ridiculousness to remain there.

Amber was seventeen, crying for a life she knew nothing whatsoever about – at thirty-seven she would be thanking her for saving her from it. It was ludicrous even to think of comparing the drudgery of making her own way with the status and comfort that would be Amber's if she did as she was told.

Not that it mattered what Amber thought or how much

she protested. Blanche would do what she had decided she would do.

'Art school?'

Amber could feel her grandmother's steely gaze virtually pinning her into the uncomfortable chair in which she was struggling to sit bolt upright.

Amber hated the décor of this room. Everything about its Edwardian heaviness was overpowering and intimidating, from the puce-coloured wallpaper and matching velvet soft furnishings to the polished mahogany furniture.

'Formidable' was how most people described her grandmother, but Amber could think of other words: formal; forbidding; *frightening*. Her mother and father wouldn't have been frightened, she reminded herself. She took a deep breath.

'It's what I've always wanted.'

Her words, more anguished than defiant, seemed to fall through the cold silence that chilled the room, despite the good fire burning in the marble fireplace: Carrara marble from the famous quarries in Italy, chosen for its perfection, just like everything else in her grandmother's life. Not that she seemed to gain pleasure from the craftsmanship. It was just the status that owning it conferred on her that mattered.

'You are seventeen years old, Amber, far too young to know what is right for you.'

Her grandmother's words spiked fear into Amber's heart, panicking her into bursting out, 'It is what my parents wanted for me. My father talked about it often, and when I do marry, I shall marry someone whom I love and who loves me as much as my father loved my mother.'

Too late she realised her mistake. Her grandmother's face had set into an icy cold mask.

'Your father? Your father, Amber, was a penniless immigrant

who married your mother for her money – or rather, for my money.'

As always when she was angry, her grandmother's voice had quietened to a barely audible whisper that still somehow hurt the ears.

For her father, though, Amber was determined to overcome her fear of her grandmother's anger, and defend him.

'That's not true. My father loved my mother.'

Ignoring her, Blanche continued remorselessly, 'I warned her what would happen when she defied me to marry him, and I was right. When he lost his job she had to come begging to me, pleading with me to give him work. Your father didn't love my daughter. Your father loved my money and my mill.'

'He did love her. They were so happy together. My mother said so. She said my father was gifted, a true artist.'

'He was nothing but a third-rate failure, who would have ruined the mill with his ridiculous ideas, if I had allowed him.'

Amber felt as though she was choking, all too conscious of her own overheated emotions whilst her grandmother remained calm and cold. Her parents *had* loved one another, she knew that. Before the factory where he had worked in London had closed down, their small house had been filled with the sound of her parents' laughter. Amber could remember how her father would bring home his friends, fellow artists who would sit around her mother's kitchen table, drinking her soup and talking. Those had been such happy times and Amber treasured their memory.

There had been less laughter when her parents had been forced to move back to Macclesfield, but there had still been warmth and love in the house her parents had insisted on renting rather than live in Denham Place with her grandmother. Her father had loved reading, and on winter evenings they would gather round the fire and he would read aloud, very often from one of Charles Dickens's wonderful books set against a background of the dreadful circumstances in which the poor lived. How could her grandmother try to destroy the memory of their love by denying its existence?

Her grandmother was wrong too when she said that Amber's father would have ruined the business. He was the one who had saved it. Amber knew that. It was because of his designs that Denby Mill's agents in London were able to report that their new silk had sold out within days of being available, with repeat orders for more. There had been fierce arguments about his designs and his desire to follow the direction of the Arts and Crafts Movement, and her grandmother's dislike of change and innovation. It was through her father that the mill had secured its valuable contracts with that movement and with the Church of England to supply it with the rich ecclesiastical silks that were especially woven.

Amber struggled desperately to hold back her angry tears. 'If my parents were alive they wouldn't let you do this.'

'That is quite enough.' Her grandmother stood up. 'I don't want to hear another word about your father or this nonsense about art school. I am the one who will decide your future, Amber. No one else.'

'You're a snob! You're only doing it because of Barrant de Vries, because people laughed at you because he wouldn't marry you . . .'

Amber recoiled as Blanche stepped forward, striking her across the face, the shock of the blow silencing her into horrified awareness of what she had done. Her cheek stung and her heart was racing.

Two red coins of angry colour burned on her grandmother's face and her breathing was rapid and shallow.

'How dare you speak to me like that? In my day you would have been whipped for your insolence. You will go to your room and you will stay there until I give you permission to leave it.'

Half blinded with tears, Amber fled, leaving Blanche alone in the room.

For several minutes after Amber had gone Blanche didn't move. Anger, seared with pride, burned inside her that her granddaughter, a child she believed to be so much less than she herself had been at her age, should have dared to speak to her in such a way and of something so intimately connected with her own past.

Blanche stiffened. For forty-four years she had lived with the memory of Barrant's humiliation and rejection of her and not once in that time had anyone ever dared to refer to that humiliation to her face.

She walked over to the window and stood looking out. She was sixty-one years old and not a day had gone by since Barrant had laughed at her and told her that he would never ever marry a mill owner's daughter when she hadn't weighed out on the scales of her life that insult and sworn she would make sure that one day those scales would weigh in her favour, even if she had to fill them grain by grain, retribution by retribution, to make sure they did so, and that Barrant would die sick to his heart with the knowledge of what his arrogance had cost him.

She hated him and she couldn't wait for the day when her grandson and her granddaughter took social precedence over his – as she was determined they would do.

Jay Fulshawe saw Amber come running from her grandmother's study in such obvious distress that he immediately guessed what had happened. His heart ached for her. So her grandmother had broken the news to her. Poor child, she would take it very hard.

She was still at the age where her feelings were open for all to see, mirrored in the dark golden eyes that were now so shadowed with her despair. Quick-witted and warm-natured, she was a great favourite with her grandmother's household staff. Since she had come home from boarding school, Jay had found himself listening for the sound of her laughter, and smiling when he heard it. Unlike some, Amber's mischievous sense of humour bore no malice or unkindness. She was so passionate about everything she believed in, and so very vulnerable because of that passion. Jay hoped that life would not punish her for it. She was still so very young.

'Amber . . .' He spoke her name gently, reaching out to her where she stood in tears in the hall, but she shook her head.

'You knew, Jay,' she accused him bitterly. 'You knew what my grandmother was planning and yet you said nothing.'

How could Jay not have told her? Amber had known him virtually all her life, and thought of him more as a friend than her grandmother's employee. He had been at Eton with Greg and he had spent many of his holidays in Cheshire. His parents lived in Dorset where his father, the third son of a 'gentleman farmer', was a clergyman. It was rumoured that once his wife had given birth to his son and heir, Barrant de Vries had lost all interest in his two daughters, and that he hadn't cared who they had married, although some said that the reason they had not done better for themselves was because there had been no money. In the aristocratic circles in which the de Vrieses and their kind moved and married, a bride's dowry was almost as important as her breeding.

Jay was more serious-natured than Greg; dark-haired,

tall and leanly athletic, with a calm, measured way of speaking and a slightly quizzical smile that often made Amber itch for her sketchpad and her charcoal to try to capture it.

Jay wasn't smiling now, though. 'It wasn't my place,' he answered her quietly. 'I'm so very sorry, but it may not be as bad as you fear.'

'You mean that no one with a title will want to marry me and that I'll be rejected like your grandfather rejected my grandmother?' Amber retorted bitterly.

So she had finally heard that old story. Jay had wondered when she would. It was fairly common knowledge locally, after all. His cousin Cassandra had enjoyed regaling him with it when she had heard it from the Fitton Leghs, not realising he had already heard it, but then Cassandra had inherited that flawed de Vries pride, which he personally found so warped and destructive.

Jay put his hand on Amber's arm, but she shook him off.

Amber ran up the stairs and along the landing until she had reached the welcome security of her bedroom. Her grandmother might consider it a form of punishment to say that she had to remain here, but she preferred to be here and on her own with her despair.

She tensed as she heard a brief knock on the door, but relaxed when Mary, the parlour maid, came in. Mary was twenty-five and courting a grocery assistant in Macclesfield. She had a bubbly personality and a warm smile, but now she was avoiding looking at her, Amber saw, as she went towards the desk and said apologetically, 'The mistress says as how I was to come up and remove your drawing things, Miss Amber.'

Amber's face burned hot with humiliation and grief. Her grandmother must have guessed that she would want to find solace in her drawing. Well, if she thought that she would apologise in order to get them back, she was wrong!

It was growing dark by the time Jay negotiated the rutted carriageway to Felton Priory in the shooting brake with which Blanche Pickford had provided him as her estate manager. She had informed him he may use the motor car 'for a certain amount of private motoring, since I dare say you will want to see your grandfather, and he is not obviously able to visit you.'

Had those words been a kind gesture on Blanche's part or an unkind underlining of the fact that Barrant was confined to a wheelchair? Jay knew which his grandfather would have chosen to believe.

Dusk cloaked the shabbiness of the house and its surrounding parkland. Unlike Denham Place, Felton Priory could never be described as an architectural gem, being a haphazard mixture of differing periods and personal styles, refronted by the fifth Viscount in a pseudo-Gothic style of outstanding ugliness.

With typical arrogance, or perhaps artistic blindness, Jay's grandfather insisted on considering Felton the premier aristocratic residence in Macclesfield, if not Cheshire, and Jay was good-humoured enough to indulge him, although in truth Jay much preferred the handsome Dorset rectory where he himself had grown up.

Jay considered himself fortunate that the de Vries inheritance of pride and arrogance had passed him by.

He parked the shooting brake on the gravel forecourt, taking the steps to the heavy portico with lithe strides.

His grandfather's butler opened the door to him. Jay had telephoned ahead to warn him of his visit, knowing that Bates, older than his grandfather by a good ten years, and rheumatic, found it increasingly painful to walk the long distance from the warmth of the butler's pantry to the main entrance.

'Good evening, Master Jay,' Bates welcomed him, taking Jay's driving coat, cap and scarf.

'Good evening, Bates,' Jay returned. 'How is the rheumatism?'

'Not too bad at all, thank you. Your grandfather has had a bad couple of days, though, I'm afraid.'

'Thank you for warning me. His legs are playing up again, are they?'

'I'm afraid so.'

Despite the fact that both his legs had had to be amputated, Barrant suffered acute pain in what his doctor had described to Jay as 'phantom limbs'. When the pain was at its worst the only thing that could relieve it was morphine, which had to be prescribed by Dr Brookes.

Jay's grandfather vehemently objected to the fact that a law had been passed that meant that contrary to what had been common practice beforehand, morphine and all its derivatives could now only be obtained by doctor's prescription. As Jay knew, his grandfather wasn't the only one to feel that the government's Dangerous Drugs Act had interfered in something over which they had no right. For many of the Bright Young Things of the twenties, as the newspapers had labelled a certain fast set of rich young men and women, the law had come too late. They were already, like poor Elizabeth Ponsonby, the young socialite whose wild ways had been referred to in the gossip columns, addicted to both drink and drugs, and as with prohibition in America, all the law had done was drive the supply and purchase of intoxicants and narcotics underground.

'Your grandfather's waiting for you in the library, Master Jay.'

Felton Priory's library was a large rectangular room, which Jay's grandfather had made his personal domain after his accident. A Chinese lacquered screen discreetly concealed the bed, which Jay had had brought downstairs so that his grandfather could 'rest' when he felt like doing so, instead of having to use the cumbersome dumb waiter to transport him and his wheelchair up to the second landing that gave access to his bedroom.

'Ha, here at last, are you?' Barrant greeted Jay. 'I dare say that Blanche works you hard and wants her pound of flesh from you. Bates,' he roared at the butler, 'bring me a brandy – and make it a large one.'

Jay looked at his grandfather with concern. 'I thought that Dr Brookes had forbidden you to drink brandy?'

Barrant gave his grandson a saturnine look. 'No doctor tells me what to do. If I want a brandy I'll damn well have one. Anyway, what does he know? Young fool. His father was bad enough. Thought he'd end up killing me before he retired, but the son's even worse.'

The old man was obviously having a bad day.

His hair, once as thick and dark as Jay's own, was white now. Pain had carved deep grooves in the flesh at either side of his mouth, and hollowed out the features beneath the high cheekbones. Fierce passions still glittered in the dark blue eyes, though driven, Jay suspected, by frustration and arrogance.

Barrant took the brandy Bates had brought him without any acknowledgement, waiting until the butler had left before saying sharply, 'So the Pickford boy is putting himself up as a candidate to take over Barclay Whiston's seat, is he? That will be Blanche's idea, of course. He won't get it. Too much of a lightweight, and no amount of money is going to alter that. He's not the man his father was.'

31

A look Jay couldn't interpret crossed his grandfather's face. 'Get on well with him, do you?'

'Everyone gets on with Greg,' Jay answered calmly.

'Cassandra don't think much of him.'

Though Jay didn't say anything, Barrant still grunted and said, 'You're right, it's time Cassandra found herself a husband. No looks to speak of, but she's got de Vries blood in her veins. Too sharp in her manner by half, though. No man wants a wife with a tongue like vinegar. Don't know where she gets it from. Certainly not from your grandmother. She was as meek as milk.

'Cassandra was telling me that Blanche is sending the girl to London with some fool idea of thinking she can buy a title for her.'

'Amber is to be presented at court, yes.'

'Good-looker, is she?'

'Yes.'

Barrant grunted again. 'She's still trade, though. Your grandmother was a Fitton Legh. Her ancestors came over with the Conquest, just like the de Vrieses. It's good blood that counts in a marriage, not good looks. Like to like. You remember that when your time comes. Not that you're a true de Vries, since it's its father's name a child carries and not its mother's.'

The bitterness in his grandfather's voice was as familiar to Jay as the reasons for it. Barrant de Vries had never got over losing his son and he never would. His grandfather would have valued him far more, Jay knew, if he had been born to Barrant's son and not one of his daughters.

'You're getting bored with me, I know you are.' Her voice was fretful, rising dangerously towards hysteria.

Greg wished he had not come. He had turned down an invitation to drive into Manchester to a new nightclub that had just been opened.

32

'Of course I'm not.'

'Yes you are. You didn't even call me your dearest darling like you used.' She was pouting now, tears swimming in her large blue eyes.

Greg could feel his heart sinking as fast as his irritation was rising.

The bedroom smelled of scent and sex, both of them somehow equally cloying. The feeling of being trapped in a situation he no longer wanted, which had been growing on him for several weeks, now intensified. He hadn't realised in the first thrill of his lust for her that her extraordinary beauty cloaked such a clinging and possessive nature. His desire for her had blinded him to the dangers.

An affair with a married woman was something that a young man in his position did, so far as Greg was concerned. He had been momentarily obsessed by his lust for her, it was true, and in that moment he had perhaps made rash promises to her, but now Greg was bored and ready to move on. She, though, was making it clear that she was not ready to let him go.

Somehow their, to him, casual affair had in her eyes – and words – become something very different. Something that Greg had never intended and most certainly did not want.

'You said you loved me, but you were lying,' she accused him. 'How can you be so cruel? Isn't what I already have to bear enough? Must I be punished even more by having my heart stolen with false promises of love?'

She was pacing the floor of the bedroom now, her behaviour becoming wilder by the minute, the white marabou-trimmed silk peignoir she had pulled on when they had left her bed, swirling round her. The silk clung to her naked body beneath, but that knowledge no longer excited him as it had once done.

Her behaviour was making Greg feel on edge. He had never imagined at the start when she had been so cool with him, teasing and tantalising him, that she would become like this, practically begging him.

She stopped in front of him, reaching for the martini she had insisted he make for her earlier, even sending for her maid, whilst he had had to conceal himself in her bathroom so that she could bring up the ingredients and a cocktail shaker.

Greg had warned her then that she was taking too many risks but she had flown into a wild outburst of tears, accusing him of no longer loving her and reminding him that once he would have risked anything for her.

Now she drank greedily from the glass she was holding. Her face was flushed, her gaze unfocused.

'I know,' she told him brightly, 'I'll ring Nurse and she can bring Baby in.'

'No!' Greg couldn't conceal his horror. 'No, I don't think that's a good idea.'

'Why not? After all, he's—' She broke off and flung herself down on the bed, its covers crumpled from their earlier lovemaking, remembering the first time he had made love to her here in this room, their passion for one another so intense that they hadn't even made it to the bed. She had known that he would call and she had been so wildly excited. She had worn a softly draped dress by Chanel, over a silk satin chemise and matching French knickers, her stockings held up by silk garters, every item of clothing chosen for the speed with which it could be removed, although she had not told Greg that.

He had taken her in his arms the minute they were inside the room, leaning back against the door to close it and holding her against him, his hands stroking and kneading, exploring her with an avid hunger that had matched her

34

own need. He had groaned out loud when she had teased his erection through the fabric of his trousers, shaping it and then running her fingertip along its length as though to measure it, pouting up at him, wanting to excite and torment him.

He had retaliated by nibbling the flesh just below her ear and stroking the soft curves of her breasts hidden from his view by the Chanel dress. When he had found the edge of her chemise bodice he had teased the flesh above it and then slowly eased it lower until her bare breasts were pressed against the fabric of her dress, her nipples swelling tightly when he pinched and toyed with them.

She hadn't stopped him when he had pulled up her dress, and then lifted her in his arms, bracing her against the bedroom door, her arms and legs wrapped around him.

He had taken her quickly and fiercely, not even bothering to remove her knickers, simply pushing the loose legs to one side after he had unbuttoned himself.

She had screamed with excitement and pleasure, urging him deeper, panting and clinging to him as he thrust into her.

He had come too quickly for her, but she had pretended that she had had her own orgasm, putting him first – as she had done so many times since, she thought now, giving in to self-pity, before begging him, 'Tell me you love me, Greg.'

'You know that I do,' he lied uncomfortably.

'Say it. I want to hear the words.'

'I love you.'

'No, I want you to say it properly and mean it, like you used to.'

Her voice had begun to rise again. If she kept on like this someone would hear her. Greg began to sweat, the room felt like a prison and she his gaoler.

'It's late. I must go.'

'No.' She turned and ran to him, gripping the lapels of his jacket, clinging to him, pushing her body into his, grinding herself against him. 'I want you to stay.'

'You know that I can't.'

'Because of her: your grandmother. I suppose she has already picked out a wife for you.'

'Not as far as I know.'

'But you wouldn't mind if she had.'

'This is silly talk . . .'

'You think I'm silly? You didn't think that when we first met. You loved me then. Remember? Tell me again what you thought the first time you saw me?'

It was a ritual he had enjoyed in the early days of their affair, but one that no longer held any appeal for him: a series of hoops through which he now had to jump before he could escape.

'I thought you were the most beautiful woman I had ever seen,' Greg told her obediently.

'And what did you say to me?'

'I said that I idolised and adored you, that I wanted you and loved you . . .'

'And that you would love me for ever,' she finished triumphantly. 'You couldn't get enough of me . . .'

It was true, Greg knew. There'd been times when he'd been so consumed by his own desire for her that he'd come almost the minute he was inside her. Hurried illicit couplings in dark corners and shadowy corridors, which their mutual lust had turned into fevered erotic encounters, like the time they'd been in the music room, whilst her husband attended to some business with his steward and she had gone to sit on the piano stool and told him to come and turn her music for her, waiting until he was standing next to her to lean over and unfasten his trousers,

36

one hand expertly stroking his cock, the other picking out notes on the piano keys, whilst her tongue flicked busily against the tumescent shiny head.

'I've always wanted to play on an organ,' she had told him mock innocently.

He had taken her quickly and urgently, pushing up her skirts when she had arched over provocatively, presenting him with the rounded shape of her behind, plunging himself deep into the warm wetness of her waiting cleft, driving them both into a swift fierce orgasm whilst they heard the voices of her husband and his steward growing louder as they approached the music-room door.

Yes, there had been good times, but Greg did not want to be reminded of those now.

'You said that, Greg,' he could hear her insisting. 'You said you would love me for ever and that you would never leave me.'

'Well, I'm afraid I must leave you now, my sweet,' he told her, taking refuge in a rueful smile and making the words teasingly light. 'Because I certainly cannot stay all night.'

'But I shall see you tomorrow?'

When he hesitated she burst out, 'I must. I must see you, Greg. If you don't come and see me I can't be responsible for what I might do.'

It wasn't the first time she had threatened him, but now her threats merely irritated rather than alarmed him. After all, she had even more to lose from their affair being exposed than he did.

Later, as he drove home, he reflected enviously on Amber's imminent departure for London. What he wouldn't give for the opportunity to spend several months there, especially now.

Chapter Three

Amber was in disgrace, of course. It was over two weeks since her birthday and her grandmother was still treating her coldly, speaking to her only when she had to.

'Do you think that Grandmother loved Barrant de Vries, Greg?' Amber asked her cousin.

It was after luncheon and they were in the billiard room, Amber sitting cross-legged in the window seat whilst Greg chalked a cue before leaning over the table and carefully aiming it at one of the balls.

'How the devil should I know?' he responded.

If her grandmother had loved Barrant de Vries, why did she hate him so much now, Amber wondered. If she had loved him then it was a very different kind of love from the love her parents had had for one another.

'Grandmother still isn't talking to me. Oh, Greg, I wish I didn't have to be presented.' Amber shivered.

'Come on.' Greg tried to jolly her out of her misery. 'It might not be as bad as you imagine. I thought you girls liked wearing pretty frocks and going to balls. You wouldn't catch me turning down the chance to have some fun in London, I can tell you that.' His eyes lit up. 'There's the Kit-Cat Club, and the Embassy and the Slipper. Places where a chap can *really* enjoy himself. Perhaps I should have a word with Grandmother, see if she'll let me go with you, then I can scare off all your unwanted admirers.' He put on a mock ferocious face.

Amber giggled.

'Look, I'll tell you what. I've got to drive over to Fitton Hall later; you can come with me, if you'd like. It will cheer you up a bit.'

Greg was so very kind. She was lucky to have such a thoughtful cousin.

'I thought Grandmother said at breakfast that Lord Fitton Legh was in London on business,' Amber reminded him.

'Did she? I don't remember, but anyway, it doesn't matter if he isn't there. I'm only returning some books to Lady Fitton Legh on Grandmother's behalf.'

Amber nodded. She looked forward to seeing Caroline Fitton Legh again. It had caused quite a stir locally when Lord Fitton Legh had married an American heiress twenty years his junior, and not much older than Amber herself was now.

Blanche was on the same charity committee as Caroline Fitton Legh and the Dowager Marchioness of Cholmondeley.

The Dowager Marchioness had invited Amber to a children's party the previous Christmas. Amber remembered that there had been a good deal of gossip at the party amongst the adults, accompanied by arched eyebrows and the words '*pas devant les enfants*' used about the fact that the Duke of Westminster had invited Gabrielle Chanel, whose clothes her grandmother loved so much, to stay at Eaton Hall. Amber had innocently asked Greg later why the adults hadn't thought it appropriate for them to know about Mademoiselle Chanel's visit to Eaton Hall, to which Greg had laughed and then shocked Amber by telling her, 'Because she's the duke's mistress, silly.'

It wasn't the scandalous behaviour of the Duke of Westminster that occupied Amber's thoughts now though, so much as the Fitton Legh marriage. Had Caroline's parents wanted her to marry someone with a title? Was that why she had married Lord Fitton Legh, who was so much older than she? Amber gave a small shiver. Was that what was going to happen to *her*?

Amber hurried downstairs. Under her cream silk jacket she was wearing her 'best' chocolate-brown afternoon frock. The December sunshine picked out the pattern of small cream diamonds on the fabric. Although her dress was new it was still very schoolgirlish in design, with its high square neckline banded in cream silk, its skirt short and pleated. Her brown patent shoes matched her handbag, and had low heels and a Mary Jane strap across the front. Her cream cloche hat was decorated with a brown petersham ribbon and a single chocolate-brown silk flower. Amber had pulled it low down over her curls and slightly to one side, copying the way the models sketched in *Vogue* wore theirs. Cream leather gloves completed her outfit.

When Amber reached the hallway she found that Greg was already there, striding up and down impatiently as he waited for her.

Like her he had changed his clothes, and was now wearing a tweed suit with the Oxford bag-style trousers, so wide that only the toes of his brown leather brogues were visible. He was carrying his hat and his thick fair hair was firmly slicked back instead of flopping in his eyes in its normal manner. He looked very handsome.

'Ready, old thing?'

Amber nodded, placing her hand on the crooked arm he extended for her with a teasing grin, whilst Wilson, her grandmother's butler, gestured to one of the maids to open the door for them. It made her feel so grown up and proud to be going out with Greg to pay an afternoon call.

Greg's bright red roadster, the Bugatti he had coaxed their grandmother into buying for him when he had come down from Oxford, was parked on the gravel outside.

While Fitton Hall lay to the east of Macclesfield, in the lee of the Derbyshire hills, Denham Place lay to the west. The two fine houses were separated not just by the town of Macclesfield itself but also by the pretty village of Alderley Edge, where the railway had originally ended and where all the wealthy railway barons lived. There was a short cut that would have taken them down a narrow winding country lane often busy with farm vehicles, but Greg was driving them the longer way round, along the better roads, and as they drove past Stanley Hall and then up the hill from Alderley to the Edge itself, Amber held her breath a little. There were so many stories about the Edge and its magical properties. It was said that no bird was ever heard to sing there, and by some that the wizard Merlin had lived deep in the caves beneath and that he slept there still, guarding King Arthur's sword.

As they approached Macclesfield, Amber touched Greg's arm.

'Can we go past the mill, Greg, please?'

'I don't know what you see in that dull place,' he complained.

Denby Mill had been built in the neo-Palladian style, which had been very popular amongst mill owners of the time. Several mills in the town were built in the same style but Denby Mill was by far the largest, and the most profitable.

Amber's mother had explained to her that the reason for their family's success was that their ancestor had married an heiress, whose father had been a wealthy Liverpool ship owner. With his wife's money he had not only built himself a new mill, he had also invested in the construction of railways and canals.

Blanche Pickford had inherited a second fortune through a bachelor uncle on her mother's side of the family to add to the fortune she had received on her father's death.

Amber's mother had also told her that it was through his wife's family that their ancestor had become interested in the Far East, explaining that he had copied onto his silk a design from a painting that had come originally from China, and this had become their famous Denby Mill 'Chinese Silk' fabric, which was first shown at the Great Exhibition, and which Queen Victoria herself had admired.

Like others in his position Josiah Denby, their ancestor, had used some of his wealth philanthropically to help the poor of the town, setting in place a tradition that had been kept up through each generation.

As a child Amber had loved listening to her mother telling her stories about her family.

There was a statue of Denby in the wrought-iron-rail-enclosed garden to one side of the mill. As they drove past now, Amber smiled to herself, remembering how, when she had been younger, she had wished that he might have done something more exciting like Miss Brocklehurst, who had travelled to Egypt and brought back with her many Egyptian artefacts, including a mummy, all of which were housed in a museum in West Park where the townspeople might go and marvel at them.

Once they had driven through the town and its mills Greg took the road that led towards Fitton Hall, and the Forest of Macclesfield.

It wasn't long before Greg was driving down the long tree-lined road that led to the Hall, pausing at the lodge by the gates whilst someone came out to open them.

The Elizabethan house and its gardens were renowned for their beauty. It was said by some that Shakespeare's Dark Lady of the Sonnets had been one of the Fittons, and there were tales too of a past tragic event when a Fitton bride, forced into a marriage she did not want, had drowned herself in one of the pools that lay between the house and the village church, rather than leave her much-loved home to go with her new husband.

'Oh, Greg, it is so very pretty, isn't it?' Amber exclaimed, as she looked towards the timber-framed exterior of the house, with its mullioned windows, whilst Greg brought his motor car to a halt outside the main entrance.

A manservant opened the door to them.

'Good afternoon, Mr Pickford.'

The obvious recognition of her cousin surprised Amber a little, although she was too interested in their surroundings to dwell on it.

She gazed round the panelled hall in awe. Could that embroidery she could see on the cushions be the original Jacobean crewel work? She longed to go over to examine it more closely, but the servant was waiting for them to follow him.

The hall had a stone floor with a carpet laid over it and in its centre was a highly polished table on which there was a beautiful arrangement of hothouse lilies and roses, their scent filling the air. A flight of stairs led up towards a galleried landing, its balustrade intricately carved with fruits and leaves in the style of Grinling Gibbons. Dark, heavily framed portraits of past Fitton Leghs looked down on the visitors from the walls, whilst the vast fireplace was surely almost tall enough for a person to stand up in.

'Come on,' Greg hissed impatiently, tugging on Amber's arm as she paused to take it all in.

Obediently she followed the manservant down a passageway of linen-fold panelling, which opened out into the house's original Great Hall. From two storeys high, its windows overlooked the green lawns that sloped away from the house, with the wall decorated with pieces of armour and swords, and the arms of the Fitton Leghs.

Amber studied them intently. Her father had been commissioned by Lord Fitton Legh's late mother to incorporate the arms into a design for table linen for the four hundredth anniversary of the granting of the manor to the family. Amber remembered watching him working on the commission, tracing the various armorial crests and then working them into a variety of potential designs, his forehead furrowed in concentration, before he broke off to summon her mother to come and give him her opinion.

The heavy curtains that hung at the windows were embroidered with a pineapple design, which, Amber knew from what her father had taught her, meant that they had probably been commissioned by the Fitton Legh whose bride's fortune had come from the West Indies trade.

An old refectory table ran the length of the room. On the wall opposite where they had entered the hall was an intricately carved screen, above which was a minstrels' gallery.

'Come *on*.'

'Sorry,' Amber apologised. 'It's just that it is all so wonderful. I could stay here for hours.'

Beyond the Great Hall the corridor widened out into a large rectangular hallway of a much more modern design and Amber realised that they had entered that part of the house that had been designed by Robert Adam. The walls were painted a soft duck-egg blue and the plasterwork picked out in white. Matching niches held busts of what Amber presumed were past Fittons.

Several sets of elegant mahogany doors opened off this hall. The servant pulled open one pair of them and then announced the visitors.

The room was painted a straw colour, its Regency furniture upholstered in satin of the same colour, so that the room seemed to be aglow with a soft warm light.

Lady Fitton Legh was seated on a small sofa with Cassandra. Cassandra, Amber knew, was staying with the Fitton Leghs, to whom the de Vrieses were connected, Barrant's late wife having been a Fitton Legh. As a child Cassandra had not spent as much time in Cheshire as Jay had done and therefore Amber did not know her very well.

Cassandra was two years older than Amber. Her parents lived near Brighton and, according to Jay, it had been on a visit to her grandfather the previous Christmas that Cassandra had been entertained by the Fitton Leghs and had then been invited to come and stay at Fitton Hall by Lord Fitton Legh as a companion to his wife.

As soon as she saw her visitors, Lady Fitton Legh jumped up from the sofa and then hurried towards them, exclaiming with obvious delight, 'Greg, what a lovely surprise!'

In contrast, Greg sounded oddly stilted and not one little bit like his normal relaxed self as he acknowledged her welcome, quickly stepping back from her, as he told her, 'My grandmother charged me with the task of returning some books to you, and I have brought my cousin, Amber, with me.'

Each time she saw Caroline Fitton Legh, Amber marvelled afresh at her beauty. Her eyes, large and darkest violet, dominated the delicacy of her face; her lips were soft and full, and at the moment seemed to be trembling slightly, making her look both sad and vulnerable. Her skin had a lovely light tan like the models in *Vogue*, which made Amber immediately long to exchange her own peaches-and-cream English complexion for it. Her hair was dark and cut, in the prevailing fashion, close to her head and perfectly waved. The frock she was wearing was the same shade of silk as her eyes. Amber didn't think she had ever seen anyone so slender or so delicate-looking. The rings on her marriage finger looked huge and heavy on such a delicate hand.

Cassandra, who had remained seated, now stood up and made as though to stand between them and Caroline. Cassandra was, Amber saw, frowning at them. Poor Cassandra, Amber thought sympathetically. Lady Fitton Legh's beauty only underlined Cassandra's lack of it. Tall and thin, with a frizz of ginger hair, Cassandra had a reputation for being abrupt and awkward, in both her manner and her movements. Even Jay had admitted to Amber that he found her difficult to get on with, and that they were not very close.

It was obvious that she didn't welcome their arrival. She was looking resentfully at them, her face flushing with anger.

'You must both stay for tea,' Lady Fitton Legh insisted. 'Cassandra and I were feeling quite dull. You must tell us some of your silly jokes, Greg, and make us laugh.' She rang for tea as she spoke.

Amber hadn't realised that her cousin knew Caroline well enough to tell her jokes.

'I do so love the ceremony of English afternoon tea,' said Lady Fitton Legh, laughing. 'Greg, you must come and sit beside me to observe that I keep to all its little rules.'

But instead of accepting her invitation Greg pushed Amber forward, saying cheerily, 'I think it's best that Amber sits with you. I am far too clumsy and all too likely to jolt something or other, aren't I, Amber?'

'Is it true, Miss Vrontsky? Is your cousin really as clumsy as he says, or is he just teasing us?'

To Amber's relief, before she was obliged to answer her, the doors opened to admit the butler, two footmen and a maid, who went about the tea-serving duties with well-orchestrated ease, the butler turning to the footman first to remove the spirit lamp for the kettle from the large silver tray he was carrying, and then once he had lighted that and placed the kettle on it, the teapot. All had to be set in exactly the right position and in exactly the right order on the crisply laundered tea table cloth that covered the table next to the sofa, whilst the maid covered another table with a cloth and then set about placing on it the china from the tray carried by the second footman.

The footmen disappeared back into the hall and then returned with the tea trolley itself, laden with tiny crustless sandwiches, and a large selection of teabreads and cakes. Not that Amber could eat a thing. She felt so nervous and overawed.

Over tea Amber tried politely to engage Cassandra in conversation whilst Lady Fitton Legh entrusted several messages to Greg for their grandmother, but it was hard work when Cassandra would answer her with either a wooden 'Yes' or 'No'. Amber was relieved when Lady Fitton Legh finally rang for the tea things to be removed.

However, her hope that they might be about to leave came to nothing when Lady Fitton Legh said sweetly, 'Greg, Lord Fitton Legh will be very cross indeed with me if he learns that you were here and I cannot give him a full report of your meeting with the Selection Committee. Cassandra, why don't you take Amber into the music room so that she may hear the piece that you have been practising? Cassandra is a most accomplished pianist, Amber.'

For a moment Amber thought that Cassandra might actually refuse, she looked so furiously angry, but then she stood up abruptly, her face burning a bright hot red as she rushed towards the door, ignoring Amber, who had to run to catch up with her.

Once they were in the music room Cassandra continued to ignore her, much to Amber's discomfort. Seating herself at the piano she raised the lid and then brought her hands down on the piano keys in a loud clash of jarring discordant notes, that set the crystals on the light fittings trembling.

Whilst Amber was still recovering from her shock, and without a word of explanation for her odd behaviour, Cassandra then started to play the piano very loudly, making it impossible for them to converse. Amber wished Greg would hurry up and rescue her.

While she played, Cassandra's face remained bright red and her eyes were glittering strangely. Amber had no idea what to do. Such behaviour was completely outside anything she was used to. At school they had been subjected to a very strict regime, which had not allowed for any expression of personal feelings in public. It was, they had been taught, not the done thing for a lady to betray her feelings.

As abruptly as she had started to play, Cassandra stopped.

'You know that your cousin is in love with Caroline, don't you? Not that she would ever look at him. She laughs about him. We both do.'

Amber didn't know what to say. She felt acutely uncomfortable and, if she was honest, just a little bit afraid of Cassandra.

'You must tell him to stop coming round here and pestering her. He will be in a great deal of trouble if he doesn't.'

'I'm sure you are wrong. Greg is merely being polite,' Amber told her valiantly.

'No, I am not wrong. I have seen the way he looks at her. I have heard the lies he has told, the excuses he has made to see her when he has no business to be here.'

She slammed the lid down on the piano, stood up and then without saying another word she swept out of the room, leaving Amber to stare after her in bewilderment.

*　　*　　*

'There, are you feeling a bit more cheerful now?' Greg asked Amber as they drove home.

Amber looked at her cousin. He was watching the road as he drove.

'Greg, Cassandra said the most peculiar thing to me.'

'What kind of peculiar thing?'

'She said that you were in love with Lady Fitton Legh.'

There was a small pause and then Greg laughed rather too loudly.

'Lord, what rubbish you girls do talk. Of course I'm not. Lady Fitton is a married woman. I dare say the truth is that Cassandra has a terrible schoolgirl crush on Lady Fitton Legh herself. You know what you girls are like,' he teased. 'You are always having a pash on someone.'

His words made sense and brought Amber grateful relief.

There had been something about the events of the afternoon that had left her feeling uncomfortable.

Lady Fitton Legh was so beautiful that it would not after all have been extraordinary if Greg *had* fallen in love with her, but Amber was glad that he had not.

As he had said himself, Caroline Fitton Legh was married, and the last thing Amber wanted was for her cousin to have his heart broken through falling in love with someone who was forbidden to him, and who could never return his feelings.

Chapter Four

'Now, Amber, I trust that you have had time to reflect on your bad behaviour and the apology you owe me?'

Why should she have to apologise for saying that she didn't want to be presented when she didn't, Amber thought indignantly, but somehow instead of stating her rebellious feelings she found that she was bowing her head and saying dutifully, 'Yes, Grandmother.'

'Very well, we shall say no more of the matter,' Blanche told her graciously, pausing for a few seconds before continuing, 'Now, you will be leaving for London early in the New Year. All the arrangements are in place.'

'But, Grandmother, I don't see how it can be possible for me to come out. You can only come out if you have someone who has already come out to present you.' Amber was stumbling over the words in her desperation. This was the hope she had been clinging to: that it would be impossible for her to be presented.

What she had stated was, after all, the truth. And it was a truth that Amber had had reinforced over and over again when she had been at school. Her grandmother might have far more money than the families of most of the other girls at school with her, but they had something far more important. They had 'breeding' – connections and titles – and some of them had been very quick to let her know how far beneath them socially they considered her to be. Some, but not all of them. Not Beth – or rather Lady Elizabeth Levington – her best friend, and Amber knew she would always be grateful to her for the kindness she had shown her.

Amber had even laughed about the fact that she would not be coming out with Beth, saying truthfully to her that she was glad that she wouldn't have to. From what she had heard, the season was little more than a cold-blooded way of marrying girls off to someone suitable as quickly as possible.

'I am well aware of the rules that apply to a débutante's presentation at court, Amber.' Her grandmother's voice was tart now as well as cold. 'It has already been arranged that Lady Rutland will be presenting you at one of the season's formal drawing rooms alongside her own daughter.'

Amber felt sick. The hope she had been clinging to was no barrier at all. Now what was she going to do? There was no point telling herself that she could defy her grandmother; she knew she couldn't. She would be packed off to London and Lady Rutland, whether she liked it or not.

Lady Rutland? The name was familiar. How . . . ? And then she realised, and her despair increased. Lady Rutland was Louise's mother! She was going to be coming out with the Hon. Louise Montford, who disliked her so much and who had been so horrid to her at school.

From the past she could hear Louise's words echoing inside her head.

'Vrontsky? What kind of name is that?' Louise had taunted her on her first day at school.

'It's my father's name. A Russian name,' Amber had replied proudly.

Louise had loved to mock her at school by referring to her as 'the Macclesfield mill girl', drawing attention to her lack of 'family' and 'breeding', whilst continually boasting of her own.

Amber couldn't believe that Louise's mother was going to bring her out. From what Beth had said, Louise's mother was even more of a snob than Louise herself; both arrogant and proud. Proud but poor.

An ice-cold suspicion lodged itself in Amber's thoughts. She had learned in these last short weeks since her birthday not to take anything at face value any more. Had her grandmother bought Lady Rutland's sponsorship of her just as she intended to buy Amber a titled husband?

Her grandmother was still talking but Amber had stopped listening. She had thought when her grandmother had first told her why she was sending her to London that things couldn't get any worse, but she had been very wrong.

It was a relief to be on her own as she walked along the trellised pathway across the shadowy formal garden of her grandmother's house. During the summer the trellising was smothered in richly scented roses, but now it was the crisp smells of winter that perfumed the dark evening air.

The sound of someone walking swiftly along a second gravel pathway, bisecting her route, had her stopping apprehensively, only to relax when the other person stepped out of the shadows and into the moonlight. Jay.

He was taller than Greg, with grey eyes that lightened when he was amused, but which Amber had on occasions seen darken to the colour of wet slate. Jay was only two years older than Greg, but there was something more mature about him.

The sturdy plainness of Jay's workmanlike plus fours and tweed jacket suited him, even though Amber knew that Greg would have raised an eyebrow to see such clothes being worn out in the evening. But somehow Jay wasn't

52

the kind of man she could envisage wearing a fashionably cut dinner jacket. With Jay, Amber was always aware of a sense of quiet purposefulness and dependability that drew her to him in a way she didn't really understand.

'I just came out for some fresh air and to . . . to think,' she told him, even though he hadn't asked for an explanation of her presence in the garden.

He inclined his head towards her and as Amber looked up at him she saw that his eyes looked dark.

Her voice trembled. 'Jay, have you ever wished for something so much that it hurts? I want to learn to be a designer, so that I can work at the mill with our silk. That has always been my dream.'

'We all have dreams.' His words, quiet but somehow heavy, checked her.

'What are your dreams?' she asked him curiously. 'I suppose you must wish that you could inherit your grandfather's title.'

'No, I do not wish for that.' His voice was firm and sure. 'My love is the land, Amber.' He bent down, scooped up some earth from the flowerbed and let it trickle through his fingers. 'This is life, Amber, this humble soil. We walk on it and ignore it, and take it for granted, but in reality it is a miracle. When we nourish it with love and care it pays us back tenfold. My great-grandfather on my father's side was a farmer, and I have, I think, inherited his nature. I am far happier with that inheritance than I could ever be with the de Vries title.'

'I wish my grandmother could be more like you. To her, having a title is all that matters.'

Jay looked at her. 'Never fear, Amber, one day you will be able to tread your own path and make your own decisions.'

The smile he gave her illuminated his whole face, turning his eyes the colour of molten silver, and for no reason she could think of, Amber's heart started to beat far too heavily and fast. She felt as though she was standing on the brink of something very important. Something she wanted to reach out for but at the same time feared. Without quite knowing what she was doing she took a step towards him, and then very quickly two steps back, half stumbling as she did so, so that Jay reached out to steady her, his hand on her arm. His fingers were long, and his nails clean and cared for. A *gentleman*'s hands. The words slipped through her head. She looked up at him, studying his face. The shadowy semidarkness threw into relief the strength of his bone structure, drawing him in light and shade, planes and hollows. He was looking back at her just as intently, the silence between them intense and compelling.

Amber had an extraordinary yearning to reach out and touch him; to trace the shape of his jaw and the curve of his cheekbone. She was breathing too fast, both shocked and excited by her own feelings.

'Jay . . .'

The moment she spoke his name he released her and stepped back.

'You had better go in. It's getting cold and your grandmother will be wondering where you are.'

'Yes.'

He was turning away from her.

'Jay!'

He stopped and looked at her.

'I just wanted to say that I hope whatever your dreams are that they will come true for you.'

He hoped that they would – for her sake – but he feared that life might not be that kind.

Chapter Five

January 1930

Amber and her grandmother arrived in Cadogan Place late in the afternoon, when the trees were a dull silver grey with a combination of frost and icy fog, their poor skeletal branches reaching upwards like the hands of the children the new arrivals had seen begging as they had driven through the streets from Euston Station.

A butler, bent over with age and with a drip at the end of his nose, let them into a hall that, whilst elegantly proportioned, was so cold that Amber shivered inside her winter coat, although she noticed that her grandmother did no more than discreetly draw her furs closer to her body. Since Amber was too young, in her grandmother's view, to carry proper furs as they should be worn, her coat collar was merely trimmed with mink.

Lady Rutland received them in her private sitting room on the first floor, which smelled faintly of old furniture and damp. It was not Louise's mother, tall and thin, with a rigidly straight back and a voice as chilly as the room, who took control of the conversation though, but Amber's grandmother, with her cut-glass accent and her cool demeanour.

It had been arranged that Blanche would stay in London for one week in order to ensure that everything was properly in place for Amber's eventual presentation, at one of the late April drawing rooms, and Amber was not really surprised, knowing her grandmother as she did, that when the end of the week arrived and her grandmother was stepping out of the house in Cadogan Place and into the chauffeur-driven Bentley she had hired for the duration of her visit, not only had a lady's maid been engaged for Amber and Louise to share, but also appointments been made and undertaken at couturiers and a court dressmaker, and every detail of Amber's new wardrobe meticulously discussed with them. Both girls had been enrolled at the Vacani School of Dancing for deportment and formal presentation curtsy lessons, and with the Comtesse du Brissac for conversational French, etiquette, and 'the social graces'. Her grandmother had also managed to transform the icy-cold house they had walked into only a matter of days earlier, where unappetising food was served and the bed linen always felt damp, into one in which fires burned in every room, including the girls' bedrooms, meals appeared on time and were delicate enough to tempt the smallest of appetites, extra servants had been engaged with a proper smartness and briskness about them, and a brand-new furnace had been installed to ensure that in future the ladies of the household could enjoy proper hot baths. A chauffeur-driven Rolls-Royce had also been hired for the duration of the season, and accounts opened for Amber at those stores where she might need to purchase small personal necessities during her stay.

Now as her grandmother prepared to leave, she looked sharply at Amber and reminded her, 'You will remember, I hope, that you are my granddaughter and that I expect you to behave accordingly. You will obey Lady Rutland at all times. Do you understand?'

'Yes, Grandmother,' Amber replied obediently. What after all was the point of her saying anything else?

When Blanche embraced her she dutifully kissed her grandmother's cheek. She could sense that her lack of enthusiasm and gratitude irritated her grandmother but she was not going to pretend that she wanted the future her grandmother had planned for her.

Blanche released her and stepped back, warning briskly, 'Remember what I have told you, Amber. I have no wish to receive any complaints about your behaviour from Lady Rutland.'

'No, Grandmother.'

Amber could hear the impatience in her grandmother's exhaled breath, as she indicated that the waiting servant was to open the door.

Amber watched until her grandmother's car was out of sight. She wasn't going to miss her – not one bit – but she did feel unexpectedly alone.

Blanche had been gone just minutes when Louise launched her first attack on Amber, following her upstairs to her bedroom, and standing in the doorway, blocking Amber's exit.

'You needn't think that I'm going to pretend that I want you here or that I like you,' she informed Amber nastily, 'because I don't. No one will speak to you or have anything to do with you. You know that, don't you? I shall tell everyone what you really are.'

'And shall you tell them also that my grandmother is paying your mother to bring me out?' Amber asked her quietly.

Louise's cheeks burned bright red, revealing to Amber that she had scored a hit, and to Amber's relief Louise turned on her heel without another word.

That exchange was to set the tone for the whole of their relationship.

If Lady Rutland knew of Louise's hostility towards Amber she gave no sign of it. Lady Rutland was not what Amber would have called a loving mother or partisan in any way on her daughter's behalf, and it seemed to Amber that she treated Louise every bit as coldly as she treated Amber herself. Not that Louise seemed to care about that, or the fact that her mother was scarcely ever there since she had a busy social life of her own. Louise's mother certainly didn't ensure that the two girls were chaperoned as carefully as Amber knew her own grandmother would have done.

Amber longed to be able to go home to Macclesfield. She missed Greg's teasing and his silly jokes, and she missed Jay too. She had been dreadfully homesick when she had first been sent away to school, but this was different. When she had been at school she had believed she had something to look forward to, a future she could choose for herself. Now she dreaded what lay ahead.

A maid had been hired to escort the girls to their various lessons, but it seemed that Lady Rutland had found her something else to do because within a week of her grandmother leaving, Amber found that she was having to make her own way to the comtesse's small house down behind Harrods, and without Louise, who had declared that she had no need of any instruction in conversational French or 'the social graces'.

Since the comtesse was reluctant to exchange the warmth of her fireside, Amber quickly discovered that her lessons in 'social graces' involved little more than listening to the comtesse's friends talk over afternoon tea.

It was a lonely life for a young woman.

Amber was aware that Lady Rutland took Louise to lunch and tea parties from which she was excluded – Louise was only too keen to tell her about them, smirking when she explained that they were 'family' invitations and that 'naturally' Amber wasn't invited, and yet at the same time making it obvious that this was just a fiction and that in reality the parties were being given by the mothers of the other débutantes who would be coming out that season, and who didn't want to invite Amber.

Shrewdly Amber wondered how much of that was because of her background and how much because Lady Rutland herself did not want her included, because her presence was a reminder of her own financial problems.

Her grandmother would feel that Lady Rutland was not keeping to her side of their bargain, Amber knew, but she didn't care about not being invited to the pre-season parties. In fact, the truth was that she was glad that she didn't have to go.

Despite the cold winter wind, Amber's footsteps slowed as she approached the Vacani School of Dancing for her late morning lesson.

She had come to dread the hours she had to spend here. Not because of the teachers – they were kindness itself – but because some of the girls, a group led by Louise, had been quick to see how difficult Amber was finding it to master the curtsy, and delighted in mocking her behind the teachers' backs.

Now Amber dreaded the lessons and her own humiliation. It seemed the harder she tried, the more impossible it was to place her feet in the correct position alongside the barre, holding it with her right hand, and then sink down and rise up again smoothly, with her back straight, as all the débutantes had to do to their teachers' satisfaction before being allowed to move on to the next stage.

Louise curtsied as though she had been born doing it, which in a way, of course, she had – or at least she had been born to do it, Amber acknowledged miserably as she removed her coat in the cloakroom and changed into her indoor shoes, before making her way into the classroom.

It didn't matter how patient and kind Miss Marguerite was, Amber just knew she was not going to be able to perform a proper curtsy, and that she would disgrace herself and, more importantly, her grandmother. She shuddered at the very thought.

Today she seemed to be struggling more than ever. At last, though, the lesson was over, but not Amber's humiliation.

Louise walked past her arm in arm with one of the other débutantes, pausing within deliberate earshot to announce in a loud voice, 'Of course the Macclesfield mill girl can't curtsy properly. She hasn't got the breeding. Have you seen her dance? She's like a cart horse.' Louise mimicked an exaggerated imitation of someone dancing clumsily, before doing a wobbly faked curtsy and then falling over. 'It's like Mummy says: you simply can't turn a sow's ear into a silk purse, or a silk mill girl into a member of the aristocracy.'

One of the other girls tittered and then another giggled openly, whilst even those who were not part of Louise's set turned away from Amber – as though she had the plague or something, Amber thought wretchedly. Just like Barrant de Vries had rejected her grandmother? It was a strange sensation to feel that she had something in common with that formidable old lady.

Blanche's letters to her were full of commands to do what she was told, and to remember how very fortunate she was. It was hard to imagine someone as controlled and determined as her grandmother ever allowing anyone to reject her.

In the cloakroom Amber was once again ignored whilst the other girls chattered together. Amber could hear Louise's voice quite plainly.

'I'll see you at Lady Wilson-Byer's lunch party, Anthea?

60

I think most of us have been invited, haven't we? Oh, except you, of course, Amber. Sorry. Mummy did say to tell you that you'd have to amuse yourself today. I forgot.'

She would not cry, Amber told herself fiercely, bending her head over her outdoor shoes as she fastened them.

She was supposed to be going to Norman Hartnell for a fitting for one of the new dresses she would wear once the round of pre- and post-presentation parties began properly, but Amber headed instead for Piccadilly and the National Gallery.

In such an alien and unwanted new world, the National Gallery, which she had visited so often with her parents, had become her private refuge, and normally just breathing its air was enough to calm her, but today the humiliation stung too badly for that panacea.

She stood in front of her father's favourite portrait of Lorenzo the Magnificent, trying as she always did to look at it with his eyes and expertise. He had loved it because he could almost feel the weight of the fabric – Florentine silk, dyed in Bruges, its colour set with alum – and she could hear his voice now and see his smile.

'The Medici never did manage to gain control of the alum trade from the Pope,' she said out loud, lost in a past that was far happier than her present.

'And was that God's will, do you suppose, that the might of the Pope's prayers should outweigh the Medici's Machiavellian negotiating powers?'

Amber jumped. She hadn't even realised that she herself had spoken aloud, never mind that a man standing behind her had overheard and was now replying.

Blushing self-consciously she shook her head.

Laughing, her new companion told her, 'Personally, I think it a shame that the Medici didn't succeed, but then

I've always had a soft spot for them, especially old Lorenzo. He knew to a nicety how to combine self-interest with piety.'

Amber had never seen such a physically beautiful human being. He was almost too perfect, surely far too beautiful for a man: tall and slender, with very dark wavy hair, brilliantly green eyes and very pale skin. His profile made the artist within her catch her breath. He was dressed in a suit that fitted him like no suit she had ever seen any man wear before, the fabric so fluid and yet so perfectly cut that her greedy gaze wanted to absorb every detail of it. What was it? Wool with silk? She ached to reach out and touch it.

'Do you have a particular interest in the Medici?'

His voice was as rich as the best quality velvet, changing tone and colour, warming and cooling in a way that mesmerised her.

'Not really. My father loved this painting, although he said that there were others he had seen in Leningrad that were even better. My parents used to bring me here and tell me all about the history of silk.'

'Silk?' He was being polite.

'I'm sorry. I'm keeping you and being very dull.' She made to move away, but he shook his head and told her firmly, 'No such thing. I confess I know very little about the history of silk. Look, there's a bench over there; let's go and sit down and you can enlighten me.'

Amber opened her mouth to refuse politely, but somehow she found that before she could do so she was seated next to him, answering his questions about her family and her home, and confiding in him in a way she could never have imagined herself doing with a stranger.

'So your grandmother refused to allow you to go to art school and instead she has sent you to London to learn to curtsy so that you can be presented at a drawing room under the auspices of Lady Rutland, and thus find a titled husband,

62

only you won't be able to do so because you can't curtsy?' It was an admirable précis of her garbled explanations.

'Yes,' Amber admitted. 'Louise – that's Lady Rutland's daughter – says it's because I'm not . . . because I haven't got . . . well, she says one needs breeding in order to be able to curtsy properly.'

'Ah, breeding. Your friend, it seems, has yet to learn that true breeding is a state of mind and cannot be conferred via a coronet.'

He was making fun of her now, Amber was sure of it, but he looked serious.

'Should we introduce ourselves?' he asked her. 'You are . . . ?'

'Amber,' Amber told him shyly. 'Amber Vrontsky.'

He reached for Amber's hand, taking it in his own as he stood up and then made a small half-bow.

'Pray allow me to present myself to you. I am Herr Aubert,' he told her, adopting a stilted foreign accent that made Amber giggle, in spite of herself. 'I have the honour to be the world's best teacher of ze Austrian Curtsy, if you will allow me to demonstrate.'

And then, before Amber could stop him, he released her hand and sank into a perfect curtsy, complete with a simpering expression on his face that made Amber want to laugh again.

'Come now, Miss Vrontsky, enough of this unseemly levity. You will pay ze attention and copy me, if you please.'

The gallery was empty and, somehow or other, Amber found that she was on her feet too and joining in the game. She dropped into a deep curtsy and then rose from it as effortlessly and as perfectly as though she had been doing it for ever.

Half an hour later, breathless with laughter as her unusual and unrepentant 'teacher' insisted she repeat her curtsy half a dozen or more times, Amber shook her head and protested, 'I can't do any more. I've got a stitch from laughing so much.'

'Laughing? What is this laughing? You are here to learn ze curtsy. You do not laugh.'

When she did, he feigned outrage, and told her firmly in his normal voice, 'And now I think we should celebrate your great victory over the curtsy with tea at the Ritz.'

Amber's face fell. 'Oh, no, I couldn't.'

'Of course you can, and you shall.'

It was very wrong of her to go with him, of course, but somehow or other it was impossible to refuse.

They took a cab to the Ritz, and as they entered, the doorman bowed and said, 'Good afternoon, Lord Robert. Mr Beaton is waiting for you at your usual table.'

'Thank you, Mullins,' he responded, instructing Amber, 'Come, child.'

Lord Robert, the doorman had called him, Amber noted.

Amber had been to the Ritz before, with her grandmother, but she was still awed by its magnificence.

As they approached the table occupied by another young man, two waiters sprang forward to pull out chairs for them.

'Cecil, my dearest.' Lord Robert was speaking in a lazy drawl now, and it seemed to Amber that his whole manner had changed subtly. No longer was it teasing and amused but instead, languid and elegant. 'I am sorry to be late but you will forgive me when you learn that I have been the saviour of this poor wretched child.'

'It is not a child, Robert, it is a young woman,' the other man's voice was waspish.

'Ah, yes, but a young woman who studies Lorenzo's portrait because she wishes to analyse the quality of his silk coat. I suspect she fears that such a vivid shade owes more to the artist's palette than the dye shops of Bruges.'

'Indeed.' This was said with a sharp glance in Amber's direction.

'Cecil here is obsessed with colour, princess – the poor models he photographs for *Vogue* are driven to madness by him.'

Cecil? This was Cecil Beaton! She was actually in the presence of the great photographer whose work she had gazed at with such admiration in *Vogue*. Amber was tongue-tied with awe.

'You are talking nonsense, Robert. Now tell me properly, who is this child?' the photographer demanded.

Amber gave Lord Robert a pleading look but it was no use.

'She is Amber Vrontsky, her father was Adam Vrontsky, and she is to be one of this season's débutantes. I found her in tears in the gallery over the ordeal of The Curtsy. However, now all is well, isn't it?' There was a look of wicked amusement in the beautiful man's eyes.

'A Vrontsky? Indeed?' Cecil Beaton's gaze had narrowed. 'Well, child, was your father the prince or the count, because I recollect that they share the same name.' He was opening his cigarette case as he spoke to her, offering it to her. Amber shook her head, watching as he turned to Lord Robert, who took one of the Black Russian cigarettes.

'My father was neither,' she told the photographer, who was watching her, his eyes narrowed as he blew out a cloud of strongly scented smoke. 'He was an artist and fabric designer.'

She held her breath, waiting for the familiar disdain, but after the merest indrawn breath, Cecil Beaton said smoothly, 'A prince amongst men indeed then.'

'Yes, he was,' Amber agreed proudly. 'And I wish more than anything else that my grandmother would have let me go to art school as he wanted.'

'You wish to become an artist?'

'No,' Amber replied. 'I want to do what my father did and create new designs for our silk – my grandmother owns a silk mill.'

The tea things arrived, and after their tea had been poured the two men began discussing a social event they were both attending, leaving Amber free to study her surroundings, whilst keeping one ear on their conversation. Here and there she managed to grasp a name, only to recognise with awe that it belonged to someone famous, but for Amber, far more exhilarating and exciting than the conversation were the women's clothes, and her senses fed greedily on them. What had previously been only sketches and photographs she had seen in *Vogue* had come alive, moving with the bodies they were adorning. She felt a pang to see Chanel's jersey demanding obeisance to its dominance, as virtually everyone seemed to be wearing it, but then she saw a woman walking in wearing Schiaparelli and she was lost, her breath catching and her gaze bewitched by the fluid movement of the silk dress with the most beautifully cut and elegant matching silk jacket worn over it. Everything and everyone else was forgotten as Amber absorbed every detail, her heart pounding in homage to both the fabric and the creative genius of the designer.

'You prefer the Schiaparelli to the Chanel?'

Amber was startled. She had been so engrossed in the outfit that she hadn't seen Cecil Beaton turn towards her.

'It's silk,' she told him simply, 'and the colour . . .' She shook her head, unable to find the words to explain the effect of seeing such stunningly vibrant colour at first hand instead of merely seeing a sketched impression of it in a magazine. It was so strong, so powerful, that it almost had its own physical presence. To get an acid yellow so pure was a work of art in itself.

'I was wondering what dye they used. I've seen the outfit in *Vogue* but I hadn't realised how different the reality would be.' Just in time she realised that the photographer was looking slightly offended and assured him truthfully, 'Your photographs are wonderful and truly capture the reality in a way that a sketch cannot.'

Lord Robert had summoned a waiter and was ordering cocktails.

'Dubonnet and gin for Mr Beaton and myself,' he told the waiter, 'half and half, and shaken very cold, and, er, a lemonade for the young lady.'

'That is why photographs are the future of fashion magazines.' Cecil Beaton was smiling approvingly at Amber now. 'I keep on telling *Vogue* this, but do they listen to me? No, they do not, because they cannot move with the times. They are fools, but I shall be proved right. The camera can capture reality so much more sharply and clearly than a workaday draughtsman with his tubes of paint. Schiaparelli's gowns are a case in point. As you have just said, it is impossible to replicate the true colour of her clothes without a camera. She is, of course, a true artist and a gifted one, but be warned, child, if you are looking to her for the future of your silk, then you are looking in the wrong place. It is my belief that Chanel, with her practical jersey and her clever mock simplicity, holds the key to the future of fashion. If you will take my advice you would be wise to direct your attentions towards silks that can be used to ornament the home rather than the human body.'

He took a sip of his cocktail and then another, putting down his glass to light another cigarette before continuing, 'We are entering a period of great change, and not just in clothes. Interior design is what you should be watching. It's there that there will be the greatest demand for new and innovative fabrics. Having one's home redone by a top designer is already all the rage in New York; people with the money to pay for it want a look for their home that is unique to them, but at the same time recognisable by the *cognoscenti* as being overseen by an expert, and having "style". That is where you should be looking in future.

'You should talk to Lees-Milne about it. He is mad about houses and knows all the best of them. Art school is all very well but it cannot give you the gift of a good eye or the true sense of knowing what is right and what is not if you do not already possess them, but something tells me that you do. Let your passion guide you. Passion should never be underestimated or ignored.'

Amber listened to him, awed and humbled that he was prepared to take the time to give her the benefit of his advice. Suddenly her future, which had seemed so bleak and oppressive, now seemed full of wonderful possibilities.

Shyly she confided to him, 'My father used to say that we hadn't moved with the times and that—' She broke off as a ravishingly pretty woman, wearing a softly flowing loose dress, escorted by a slender foppish-looking young man with faunlike features, came towards them, exclaiming, 'Robert and Cecil, how fortunate! I need you both to help me, and as you can see, Cecil, I have already commandeered your assistant. I found him in the foyer and rescued him from a pack of young ladies. Bryan and I are planning a party, for after the baby, you understand.'

Amber couldn't stop looking at her. She was dressed for the evening, in a gown of gold lamé over lace, over crêpe satin, over which she was wearing a brown velvet evening coat with a lining of peach satin fulgurante. On her feet she was wearing shoes of silver tissue flecked with gold. In her prettily waved golden-blonde hair were diamond stars that twinkled in the light of the chandeliers. On her fingers and wrists were more diamonds, and her lips were painted rose-brown to complement the colour of her gown and coat.

'What, another party?' Lord Robert was demanding, as he summoned a waiter, instructing him, 'Mrs Guinness will join us for tea.'

Amber was acutely conscious of how out of her depth she was.

Lord Robert was still talking with Mrs Guinness.

'It's just as well you have married the Guinness millions and that Bryan is so adoring a husband, Diana,' he teased her, before turning to the young man standing with her to tell him, 'Saville, you must sit here next to Cecil, for if you don't he will sulk with me.'

Whilst the young man made his way to the seat, far from being offended by Lord Robert's teasing, Mrs Guinness simply laughed and told him, 'Well, so he should be, since I hope very soon to give him an heir.'

Amber blushed a little to hear her speak so openly of her condition.

'Then let us hope that it *is* a boy and that you deliver him on time and with far less fuss than poor Evelyn Waugh is making over his new book,' Lord Robert grinned.

Mrs Guinness shook her head. 'Robert, that is very wicked of you.'

'Wicked, perhaps, but also true,' Lord Robert insisted. 'Harold Acton told me that when he asked Evelyn what this new book of his was about, Eve told him that it is a welter of sex and snobbery.'

Mrs Guinness gave a trill of laughter. 'Oh, that is too naughty of him. He and Nancy are taking bets on which of them will have their new book denounced as a "sewer" first by Farve.'

How very pretty and gay she was, Amber thought enviously. It was no wonder that the men were gazing at her so admiringly.

'Now, Robert, I want you to listen to me,' she was saying firmly.

'Very well then,' he agreed, 'but first, Diana, most beauteous of all the beautiful Mitford sisters, pray allow me to introduce my protégée to you.'

'Your what?' she exclaimed merrily.

Amber's face burned, as much with self-consciousness at finding herself in the company of someone she had read about in the pages of *Vogue* and the social gossip columns, as with the idea of being Lord Robert's protégée.

It was Cecil Beaton who answered Diana Guinness, telling her drolly, 'Miss Amber Vrontsky. Robert found the child in the National Gallery and has been teaching her to curtsy.'

The blue eyes widened their gaze resting on Amber's flushed face. 'Oh, the curtsy. Yes, indeed, it is perfectly horrid. Muv threatened to ask my sister Nancy to teach me, but luckily for me Nancy made Muv cross with one of her teases so I went to Miss Vacani instead. You poor child,' she addressed Amber directly for the first time, 'and so pretty too. You will be besieged by admirers. You must come to one of my parties. I shall send you an invitation.'

'What do you think of London so far, Miss Vrontsky?' Cecil Beaton asked.

'When I am in the art galleries or looking up at the wonderful architecture, I think London is the most magnificent city there could be, and I feel very proud.' Amber's voice faltered slightly as she continued, 'But then when I look at all the poor people begging on the streets and I read in the newspapers that there is no work for them I feel ashamed.'

There was a small silence and then Cecil Beaton said softly, 'Out of the mouths of babes . . .'

She had spoken too frankly, Amber realised guiltily. Greg

was always teasing her for doing so, but her parents had instilled in her a respect for honesty and truthfulness.

'The truth can sometimes hurt,' her mother had told her, 'but deceit causes a far more painful wound.'

Cecil Beaton and his young assistant were discussing some sketches the photographer had submitted to *Vogue*. From his pocket he withdrew a small sketchpad and a pencil, using it to underline the point he was making.

Amber watched, both fascinated and envious, unaware of how clearly her face revealed her feelings. How fortunate Saville was to have such an apprenticeship.

Amber's head was beginning to spin slightly, from the air around the table, rich as it was with cigarette smoke, and the headiness of the conversation.

The tables around them were filling up, the sound of laughter growing louder, the tea cups replaced by champagne glasses.

'Robert, I think perhaps it's time you returned your protégée to Lady Rutland, before both you and she get into trouble,' Cecil Beaton warned, tearing a page from his notebook as he spoke.

'Yes, I must go,' Amber agreed, suddenly realising the time with an icy feeling of dread. 'Thank you for my tea and for being so very kind . . .' She was scrambling to her feet as she spoke, all too aware of the shortcomings of her appearance amongst so many beautifully dressed and sophisticated people, and the fact that she was going to be horribly late getting back to Lady Rutland's. Her heart gave a small flurry of anxious beats. What on earth was she going to say to Lady Rutland? She shouldn't have stayed out so long, she acknowledged guiltily. In fact she shouldn't have come here at all. But she was glad that she had.

'Here, child, this is for you – a small memento.'

Her dread disappeared, to be replaced with a mixture of

71

delight and awe as she stared down at the small sketch Cecil had given her. There in front of her they all were – small but oh so accurate caricatures of themselves on paper, seated around the table. Underneath the sketch he had written, 'Miss Vrontsky takes tea.'

'Oh, thank you,' Amber choked, unable to say any more. It seemed impossible that she who had pored over Cecil's witty society sketches should now possess one that included herself.

The head waiter was summoned and requested to ensure that she was put safely in a hansom cab. The gentlemen stood up and bowed formally over her hand, and then she was being escorted away from the table.

She had just reached the main entrance when Lord Robert came hurrying after her.

'If there should be any repercussions from Lady Rutland, make sure you refer her to me,' he told her.

His thoughtfulness after the misery she had felt was almost too much for her. 'You're all so kind,' she told him emotionally,

Lord Robert watched her leave. She had so much to learn. She didn't even know yet that society was divided into those who did accept and mingle with classes other than their own and those who did not and would not ever.

He, of course, belonged to the former group; his world embraced all those who had wit, and style, and most of all beauty. It was a world that was sophisticated, amusing and moneyed. It was also a world that had its dark underside, since it was the world of the louche, the raffish, the brazen and the fallen – the world of those who preyed on beauty and those who bought and sold it. It was into that world that Amber, with her beauty tethered by her grandmother's wealth and desire for a title, would be welcomed. Could she survive it or would it destroy her?

Poor child, he felt for her. After all, he knew what it was like to have a powerful cruel grandparent. His own grandfather had . . . but no, he must not allow himself to think of that.

Amber knew she would never forget today. She was filled with a new sense of hope and happiness. Oh, but she still couldn't help envying Cecil Beaton's young assistant. How very lucky he was.

Inside the cab, as it carried her back to Cadogan Place, Amber fluctuated between anxious fear of what Lady Rutland was likely to say to her, and a stubborn refusal to wish that she had not gone with Lord Robert.

The happiness the afternoon had brought was worth braving Lady Rutland's wrath ten times over. She would never forget what a lovely time she had had and how kind everyone had been, but most especially Lord Robert. A pink glow warmed Amber's face and her heart started to beat a little bit faster. Lord Robert was such fun, and so handsome. She was hardly likely to see him again, of course, but if she did . . .

Chapter Six

It was gone six o'clock by the time Amber got back to Cadogan Place, the lunch Lady Rutland and Louise had attended long over.

A sympathetic-looking maid informed Amber that she was to present herself immediately to Lady Rutland, but before Amber could do so, Louise came into her room without bothering to knock, and looking very smug.

'Mummy is absolutely furious with you,' she informed Amber gleefully. 'She is going to write to your grandmother and tell her that because of your behaviour she can't possibly present you.'

Amber's first guilty thought was that someone must have seen her at the Ritz and somehow or other managed to inform Lady Rutland. However, Amber's fear was put to rest when Louise continued, 'Mummy says she couldn't possibly endure the shame of presenting a débutante who can't curtsy.'

Amber exhaled shakily in relief. Innocent though she was, she was well aware that accepting an invitation from a strange man was a far more damaging social crime than not being able to curtsy. Not that she cared. She wouldn't have missed her wonderful afternoon for anything.

Lady Rutland was seated in front of the small campaign writing desk, which she had informed Amber and Blanche she had inherited from an ancestor who had fought at Waterloo.

Amber still blushed to remember how her grandmother had responded coolly, 'Really, it looks more Victorian than Georgian to me.'

Although the footman had announced Amber, Lady Rutland continued to study the letter on the desk in front of her as though Amber simply wasn't there, so that it was a good five minutes before she finally turned round and announced coldly, 'One of the things that separates the upper classes from those lower down the social scale, Amber, is an awareness of the importance of certain values. The upper classes do not tell tales. It is simply not done. I have a letter here from your grandmother. In it she expresses concern because, as she puts it, "My granddaughter does not appear to be attending as many pre-presentation social events as I would have expected."'

Amber was mortified. Jay must have said something to her grandmother. Before she had left Denham she had pleaded with both Greg and Jay to write regularly to her. Greg was an unreliable correspondent, his letters stilted, betraying his desire to be enjoying his life rather than writing about it, but Jay's letters were informative and interesting, just as though he was actually having a conversation with her, and gradually Amber had found herself writing more and more openly to him about her life here in London.

Even though Jay had written back to her in a very serious manner that since her grandmother was paying Lady Rutland to bring Amber out, she was in effect taking money for something she was not doing, it simply hadn't occurred to Amber that Jay would say anything to her grandmother.

Now Amber understood why her grandmother's most recent letter had requested a list of all those social events Amber had attended.

'You will find that society does not like sneaks, Amber. I had hoped to protect your grandmother from the unpleasant news that her granddaughter has made a laughing stock of herself by not being able to perform a court curtsy, and that several society mothers have declined to invite you to their parties. However, now, thanks to your own foolishness, I have no choice but to inform her of the truth.'

'I know that Louise is hoping that my grandmother will change her mind and that I shall be sent back home,' Amber told Lady Rutland bravely, 'but I shall not mind if she does.'

Lady Rutland didn't look as pleased to hear this as Amber had expected. In fact she looked extremely displeased.

'There is no question of your returning home, Amber. I am simply warning you of the consequences of tale telling. In this instance I am prepared to give you a second chance. As it happens I had already been busy on your behalf begging some of my dearest friends to include you on their guest lists as a personal favour to me, and I hope to be able to write to your grandmother within a few days with a list of the pre-presentation invitations I have accepted on your behalf.'

Lady Rutland's unexpected about-turn confused Amber at first. She had expected to be sent home in disgrace but here she was being told instead that Lady Rutland was planning to take her to the very kind of parties from which she had previously been excluded. It was almost, Amber recognised, as though Lady Rutland were afraid of her grandmother.

'At last. I have been in a fever of anxiety waiting for you. I telephoned you over an hour ago and told you that I must see you immediately. How cruel you are to me, Greg.'

She had run to him, attempting to fling herself into his

76

arms, but Greg held her off, his fury born of irritation and fear.

'Caroline, you know we agreed that we would never telephone one another. Fortunately it was only Jay who picked up the receiver, and I managed to spin him some tale about you having a message for me from Lord Fitton Legh.'

She obviously hadn't liked being pushed away, because now she was pouting in that pseudo-baby way he had once found so adorable but which he now detested. She was twenty-three, for heaven's sake, not seventeen.

'Now what the devil was it that was so important you had to take such a risk and drag me over here?'

'You haven't said that you love me yet.' Now she was being coquettish, and he found that equally unappealing.

'Caroline—'

'Say it.'

'Now listen—'

'Say it, Greg. You must say it otherwise I can't bear to tell you.'

She was crying now, her voice starting to rise. Greg looked anxiously towards the door to her bedroom.

It was one thing to be in here with her by prearrangement when there was little chance of their being disturbed, and their relationship was a secret known only to the two of them, but Cassandra, who had been waiting for him outside on the drive and who had taken him into the house via a side entrance, had plainly known what was going on. And equally plainly did not approve, if the look of angry contempt she had given him had been anything to go by. Well, he wasn't here by his own wish. In fact, if it was left up to Greg he would be happy never to see Caroline Fitton Legh again. Very happy, in fact.

Dash it all, what exactly did a chap have to do to make it clear that he wasn't interested any more? Caroline was no ingénue; she knew the rules of the game they had been playing. She had to do, married as she was to a man old enough to be her father, and one who, according to what Caro had told him, wasn't up to much in the bedroom department.

'Say it,' she was insisting.

If there was one thing Greg hated it was having his hand forced. His was an easy-going nature, but with a core of stubbornness. He didn't love her any more and he was damned if he was going to say he did.

'I'm not playing games,' he told her. 'I've got things to do.' Greg headed for the door.

His hand was on the door knob when Caroline said softly, 'You were happy enough to play games with me once, Greg, and if those things you are so eager to do include that silly political career, well, you'd better think again. There's to be a child.'

His hands were clammy now and the door knob slipped in his grasp.

'I'm honoured that you've told me, but surely that's something between husband and wife,' he blustered.

'Or between the mother and the father of the child?' Caroline suggested.

Greg was panicking now. 'Look, Caroline, this has gone far enough. What you and I shared together was fun and I shall always remember it, and you, with affection and . . . and tenderness. But we've both always known that all we could ever hope to share was an interlude of mutual pleasure.'

He was sweating profusely now and she wasn't saying a word, just standing there staring at him in that damnably unnerving way she had.

'We both knew that it had to end, and all the more reason now that you and Lord Fitton Legh are to have another child.'

'No! This child is not my husband's.'

78

'For God's sake,' Greg protested anxiously, 'what's the matter with you, Caroline? You know the child has to be your husband's. There can't be any choice. Think of the social disgrace. He would divorce you, and—'

'And then you'd have to marry me.' She gave a dismissive shrug. 'Divorce isn't so very bad. My father got divorced from my mother so that he could marry his lover.'

'That may be all very well in America,' Greg told her, 'but it's different here.' His belly was churning sickly. 'You don't really think that my grandmother would countenance me marrying you, do you?'

It was the wrong thing for him to have said, Greg realised too late. She almost flew at him, clawing at his face, her own contorted with rage.

'Your grandmother! Do you think that I don't know now that you're just hiding behind her? Do you think that I haven't been told about that girl in Macclesfield you've been seeing? How could you, Greg? A common little nobody whose father makes his money from pork sausages. But then I suppose I shouldn't be surprised, given your own lack of breeding.'

Her insult stung Greg.

'You can say what you like,' he told her. 'Maisie's a hell of a lot more fun than you are, and as for breeding, the only breeding you can lay claim to is the kind you get from what's in your belly.'

He heard the crash of the mirror she had picked up off her dressing table hitting the door behind him as he escaped into the corridor.

'Lady Rutland wants to see you in her sitting room, miss.'

Amber's heart sank. Not again. What had she done now?

'Thank you, Alice.' She dismissed the maid, ignoring the look Louise was giving her.

This time Lady Rutland wasn't alone. Two other people were with her, one of whom, a young woman wearing a startling large and ornate hat, Amber thought was puzzlingly familiar in some way. The other, an elderly man hunched over a walking stick, was wearing a black donnish-looking gown over a very hairy tweed suit.

'Ah, Amber,' Lady Rutland greeted her. 'You are fortunate in that your grandmother seems tireless in her efforts on your behalf. Professor Roberts here informs me that Mrs Pickford has instructed him to give you lessons on the history of London's famous buildings. I have to say that I would have thought that Mrs Pickford might have informed me of this decision, but I dare say she has other and more important things on her mind. Personally, I cannot see what advantage it might be to a débutante to study history but then I dare say that is because when one's ancestors have played such a predominant role in the history of one's country there is simply no need. History is one's family.'

There was an odd choking sound from the professor, and as Amber looked at him anxiously he lifted his head and looked straight at her, giving her a big wink unseen by Lady Rutland.

Lord Robert! What on earth were Lord Robert, and yes, she could see it now, Cecil Beaton's assistant, Saville, doing here, and dressed up in such a way?

'Quite so, my dear Lady Rutland,' the professor was agreeing in a quavery voice. 'Let me see, it was Sebastopol where your grandfather fell, I believe, and his cousin the marquis was with the Light Brigade, as I recollect. A most distinguished military history, although my own expertise lies more in the field of political history. I seem to think that there was a record somewhere of an argument between one of your ancestors and William Pitt the Younger, would you know anything of that?'

When Lady Rutland, lost for words for once, simply shook her head, Lord Robert sighed and said, 'Pity . . .' before turning to Amber and asking, 'This is the child, then?'

'Yes,' Lady Rutland confirmed.

'Well, I hope she proves to be a good student although my experience is that young girls have a tendency to foolishness and an overfondness of things of little importance. We shall start her lessons with a walking tour, if possible immediately.'

'Well, yes, of course, Professor.' Lady Rutland was all compliance.

Amber badly wanted to laugh.

'Well, child, you heard Lady Rutland. Go and get your outdoor things. You will see, Lady Rutland, that I have taken the liberty of providing Miss Vrontsky with a chaperone? I shall not introduce you. It would not be worth your while. She knows nothing of the history of the great families of our country.'

'What's going on?' Louise demanded when Amber raced upstairs to get her outdoor clothes. 'What did Mummy want? Why are you putting your coat on, Amber? Amber, answer me,' she demanded, but Amber merely shook her head and almost danced back down the stairs and into the hallway, where 'the professor' and 'her chaperone' were waiting.

'I couldn't believe it when I realised it was you, Lord Robert,' Amber laughed once they were outside and out of view of the house.

'And I can't believe that I have to wear this beastly hat,' Saville complained.

'You said that you had always fancied the stage, Saville,' Lord Robert told him cheerfully. 'You should be grateful to

81

me for giving you the opportunity to have an off-stage run. Besides, you would not have had to wear the hat if you were not sporting half a day's growth of beard.'

Whilst Saville retreated into a sulky silence, Lord Robert told Amber, 'It is Cecil you have to thank – oh, and Diana, she was party to it as well, when Cecil decided that you should be *his* protégée. Saville and I are simply the instruments by which his plan is to be conducted. Sadly, I'm afraid that Saville is on loan to us only for today, Cecil has refused to be without an assistant for any longer. But no matter, I am sure we shall do very well just the two of us, unless of course you wish me to find another chaperone for you?'

His smile was still teasing but Amber's heart had started to flutter with a delicious heady excitement that was both unknown to her and yet at the same time something she immediately recognised. Was Lord Robert actually flirting with her? Amber rather thought that he might be.

'It was clever of you to remember all about Lady Rutland's ancestors. She was very impressed.'

Saville gave a snort of derision.

'Now, Amber, let us get down to business,' Lord Robert told her, ignoring Saville. 'Cecil has given me instructions that you are to become knowledgeable in a wide variety of matters of fashion. He has made arrangements for us to visit the offices of *Vogue* magazine; although I suspect that will be more of a penance than a pleasure, knowing Cecil. I am to take you to shops and educate you as to architecture and design, and Cecil has told me to tell you that he will be setting you tests to ensure that you are studying diligently.'

Amber was overwhelmed. 'He is too kind. Why should he go to so much trouble on my account?'

Lord Robert looked down at her. There was no point in explaining that Cecil Beaton was part of a world in which the whim of the moment was all – or at least on the surface it was. Cecil worked hard, and if he chose to affect a nonchalance that made it look as though he did not, then that was his affair.

To tell Amber that it had been amusing to drink cocktails and discuss what could be done to help her, and even more amusing to hatch a plan that involved drama and dressing up, would be cruel.

'Since Cecil has to travel such a lot, the day-to-day management of your education must rest with me, your professor,' Lord Robert informed Amber, his hands gripping the edges of his gown. 'So, today we shall explore the modern phenomenon that is Selfridges.'

Selfridges! Amber's face lit up. She had heard of the famous store – everyone had – although Lady Rutland claimed that it was vulgar and she shopped only in Harrods.

'They have the most wonderful parties there,' Amber told Lord Robert excitedly. 'I read about one in the *Express*.'

'Amber, you must not believe everything that Lord Beaverbrook says,' Robert told her, tongue in cheek.

'I'm not going to Selfridges looking like this,' Saville told them petulantly.

'Very well then, my dear, do not come,' Robert answered him.

Looks passed between them that Amber did not understand, mocking on Robert's part and angry on Saville's.

They spent over two hours in Selfridges, going up to the roof garden to see where the bulbs were poking their heads through the earth, and to sit in the café and drink tea, before going back down to watch one of the famous Selfridges models displaying a new collection of jewellery.

'What do you think of it?' Robert asked Amber.

She hesitated and then admitted, 'It is very pretty. The diamonds sparkle so much, but . . .'

'But?' Robert encouraged her.

'It is not to my taste. I should prefer something a little less . . . shiny.'

Robert nodded approvingly. Cecil had been right: the child had a good eye and good taste, although what exactly she would be able to do with them, given her situation, he wasn't sure. She certainly wouldn't be making a career as one of Cecil's assistants. She lacked a very important qualification for that. She wasn't male.

Amber's eyes rounded when she recognised a familiar face.

'That's the Prince of Wales,' she whispered to Lord Robert in awe.

'Yes, indeed.' Robert glanced at the Prince and saw that he was with his mistress, Freda Dudley Ward. The Prince had a taste for outspoken American women – outspoken married American women – although he wasn't going to say anything about that to Amber, who was still in many ways too sweetly naïve.

An hour later, Lord Robert returned an exhausted but very happy Amber to Cadogan Place.

Two nights later, as she lay in bed, Amber decided that she was happier than she had ever thought it was possible to be. Yesterday she had been taken to Selfridges by Lord Robert and today she had performed her curtsy perfectly.

Unexpectedly, and thanks to Lord Robert, London and her new life had become far more exciting and fun than she had ever believed possible. How lucky she was to have met Lord Robert and how kind he was to have befriended her in the way he had. Amber couldn't wait for their next meeting.

Chapter Seven

'It's intolerable and if I had my way he'd be thrashed within an inch of his life.'

Blanche Pickford looked at her visitor, schooling her expression not to betray the fury she was feeling.

'I agree, Lord Fitton Legh; it is indeed intolerable when a married woman lies to her husband in an attempt to conceal an affair. As for your wish to thrash my grandson within an inch of his life, all I can say is that it takes two to commit adultery.'

Her neighbour's already mottled skin turned almost purple with rage. 'You have not heard me correctly, obviously, madam. It is your grandson who attempted to force himself on my wife. Dammit all, woman, there was a witness. Cassandra saw everything.'

'Yes, so you said,' Blanche agreed, adding pointedly, 'Your poor wife, she must have felt very beset, having two ardent supplicants for her favours.'

Lord Fitton Legh looked as though he might explode. 'Allow me to tell you, madam, that your reaction betrays your class, or rather your lack of it,' he sneered. 'Any person of breeding would understand—'

'What? What is there to understand other than that my grandson and your wife have been having an affair under your nose? Is blue blood thinner than red? Do you wish me to understand that persons of breeding do not have affairs? Come, Lord Fitton Legh, let's be plain with one another. You wish to see my grandson punished.'

'Punished? I shall see to it that he is ruined. You can make up your mind to that. You won't be foisting him off on the county as a prospective parliamentary candidate now, Mrs Pickford. When people learn of the way he has insulted my wife— Oh, you may look at me like that, but Cassandra is prepared to swear on the Bible that the crime was all his. My wife had confided to her how upset she was about your grandson's ungentlemanly manner towards her, and naturally when Cassandra heard my wife cry out she hurried to her aid, only to discover your grandson on the point of assaulting her.'

'Shocking indeed, and I dare say a total pack of lies. Whilst it is none of my business I would caution you against making your story public, Lord Fitton Legh. There are always those who believe that there is no smoke without a fire and, after all, Lady Fitton Legh is a very beautiful and high-spirited young woman married to a much older husband.'

'Why, you . . . I'll ruin him, I tell you. He won't be able to show his face in Cheshire for the rest of his life.'

'I understand your feelings. Greg has behaved badly. I am quite prepared to punish him for that by banishing him from Cheshire – and indeed from England – for a time. However, I am not prepared to stand by and see him ruined.'

'You can't prevent it.'

'Such a pity that you should have to face this additional worry. I hear that your father-in-law has lost a very great deal of money on Wall Street recently.'

Blanche paused and looked down at her hands, as though more intent on studying them than continuing their discussion, before lifting her gaze to Lord Fitton Legh's face and continuing almost gently, 'You yourself are currently rather, shall we say, overextended – so much so, in fact, that you have had to mortgage Fitton Hall.'

'You can't possibly know that.'

'Oh, but you see I do. You know, it is always rather foolish, I think, to let young people have their head without checking them, especially a certain type of young person. I am thinking of poor Cassandra here. One does not like to say too much, of course, but there has been talk about her preference for her own sex. I dare say there will be those who will wonder about the true provenance of her story with regard to my grandson. So sordid and unpleasant. But alas, it is too late now to remedy the situation. However, I'm sure that, two older and wiser heads together, between us you and I can come up with something more balanced and closer to the truth. A young man, foolish and impressionable, falls in love with a devoted and beautiful young wife. A regrettable situation but understandable. Of course, neither of them has any intention of giving way to their feelings. They are, after all, very honourable. Sadly, though, events conspire to throw them into one another's company, a foolish moment of weakness on the part of the young man, allied to loneliness on the part of the devoted wife, lead to an embrace, which is instantly regretted by both parties. Unfortunately, though, this embrace was witnessed by an overexcitable young woman who has yet to learn the ways of the world.

'Those with wiser heads decide that the young man should be sent away in order to learn the error of his ways; the devoted wife remains exactly that, of course. The young man – naturally and honourably – says nothing of the fact that the lonely wife invited him into the privacy of her private quarters and without a chaperone, knowing that her husband was absent. He, however, did admit this folly on her part to, shall we say, his family. But why torment the poor girl with the threat of even more shame than she must already bear? She has learned her lesson, we must suppose.'

'That's blackmail.'

'No, Lord Fitton Legh,' Blanche corrected him coldly. 'It's self-preservation. I understand that your pride has suffered a severe blow, but I am sure that the application of a comfortable sum of money – enough, shall we say, to pay off your creditors and enable you to keep Fitton Hall – will aid its speedy recovery.'

Blanche waited for half an hour after Lord Fitton Legh had left before removing the photograph frame she always kept in the top drawer of her desk. A young man looked back at her from his photograph. Her son. Greg's father.

'You should have lived,' she told him, her throat dry, like her eyes. 'If you had lived none of this would have happened.'

When she had replaced the photograph in her desk drawer she rang for Wilson, telling him, 'When Master Greg comes in, tell him that I wish to see him.'

God, but it felt good to be finally free of Caroline. Three whole days had passed now without her making any attempt to contact him. Greg felt positively light-headed with relief. In fact, he felt so good he wanted to celebrate. With Maisie, he decided with a grin, as he climbed out of his Bugatti and hurried into Denham, too impatient to wait for the butler to take his cap and his coat, and hurling first his cap and then his coat in the direction of the coat-stand with a neat overarm action, and a cheery 'Howzat?'

His coat missed, but his cap landed neatly on one of the hooks.

'Good catch, eh, what?' He congratulated himself as Wilson bent to retrieve his coat.

'Mrs Pickford said to tell you the minute you came in that she wants to see you,' the butler informed him.

'Does she so? Well, I'd better toddle along and see what she wants then, hadn't I?' Greg laughed.

'Well, Gregory, is there anything you feel you might want to tell me?'

Greg moved his weight from one foot to the other. It was always wise to be cautious when his grandmother called him 'Gregory'.

'Not really, Grandmother, unless it's that I wouldn't mind nipping off to London for a few days. See how little Amber's getting on, you know.'

'Well, I'm delighted to hear of your concern for your cousin, Gregory, delighted but somewhat surprised, since by your own behaviour you have placed your family in a situation that threatens all our reputations.'

Greg's stomach plunged. He was quick-witted enough to know where the conversation was leading.

'I refer of course to your affair with Caroline Fitton Legh. Lord Fitton Legh came here to see me earlier.'

Fitton Legh knew? Greg grew pale.

'Apparently Cassandra urged Caroline to confide in him, having found you both *in flagrante*, although as I understand it, the *flagrante* was more on your part than Caroline's, since according to Cassandra you were assaulting her.'

'That's a lie.'

'And the affair? Is that also a lie?'

Greg didn't dare say anything.

'So then, I take it that you *were* having an affair with Caroline Fitton Legh.'

'It was nothing, just a bit of fun.'

'On the contrary, it was far from nothing. It will be impossible now, of course, for you to hope to be selected to replace the sitting MP when he retires; Lord Fitton Legh will see to that. The Fitton Leghs are too well connected for their influence to be ignored, Gregory, and I am disappointed that you didn't have the intelligence to think of that before becoming involved with her. Lord Fitton Legh has demanded that you leave Cheshire, and in the circumstances I agree with him that that would be a good idea. Were it not for that wretched girl Cassandra being so quick to spread the tale, it might have been possible to mend matters, but unfortunately things have gone too far for that. Now Lord Fitton Legh's pride demands retribution in the form of your banishment. I have to say that I am most seriously displeased with you, Gregory.'

'It wasn't my fault,' Greg protested. 'It was Caroline who began it, I swear it, Grandmother, and then when I tried to end it she wouldn't let me.'

Blanche looked at him and then said calmly, 'Whilst I was waiting for you to return, I wrote to Henry Jardine in Hong Kong on your behalf, asking him if he could find you a place in his business. It will be good experience for you. Jardine is a first-rate businessman, the raw silk for the mill is shipped via him, and our families have known one another for three generations. Whilst I don't expect you to involve yourself in trade, Gregory, it is always wise for a person to know how to handle money, as I am sure Lord Fitton Legh would agree.'

Blanche's loathing of trade had meant that she refused to invest in the stock exchange. Her wealth was all in cash – held in the same bank vaults as that of the royal family.

'Hong Kong?' Greg was about to object but then he remembered that he had heard some interesting tales about the fun enjoyed by the ex-pat community living there. Hong Kong couldn't possibly be as dull as Macclesfield.

Greg found it easy to shrug off anything unpleasant, so long as he wasn't constantly reminded of it.

'I take it there isn't anything else you wish to tell me with regard to your affair with Caroline?' his grandmother was asking him.

Greg thought fleetingly of Caroline's claim that she was having his child and then dismissed it. If she was breeding then if she had any sense she would insist that the brat was her husband's, Greg decided. That being the case, there was no need for him to mention it to his grandmother.

In fact, he congratulated himself a couple of hours later, he had come off pretty well, all things considered. His grandmother was being frosty with him now but she would soon come round. And as for being banished to Hong Kong, he reckoned it would be a piece of cake, and he'd have a fine old time.

'So, Fitton Legh is forcing Blanche to send her precious grandson to Hong Kong. Bit of luck, eh, Cassandra catching him out like that? Mind you, I'd warned her to keep an eye on him when she said that he'd taken to calling when Fitton Legh wasn't there. Plain as the nose on Cassandra's face what was going on.'

As Jay listened to his grandfather he recognised that he was in high glee over Greg's disgrace. Jay certainly couldn't remember when he had last seen him in such good spirits.

He'd obviously been drinking quite heavily, as the decanter on the table beside him was nearly empty. Jay frowned to see it, knowing that his grandfather had been warned to moderate his drinking for the sake of his health.

The gossip about the affair had spread fast, of course, but it had come as no surprise to Jay, who had guessed exactly what was going on.

'It's a pity you aren't more of a de Vries, Jay,' Barrant told him. 'If you were only half the man your uncle was, you'd have had the Pickford granddaughter falling for you and then we could have brought her down as well.'

Jay had felt many things for his grandfather over the years – compassion, pity, frustration, love – but this was the first time he had felt anger and contempt. He accepted that his grandfather would take pleasure in Greg's downfall because it was also Blanche's downfall, but it had not occurred to him until now to suspect that Barrant might actually have deliberately meddled and stoked the fire that had burned Greg, via Cassandra. Now, though, with Barrant's tongue loosened by triumph and brandy, Jay was unwillingly aware that his grandfather could be more manipulative than he had previously considered.

'If that's what you have in mind then you'd be better off suggesting it to Cassandra. She obviously has more of a taste for betrayal than I do,' Jay told him grimly, adding for good measure, 'Although whether or not that is a de Vries characteristic I dare say you will know better than I, Grandfather.'

Let his grandfather make what he liked of his comment. If Barrant didn't know by now that Cassandra preferred her own sex to his then perhaps it was time he found out. After all he had shown no mercy for the vulnerabilities of others so why should any be shown to his? His suggestion with regard to Amber was as unthinkable as it was distasteful. The anger Jay felt at the thought of Amber being harmed or hurt in any way burned in his chest. He was glad that she was in London and out of reach of his grandfather's malice.

Chapter Eight

Spring 1930

Amber was so happy. She felt as though her happiness was bursting out of her in the same unstoppable tide that had all the signs of spring appearing in Hyde Park. She was enjoying herself so much. Her happiness fizzed and bubbled inside her, and all the more so on days like today when she was with Lord Robert.

So far, as 'the professor', Lord Robert had taken her to the *Vogue* offices, where she had glimpsed Mrs Alison Settle, *Vogue*'s Editor, and been introduced to Madge Garland, the Fashion Editor, who had asked them rather pointedly to 'remind Cecil, when you see him, that I am still awaiting the sketches he promised me'.

They had gone to the British Museum, where Cecil had given instructions that they were to look at all things Egyptian. But best of all, so far as Amber was concerned, had been their visit to the Royal Society of Arts behind the Strand, where she had gazed in wonder at the architecture and listened to a lecture on its provenance. Lord Robert had promised her that he would take her to West Wycombe, the village recently bought by the society in order that it could be preserved for future generations.

He had set her 'homework', which consisted of instructions

such as 'design a south-facing room setting for a blonde socialite who wears only Wedgwood blue', or 'Lord R. wishes to have new curtains for his drawing room – the theme is Egyptian Napoleonic – show three different styles.'

Sometimes his instructions were accompanied by little sketches similar to the ones he sketched for *Vogue*; other times they were just rough notes, but Amber adored receiving them almost as much as she adored being with Lord Robert – especially when they were on their own, without Saville, as they were today.

Amber looked adoringly at Lord Robert, dressed as usual in his academic 'disguise'.

The days were flying by now, what with the pleasure of her outings with Lord Robert to look forward to, the Comtesse du Brissac's French conversation, the Constance Spry flower-arranging classes she and Louise were now attending, and of course the deportment classes, which no longer held any fears for Amber now she had mastered the curtsy.

Add to that the social events she was also now attending and there were hardly enough hours in the day, as she had just complained to Lord Robert.

'Lady Rutland is treating you better now, is she?' he asked.

'Yes,' Amber confirmed. There was no point in spoiling the day by confessing to him how uncomfortable and out of place she felt at these social events and how conscious she was of the chilly looks she received from the mothers of other débutantes, the stiff silences and awkward pauses, when those débutantes refused to talk to her. Louise didn't help, of course. She had made it plain that she despised Amber, and of course her close friends had followed suit.

In some ways Amber didn't blame them. She was, after all, an outsider amongst them. She suspected she would have felt alien even without Louise's unpleasantness.

'I had a letter from my cousin Greg this morning. He's going to Hong Kong. My grandmother thinks it will be good for him, he says,' she told Lord Robert, deliberately changing the subject. 'It was a shock because he had been going to be a Member of Parliament. He writes that he thinks that Hong Kong will be much more fun than becoming an MP.'

Since Greg himself had written so enthusiastically about the change of plan, Amber could only be pleased for him. But she'd miss him so much, knowing he was halfway across the world, and somewhere unknown to her, where, unlike at Macclesfield, she would be unable to picture him mentally.

'I dare say he is quite right,' Robert agreed. She was so innocent. Frighteningly so at times, he acknowledged. Being with Amber was like drinking a glass of clear pure water: a shock at first to the system when one was accustomed to far more intoxicating substances, but somehow it left a yearning within one to return to its simplicity and goodness.

'I'm pleased for Greg, but disappointed for myself as I was hoping he would be at the dance Lady Rutland is to give after the presentation,' Amber admitted. 'At least then I would have known that I'd have someone to dance with.'

'You will most definitely have someone to dance with.'

Amber looked at him. 'You mean *you* will be there?' Her eyes sparkled.

'I wouldn't miss it for the world,' Robert told her, realising as he said the words that they were true.

They were in Selfridges, and soon it would be time to leave since Amber had a fitting for her presentation dress. As always, though, she wanted to draw out the precious minutes she spent with Lord Robert and so she begged him, 'Tell me again about the party when they had a treasure hunt and the clues had everyone running into Selfridges and jumping over the counters.'

Robert shook his head and laughed. 'Those were foolish times – I should never have told you about them.'

'I'm glad you did. They must have been such fun.'

'Come now, it's time you were back in Cadogan Place,' Lord Robert told her firmly.

'Are you ready yet?' Louise asked Amber aggressively, 'only I'm not waiting for you if you aren't, and Mummy said to tell you that you're to come with us to a tea party later.'

Amber didn't mind so much about going for her gown fitting, but she would much rather not have been going to the tea party.

The gowns were being made by Reville in Hanover Square, the same court dressmaker who had not only made Lady Rutland's own gown a generation before, but who had also been one of Queen Mary's favourite dressmakers. Although Amber's grandmother had been content to let Lady Rutland choose the dressmaker, she had insisted on selecting the fabric for Amber's gown herself. It was *de rigueur* that débutantes wore only white or the palest of pastel-coloured gowns. For Amber's gown her grandmother had chosen a silk for the underdress that was neither white nor cream but somewhere in between, over which was to go lace sewn with tiny pearls so that it looked as though the entire skirt of the overdress was made from mother-of-pearl. To complement the fabric Blanche had specified that the dress itself was to be made in the simplest of styles, little more than a narrow full-length shift at the front, but at the back from the base of Amber's spine the overskirt was split to reveal a fan of plain satin pleats that formed a small train.

Louise had laughed mockingly when they had gone for

their first fittings, twirling around in her own far more full-skirted and fussy gown, with its daringly peach underskirts showing through the heavy lace overdress, but now as they both watched the undeniable elegance of Amber's gown emerging from the seamstress's clever fingers, Louise's mockery had given way to scowls.

Not that their presentation gowns were the only new clothes the girls had. Amber's grandmother's letters were full of detailed instructions about which shops Amber was to visit in order to be fitted for the outfits Blanche had already discussed by telephone with the shop manageresses. Invariably Louise too had a new outfit paid for by Blanche, but Louise's choice was her own, and Amber was beginning to recognise that whilst her grandmother had 'good taste', Louise clearly did not.

Now as she brushed her hair, and thanked her maid for helping her, Amber acknowledged that she didn't much care whether Louise waited for her or not.

She had had such a wonderful time this morning with Lord Robert. She hugged her pleasure to herself, wrapping it around her. What did Louise's unkindness matter when she had such a wonderful friend in Lord Robert?

The fitting didn't take very long, although Louise complained that her dress had been trimmed with the wrong lace. On their way back Amber insisted on calling in at Hatchards to order a copy of Evelyn Waugh's new book.

It was only after she had completed giving her order that she realised that Louise was now in conversation with a man who must have come into the shop after them. Although she didn't know why, something about the way Louise was behaving made Amber feel uneasy and uncomfortable. When Louise didn't make any attempt to introduce Amber to her companion she felt relieved.

98

Louise was plainly enjoying the encounter, though, and in the end Amber left the shop without her and was several yards down the street when Louise finally caught up with her, out of breath but looking like the cat who'd got the cream.

The tea party was being given by Lady Wyesnaith at her Carlton Terrace home. Louise had chosen to wear a very close-fitting satin sleeveless dress in bright blue – almost the same shade as her eyes – with a deep V neckline, whilst Lady Rutland was wearing her customary rusty black beneath her furs.

Amber, without anyone to guide her, had asked her maid uncertainly, 'What should I wear, do you think?' and she had guessed from the pleased look Louise had given the softly draped, very simple pale amber frock, with its toning silk velvet jacket embroidered with amber bugle beads Amber had chosen, that Louise considered her own outfit to be far superior.

Since Lady Wyesnaith was presenting her own daughter at one of the court presentations, the tea party was one of those events, given by the sponsors of débutantes, ostensibly for the girls to get to know one another and the mothers to check diaries to ensure that no important débutante balls clashed, but in reality for the mothers to check out the competition their daughters might face amongst the other girls and to tailor their guest lists accordingly.

Amber, who had listened diligently whilst the Comtesse du Brissac instructed them on the importance of small talk and how one should engage in it, did her best when Lady Rutland abandoned her at a tea table with one spare seat without introducing her, but Amber knew from the silence that her intrusion was exactly that, which made the hand she felt on her arm and the familiar voice of her best friend from school, exclaiming happily, 'Amber, I can't believe it's you. How wonderful!' all the more welcome.

They had agreed, at Amber's suggestion, during their final term together at school that they would not write to one another. Amber had believed then that their paths lay in very different directions and, knowing how conservative Beth was, she hadn't wanted to embarrass her schoolfriend by clinging to their friendship when there was such a wide social divide between them. Now, of course, things were different – at least for the present, and whilst Amber was mixing in the same social circles as her schoolfriend.

Within seconds Amber was being spirited away to be introduced to Beth's mother, who greeted her with such genuine kindness that Amber felt close to tears.

The Countess of Levington was an older and worldlier version of her daughter. They shared the same features, and good clear English skin, although Beth's hair was fairer than her mother's. Looking at Beth's mother, Amber could see quite plainly what Beth herself would be in years to come. It was plain that the countess was a loving parent.

A brisk nod of her head confirmed that yes, the countess did indeed remember Beth talking about Amber, her friend from school.

'Your father was, I believe, Russian?' she questioned Beth, with practised ease.

'What are you doing here?' was Beth's first question once they were on their own. 'I thought you wanted to go to art school!'

'I did. But my grandmother wouldn't let me. She's paid Louise's mother to bring me out.'

There, she had said it, and she was holding her head high, even if inside she was dreading what Beth might think.

To her relief Beth's only comment was a sympathetic, 'It must be horrid for you, having to live with Louise.'

Amber gave a heartfelt sigh. 'It is.'

Beth gave her arm a small squeeze. 'Never mind. I'll ask Mummy to make sure that we get invited to the same things. Finishing school in Paris was *awful*, worse than school, and now I still have to go to the Vacani School to learn to curtsy, and you know how clumsy I am.'

'We've done that,' said Amber. 'I was hopeless at first.'

'Oh, were you? That's much better than getting it right first go.'

When Amber looked unconvinced, Beth told her, 'Mummy says that it's always the girls who get the curtsy right from their first class who go and do something silly when they're presented. Oh, watch out, here comes Louise,' she warned.

'What are you two talking about?' Louise demanded suspiciously.

'I was just telling Amber how lovely it is to see her here.'

'She's only here because my mother has taken pity on her,' Louise told Beth sharply.

Amber and Beth exchanged knowing looks.

The three of them, although they themselves did not know it, made an attractive picture standing together, Beth with her soft light brown hair and her sweet expression; Louise, the tallest of the three of them, the most 'knowing', her short bobbed hair as sleek and dark as a raven's wing, and her blue eyes fringed with long dark lashes. But it was Amber, with her strawberry-blonde hair, her dark gold eyes and her perfect bone structure, who lifted the visual appeal of the trio above mere prettiness to true beauty.

'You'll be having a coming-out ball, I expect?' Louise asked Beth.

'Yes,' Beth told her, 'Mummy's already worrying about finding enough young men to invite, especially if there are

101

other balls on the same night. It would be awful if there aren't enough men for us to dance with.'

'Debs' delights, you mean?' Louise looked scornful. 'Who wants to dance with them? Not me. I want to dance with a *real* man, someone exciting and . . . dangerous.'

'From the warnings the comtesse has been giving us about not getting into cabs on our own with debs' delights it sounds as though they *are* dangerous.' Amber pointed out.

'What? Because they might try to steal a kiss?' Louise tossed her head. 'Well, personally I think I'd rather like to know what it's like to be kissed, wouldn't you?'

Whilst Beth looked shocked Amber replied honestly, 'It would depend on who was doing the kissing.'

'Well, yes, of course. He'd have to be handsome, and rich, although I suppose in your case, Amber, all that would matter was him having a title.'

'She's such a cat,' Beth said angrily after Louise had gone. 'She hasn't changed at all.'

Amber said nothing. After all, what could she say when Louise's comment had been the truth, at least as far as her grandmother was concerned?

'I'm so pleased we shall be coming out together,' Beth told Amber warmly. 'I've been dreading it, but now it's going to be fun. Oh, look, Mummy wants us.'

Amber hung back.

'What is it?' Beth demanded.

Uncomfortably Amber explained how she'd been excluded and ignored, adding that she didn't want to put Beth in an embarrassing position by clinging on to her.

'I shouldn't be surprised if it's Lady Rutland people want to avoid and not you,' Beth told her firmly. 'She isn't very well liked, you know.'

And not as well connected or socially powerful as Beth's

mother, as Amber soon discovered, after Beth had insisted on dragging her over to her mother.

People who had ignored her when Lady Rutland had introduced her were now being astonishingly pleasant. Girls who had previously turned their backs on her were now smiling at her and making room for both Beth and Amber to join them round tables set up for tea.

Engrossed in conversation, Amber only noticed the dark look Louise was giving her when she happened to glance up and see her, standing by the door with one of her own coterie of friends.

Seeing her look at Louise, the girl sitting next to Amber told her conspiratorially, 'That's Louise Montford. She's fearfully fast, you know. My brother met her at a house party over Christmas.'

'What do you mean?' Amber asked her curiously.

The other girl gave her a coy look and then told her breathlessly, 'Well, when they were playing hide-and-seek one evening, no one could find Louise for ages, and then when they did find her in one of the boots cupboards she swore that she'd been on her own but someone else said that they'd seen one of the boys sneaking away from the cupboard just before they found Louise. And then another night she went and joined the boys in the billiard room after supper, and she was the only girl there. One of the boys, Edward Fearton, told my brother that she'd let him kiss her and that she'd sat on his lap and let him put his hand on her knee. If she isn't careful she's going to get herself in an awful lot of trouble.'

Amber digested these confidences in silence. It was true that the kind of behaviour the other girl had just described was very fast and not acceptable at all for a young unmarried girl. There was a certain wildness about Louise at times, she admitted, as though the other girl enjoyed taking risks and breaking the rules. But the reality was that Louise could not afford to flout convention, not if she was to make the kind of marriage her mother needed her to make to repair their family finances, to someone of equal social standing to her own, and with money: the kind of man that every mother wanted for her daughter and the kind of man too who could take his pick of socially acceptable well-brought-up young women when looking for a wife. The kind of man who was not likely to choose a young woman with the wrong kind of reputation.

'I suppose you think you're something special now just because Beth has taken up with you,' Louise challenged Amber later when they had returned to Cadogan Place. 'Well, you aren't. You're still just a Macclesfield mill girl. What was Julia Smethington-Blythe saying to you about me? And don't say she wasn't because I know she was. I could tell from the way she was whispering to you.'

'She mentioned that her brother had met you at a house party, that's all,' Amber answered diplomatically.

'Oh, him. He was a *complete* drip. He couldn't even dance, and his teeth stick out.'

Louise scowled. She hated Amber almost as much as she hated the life that being poor imposed on her. Louise craved luxury and excitement; she wanted to sweep into the most fashionable places wearing the most expensive clothes and jewels, on the arm of a handsome man and looking so wonderful that people turned to stare at her.

Louise had never known a time when money hadn't dominated her life. Her mother rarely spoke of anything other than their lack of it. Louise had only been able to attend the exclusive girls' school she had because a relative had paid the fees.

Mummy was always irritatingly vague about the exact

relationship between her and 'cousin Hugh'. So much so, in fact, that Louise was beginning to wonder if they were lovers.

Louise was extremely interested in people's sexual relationships, and all the more so if they were illicit. In fact, Louise found the whole idea of sex very exciting. It must be rather fun to be the mistress of a very rich man; a man who was prepared to indulge one's every whim and shower one with clothes and jewels. First, of course, she would have to be married: a rich husband and then a rich lover. She hated being only seventeen and treated like a child. She couldn't wait to be grown up and free to do whatever she wanted.

The invitations were mounting up on the mantelpiece in the drawing room of the house in Cadogan Place, and all the more so, Amber suspected, since Beth's mother had kind-heartedly taken Amber under her wing.

Some mothers might be having to cut corners, but of course, thanks to Amber's grandmother, there was no question of economising for the ball Lady Rutland was giving for Louise and Amber, after their formal presentation.

Lord Cadogan had given permission for the private gardens to be used, and a marquee was to be erected there, whilst decorators had been set to work refurbishing the reception rooms.

Some families were hosting private dinners before their balls but Lady Rutland had eschewed this idea, much to Amber's relief.

Along with everything else she had managed to organise during her week's stay in London, Amber's grandmother had chosen both the flowers for the ball and the supper menu – a copy of one chosen by the Duke of Westminster for a ball at Eaton Hall he had given for Royalty – even though she herself was not going to be present.

Amongst the invitations arriving at Cadogan Place was one from the Hon. Mrs Guinness to attend a ball at 10 Buckingham Street, which had caused Amber a pang of anxious guilt, and worry that Lady Rutland might wonder how Diana Guinness had come to be sending them an invitation, or even worse, that somehow or other it might come out that she had met Amber at the Ritz, until Lady Rutland had remarked that there was a family connection between her own late mother and Diana's family, the Mitfords.

'We have been invited as well,' Beth had informed Amber, when Amber had told her about the invitation. 'My mother's family are connected to the Guinnesses, although Mummy is a bit concerned about me going.' Beth had pulled a small face. 'I don't think Mummy approves of the fact that Diana is so very modern, but I think she is such fun. My mother's godson is part of that set and he says that she gives the most wonderful parties.' Beth giggled. 'To be honest I don't think that Mummy always approves of Teddy either, but of course she can't say so, and since he has insisted on accompanying us she can hardly refuse. I'm looking forward to it.'

'So am I,' Amber had agreed fervently.

It was nearly a week since she'd last seen Lord Robert, and she missed him dreadfully, although he had warned her that he was having to go away for a few days.

She may have told Beth that she was looking forward to the Guinness party, but right now, as she stood in front of her bedroom mirror whilst Renton finished fastening the buttons of her kid gloves, prior to Amber leaving for the ball, Amber acknowledged ruefully that what she was actually feeling came closer to nervousness.

Amber's Norman Hartnell gown was a soft eau-de-Nil.

The bodice was trimmed with rows of tiny crystal drops that shone in the light, and was modestly high-necked, but the skirt was rather dashingly cut on the bias.

Over it Amber would be wearing a matching draped satin bolero jacket several shades darker than her dress, but lined in exactly the same eau-de-Nil satin.

Her hair had been dressed in soft curls, the pins securing it decorated with small individual crystals to complement those on the bodice of her dress.

Her matching satin purse was just the right size to hold a dance card, a handkerchief and a small bottle of scent. Lady Rutland did not approve of makeup, although Amber knew that Louise ignored her mother's disapproval and wore lipstick.

'Are you sure I look all right, Renton?' Amber asked her maid anxiously. She had found the maid a little stern and formidable at first, but she had quickly come to value her judgement and her good taste, and had soon found that she was turning to Renton for the answers to her questions on matters of etiquette in high society with which she was unfamiliar, rather than Lady Rutland. Renton, Amber had learned, had grown up on the estate of the Earl of Radsbury in Norfolk and had gone into service with the countess at fourteen, determinedly working her way up through the household hierarchy until a vacancy as a lady's maid to one of the countess's friends had brought her to London, and then to Cadogan Place when her previous mistress had died.

Renton had told Amber that she had been on the point of returning to Norfolk to share a cottage with her sister, who was now retired, when she had been interviewed by Amber's grandmother.

'I could see straight away that Mrs Pickford knew what was what,' Renton had told Amber, surprising her with the approval she could hear in her voice, 'and that she knew how to treat a person properly.'

Amber acknowledged that she was glad that her grandmother had chosen Renton to be her maid.

'You look just as you should,' Renton told her now, giving Amber one of her very rare smiles. Amber felt that, in her own way, Renton was every bit as formidable as her grandmother.

The road outside the Guinnesses' house was filled with chauffeur-driven cars conveying guests to the party, but whilst Louise was anxious to get out of the car and impatient at the delay, Amber was content to gaze wide-eyed at people whom she recognised from the newspapers and the society magazines; people like Emerald Cunard, who was wearing what Amber knew immediately must be a Schiaparelli gown, white satin with a black satin cape. Eventually their car was close enough to the entrance to the house for them to get out, Lady Rutland's gown of puce satin rustling stiffly as they climbed the front steps.

Once inside, a smiling maid offered to relieve them of their wraps.

Amber's eyes widened when she saw how low-cut Louise's rose-pink gown was, surely much lower than when they had had their fittings.

The elegant reception room on the first floor was filled with so many people that the sheer volume of their conversation made it impossible to hear the music from the quartet playing in the antechamber.

A waiter carrying a tray of glasses came towards them. 'Cocktail, madam?'

Amber looked uncertainly at the bright green liquid, but Louise was already reaching for a glass whilst her mother, who was engaged in conversation with another chaperone, had her back to her. She had finished her drink and picked up a second by the time Lady Rutland joined them.

Amber was relieved to see Beth, but her relief turned to amazement and delight when she saw who was standing at the countess's side.

Lord Robert!

Confusingly, though, the countess was asking Lady Rutland if she might introduce 'her godson' and Amber had no idea what to say when the familiar hand, white-gloved tonight, of course, took her own.

'Amber, my dear, please allow me to introduce to you my godson, Lord Robert Devenish, the Earl of Montclare. Teddy, Miss Amber Vrontsky.'

Amber held her breath, praying that Lady Rutland would not recognise in Lord Robert Devenish the professor who had been attending Cadogan Place, whilst her own head spun dizzily with the shock of discovering that 'her' Lord Robert was also Beth's 'Teddy'.

Lord Robert was smiling at her. 'Miss Vrontsky, I do hope I can look forward to the pleasure of dancing with you later?'

He had that mischievous look in his eyes that Amber now knew so well. Her heart was beating giddily fast.

Before she could answer him, though, the countess said firmly, 'You may dance with Amber, Teddy, but you are not to introduce her to those rackety friends of yours.'

'Cecil would be most hurt if he heard you describing him as merely rackety, Aunt Phoebe. He likes to think of himself as positively dissipated,' replied Robert, laughing.

The countess gave him a reproving look. 'Well, I dare say that your grandfather would agree with him.'

Immediately his expression changed, the amusement dying out of his eyes, to be replaced by a hard blankness that made his handsome features look as though they had been carved from stone. Amber was shocked. She had never seen him look so formidable and withdrawn.

'Louise's gown is fearfully low-cut, isn't it?' Beth whispered to Amber under cover of her mother's conversation with 'Teddy'. 'I'm surprised her mother allowed it.'

'It wasn't like that when we went for our last fittings,' Amber whispered back.

'It makes her look very fast. No wonder George Ponsonby's made a beeline for her.'

Amber looked over to where Louise was standing talking to a dark-haired man of medium height. As it had done before, something in Louise's manner made Amber feel uncomfortable.

'Just look at how close to him she's standing.' Beth looked scandalised. 'Mummy was talking about George Ponsonby last week. She says that he's a fortune-hunter and an adventurer, and not to be trusted. There was a terrible scandal a couple of years ago when this poor girl had told all her friends that they were going to be engaged, and then he just dropped her. Her family had to send her abroad. There was talk of . . . you know . . .'

'What?' Amber demanded, puzzled.

Beth leaned closer to her. 'People were saying that she was going to have a baby and that was why she had to go abroad.'

They both looked at Louise, who was now dancing with George Ponsonby. He might be handsome, but he was one of those men who somehow looked too smooth and polished, his smile too ready, and his hair too brilliantined. He was holding Louise very tightly but, far from looking uncomfortable, she seemed to be revelling in his attention.

'Mummy said earlier that Louise's manner is far too forward and that it's already causing comment,' Beth added.

* * *

110

Louise was dancing with George Ponsonby again when Lord Robert guided Amber out onto the dance floor a little later.

'Why does Beth's mother call you Teddy?' she asked him.

'It was my mother's nickname for me when I was a baby. She died when I was two, and since Aunt Phoebe was her best friend she still uses it.'

Amber gave him a sympathetic look. 'It must have been horrid for you having to grow up without her.'

'Yes, it was rather.'

His voice was clipped and Amber guessed he wanted her to change the subject.

'I was so relieved that Lady Rutland didn't recognise you.'

'Lady Rutland is the kind of person who only sees what she wants to see.'

He was an excellent dancer. Amber felt quite light-headed with the ease with which he swung her round as they glided across the floor.

As he whirled her round, Lord Robert told her, 'Cecil's over there with Diana, and Ralph Seaforde. I shall be in fearful trouble with Aunt Phoebe, though, if I take you over to join them.'

Amber looked in the direction he was indicating. Ralph Seaforde was tall and willowy, with dark hair and slightly olive skin. He turned to look at them, and for some reason Amber felt herself recoil, which was silly because he wasn't even looking at her. He was looking – staring, really – at Lord Robert . . .

The ball was over and they were on their way home. Amber was so tired she could barely keep her eyes open and her feet positively hurt from all the dancing she had done.

Although the ball had been very exciting, and she had danced with Lord Robert, somehow the evening had left her feeling confused and not as happy as she felt she ought to be, although she couldn't explain to herself just why she felt the way she did, except that it had something to do with Lord Robert and the way he had seemed different somehow, distant almost at times, and not the kind teasing Lord Robert she knew and liked so much, she acknowledged. Not for the world did she want to admit that the evening – and Lord Robert – had left her feeling slightly forlorn and deflated.

Louise, on the other hand, wasn't tired at all. She was positively fizzing with excitement and energy, her face flushed and her eyes sparkling. George Ponsonby was exactly the kind of man she liked: wickedly handsome and dangerous, and with that look about him that said that he could introduce her to the most interesting and exciting things. Just thinking about him brought Louise a sharp thrill of excitement. She had had her fill of kissing inexperienced boys in broom cupboards, and watching the effect she had on them when she teased them with promises she had no intention of keeping. That was schoolgirl stuff, and she wasn't a schoolgirl any more. She was a woman.

Chapter Nine

'Do you ever wonder what our futures really will be, Amber?'

They were at a tea party at the Savoy and it was the day after a luncheon at which they had all been entertained and scared by a fortune-teller hired by their hostess to keep her guests entertained and amused.

Louise predictably had been the first in the queue to step into the small brightly coloured tent, erected in the drawing room, inside which the fortune-teller had been seated.

'No,' Amber answered Beth, teasing her, 'because I already know what yours will be. You will be engaged before the end of the season to a very suitable and delightful young man with a title and a fortune. He will have a large estate in the country and a handsome town house in London, and once you are married you will have lots of deliciously pretty little girls and handsome little boys.'

'And I know what yours will be,' Beth countered. 'You will meet a wonderfully handsome and wickedly dangerous artist, who will fall passionately in love with you, and you with him. He will offer you his heart and his hand. You will refuse him at first, but then once he has proved himself to you, you will accept him and then together you will design the most wonderful silks. I wonder what the fortune-teller told Louise – she was in there for ever.'

'I don't know,' said Amber, 'but whatever it was it must

have pleased her because she has been looking very secretive and smug ever since.'

'I'm getting really nervous about our court presentation and I'll be glad when it's over. I'm so pleased that we'll be at the early courts instead of having to wait until June, aren't you?'

They were to be presented the following day, and Amber agreed, swallowing back her own fear.

'Lady Rotherford, my godmdother, has accepted Mummy's invitation to my ball.' Beth flushed slightly. 'Her son, Alistair, will be escorting her. I haven't seen him for ages, but he used to be such fun, but of course we've got your ball first. Did I tell you that Teddy has insisted on escorting Mummy?' Beth gave her a teasing look. 'Do you know what I think? I think that Teddy could be falling in love with you. He'll be a duke when his grandfather dies, you know, and he's fearfully rich.'

Amber laughed. 'Of course he isn't,' she denied.

The truth was that she rather thought she might be falling in love with *him*, Amber admitted. Not that she was going to say that to Beth, just as she hadn't admitted that she had already known Lord Robert before Beth's mother had introduced them. It was her secret alone, and one that gave her a warm glow every time she thought of him.

'We've had fun together, haven't we?'

Amber nodded.

They were in the rooftop café in Selfridges, Lord Robert in his disguise.

'I hadn't realised that you and Beth were such good friends.'

Suddenly Amber felt anxious. 'It doesn't make any difference, does it?'

'Of course not. You're so busy now that you won't have time for your old professor soon.'

Amber was about to protest when Lord Robert continued, 'Which is just as well. I suspect that we would be found out if we continued with our little game much longer, and whilst it has been both delightful and inno-cent, the last thing I want is for your reputation to be called into question.'

Amber's hand trembled as she put down her china cup. 'Yes, yes, of course. You are right. I know that.'

She did. Amber had learned a very great deal about life during the short time she had been in London. If Beth had been shocked and disapproving about Louise dancing with George Ponsonby, then how much more so would she be if she knew that Amber had been out on her own with Lord Robert? London society loved to gossip, and that gossip could be cruel. A young unmarried girl's reputation must not be tarnished by any trace of scandal.

The loving gentleness of her parents and their marriage seemed a world away from the things Amber saw around her now. People spoke openly of the Prince of Wales's mistress, a married woman, of course. There were so many different rules to be learned and codes to be understood. She had been shocked when she had learned that Diana Guinness, whom Amber had been inclined to hero-worship, talked openly about Evelyn Waugh's devotion to her and had allowed the author virtually to move in with her and Bryan whilst he recovered from his divorce.

In society, once a woman was married and had given her husband an heir, it was, Amber had learned, deemed perfectly acceptable for her to take a lover. Even Beth, who was so prim and proper, spoke openly of relationships between couples who were not married.

A man who was a member of the aristocracy could and

did expect his mistress to be invited to the social events he might be attending and as his partner, provided her pedigree made her socially acceptable to his hostess. They could even be invited to house parties together, but must always be given separate, but conveniently close, rooms. The Prince of Wales when conducting an affair always chose to surround his mistress with a handful of his close friends, sometimes including her husband.

Then there was the other kind of mistress, the ones that men set up in discreet expensive houses in St John's Wood where they visited them. These mistresses were often showgirls of one sort or another. They could accompany their aristocratic lovers to Cannes or Monte Carlo; attend the Grand Prix, and louche parties with them, but they could not accompany their lovers to the kind of formal society events to which a man could take his aristocratic mistress.

There were aristocratic wives who had originally been on the stage, but they were few and far between.

One thing that was non-negotiable, though, was that a young woman who was not married had to preserve her reputation at all costs.

Amber was very close to tears and she was terribly afraid of disgracing herself. She mustn't embarrass Lord Robert by creating a silly scene. She'd miss him so much – he had been so very kind to her – but she was just a young inexperienced girl and he was worldly and so handsome that he could have any girl his heart desired. She couldn't possibly expect him to fall for her, she thought miserably as the dusk started to gather over Oxford Street. That would be the stuff of fairy tales, and she was far too sensible to allow herself to believe in those.

Louise shivered as she waited in the doorway of Harvey Nichols, as much with excitement as impatience. They had chosen this rendezvous because, as George had said, if anyone was to see them Louise could simply claim that she had been shopping and that they had bumped into one another.

She had known from the minute he had looked at her in that meaningful way at the Guinness ball that she would have to see him again. If he hadn't suggested it himself then she would somehow have found a way to make sure that their paths had crossed again.

Louise shivered once more, this time only with excitement. It had made her feel so important when George had singled her out for attention. She knew all about his reputation, of course, but that had only made him seem all the more attractive.

He thought that he could seduce her, but instead she intended to make him fall in love with her. Louise had discovered at a young age how easy it was to manipulate men, and how exciting. There was something in her that craved excitement.

Louise longed for the day when she would be one of those fêted beautiful women whose lives were spent in luxury, their every whim indulged. The life Louise longed for wasn't the one her mother planned for her: a dull boring life of wifely duty to some equally dull and boring man of equal social status to her own to whom she would be expected to be grateful for marrying her, despite the fact that she did not have a dowry. No, what excited Louise was the kind of life she had seen lived by the beautiful young women escorted and indulged by their rich, often much older, lovers; a life that would allow her to dress in beautiful clothes and jewellery and to be part of the fast set that spent their lives in a social whirl of pleasurable activity, that took them from the casinos of the French coast to the louche nightclubs of London, travelling in fast cars and sleek yachts, sleeping in the most luxurious hotel beds, eating the most delicious food and always being on show so that she could be admired; desired by men and envied by her own sex, but always the sparkling glittering centre of the 'in' crowd.

Her lover would adore her and lavish her with gifts – a racehorse or two; jewellery, of course; a pretty town house, and a villa in the South of France. Nothing would be too much, her every wish would be granted. And of course there would be other men, young, deliciously handsome men who would also lust after her and adore her.

She wanted it all. She would have it all, Louise promised herself fiercely.

Her relationship with George Ponsonby was simply the place where she would start.

She couldn't marry George, of course. She didn't want to. He wasn't rich enough, for one thing, but it would be a triumph to be able to claim him as her conquest, especially when he had such a bad reputation. She'd be hailed as the woman who'd finally tamed him.

A taxi was pulling up; George got out and smiled at her. Louise didn't smile back.

'You're late,' she told him petulantly. 'I was just about to go home.'

His mocking 'Liar' brought a flash of temper to Louise's eyes.

'You and I, my dear, are two of a kind. We know what we want and we don't let it go when we've found it. Now, do you really want to go into Harvey Nichols or shall we find somewhere more private? There's a club I know not very far away where they make the most wicked cocktails.'

'That's silly,' Louise told him, refusing to give in to the intoxicating sensation she could feel inside herself. This was so very exciting, because it was so very dangerous. She was playing with fire and she knew it.

George smelled of the sandalwood cologne he always wore, stronger than was considered 'British and gentlemanly'. He was wearing a dark grey suit with a pink chalk-stripe, over a white shirt and with a maroon silk tie. He looked, Louise knew very well, just that little bit too smart, his clothes just that little bit too well fitting, his hat tilted just so at a slightly rakish angle and his confidence very evident in the swagger with which he walked.

'How can a cocktail be wicked?' she responded.

'Come with me and I'll show you.'

Chapter Ten

'But you can't have been as terrified as I was; I promise I was literally frozen and unable to move . . .'

'I was frightful . . .'

'Well, you were lucky. I was shaking all over and I was sure that my combs would come out and my headdress fall off.'

'I can't even remember if I did curtsy, I was so scared . . .'

The ordeal of their presentation was finally over. Amber, Beth and Louise, along with their fellow debs, had had their names called in stentorian tones by a liveried member of the royal household and had made their formal curtsies to the King and the Queen, the photographs had been posed for and taken, and their relief now scented the air as intoxicatingly as a heady wine.

Their voices high-pitched with relief and excitement, the girls all vied with one another with their tales of how terrified they had been.

Amber felt almost light-headed with a relief that she knew went deeper for her than it did for the other girls. They had grown up knowing the role they were to play and that their formal presentation would be part of that role. For her it was different. She had felt awkward and ill at ease, intimidated sometimes by the other girls, especially in the early days, and afraid of what her grandmother's ambitions would mean for her. Afraid too of letting her grandmother down. But now at least that hurdle had been overcome, and she need not fear her grandmother's anger on that account.

She had no idea what the future held, but at least the ordeal of her unwanted presentation was now behind her, Amber acknowledged. She hardly dared let herself think too much about the future and her own hopes. They made her feel too vulnerable and afraid, knowing what her grandmother wanted for her. It would take a miracle to give her the future she wanted, woven with the kind of love her parents had shared, and her own passion for silk, into its every weft and warp.

Tired chaperones were chivvying their charges towards waiting cars, wishing they might return home to bed instead of having to go on to one of the evening's many balls, but only one ball could be the highlight of the season, the one that everyone would remember and use as a yardstick to measure the others against. Lady Rutland, of course, hoped that it would be her ball, just as every other hostess hoped that it might be her own. It was the social diarists in the society papers, though, who would pass judgement and decide.

Whilst they had been at court waiting to be presented, an army of magicians had been working their magic on Cadogan Place, preparing everything for their coming-out ball, or so it seemed to Amber when she saw the tiny lights shimmering in the trees and ornamenting the marquees, through the car window.

Lady Rutland didn't allow her time to marvel, though, bustling the debs inside and into Renton's efficient care, warning their maid that their guests would be arriving for the ball in just over an hour.

'Don't worry, your ladyship, everything is organised.

121

Cook's sent up a bit of supper for them to have before they get into their ball gowns.'

From her bedroom window Amber could look down into the gardens. She could hear the musicians tuning up. Her tummy was churning too much for her to be able to eat the light dish of baked cod sent up by Cook. The scent of fresh paint still permeated the house, even up here in her bedroom. It was a wonderfully balmy evening, a perfect evening for a ball, in fact.

Renton came bustling in, shaking her head when she saw that Amber hadn't eaten her supper.

'I'm sorry, Renton,' Amber apologised, 'I just can't.'

'Well, that makes two of you, because Miss Louise has left hers as well. Now come on, let's get you out of that court dress and into your ball gown.'

'Oh, Amber, this is all so beautiful,' Beth gasped appreciatively two hours later, as they stood side by side in one of the marquees, flushed and breathless from dancing, and they drank the silver and black champagne cocktails that had been specially created for the ball.

The interior to the marquee had been lined with mother-of-pearl silk, and tied with white and black ribbons and bunches of white and silver flowers to match the huge urns of white and silver flowers outside. The black satin ceiling was covered in clouds of white tulle studded with tiny silver stars. Black and silver cloths covered the tables and the lights shone softly on the silver-gilt chairs, their backs tied with black and white satin ribbons and small posies of white gardenias and silver-painted foliage. It was a simple colour scheme and Amber had worried that it might seem dull after the exuberance of the many costumed and themed balls that were all the rage. But it looked simply magical.

Even the gowns Amber and Louise were wearing had been chosen to harmonise with the colour scheme. Louise was wearing a gown of silver lace, over an underdress of white satin with a daringly plunging back, so that her creamy skin was revealed through the lace. She had her hair newly shingled, which suited her, but she was sulking because her mother had refused to invite George Ponsonby.

Amber's gown was in the bias-cut style of Vionnet, in four-inch bands of white satin, white seamed with narrow bands of tiny silver tissue stars. Amber too had had her hair shingled, but in a much softer style than Louise's, and two pretty diamanté clips in the shape of hearts kept her curls in place.

Later, when Amber actually overheard Emerald Cunard remarking approvingly to someone that the pale colours of the debs' gowns and the white theme of the marquee reminded her of the elegance of one of Syrie Maugham's famous white room schemes, Amber's heart swelled with so much pride that she thought it might burst.

Even Lady Rutland was smiling for once, graciously accepting everyone's praise, although privately Amber knew that it was her own grandmother who should have been receiving it for she had been the one to plan everything. It bewildered Amber that someone with such a strong sense of style as her grandmother should turn her back on the fabric that to Amber possessed more of that quality than any other.

Even though the ball was far from over, it was already being pronounced a success. Amber could have filled her dance card twice over, thanks to the good offices of Lord Cadogan, who had generously stepped in to act as a male presence at the ball, and had also conjured up a score and more dashing young men with the right kind of pedigree from the Blues and Royals, who could be seen dotted here and there amongst the guests, their dress uniforms making a vivid splash of colour against the ladies' gowns and the men's evening dress.

Amber had danced with several of them herself, but best of all had been dancing with Lord Robert, who had kept his promise to come to the ball.

Lord Robert . . . There was a tiny bruised place in Amber's heart now when she thought about him. She wasn't going to be silly about it, she had told herself. And it would be foolish to give any meaning to Beth's statement that he was falling in love with her. He must know so many pretty girls – prettier than she, and far more suitable. He was twenty-seven after all, a full ten years older than she. But he wasn't married, a tiny voice in her head said . . . Amber's heart gave a little thump, and then another as she looked up and saw that he was coming towards her.

'I hope you are going to save me another dance,' he told her.

Amber wanted to say that she would have saved him *all* her dances, had he asked.

'Only if you promise that you will take me to West Compton,' she told him.

She could see that she had struck the right note because his eyes had that lovely warm twinkle in them.

'I've just been speaking with Diana and she said to tell you how lovely you look and how much she's hoping you can be friends.'

'Oh, that's so kind.'

'And Cecil says that he is extremely cross that your grandmother has not asked him to take a formal photograph of you, but that he is going to anyway, and that he intends to tell Lady Rutland so.'

Amber was becoming quite used to the flamboyant way of speaking and dressing adopted by Lord Robert's set, even if something about the way that Ralph Seaforde watched Lord Robert all the time made her feel uncomfortable.

Both Lord Robert and Cecil had sent her corsages to wear, but instead she had worn the one that Jay had sent for her, laughing when Lord Robert had teased her about her secret admirer. She had been so thrilled this morning when the flowers had arrived with a small note to say that they were from Jay, and even more touched when she learned from Renton that he had actually telephoned and asked to speak to her to solicit her advice on what kind of corsage would be most appropriate.

Dear Jay. She wished that he and Greg could have been here. Lady Rutland and Louise weren't her family, after all. In fact, she felt closer to Beth's mother, and it had been the countess who had discreetly checked that she was holding her bouquet properly before she was called in to make her curtsy, and who had produced a clean handkerchief for her for those tears afterwards, as well as one for Beth.

Louise wasn't enjoying the ball whatsoever. In fact she was very angry. With George and with her mother. Before she had learned that George was not going to be invited and that nothing she could say would change her mother's mind, she had told George that she expected him to come and dance with her, but he had refused, saying that he had a prior engagement.

'Then you must break it,' she had told him imperiously.

'If I do that then it will have to be worth my while to do so,' he had responded.

She had known what he meant, of course, but she was not so stupid as to let him trick her like that.

When she hadn't responded he had continued, 'You would have to promise me something very special.'

'You know I can't do that.'

He had smiled at her then in a way that she hadn't liked, saying smoothly, 'Well now, I dare say your mother has been warned not to allow the heiress to meet any fortune-hunters. She's a pretty-looking piece, I must say, and very tempting even without the grandmother's money. Almost makes me wish *I* had a title.'

Louise had been so angry that she had tried to hit him, but George had been too quick for her, twisting her arm behind her back so painfully that she had cried out.

And that was when he had kissed her. God, but it had been so exciting. And it had made her so angry. She was still angry. Angry and on edge, and desperate for one of the cocktails to which George had introduced her. And another of those passionate kisses . . .

These weeks in London had opened Amber's eyes to so much, she thought as her partner thanked her for their dance and bowed. Her parents' love for one another was still her ideal, but she recognised now that for most young women of Beth and Louise's class the right husband was considered more important than love, especially by their families. The right marriage, a good marriage, was a necessity if they were to enjoy the position in society to which they had been born.

Diana Guinness, for instance, made no bones about how much she enjoyed her husband, Bryan's, wealth. Without the advantage of a good marriage how were one's sons and daughters to be provided for and their futures in turn secured? If the benefits of social advantage were not worth having, then why were so many mothers anxious to push their daughters up from the middle class, and why did society look down on them and mock them for their ambitions? Social privilege was a fiercely guarded territory and just as subtly out of bounds to those who did not have the

126

right credentials to enter it as Lord Cadogan's gardens were to those who could only stand and stare in through the iron railings.

To marry well might not be what *she* wanted, but she could understand now why so many girls did, Amber acknowledged ruefully, as she left the marquee to slip outside and make her way along one of the paths through the shadows of the garden so that she could enjoy the cool air.

Even Beth had confided to her that she was anxious not to disappoint her mother and that she hoped that by the end of the season she would have received an acceptable offer of marriage from someone she could grow to love.

Love. Amber didn't want to think about love. It had been so wonderful to dance with Lord Robert. He was such fun and she felt so happy when she was with him, so free . . .

A movement beneath the trees caught her eye, as two figures emerged from the darker shadows. Something about the stiffness of their bodies told her that there was discord of some kind between them, and so she held back, not wanting to intrude. She realised with a jolt that it was Lord Robert and Ralph Seaforde.

Seaforde said something to Lord Robert, and then started to walk away from him, but Lord Robert went after him, catching hold of his arm to stay him. At first Ralph Seaforde shrugged him off but then Lord Robert stepped in front of him blocking his path.

It was obvious now that they were quarrelling, even though Amber couldn't hear what was being said. And then suddenly, so suddenly and so shockingly that Amber could not believe what she was seeing, Lord Robert reached out to Seaforde and embraced him, taking him into his arms and holding him, kissing him on the lips. As though he were kissing a woman and not another man . . .

Amber recoiled in disbelief, wanting to look away and yet unable to do so. Surely she could not be seeing what she was seeing? It wasn't possible! She must be wrong, must have misunderstood. But she knew she had not done. She blinked, her eyes dry and sore as though somehow what she had seen had burned them. There was a horrible miserable feeling in the pit of her stomach. All she wanted to do was blot out what she had seen and get away, but as she moved, Amber heard Lord Robert call out her name. He must have seen her!

She panicked. She couldn't stay to speak to him, not after what she had seen. She turned, running blindly through the darkness, her heart pounding.

He caught up with her within a few yards, taking hold of her arm and telling her urgently, 'Amber, I'm so sorry. What you saw . . . You won't understand.'

'You're wrong, I do understand,' she told him almost fiercely, before wrenching her arm free and hurrying towards the lights of the marquee.

This time he didn't follow her and she told herself that she was glad.

Of course she had understood. She wasn't a complete fool, no matter what he might have thought. Greg had told her about 'it' in that boastful way of schoolboys towards younger relatives, and wanting, of course, both to shock her and show off his own newly acquired knowledge. She had been shocked and disbelieving then, but now she understood. Robert was one of those men who preferred his own sex.

How silly she had been for so nearly falling in love with him. And it had only been *nearly*, Amber told herself firmly. Nearly, that was all. Nothing more. So there was no reason for her to feel so humiliated. As her grandmother had felt humiliated when Barrant de Vries had rejected her? To her

128

own surprise Amber felt tears stinging her eyes at the thought of her grandmother as a hurt and vulnerable young girl. Had Blanche ever been that? If so, it certainly didn't show now. If she had then Blanche had somehow grown a tough second skin to cover her sensitivity.

It was pointless her attributing sensitive feelings to her grandmother she may never have had or comparing herself with her, Amber told herself. Lord Robert had not rejected her. He had been kind to her. It was silly of her to feel such a painful sense of loss.

The band were still playing the same number that they had been playing as she left the marquee, the coloured paper lanterns were still throwing out their soft light, other girls were still giggling and flirting with their dance partners. None of that had changed and yet within *her* Amber knew that something had been altered for ever.

It wasn't just because she could so easily have fallen in love with Lord Robert; it was more than that. Something inside her flinched from what she had seen. It could not be forgotten, though, any more than the wrong dye could be washed out of a piece of silk. A clever designer might be able to find a way to incorporate the dye into a new design and so disguise it, but it would never be hidden from their eyes, no matter how well concealed it might be from those who did not know.

How frightening love could be, and how painful. How confusing and difficult to understand. People were not always what they seemed. Poor Lord Robert, he had looked so anguished.

She felt so different now – older, somehow, and more grown up; stronger too, Amber recognised, because she must be strong, for her own sake. But how could she be strong when she felt so hurt; so betrayed? She had trusted Lord Robert and believed that they were friends, and yet all the time she thought she had known him she had not known him at all. That made her feel very alone. Lord Robert and the friendship she had believed they shared had become a symbol, a touchstone almost for her of her future and all that she hoped it might be. She had told him her dreams for that future, trusted him with them, believed that there was a special bond between them. But how could there be when she had not known something so important about him? She had not known him at all. All she had known was a chimera, a fiction. How could she ever trust her own judgement again?

Was this what growing up was? Learning not to trust others, learning not to rely on them or to accept them at face value? Learning to accept that where there was love there was also pain? Could she bear all of that? Sorrowfully and with a heavy heart Amber acknowledged that she must bear it.

Never again would she put her feelings on such open display, she promised herself. That Amber was gone. The Amber that would grow from her would be different; wiser, and less vulnerable. Less ready to trust so easily.

Chapter Eleven

The weeks were flying by so fast now, that Amber felt she barely had time to draw breath.

Under the strict chaperonage of the countess, she and Beth had attended luncheon parties, fashionable race meetings, afternoon teas and, of course, night after night of parties and coming-out balls.

A group of debs, including Beth and Amber, had even been taken to the Kit-Cat Club where they had all sat excitedly together, trying not to look too awed to see the Prince of Wales there with his entourage.

Amber had looked to see if she could see Lord Robert, even though she knew from Beth that he was visiting friends in Yorkshire. She hadn't seen him since the night of the ball, and although she had tried not to do so, she still missed the fun they had had together, even if she no longer felt that little flutter of her heart whenever she thought of him.

Someone she and Beth were sure they had seen at the club, though, had been Louise seated in a corner with her escort, whom Beth swore was George Ponsonby.

'Louise will ruin her reputation; no one will want to marry her,' Beth had prophesied.

Although Amber and Louise slept under the same roof,

Amber and Beth had been so busy attending the functions to which they had both been invited that Amber barely saw Louise any more.

She and Beth had tried their first cigarette, giggling together as they did so. Poor Beth had been dreadfully sick and Amber had felt almost as unwell.

It was hard to believe that it was over a month since her own ball, Amber thought, as she sat down to her breakfast, having said 'Good morning' to Lady Rutland.

Amber was drinking her coffee when Louise came in and sat down at the table, immediately lighting up a cigarette. Her nails were varnished a deep shade of red and the way she inhaled and then blew out a cloud of cigarette smoke was incredibly sophisticated, Amber thought slightly enviously.

Lady Rutland, who had begun to frown disapprovingly the moment Louise had lit her cigarette, announced sharply, 'Amber, if you have finished your breakfast, I would like to speak with Louise alone.'

Although she had closed the door as she left the breakfast room Amber could still hear Lady Rutland telling Louise angrily, 'Put that cigarette out at once, Louise. I will not have you smoking at the table, and what is this I have heard about you being seen in some nightclub with a man?'

Not wanting to eavesdrop Amber hurried upstairs.

She had been in her bedroom a matter of minutes when Louise burst in without knocking, plainly in a furious temper.

'It was you who told Mummy about me being with George at the Kit-Cat Club, wasn't it, you little sneak?'

'No,' Amber defended herself. 'It wasn't.' Louise no longer had the power to intimidate her. Her confidence had soared since Lord Robert had taken her under his wing and Beth had returned from her finishing school in Paris to renew their friendship.

'You told her because you're jealous,' Louise stormed, ignoring Amber's response. 'You want him for yourself. Well, you're wasting your time. George would never look at someone like you, whose family are in trade.'

Amber didn't bother dignifying Louise's insult with a response. It was laughable that Louise should think she was interested in George Ponsonby. Amber thought he was selfish and self-serving, and didn't find him in the least bit attractive.

'Mummy can say what she likes,' Louise continued angrily, 'I'm not going to stop seeing him.'

Louise had gone before Amber could say anything, slamming the door behind her.

'I can't imagine ever doing something that Mummy had forbidden me to do,' Beth told Amber, after Amber had related the incident to Beth later in the day.

They were in the countess's private sitting room in the Levingtons' Belgrave Square house, waiting for the countess, who was to accompany them to a luncheon party at the Savoy Hotel.

There was a copy of *The Times* on the countess's desk, and Amber noticed that its main story contained yet more bad news about the growing number of unemployed. Jay had mentioned in his last letter that several of Macclesfield's mills had had to lay men off because of the slump in trade that had followed the previous year's Wall Street crash.

One could see poor people begging everywhere in London, and the Labour government seemed no more able to mend matters than the Conservatives had been.

'Mummy will be here soon,' Beth told Amber. 'There's something she wants to discuss with you, but I'm not supposed to say anything. Oh—'

Beth stopped speaking as her mother came into the room and looked at them, shaking her head at Beth wryly, before turning to Amber to smile and say, 'Amber, my dear, the débutante dances will soon be at an end, and I was wondering if your grandmother has discussed her plans for you for the summer?'

'Grandmother hasn't mentioned anything in her letters,' she answered the countess shyly, not sure where the conversation was leading.

'Very well, in that case I shall write to her to ask her permission for you to accompany us to the South of France next month – that is, of course, if you are happy for me to do so?'

If she was happy? Could it really be in any doubt?

'Oh, yes. Yes, thank you,' Amber responded fervently.

How could she not be thrilled at the thought of spending the summer in the South of France, and with Beth, her best friend in the whole world?

She gave Beth a look of gratitude, which Beth returned with an excited smile.

The countess went on to inform Amber that their party was going to include Beth's father, the earl, and their eldest son, Henry, Viscount Hollowes, both of whom were currently in Australia where, as Beth had already told Amber, her father had business interests in a sheep station and in mining. They would also be joined by the nursery party, comprising Beth's two younger brothers and the baby of the family, her sister, Arabella, and that they would be staying in Juan-les-Pins where the earl was renting a villa for the summer.

'I'm so happy that you'll be coming to the South of France with us,' Beth confided excitedly to Amber later over luncheon. 'It's going to be such fun.'

'Yes,' Amber agreed.

She could hardly take it in that she was to visit the South of France, the haunt of so many famous artists. She couldn't wait to see the places and the colours that inspired them. It would be a relief not to be constantly looking over her shoulder to see if she could see Lord Robert too.

The South of France. How very lucky she was to have such a good friend as Beth and how grateful she was to the countess for inviting her to join them.

'But you said you were going to take me somewhere exciting, not some dingy horrid hotel in Brighton,' Louise objected, taking several nervy drags on her cigarette.

They were standing in the bedroom of the hotel and although she had known all along what George had in mind, now that she was confronted with the unattractive reality of their surroundings, defying her mother for the delicious thrill of taking such a dangerous risk no longer seemed either exciting or glamorous. And, in fact, somehow George himself no longer cut the dashing figure here in these drab surroundings as he had done in the prim drawing rooms of Mayfair and the correspondingly louche night-clubs.

In fact, if she was honest with herself, what Louise actually felt right now was not excitement but distaste. She had hated the way the man in reception had smirked and looked her over when George had registered them as Mr and Mrs Smith, but she had been too shocked by the fact that he had done so to object.

When George had suggested driving her down to Brighton for 'something special at a discreet little place I know', Louise had envisaged herself sweeping into a glamorous establishment where heads would turn admiringly in her direction and suave handsome men would leave their companions immediately to demand an introduction to her.

They would have lunch – with champagne, of course – and then cocktails in a piano bar.

Carelessly Louise had ignored the small problem of how she was going to manage to stay out so late without explaining her absence to her mother.

Now, faced with a bedroom smaller than her maid's at home, its wallpaper peeling, and the smell of damp and greasy cooking pervading everything, the issue of her mother's likely reaction to her absence suddenly became vitally important.

'I really can't stay,' she told George, affecting insouciance. 'I had no idea it would take us so long to get here. Mummy will be simply furious if I'm not back in time for cocktails at the Edales.'

'Really?' There was a look in George's eyes that warned Louise he was not going to take 'no' for an answer.

How exciting. And how powerful it made her feel to know that he wanted her so much.

'Yes, I want you to take me home now,' she told him.

'And I want – you,' George responded.

Louise tried to sidestep him as he came towards her but the bedroom was too small and all he had to do to throw her down on the bed was take hold of her arms and force her backwards.

'No, George. You mustn't,' Louise protested, feigning anger. This was just as she had imagined it would be: the delicious feeling of power and wantonness, the knowledge that George was overwhelmed by his desire for her. If she could do that to George then how much more easily would she be able to manipulate someone older – and richer. Avarice gleamed in her eyes.

'It's too late to play teasing games now, Lou,' George warned her. 'You've been coming on to me for weeks, and you know it. Stop worrying, you're going to love it. Your kind always does. Careful, you don't want me to go tearing that pretty blouse you're wearing, do you? What would Mummy say?'

She was genuinely angry now – she hadn't planned for things to go this far. Teasing George was one thing, actually letting him do 'it' was another.

Somehow Louise managed to fight him off and push her way past him to the door, but it was locked and whilst she struggled helplessly with it he caught hold of her, dragging her back to the bed.

This definitely wasn't what she wanted or how things were supposed to be. George was tugging at her clothes, undressing her swiftly and expertly, despite her protests and struggles, until all she was wearing was her pale pink silk chemise and her matching French knickers with their lacy edging.

Automatically when George let go of her and stood up to remove his own clothes, she lifted her hands to cross them over her breasts. She wasn't going to let him know that she was apprehensive. Men like George didn't feel any sympathy for women who cried and pleaded; a woman had to stand up to a man like George. Louise knew that instinctively.

She might be nervous but she was still curious enough to risk a look at him. She hadn't seen a man naked before, not properly, although she was familiar with the feel of that thick jut of flesh rearing up in swollen urgency, having allowed George to put her hand on it on several occasions, including one time when he had unbuttoned his trousers and pushed her hand inside his underwear to really touch 'it'.

She hadn't expected that it would look so ugly, nor have that awkward-looking pouch of flesh hanging beneath it.

'Like what you see?' George asked. 'Want a closer inspection?'

She tried to look nonchalant as she gave a small shrug, but she was wasting her time, she realised, because George was more interested in pushing down the straps of her camisole to bare her breasts, before cupping them in his hands and then kneading them and tugging almost painfully on her nipples.

She relaxed a bit when he started to kiss her – she was, after all, on familiar territory here – but when he transferred his mouth from her lips to her breasts she tensed again and then tensed even more when she felt him tugging – sucking – on her nipples, first one and then the other. An unfamiliar sensation zigzagged right through her body, causing a dull ache low down inside her that began to grow in intensity. George's teeth suddenly raked her nipple, causing her to cry out and jerk away from him, but he pulled her back, sliding his hand into the open leg of her knickers, and touching her almost roughly where she had secretly and daringly touched herself before but never like George was doing, working his fingers into her, ignoring her protest that he was hurting her, rubbing that special magical place she had found during her own explorations until suddenly Louise wasn't thinking about how she could bend George to her will any more because she wasn't capable of thinking anything, only doing; arching her back, moaning and crying out, protesting when George abandoned the source of her pleasure and instead pushed a pillow beneath her hips and then rolled on top of her, raising her knees and then pushing slowly into her, ignoring the stiffening that accompanied her demand for him to stop.

But he refused to stop, and then miraculously the pain disappeared, and the sensation of him thrusting deeper and faster inside her became a challenge she felt driven to meet, and then a need that had her crying out to him.

When he groaned and tensed Louise wondered what was

happening, fearful that something was wrong, and even that he might be stuck inside her, but before she could panic, he groaned again and pumped furiously into her, before exhaling in satisfaction and slumping over her.

It hadn't been at all like she had thought it would be. George had been so rough, too rough at times. And all that sweat and hard work, and that sticky wetness she could feel leaking from her now that George had removed himself from her.

'There, I told you you'd like it, didn't I?'

Louise was sitting up in bed, the sheet dragged up to cover her breasts whilst she smoked the cigarette George had just lit and passed to her. George was lying beside her, his head propped up watching her with a smug expression on his face.

'No, I didn't like it at all,' she denied sharply. She was still angry at having her hand forced.

George laughed. 'No? Then what was all that, "Oh, George, please, oh, George. Oh, oh . . ." all about then?' he laughed.

She had enjoyed it, Louise admitted, but she was still furiously cross with George. After all, this was not the kind of place in which she had expected to lose her virginity. She deserved better. But she'd make him pay . . .

Chapter Twelve

Lady Rutland wasn't at all pleased that Amber had been invited to the private pre-ball dinner party Beth's parents were hosting on the evening of Beth's coming-out ball, when Louise had not, but since her grandmother had not only written to her saying how delighted she was that Amber had been invited to accompany Beth to the South of France, but had actually also telephoned her as well, Amber had felt justified in ignoring Lady Rutland's crossness.

Lord and Lady Levington's Belgrave Square house was far grander than Lady Rutland's in Cadogan Place; the flowers to decorate the ballroom had been sent up from the hothouse at Chevenely, their country estate, having been expressly grown for Beth's ball.

Since it was the first time she had met the Earl of Levington Amber had been worrying that she might not earn Beth's father's approval, and that the invitation to the South of France might be rescinded. However, to her relief Lord Levington had treated her most kindly, putting her at her ease straight away.

Amber had been partnered for dinner by Beth's elder brother Henry, Viscount Hollowes. Fresh-faced, with Beth's soft brown hair and his father's hazel eyes, his manner slightly awkward and intense, Henry had talked earnestly to Amber about Australia over dinner.

'Henry isn't really used to girls,' Beth had confided to Amber. 'Mummy thought it would be good for him to stay here in London whilst I was doing the season, but Daddy said that it was more important that he went with him to Australia.'

Beth looked truly radiant tonight, as much because of the presence of her godmother's son, Alistair, as anything else, Amber suspected, watching her friend later as she was whirled round the dance floor in Alistair's arms. Sturdily built, with red-gold hair and bright blue eyes, the Hon. Alistair McCrea might not appear as glamorous as some of the more polished debs' delights, but there was a reassuring quality about him. He was the kind of young man who would take his responsibilities very seriously, Amber could see, and those responsibilities would naturally include his wife. Ultimately he would inherit not only his father's title and Scottish lands but also a small Hertfordshire estate that would come to him via a great-uncle on his mother's side of the family, Beth had confided to Amber, and Amber suspected that Beth was halfway to falling in love with him already.

Lucky Beth, Amber thought, to be able to fall in love with someone so suitable. But then Beth was the kind of girl who wanted to please her parents, especially her mother to whom she was extremely close.

With something as very exciting as the South of France to look forward to Amber could almost forget the scene she had witnessed the night of her ball, and how much she missed the fun she had had with Lord Robert. Almost. But not entirely.

Beth hadn't mentioned him recently and Amber had not liked to ask, afraid her enquiries would give her away. Diana and Bryan Guinness were here at the ball in a group that included Diana's brother, Tom Mitford, Jim Lees-Milne, Oswald Mosley and his wife, and the novelist Evelyn Waugh, all of whom Amber recognised, having either been introduced to them or had them pointed out to her on previous occasions.

Amber saw them whilst she was dancing with Henry, and trying not to feel uncomfortable about the way he was looking at her so intensely, without saying a word. They were all crowding around Oswald Mosley, a very good-looking man in the mode of Rudolph Valentino, who all the popular papers were lionising because of his decision to resign from Ramsay MacDonald's government over the rejection of what was being termed the Mosley Memorandum: a document that set out plans for large-scale public work programmes to provide jobs and an income for the poor and out of work. Personally Amber thought that anything that relieved the dreadful situation whereby men were unable to find work to support their families should be praised and put in force as soon as possible. Not that she knew very much about politics, of course.

They were almost level with the group when Diana, who was standing next to Mosley, suddenly screamed, and then laughed, shaking her head as she exclaimed, 'Oh, you beast, Mosley,' before turning to her husband and telling him, 'He has just dropped something icy cold down my back, Bryan.'

'Oh, no, poor you,' the pretty brunette clinging to Tom Mitford's arm protested, whilst Oswald Mosley opened his fist to reveal some of the small pink puffballs that had decorated the supper tables.

'It was only one of these, iced with champagne,' he was drawling, obviously enjoying the tease. 'You were so deliciously hotly defensive of my Memorandum, Diana, that I felt it my duty to cool you down before you burned poor Ramsay's reputation to cinders.'

The dance had come to an end, and Amber was rather relieved to be able to wriggle free of Henry's tight grip.

'You must go and find your next partner,' she reminded him gently when he showed no sign of moving from her side.

His blurted, 'I'd much rather dance with you,' made Amber feel freshly uncomfortable.

And when a familiar voice drawled, 'Ah, but Miss Vrontsky is engaged to dance this dance with me, I'm afraid, Henry old chap,' she was too relieved to feel self-conscious when she turned to look up at Lord Robert.

'I take it that you were not wanting to dance with him again?' he asked once Henry was out of earshot.

'Not really,' Amber admitted, 'but you need not stay and dance with me if there is . . .' She stopped, floundering uncomfortably.

'I want to dance with you very much.'

Now she was blushing, Amber realised in vexation.

'But I think we should stroll instead,' Lord Robert suggested, offering her his arm. 'We can talk more easily that way.'

Lord Robert obviously knew the house well, Amber realised, because he soon found a small anteroom to the ballroom, its doors open to a balcony just wide enough for two people to stand and enjoy the evening air.

'I'm sorry I was so silly about . . . about things,' Amber told him.

'You weren't silly. In fact, I doubt you could ever be silly, Amber.' When she looked at him, her eyes wide with uncertainty, he told her, 'I should not have behaved in the way that I did. Some things should remain private. Not seen and not heard.'

'I dare say that it isn't always easy not to betray one's feelings, when they are very strong.' Now Amber was looking

143

out into the darkness, unable to bring herself to look directly at Lord Robert.

'You are as compassionate as you are kind. I loved foolishly and I paid the price for it.'

His words made Amber feel intensely sad for him.

'I used to think that loving someone meant that person would be happy like my parents were happy, but love isn't always like that, is it?'

'No, it isn't. Love can be many things, some of them damnably painful. I hope that when you find love it will be the kind of love your parents shared.' He paused and then said abruptly, 'I have missed you and our outings together.'

'Have you?' Now Amber turned to look at him. 'I have missed you too. I thought you must be cross with me because—'

'No. If I was cross with anyone it was myself.'

He reached for her hand and held it gently. 'Shall we be friends again?'

'Oh, yes.'

They looked at one another, and smiled.

'Cecil *will* be pleased. He considers that you have great promise, you know, and would, I think, like to see you as another Syrie Maugham.'

Amber's eyes widened at the compliment. Syrie Maugham, the former wife of the famous playwright, was currently the most fashionable interior decorator.

'My grandmother would never allow me to set up in business,' she told Robert sadly.

'No, I dare say not, but your husband might if you choose him carefully, and he is rich enough,' he told her.

Amber laughed. 'So now I must find a titled husband to please my grandmother and a rich one to please Cecil.'

Robert looked at her. 'I hope you will find a way to follow your own heart, Amber, for if anyone deserves to it is you.'

144

His kindness brought Amber near to tears, and as though he sensed how close she was to being overwhelmed by her emotions, Lord Robert said teasingly, 'We'd better get back to the ballroom before Henry sends out a search party and you are accused of attempting to sully my reputation by enticing me out onto this balcony.'

Amber laughed again. She was so pleased that they were friends once more, but even better, she had realised standing on the balcony with him that he was now just dear Robert, her friend, and nothing more. Her former feelings had disappeared and she recognised them for what they were: her first proper infatuation. Who could blame her when he was so handsome and so exciting? But she knew that when true love finally showed its face, she'd know it in a heart-beat.

Chapter Thirteen

In less than a week they would be leaving for the South of France, and the Belgrave Square mansion was busy with preparation.

'Now, my dears,' the countess informed Beth and Amber, 'whilst the little ones will be going straight to Juan-les-Pins with Nanny and the servants, the three of us will be staying in Paris for a short time before joining them. You will both need clothes suitable for the South of France and these, of course, are best bought in Paris.'

Paris! Amber and Beth exchanged thrilled looks.

'Oh, Amber, I am just so excited,' Beth burst out after her mother had been called away to take an urgent telephone call. 'It's going to be such fun. We shall need new tennis dresses, and swimming togs. Oh, and I do hope that Mummy will let us have some of those new pyjama suits that *Vogue* says everyone is wearing.'

Amber was still thinking about the excitement of going to the South of France half an hour later as she went up the steps to the front door of Lady Rutland's house in Cadogan Place. Louise and Lady Rutland were, she knew, out visiting an elderly cousin of Lady Rutland's who lived in Richmond.

'There's a visitor to see you, miss,' the butler told her as he let her in. 'A Mr Fulshawe. He said to tell you that he's here on your grandmother's behalf. I've put him in the library.'

Jay was here and on her grandmother's behalf? How ominous that sounded. Amber quickly walked across the hall and pushed open the library doors, trying to quell her anxiety as she did so.

Jay was standing in front of the unlit fire. He was wearing city clothes and, she realised with sudden surprise, he did not, as she had imagined, look out of place in them at all. Far from it. He looked, in fact, very handsome and smart.

'Your grandmother instructed me to come,' he told her. 'I'm afraid I have some bad news for you.'

'Bad news?' Her mind raced. What did he mean? She searched his face but there was no clue to be found there. 'What is it? What's happened? Is it the mill?'

He was shaking his head.

'Greg?' Anxiety sharpened her own voice. 'It is Greg, isn't it?' she demanded when she saw the small movement he made. 'Something's happened to him. What, Jay? Oh, please tell me.'

'It isn't Greg, although in a sense it does concern him. It's Caroline Fitton Legh.'

'Caroline?' Amber repeated blankly. Jay had come all the way to London to tell her something about Caroline? Her anxiety for Greg had eased back, and now she felt confused.

'There is no easy way to tell you this, Amber. Caroline is dead.'

Of all the things she might have been dreading hearing, the death of Caroline Fitton Legh had not been one of them. She was – had been – so young and so very alive. It seemed impossible. Amber remembered how beautiful she had looked the afternoon she and Greg called on her at Fitton Hall. She had been so kind, so very friendly and warm. Amber was perplexed. How could she have died? She suddenly

147

remembered what Cassandra had said: that Greg was in love with Lady Fitton Legh. But Greg had laughed when Amber had told him that.

Her heart was beating uncomfortably. She felt somehow afraid.

'But how?'

'An accident,' Jay told her briefly.

'Does my grandmother want me to go home for the funeral? Is that why you are here?'

Jay shook his head. 'Lord Fitton Legh has announced that there will be only a small private family ceremony.'

'I can hardly believe it,' Amber admitted. 'Everyone must have been so shocked. Especially poor Cassandra.'

There were dark shadows beneath Jay's eyes and a certain hollowness to his face.

'Amber.' He stopped and exhaled. 'Your grandmother has charged me with . . . that is to say, there is something she wishes me to tell you. Come and sit down.'

Obediently Amber sat down in the chair he was holding, waiting uncertainly whilst he took one opposite her. There was no fire in the grate and the room felt cold. This side of the house did not catch the sun.

'You will know, of course, that Greg is on his way to Hong Kong.'

'Yes, of course,' Amber agreed. 'He seemed pleased to be going when he wrote to me about it, although I don't understand what that has to do—' She broke off when Jay held up his hand to stop her.

'There is no easy way to tell you this and I would rather not have been the one to do so, but your grandmother believes you should know, and I confess that I share her feelings. You are bound to hear of it anyway when you return to Macclesfield, and no doubt so well embroidered that you will not be able to tell truth from fiction.'

148

Amber's stomach was churning nervously. She had no idea what it was that Jay had to tell her but she did know that it was something unpleasant.

Jay looked at Amber. There hadn't been a minute on the train journey south – first class at his employer's insistence – when he hadn't been thinking of this meeting and what he would have to say, how much he might have to say and how he was going to say it.

It had shocked him to realise how much Amber had matured in such a short space of time; the way she had received him, her manner, her composure now as she controlled her emotions; the girl he had known had gone, and a calm and assured young woman had taken her place.

He took a deep breath. 'The reason your grandmother sent Greg to Hong Kong was because he and Lady Fitton Legh had been involved.'

Amber absorbed the careful words and then looked at Jay. 'Do you mean that they were having an affair?' she asked.

'Yes.'

'Grandmother sent Greg away because she discovered that he was in love with Lady Fitton Legh?'

'No. That is to say, I don't think it was a matter of their being in love, so much as a matter of chance and circumstance, throwing them into one another's company.'

'Yes,' Amber acknowledged.

Jay was amazed she seemed so calm, so unmoved by this latest news. My, but she was a world away from the girl he had known so well.

'Unfortunately it was Lord Fitton Legh who first discovered the affair – not your grandmother – and there was some gossip about it before your grandmother was able to prevail upon him to see the wisdom of the matter being kept as private as possible. Whilst he demanded that Greg be punished by banishment from Cheshire, I think that both your grandmother and Greg himself were happy that he should distance himself from events.'

Greg had been happy about going to Hong Kong – Amber knew that from his letter to her – so obviously he hadn't loved Caroline. She remembered now how she had sensed his discomfort the afternoon they had paid their call, and how too she had thought Lady Fitton Legh's manner towards him more intimate than seemed proper. Had she perhaps cared for Greg more than he had for her?

'I don't understand. What has Greg going to Hong Kong to do with Lady Fitton Legh's death?'

Jay sighed. He had known they would reach this point.

'Lady Fitton Legh was to have had a child.'

Amber guessed immediately what he was not saying. 'Greg's child?' she demanded.

'I don't know.'

'But it is possible that it could have been Greg's child?'

'Yes,' Jay admitted. What else could he do? The whole of Cheshire was thick with gossip and supposition, and Cassandra had sworn that Caroline had told her that the child was Greg's and had accused him of abandoning her.

'Does Lord Fitton Legh know that it could have been Greg's baby?'

'I should think so, yes.'

'Oh, poor Caroline.'

'Her situation was an unhappy one.' Untenable was the word he should have used, Jay thought.

'What happened?'

'She drowned, in the lake. Cassandra found her and raised the alarm but it was too late. It is believed that she must have stepped off the path onto the grass, slipped and been unable to save herself. There had been rain, and the pathway and bank were muddy.'

Amber swallowed hard. A tragic accident, or had Lady Fitton Legh, unable to face the gossip and disgrace of bearing a child that might not be her husband's, taken her own life? Had she perhaps loved Greg even though he had not loved her? How must it feel to love a man and be abandoned by him in such circumstances? Amber shuddered.

Seeing it, Jay wondered if he had said too much.

'You are shocked, I know,' he tried to comfort her. 'But it is better that you know the truth rather than hear all manner of wild tales. I know how much Greg means to you.'

'But what is the truth?' Amber asked him. 'How can we know? She must have felt so desperate and alone to take her life and that of her child.'

Jay reached for her hand and held it within his own. Caroline Fitton Legh had been shallow and selfish, much like Greg in many ways. Amber, on the other hand, felt things very deeply for others as well as for herself.

'We must accept that it was an accident, Amber, for Lady Fitton Legh's sake as much as that of anyone else.'

Amber nodded. Everyone knew, of course, that it was against the law to commit suicide and that a person doing so could not be buried in consecrated ground, or even have their burial place marked.

'I'm glad that it was you who told me, Jay.'

'We should talk of happier things. I have brought you something that I hope will please you and give you some comfort,' he told her with a smile. 'Your grandmother has charged me with the task of cataloguing various items and papers she has kept over the years, and amongst them I found this.'

As he spoke he was reaching into the attaché case he had placed on the leather-covered mahogany desk, and removing what looked like a thick sketchpad.

As he handed it to her Amber's hands shook.

'I think this must have been your father's.'

Her senses were already recording the familiar scent of lavender water and tobacco mixed with graphite and paper coming from the pad even before she had seen her father's signature across the front. Holding it tightly to her chest, she looked up at Jay, her eyes blurring with fresh tears.

'Thank you, oh, thank you, Jay.' And then she put the sketchpad down on the desk and hurled herself into his arms.

This time he didn't stop her, comforting her whilst she cried.

'I shall never give up on my dream to do what my father wanted me to do,' Amber told Jake passionately after he had released her and handed her a clean handkerchief.

'So no handsome young man has touched your heart whilst you have been in London?' Jake teased her.

'No.'

'Are you sure? Only your letters often mention a certain Lord Robert.'

Amber wound his handkerchief between her fingers. 'I do like him, and we are friends, but only friends. I saw him kissing another man, and I do know what that means. Love can be so frightening sometimes.'

The words were out before she could stop them, causing her face to burn.

'Yes,' Jay agreed soberly. 'It can.' He paused and then added, 'Such a love as Lord Robert's, in this country at least, is against the law and punishable by imprisonment, and so it is rarely spoken of.'

'I would not do so to anyone but you, Jay,' Amber told him, sensing that he was giving her a warning. 'Somehow I always feel I can tell you anything.'

'I hope you will always feel like that.'

They looked at one another in silence, and it was Amber who was the first to break it.

'How long are you in London for?'

'I return to Macclesfield today.'

'So soon?' Her heart sank.

'Yes, in fact I must go now if I am to catch my train,' he said, getting ready to leave.

On impulse Amber turned to him. 'You will keep writing to me, won't you?' When he made no response, she begged him urgently, 'Please, Jay, you must. There is no one else I can trust. You are the only person who understands how I feel about . . . about things.'

She meant about her parents and the way in which her dreams had been taken from her, Jay knew. His heart ached for her, and not just his heart. He closed his eyes. For both their sakes he should refuse her request. She was not a child any more and he didn't know how much he could trust his ability to maintain the old easy relationship they had shared when she had been.

His body had told him even before she had left Denham for London what his mind had not wanted to accept. He had felt it that time when he had held her and had wanted to go on holding her. As he wanted to hold her now and go on holding her.

'It would be better, I think, if I did not,' he told her quietly.

'Better? Better for whom?' Amber demanded emotionally. 'Not for me, Jay. It's bad enough that my grandmother won't allow me to do what I want to do, without not knowing what's happening at home and at the mill. Are the workers still on full time? Is the order book full? I know Grandmother doesn't care what happens to the mill, but I care, Jay, and I thought you cared too.'

She was too young and too unknowing to realise what she was doing to him, or how much her passionate outburst was tearing him apart with conflicting needs and the burden of his own guilt.

If he gave in she would believe that he was helping her, but he knew that then he would be indulging himself by keeping her close to him, by strengthening the bond between them, by holding her in his heart where he had no right to want her to be.

'Jay, please,' Amber begged him. She didn't know why she needed so desperately to cling on to the contact between them, but she did know that the thought of losing it – losing Jay from her life – was more than she could bear. Tears burned the backs of her eyes but she refused to let them fall. She wasn't a child any more, after all. She had been wrong in her assessment of the strength of the bond of friendship between her and Lord Robert; she couldn't endure it if she was wrong about her bond with Jay as well. She needed to be assured that it was strong and that she could rely on it and on him.

'I need you to write to me,' she told him. 'If I can't rely on you, Jay, then I don't think I will ever believe again that I can rely on anyone. Please promise me that you will keep in touch with me.'

How could he deny her? He couldn't.

'If that is what you wish,' he told her.

'Yes, yes, it is.'

'Very well then.'

They looked at one another, and then impulsively Amber ran to him. Another moment and she would be in his arms.

As Jay stepped back from her Amber realised what she was doing and stopped dead in her tracks, blushing. Poor Jay. She would have embarrassed him dreadfully if she had flung herself into his arms like a child.

She stretched out her hand towards him and touched his sleeve briefly as she told him softly, 'Thank you, Jay.'

* * *

154

'You will have heard, of course, that Lord Fitton Legh has implored me to remain at Fitton to care for the child?' Cassandra demanded importantly, as she descended the wide stone steps of the main entrance to their grandfather's house. The late spring sunshine burned her hair the colour of fire, and whether by accident or design, Jay did not know, she had started to address him whilst she was standing on the top step and he was just mounting them so that they were on a level with one another.

'Yes, Cassandra, I had heard that,' Jay agreed.

'Lord Fitton Legh has asked his second cousin Elaine Fitton to come to Fitton Hall in order to provide me with a female companion. She is, of course, far too elderly to take charge of the child.'

Jay's heart sank. Cassandra was obviously delighted to be boasting about her new role but nothing she had said had indicated that she felt any warmth towards Caroline Fitton Legh's young son – far from it.

'It is a pity that Lady Fitton Legh is not alive to care for her child herself,' he told her, unable to keep his own feelings out of his voice.

He had never particularly liked Cassandra, but something about the way she was behaving disturbed him, although he wasn't able to say why. She had been close to Caroline, and yet she seemed disconcertingly unaffected by her death, especially since she had been the one to find her, which alone was surely enough to have had a profound effect. In anyone else he could have thought that this detachment was a means of protecting herself from her anguish, but Cassandra wasn't like that. She was very much a victim of her own emotions and showed what they were.

'She had no one to blame for what happened to her other than herself,' she announced self-righteously. 'I tried to help her. I warned her what would happen once Lord Fitton Legh found out she was carrying another man's child.'

Her smugness filled Jay with distaste. Where was the compassion she ought to have felt?

'That is merely supposition,' Jay reminded her.

'No, it is not. She told me herself that it couldn't possibly be her husband's. She was a fool.' Cassandra's voice rose with her anger. 'All she had to do was get rid of the child. There are doctors, everyone knows that, and she could have afforded it despite the fact that her father had lost so much money. All she would have had to do was sell a few pieces of that frightful jewellery her parents gave her when she got married. She was hardly likely to wear it any more, after all, not with Lord Fitton Legh refusing to allow her to socialise after the disgrace she had brought on herself.'

There was real vindictiveness in Cassandra's voice. And something more?

Jay didn't know why, but gradually, listening to his cousin's outburst, he had begun to feel uneasy.

'She should have listened to me,' Cassandra went on fiercely. 'I told her what would happen if she didn't get rid of the child. I told her she would be disgraced and that Lord Fitton Legh would not accept it as his, once he knew. I told her too that everyone would know that she had whored herself and broken her marriage vows.'

Cassandra's almost gloating satisfaction repelled Jay. He wanted to refuse to listen to her and walk away. There was something alarming as well as distasteful about her whole manner.

'She was the one who chose to ignore my warning. I would have helped her, gone with her, she knew that. It was her own fault. It didn't have to be like that. It was her choice.'

Cassandra sounded virtuously critical now, increasing Jay's sense of disquiet. This was not the attitude of someone who had purported to be a friend of the dead woman but rather someone who had felt she had the right to sit in judgement over her, and who had resented her. Jay frowned, reluctant to pursue such a course of inner questioning and yet at the same time feeling morally obliged on Caroline's behalf to do so.

Her own fault. Those callous-sounding words stirred something unwanted and not to be thought of in Jay's mind. His suspicion that Cassandra's cruel behaviour and her refusal to help Caroline might actually have been a contributory factor to Caroline's death refused to be dismissed.

'If Caroline did confide to you that her husband was not the father of her child,' he began sombrely, 'then . . .'

'Then what?' Cassandra challenged him. 'I should have lied for her like she wanted me to and pretend that she had sworn to me on oath that the child was Lord Fitton Legh's? Why? Why should I? I told her that I wouldn't.'

So his suspicions had been right. Jay was too shocked to conceal what he felt.

'Cassandra, if what you are saying is true, then you must surely realise that it is possible that you helped to drive Caroline to her death.'

A peculiar look crossed his cousin's face – not triumph, and certainly not guilt, but something that twisted Jay's heart with horrified certainty that not only was Cassandra aware of the truth of what he had said but that somehow she had managed to convince herself that she had been justified in doing what she had done.

Hard on the heels of that awareness came another, equally unwanted and discomforting.

Cassandra was claiming that she could not and would not lie to help Caroline, and yet surely she had already done so in claiming that Greg had been forcing himself on Caroline?

There was something here that Jay didn't like, something unwholesome and rank with deceit and ill feeling. As little as he wanted to become involved, he felt he had a duty to do so. Amber had been so distressed by what had happened. For Greg, naturally, her loyalty to her cousin was always paramount, and for Caroline Fitton Legh and her child, even though, unlike Cassandra, she had not been intimately acquainted with Caroline. Instinctively Jay flinched from the word 'intimate' and its unpalatable connotations. One of the reasons Cassandra's mother had been so happy to accept the Fitton Leghs' invitation on Cassandra's behalf had, according to Jay's own mother, been because of the concern that had been felt about the intensity of a friendship Cassandra had struck up with a woman who had moved into the area and who, it was rumoured, 'worshipped at the altar of Lesbos', as Jay's mother had delicately put it.

Jay took a deep breath. 'You say that you refused to lie for Caroline—'

Before he could finish what he had been going to say, Cassandra said fiercely, 'How could I? Morally it would have been wrong.'

'And yet you did lie for her when you told Lord Fitton Legh that you had gone to her aid and found Greg assaulting her.'

Cassandra's mouth tightened. It was quite plain that she didn't like what Jay had said.

'That was different. Greg deserved to be punished,' Cassandra defended herself. 'Caroline wanted to pay him back. She wanted to see him disgraced and shamed, and he would have been if it hadn't been for his grandmother. I can't understand how you can demean yourself by letting her buy you, Jay, you a de Vries! Grandfather feels the same. He says you've no pride or self-respect. He says that you are a traitor to your name and that you think more of Blanche Pickford than you do your own family.'

'My name is Fulshawe – not de Vries,' Jay pointed out hardily. 'And as for my pride and self-respect, I have enough of both to consider myself a better man for earning my own living, however humble that living may be.'

Jay knew perfectly well that it irked his grandfather that he refused to discuss Blanche with him, and behave as though he was some kind of spy gathering information against her that showed her in a bad light because he knew it would please Barrant.

'You are a de Vries, Jay, and I agree with Grandfather that it is shameful that you allow Blanche Pickford to order you around.'

'There is nothing shameful about honest work. You should not encourage Grandfather to cling on to his animosity towards Blanche, Cassandra.'

'He doesn't need encouragement. He hates her.'

'As you hate Greg Pickford?' Jay suggested drily.

Cassandra's face burned an angry red. She had never been good at concealing her feelings. Her skin always gave her away, flushing hot with temper. Jay looked at her.

'Caroline made me do it. You don't understand. I loved her.'

There was real emotion in her voice now, a mixture of pain and bitterness that Jay suspected echoed her true feelings for Caroline.

'She said she loved me.' Cassandra was sobbing now, her face blotched scarlet. 'She said it would serve him right, and that she was sorry she had hurt me. It was me she loved until Greg Pickford came between us. I had to make her see that, Jay.' Cassandra's voice had become harder. 'I had to make her understand how much she owed me. There had to be payment for that, and punishment for her. You do see

159

that, don't you? Caro did, once I'd explained it all to her. She betrayed me, after all, and not just me but our love. She let him put that thing of his inside her and then leave his disgusting seed in her. It had to be expelled. She couldn't possibly have let it bear fruit. I told her that, and she promised me that she would do as I'd said. But she was lying. She tried to trick me by pretending that she'd get rid of it, and then she said that it was too late.'

Jay listened in shocked revulsion. He had begun to suspect that Cassandra had a passionate crush on Caroline but he had never dreamed that his cousin harboured thoughts of deeds as evil as the ones she was now revealing.

'I wanted her to love me best, she knew that,' Cassandra continued, patently oblivious to Jay's disgust. 'She swore to me that Greg Pickford meant nothing to her and yet she refused to get rid of his child. She's better off dead, Jay. For her own sake. She would never have been able to stand the disgrace.'

Better off? It was sickeningly plain to Jay that Cassandra actually believed that. To the extent that she had threatened and refused to help Caroline with the intention of hounding the poor woman to her death? It was a horrifying thought, but his suspicions could not be dismissed.

'Do you know what you are saying?' Jay demanded. 'Do you know what you have done? It is my belief that you are as responsible for Caroline's death as surely as though you had pushed her into the water and watched her drown yourself. And you did it out of jealousy because she chose Greg over you. She had her faults, I don't deny that, but to destroy her out of some jealous pique because she did not return your feelings . . .'

'You are not to say that. She did love me, she did. She promised me she would get rid of the child and we would be together.'

160

She launched herself at him, raining blows at his face, trying to claw his flesh, her fury giving her so much strength that it was several seconds before Jay could hold her off. She was panting, her face contorted with rage and pain.

'She cheated me because she thought I loved her so much that I would give in, but I did not. I could not.'

'You drove her to her death,' Jay accused her flatly.

'No. You are not to say that. It is not true. You will be sorry that you have said that to me, Jay,' she warned him. 'Somehow I shall make sure of that.'

She rushed past him, and got on to the bicycle she had left leaning against the steps, pedalling furiously down the drive, leaving Jay feeling sickened and horrified.

For all her faults Caroline Fitton Legh had not deserved to be hounded to her death in the way he suspected that Cassandra had done. Cassandra might choose to believe that 'love' excused her from any guilt or responsibility for her actions, but Jay thought otherwise.

There was nothing that could be done, of course – Cassandra had not after all physically killed Caroline Fitton Legh – but his cousin's behaviour left him not just shocked but sickened.

Chapter Fourteen

Paris. Amber could scarcely believe she was really here. They were staying at the George V Hotel, which had been open for only two years and which had been built in honour of King George, before continuing their journey to the South of France, on *Le Train Bleu*, the all-first-class night train from Paris to Marseille, and the Côte d'Azure.

Since they were travelling alone without a male escort Lady Levington had decided that it would be better for them to have a suite at the George V rather than several separate rooms.

Even though she was now familiar with the opulence of both the Ritz and the Savoy, Amber was awed by the splendour of the George V. She was seated in front of her bedroom window, her sketchpad on her lap. Beth and Lady Levington were resting after their journey but Amber was far too excited to sleep.

The first thing she had unpacked had been her father's notebook, the contents of each page so familiar to her now and so loved by her. He would have adored Paris. Both her parents would. What images would he have most wanted to capture? The Eiffel Tower, the women in their summer clothes? Amber longed to go out and explore. Was it selfish of her to want to do so alone, at her own pace, so that she could just stand and gaze and absorb everything?

Cecil had sent her a brief note instructing her to 'look beyond the obvious', and then 'superimpose it on the obvious – then you will have the beginning of a hint of what makes Paris the gourmet feast to the senses that it is'.

Amber wasn't sure she understood what Cecil meant. When she had said as much to Robert he had laughed and said that she wasn't to worry, sometimes even Cecil didn't understand what he himself meant.

What would her father, whose sketches of Classical Greek and Egyptian motifs were so expertly detailed, want to record if he was the one sitting here? Was it foolish of her to want to drape her father's columns in folds of silk printed with Greek urns and Egyptian hieroglyphs?

If she were ever to have her own premises as an interior decorator she would dress her windows with a single piece of furniture, a chair or perhaps a small desk – not polished wood but painted in a colour that complemented the fabric that would be draped over it; it would be the fabric that was centre stage, everything else merely a backdrop. People would stand and stare, unable to drag themselves away, bewitched by the spell of the fabric.

Amber laughed at herself. She was in Paris, with all that it offered. She should not be wasting her time daydreaming. Oh, but she did so long to go out; she had her guidebook and— But Lady Levington had said that she and Beth were not to leave the hotel without her, Amber reminded herself sternly. She didn't want to be sent home in disgrace on her very first day. A yawn caught her unawares, and then another. She hadn't felt tired but maybe it would be as well to have a rest. Lady Levington had warned them that their time in Paris was short and that there was a great deal to be done.

* * *

163

'I do hope that Alistair will visit us in Juan-les-Pins,' Beth whispered excitedly to Amber as they waited behind Lady Levington for the doorman to hail them a cab.

Alistair had written to Lady Levington before they had left London to say that he would be passing through Juan-les-Pins on his way to Florence, and asking her permission to call on them.

'Not that I shan't be perfectly happy with your company, dearest Amber,' Beth assured Amber as Lady Levington ushered them into their cab, whilst the doorman gave instructions to take them to number 31 Rue Cambon, 'for I shall, of course.'

But she was not Alistair, Amber acknowledged, and it was plain to her that Beth was already in love with her old playmate.

Number 31 rue Cambon was the address of the Chanel salon.

'We are merely taking a look,' Lady Levington warned as they stepped out of the cab into the morning sunshine and gasped with delight at the sight of the famous boutique.

Lady Levington had already told them both that she planned to order the vacation clothes they would need from small discreet dressmakers tucked away down narrow little streets, who understood perfectly the requirements of clothes suitable and *comme il faut* for very young ladies: pastel frocks in cool muslins, carefully discreet bathing suits, and new tennis dresses.

She would remember the special smell that was Paris for the rest of her life, Amber decided as they all stood on the pavement outside the Chanel salon. It was completely different from London, unique and somehow racy and yet sophisticated and elegant at the same time, a mixture of perfume, bread, coffee and cigars, bound together with something else that Amber could not identify but which she knew instinctively could not possibly be found anywhere else but Paris.

Frenchwomen, dressed so chicly that one could only admire them with awe, walked past in their beautiful clothes, accompanied by tiny little dogs on jewelled leads. To hear French spoken all around them was an experience that alone sent a thrill of excitement down Amber's spine. Thanks to the comtesse her understanding of spoken French and her ability to speak it fluently herself had improved dramatically, and it gave her a quiet sense of pleasure to listen to the French conversation going on all around her and realise that she could understand it.

She could quite happily have stayed here outside the salon, just watching everyone, but once they were inside everything she had seen on the street faded into insignificance. Mirror revetments turned the salon into an endless space filled with unspoken possibilities. Here and there a garment hung as though left there carelessly, and yet somehow catching the eye and holding the attention. Amber longed to examine them more closely.

Lady Levington, though, was in no mood to linger, and swept them up a flight of stairs where *vendeuses* were summoned to attend them. A few murmured words from Lady Levington, and a firm clap of a *vendeuse*'s hands, and it seemed to Amber only seconds later they were being shown outfit after outfit.

Amber immediately lost her heart to a pair of flared beach pyjama trousers, in sea-turquoise-coloured silk, embroidered around the hem with scallops of seashells, the trousers worn with a brief gilet over a thin vest, whilst on her head the model was wearing a broad-brimmed sunhat.

There were yachting outfits, tennis dresses, sporty clothes of every type, as well as beautifully elegant evening gowns

165

in Chanel's signature black, which Lady Levington decreed were far too old for such young girls.

Amber couldn't help looking longingly at them, though: simple fluid slips of jersey with fluted flirty hems cut in such a way as to make any woman who wore them feel she was at her absolute best.

Shoes for the daytime, with low heels and neat little T-bar fronts, in black and white were paired up together on the floor at an angle that made them look as though someone had just stepped out of them, whilst on their own raised dais there were evening shoes in black kid, shimmering with pearls and diamonds, teamed with matching clutch bags just large enough for a handkerchief and a lipstick.

It was one of Chanel's leather quilted bags that Amber longed for, though, unable to resist stroking the wonderfully soft leather and causing the saleswoman to state in swift polished French that it was the perfect bag for a young girl, an heirloom of a bag that she would cherish all her life.

Lady Levington shook her head over the price, but Amber couldn't bear to put it down. In the end, although she knew that Lady Levington did not really approve, Amber did the most grown-up thing she had ever done, and announced that she intended to buy the bag for herself with some money her grandmother had given her.

Waiting for it to be wrapped – and refusing to agree to have it sent to their hotel because she still couldn't really believe it was hers and that it wouldn't disappear if she let it out of her sight – first in its own soft fabric cover, then in several layers of tissue, then in a smart Chanel box, which was tied with black and white Chanel ribbon before being placed in a Chanel bag, Amber felt as though her heart might burst with the pleasure of owning something so beautiful.

Before they left Lady Levington allowed the girls to choose

for themselves one of the designer's trademark camellias to be worn as a brooch on a coat or a dress, or on a slide as a hair ornament.

Beth chose one in a pretty soft pink whilst Amber, after some indecision, opted for one in cream.

When they eventually left the Chanel salon Amber felt as though she was walking on air, hugging to herself the knowledge that no matter what happened to her in her life, no one would ever be able to take from her the pleasure of buying her Chanel bag.

After leaving Chanel, they walked along the Rue de la Paix where they stopped to look in the windows of the famous jewellers Cartier, where the plain Tank Americaine watches drew Amber's eye.

One shop, tucked away in the same street as Cartier, sold nothing but silk scarves, and once inside it even Lady Levington was tempted into buying an elegant silk evening scarf in jade green, decorated with hand-painted lotus blossoms, whilst Amber fell for one in Fortuny-style pleats in various shades of creams and golds.

At Jeanne Lanvin they were shown jersey golf clothes, and at Vionnet, Beth and Amber traded longing looks over the designer's bias-cut, fluid silk evening gowns.

But in the end it was to the discreet little dressmakers down the side streets that Lady Levington prudently gave their business, informing the girls that they were far too young to be wearing couture.

She did, though, allow Amber to quickly sketch the Chanel outfit she had fallen in love with for one of the dressmakers, who confirmed that she could make up something similar for her.

Sample garments were produced for the girls to try on, and Amber had to admit that they were every bit as elegant and smart as anything they'd seen in the couture houses.

For Amber, Lady Levington ordered a cream silk linen panelled skirt, which was to be teamed with its own matching blouse with a contrast trim on the neckline in navy. In addition there was a navy, red and white striped jacket, and then a darling little sweater in a pretty shade of green with cream silk bows appliquéd on it, plus another sweater in lemon yellow, appliquéd with navy silk bows.

Beth was to have a similar collection, but her skirt was to be French blue. They would do for informal outings, and sporty occasions, Lady Levington announced.

For more formal daytime wear there were afternoon dresses, three each, in pretty pastel-coloured silk and linen.

Curious about the provenance of the bales of fabrics the dressmakers produced for their inspection, Amber asked them in her neat French where they bought them from, and how they chose them.

'You were thinking of your silk mill, weren't you?' Beth teased her later when they had emerged from the narrow alleyways and returned to the Rue du Faubourg St-Honoré.

'They buy their silk from Lyons, not England,' Amber told her.

Then, of course, there were their new evening gowns, not properly grown up but certainly with that French *élan* about them that made Beth and Amber's eyes light up.

Silk chiffon over satin cut on the bias, in sugared-almond colours – the prospect of wearing something so up to the minute delighted them both, although Lady Levington took a little persuading that the low backs of the gowns were truly suitable for young girls.

'But see how the silk chiffon will cover any bareness,' the saleswoman pointed out, soothingly reassuring her.

After a light lunch in a café that had been recommended to Lady Levington, and which had a separate room for ladies only, which could not be looked into from the street, Lady Levington took the girls to Galeries Lafayette, where she bought them silk chemise and knicker sets trimmed with delicate lace, stockings, garter belts and handkerchiefs, before announcing that it was time to return to the hotel.

Of all her purchases her Chanel handbag was her favourite, Amber admitted. Her first fashion purchase for herself.

The stay in Paris flew by in a whirl of shopping, quickly followed by the delivery of exquisitely presented boxes of tissue-packed clothes, shoes and hats. New trunks had to be ordered from Louis Vuitton to accommodate all the purchases, and as the day for departure drew near, the maids were kept busy carefully repacking the new clothes in them.

There was barely time to do more than take a brief carriage ride in the Bois du Boulogne, followed by an equally brief visit to Versailles, where they were shown round the palace, now sadly only a shadow of its former glory, and nothing like Amber had imagined. The French Revolution had led to the palace being looted, and now it had the shabby air of somewhere deserted and unloved.

It was, though, possible to use one's imagination to picture how it might once have been, the Hall of Mirrors illuminated by hundreds of candles, their glow reflected infinitely, the courtiers moving through the formal steps of a formal dance, whilst those who were not dancing gossiped and looked on. But even imagining that was shadowed for Amber by the thought of the fate that had awaited poor silly Marie Antoinette, who had said that her husband's starving people should 'eat cake' when she was told that they could not afford to buy bread.

Thinking about Marie Antoinette reminded Amber of the plight of the poor at home, making her feel guilty about the fact that she was in such a fortunate position. Her grand-mother always said that it was important to be aware of one's responsibility to those less well off and, remembering that now, Amber made a vow that she would do exactly that.

The night before they were due to leave for Juan-les-Pins, Amber was so excited she could not sleep. Once again she opened her father's sketchbook, her eyes filming with tears. Here on these pages were sketches not just of some of his designs but of her mother and of Amber herself, swift char-coal likenesses, a few lines, no more, but enough to capture them faithfully.

As much as she had admired the fabrics she had seen since she came to Paris, to Amber, her father's designs still had a special freshness; her favourite sketches were those incorporating Roman coins and Greek heads, using clas-sical themes in rich colours; winged horses, manes flying, and heraldic symbols, ideas he had jotted down, which she knew he had used later to translate into elegant designs.

Her own sketches – minute Arc de Triomphes, and Eiffel Towers, elegant women in fitted dresses wearing large hats and walking tiny poodles, *tabac* waiters with waxed mous-taches and pristine white aprons stretched over round stomachs – which she had envisaged as witty and gay when she had written beneath them 'Paris at Play', seemed so lightweight in comparison. She closed the sketchpad, feeling rather downhearted.

As might have been expected at such a popular time of the year the majority of their fellow passengers on *Le Train Bleu* were also English, and as Amber discovered over dinner in the dining car, the ladies seemed to be taking the oppor-tunity to show off new clothes. Even Lady Levington wasn't immune to this temptation and was wearing a Lanvin dress with a matching jacket that she had bought earlier in the week.

Observing the elegance of their fellow diners as they were shown to their table, Amber was glad that Lady Levington had insisted that she and Beth dressed in one of their new outfits – pretty silk evening dresses from one of the 'clever little dressmakers' whose names and addresses were fiercely guarded by those privy to them. Lady Levington had admitted to the girls that she had obtained her list from the wife of the British Ambassador to whom she was distantly connected.

Since this was France, Lady Levington permitted them each to have a glass of white wine with their dinner, although she drew the line at following French custom to the extent that she was prepared to permit the rather plump gentleman who was trying to strike up a conversation with them to do so, and made it frostily clear to him that his overtures were not welcome. Whilst this was going on Amber did not dare to look at Beth in case she gave way to a fit of giggles.

Monsieur was extremely fat, and there had been an ominous creaking when he had bowed low over Lady Levington's hand, hinting that he might actually be wearing a corset of some description.

After dinner, when some of the gentlemen retired to the smoking car, Lady Levington insisted that Amber and Beth must retire to their *wagons-lits* for an early night.

Amber got out her notebook, too excited for sleep. She could hardly believe that she was on her way to the South of France. It seemed too marvellous to be true. She just wished that there was someone to share this excitement with, who would truly understand. Beth was a dear but she didn't have Amber's own passion for the artistic side of life. Lord Robert would have understood, and so would Jay.

171

Jay! She would write to him now this minute, Amber decided. At least then she would feel that she was sharing her excitement with someone who understood her.

She wrote so much that her wrist started to ache. Her only disappointment, she told Jay, was that she would not see Lyons, as they would pass through it during the night. It would have been interesting to have explored because of its historical connection with silk.

Dear Jay. Unlike Louise, who was also well born but without money, Jay never showed any sign of bitterness about that fact. Amber had learned from her stay in London that many members of upper-class families, who had lost their money after the war, through death duties in the main, thought it beneath them to work for a living. Did Jay ever feel resentful about his own situation? He had said not, Amber reminded herself, and at least he was free to choose his own path through life. He could marry whoever he chose, and because he loved her.

She wished she too could have that choice. If Blanche had not been so very wealthy maybe she would have. But the price she had to pay for having a wealthy grandmother was that Blanche wanted to use that wealth to buy Amber the husband and the title she herself had been denied, even though that was not what Amber wanted.

Chapter Fifteen

'Still at work, Jay?'

Jay looked up from the ledgers he was studying in what was known as the steward's room of Denham Place, and which was in effect his office as estate manager. Jay felt very much at home in this good-sized comfortable room, and appreciated the fact that Blanche had allowed him to make it his own territory. Warm dark green curtains hung at the windows, and in addition to the large desk and chair there was also a handsome leather fireside chair and a comfortably sagging Knole sofa covered in green velvet.

'By choice, Mrs Pickford. I've been studying the yearly yields for Denham's arable lands.'

Blanche didn't often come in search of him, normally either sending for him or appointing a time when she wished him to attend her in her own study when there was something she wished to discuss with him.

'We are making a profit, I trust?'

Jay smiled. 'Yes indeed. Last year's yield was up on the previous year, and I am hoping for another increase this year. I've been wondering as well if we shouldn't be thinking about improving our breeding stock of cattle. Buying a champion bull would be expensive I know, but worthwhile in the long run.'

'Prepare some figures for me and I shall take a look at them,' Blanche said.

Jay kept his office in immaculate order. Blanche paused and bent down to pat the aged spaniel asleep in its basket.

'We have a new member of the household, I see.'

'My grandfather's old gundog,' Jay told her calmly. 'He's far too old to work now, of course, and he's gone lame. My grandfather felt it was best to have him put down, but I got the vet to take a look at him, and he reckons he just has a bit of rheumatism. Might as well let the old chap live out his life in comfort.'

Blanche already knew all about Barrant's curt order that his dog was to be shot, and the fact Jay had not only paid for the vet to take a look at him out of his own pocket but that he had also paid for his treatment and bought him the warm sheepskin that was now lining his new basket.

'If we're talking about the dog, then I agree; if we're talking about your grandfather then the shotgun would have been my preferred option,' she told Jay drily.

'I'm increasing your wages from the beginning of next month, Jay. No, don't thank me,' she stopped him. 'My father believed in the old maxim that a good workman is worthy of his hire and so do I. You'll be aware that many of the mills in Macclesfield are laying people off?'

'Yes.'

'I have no liking for Denby Mill, as I'm sure you know, and would happily see it closed down. However, I feel I have a duty to the workforce there. Tomorrow I want you to go down to the mill and tell the manager that no one is to be laid off from Denby Mill, and that wages are to be slightly increased.'

Jay was not as surprised by Blanche's instructions as he knew others might be. He had come to know his employer well, or at least as well as she allowed anyone to know her, and he knew that for Blanche Pickford charity wasn't just a matter of sitting on a committee.

It saddened Jay that Amber had never been allowed to see behind the cold façade that Blanche often showed to the outer world. He wondered sometimes if Blanche unbent with him because his status as her employee meant that he was not in a position to criticise her, but he hoped that it was because she knew that she could trust him, and because she respected his desire to make his own way in the world.

He had guessed when she had given him the job initially that her decision rested in part on who he was rather than his qualifications for the position, but as he had discreetly made plain to both her and his grandfather, he was his own man and he did not intend to be used by either of them to foster their animosity towards one another.

Barrant was his grandfather, Jay loved him, but that did not mean he was unaware of Barrant's faults. Blanche was his employer but that did not mean that he could not respect and admire her, and be aware that his grandfather must have hurt her.

Blanche had turned to leave but suddenly she stopped and turned back to him, saying abruptly, 'You don't approve of my plans for my granddaughter, do you?'

'She is very young and idealistic, and I imagine the prospect of a marriage based on practical issues must seem daunting to her,' Jay responded as tactfully as he could.

Blanche inclined her head in acknowledgement of the truth of his words. 'They are as much for her sake as my own,' she told him guardedly.

Amber had no idea what real life was all about. She was a dreamer, idealistic, and stubborn. There was so much that a woman could achieve in the right marriage, so much that she could do in the wider world if her husband had power and influence, and was prepared to share that with her.

Blanche herself had been denied the chance to be all that she could have been, and that was not going to happen to Amber.

Changing tack, Blanche said, 'Your cousin Cassandra is staying on at Fitton Hall, I hear.'

Jay stood up. 'Yes.'

'I dare say then that ultimately we can look forward to another de Vries–Fitton Legh marriage. That should please your grandfather, history repeating itself. He took a Fitton Legh bride himself.'

Barrant de Vries was a fool for not valuing his grandson more, Blanche decided. But then Barrant never had valued those whom he should have done, Blanche thought bitterly after she had left Jay. She could have given him so much, but he had rejected her. Amber was not going to suffer a similar fate – or its consequences. She would have the life that Blanche had been denied.

Blanche had high hopes of the Levingtons' son. She had made some discreet enquiries following Lady Levington's invitation to Amber. Two young people thrown together for the summer – it was almost inevitable that there would be a romance.

Chapter Sixteen

Even before their train had drawn to a halt in the station at Juan-les-Pins, Amber knew that she would never forget the sights and smells of the South. With each mile that had taken them deeper into its sensual embrace she had become more intoxicated. Aix-en-Provence, even though seen merely from the window of their *wagons-lits*, had literally seized her heart and, she half suspected, stolen it for good. She was entranced, bewitched, lost in the magic of the Midi, her mind filled by its colours. She could feel her senses opening up to it and drinking it in until she was dizzy with the beauty of it.

Lord Levington and Henry had driven down to the station to meet them, Henry beaming with pride over the new Bugatti car his father had given him as a coming-of-age gift.

There was much enthusiastic talk on the part of father and son with regard to Le Mans, the motor car race, interrupted by concerned questions from Lady Levington as to the health of her younger children. Amber, though, was content to stand aside from their family conversation and simply hold to herself in beatific silence, revelling in the sheer pleasure of being there.

She could hear Lady Levington questioning her husband about the villa and its suitability for their purposes.

'Top hole in every way,' Lord Levington assured her. 'Mind you, I was a bit concerned when Benson informed me that we've got the owner's godson staying in a cottage in the gardens. Turns out that the agent neglected to inform us that this Jean-Philippe fellow lives there. He seems a decent sort, obviously well connected, since the owner of the villa's his godmother. No need to worry about him, though. Keeps himself to himself. Dabbles with paint.' Lord Levington gave a small sigh and then added, 'Well, at least it's not poetry. Apparently he's working on something for some Academy showing or other. Anyway I've told him that he'd better come up to the house for dinner tonight and introduce himself to you so that you can look him over for yourself.'

'Indeed he had,' Lady Levington agreed coolly, obviously not entirely pleased about the idea of their new neighbour.

By contrast, the thought of living so close to a young man who sounded as though he must be an artist filled Amber with an awed delight that she hugged to herself.

The luggage was loaded onto a waiting dray by the servants, sweating in the stillness of the late afternoon heat.

Henry wanted to show off his new car and its prowess, but Lady Levington insisted that Amber and Beth were to join her in the Bentley.

''Fraid there might not be room for all of us, Phoebe,' Lord Levington warned her. 'One of the girls will have to go with Henry.'

'You go, Amber,' Beth urged her. 'Henry drives too fast for me and makes me feel quite sick.'

The Bugatti was dark blue, the sun glinting off its polished bonnet and shiny wheels. The hot sun strengthened the odours of leather, paint and petrol, mingling them with the scent of dust and pine.

As the road wound up from the station through the town

and beyond it into the hills, Henry was forced to moderate his speed to the sharpness of the many bends and the traffic of donkeys, carts and other cars. The winding nature of the road afforded Amber tantalising glimpses of the sea down below them, through the stone pines that shaded the hill-sides. They drove past high white-painted walls and wrought-iron gates with scarlet geraniums frothing through them, and onto the dusty road.

'Here we are,' Henry shouted to her above the roar of the engine and the rush of the wind, as he turned in through a pair of open gates and along a driveway scattered with rose petals, whilst Amber caught her breath in delight.

Villa Florentine, with its stucco walls painted a dazzling white, was as beautiful and as ornately Italianate as its name suggested. It resembled a storybook illustration of a house, all turrets and towers, with high arched windows, and wrought-iron balconies, the cool purity of its white walls heated by the passionate tumble of scarlet hibiscus and purple bougainvillaea.

Terracotta jars the height of a small child decorated the stone steps leading to the columned portico, bright red geraniums tumbling from them, formality and informality married together in a way that awakened the senses.

The hallway beyond the porticoed door was welcomely cool after the heat outside. The black and white marble-tiled floor, which looked like a chessboard, echoed to the sound of their movements and voices.

Black marble statues filled the arched niches set into the alabaster-covered walls. A wrought-iron staircase curled upwards past pseudo-medieval windows.

The lady's maid Amber was to share with Beth arrived to sweep them upstairs to their rooms, on the second floor of the villa next to one another and with views overlooking a wide terrace, beyond which was a swimming pool, and then elaborate Italian-style gardens dropping down towards the Mediterranean itself. From her own window Amber looked discreetly for the cottage in which Lord Levington had said Jean-Philippe was living, but disappointingly she could not see it.

It was early evening before Amber saw her hosts again. Lady Levington had suggested that she might want to spend the afternoon supervising her unpacking, resting and writing to her grandmother to inform her of her safe arrival.

Since they were dining *en famille* Lady Levington had said that there was no need for Beth and Amber to wear evening gowns, but their long journey and the heat of the day had still necessitated a cooling wash and changing into fresh simple dresses. Amber chose one of pale blue silk embroidered with flowers made from small pearl beads, the edges of its handkerchief-hem skirt sewn with the same small beads. Over it Amber wore a matching white bolero lined in the same pale blue silk. A pretty pearl-decorated hairclip secured her curls, which she had had to brush ruthlessly to remove the tangles caused by the drive up to the villa in Henry's open-top car.

Beth's parents and Henry were already on the terrace drinking martinis when Amber walked through the open French doors to join them, their conversation accompanied by the chirping sound of the crickets.

Lord Levington offered to mix Amber one of his specialities – a White Lady.

'I am not sure that the girls should be encouraged to drink cocktails,' Lady Levington protested.

'I shan't make it very strong,' the earl reassured her, giving Amber a kind smile.

She sipped it hesitantly, relieved to find that he had been as good as his word. She had quickly learned that some of the more unscrupulous debs' delights were inclined to produce drinks that were far stronger than they were supposed to be, luring girls into shadowy conservatories or outside into darkened gardens with a glass of what was supposed to be lemonade and the promise of some cooling air after the heat of a ballroom, only for the girl to discover once she had drunk her 'lemonade' that she was in no position to defend herself, and that her drink had contained something much stronger – normally gin – allowing her escort to take advantage of her intoxicated state.

'Never accept a drink from anyone unless you have seen it poured or selected it yourself from a tray carried by a waiter,' was the advice that the more worldly-wise girls shared with those who were less so.

Beth had just come hurrying through the French doors to join them when the butler came out onto the terrace to announce the arrival of the Levingtons' dinner guest.

Amber's fingers tightened round the stem of her glass, butterflies of nervous excitement fluttering giddily inside her stomach. Already in her mind's eye she had pictured Jean-Philippe, modelling him on her father, and adding a dash of French elegance, imagining a person with great charm, dark-haired and dark-eyed, with long narrow artist's hands.

But the man now standing conversing with the earl and countess was nothing like that at all. He was tall, yes, but with great broad shoulders and a muscular chest, the contours of which could be seen quite plainly beneath the thin smock-like shirt he was wearing. Where Lord Levington and Henry were clean-shaven, he had a small pointed beard, his skin was swarthy, his thick dark hair worn in almost shoulder-length curls like a cavalier. No, Amber corrected herself as he turned his head and looked at her and she saw the flash of the gold earring he was wearing in one ear, he was not a cavalier, he was a gypsy, or maybe a pirate, merciless, ruthless and dangerous. Automatically she turned her back on him, but not before she had seen the white flash of his teeth as he smiled mockingly at her. Her hand was trembling. Her face felt hot but she was shivering. She had never seen such dark eyes, almost black, and his hands, not an artist's hands but an artisan's, wide and square and . . . and powerful. He would paint in thick heavy strokes, she decided, not pale watercolours or even oils, and in clamouring sensual colours that drugged the senses, stealing away reason.

Beth was tugging on her sleeve, round-eyed with awe and excitement.

'Do look, Amber,' she begged in a whisper. 'Isn't he handsome?'

Handsome, with those too bold eyes and that gypsy pirate face, that too muscular body and that ridiculous earring?

'No,' Amber denied sharply. 'I do not think him handsome at all.'

Amber could hear Lady Levington laughing, followed by Jean-Philippe speaking. His voice was like the warm treacle her grandmother's cook used to heat to put on Amber's porridge in the winter, almost too rich so that Amber's stomach flinched from the taste of it as much as it longed for it.

It was late, gone midnight, and Amber's head was aching. Jean-Philippe might have departed physically over an hour ago, apologising yet again for his presence in the cottage, but he was still dominating the conversation, as if he had been there.

Amber had no logical explanation for why she felt so antagonistic towards him or why it was such a relief when he had left. All she could understand was that something about him jarred her so powerfully that it frightened her.

182

He would not intrude on them, he had assured Lady Levington. He had important work to complete, on which he would be working virtually day and night.

Day and night. Amber shuddered. There was something about the connection between those dark eyes and the dark hot velvet darkness of the Mediterranean night that raised a rash of gooseflesh under her skin.

Lord Levington and especially Lady Levington had been evidently impressed by him, and Beth too had responded to his Gallic charm.

Henry, though, did not seem to share his family's admiration for Jean-Philippe, Amber had noticed. So she was not completely alone in her feeling of wary discomfort. Thank heavens for that.

'You are late.'

'But you have waited.' Jean-Philippe laughed as he slid his hands over Marianne's smooth bare shoulders and then bent his head to kiss the red ripeness of her pouting lips.

'My husband will be back very soon. You had better leave if you don't want him to catch you here with me.'

'How can I leave now when you are presenting me with such a feast of sensual delight?' Jean-Philippe teased her, slipping his hand into the loose neckline of her blouse. Her breasts were round and full, their flesh smooth and sun-ripened, her nipples dusky and engorged. It was barely six weeks since she had weaned her fourth child, and her breasts still held the heady scent of milk and fecundity.

She had been feeding her child the first time he had seen her, deliberately allowing the unfastened top of her dress to fall open so that he could see the baby's greedy suckle, and she had been slow to cover herself when she had removed him from her breast.

Her husband was the local baker, rising early and spending

his evenings drinking in a nearby *tabac*, leaving her untended and eager for the kind of pleasure Jean-Philippe was only too happy to supply.

He released her to pull a chair from the table and sat down on it whilst she stood watching him, her hands on her hips. Drawing her closer, he pulled down her blouse to fully expose her breasts and set about licking and tugging on them with his tongue and his lips, sharing his attentions equally in a speedy rhythm until he felt her shudder fiercely in pleasure.

His own brief grunt was the only acknowledgement he gave of her arousal – that and the swift movement of his hands beneath her skirt to her thighs, heavy and hot, the place between them wet and ready.

He slid his hands round to her buttocks, kneading them, asking her mockingly, 'Would your husband give me a job, do you think? Certainly something is rising well around here.'

She didn't answer him. She took her pleasure as greedily and selfishly as though she were a man, closing her eyes, making guttural noises deep in her throat as she urged him on. His fingertip slid expertly through her wetness, finding the place that made her tense and arch and then buck frantically in the grip of her climax.

Releasing her, Jean-Philippe stood up, unfastening his trousers. Without any need for words she leaned forward, her hands either side of the seat of the chair he had just vacated, gripping it, her legs apart.

Jean-Philippe went behind her, pushing up her skirts. Her buttocks were soft and fleshy, her stance exposing the cleft between them, and beyond it the fleshy opening to her sex with its still swollen lips drawn back in offering, the dark bush of her body hair a tight mass of wet curls.

He stroked into her slowly, enjoying both the sensation

and the sight of the dark-veined head of his penis sliding into her wetness, and then out again as he slid it the length of her slit to her clitoris, and then back again and in, and out, and then in deeper, fully in, penetrating her fiercely and fully so that she cried out in eager pleasure, protesting when he pulled back to tease her with the sliding caress of his head between her lips.

Between the *tabac* and the kitchen was the bakery, with its ovens and its shop frontage that ran the length of the house, and as Jean-Philippe played with her clitoris he could hear the sound of the bell on the shop door.

'My husband,' Marianne warned him, groaning when Jean-Philippe simply thrust powerfully into her, catching her up in his rhythm as he leaned forward and whispered, 'Do you really want me to stop? Can you bear it now? You can't, can you?'

She was moaning and trying to smother the sound as his strokes increased in speed and depth. Jean-Philippe felt the excitement that came with risk burn through him, and he thrust harder and felt her muscles latch on to him and tighten in a furious burst of spasms. On the other side of the wall he could hear the footsteps of her husband coming closer. He thrust into his own orgasm and then again, letting it take him, savouring the explosion of pleasure and the release that came with it.

The handle on the door rattled. Jean-Philippe patted Marianne's bottom and pulled down her skirt as the door started to open. As Marianne's husband stepped into the kitchen Jean-Philippe sat down on the chair.

'Ah, Monsieur du Breveonet, you are here,' the baker grunted.

'Yes, Jacques, your good wife promised me some of her special conserve. I believe its flavour and perfume are beyond compare,' he added softly, looking at Marianne as he spoke.

The smell of her sex was still on his hands, and it amused him that she could not walk for fear of what he had deposited inside her running down her legs to betray her.

He was still grinning to himself half an hour later as he walked back to the cottage.

Chapter Seventeen

Greg was having the time of his life in Hong Kong, or at least he had been doing since he had run into Lionel Shepton, an acquaintance from Oxford. Lionel's parents had been missionaries. After their deaths in Africa the Church had paid for their orphaned son's education, on the understanding that Lionel would follow in his parents' footsteps, but Lionel had had other ideas. Not for him a life of good works and poor pay. Lionel had seen how some of his contemporaries at Oxford lived and had quickly resolved that he was far more suited to their fun-loving way of life than he was to the Church.

He had originally come out to Hong Kong with a rich friend, who'd since moved on. He was popular with women, well-mannered, good-looking and charming, and he was careful to keep from the smart social circle of the exclusive Peak Club, in which he moved courtesy of the rich friend, the fact that he made a living introducing young men like Greg to the pleasures of the darker side of Hong Kong life: prostitutes, drugs and gambling, and all run by Hong Kong's notorious Triad gangs.

Blanche loved Greg and she had seen to it that he would be provided with a generous allowance whilst he was in Hong Kong, far more than the modest salary he was now being paid for 'working' for Henry Jardine in the offices of his shipping company. Jardine and his wife, Jane, owned a large house on the Peak, with a small bachelor guesthouse in its grounds – Greg's new home.

Greg and Lionel first renewed their acquaintanceship at a cocktail party held by the Governor of Hong Kong – a dull, stuffy affair Greg had considered it until he had quite literally bumped into Lionel.

The exchange of histories since leaving Oxford, mutually edited before being passed on, made it apparent to both of them that what had been mere acquaintanceship should now become a friendship.

Jardine, at a loss to know how best to entertain a bored young man who had made it obvious that he neither needed nor wanted to work, was initially relieved by their camaraderie.

Much of British Hong Kong's respectable social life was focused on the Peak Club, which vetted everyone applying for membership and made it quite clear that certain races, including the Cantonese, would never be granted access. Tea dances and bridge, followed by dinner were the order of the day at the club; well enough in their way, but as Lionel pointed out to Greg within a week of their meeting, there were more amusing ways for a young man to entertain himself.

Greg was quick on the uptake.

'I could do with a woman,' he had told Lionel frankly. 'And not one who's looking for a ring on her finger, if you know what I mean.'

Lionel most certainly did. Hong Kong's complex system of licensed brothels for each and every different class of customer, might now be against the law, but that didn't mean that they had ceased to exist.

Prostitution, like so much else, was now controlled by the Triads. Chinese girls were taken from poor villages and brought to Hong Kong, some to be shipped overseas, some to remain in Hong Kong itself, all of them bought for pitifully small sums of money. And all would earn that sum back many thousands of times for those who 'owned' them during their short working careers.

Once Greg knew that he could list his preferences and requirements just as though he was putting in an order for any other commodity, his original hesitation gave way to an almost overreaching self-confidence. Why restrict oneself to the taste of a single fruit when one could enjoy so very many differing 'flavours' – and all for such a reasonable price?

Very soon he was thanking Lionel for putting him wise, and enjoying the fawning subservience of the madams running the brothels.

One of Greg's favourites was a very upmarket affair catering to a wealthy clientele. To the uninitiated the Shangri La Residence looked like a smart discreet hotel from the outside. A pair of large muscular doormen wearing blue and gold livery flanked the carved satinwood double doors, which remained closed unless the man entering knew the correct current password. New clients had to ask for Madame S. Once inside the ornately decorated hallway a beautiful receptionist, in a cheongsam so tight that she must have been sewn into it, came forward to bow and ask the client what his desire for his visit was.

The brothel extended to all five floors of the tall narrow building, with each floor providing a designated 'type' of sex, starting with the basement, which was reserved for those whose tastes ran to bestiality – situated in the basement, so Lionel had told Greg with a grin, because it was easier to accommodate the animals at that lower level.

There was a macabre in-joke amongst men who were regular visitors to the Shangri La that the smell of roasting meat from the food shops close to the brothel signified that a client had enjoyed a particularly violent form of pleasure, and that the animal now being cooked had come from one of the basement rooms.

Each floor was designed to the same pattern: a series of small individual pleasure rooms, some with large 'windows' that looked out into a 'viewing area' for those clients who enjoyed voyeurism, and a large communal room for 'shared pleasures'.

Greg's favourite activity was paying for two or sometimes three girls to pleasure him whilst at the same time carrying out lesbian acts on one another.

There was one house girl, a tall broad-shouldered Scandinavian blonde with large high breasts and nipples the size of coat pegs, who drove her strapped-on dildo into the other girls with particular enthusiasm.

The torture chambers, also down in the basement, were somewhere that didn't tempt Greg, although he wasn't averse to a bit of punishment when he was the one administering it to one of the girls. Nothing too much, just smacking her around a bit and making sure she knew who was boss. There was nothing quite like the pleasure of bringing down a small cane on the bare backside of a girl who wasn't working her tongue and her lips round a chap's dick well enough, especially when he was paying for the privilege.

When Henry Jardine heard on the grapevine what Greg was doing, he took him to one side and informed him that the done thing for a young man in his position was to buy himself a clean girl and set her up as his mistress.

'Many of the girls in the brothels have syphilis,' he told Greg uncomfortably. 'And I'd be doing you an ill favour if I didn't tell you that. In fact I'm surprised that young Shepton hasn't done so already. The other thing is, well, our sort just don't go down to that quarter. It isn't done. Bad form, you know. Hong Kong is a small place and people talk.'

Henry Jardine's well-meant advice infuriated Greg. He didn't like having a dried-up old stick like Jardine making out that he wasn't sharp enough to know what was what.

Lionel, on the other hand, was irritated by Greg's stupidity in not recognising the need to at least pay lip service to the 'rules'. Lionel had been careful to keep the two worlds he inhabited entirely separate – after all, he needed his social acceptability to meet his victims. Normally once they were hooked into the life to which Lionel introduced them, the last thing they wanted to do was talk about it, especially to those they knew would disapprove.

And so to punish Greg for prejudicing his own position he took him to one of the Triad-run gambling dens that flourished by trapping foolish young men.

Hooked by the heady adrenalin-fuelled triumph of his 'beginner's luck', Greg failed to see the small nod the Chinese standing in the shadows gave Lionel, or the money that changed hands. He was far too busy congratulating himself on his early success and skill.

It was late when they finally left the club, Lionel's arm round Greg's hunched shoulders as he comforted him.

'Never mind, your luck's bound to turn. Look at how well you were doing at the outset.'

Greg blinked in the pre-dawn light. His eyeballs felt sore and his head felt heavy. He had lost count of the number of IOUs he had written on Lionel's assurance that the full amount would be next to nothing and that this next hand was bound to be a winner.

'And don't worry about Chung Hai. He's a decent sort and will run a tab for you so that you can settle up with him when you get your allowance. Fancy a pipe before we head back to the Peak?'

Greg shook his head. He couldn't think straight as it was, without making things worse by visiting an opium den.

Chapter Eighteen

The days were flying by, filled with all manner of social entertainments. With Henry to escort them, Lady Levington permitted Beth and Amber more freedom than they had had in London, and within a week they were part of a group of young people staying in the smart villas scattered about Juan-les-Pins, all intent on having fun.

Most days Henry drove them down the Promenade des Anglais coast road, where they might drive into Cannes along the Croisette, so that they could meet up with their new friends for lunch at the art nouveau Carlton Hotel or the art deco Hotel Martinez before strolling along the Croisette itself, or if they preferred, they could drive into Antibes for cocktails at the Hôtel du Cap, with its acres of garden and its spectacular swimming pool.

Life was as heady and hedonistic as the cocktails Amber was learning to drink, and the compliments of the charming young French boys who spoke English with a delicious accent. But at the back of her mind was always the stark reality of the tragedy that had sent Greg into exile, and her grandmother's own expectations for her.

Amber knew perfectly well from her boarding school days how upper-class girls were expected to behave, but knowing how to behave to fit in with the set in which she was mixing, and feeling comfortable doing so, were two very different things.

The rigid formality of the upper-class way of life, with its artifice and its 'rules', seemed so false and unnatural after the home life she had known with her parents. She felt as though she were playing a role to suit other people rather than simply being herself, and she hated the falseness of that. It chafed against her and made her feel that she was an outsider who did not really fit it.

It was a relief to open her sketchbook and escape into her own private world.

Wherever she went Amber took her sketchbook with her, trying to capture the images filling her head and firing her imagination: blue silk shot through with turquoise, the colour of the Mediterranean, sprays of bougainvillaea and geranium against terracotta and white, and then in contrast the old buildings of the medieval towns of St-Paul-de-Vence and Mougins, jewel colours against worn stone, soft silken beauty on bare rock, the patterns and colours of nature translated into fabrics that would capture the essence of everything that the South of France was.

She and Beth coaxed Henry to get up early one morning and drive them to Grasse, where they visited the famous flower market and then bought perfume, giggling self-consciously together at the passion of the 'nose' at the small perfumery, when he spoke with deliberate sensuality of the impossibility of his desire to capture the elusive fragrance of a woman's skin.

Amber's skin tanned a warm gold, and freckled Beth sighed in envy. The young Frenchmen grew ever more ardent with their compliments.

One evening Lord and Lady Levington took them to the casino in Monte Carlo, where Amber won fifty pounds at *chemin de fer* with traditional beginner's luck.

There were yachting parties and picnics, supper parties and impromptu dances held after dinner on the terraces of elegant villas; so many things that she could barely describe them all in the letters she wrote home to both Jay and her grandmother. Whilst her letters to her grandmother were stilted dutiful accounts detailing the things she felt her grandmother would want to hear: the names – and titles – of the people to whom she had been introduced – in her letters to Jay, Amber was able to give rein to her joy in the intoxicating beauty of her new surroundings. She filled page after ecstatic page with detailed descriptions of the places they had visited, barely mentioning the people she had met. Pleasant though they were, they could not compare with the effect on her senses and her emotions of the South of France itself.

She didn't mention Caroline. What Jay had told her had been put away carefully somewhere at the back of her mind as too painful and shocking to think on.

To her own confusion, she was almost glad that the distance between them meant that as yet she had received only one very brief letter from Greg, forwarded to her from Macclesfield, and not containing any reference to Caroline at all, but instead simply telling her that he had arrived safely. Now, with her own knowledge lying between them, Amber found that her letter to Greg telling him about the changes in her life had been hard to write – almost as though she had been writing it to a stranger.

Twice Lady Levington invited Jean-Philippe to join the family for dinner, and on both occasions Amber felt the same sharp antagonism she had felt on first seeing him. He had a carelessness about him; an arrogance, in the flash of those dark eyes, whenever his gaze rested on her. He was ridiculous with that mane of thick curls, and that reckless edge of danger, a folly of a man whose only art probably lay in the bold strokes with which he had drawn himself. He was an offence, an affront to real art, a predatory poseur who was flirting and flattering his way into Lady Levington's good graces, but Amber wasn't taken in by him.

'But how can you not like him,' Beth protested one evening when he had had dinner with them, 'when he is so very handsome, and an artist?'

'I just don't,' was all Amber could tell her.

Towards the end of their second week at Juan-les-Pins, Alistair and his parents arrived, *en route* for Florence, and it quickly became plain that both sets of parents' hopes for a match between their children were going to be realised. Beth drifted from hour to hour in a haze of Alistair-drenched delight, and Amber wasn't surprised when it was decided that instead of continuing to Florence with his parents, Alistair would stay on in Juan-les-Pins as the Levingtons' guest.

Now when they went out it was Alistair who drove Beth, so that they could be alone, leaving Henry and Amber to pair off. Amber didn't want to say anything – Henry was the Levingtons' son, after all, and Beth's brother – but increasingly something about his manner towards her was making her feel uncomfortable. He had taken to appearing silently and unexpectedly whenever she was on her own, almost as though he had been watching her. And when he was with her he would stand uncomfortably close to her, his unwavering gaze fixed on her.

One evening after a party at the Hôtel du Cap, instead of allowing Amber to go inside once they had returned to the villa, Henry grabbed her hand and insisted that she walk through the villa gardens with him, into the darkness where the formal gardens ended and the steps that led down to the beach began.

He had been in an odd mood all evening, scowling and

getting cross when one of the French boys had flirted with her, and Amber would rather have gone straight inside. Henry had drunk several Blood and Sand cocktails, downing the mix of whisky, orange juice, cherry brandy and vermouth in a few quick swallows before calling for another, and she had been frightened by the speed at which he had driven back.

'I really think we should go straight in,' she told him.

'Not yet.'

Henry was still holding her hand and before she realised what he intended to do he made a grab for her, pushing her back against the low wall behind her and trying to kiss her.

Amber managed to turn her face away so that his lips touched only her cheek. Alarmed and upset by his behaviour, she pushed him away, relieved when he released her, allowing her to run back through the garden towards the villa.

She didn't see Jean-Philippe until it was too late and he was standing in front of her, blocking her path.

'So, the virgin runs from her would-be lover, too afraid to be kissed,' he mocked her. 'Poor Henry, he is on fire for you, but you are oblivious to him.'

'Let me past.'

Somehow Amber managed to sidestep him, her heart pounding as she fled towards the villa. She was beginning to realise that men were not all, as she had so innocently imagined, made in the same mould as her father. Even Greg had been overcome with lust. The forceful intent and anger that had accompanied Henry's embrace had frightened her, and now Jean-Philippe's mockery left her feeling that she was better off not having anything to do with the male sex at all.

The next morning at breakfast, when Henry sat opposite her and stared at her throughout the meal without saying a word, Amber felt uncomfortable and somehow slightly afraid. Would he say something about her to his parents? Ask them to send her home out of spite, perhaps? She hoped not. She would hate that.

She was walking in the garden a little while later when she saw Lady Levington coming towards her.

'Amber, my dear, there you are, good,' her hostess greeted her. 'Come and sit down for a moment. There is something I wish to discuss with you.'

Obediently Amber took a seat on the garden bench next to Beth's mother.

'Lord Levington and I are a little concerned that Henry could be getting rather too fond of you. Young men of Henry's nature are rather prone to imagining themselves in love, and you are an exceptionally pretty girl.' Lady Levington gave a faint sigh that made Amber feel guilty, as though she had done something wrong.

'It is unfortunate that you have been thrown so much together,' Lady Levington continued. 'I should have realised. You're a charming girl, Amber, and I know you are far too sensible not to understand that Lord Levington and I have . . . certain hopes for Henry's future.'

Amber knew exactly what she was inferring: a suitable girl from the right kind of background. Not a girl like her. Amber's face burned with humiliation.

'Of course, I know that you are not the kind of girl to misunderstand a foolish young man's calf love, Amber, and I have said as much to Lord Levington.'

'I have never thought of Henry as anything other than Beth's brother,' Amber told her quietly. 'It is the only way I think of him.'

'Well, of course.' Lady Levington was looking more relaxed now. She patted Amber's hand and smiled at her. 'I just wanted you to understand why Lord Levington and

I feel that it would be better if the two of you were not to have any more contact with one another.'

There was a clammy, unpleasant feeling in Amber's stomach. 'You are sending me home?' she guessed.

Immediately Lady Levington reassured her, 'Oh, my dear, no such thing, of course not. No, nothing of the sort, for as I have already said, we lay no blame on you. It is simply a matter of nipping in the bud a situation that could become difficult. In a couple of days Lord Levington will be joining some friends who have invited him to sail on their yacht, and Henry will be accompanying him. When they return Henry will escort Beth to Florence, where she is to stay with Alistair and his parents.' She patted Amber's hand again. 'I shall enjoy having your company in the absence of Beth and my husband. Now, a word of warning: it may be that Henry will suggest that you correspond with one another.'

'I shall tell him that I would rather not,' Amber said quietly.

'There, I knew you would understand. I'm glad we've come to this arrangement. What a lovely morning it is.' The countess was all smiles now.

'Yes.' Amber felt as though her tongue were stuck to the roof of her mouth. It was silly of her to feel so upset. Of course Lord and Lady Levington did not want her as a daughter-in-law. Nor had it ever occurred to her to think of herself in that role; not for one minute. It was just that hearing Lady Levington speak to her in such a way had shown her a reality that hurt. She had believed that the countess liked her and cared about her, and that their differing social class wasn't important. But she had only been deceiving herself and now she felt humiliated and betrayed – by herself for not realising the truth. Beth's mother was just like Lady Rutland and her friends in reality, concerned solely with appearances and convention.

Lady Levington had returned to the villa but Amber couldn't face going back. Not yet. She got up from the bench where she had been sitting and walked slowly through the garden, oppressed by the sombre weight of her own thoughts as she started to walk down the stone steps leading to the villa's private beach. At least she could be on her own there. It was too early in the day for the nursemaids to bring the nursery party down to play.

Lost in her own misery, Amber walked along the sand, her head down, the morning sun warm on her back. She and Henry had planned to drive to Antibes later in the morning. Of course she would not be doing that now.

She looked up, blinking away her threatening tears and then stiffened, her attention caught by a movement in the sea, an arm, brown and thickly muscled cleaving the foaming waves, then another, a head of thick dark hair, shoulders broad and gleaming where the sunlight met their sea-wet flesh.

Without thinking, Amber moved back into the shadows of the rocky outcrop that had broken free of the cliffs.

The artist was swimming. His cottage had its own access to the beach, she remembered him telling Lady Levington. He was standing up now, water spraying from his flesh as he shook himself. His chest was barred with thick dark hair. It arrowed down, running over his flat stomach as he strode naked out of the sea. Naked . . .

Amber wanted to turn and run but she couldn't. She was transfixed, trembling with shock and unwanted knowledge. Male statues did not look like this, with thick dark body hair and powerful thigh muscles that, as he walked, made what was not concealed by the thicker growth of body hair above it sway and bounce, drawing her attention to its primitive sexuality even though she wanted so desperately to look away.

He had reached the sand now, and was turning away from her, no doubt heading for the steps that led up to his cottage, walking across the sand, his buttocks taut and hard, their contours and flesh so very different from the softness of her own. Her heart was hammering with a fast insistent beat driven by her anger that he should display his nakedness so arrogantly in the purity of the morning and her own privacy. His behaviour was an affront to decent respectable people; the children could have seen him – she *had* seen him – and now she felt uncomfortable and horribly embarrassed. He still had his back to her and had reached the steps that led to his cottage, leaving her free to escape via the steps that led back to the villa.

The sun had strengthened whilst she had been in the shadows, its glare dazzling her as she stepped into it. Her feet slipped on the loose pebbles, sending them rolling noisily together. Startled, Amber looked over her shoulder.

He had stopped and was turning to look towards her. She started to run, not knowing why she was doing so, knowing only that she must, but the dainty shoes she was wearing weren't designed for running on sand. His shadow darkened hers and then covered it, just as he grabbed hold of her, the impetus sending them both falling into the soft sand, his body over hers, his breath harsh in her ear whilst her own caught in her throat as her heart raced. He was a barbarian, a corsair, a brigand who lived by no one's rules but his own.

'*Mon Dieu*, if it isn't the little virgin.' He was laughing at her.

'Let me go, you beastly man.'

'Ah, beastly, is it? *Vraiment*, I dare say that there is something of that in me, since a beast is driven by his instincts more than his intellect. Why were you spying on me?'

'I wasn't doing any such thing,' Amber denied. 'And . . . and you had no right to be . . .'

'To be what? Swimming, *oui*?'

She could feel the amused gust of his breath against her face. He was laughing at her, she knew. His hair, salt-rimed and damp, was tightening into tangled curls. If she were to put her hand to them, would they curl round her fingers, binding her to him? His eyes weren't black after all, she discovered, but very dark brown. He smelled of salt and sea, and something that was alien and dangerous and only of him. The scent of him was overpowering her, stealing away her willpower and her senses, whilst his proximity forced her to keep breathing it in.

The weight of his body, which had at first been merely an imprisoning mass, was now becoming identifiable entities: a hipbone pressing into the softness of her own flesh; a thigh, muscular and coarse with salt and sand and body hair, thrown across her body, pinning her down; a throbbing hard heat that pulsed against her thigh. Her body quivered, shuddered as she sucked in more air. He rolled from her. Immediately Amber scrambled to her feet and ran, ignoring the laughter she could hear as she reached the steps and hurried up them.

Her skin was raw and dusty with sand, her sundress damp with sea water. Her flight had tangled her hair. Small sobs impeded her breathing.

Beastly, beastly man! How she loathed him. To her relief there was no one to see her as she entered the villa and went straight to her room.

That evening they were on the terrace, drinking the pre-dinner cocktails Lord Levington had just mixed for them. Henry, Amber learned, had gone out on his own with some friends. Gone out or been sent out because of her?

'I've invited Jean-Philippe to join us for dinner tonight. I feel so sorry for him, living on his own as he does, poor boy.'

Amber almost choked on her drink. She was horrified at the thought of having to make polite dinner table conversation with the artist, knowing all the time what had happened earlier and how he would be secretly laughing at her, but there was nothing she could do.

It was too late now for her to claim a fictitious headache that might have kept her away from the dinner table, far too late she admitted, as Jean-Philippe joined them on the terrace, his dark curls and the gold ring in his ear gleaming in the soft evening light.

At Amber's side Beth gave a soft sigh, and whispered, 'He is just so romantic-looking, like Lord Byron, or—'

'Lord Byron was not romantic. He abused his wife and broke his marriage vows,' Amber told her defiantly.

'You'll never guess what Alistair has told me,' Beth whispered.

'That he loves you,' Amber teased her.

'No.' She made a face. 'About Louise. Amber, she has done the most shocking thing. She was seen coming out of George Ponsonby's lodgings.' Beth paused and then added significantly, 'In the *morning*. Alistair didn't want to tell me at first, but apparently it is all over London and *everyone* knows. Louise is totally ruined now and no one will have anything to do with her. Isn't it dreadful?'

'Yes,' Amber agreed. Right now she really couldn't care less.

Lady Levington was laughing at something Jean-Philippe had said to her.

'I have a favour to ask you, Lady Levington.'

He was looking at *her*, Amber recognised, as her heart kicked painfully against her ribs, fixing his gaze on her as he spoke to Beth's mother.

'I would very much like your permission to use Miss Vrontsky as a model.'

Amber could feel her cocktail splashing onto her wrist as her hand shook.

Lady Levington was frowning.

'Everything will be *comme il faut*, I do assure you. It is only Miss Vrontsky's head that I wish to paint, nothing more. *Et naturellement* she will be properly chaperoned.'

Lady Levington's smile had returned. 'Well, of course, the decision must be Amber's . . .'

'Oh, Amber, how exciting to be an artist's muse,' Beth was enthusing. And then before Amber could stop her she was telling Jean-Philippe, 'Amber's father was an artist, wasn't he, Amber?'

'A graphic designer, actually,' Amber corrected her, lifting her chin proudly as she looked into Jean-Philippe's mocking brown eyes. 'My family are in trade. My grandmother has a silk mill.'

There, let him – let them all – look down on her as much as they wished.

'Amber wants to follow in her father's footsteps but her grandmother would not allow her to study art. Perhaps Jean-Philippe can help you . . . teach you something, Amber . . .'

'*Bien sûr*, I should be delighted to teach Miss Vrontsky as much as I can.' His voice was smoothly polite but it hid danger, Amber was sure of it.

She wanted to refuse, but her pride still stung from her morning conversation with Lady Levington. The countess was happy for her to model for Jean-Philippe because her presence was causing problems that had resulted in Lord Levington deciding that it was necessary for him to remove Henry from her company. She obviously didn't want a mere merchant's daughter for a daughter-in-law, and Amber

204

suspected that she would certainly never have allowed Beth to model for Jean-Philippe.

'So, then it is agreed. You will come to my studio tomorrow morning. I like to work early when the light is at its best, so you must be there for seven. I shall arrange a chaperone for you. *Certainement*, Madame Brun will have someone suitable she can spare.'

Chapter Nineteen

Amber had been awake before dawn. In fact, she had hardly slept, getting out of bed more than once to pace the floor and then sit holding her father's sketchbook as though somehow it could protect her.

Jean-Philippe was humiliating her by saying that he wanted her as his model, Amber knew.

At six o'clock the maid brought Amber her *café au lait* and a croissant, and offered to help her dress. Amber shook her head. She didn't want her to witness her apprehension and report it back to the servants' hall. The rich scent of the coffee made her feel nauseous and she could do no more than nibble at the croissant.

She dressed simply in a pleated skirt and a matching silk knit twinset, not having any idea of exactly what would be expected of her or how long the sitting would take.

When Monsieur Lafitte had arranged life classes for them at school, the models had all been children – impatient of having to sit still and eager to wriggle away just as soon as they could.

It was half-past six. She had no excuse to delay any longer. Under other circumstances she could almost have welcomed the necessity of getting up so early – the perfection of the new morning in all its untouched purity was a sight to behold. The sun was risen, casting its light over the gardens and beyond them to the quiet sea. The air was tangy with the scent of the pines and of the lemon trees that grew in the gardens. Only later in the day would the roses give up their scent to the heat of the sun.

A lizard scrambled across the path in front of her, disturbing the small stones. Amber stopped walking and looked back at the villa. Reluctantly she continued to walk towards the cottage hidden away in its own small private garden close to the cliff top, its white walls smothered in bougainvillaea, the sun warming the terracotta tiles of its sloping roof. The cottage lay to the north of the villa, and close to the wilder territory of the pine forest. Its shuttered windows showed no sign of life. The sun was now sending glittering rays of light darting over the waves. Shading her eyes from the bright light, Amber headed for the doorway almost concealed by the climbing roses smothering it. It was hard to picture a man like Jean-Philippe living in such a place.

The door was open. Hesitantly, she knocked, expecting her knock to be answered by a domestic servant of some sort – preferably the chaperone Jean-Philippe had assured Lady Levington he would provide – but it was the artist himself who pulled back the door and beckoned her in.

The cottage was older than the villa, its floors plain stone and its walls roughly rendered. The door opened straight into a large low-ceilinged kitchen, its beams hung with bunches of herbs. The smell of paint and turpentine filled the room, making Amber catch her breath at its sharp sting.

Jean-Philippe was dressed in a loose white smock worn over a pair of trousers cut off at the knee to reveal the muscular strength of his sun-browned calves. His feet were bare and dusty. He smiled as he saw the way Amber was looking round the kitchen.

'It may lack the grandeur of the villa but this cottage has

something that the villa does not possess. There is nothing between it and the headland to the north, and my studio faces in that direction. The morning light is the purest I have ever seen. Trying to catch its luminescence could drive a man to madness. I was just about to have some coffee – do you want some?' he asked her, gesturing to the coffee pot and the cups with it.

Amber shook her head, watching as he filled one of them. His hands, large and square as they were, were surprisingly deft and flexible.

He picked up the cup and drank quickly from it.

'So, they plan to send your lovelorn admirer away from you, *n'est-ce pas?*'

'You said you wanted me here early so that you could take advantage of the morning light,' Amber reminded him, ignoring his question.

He drained his coffee cup and put it back on the table, commanding her, 'Come,' and then leaving her to follow him as he made his way down a narrow windowless passage and into the room beyond.

Amber had seen studios in London especially designed to provide those who worked in them with the best quality of light but the light pouring into this room was so intense that it literally took away her breath.

'*Ah. Oui*, you feel it here, don't you?' Jean-Philippe told her, thumping his chest over his heart. 'It seizes you and commands you and then it mocks you when you fail to capture it.'

Several canvases were stacked against the internal wall, their contents hidden. The room smelled of paint and sweat, turpentine and dust, colour dyes and varnish; it smelled, Amber thought helplessly, of her father. She looked towards the window, not wanting to let Jean-Philippe see her weakness.

A large canvas on an easel dominated the room, a cloth draped over it, the familiar paraphernalia of the artist grouped around it, and a chair made ready, she assumed for her to sit in as his model whilst he worked. At one end of the room was a bed.

'Beth said that you were preparing a canvas for an Academy exhibition.' It was better that she made polite small talk than let the atmosphere or the man overwhelm her.

'It is a fool who subjects his genius to the pedestrian view of those who call themselves art critics. How can they have any true understanding of what it is to be an artist? They cannot think above patrons and money. And they force the artist to submit to them. But it is necessary to exhibit, to sell oneself into the marketplace. Go and sit over there in that chair. I shall tell you how I wish you to arrange yourself.'

He was removing the soft cotton smock he had been wearing, tugging it over his head, the movement of the muscles in his torso catching the light as sharply as Amber was catching her breath.

'You told Lady Levington that there would be a chaperone,' she reminded him.

He shrugged, carelessly rolling his discarded shirt into a ball and tossing it into a corner. 'There is no need for one,' he told her arrogantly, 'and some foolish woman chattering would only disturb me. There is a quality about your features that intrigues me. It isn't medieval, and yet they possess some of that legacy, and something more pagan as well. Perhaps it comes from your Russian ancestry. Purity allied to passion, innocence to sensuality. The disapproval with which you look at me cannot hide from me that you want it too, Mam'selle Amber Vrontsky.'

He was coming towards her. She wanted to leave, to get up and go, now, whilst she still could.

'I had intended to paint you against the simple back-drop of these walls, innocence married to simplicity, but last night I realised that I was ignoring something vitally important. The innocence you wear is merely a mask that society has imposed on you. Now where did I put it? *Ah, oui*, there.' He was reaching into an ancient trunk behind her chair and removing a length of fabric. '*Maintenant . . .*'

He was standing far too close to her, the hot scent of his body repelling and dizzying her as he unravelled the bolt of fabric and then dropped it onto a low table in front of her where it pooled in rich folds.

Silk, and like none she had ever seen before. She looked down at the shimmering waves of dark blue-green fabric, embroidered with scarlet dragons breathing fire, their jewelled eyes burning in the light.

Unable to stop herself, she reached out and touched the material. It felt warm beneath her fingertips, alive, breathing as only the best quality silk could. If she closed her eyes she could almost hear her father's voice as he told her about such a silk, reputedly only woven for Chinese emperors, priceless and now rarely found outside the collections of the extremely wealthy.

Maybe she was wrong; maybe this was a lesser kind and not an Emperor silk, but the moment she touched it Amber knew that it must be.

'Don't move.'

She had been so entranced that she had almost forgotten Jean-Philippe, who had reached for a sketchpad and was kneeling in front of her, his hand moving swiftly over the paper.

'That look of mingled homage and longing is perfect.'

Amber flinched, the silk slithering heavily through her fingers as she relinquished it. Jean-Philippe's words made her feel as though she had exposed an intensely private part of herself to him.

'This is even better than I had hoped. I shall call the painting *The Silk Merchant's Daughter*, and we shall see if those dullard critics are able to connect my choice of the word "merchant" with that look of longing in your eyes. Only those who know the true value of something are able to feel the strongest desire to possess it.'

'Where did the silk come from?' she asked him, refusing to react to his comments.

'It belongs to my . . . my godmother. As soon as you mentioned last night that your family owned a silk mill, I knew I had to paint you against this fabric.'

Amber sat stiffly, refusing to look at him. It angered her to know that he was deliberately manipulating her feelings. She hated the fact that he could read her so well; she felt at such a disadvantage.

'So you don't miss him then, the moonling who does not know how to kiss you properly?'

The unexpectedness of his change of subject caught her off guard.

'Shall I show you what a kiss should really be?'

His voice was softer now but still taunting. Amber's face burned when he put down his sketchpad and came towards her. She was trapped in her chair, unable to escape, unable to do anything when he leaned towards her and cupped the side of her face in one of his large square hands, his fingers splayed out across her throat, like burning brands.

His head blotted the light, his mouth on hers making no allowances for her own ignorance. It was, she recognised, as much a raw statement of his maleness and his own pride in it, as his nudity had been the previous day. The darting movement of his tongue breached the closed line of her lips. He tasted of salt and spice. Her heart was hammering against her ribs. His free hand was on her shoulder, his thumb rubbing softly against her collar-bone. Her body felt heavy and yet somehow weightless as well.

Abruptly he moved away from her, releasing her.

'There, are you happy now that your curiosity is satisfied?'

'I wasn't curious,' Amber told him angrily

'Of course you were. I could see it in your eyes. It was there yesterday on the beach too.'

'No,' Amber denied, but he was ignoring her, returning to his easel, commanding her to pick up the silk again as she had done before.

For three hours he worked in silence, which was broken only when he barked at Amber to keep still when her aching arm trembled, and then threw down his brush in angry displeasure when she couldn't stop the tremor, or when he came over to her to reposition her as he wished her to be, the movement of his hands on her body now clinical and impatient.

He worked on in silence. The sun rose and the air in the studio became overcharged and drained of oxygen, sapped by his furious activity and Amber's tension. Amber was beginning to feel light-headed in the heat of the studio. Her muscles ached, but she didn't dare move again.

Finally Jean-Philippe put down his brush, and told her she could relax.

'Tomorrow you must do better and keep still.'

Amber stared at him in disbelief. Did he really dare to believe that she would come back after the way he had behaved towards her?

She was trembling as she skirted past him, not trusting herself to speak.

*   *   *

212

It was five o'clock. Sleep had eluded her for much of the night. She might as well get up because she wasn't going to be able to sleep, Amber acknowledged.

She had returned to the villa yesterday determined not to pose again for Jean-Philippe but he had outwitted her, turning up just before dinner to charm Lady Levington, and cause Henry to glower at him, before Amber had had the chance to tell her about her decision.

How easily and fluently he had lied, claiming that Amber was providing him with the inspiration he had needed and that it was now impossible for him to finish his work without her. How subtly and cleverly he had given Lady Levington the impression that Amber had benefited from his advice and help, and was eager to return for more, inferring that this advice had been of a cerebral nature whilst slanting suggestive looks at Amber. He was hateful, and loathsome, and it was because she was so very angry that her heart was jumping around inside her chest the way it was and she hadn't been able to sleep properly last night.

It was impossible now for her to tell Lady Levington that she didn't want to model for Jean-Philippe any more, not without giving a very good reason. And she certainly could not do that. It was her reputation that would be ruined if Lady Levington knew that Jean-Philippe had kissed her. She should have left the moment she had realised that there was no chaperone for her. The fact that she had not done so put her in a very vulnerable position and cast her in a doubtful light. It was too late for her to complain now, and Jean-Philippe well knew that.

Jean-Philippe opened the door as soon as she knocked. Amber could feel him scrutinising her but she refused to look back at him.

'You have had breakfast?'

'I wasn't hungry,' Amber answered him tightly.

He made a noise somewhere between mockery and irritation. 'You must eat. Sit down.'

'I don't want anything,' Amber protested, but it was no use, he was pushing her down into a chair at the kitchen table and filling a large cup with coffee and hot milk from the old-fashioned stove.

'Drink that,' he told her, putting the cup in front of her and then pushing a basket of croissants towards her. 'I do not begin work until you have eaten,' he warned her, 'and if I miss the morning light I shall be very angry indeed.'

Once she started to drink it she discovered that the coffee's rich bite stirred her body and brought it to life.

'*Maintenant*, we go to work,' Jean-Philippe told her as soon as she had finished.

The chair had been removed, and the silk spread as it had been the previous day over the low table.

'I want you to kneel here on the floor,' Jean-Philippe told Amber, 'and reach for the silk like so, holding it close and with passion.'

Amber did as he instructed, tensing when she saw him frown.

'*Non!* That is no good. You must imagine that you have come here in your father's absence and discovered this most beautiful of all fabrics that he has kept hidden from you. You know he will not allow you to have it, and that he will be angered by your desire for it, but you cannot help yourself. When you touch it, you yearn for it; you hold it to your skin as though its touch were that of a lover; your desire to possess it overwhelms everything else.'

Amber reached for the silk again. It was beautiful and so rare, silk like this could only be found once in any lifetime, but it could never be hers, no matter how much she longed for it.

Lost in her own feelings she dropped the silk in shock when Jean-Philippe reached out and unbuttoned the neckline of her sleeveless top, pulling it down to expose the flesh of her shoulders and throat.

She tried to pull away but he shook his head, telling her curtly, 'This is how it must be, the silk against your skin as you succumb to your own passion for it; your senses are possessed by it.'

Hadn't her father always said that silk should be enjoyed with more than merely one sense? Amber shivered as she felt the cool stroke of it against her bare skin. Somehow it had fallen so that one of the embroidered dragons seemed to be curved around the swell of her breast, so that a finger tracing the dragon's outline would stroke against her flesh. What would it be like to bear such sensuality? The softness of silk under the hardness of an artist's callused hand? Soft colour warmed her throat and face, her chest lifted sharply on her indrawn breath and her eyes burned dark with awakening desire. Amber rested her cheek against the cool fabric lost in her own mystery.

'*Oui*. That is it exactly.'

Jean-Philippe's triumphant words brought Amber out of her dream, to the discovery that she was afraid of what was happening to her and the feelings she was experiencing. She dropped the silk, pushing it away from her, and pulled up the bodice of her dress.

In two quick strides Jean-Philippe was in front of her, his hands manacling her upper arms.

'Go back to what you were doing. It was perfect.'

'I don't want to do this. I want to leave.'

'You cannot. I will not let you.'

Amber looked at him and then shook her head in denial of what she could see in his eyes, but it was too late. He was kissing her fiercely.

215

She was trembling violently, too weak to move, letting him lift her to her feet and then slide his hands into her hair as he covered her face in passionate kisses.

'See what you have done to me. How you have broken me on the wheel of the enchantment you have cast over me. You are the most beautiful creature I have ever seen, a virginal seductress who has stolen my heart and my will. You are all I have thought of since the moment I saw you. You possess my nights and steal from me my days. I cannot exist without you. You are my meat and drink, and my life itself. See how you turn me from an artist to a mere man.' His hand took hers and placed it on that part of him she had seen so shockingly when he had come from the sea naked. She could feel its life force thudding through it and she could feel too within herself an innate response: an ache that beat unsteadily in time with her ragged breathing.

'You mustn't say such things to me.'

'Ah, how pitiful it is that the passion nature has given you in such abundance should be constrained by something as ugly as convention. How I shall enjoy freeing it from such a cruel and painful restriction, and how you shall enjoy it too, my love. You tremble and look at me in disbelief but I assure you that it is true. See . . .'

Before she could move he had pulled down the top of her dress to expose the upper curves of her breasts. Out of the corner of her eye Amber thought she saw a movement outside the window, but when she turned her head to look more closely there was no one there.

She turned back towards Jean-Philippe to demand that he release her but it was too late.

He bent his head, his tongue working on her flesh, making her shudder beneath the onslaught of her body's response to him. A wildness she didn't recognise had entered her, possessing her and glorying in the tug of his teeth on the

216

fabric covering her breasts as he pulled it away to expose them to the pure northern light of the morning, pearl flesh crowned with rose-madder nipples puckering into hardness beneath Jean-Philippe's touch.

'I have waited so long for you to come into my life, *ma chérie.*'

Such sweet words crooned against her skin and poured into her lonely heart.

'Wanting you, and waiting for you to want me has driven me to madness.'

'I didn't know.'

'I don't believe you. You must have seen it from the first. I couldn't disguise it if I tried.'

'You frightened me.'

'A virgin's fear that in reality is more excitement than real dread. You have dreamed of me at night, *n'est-ce pas? Oui?* Have you dreamed of me at night? Did you take me down into the secret place within you in your thoughts and those dreams? Did you know secretly how much I willed you to want me, sending you my desire from my lonely bed and imagining you waking from your own sleep at its command to receive it? Did you dream of me in the darkness with you?'

Had she done, and not wanted to admit it? It seemed impossible now, with her body singing and yearning beneath his touch, that she could not have done so. Not when he spoke to her like this, as though they were already bound together.

'*Vraiment.* How very perfect you are. My eternal muse, perfect in every way, although since I am merely mortal I shall never be able to capture your perfection the way the light is drawing it now.'

Amber shuddered as his hands smoothed the path of the morning sunlight on her bare body, sloughing off the restrictive inhibition of her clothes.

He filled her senses, flooding them and her with swooning pleasure. Jean-Philippe lifted her in his arms and carried her to the bed.

She was lying against the silk, a fold of it draped beneath her breasts. It caressed the heavy unfamiliar languor of her parted thighs. Through half-closed eyes Amber watched as Jean-Philippe worked behind his easel, his brush moving swiftly. He was naked apart from the cut-off trousers he had worn the previous day. Her languor became a sweet pang that made her move restlessly on the bed.

Jean-Philippe put down the brush and came over to her.

'If you must disobey me and move, then you will have to pay the price.' His voice was thick and rough, making her shiver with pleasure even before his lips plucked at her nipple and his hand rubbed the silk against the soft hair covering her sex.

How could she ever have thought those fingers clumsy and unskilled? Her body rose and surged, her sharp cry stolen from her by his kiss so swiftly that she barely knew that it was gone.

He poured her red wine and watched it stain her mouth and darken her eyes with sensuality, and then he told her that he must return to work and that she was not to tempt him further.

It was he who tempted her, Amber protested breathlessly when he left the easel yet again to rearrange her limbs and stopped to tease her into trembling longing.

'Tonight you will dream of me and tomorrow I shall make your dreams reality,' he told her when he had taken away the wine and helped her to dress.

Amber had just reached that point in the curve of the path where she was out of sight of the cottage and not yet in sight of the house when suddenly Henry stepped onto the path in front of her, blocking her way.

'Henry! I thought that you and Lord Levington were due to leave this morning?'

Ignoring her question Henry told Amber in a hoarse voice, 'I saw you with him. I saw you letting him fondle you. Whore.' As he screamed the word at her, spittle coated his lips and his eyes filled with tears.

Amber was terrified. She tried to dart past him but he moved faster, grabbing hold of her, dragging her to the ground and pulling at her clothes, smothering the flesh he exposed with hot wet kisses that made her shudder with horror.

'Henry, you mustn't do this.' She must make him see sense; if she didn't she would not be able to save herself.

'Why not? You let him. You're mine. I loved you but now you've spoiled everything – whore, whore.' He was shaking her, banging her head back against the sandy earth behind her so that she felt dizzy.

'I will tell Jean-Philippe,' she told him.

As abruptly as he had taken hold of her, Henry released her and went stumbling back up the path.

Shocked and nauseous, Amber gulped in breaths of clean fresh air and tried to smooth her clothes and hair. She couldn't tell Henry's mother. She would not want to believe her; no one would believe her. She looked down towards the cottage, and then, before she could change her mind, she ran back down the path but when she got there, there was no sign of Jean-Philippe.

Henry had said that he'd watched them. Amber's stomach roiled, sickness clawing at her throat. She had been right in thinking she had seen something at the window.

Fortunately when she got back to the house she was able to slip in through the side door without meeting anyone.

In her room she stripped off her clothes and ran a bath, immersing herself in the water and scrubbing at her skin.

She longed to be with Jean-Philippe so that she could tell him what Henry had done and so that she could feel safe.

To her relief, by the time Amber felt composed enough to go downstairs, Henry and his father had gone.

It was halfway through the afternoon when the nursery nurse came hurrying to find Lady Levington, who was sitting with Amber, to tell her that little Arabella was very sick.

Within an hour a doctor had been summoned. Arabella had a bad fever and must be kept in bed, Amber learned from the nursery maid sent down to tell her that, with Arabella crying constantly for her mother, Lady Levington didn't want to leave the nursery, which meant that Amber would be left to her own devices until Arabella recovered.

Amber assured the nursery maid that she understood and that of course Lady Levington should not give her a moment's thought.

It was just as well that Jean-Philippe has asked her to sit for him, for it would have meant that she would be alone and bored, said Lady Levington later, when she eventually came downstairs to apologise to Amber, and give instructions to the kitchen staff on the special food to be prepared for the invalid.

Amber said nothing. What, after all, could she say?

Her thoughts, like her feelings, were in a maelstrom of intense confusion. She could scarcely believe what had happened; what she had felt; what she had wanted; the emotions she had experienced, all of it so new and un-expected that it had left her in a fevered daze that swept her to the heights one minute and the depths the next. What he had done in the eyes of the world was very wrong, she knew that, and yet she could not regret it. It belonged in the most private sanctuary of her thoughts and her feelings. Unexpectedly she could even now understand Caroline and Louise's reckless behaviour. Not that her situation was the same as theirs. She loved Jean-Philippe and he loved her, and they were free to love one another. All they had done was anticipate the vows they would ultimately make to one another, because the intensity of their feelings had over-whelmed them.

The baker's wife tossed her head and pretended she didn't know what Jean-Philippe had come for, but he knew perfectly that she wouldn't deny him for very long, and he was right.

The virgin and the fecund mother – he would have them both and he would pleasure and satisfy them both. He followed Marianne into the small room off the kitchen where she kept the herbal remedies she made, pulling up her skirt with one hand whilst pulling down her blouse with the other, working on her energetically and expertly with his fingers, whilst plunging his tongue into the hot wetness of her mouth in imitation of the manner in which he would be plunging himself into her heat before too many minutes had gone by. And all the time he'd be thinking of Amber.

Chapter Twenty

Left to her own devices, Amber wandered through the sun-bathed warmth of the villa's gardens, smiling because her body was flooded with happiness.

So this was love? How very different it was from what she had been expecting. Not a bit like what she had thought. Had her parents felt like this? She had never imagined or guessed. They had kept the passion they must have shared hidden from her, and a secret between them. Amber didn't think she could ever do that. Her love for Jean-Philippe possessed and obsessed her. It touched every single thing she did and was, like the power of the sun overhead, stretching into every corner, illuminating everything, and changing the whole landscape. Its power was so great that there was no escaping or avoiding its impact.

Falling in love with Jean-Philippe had quite simply changed her whole world. Already she was imagining their shared future together, her love overriding all the difficulties her grandmother would undoubtedly put in their way. They would live in Paris, in an apartment with views of the Seine and huge north-facing windows in the *atelier* where they would both work, Jean-Philippe on his paintings, and she on the fabrics she would design.

In the summer they would come here to Juan-les-Pins to stay in the cottage where they had first known their love.

How proud she would be to introduce Jean-Philippe to Lord Robert and to Cecil. And to Jay? Now her thoughts became troubled. Somehow she couldn't imagine introducing the pair. They came from different worlds. Jay was dependable, loyal and reliable, while Jean-Philippe was wild, temperamental, unpredictable.

Jay belonged to Macclesfield; Jean-Philippe belonged to the sun and to France. Jay might not be able to understand or appreciate him. But Jay would always be her friend, Amber told herself quickly. Nothing would change that. Nothing.

Wandering through the garden thinking about Jean-Philippe was sweetly pleasurable, but what she really longed for was to be with him. Now and for ever. In fact, she was in a fever of urgency to be with him, Amber admitted. Every second spent away from him was a second wasted. How foolish she had been to imagine that she disliked him. She almost wanted to laugh out loud now at the silly unknowing girl she had been.

They were meant to be together, it was their destiny. How could it not be when circumstances had brought them together in such an extraordinary way? A small thrill of shock went through her to recognise how easily they might not have found one another.

Jean-Philippe, Jean-Philippe, Jean-Philippe. Even whispering his name to herself had the power to entrance and delight her. She said it again, adding his surname and then adding her own name to that: Madame du Breveonet; Madame Amber du Breveonet, wife of Monsieur Jean-Philippe du Breveonet. Her heart was skipping giddily with joy.

She wanted to give him all of herself so badly – her love, her happiness, her future and, of course, her body.

She said as much to him the next day, drinking the coffee he had made her after he had drawn her into the darkness of the kitchen and kissed her, his hands roving her body.

'*Bien*, come with me,' he commanded her, taking her hand.

Wonderingly she let him lead her up a set of narrow stairs and into a bed chamber. The room smelled of him, and of sleep. His scent intoxicated and weakened her. She couldn't resist him even if she wanted to.

The bed was high and old-fashioned, the room's windows overlooking the sea.

'I have been thinking of you all night,' he whispered to her as he languorously undressed her. 'You fill my thoughts so that I can't work, so that nothing else matters but you and this.'

When he kissed her nothing else mattered to her but him.

The way he touched her dizzied her, sending the most thrilling feelings cascading through her, lifting her to almost unbearable heights of pleasure. His lips on her throat, his tongue stroking the flesh behind her ear whilst his hand cupped her naked breast and then his thumb and forefinger plucked at her nipple, aroused such intense sensations inside her that Amber felt as though she simply could not contain them.

An ache began to build up low down in her body, a dragging heavy feeling that began to grow in intensity with each touch of Jean-Philippe's hands on her body. Just the sensation of his breath against her skin was enough to heighten her arousal, making her want to reach out in turn to touch him, to breathe in the warm spicy scent of his skin, to press her hot face against his chest, in need and also in a shy, self-conscious need to hide her face, after she had cried out in pleasure at the feel of his lips and then his mouth on her breast.

'Taste me,' he urged her softly, lifting his hands to hold her face against his chest. 'It's easy, just place your lips against my skin.' When she had done that and trembled at the salt taste of his flesh and the tickle of his body hair against her lips, he commanded her softly, 'And now with your tongue.'

It shocked her to discover how much it pleased her to feel him tense and then murmur, '*Oui, chérie, oui* – now lower, aaahhhh. *Oui . . . vraiment*, that is good,' as she shyly followed his instructions, all the time the heavy weight of her own desire pressing even more demandingly low down in her body.

When he touched her intimately with his fingers, parting the lips of her sex and then stroking her gently with his fingertip, Amber cried out in hot delight.

'*Bien*, you are so hot and wet, so ready for me, *ma petite*.'

His fingertip circled a place so sensitive to the pleasure of his touch that Amber shuddered violently, longing for it to remain there instead of stroking along the length of her, although that too was very pleasurable, especially when Jean-Philippe started to kiss her nipples at the same time, drawing first one and then the other into his mouth as his finger slid gently inside her.

Instinctively Amber tensed, making Jean-Philippe laugh.

'*Vraiment*, if you hold me as tightly as that when it is my cock that is inside you, you will make me a very happy man, but first we must prepare this little treasure of yours to receive it, *n'est-ce pas*?

He was kissing her nipples again, sliding his finger deeper and stroking her as he did so. A feeling of hot urgent need filled her; an ache that went deep inside her, a pulse that was now beating suffocatingly fiercely, welcoming, wanting the sensation that came from feeling slightly stretched and filled by the rhythmic movement of Jean-Philippe's fingers; wanting to respond to it, to move with it, and in counter-point to it, so that she could take that feeling deeper within herself.

Jean-Philippe was moving over her, lifting her so that he could place a pillow beneath her hips. Amber watched him, trembling slightly, half dazed by her own passion, keyed up and impatient for him to touch her again, the normally pale flesh of her chest suffused with the colour of her arousal.

He kissed her fiercely, and then slowly and lingeringly, his hand between their bodies, between her legs, stroking her again, touching that special place, making her arch up in longing and then gasp, her eyes widening as she felt him thrust firmly into her, filling her and stretching her, her whole body filled with the pleasure that radiated out from the sensation of him moving within her. The pleasure was like a rainbow, making her want to pursue it to its end, intent only on doing so, heedless of anything else, so that when the pain came, sharp and spiking, seizing her in its grip, by the time she had cried out and gripped his arms, it had gone and his increasingly powerful thrusts were taking her with him on a journey that his flesh already knew and hers knew only that it must know.

The sensation of him tensing and then suddenly moving very quickly and fiercely, followed by the gasps of pleasure he shuddered into her skin, left her confused and aching, no longer a virgin, but somehow not yet a woman, until he touched her again, stroking that special place, holding her and watching her as the pleasure built up inside her until it was like a dam that had to burst in a huge flood of pleasure that made her cry out in awe.

'I love you,' she told him shyly, as he held her, after he had dried her tears and kissed her.

'My little virgin who is a virgin no more,' he teased her as she lay against the pillows in the aftermath of his possession. 'Sleep now,' he told her, his teeth white against the olive warmth of his skin as he laughed, a pagan buccaneer who had captured what he wanted.

When she woke up he was sitting cross-legged on the bed, sketching.

'What are you doing?' she asked.

'Preserving a very special memory,' he told her lightly. 'I never want to forget today.'

'You're drawing me now?' For some reason that upset her. 'Can I see?'

'There is nothing to see. Just a few lines that only have meaning for me. Are you going to stay there and tempt me to come back to you?'

He put aside his sketchbook and came to her, and very quickly Amber forgot that she had ever been upset.

How wonderfully marvellously magically and perfectly happy she was. She had never imagined life could be like this. For the first time since her parents had died she felt complete and whole again. Jean-Philippe had taken away the emptiness inside her. Sometimes after they had made love and he was asleep, she would lie next to him watching him, filled with so much love for him, so much happiness that she felt as though her heart could barely contain it.

They were two halves of one whole, Jean-Philippe told her, and destined to be together. His words echoed her own feelings. She felt sure that somehow her parents were responsible for bringing her to him, an artist like her father, a man with whom she could share the deepest part of herself.

They had not as yet spoken of any detailed practical plans for their future, there was no need, because Amber knew that they were meant for one another and that nothing could keep them apart, not even her grandmother.

Jean-Philippe had told her, though, that they would live in Paris, in an apartment with views of the Seine, and Amber had laughed because his words so exactly matched her own daydreams.

He would exhibit *The Silk Merchant's Daughter*, and the critics would fall over themselves to praise his work. Amber would bring him luck, he had told her, and rich patrons who would all want to buy his paintings.

He was exultant, excited, laughing as he pulled her to him and kissed her and told her that he loved her.

'I want us to be together always,' she had told Jean-Philippe solemnly, lying in his bed in his arms.

'And so we shall be,' he answered her. 'It could not be any other way for I could not live without you.'

The days drifted by in a haze of love and discovery, and joy clung to Amber like a luminescent cloud of delight.

Little Arabella grew better and Lady Levington emerged from the nursery, apologetic towards Amber for neglecting her.

Jean-Philippe became a regular dinner guest. Lady Levington treated him very much as though he were her own godson.

It was both heaven and hell for Amber that he was there, and a form of sweet torture: heaven because they were in the same room as one another, and hell because, as Jean-Philippe had warned her, it was not safe for them to betray their feelings for one another, because if they did Lady Levington was bound to put a stop to them being alone together. She plainly assumed that Amber was being chaperoned by Jean-Philippe's non-existent housekeeper, as convention demanded.

Amber knew that she had never properly understood before what happiness was, or her own passionate nature. Just the small reality of writing Jean-Philippe's name in her letters home to her grandmother and Jay, even though she was saying nothing more than that he had escorted them somewhere, filled her with almost unbearable delight.

Lord Levington, Henry and Beth were all due to return to the villa, but it was someone else altogether whom Amber found standing on the terrace with Lady Levington, one evening before dinner, after she had had to race through her toilette because she had lingered for so long with Jean-Philippe. She only just managed to check herself from running to him, she was so delighted to see him.

'Robert!'

He was, he explained, staying with friends in Cannes and just had to stop by.

'Cecil asked particularly to be remembered to you,' he told Amber, who laughed and shook her head.

'I am sure he did no such thing. He must know that I would never forget him. I am so grateful for his kindness to me.'

Lord Robert was making Amber laugh with his droll description of the *mal de mer* he had experienced when his friends had insisted on taking him sailing, when Jean-Philippe arrived to join them for dinner.

Amber's heart flooded with love and pride when Lady Levington introduced Jean-Philippe to Lord Robert. She wanted to tell Lord Robert how much she loved Jean-Philippe, but of course she could not with Lady Levington there.

'It is Jean-Philippe's godmother who owns the villa, Teddy,' Lady Levington explained.

Lord Robert had been smoking and now suddenly he

frowned and then looked away from them all, making a great play of stubbing out his cigarette.

'Jean-Philippe is an artist,' Lady Levington continued.

'And which school do you favour, Monsieur?' Lord Robert asked Jean-Philippe.

'None. I prefer to make my own mark and follow my own path.'

Amber could hear the prideful anger in Jean-Philippe's voice and instinctively she moved closer to him, her look towards Lord Robert one of protective indignation.

To Amber's distress Lord Robert's presence seemed to have introduced an edge of tension to the evening, although she could not understand why. She desperately wanted him and Jean-Philippe to like one another, but if they could not then her loyalty must lie with Jean-Philippe, her soul mate and her love.

Once dinner was over Jean-Philippe announced that he must return to his cottage, and as soon as she could after his departure, Amber too excused herself, fibbing that she had a headache so that she could hurry down the narrow path after him.

He was waiting for her by the cottage door, drawing her inside with him and kissing her fiercely, and of course she stayed with him far longer than she had intended.

It wouldn't matter, though, she reassured herself as she walked back. Lady Levington would probably welcome the opportunity to have Lord Robert to herself, and hopefully it would give Lord Robert time to get over his peculiar mood.

She had almost reached the terrace when Lord Robert stepped out of the shadows on the path in front of her, bringing her to an abrupt halt.

He was smoking, she noticed, and as abruptly as he had done earlier in the evening he put out his cigarette without finishing it, almost as though he had been smoking simply to pass the time whilst he waited for her. That, of course, was impossible. He could not have known she was outside, after all. She and Jean-Philippe might love one another, but Amber was well aware that in the eyes of the world it was not acceptable for them to be alone together unchaperoned, and it was certainly not acceptable for her to have given herself to him as she had. Not that she regretted doing so, not for one minute. She had her father's passionate Russian blood running in her veins, after all, and loving Jean-Philippe as she did meant that it was impossible for her not to show him that love.

'Walk with me, Amber? There is something I need to discuss with you, and it is best said in private, I think.'

Amber had a feeling of foreboding, and wanted to refuse, but Robert was already cupping her elbow and directing her steps along the path that led to the formal gardens.

'My godmother tells me that you have been sitting for Jean-Philippe.'

'Yes,' she agreed nervously.

'He will have told you, I expect, something of his life?'

Now Amber was confused. She had thought that Lord Robert was going to ask her who had chaperoned her at the cottage, and she had known that she was not going to be able to lie to him.

'I know that, like me, he lost his parents at a young age and that he has been living here with his godmother.'

She could hear Lord Robert exhaling. 'He has told you that? He has said specifically to you that Mrs de Wittier is his godmother, and described her to you as that?'

Amber's confusion grew. 'Yes. Why should he not when it is true? Lord Levington told us that when we first arrived.'

'And you and he are lovers?'

Amber couldn't hide the betraying catch of her breath

even if the shadows were concealing the rush of colour to her face.

'We do love each other, yes,' she admitted proudly.

'You mean he seduced you.'

'I mean that I love him and he loves me.'

'He isn't free to love you, Amber. And Mrs de Wittier is not his godmother. He is her lover.'

'No, that's not possible,' Amber denied, shaking her head. 'He loves me, he has said so. And anyway, I have seen a photograph of her. She is older, older than Lady Levington.'

'A good deal older,' Lord Robert agreed, 'but nevertheless he has shared her bed and will be expected to return to it once she comes back from Paris.'

'No, it isn't true. You're just making it up. I do not believe you. I won't . . . Jean-Philippe loves *me*.'

'Maybe he does. After all, his relationship with Mrs de Wittier is merely a business arrangement via which she pays him to share her life and her bed. It is a well-established tradition in a certain stratum of society. A wealthy older woman pays a handsome young man to be her lover – such a young man is known as a gigolo. For form's sake Mrs de Wittier may have passed Jean-Philippe off as her godson, but I assure you that amongst her friends it is well known exactly what he is. There was much talk of it in Cannes amongst the friends I am staying with. It seems the only reason Jean-Philippe is here and not in Paris with Mrs de Wittier is because she is entertaining some strait-laced members of her American family.'

Amber felt sick with disbelief. 'No, that isn't true,' she repeated. 'You must be mistaken. Your friends must have been talking about someone else. I know Jean-Philippe. He would not . . .' Amber's emotions suspended her voice.

'I am very sorry, Amber. I wish I could have spared you this.'

'No you don't. If you did you would not have told me.'

'Child, I could in all honour do nothing else. Even if I had not seen for myself this evening how you follow his every word and movement with your heart in your eyes, my godmother's comments about you sitting for him would have prompted me to do so. My godmother has, of course, been as deceived as you have yourself since she also patently believes him to be Mrs de Wittier's godson.'

'Have you told her that he isn't?'

'I wanted to tell you first.'

'Well, now you have told me, but I don't believe you. When I tell Jean-Philippe what you have said to me I know he will say that you are wrong.'

'I'm sure he will, but when he does, Amber, for your own sake ask him if he is willing to make that denial in my presence and to my face. Don't look at me like that. I promise you I only have your best interests at heart, even though you might find that hard to believe.'

Amber stumbled away, unable to believe what she had heard. Her world – the world that was so full of promise and possibility – had now come crashing to the ground.

Chapter Twenty-One

She had slept only fitfully and wished that she had not slept at all because her repose had been tormented by hideous nightmares in which Jean-Philippe had been torn from her by Lord Robert and her grandmother.

What Lord Robert had told her wasn't true. It couldn't be. His friends were mistaken.

It was only four o'clock but she couldn't wait any longer. She dressed quickly, her fingers clumsy over buttons and fastenings.

An unexpectedly cool breeze made her shiver as she picked her way along the familiar path. The sun was only just rising above the hills behind the villa. It would be stroking long fingers of gold against Jean-Philippe's sleeping body.

Jean-Philippe never locked the door to the cottage. She slipped inside and then leaned against the door, trying to steady the painful thudding of her heart. Why was it beating like this? There was after all nothing for her to fear. Jean-Philippe loved her. He had said so over and over again.

They may not have made exact plans, but Jean-Philippe had talked openly and excitedly of their future, of taking her to Paris, of begging her grandmother to let them marry, things he would not have done if what Lord Robert had heard was true.

The wooden stairs were old and creaked under her slender weight, as though grudgingly accepting her presence.

The bedroom door opened easily, the morning sun slanting through the windows just as she had known it would. Jean-Philippe was lying on his back asleep. The sunlight streaked his bare torso gold where he had pushed away the bedding.

Her love for him overwhelmed her. It filled every part of her, every cell and nerve ending so that her whole body was her love and beat to the pulse of it.

He was everything to her, an affirmation of her parents' love for one another and for her, a promise for the future.

As though her heart had called out to his he opened his eyes and smiled at her, holding wide his arms, waiting for her to run to him as she always did.

'You're early.'

'I couldn't sleep.'

He laughed softly, wickedly almost, in that way that made her heart lurch into her ribs and her toes curl in sharp expectation.

'My sensual ex-virgin, how very sweet and delicious you are. *Certainement* a dish that no man could ever tire of. Come here.'

'There's something I have to ask you.'

He yawned and stretched, making her heart turn over with aching longing. Amber had to fight not to run to him and throw herself into his arms – anything to make it possible for her not to have to say what she knew had to be said.

'What something?' His voice was lazy with sleep and satisfaction.

'Lord Robert says that Mrs de Wittier is not your godmother and that you are her gigolo.'

Jean-Philippe threw back the bed covers, swung his feet

235

to the floor and strode towards her. 'What is this?' he demanded angrily. 'He lies to you and you believe him? I thought you loved me?'

'I do.' She was almost in tears, relief battling with anguish because she had made him angry.

When he saw her distress Jean-Philippe's face softened and he took her in his arms.

'You are everything to me, Amber, I promise you that.'

'And you will tell Lord Robert that he is wrong, and that Mrs de Wittier *is* your godmother?'

Amber could feel him tensing.

'Why should I have to say anything to him? Isn't my word good enough for you?'

Amber stepped back from him and looked up into his face, searching his expression whilst her heart hammered against her ribs.

'Mrs de Wittier *is* your godmother, isn't she, Jean-Philippe?'

'I do not have to prove myself to anyone. If there are those who choose to misinterpret our relationship then that is their concern, and there is nothing I can do about it.'

He was avoiding meeting her gaze directly, Amber recognised, just as he was avoiding answering her directly. A sick clammy fear began to crawl through her body.

He turned away from her, and then back again. 'Look, Amber, even if it is true what Lord Robert has told you, what difference does it make to us? She has no rights over me, no matter what she chooses to think. She does not own me. I am a free man. She cannot change anything between us. No one can.'

What she was hearing didn't make any sense, and yet at the same time it made horribly clear sense. She wanted to cry out that she didn't want to hear any more but she couldn't.

It was true. Lord Robert had been right and she had been wrong.

When had it gone so very cold that her blood seemed to have turned to ice; an ice that froze her heart with its painful reality? Jean-Philippe, her god amongst men whom she had put high on the summit of her love, was merely mortal after all.

'So it is true then?' How calm and gentle her voice sounded, so very different from that screaming sobbing voice inside her.

'She tricked me into it, offering to help me, pretending she wanted me to paint her portrait, bringing me down here and then refusing to pay me what she had promised. I had no choice. But it is over now.'

'Then you will leave here with me today and we will go to Paris together, live our own lives together?' Amber pressed him quietly. There was no passion in her voice, no hope or conviction because she already knew his answer.

'I cannot leave until she has paid me what she owes me. She is a witch, a harridan who torments me and makes me dance to her tune. *Mon Dieu*, you cannot imagine how much I hate her. But I love you, my sweet Amber. I swear that to you. I love you.'

She walked back the way she had come.

Lord Robert was standing on the path ahead of her, watching her, waiting for her, she recognised, as her composure broke and his arms closed round her, holding her.

'I'm so sorry, so very sorry,' he told her. 'I would have spared you if I could. After all, I well know the pain of loving where I can only be hurt.'

'I must go back to the house.'

'Not yet. There is something more I want to discuss with you – a proposition I want to put to you.'

He had tucked her arm through his own so that Amber had no option but to walk alongside him.

'I want you to marry me, Amber.'

Chapter Twenty-Two

'Marry you? I don't understand. Why would you want me to marry you? You don't love me, there's no reason . . .'

'Actually, there is a reason. You see, I have to marry before my thirtieth birthday if I wish to inherit the fortune my maternal grandfather has left me. And as for me not loving you, whilst it is true that my nature precludes me from loving any woman in a physical sense, I care a great deal about you, Amber. I admit whilst the need to secure my inheritance has been occupying my thoughts a great deal recently, until last night the thought that the solution might be for *us* to marry had not occurred to me. However, once it did, the more I thought about it the more I recognised how sensible it would be for us to do so, since I need a wife in order to obtain my inheritance and you need a titled husband in order to please your grandmother and protect your reputation.'

Amber shivered inwardly. Lord Robert's warning about her reputation had made her sharply aware of the danger she was in. She only had to remember Beth's comments about Louise and Caroline Fitton Legh's death to know what her own fate would be if her relationship with Jean-Philippe became public.

Honesty, though, compelled her to say shakily, 'But you could marry anyone.'

'No, Amber, I could not. Certainly there are men of my persuasion who do marry, and who can perform their marital duties, if only reluctantly, but that would be an abhorrence to me. I will be frank with you. Whilst I can and do like and admire you – yes, and even love you as a friend – I can never be a proper husband to you. Since you already know the nature of my desires I can say this to you, and since too I know that you have already given your heart to someone else I can be sure that there is no danger of you falling in love with me.

'I do know how you are feeling, believe me. I have been there and had to face that pain you are now facing, and that feeling that one's whole life is over and not worth living. You can't imagine that anything could be worse than your present despair but it can be, Amber. Have you thought yet of what your fate will be if there are to be repercussions from your relationship with Jean-Philippe? If you were to find yourself carrying his child?'

Amber could feel the blood draining from her limbs.

'We cannot afford to delay. We must be married as speedily as possible.'

'You cannot mean that you would marry me knowing that I could be carrying Jean-Philippe's child?'

'I assure you that I do.'

'But if there was to be a child, and it was a boy . . . ?'

'Then I shall have provided myself with an heir and will be very well thought of for having done so. My grandfather in particular will be delighted if it should turn out that you are with child.'

Until Lord Robert had raised the spectre of a potential child Amber had taken little interest in his proposal to her other than to think it impossible that he should want to marry her, but now a second and a very real fear had been added to the agony of Jean-Philippe's betrayal of her.

The sun was warming the beach now, and it was too late for her to wish that she had given in to that urge she had felt as she left the cottage, to walk out into the sea and simply drown herself along with her sorrows.

Inside the villa the household would be waking, and she would be missed. Like someone waking from a dream she saw with frightened clarity the risk she had run and the danger she was now in.

'Poor child,' Lord Robert told her gently. 'Life is so very cruel, especially to the valiant and the innocent, but it need not be as bad as you fear. We shall deal very well together, you and I, Amber. Marriage to me will give you the freedom to choose what you will do with your life – within reason.'

'I could study graphic design?'

Lord Robert inclined his head. 'If you wish.'

A tiny spear of hope unfurled inside her and then withered.

'But we can't just get married. No one will let us. Lady Levington—'

'I assure you that once I have intimated discreetly to my godmother that I fell in love with you in London and that, regrettably, after being separated from you for so long, last night my ardour overwhelmed me, she will understand perfectly the need for us to be married without any delay. I shall speak to the Ambassador in Paris. It is probably best that we are married there, by special licence. Your grandmother will, I am sure, be delighted to learn that you are about to marry the heir to a dukedom and will give us not just her consent but also her blessing. Henry, though, I suspect will be another matter.'

Henry!

'What is it?' Lord Robert demanded when he saw her expression.

Amber didn't want to tell him but her own honesty compelled her to do so.

'He hurt you and threatened you? Well, you may rest assured that he will not do so again.'

Amber trembled, not far from tears when she recognised that Lord Robert's concern was all for her. It hurt so badly to know that Jean-Philippe had betrayed her; he had been the one she had thought would want to protect her from Henry.

She was very lucky, she acknowledged. Lord Robert was offering her so much: the protection of his name, and the security that would give her – and her child if there should be one. She thought again of Louise and Caroline Fitton Legh, and of Henry, and she knew there was only one decision she could make and one answer she could give Lord Robert. Who else would help her? Her grandmother certainly wouldn't.

But a part of her still ached and wept in despair for what she had had so cruelly snatched away. It seemed impossible that such a thing could be happening. This time yesterday the only future she contemplated had been one with Jean-Philippe.

As though he knew her thoughts, Lord Robert told her gently, 'It will all be for the best, I promise you.' He reached for her hand and held it comfortingly. 'We'd better go back to the villa and break our news to my godmother.'

Blanche had read Lord Robert's letter not just once but twice. It had arrived with the rest of the morning's post, which had included letters from Amber and Greg, neither of which she had as yet read. The breeze coming in from the open window ruffled the writing paper slightly, despite its thickness. Automatically Blanche reached out and placed her hand on it, frowning when she realised that her fingers were trembling.

It was the unexpectedness of Lord Robert's announcement that he was marrying Amber that was responsible, nothing else. How could it be, when this was obviously such an advantageous marriage for Amber and for the family, far far more advantageous than anything Blanche had hoped for, even if Lord Robert had announced his intentions as a statement, rather than made a request for her permission to the marriage.

Every question a bride's guardian might have wanted to ask had been anticipated and answered. Lord Robert had included the details of his bankers – the same as her own – so that Blanche could check on his financial stability; a letter from the British Ambassador confirming his identity, a legal document making the most generous of financial arrangements for Amber's future, and a declaration of Lord Robert's desire to ensure that Amber was as happy in their marriage as he knew he would be.

What Lord Robert had not addressed was a request for her presence at their wedding.

'We are both agreed that we consider it essential that we become man and wife as quickly and quietly as that can be arranged,' he had written, 'with no fuss and, more importantly, no delay.'

There was only one reason why they would need to marry so speedily, and that was that either they knew that Amber was carrying a child or they thought that she could be.

Blanche hoped that it was the latter. She certainly couldn't write and ask them, and if she was right and they were already lovers, then the faster they were married the better – for Amber's sake.

It might sting Blanche's pride that she had not been asked to travel to Paris for the wedding, but she certainly had no intention of letting anyone else know that.

She reached for Amber's letter, opening it and reading it swiftly.

After informing her grandmother that she was to be married and asking her to read Lord Robert's letter for all the practical details, Amber's letter continued,

I hope that you will forgive us for the haste with which everything must take place, and I know that when you meet him you will be happy to welcome Robert into our family, and be as happy with my marriage as I am myself. I love and respect Robert, and have every confidence in our future together. Robert's title means that I am confident too that you will feel that I have fulfilled your hopes and wishes for me.

Since ultimately her granddaughter would become a duchess, there was no denying that she had, Blanche admitted.

She got up from behind her desk and walked over to the window. In her mind's eye Blanche could see herself at seventeen, wildly in love with Barrant de Vries. What kind of letter would she have written to her father if Barrant had insisted on marrying her at such short notice? Not one that was so calm and businesslike.

But loving Barrant so passionately had not brought her happiness; instead it had brought her only pain, Blanche reminded herself. She had done what she thought best for Amber to avoid her experiencing the same anguish.

She looked towards the door of her office. Jay would be back shortly. The old gun dog had died in the night and Jay had taken it to bury it in the Denham pets' graveyard. There were stones there bearing the names of dogs, horses, and even a parrot owned by those who had lived at Denham over the generations. Blanche had found herself turning more frequently to Jay as someone she felt she could discuss certain things with, not because she wanted his advice – Blanche would never put herself in a position where she needed advice from anyone else – but because he had a sound and wise head on his shoulders, much more so than Greg, and far more than she might have expected for a de Vries. Jay obviously took after the paternal side of his family.

It was true that originally Blanche had hired Jay to taunt Barrant, but his diligence and quiet, knowledgeable confidence had won her respect, just as now he was winning her trust.

She was about to go in search of him when she remembered that she had not yet read Greg's letter.

It was lengthy and rambling, filled in equal measure with complaints against Henry Jardine and praise for 'my good friend Lionel Shepton'.

Greg was bored by Hong Kong, he had written. He was planning a visit to Shanghai, but he was short of money; he had made a loan to his friend whose own funds had not arrived as anticipated, and now Greg desperately needed money himself. Would his grandmother please send him some? Blanche sighed. Her plans for Amber might look as though they were going to work out satisfactorily, but where Greg was concerned it was a different story altogether.

Jay leaned on his spade. It was going to be a hot day, the sun was already dispersing the faint mist that lay across the valley below Denham and he could feel the warmth in its rays.

He had woken up in the night, compelled without knowing why to check on the old dog, and had found it waiting for him, raising its head to look at him with eyes that could barely see, its tail managing one last thump as he had slipped away whilst Jay stroked him.

The dog hadn't been his, but that hadn't mattered: they had shared these last months together and the dog, like the polite beast it was, had waited to say its final goodbye to him.

In return Jay could only accord it the same respect. He had buried him in a sheltered spot amongst others of his kind, and he would have a stone carved with his name to mark it. He would miss his company, Jay acknowledged, as he headed back to the house.

The post had arrived in his absence and Jay's heart leaped in a sudden fierce surge of emotion as he saw Amber's handwriting. Merely the sight of it, when he had just had to perform such a sad duty, was almost as comforting as hearing the sympathetic words he knew she would have offered had she been here.

It was only in moments of weakness such as this one that he allowed himself the emotional luxury of thinking of her so personally, and as a man who loved her and always would love her. He had known from the start that there was no future in his love for her, and that no matter how much Blanche might value him as her estate manager, she would never permit him to court Amber. Rather she would dismiss him on the spot if she thought he might attempt to do so, and knowing that, and that he was not in a position to offer Amber any of the things she deserved, Jay had made sure that he never said or did anything that might encourage her to think of him as anything other than a friend.

He wasn't vain enough to think that Amber would have fallen in love with him simply because he loved her, but she was young and vulnerable, and she had been ready to turn to him for comfort, and being such a sweet-natured girl, she could easily have been persuaded by a manipulative man that what she felt for him was love. That would not have been fair to her, even if Blanche had been willing to allow him to court her. Amber was so very young, and knew so little about life or even herself. Jay hoped that when the time came when she did fall in love and marry, he would be strong enough to stand back and be glad for her sake. In the meantime he had the bittersweet pleasure of her letters and her trust, and his starving heart took sustenance from that.

He opened the letter and sat down to read it.

'Dear Jay, I am writing to tell you that I am to be married to Lord Robert.'

The shock of the words, so unexpected and so unwelcome, was like a blow to his heart. Before he realised what he was doing he had crushed the letter in his hand. Then Jay looked at the ball of paper and placed it on his desk, smoothing it out with fingers that trembled.

He read it again, and saw with a sickening jerk of pain what he had overlooked before, and that was that Amber's letter hinted at the reason for her marriage without spelling it out. She had fallen in love with and been betrayed by someone else, Lord Robert was rescuing her from the consequences of that; he was her saviour and she was grateful to him. One sentence, making reference to Lady Fitton Legh, her disgrace and then her death, told Jay what Amber's real fear was. She had written,

You will be very shocked, I know. I am so very ashamed and will understand if you think me sunk beneath all reproach now. I am so very lucky that Lord Robert is prepared to save me from the consequences of my own folly. I shall understand if you no longer want anything to do with me, Jay, for I have truly behaved very badly indeed.

Jay ached with anguish for her. His darling, darling girl. He understood perfectly well why she felt grateful to Lord Robert. And he knew equally well that he would have given anything and everything to have been the one to have taken care of her.

Standing up, he went over to the fire and fed Amber's letter to the flames, watching it burn as the pain of his love for her burned its way through his heart.

Blanche walked into the room just as Jay was on his way back to his desk.

The dog's basket, she noted as she entered his office, had gone.

'Amber is to be married,' she told him without preamble.

Jay nodded. He couldn't trust himself to speak.

'Lord Robert has written to me to say that he wishes them to be married immediately, in Paris at the British Embassy. There will not be time for me to arrange to attend the wedding. I would, though, like to reassure myself that Lord Robert's credentials are as excellent as the references he has given me seem to suggest.'

Should he tell Blanche about Lord Robert's sexual orientation? What good would it do if he did? The last thing he wanted to do was harm Amber in any way. She had made it plain in her letter that she now needed the protection and respectability of a husband, so doing anything that might delay or stop the marriage would not be in her best interests. She knew what Lord Robert was, after all, and she liked him, Jay knew that.

It wasn't just the old dog he would no longer have to keep him company; he would no longer have his private impossible dreams either, Jay acknowledged.

Two weeks after he had proposed to her, Amber and Lord Robert were married by special licence in St Michael's

Church in Paris, the 'official' church of the British Embassy. Amber wore a Vionnet wedding gown sewn with pearls and tiny diamonds, and the lace veil that Devenish brides had worn for several generations, couriered to the British Embassy in Paris, along with some of the family jewels.

Lord Levington gave her away, and Beth, wearing a plainer version of Amber's wedding dress in a pretty shade of lavender blue, was her only attendant, whilst a young diplomat from the embassy performed the office of Robert's best man.

Beth, much to Amber's relief, had been thrilled to learn that Amber was marrying Lord Robert, and had even teased Amber that she had guessed all along that Amber might be falling in love with him.

It had been easier – and safer – to let her go on thinking that.

Amber had, everyone agreed, been remarkably calm. Only she knew of how nearly she had broken down when she had heard the compelling time-honoured words of the marriage service ringing sombrely in the awesome silence of the church. That had been such a painful moment, and one in which she had longed desperately for the comfort of her parents.

And for Jean-Philippe? she had asked herself as Robert slipped his ring onto her finger.

No! Jean-Philippe had lied to her and betrayed her. She had loved him, but now she must not. But neither could she hate him as her grandmother hated Barrant de Vries.

She hadn't seen Jean-Philippe since that dreadful scene when she had confronted him with what Lord Robert had told her, and nor had she wanted to. She never wanted to see him again. In fact, she wanted to forget that she had ever known him at all.

Had her grandmother felt the same gratitude for Henry

Pickford that Amber herself felt for Robert? Amber didn't want to think that she was like her grandmother in any way.

Robert was inclining his head, his lips kind and warm as they brushed her own. They were married. It was done. She was safe.

Robert was guiding her back down the aisle whilst the organist flooded the church with the swell of Handel's triumphal music.

Although the sanctity of a church was not the place to think of such things, she had been having dreadful nightmares about Caroline Fitton Legh. How wretchedly unhappy and afraid she must have been, deserted by Greg and abandoned by her husband. What a terrible price to have to pay.

Amber was so very lucky. Robert had saved her from the shame and disgrace that Louise was currently experiencing and potentially from the even more dreadful situation Caroline Fitton Legh had been in, and into which Jean-Philippe had led her without a single thought for her. In such circumstances it was always the woman who paid the price, not the man.

She would never forget what Robert had done for her and she would never cease being grateful to him, Amber told herself passionately, making a solemn inner vow that from now onwards her love and her loyalty belonged only to Robert.

The church doors were flung open to admit the sunshine and allow them to step out into it.

Caught up in the intensity of her own emotions, Amber turned to look at Robert, her heart overflowing with gratitude, and it was that moment captured by Cecil's camera and skill that produced the photograph that later accompanied the hail of excited pieces in the society columns of

250

the British papers announcing their marriage. A young girl looking adoringly into the face of her new husband. Who seeing that look could not be touched by it?

After the church ceremony, the Ambassador hosted a wedding breakfast for them at the British Embassy. Whilst Lord and Lady Levington had outwardly been supportive, Amber suspected that neither of them, but especially Lady Levington, really approved of Robert marrying her. How could she when after all she had not thought Amber good enough to marry her own son? And Robert, as the heir to a dukedom, was higher up the peerage than Henry.

Not that anything had been said, and certainly Lady Levington had done everything she could to help arrange the wedding. However, there was a distinct coolness there, and it was one Amber suspected that she would encounter from others as well.

In the eyes of Robert's world she had done very well for herself in marrying him, and that would be resented by mothers with well-born daughters to marry off. She had been tolerated when she had merely been 'Beth's friend from school', but now that she was Robert's wife was she constantly going to encounter subtle animosity from those who had thought themselves above her but over whom now, thanks to her marriage to Robert, she would take social precedence?

That was the least of her worries, Amber admitted. She had been relieved when Henry had stayed on with his friends instead of coming to Paris. She couldn't bear to think of the way he had behaved and what he had done. Robert had told her that he had warned Henry that it would be the worse for him if he ever breathed a word about Amber and Jean-Philippe, and he had assured her that, given his own behaviour, Henry would not dare to say anything to anyone else.

251

Robert had told the Ambassador that they didn't want any fuss, but there were still toasts, cards to be read and wedding gifts piled up for them.

Amongst the cards, Amber found one from Jay, wishing her every happiness.

Dear Jay. Amber was so very fond of him. He had been a true and kind friend to her, and someone she had always felt able to confide in. There was a card from her grandmother for both of them, and a cool typically distant letter for her, in which Blanche announced that she was looking forward to seeing them on their return and to meeting Robert at last.

The party went on longer than Amber had expected and she was relieved and grateful when Robert announced calmly that it was time for them to leave.

They spent a week in Paris after the wedding, staying at the George V in a suite so huge that their bedrooms were separated by two large salons, whilst the Levingtons returned to Juan-les-Pins, and Cecil Beaton left for London.

As Amber had learned during her season and whilst staying at the villa, it was considered quite normal amongst the aristocracy for married people to have separate bedrooms. Even Diana Guinness had had her own bedroom and not shared one with her husband, Bryan, and they had been very much in love. So there was no reason for her to feel at all self-conscious about the fact that she and Robert had their own rooms, or to worry that people might think it odd in a newly married pair.

A peer's wife needed a rather different wardrobe from that of an unmarried débutante, Robert informed Amber, when she protested about his insistence that she was to have whatever new clothes she desired.

And it wasn't just clothes that Robert bought her. The first morning after their marriage he took her to Cartier, saying that she must have jewellery of her own and not just the family heirlooms she would be obliged to wear on formal occasions. His wedding gift to her was a pair of white and black diamond snake bangles with yellow diamond eyes that privately Amber felt were far too dramatic for her to feel comfortable wearing.

The London house in Eaton Square, virtually unused since his grandfather had retired to live full time at Osterby, the huge stately home that was the country seat of the family, would be their home, Robert told her, adding warningly, 'But it is far from fit to live in at the moment. So in the meantime we shall have to make do with Cheyne Walk, where we shall be very cramped.'

Naturally their marriage was the subject of a great deal of interest amongst the English upper classes living in and visiting Paris, and of course the newly married couple were fêted and invited to all manner of events, at which Robert was everything that a newly married man should be to his bride – attentive, tender and apparently in love with her.

The night before they were due to leave Paris to return to London they attended a dinner as guests of the British Ambassador. Amber had already met most of the other guests; most but not all, and her stomach churned with despair when she saw Jean-Philippe walking into the room accompanied by the woman she recognised from her photograph as Mrs de Wittier.

She was very elegant, Amber grudgingly acknowledged, and very thin, her skin drawn back tightly against the bones of a face in which her eyes were as hooded and predatory as those of a vulture. Jean-Philippe, far from exhibiting embarrassment or shame, actually sketched Amber a mocking half-bow when he saw her, his earring glinting in the light beneath the wild dark curls.

Immediately Amber's stomach cramped and the agony of the love she didn't want to feel for him flooded her. Just that one glance he had given her had been enough to burst open the locked door behind which she had pushed her memories of all those intimacies they had shared and which she could no longer endure. The physical ache inside her for him was so intense that she could scarcely bear it. Telling herself what he was, reminding herself that he was giving his body to the woman he was with in exchange for money, was a poor defence against her love. If he were to call to her, come to her, she—

'Amber.'

Robert stepped in front of her, obscuring her view of them.

'Remember where you are. Who you are now.'

Amber badly wanted to cry, but she couldn't. She was Robert's wife now and she owed it to him to behave accordingly, she reminded herself.

She could feel Jean-Philippe looking at her, willing her to look back at him so that he could torment her even more but she refused to do so, terrified of what she might do if she looked into his eyes and saw longing for her in them. Jean-Philippe did not love her. He could not do so to have lied to her as he had. But neither could Robert be the husband to her she had always hoped for.

After that it seemed as though the evening would never end, and when at last it did, Amber could not have been more thankful.

The next morning Amber woke up feeling nauseous and unwell.

The sight and smell of the breakfast Robert was eating had her excusing herself from the table and rushing to the bathroom.

When she returned, Robert grinned at her and told her that he hoped the baby would wait a respectable eight months before making its arrival, whereupon Amber duly fainted.

When she came round, she protested that it was the upset of the previous evening and the fish she had eaten that had unsettled her stomach, that was all, but Robert refused to be convinced, and began immediately to be extremely protective and to treat her as though she were made of the most delicate china.

Three days after their return to London, they travelled to Macclesfield to attend the post-wedding party Blanche had insisted on giving, and of course to allow Blanche to meet Robert.

Amber was disappointed to discover that Jay wasn't at Denham, having taken some holiday leave owing to him to visit his parents in Dorset.

Amber had known that Blanche would approve of Robert – how could she not do when he filled all her criteria as a grandson-in-law and was so very kind and charming into the bargain? What Amber had not anticipated, though, was that Robert would take equally well to Blanche.

Just before their departure, Blanche came up to their room where Amber was writing a letter to Beth whilst Robert enjoyed the comfort of Denham's library.

'I am so very pleased and happy for you in this marriage, Amber,' Blanche told her. 'Robert is everything I could have wished for you in a husband, and more.'

'You mean because he will make me a duchess?' Amber couldn't resist asking drily.

'Robert's breeding would speak for itself, no matter what his title,' Blanche told her coolly. 'No one could fail to be aware of it. You are very fortunate.'

'Am I?' Amber realised too late that the sharpness of her voice was giving away more than was wise. 'I mean, yes, I am, aren't I?' she corrected herself.

Blanche frowned. She had known the moment she had met Robert, and before she had seen the looks of approval and respect being exchanged by her guests at the party she had given for the newlyweds, that no one meeting Robert could fail to be impressed by him, and not purely because of his title and his wealth, and she had been right.

More than that, though, Blanche had been delighted by Robert's charm and his obvious good nature. It was plain to her how much he thought of Amber and Blanche knew she need never have any fears for her granddaughter's future. But she also knew that Amber wasn't happy. She was too thin, too on edge, too defensive and angry, even though she was trying hard to hide that anger, and nothing had been said about the reason for their immediate marriage.

'Amber, I am rather concerned about you.'

'No you aren't. You have never been concerned about me. You wanted me to marry someone with a title. Well, I have done so. You can wash your hands of me now.'

Before either of them could say any more Robert walked in, bringing their conversation to an abrupt end, much to Amber's relief. She was glad that they were returning to London in the morning but disappointed that she had not seen Jay. She had been so looking forward to seeing him. The house had seemed empty without both him and Greg, although she had had a letter from Greg offering his best wishes on her marriage, and apologising for not sending a gift but explaining that he was rather short of money.

'And you do not mind working for Mrs Pickford when your grandfather's estate is so close at hand?' Lydia asked.

'No, why on earth should I?' Jay responded as he held out his hand to help her over the stile.

Lydia's grandmother lived in the same small market town as his parents, and they had known one another most of their lives, although it had been several years since Jay had last seen her.

Her obvious admiration for him should, Jay knew, have provided a welcome balm for his aching heart and certainly one he should have appreciated had he any sense, but who when in love possessed that advantage? Lydia was not Amber, and Jay found that Lydia's intensity and the suddenness with which her mood could change from almost overexcited happiness to stark despair off-putting, even if he did feel sorry for her.

She had told him that her father's remarriage after the death of her mother had devastated her and that she was very upset by her stepmother's animosity towards her, confiding a little reluctantly that her stepmother didn't treat her at all well and seemed to want to drive a wedge between her and her father, and naturally Jay had sympathised with her in her distress.

They had met by chance today when Jay had been out walking, and although he was too polite to show it Jay would have rather had the solitude of his own company.

'I must get back, otherwise you will grow bored with me,' Lydia said now.

'Nothing of the sort,' Jay responded, more because he knew it was what she expected than because it was what he felt.

'Will you walk back with me? Only I never feel quite comfortable walking through the wood.'

'Of course I will,' Jay assured her, falling into step beside her.

They were having good weather, although perhaps a little

too warm for walking very far, and when they reached Lydia's grandmother's house and Lydia offered him a cool drink before he went home Jay gladly accepted, following her gratefully into the kitchen of the neat house.

He was slightly surprised when Lydia dragged a chair over to one of the cupboards and insisting on climbing onto it to get a glass, even though he had offered to do it for her, keeping up a stream of chatter as she did so. Her overvivacious manner was wearying and Jay longed to escape.

'You can hold the chair for me, though,' Lydia started to giggle, 'but you must promise not to look at my legs.'

'Lydia, please let me get the glass,' Jay begged her, but it was too late. Lydia wobbled on the chair and lost her balance, tumbling straight into his arms.

Jay was just wondering if her tumble had been more deliberate than accidental when Lydia confirmed his suspicions by flinging her arms round his neck and kissing him.

Jay had never imagined himself in this kind of situation, and felt extremely uncomfortable. He didn't want to hurt Lydia but he had no romantic feelings towards her whatsoever. However, worse was to come.

'Oh, isn't it wonderful that we've met again?' Lydia breathed happily. 'I never imagined when we were children that we'd fall in love with one another, did you?'

In love?

'Lydia, I'm sorry but—'

'You mustn't be sorry.' Her voice was low and worryingly intense. 'I— oh.'

Behind him Jay heard the back door open, and then Lydia was saying excitedly, 'Grandma, isn't it wonderful? Jay and I are in love and we're going to get engaged.'

There was nothing Jay could do. It was impossible for him to correct her, or deny what she had said. He was trapped both by his own moral code and by Lydia's intensity. How could his life have taken such a wrong turn?

Chapter Twenty-Three

Two months after their return from Paris, and at Robert's insistence, Amber paid a visit to an eminent obstetrician in Harley Street, who confirmed that Amber was indeed pregnant.

She had left the doctor's chambers and was about to get into the smart new chauffeur-driven Bentley Robert had insisted on providing for her when the sight of a woman emerging from another surgery a few doors away made Amber pause. Despite the fact that the woman was heavily wrapped up in a coat and a hat with a veil that obscured her face, something about the way she moved gave away her identity.

'Louise.' Amber felt the girl stiffen as she put her hand on Louise's arm. 'I thought it was you.'

Beneath the veiling Louise's face looked pale and her eyes slightly sunken. Her arm felt thin but her eyes blazed with the hostility that Amber remembered so well.

'And I suppose you thought as well that you'd do a bit of gloating, did you, since I am in so much disgrace, and unlikely to ever find a husband, especially now?'

Amber didn't know what to say. She had approached Louise automatically and without giving any thought to the gossip she had heard about her and her relationship with George Ponsonby. It had certainly not been her intention to gloat about her own unexpected social elevation.

However, before Amber could tell her this, Louise was continuing sharply, 'How wise you are to have married so well, and how unwise I have been to have loved so foolishly.'

Louise's words couldn't help but strike a chord in Amber's own heart. To her own surprise, Amber discovered that she actually felt sorry for Louise. She sounded so defeated, so low, and so very unlike the arrogant, confident girl Amber remembered.

Impulsively she suggested, 'I was just on my way home, why don't you come with me? We could talk properly then.'

Immediately Louise was sharply defensive. 'Talk properly? What about?'

'We may not have been friends, Louise, but we came out together, and that has to mean something,' Amber told her quietly.

To her dismay Louise's eyes filled with tears.

'You can say that now, but when the truth comes out, as it is bound to do before very long, you won't want to know me. No one will, not even my own mother. Of course I can make some excuse and disappear into the country for the necessary length of time but no one will be deceived, and socially I shall be ruined, as no doubt everyone thinks I should be. I had hoped that I could be wrong and have mistaken the signs but it seems I have not. As the good doctor has explained to me, the package I am carrying will soon be unreturnable, and since the cost of returning it, as he puts it, is far, far more than I can find, there is nothing for it but for me to quite literally bear the results of my folly.'

Louise was trembling now, and weeping openly, and Amber couldn't blame her. After all, she knew all too well how she would have felt in her shoes, and how easily she might have been in them. A sense of fellow feeling drove out Amber's old dislike of her.

'Get in the car,' she instructed her, refusing to take no for an answer, and then once Louise had given in and was seated next to her in the Bentley, Amber instructed the chauffeur, 'The National Gallery, Harris.'

'Why on earth are we going there?' Louise demanded.

'So that we can talk without anyone overhearing us,' Amber answered.

They were there for over four hours, but no matter what suggestions Amber made, Louise remained adamant that what she wanted was to have the child she was carrying aborted.

'Don't you see, it's the only choice if I'm to have any chance of continuing to be accepted socially. Without a husband to give this child a name, I cannot have it.'

Amber thought of the child she herself was carrying and wanted to weep.

'There must be some way . . . someone . . .'

'No, there is no other way, and the only someone who can help me is the doctor who will do nothing for me unless I pay him a hundred pounds.' She laughed mirthlessly. 'Although how I am supposed to find such a sum of money I do not know. I certainly do not have it. George Ponsonby, who should surely help me, has given his servants orders to refuse me entry to his rooms and will not answer my letters or telephone calls. Besides, Georgie boy is shortly to announce his engagement to a wealthy tradesman's daughter.'

'But he has a responsibility towards you,' Amber protested.

'He does not think so, and in fact I suspect he thinks I should take the honourable way out and do away with myself as well as the child.'

Amber felt acutely sick, and not just on her own account.

Caroline Fitton Legh's tragic end hovered in her thoughts like a pale ghost.

Fresh tears were welling in Louise's eyes. 'I would pawn the family tiara, except that it is already paste since the real one was sold to pay my father's gambling debts.'

They were almost level with the painting of Lorenzo Amber had been studying when she had first met Robert. Automatically she paused to look at it. Would she do things differently if she could go back in time to that first meeting with Robert, knowing what she knew now? Would she choose to walk away from him? But that would not have prevented her from meeting Beth again, would it, and that in turn would have led to her meeting Jean-Philippe. Robert was her saviour, not her enemy. Without him her situation would be just as bad, if not worse, than the one Louise was in.

'I am boring you, I can see,' Louise said huffily.

'No. Not at all,' Amber denied truthfully. 'I was just wishing . . .'

'What? After all, why should you have any sympathy for me? Beth certainly wouldn't have.'

There was nothing Amber could say, either to refute Louise's comment about Beth or to explain her own sympathy.

'There must be another way.'

'What other way? People are gossiping about me behind my back already. If I were to disappear to the country now – even if I had somewhere to disappear to – that would be as good as putting a notice in *The Times* social column.'

Louise looked and sounded wretchedly desperate.

'I will give you the money.'

Louise went white and clutched at the back of a seat for support, so obviously and genuinely shocked that Amber knew beyond doubt that she had not been expecting, never mind angling for, such an offer.

'You? But why should you do such a thing for me?'

Louise looked close to breaking down completely.

Amber reached for her hand and Louise let her take hold of it. It felt icy cold within Amber's own. Of course it was impossible for her to explain to Louise why she felt the way she did and to say that just listening to her and seeing her despair brought home to her how very lucky she was. When Louise's fate could so easily have been her own, how could she not put aside the past and the animosity that had existed between them and reach out to help her?

'Robert makes me a generous allowance but I do not carry large sums of money around with me. I shall need a few days to organise things. In the meantime, why don't you come and stay with us? We could call on your mother now and I could ask her to spare you to me to keep me company. But first I think I should tell you that I am to have a child myself, so if you feel that my condition will make things too hard for you to bear—'

'What is too hard for me to bear is the thought that I was ever fool enough to believe that George Ponsonby loved me. I am not the maternal type, Amber, and I never shall be. You and every other woman in London could be expecting a so-called happy event, and it would still not make me feel any differently. More than anything else I want to be free of . . . this . . . this wretched *thing* that could destroy my life.'

Louise was upstairs resting in the best guest bedroom, while Amber was downstairs in the library with Robert. She had made up her mind to be totally honest with her husband.

'You are telling me that you want to help someone who has treated you so wretchedly in the past?'

'I can't help thinking how easily I could have been her, Robert, if you had not stepped in and saved me. I just wish there was some way I could do more.' She put her hand against her own still-flat body as though to guard the life that was growing within it, tears springing into her eyes.

'I will not have you upset over all of this,' Robert told her. 'And you are not to compare yourself with Louise. She knew very well right from the start what Ponsonby was, and in my view she has brought her misfortune on herself.'

'I have to help her, Robert. It would be on my conscience for ever if I did not. I just wish there was some way to make it impossible for her not to have to—'

'There is no way,' Robert stopped her firmly. 'People are already gossiping. Everyone knows there was an affair thanks to her own indiscretion in flaunting it. She will not be forgiven for that alone. For her to disappear now would only confirm people's suspicions. I will cover all the costs involved,' he continued. 'And I will make enquiries to ensure that she has the best available medical attention. There are certain well-qualified surgeons who do perform female operations necessitated by a variety of female complaints – in private. Afterwards, since you are so determined to help her, I think it might be wise for the two of you to spend a few weeks at Osterby. She will need to recuperate in private and we shall put it about that because of your condition you have been advised to rest.

'After that, though, Louise must make her own plans and live her own life, Amber. She is the kind of person who will always attract trouble and who will always be drawn to the darker side of life, and I will not have you contaminated by that. I hope I do not need to insist to you that you say nothing of your own history to Louise.'

'No, you don't. I shall never tell anyone,' Amber assured him.

She had been so grateful to him, and still was, but it terrified her to recognise how fine and delicate was the thread to which she was clinging for security.

Like silk. But silk was also incredibly strong, as she would have to be – as she *would* be – in order to protect her child. As strong as silk.

As strong as the child growing inside her. Jean-Philippe's child. If it was a boy would he have his father's bold pirate looks? Would he have his gift as an artist, and his charm and his cruelty?

She must not think like this. The child she was carrying was to be Robert's child, and for its sake even more than her own she must think of it as Robert's child, and a child of their marriage.

A child of their marriage? When they didn't live as man and wife? When her nights were spent alone and lonely in a marriage bed that she would never share with the man who was her husband? Never share with any man. That could never be. She could never take such a risk again, knowing the price she was already having to pay.

She must be strong and accept the payment life was exacting from her.

Robert would be annoyed if he learned that she had agreed to come here with Louise, Amber acknowledged, as they hurried into the Harley Street address via a side door. But Louise had begged her to.

It was three weeks now since Louise had first confessed to Amber the terrible situation she was in.

Amber could feel her trembling violently now as she clung to her arm. They were shown very quickly through

266

a door that was locked behind them, up a flight of stairs and into a small room that smelled strongly of carbolic.

A nurse appeared to take charge of Louise, who was looking sick with fear.

'If you want to change your mind—' Amber began.

But Louise shook her head. 'I just want it to be over with.'

'How long will she be?' Amber asked the nurse.

'As long as it takes.' The nurse was purse-lipped and disapproving.

Louise had been gone for nearly an hour when the door to the waiting room suddenly opened and two young women, over made-up and wearing too tight and too brightly coloured clothes, burst in past the receptionist, who had obviously been trying to stop them, supporting between them another girl, who could hardly stand up.

'You can't go in there,' the receptionist was protesting.

'And who's going to ruddy stop us? Not you. Look at the state she's in. She'll snuff it soon if the doctor doesn't see her, and he better had, seein' as it's him wot's gorn and messed her up like this.'

'What's going on in here?' The nurse came hurrying in, her mouth compressed into a hard angry line, only to open into a look of anxious concern, as she demanded, 'What's she doing here? She was told to stay in bed.'

'Aye, well, if she had she'd have bin dead by now. Messed her up proper, he has, and she wants sortin' out, and now. Bleeding like a stuck pig, she's been.'

From behind the closed door a shrill scream like that of an animal *in extremis* raised the hairs on the back of Amber's neck.

'He's butchering someone else now by the sounds of it. Well, I hope she has better luck than poor Maria here. Told he was the best in the business, we was. I reckon we could have got someone down the East End to do the job for half the price, and better.'

'She can't stay here. You'll have to take her to hospital.'

'Wot, and have her arrested for wot she's done? She's staying here and he'd better get himself out here to look at her if he doesn't want her dying on his carpet.'

'If I was you, love, I'd scarper now before he does the same to you,' the other girl warned Amber.

Another nurse had appeared, her gown covered in blood, and was now attending to the poor girl. The smell in the room made Amber want to heave. It reminded her of having to walk past the entrance to the abattoir they had lived near when she had been a young girl.

'Your friend is ready to leave now, if you'd like to come this way,' the first nurse told Amber, indicating that she was to follow her.

In the room beyond the closed door Louise was lying on a bed with a sheet pulled over her. The smell of blood and vomit filled the air.

'She's to go home and rest.'

Amber nodded. There was a bucket by the bed. Absently she looked into it and horror and nausea rushed over her at what she saw. She could feel herself trembling from head to foot, filled by mortal fear and anguish.

'Come on,' the nurse was chivvying Louise. 'You can't stay here.'

The life that had been torn from Louise lay motionless in the bucket, a mess of blood and flesh.

Amber wanted to look away but somehow she couldn't. Grief and anguished guilt filled her for the life that had been destroyed. In Louise's shoes she didn't think she could have borne to know that she had allowed her child's life to be taken, and yet without Robert it might not just have been her child's life she would have had to end but her own as well. Amber's face was wet with tears.

She put her hand on her own body, immediately and fiercely protective of the life she was carrying, and filled with an overwhelming need to escape from such a dreadful horrible place.

Chapter Twenty-Four

When, a few weeks short of nine months after they had been married Amber gave birth to a sturdy baby boy, who everyone said was the image of his father, it was Robert who wept tears of joy at their son's birth, and who held the child as though he could never bear to let him go, whilst Amber lay and watched, stunned. Only now could she finally let go of the terrible fear that had haunted her throughout her pregnancy, that somehow because of what had happened to Louise's child her own would be damaged in some way. To see him and hold him and know that he was whole and safe was more joy than she was able to bear.

Only when she was finally alone with her son was Amber able to study him closely, and anxiously. He had been born with a head full of dark curls – like her father, and like Robert. His eyes were blue, and when she looked at him it was her own father she saw in his features, not Jean-Philippe. As she held him close and gave in to her relief, Amber asked herself a little giddily what she had been expecting. That he would be born with an earring in his ear?

What she was doing meant that her son would be denied all knowledge of his real father. For his own sake. Robert would love him – he already did. As Robert's legitimate son he would never know what it was to be unwanted and an outcast. But might he sense something as he grew? He would not – why should he?

'I love you,' Amber whispered to him as she cradled him. 'Everything I have done and will do for you is done with love and always will be, I promise you that.'

She wished Jay could see him. She could visualise the smile he would give her when he looked at the baby. A smile that told her that he understood and that he was assuring her that she had done the right thing. They still corresponded but not in the same way. After all, she was married and Jay himself was engaged now.

Amber had been shocked at first when she had heard the news of Jay's whirlwind romance – shocked, but of course very pleased and happy for Jay, she had assured herself firmly.

Her grandmother was due to arrive tomorrow, having insisted on travelling to London to see her first great-grand-child. What would Blanche make of him?

All the way to London the pain had been there, tightening round her heart and seizing her breath. Blanche wished that Jay had not insisted on escorting her. His presence in the first-class railway carriage with her made it imperative for her to conceal what she was feeling.

How well she remembered the birth of her own first child. It had been a protracted and painful labour, with the baby presenting in the breech position. It had been the midwife who had finally managed to turn him, allowing him to be born with such speed after she had done so that she had laughed at his impatience.

Blanche had heard it said that in the first hours after its birth a baby's closest resemblance was to its father, nature's way of ensuring a child's acceptance by that father – providing he was able to see it. Henry had been away

271

when Marcus had been born. She had loved him so very much. Her first child and a son – how could she not have done so?

Even now the agony of his death was as sharp and clear as it had been the night she had woken from her sleep, knowing that he had gone. A whole platoon of brave young men from Cheshire had died that night, including Barrant de Vries's son, who had led the charge that had killed them.

Barrant had wept openly during the memorial service held at the parish church but the tears Blanche herself might have cried had been burned dry by the heat of her hatred for Barrant. She prayed that Amber would never know the grief she had known, but why should she? Amber would have the life that Blanche had wanted so passionately for herself and never had. There would be no door that was closed to her. As Robert's wife, a duchess in due time, she could if she wished become a great political hostess, shaping events behind the scenes. With the right husband she could have done so much, Blanche knew. She had yearned for all those things that being Barrant's wife could have given her. But he had laughed at her and rejected her.

Well, now she was the one who could laugh at him. It was her great-grandson who would be one of those who would lead his country into the future, whilst the de Vries line practically died out. She could have given Barrant so much – she *had* given him so much – and he had taken so much from her. Too much.

Amber waited anxiously whilst Blanche inspected the baby she was holding in her arms.

'He looks exactly like you,' she pronounced eventually, smiling up at Robert, whilst Amber released her pent-up breath on a sigh of relief.

'Amber believes he has a look of her father,' Robert told Blanche, giving Amber a mischievous look.

'A Russian émigré? Nonsense. I can see quite clearly that he has your nose, Robert. But then Amber has always been far too sentimental where her father is concerned. Jay asked me to give his best wishes to you, Amber. He is staying at his grandfather's club whilst I am here. I told him it wasn't necessary for him to escort me but he insisted.'

'Jay is here in London?' Amber was astonished.

Why did she feel such a sharp sense of disappointment that he hadn't come to see her or written to tell her that he planned to escort her grandmother? It was silly. He had his own life now. And she had hers, she thought, holding her baby son contentedly.

Six weeks after he was born, Amber's son was christened Lucius Robert Vernon Devenish, in the private chapel at Osterby, and given the courtesy title Viscount Audley. His great-grandfather attended the christening, along with Amber's grandmother. Beth was his godmother, and his godfathers were Alistair and Sir Charles Afton-Blake, a friend of Robert's from their schooldays.

To mark the occasion the earl presented his countess with a diamond necklace and the duke handed over to her a parure from the family jewels that Robert described as unbelievably ugly.

On their return to London the earl and countess gave a party that was reported in *The Times* and *Vogue* as the party of the season. Cecil Beaton photographed the new family with Lord Robert, the earl, standing proudly to one side of the countess whilst she cradled their son.

The silk had held and they were safe.

Part Two

Chapter Twenty-Five

England 1935

'But my dear girl, of course he will go to my old prep school as a boarder before he goes on to Eton.'

At twenty-two she hardly merited the description 'girl' any more, Amber reflected, but she had no intention of allowing herself to point that out to Robert, when she needed to save all her fire power for a far more important issue.

'Robert, Luc is only four, a baby still.'

'Because you insist on keeping him as one. It really won't do, Amber. Such things may be all very well in the home of wealthy manufacturers, but in the peerage we do things differently.'

Even now she was still not really 'accepted'; not even by her own husband, Amber reflected, dipping her head to hide from Robert how much his careless comment had stung her.

Was it because of who she was or what she was that she was so acutely sensitive to the fact that the society in which they moved watched her with a mixture of disdain and avid interest, waiting, she felt sure, to see how long it would be before she fell from grace? On the surface she might be accepted, but there were those who were always ready to drop those little acid comments to remind her that Robert's title could only mask that she came from 'trade'. More worrying though for Amber was the 'what' she was: namely a woman in a sexless marriage who must preserve her virtue if she wanted to preserve her marriage. Robert had made that much plain to her. He would not, he had told her more than once, countenance her having any affairs, no matter now discreet, and no matter how much accepted as a fact of life by others in their social circle.

Not that she had been tempted to have an affair; far from it, and she was still very grateful to Robert for all that he had done for her, and of course for Luc, whom Robert truly loved as his own son. That alone was worth the sexual wilderness her 'lavender' marriage banished her to.

And at least she had Jay, her faithful friend and correspondent, and married now to Lydia, with whom Amber had never been able to feel totally at ease, no matter how hard she tried. She had expected to love Jay's wife and it had been an unpleasant shock when she had discovered that she couldn't. Sadly, whilst her childhood bond with Jay had if anything strengthened, with meetings as friends in the company of their spouses on those occasions when Amber and Robert travelled to Cheshire to stay with Blanche, Amber's bond with Greg had weakened. They still wrote to one another, long newsy letters on Amber's part and short spasmodic replies on Greg's, often containing pleas for money.

Amber had been astonished when Greg had announced that he intended to remain in Hong Kong instead of returning home, and she suspected that Blanche was disappointed although, being Blanche, she had not of course said so. It was nearly six years now since Greg had left Cheshire for Hong Kong and Amber wondered when she would actually see him again.

'I promise you, he will love boarding once he gets used to it. I did,' Robert continued cheerfully.

Amber wanted to point out that the reason her husband had loved being at a boarding school was because it had allowed him to escape from the cruelty that had been shown to him, as an orphaned child, by his grandfather.

She had been horrified when, shortly after Luc's birth, Robert had warned her that their son was never to be left alone with the duke.

'He is a sadist; there is no other way to describe him,' Robert had told Amber curtly. 'He set traps for me to fall into and then punished me for what he said was lying to him. There were beatings, cruelty such as you can't imagine. He would have me locked in a trunk he kept in his room and left there sometimes for a full day and night. He used to taunt me that he might go away and leave me there and that no one would find me.'

'But why would he do such things? You are his grandson – his heir.'

'He claimed it was to prepare me for life, but it is my opinion that there is a touch of madness in him – perhaps more than a touch. If there is then all the more reason for me to be glad that Luc does not carry his blood. But, like I said, Luc is never, ever to be left alone with him, nor must he ever visit him without one of us being there.'

Robert's disclosures had shocked Amber and she had taken his warnings to heart.

'Don't let us quarrel, Amber.' Robert smiled coaxingly at her now. 'You know that I wouldn't do anything that I thought would harm Luc in any way.'

She did know that, Amber acknowledged. Father and son adored one another and were inseparable.

'It will be another two years before he goes to my old prep school anyway. I thought we'd alter the guest list for Scotland this year,' Robert added casually.

He was standing in front of the handsome fireplace, jiggling coins and keys in his pocket, trying to look nonchalant and merely succeeding instead in looking boyishly guilty.

Amber knew all the signs now, of course, after nearly five years of marriage. She had suspected earlier in the month that Robert was in love again, and now his suggestion that they change the guest list for their annual shooting party on their Scottish estate confirmed those suspicions.

The rule of celibacy and fidelity that applied to her did not, of course, apply to Robert himself, and Amber had quickly come to recognise when Robert was in the throes of a new passion.

'If you wish,' she agreed calmly, knowing what was expected of her. 'I had thought of going down to Osterby soon,' she told him. Two could play the 'let's change the conversation' game, after all. 'The sample for the King's Bedroom is ready, and of course I want to see it before I give Maurice the go-ahead to have the fabric made. Jim has offered to meet me at the factory to give me his opinion.'

The Osterby estate and its Palladian house had passed to Robert, along with the title, in 1933. Amber had been appalled to discover how badly the house had been neglected and then relieved when a thorough inspection of it had shown that the neglect was more cosmetic than structural.

She had relished the challenge of taking on the restoration of the house; it was the kind of project that was very dear to her heart.

Robert had not been happy initially when Amber had informed him of her plan to become involved with the design and production of new silks at Denby Mill. It was not fitting that his wife should be engaged in trade, he had told her, but Amber had been firm, pointing out to him that she needed to have some outlet for her unspent energy. She had made it plain exactly what she had meant, and to her relief Robert had conceded.

The dedication Amber had given to learning as much as she could about textiles and design since her marriage had enabled her to act with confidence when it came to Osterby's refurbishment.

All the paperwork relating to the original building and furnishing of the house had been gathered together for Amber to study; Cecil Beaton had been coaxed and cajoled into taking photographs of the rooms as they were, and of the faded, worn fabrics.

Amber had been determined that the refurbishment of Osterby would follow the plans for the original décor as closely as was possible, especially where Osterby's state apartments were concerned, allowing her to create a grand house that was also a home.

For their own private apartments Amber wanted to combine the classic lines of the original décor with something more suited to modern living. It had been to her father's designs that she had turned for inspiration, adding in ideas of her own to create new silk fabrics. Naturally the silk would come from her own family's mill in Macclesfield, but knowing her grandmother as she did Amber had kept the details of her designs to herself. She might have won her grandmother's approval, first by her marriage to the heir to a dukedom, and secondly by giving him a son, but Amber was under no illusions as to her grandmother's real feelings for her.

Now Amber had a new ambition, which she hadn't revealed to Robert as yet because she was waiting for the right moment.

It had been Cecil who had first suggested to her that she should think of opening her own shop. She had laughed at the idea at the time, shaking her head and saying that Robert would never allow it, but somehow the idea had taken root and grown until she couldn't stop thinking about it.

Things might not have gone any further if she hadn't happened to be walking down Walton Street, just over a month ago, and seen the empty shop for sale. She had fallen in love with it immediately, seeing its possibilities. Double-fronted with a bow window either side of the front door, it was both a handsome building and yet at the same time not so formidable that it might seem off-putting. It was true that it looked rather shabby and neglected, but that only made Amber want it all the more so that she could bring it back to life and put her own stamp on it. It had such potential and such charm. It was perfect for her purpose, and she knew she had to have it.

All she had to do now was convince Robert that the opening and running of a shop, which she planned to name Silks, was a good idea. Amber was tempted to solicit Cecil's support but he could be a dreadful gossip and Robert wouldn't take it very well if he thought she and Cecil had been discussing it behind his back before she'd consulted him.

Amber already had the most wonderful plans for the large windows. She wanted them to be just as she had visualised in Paris. The rooms behind the windows had wood-panelled walls and Amber planned to have all the woodwork painted in a light neutral colour, maybe a soft French grey, or a plain stone colour, with just one chair in one window and a large mirror in the other, both painted in something striking, perhaps black, over which a roll of silk would be draped as though it had just been casually dropped there. Maybe she would allow one or two small interesting *objets d'art*, and on small reading desks there would be open 'books' containing information on the history and the process of silk manufacture, and the designs of traditional silk fabrics, written so that those outside the window looking in could see them.

Amber's dream was that her shop would become the destination for all those who wanted the very best quality silk furnishing fabric for their homes.

It would not be easy to convince Robert, she knew. For all the legal irregularity of his own sex life, Robert could be surprisingly rigid when it came to what he did and did not think was acceptable behaviour on the part of his wife.

All in all, she and Robert got on pretty well together, although Amber often felt that of the two of them she was the one who had to make the greater concessions within their marriage. Only very occasionally did she allow herself to think of what her life could have been if she had been allowed to marry for love – very occasionally, because after all she had Luc to think of, and she could never say there was no love in her marriage whilst there was Luc. Loved by both of them and adored by Robert, but not in any way spoiled or overindulged, Luc brought the sunshine into Amber's heart with his natural enthusiasm and excitement for life, and his expressive face and his readiness to give love to those who loved him.

Initially she had watched him fearfully, worried with every development he made that he might be exposing himself as his father's child, but by the time he had reached his second birthday Amber had learned not to worry. Luc was his own wonderful individual self, no matter what had gone into the making of him. He had the sweetest nature, filled with laughter and good humour; he was, as Robert never tired of boasting, very bright and quick to learn.

Robert was a wonderful father to Luc and the bond between the two of them was one that in many ways excluded her. Luc had all Robert's small mannerisms. He stood like him and walked like him, looking up to Robert and copying him in everything he did.

Robert in his turn gave Luc not only the firm fatherly guidance that all boys needed, he also showed him his physical paternal love, with the result that Luc had none of the stiff emotional awkwardness with, and sometimes even fear of, their fathers that so many of her friends' young sons had.

As parents they were united by their love for their son as nothing else could unite them.

If Amber ever thought of Jean-Philippe now it was with anxiety and dread in case Luc grew to look like his father, or Robert turned against him.

If she was lonely deep inside herself for a love such as her parents had shared, then that was the price she had to pay for Luc's security and happiness, and therefore she would pay it willingly.

Amber was reminded afresh of her good fortune that evening when she and Robert joined their friends in the Savoy's American bar for cocktails prior to going on to the Embassy Club, and she saw Louise with her husband seated at one of the tables. Louise looked rather too thin, and was surveying the other tables with a restless edgy air that betrayed her boredom.

Amber knew that she would never forget how easily the fate that had almost been Louise's could have been her own. Now Louise had no child, and her husband was a boor of a man twenty years older than she, who made no secret of the fact that he felt he had done her a favour in marrying her. They lived on the edge of society, kept there by Louise's

284

family connections and her husband's grim determination to make the most of them. There was also a good deal of gossip about Louise not being faithful to her husband, and that the lovers tended to be rich older men who liked the idea of being able to boast that they were bedding a woman with a title.

Robert had made it clear to Amber that he did not wish her to continue to associate with Louise.

'She has disgraced herself and her family name,' he had told Amber after one episode when Louise had been openly named in a newspaper article as a 'close friend' of a certain 'well-known shop owner'. The shop owner in question had been Harry Selfridge, who was notorious for his gambling and his ongoing affair with the Dolly Sisters, twins who had a stage act. Beth, scandalised, had told Amber that she had actually seen Louise in Selfridges, being escorted through the store by its owner.

'I had to pretend I hadn't seen her. She was wearing the most dreadfully vulgar jewellery that he had obviously just given her, and far too much makeup.'

Amber, though, couldn't think of Louise without feeling incredibly guilty. Both of them had fallen in love with the wrong man, both of them had behaved recklessly because of that love, and both of them had ended up in the same situation. She, though, had been saved from the consequences of that situation by Robert, whilst poor Louise had not had anyone to rescue her.

When Amber had once said as much to Robert, he had been very angry with her, telling her that she was never to compare herself with Louise.

'You are my wife. There is a vast difference between you. Louise is a born harlot,' he had told Amber tersely. 'She had been warned against Ponsonby but she deliberately ignored that warning. Everything that has happened to her she has brought on herself. She makes no secret of the fact that any man with the money to do so may buy her presence in his bed.'

'That's not fair,' Amber had protested, but Robert had insisted, 'It is the truth, and everyone knows it.'

Robert had left their table and was talking to a young man who had just arrived, tall and fair-haired, not a day over nineteen, with what would have been a beautiful face were it not for a certain calculating sharpness to his close-set eyes.

He would break poor Robert's heart, Amber suspected. For all his intelligence and wit, something in his nature meant that Robert always seemed to end up being the one in his love affairs who loved the most. His closest friends, many of whom Amber had learned over the years were themselves either homosexual or bisexual, and no strangers to intense passion and unrequited love, did their best to protect Robert from his own vulnerability, but to no avail.

'The trouble with Robert,' Cecil Beaton had once told Amber, 'is that he will fall in love with pretty little straight boys who like teasing him into thinking that they could be homo, given the love of a homo chap, but who then change their minds at the last minute, just when poor Robert has thrown his heart at their feet.'

The five years of her marriage had opened Amber's eyes to a world she had simply not known existed. It no longer surprised or shocked her to learn that an outwardly devoted husband or a practised flirt who seemed to adore women in public, turned in private to his own sex.

Other people might speak romantically of 'love', but from what Amber had seen as well as experienced herself, physical and emotional passion caused far more pain and despair than happiness. She was determined not to allow either of them into her life ever again. The pain of loving

Jean-Philippe had seared her, sealing her heart against wanting to love again.

Now Amber sipped her White Lady and smiled warmly when Beth and her husband came hurrying in.

'We're late, I'm sorry, but Baby is teething, poor little thing, and Nanny does get so cross with her,' Beth apologised as Alistair went over to the bar to join the other men.

Beth had given birth to her third child, a daughter after two sons, the previous autumn.

'I see that Wallis Simpson is here,' Beth grimaced as she sat down next to Amber. Beth did not approve of the American divorcee who had become such a close friend of the Prince of Wales. 'Have you heard the latest news about Diana Guinness?'

Beth had turned into something of a gossip as she had matured and, fond as she was of her, Amber disliked discussing the private affairs of others, perhaps, she admitted, because she couldn't bear the thought of people gossiping about *her*.

Beth went on to talk about Diana's affair with Oswald Mosley, who was setting tongues wagging himself with his involvement in fascism. 'I don't know how Diana can be with him. This dreadful fascism is all so very shocking,' Beth continued.

'Yes,' Amber agreed.

Earlier in the week she and Robert had been discussing the situation and Robert had told her that he feared for the future of Europe if Hitler continued on his current course.

'In my opinion,' he had said, 'it's just as well that we are expanding the RAF. The working people of Germany may be ready to worship Hitler because of way he is improving the economy, but several friends of mine who have Jewish connections are increasingly concerned about his anti-Jewish stance.'

'Oh, and I almost forgot to tell you,' Beth continued, 'Pamela is pregnant again. Mummy telephoned me to tell me. Daddy and Henry are desperately hoping it will be a boy this time, for the title, you know.'

Henry had married Lady Pamela Mountjoy, the daughter of Lord Noakes whose land bordered Beth's father's, a year after Amber had married Robert. Their first child had been a daughter, as had their second, and Amber could well imagine how anxiously the family would be awaiting this birth.

She still felt uncomfortable at the thought of Henry, though, and preferred not to talk about him.

'Shall you be going to the Continent this year, Amber?' Beth asked.

Amber looked across to where Robert was gazing adoringly at his beau.

'We haven't decided yet. Robert was talking about buying a yacht. He was very taken with Daisy Fellowes' yacht last year.'

'Alistair says that yachts are incredibly vulgar,' Beth informed her.

Amber hid a small sad smile. Four years of marriage had changed Beth from the gentle girl she had been into someone far less compassionate. Someone who would definitely not have wanted anything to do with the Amber who had been Jean-Philippe's lover and who had given herself to him in such abandon. Amber was just thankful that Beth didn't know anything about that reckless passionate time in her life, and the consequences of it.

She was rather regretting agreeing to go on to the Embassy Club now, Amber admitted, but Robert had been keen, and Emerald Cunard, who had been at the same dinner party they had been attending earlier, had insisted that she must. But now the Prince of Wales had arrived with Mrs Simpson and there was a very noticeable tension in the air, with those to whom Mrs Simpson had given her approval grouped closely about the Prince, and those who had once been his friends but of whom she did not approve excluded.

'He is hopelessly besotted with her, poor little man.'

Amber shook her head warningly at the handsome bon vivant Max Leighton, as he took a seat next to her.

'You mustn't let anyone else hear you saying things like that, Max,' she warned him.

He shrugged dismissively, then drawled, 'Why not, since it is true?' He changed the subject. 'So that is Robert's new crush, is it? Very Aryan, Amber. The Führer would approve.'

'That's not funny, Max. This anti-Semitism propaganda the Führer supports is loathsome,' Amber told him fiercely.

The smile Max gave her was edged with cynicism. 'It is my belief that it will get far worse, and I am not the only one to think so. Goodness, who on earth is that gorgeous creature over there with Syrie Maugham?' he asked, changing the subject again. 'Excuse me, my dear, whilst I go and see if I can persuade Syrie to introduce me to her.'

He had only just left when a sharp clipped voice with an American accent, close to Amber's ear, exclaimed, 'What very unusual bracelets!'

Amber turned and found herself face to face with Wallis Simpson. The American divorcee was wearing an oyster satin Schiaparelli gown with emerald-green embroidery that enhanced the extreme slenderness of her narrow body. Her dark hair was cut short and elegantly waved. Enormous diamond and emerald clips that matched the necklace she was wearing flashed in her ears.

Amber could see the acquisitive look in Wallis's eyes as she looked down at Amber's black and white diamond snake bangles with their yellow diamond eyes. Amber rarely wore them; to do so in the years of the depression had struck her as an insult to those poor men without work, but since unemployment was now falling swiftly, and her own Chanel gown was almost severely plain, she had decided for once to do so.

Denby Mill had been one of the few mills that had not needed to turn off workers at the height of the depression, and Amber had been astonished at first and then deeply moved when she had been discussing that with Jay and he had told her that it was because her grandmother had given instructions that no worker at the mill was to lose their job, no matter how little work the mill might actually have. To ensure that her wishes were carried out Blanche had actually set up a fund to provide for the workers' wages. Her grandmother might not care for the mill itself, but she did care for those who worked there.

'Thank you. They were a wedding present from my husband,' she told Wallis.

'From which jeweller?' the divorcee pressed her eagerly.

'Cartier.'

'David,' Wallis Simpson called out imperiously, 'do come and look at these bangles. They are such fun.'

'Do you know, Robert, I really think that Wallis Simpson believes the Prince of Wales will marry her,' Amber confided to her husband in the privacy of their library later as she removed her bangles for him to place in the safe.

Robert yawned and shook his head. 'He won't marry her,' he told Amber firmly. 'You can depend on that. The government would never allow it.'

It was late that night, and still Amber couldn't sleep; the evening had awakened too many painful memories and with them, the ache that was tormenting her with increasing regularity. She had tried her best to deny, and then when that failed to ignore it, shocked by it and ashamed of herself

290

for experiencing it. Her knowledge of what was acceptable in terms of female sexuality and its needs had, prior to her relationship with Jean-Philippe, been limited to an awareness that it was not acceptable for a 'nice' girl even to acknowledge that she knew that sex existed, never mind have any curiosity about it – or, heaven forbid – desire to experience it. As a married woman and a mother she was obliged to live as though sex, the desire and longing it created and the fulfilment of those needs, simply did not exist. She had told herself that she could easily live like that and she had believed it to be true, but suddenly these last few weeks, an ache – no more than a small touch, gone so swiftly she had managed to convince herself it had never even existed – had begun to pursue and haunt her.

Amber lay in the darkness, tensing her body against the ache's unwanted invasion and its equally unwanted demands. This need that was now gripping her was her shameful unwanted secret, to be shared only with the dark hours of the night. During the daytime she could ignore it, by keeping herself busy, but at night . . .

She looked towards the closed communicating door that separated her bedroom from Robert's. Robert. Her husband. A small pang of emotion caught at her heart and her breath. She had thought him so magnificent and so romantic when she had first known him. She had even been on the edge of giving her heart to him until she had realised . . . She had dreamed of Robert with a young innocent girl's dreams of romantic love, all tender kisses and soft touches. But now the kisses and the touches she wanted were those desired by a woman, not a mere girl. The ache tormenting her was so hard to bear, and Robert was her husband. Other men with his inclinations had proper physical married relations with their wives, and their children were evidence of that fact, Amber reminded herself. She felt so very alone sometimes, deprived, cheated almost – cheated? How could she even think that, after everything that Robert had done for her? Tears burned the backs of her eyes.

Was it really so very wrong of her to wish that just occasionally Robert might be a proper husband to her? The communicating door seemed to draw her. She got up, pulling on a lace peignoir over her nightgown, her heart thumping with a mixture of excitement and apprehension as she walked over to the door and then opened it.

Robert's bedroom was decorated in shades of stark white and pale silver grey, very masculine and modern; the thick soft rug covering the dark stained floorboards, specially woven for him, its raised border showing silver white against the darker dove-grey background in the moonlight. Robert loved moonlight and refused to have the curtains closed on those nights when the moon was visible.

He was sleeping on his side, facing the window, his hair dark against the white pillow, his black silk pyjama-clad shoulder hunched.

A feeling of sweetness and love filled her, softening the gnawing teeth of her inner ache. Surely they could give some physical comfort to one another? She might not desire him in the way she had done Jean-Philippe, but they were man and wife, and who else should she turn to but him to soothe the need that would not let her sleep? They liked and respected one another – married couples who had far less regard shared physical intimacy. Surely it wasn't impossible for them to do the same?

Amber walked round to the far side of the bed. She looked down into Robert's sleeping face, and then reached out to touch him, cupping his face with her hand as she whispered his name.

He was awake instantly, jerking away from her touch,

sitting up in the bed, demanding sharply, 'Amber, what are you doing in here?'

'I couldn't sleep.' It was true, after all. Before she could lose her courage she blurted out, 'Robert, I ache so much inside that it hurts. I can't sleep and—'

'You aren't feeling well? You want me to send for a doctor?' He threw back the covers and stood up, switching on a bedside light and frowning at her.

'No,' Amber denied immediately. 'It isn't that kind of ache. Oh, Robert, I feel so alone sometimes, so very lonely.' She threw her arms round him, leaning into his body, her head on his chest. 'I need to be with you as your wife, Robert, as a woman is with her husband. Please . . .' Amber raised her head and pressed her lips softly against his.

She felt his body stiffen and then recoil as he grasped her arms and pushed her away so forcefully that she almost fell.

'I think you must have drunk too much champagne this evening. It is the only explanation I can think of for your behaviour.'

'Robert,' Amber pleaded desperately, 'I need you. You are my husband.'

'I will not listen to this, Amber. Please do not say another word.' He turned his back on her, then turned back to her, telling her savagely, 'You know what manner of man I am.'

'But other men like you are also husbands to their wives,' Amber protested. 'And—'

'No, they are not men like me. Do you not understand that?'

When Amber shook her head, he swore under his breath and then said cruelly, 'Very well then, I shall make you understand. To men like me the mere thought of touching female flesh in the way that you desire is one that revolts us, fills us with nausea and disgust. To hear you speak of aching, wanting, needing . . . makes my flesh crawl.'

293

For a minute Amber felt too shocked and humiliated to say or do anything, but her pride came to her rescue.

'Then if you will not be a husband to me, what am I to do? Bear in silence the ache that you are able to satisfy when and with whom you choose?'

'It is the general accepted rule that a wife may take a lover so long as she is discreet, and careful not to fill her husband's nurseries with bastards.' Robert's voice was stiff and formal. 'If you wish me to make some suitable recommendations—'

'No!' Now it was Amber's turn to recoil in revulsion. 'I would rather bear the ache and keep my self-respect than have my husband shame me by pimping for me as though . . . Isn't what you've already done enough? Do you really hate me so much, Robert?' She had to stop – she simply couldn't speak for the tears choking her voice.

'I do not hate you at all. You are my wife, by my own choice.'

Then Amber started to laugh. 'Your wife? But you would whore me to keep me out of your own bed.'

'That is enough. Hysteria I might countenance, Amber, but not vulgarity. I am sorry if I have upset you, but you should not have come in here. The fault is mine, I suppose. I should have seen to it that the communicating door is permanently locked. You must either learn to live with your . . . needs, Amber, or find a discreet means of dealing with them. Some women – the worthier sort, no doubt – immerse themselves in good works, I believe. The choice is yours. I do not wish to hear another word on the subject. Please return to your own room.'

Amber was only too relieved to be able to escape. How could she have humiliated herself like that?

The ache that had driven her into Robert's room had gone. It must never return. The thought of cold-bloodedly taking a discreet lover sickened her, even more than Robert's rejection of her had humiliated her. No, from now on she would find some other way of living her life as the wife of a man who did not want her, and it would not involve either taking a lover or pleading a second time with her husband.

Shivering, Amber got back into bed. She wished that she could close her eyes and forget that tonight had ever happened, as though it had merely been a bad dream.

'Amber, I've been thinking.'

Amber tensed. It was two days since her disastrous attempt to seduce him, and so far Robert had not made any reference whatsoever to what had happened.

'Since you are going to Macclesfield and then on to Osterby,' Robert continued with careful casualness, 'I rather think I might pop over to Paris for a few days.'

Was it relief or was it shame that was making her feel so light-headed and weak, or did it even matter? Robert was speaking again and she made herself focus on what he was saying.

'Otto has never been to Paris, poor boy – can you imagine? – and I thought he might find it amusing.'

Amber wanted to urge him not to give his heart too quickly or too completely. There had been something about the cold and calculating look she had seen in Robert's new young man's eyes as he watched Robert's face light up with love for him that had struck her as chilling.

Chapter Twenty-Six

'Jay, what a lovely surprise!' Amber couldn't conceal the pleasure it gave her to find Jay waiting for her on the platform of Macclesfield station.

'I hope you don't mind, only your grandmother had a charity committee meeting to attend, so she asked me if I would pick you up since she needed Horace and the car.'

Amber laughed. 'I would far rather be met by you than by Horace, and far rather be driven by you as well. Grandmother really should retire him. I'm not sure that he's at all safe.'

'Probably not, but since everyone local knows him and takes care to give your grandmother's Bentley a wide berth, I dare say he is safe enough.

'You've come to see the silk, of course?' he smiled at her as he opened the door of a sturdy-looking Morris Oxford for her.

'Yes. Have you seen it?' Amber asked him eagerly.

'Not yet. Maurice Westley wanted me to, but I told him that I thought you should be the first. He's thrilled with it – or at least as thrilled as a Yorkshireman can allow himself to be – and he reckons they've done a good job.'

Maurice Westley was the new mill manager Jay had found after Amber had confided to him that she felt that her grandmother's lack of interest and the previous manager's age were combining to drive the mill's falling sales even further downwards.

Jay had a way of dealing with her grandmother that got the result that Amber never could, and she had been delighted when Jay had introduced her to Westley. The Yorkshireman made no secret of the fact that he thought the manufacture of silk could never compare in importance or substance with the manufacture of wool or cotton, but he had settled down well at the mill and the workers respected him.

Thanks to Cecil Beaton's advice and her own discreet lobbying within her circle, Amber had managed to obtain several excellent commissions for the mill, including some via James Lees-Milne, whose involvement with the National Trust meant that he had become something of an expert on the interior decoration of the country's grand houses.

They had produced white silks for Syrie Maugham's interiors and they still had the ecclesiastical contracts won by Amber's father all those years ago, but it was thanks in the main to Robert that Denby Mill had received a much-needed new order for large quantities of parachute silk. It had been Robert, who, when the government had first announced in the spring of 1935 that it intended to treble the size of the RAF over a two-year period because of the growing strength of Germany, had recognised that this would mean there would be an increased demand for silk parachutes, and who had suggested through his contacts that Denby Mill should be invited to tender for these new contracts.

Securing a government contract to supply parachute silk had made a tremendous difference to their business.

'I can't wait to see the silk,' Amber told Jay. 'I have arranged to go to the mill tomorrow morning. If you can spare the time I would love it if you could come with me.'

'I shall make the time.'

Jay was one of those men who wore his good looks in the same way as he might a comfortable country jacket, Amber thought as he smiled at her. Perhaps it was a fault in her, but somehow she had grown tired of too witty, too smart men and women who existed merely on brittle quips, their lives without meaning unless they had attended the most fashionable society ball or were *au fait* with the latest gossip.

'How is Lydia?' she asked Jay.

'A little better. Dr Brookes says there must be no more children. He suspects that it is in some way the carrying and birth of a child that is responsible for her condition.'

Lydia had suffered very badly after the birth of both her daughters, and although Jay was immensely loyal to her and had said nothing of her behaviour to Amber, she had heard from her grandmother that after the birth of their second child just before Christmas, Lydia's condition had been so bad that there had been fears for her sanity as well as the safety of her baby. Amber felt desperately sorry for Jay, and for Lydia herself, but she could see from his expression that any show of pity would hurt his pride.

It must be hard, though, for a man like Jay, who loved his wife, to accept that there could be no sexual intimacy within his marriage, since no form of birth control could be completely relied upon. He could, of course, always take a mistress, but Macclesfield wasn't the kind of cosmopolitan society in which such liaisons were accepted as a matter of course.

'How is your grandfather?' Amber enquired and as they drove past the Dower House. Following his marriage, after some discreet hinting from Amber, her grandmother had allowed Jay to move into the empty Dower House, and make that his home, since it was easily large enough to house a family and had its own private garden.

'No different, really,' Jay answered. 'Your grandmother is still determined that he will have to sell her some of his land, if only for the money to stop the house falling down around his ears, and my grandfather is equally determined that he will not part with a single acre, even though he has no direct heir and the place will have to be sold after his death to pay the death duties.'

'It must be hard for him,' Amber sympathised. Stubborn old goat, she inwardly thought.

They had reached the main house and Jay brought the car to a halt outside the front door, getting out of the car himself to help Amber.

'Have you heard from Greg recently?' he asked Amber as he walked with her to the main entrance.

'Last week.' Amber was very worried about her cousin. She hadn't seen him for years now, and his letters were becoming increasingly erratic. 'He sounds so unhappy, Jay, and, well, he asked me if I could lend him some money. Of course I can and will, but it worries me that he should need to ask so much.'

'I was afraid he might do that,' Jay told her. 'Look, I don't like discussing Greg behind his back, but it seems that he's got himself into a bit of a mess.'

'What kind of a mess?'

'Gambling debts, which your grandmother has had to pay off, and apparently he's taken up with a Chinese woman as well, at least according to Henry Jardine. Your grandmother showed me Jardine's letter.'

'I do wish that he would come home. There's no reason why he shouldn't now, surely? Lord Fitton Legh has remarried, after all.'

Lord Fitton Legh had married Cassandra just over a year

after Caroline's death. Amber had been surprised, but her grandmother had pointed out that it was an old custom for the Fittons and de Vrieses to marry.

'It seems that he doesn't want to. Your grandmother has suggested it. She seems to think Greg fears that if he did come back he'd be ostracised by local society.'

'Is it that, or is it because he feels guilty about Caroline?' Amber asked. 'What happened to her must prey on his conscience so much.'

Jay doubted that it did, knowing Greg, but he didn't want to upset Amber by saying so. Instead he answered gently, 'I dare say his memories must play some part in his reluctance to return.'

'From his letters it sounds as though he lives a very busy social life in Hong Kong. He's always apologising for not writing more,' Amber told Jay. 'He'll have to come back at some stage, though. After all, he is Grandmother's heir, and I know she must miss him. She'll want him to marry and settle down.'

'What time would you like me to pick you up tomorrow?' Jay asked, changing the subject tactfully.

'Would eleven suit you?'

'I'll make sure that it does,' Jay told her, taking his leave of her with a warm smile when Wilson, the butler, opened the door for her.

Greg waited and then deliberately caught the eye of the Chinese standing as though casually close to the anonymous-looking door, so tucked away in the shadows of the gambling den that it was easy to overlook unless you knew it was there.

He'd had a rotten day. The money he'd been expecting to receive from his grandmother hadn't arrived as yet, his ruddy bank manager had had the gall to refuse to give him an advance against it, claiming that he had a prior appointment when Greg had tried to arrange to see him. And if that hadn't been bad enough, the damned tailor who made his suits had had the temerity to turn up at the office trying to dun him for the money Greg owed him.

Greg had hoped that his bad luck would undergo a sea change at the gaming table, rationalising that it had to change at some stage and that tonight would be as good a time as any.

Initially it had seemed that he was right, and he had had winnings of close on a hundred pounds in front of him at one stage, but then unfairly Lady Luck had deserted him, and he had lost the lot, plus a hundred more.

The man guarding the door nodded his head, and Greg made his way towards him.

He'd been a bit uneasy at first about visiting an opium den, but when Lionel had laughed at him his pride had forced him to accompany the other man.

Greg shook his head a little ruefully now as he slipped discreetly through the open door. How naïve he'd been imagining something out of London's notorious Limehouse slum area: the kind of thing one read about at home in the sensationalist newspapers.

The opium lounge here was nothing like that. True, the narrow flight of stairs up to the lounge from the gambling den were worn and shabby, but once the landing was reached and the guard on duty outside the door to the lounge had been given the token you were presented with in the room down below when you paid, the doors were opened, if not to heaven, as some *aficionados* of the drug claimed, then certainly to a very elegant room, where the paraphernalia of opium smoking was an art in itself.

Large low opium beds stood on the polished wooden

floors, their occupants wearing the long silk robes that one was handed to change into behind screens.

The one Greg was handed was red, embroidered with gold dragons. He smiled as he slipped it on. 'Chasing the dragon' was the euphemism the Chinese used to describe smoking opium.

Greg was shown to a bed with only one other occupant, a European, as were all the clients. Calligraphy scrolls bearing auspicious sayings decorated the walls, along with rich silk hangings, the sweet smell of the opium itself hanging heavily on the air, too precious to be allowed to escape through open windows or via a fan.

An enamelled tray containing everything he would need was passed to him, the lamp with its narrow funnel to direct the heat at the bowl of the smoking pipe lit.

The lamps themselves were handmade and intricately patterned, like the bowls containing the precious tiny lumps of the drug, and fitted into the delicately wrought silver saddle on the smoking pipe itself.

Here in this room with its rich trappings, everything was provided to elevate the experience of smoking opium to something that could only be enjoyed by the favoured few who could afford it. Such surroundings were a world away from the vile and sordid opium dens that existed in the poorest areas of Hong Kong.

Greg inhaled and let the cares of his day start to float from him, to be swiftly replaced by a growing sense of euphoria. This wasn't chasing the dragon, this was riding it, commanding it, owning it and the pleasure it could give him.

'Well, Amber, I should have thought you would be wiser accompanying your husband to Paris than coming here to order silks for your drawing room like a shopkeeper's wife.'

Her grandmother never gave an inch, Amber reflected ruefully, nor changed in any material way. She was as immaculately dressed for breakfast as she would have been for a ball, and wearing as always her pearls, her silver-grey hair elegantly crimped and waved.

'Robert has business of his own in Paris,' Amber answered, 'and as for my silk, you were the one who taught me the importance of keeping a close watch on one's household budget.'

'I don't understand this fascination for decorating that seems to have overtaken people who should know better. Every time one opens *Vogue* it's full of rubbish about Lady this or that moving her furniture. I should have thought you would have had more important things to occupy your time. An heir and a spare is the ideal. If anything were to happen to Luc—'

'Nothing's going to happen to Luc,' Amber stopped her fiercely. The thought of harm of any kind coming to her son filled her with a fierce need to protect him and an equally intense fear for him.

'You aren't God, Amber, and if there were to be another war, which there could well be, the way that Germany is rearming . . .' Blanche paused meaningfully.

Her grandmother didn't know, of course, that there could be no question of her having another child or why.

'I'm surprised that Cassandra hasn't given Fitton Legh a child of her own yet. Not, of course, that Fitton Legh needs to rely on Cassandra for an heir, since he has one, which is just as well because neither the Fitton Leghs nor the de Vrieses are good at producing sons, especially not together,' Blanche continued.

'Lord de Vries' wife was a Fitton and they had a son,' Amber felt bound to point out.

For the first time in all the time she had known her,

Amber saw what looked like an expression of pain darkening her grandmother's eyes.

'Lord de Vries had a son, certainly, but a son is not always an heir, which is why I suggest that you should spend more time providing your husband with a second son and less providing his house with new curtains.'

Trust her grandmother to insist on having the last word, Amber thought ruefully an hour later as she set out to walk to the Dower House, having telephoned ahead to warn Jay that she would meet him there rather than him having to come and collect her.

It was too lovely a morning not to take advantage of the sun shining down through the full leaf of the beech-lined driveway and dappling dancing shadows on the gravel.

Handsome black-painted metal railings kept the park deer back from the driveway and the verges beneath the trees, but Amber could see them grazing on the rolling parkland either side of the drive. Her grandmother had seen the deer at Lyme Park in Disley, and had insisted to Jay that they must have some at Denham.

Male cock pheasants, escapees from Lord de Vries' land where they had once been raised for shoots, froze as she walked past them, trying to pretend that they did not exist, and then taking off in a whirr of heavy bodies and beating wings.

Jay laughed that they were more like domestic pets than wild animals, and that that was why her grandmother had given orders that they were not to be shot, but Amber suspected her protection of the birds owed more to a desire to irritate Lord de Vries than any desire to protect his trespassing game.

Marriage to Robert and her responsibilities towards their own estate had given Amber a greater understanding of how land should be managed, and she was able to appreciate the hard work and the money that had been put into bringing the land around Denham Place into such excellent condition.

Jay had remarked to her how pleased they'd been with the current year's return on the tenanted farmlands, but he'd shaken his head when she'd said gently that he must find it hard to see Denham Place's lands thriving under his care when his grandfather's lands were suffering so badly from lack of investment and good management.

'I've never had any personal interest in my grandfather's lands, and to be truthful I suspect I find it easier to work for your grandmother than I would do to work for my grandfather. The land has never really interested him other than for its ancestral value, whilst your grandmother values her land for what it represents as a productive financial asset.'

'And yet she hates the mill and has to be coaxed and persuaded to spend the smallest amount of money investing in its future. I suppose that's because she sees land as an aristocratic investment but the mill as trade, and she is such a snob that she hates the thought of being associated with trade,' Amber had responded.

She had reached the Dower House and as Amber lifted the latch on the gate that led to its pretty private garden, a nursemaid was crossing the lawn, pushing a perambulator with one hand and holding the hand of a small child with the other.

Jay's children. Amber smiled warmly at Jay's elder daughter, wondering if she would remember her, and then laughed as little Ella broke free of her nursemaid and ran across the lawn to fling herself into Amber's arms.

Baby skin. It smelled so good and so pure, Amber thought as she swept her up into her arms and hugged her close. She had never realised until she had had Luc just how strong her maternal urges were. She would have loved to have had more children, and just holding Ella's small wriggling body whilst the little girl planted excited kisses on her face made her womb ache.

'Now, now, Miss Ella, that's enough getting yourself overexcited,' the nursemaid was cautioning.

Not just her charge but me as well, Amber thought ruefully.

'If she does it will be my fault,' Amber told the nursemaid with a smile. 'She's grown so much, and Baby too. They're a real credit to you, I can see that.'

The nursemaid looked suitably mollified. 'Well, I'm not saying that it's always easy, Your Grace. Baby has given us some bad nights just lately, what with teething an' all.'

Amber put Ella down but still held her hand as she looked into the perambulator.

The baby looked very much like Ella at the same age, and had the same large, widely spaced grey eyes – Jay's eyes. When she smiled she revealed the beginnings of two small teeth, and when she lifted up her arms, wanting to be picked up, Amber knew that she was in danger of losing her heart.

'Oh, you are just so gorgeous.'

Amber longed to pick her up but she knew better than to interfere with nursery routine, especially with the nursemaid keeping a very proprietary hand on the perambulator and obviously not really approving of the disruption of her small charges' morning, and so instead she contented herself with kneeling down to give Ella another small hug, wondering as she did so if she could possibly get away with sending some pretty children's clothes down for her from London without causing any offence to Jay's pride.

'Is Mrs Fulshawe at home to visitors?' Amber asked the maid. It would be very rude of her not to see Lydia, even though mornings were not normally the time when one paid 'visits'.

'I'm sorry, Your Grace, but Lady Fitton Legh called for her this morning to take her into Manchester.'

Jay himself appeared just as she Amber stood up, his love for his daughters plain as he pretended to be stern when Ella begged for a hug, but instead gave in and picked her up.

'I would have liked to have said hello to Lydia, but the maid says she's gone out with Cassandra,' Amber told Jay, after they had said their goodbyes to the children.

'Yes. Cassandra thought it would do her good to get out.'

'I am sure she will get better in time, Jay,' Amber offered sympathetically.

'I hope so,' he answered her bleakly, 'for the girls' sake, and her own.'

How typical it was of Jay to think of others rather than himself, Amber acknowledged.

'Ella will be so thrilled that you remembered her,' Jay told Amber once they were in the car.

'I am the one who is thrilled that she remembered me,' Amber laughed.

'Luc is very lucky to have you as his mother.'

Was he thinking of his own children and poor Lydia?

Amber said quietly, 'No, I am the one who is lucky, more lucky than I really deserve, and in so many different ways, but most of all because Robert married me.'

They looked at one another and Amber knew that Jay understood what she was really saying.

'Robert said when he proposed to me that marriage would give me a key to the door to my future, and he was right. Jay . . .' Amber paused. She didn't like discussing Robert behind his back with anyone, but Jay was a very old friend and, more than that, he was someone she trusted and whose advice she valued. 'I have seen a shop I would like to buy, for my silk. It's in Walton Street and perfect in every way. It was Cecil who suggested that I should open a shop, and I must admit that I'd love to. I haven't discussed it with Robert yet, though, and . . .'

Jay looked at her bent head.

Lydia had been in one of her overexcited moods this morning, delighted at the thought of going out with Cassandra and telling him, as she often did in such moods, that she hated him and she wished she had never married him. When her mood plunged from its height down into the depths, taking her with it, she would as she always did beg him to forgive her and tell him that she loved him and their children above all things. She would cling to him, crying and pleading, until her emotions had finally exhausted her.

'It sounds an excellent plan,' he agreed cautiously.

'But you don't think that Robert will like it?' Amber guessed.

'You know him better than I, Amber. But it is not unusual for men not to want to see their wives involved in business, and I should think that holds even more true in the case of a man in Robert's position.'

'Yes, I know what you are saying, and I had thought of that myself, but, Jay, I need something of my own, something . . .'

Something to live for, Amber knew she had been about to say.

'You must think me so selfish. Here I am with a good husband and the most wonderful son.'

'I don't think anything of the kind,' Jay assured her. 'Far from it. In fact I think it's an excellent idea. I'm just not sure how Robert will react. I'd hate to build up your hopes, only for them to be disappointed.'

'I thought I'd have a word with James Lees-Milne when we see him today, to ask him what he thinks. He's part of the same social circle as Robert, and of course he's involved with the National Trust, which means that Robert will be more inclined to respect his opinion.'

They had reached the mill. Jay was always so easy to talk with, and she'd barely noticed the miles going by.

'You're such a good friend to me, Jay,' she told him, clutching his hand.

They got out of the car and headed inside.

Jay smiled. She would never know how much more he wished in his heart he could have been to her. He had married Lydia knowing that he had no real choice. But he had told himself that it would be better to be married than to be alone, and that he would do his best to be a good husband to her.

None of that, though, had been enough to stop him loving Amber, even if he had locked that love away within himself, knowing that it could never be expressed. He had a duty to Lydia as his wife and he would never want to burden Amber with his love. Painful though it sometimes was for him to bear, he would rather have her friendship than nothing at all. He would certainly never risk telling her how he felt, for her sake more than anything else. The last thing he wanted to do was upset her in any way.

What he felt for Amber was in no way a threat to his marriage with Lydia. He had, after all, loved Amber first.

He loved their daughters totally and unreservedly, but when Lydia accused him of not loving her his guilt struck him to his heart. He had wanted to love her, but Lydia's nature made it so very difficult for them to establish any kind of true rapport. They had no interests in common, Lydia was constantly complaining about the fact that Jay, whilst a de Vries, was 'only an estate manager', and Jay suspected that

Cassandra was making things worse. Lydia always seemed more irritable and wrought up when she had been with his cousin.

Jay knew he could never feel entirely comfortable about Lydia's friendship with Cassandra. He didn't want to be the kind of husband who dictated to his wife where she made her friends but he couldn't forget Cassandra's involvement with Caroline Fitton Legh, nor could he envisage himself discussing Cassandra's 'love' for Caroline with Lydia. They simply did not have the kind of relationship that allowed that kind of intimacy.

On the face of it Cassandra's friendship with Lydia was simply that of one married woman with another. He had no way of knowing if Cassandra had exaggerated her feelings for Caroline; if they had simply been an aberration – after all she had been married now to Lord Fitton Legh for several years – or, if they had not, if her friendship with Lydia masked a deeper feeling too, and he certainly couldn't ask Cassandra herself.

All he could hope was that Lydia's mental health would improve.

The silk was everything that Amber had hoped it would be, the colours glowing jewel bright in the emblems she had spent so many hours painstakingly integrating into its design: golden pomegranates from Robert's family's ducal crest, alternating with peacocks with their fanned tails, peacock blue mingling with jade green against a background of rich crimson, and pale oyster. Its beauty made her eyes sting with tears.

'It's perfect,' she told Maurice Westley once she had enough control over her voice to be able to speak. 'It's going to be used in the King's Bedroom in the state apartments. The bedcover will be padded and the peacocks picked out in raised stitching in gold. The bed curtains will be lined with gold tissue and the one behind the bed head embroidered with the family arms.'

'Told you yet that he's become a football fan, has he?' Maurice Westley asked Amber, after they had agreed on how much fabric needed to be made, grinning at Jay, who laughed and explained ruefully to Amber, 'You'll remember Geoff Stanley, from Alderley Edge? His grandfather was one of those who put up the money for the railway?'

'Yes of course,' Amber confirmed. 'You were all at Eton together.'

'Well, his grandfather also had shares in one of the Manchester football teams, and to cut a long story short, Geoff and his cousin Ronald inherited their grandfather's football shares when he died. Geoff persuaded me to go along to one of their matches. He's got dreams of the team getting into the first division. He's renamed it Hermes Stanley. He reckons it should put a bit more speed into them than calling them something like the Rovers.'

Amber laughed. 'And have they got winged heels?'

'Not as far as I could see, although the fans are already calling the team the Stanley Wingers.'

She'd forgotten how easy it was to talk with Jay, and how much at home with him she felt, Amber recognised. Perhaps there was some truth in Louise's old taunt to her that she was a Macclesfield mill girl. Coming here was a breath of fresh air after the frenetic, almost incestuous world of London society.

Maurice Westley's assistant knocked on the open door and announced, 'Mr Lees-Milne is here.'

'Jim, it's lovely to see you again,' Amber greeted the new arrival. 'And congratulations on your appointment.

Historical Buildings Secretary to the National Trust sounds very grand.'

'Well, it isn't officially official yet,' he told her with a small smile. 'And the reality is that it's far from grand.' He looked pleased, though.

'Here's the silk,' she told him. 'What do you think?'

He studied it for such a long time that Amber began to worry, but then he looked at her and she could see his opinion shining in his eyes.

'I think it's perfect. Would you mind if I were to drive over to Osterby and take some photographs of the room, both before and after the fabric goes in? I'm starting an unofficial record of grand and country house interiors for my own interest. Cecil complains that my photographs are dreadful but secretly I think he's rather pleased that he hasn't got a rival.'

Amber laughed. 'Of course you can drive over.'

'I saw some of your fabric up at Charlton last month. The yellow silk you've used in the Marbles room.'

'Aye, we've sold many a yard of that since it was shown in *Vogue*,' Maurice Westley informed them both happily.

'It's one of my favourites, I must admit,' Amber agreed. 'I used one of my father's designs, the Roman coin one, to make a border along the edge of the silk. It worked well.'

'Yes. I've heard that your cloak-and-toga style is becoming as famous and as sought after as Syrie Maugham's white rooms.'

Amber laughed. 'I doubt that, Jim.'

She'd had the rectangular room at Osterby, which had contained several marble busts brought back from Italy by one of Robert's ancestors, repainted in a warm yellow, and the tall windows dressed in yellow silk bordered with a gold coin design, over plain Imperial-purple silk blinds, in what she'd laughingly joked was an Imperial-cloak-and-toga style, and which looked extremely stylish and effective, providing a richness that did not in any way detract from the busts themselves.

'Shall you have time to come back to Denham and have luncheon with us?' Amber asked Jim once they had left the mill manager's office.

'I'd love to but I can't. I'm due at Dolly Hetherington's, where it is freezing cold the whole year round and where I shall be obliged to eat boiled cabbage and mutton.'

'Oh dear, poor you.'

'A sacrifice I am obliged to make since Dolly is flirting with the idea of leaving both the house and its paintings to the National Trust.'

'I was hoping I could pick your brains over the feasibility of my opening a shop in London to sell Denby silk.'

'Well, I can tell you now I think it's an excellent idea. You'd certainly have no trouble attracting customers.'

'I may need you to repeat that in front of Robert,' Amber warned him.

To her relief he laughed and said cheerfully, 'I'd be happy to.'

'You really are keen on this shop idea, aren't you?' Jay commented as he drove her back to Denham.

'Yes. The more I think about it, the more I want to do it. Luc will be starting prep school soon, and since . . .' Since there won't any more children, she had been about to say but she stopped herself, and said instead, 'And since I shall have time on my hands then, it seems a logical thing to do.'

Amber didn't want to say so – it would be so disloyal to Robert after all that he had done for her – but she felt an increasingly desperate need for something worthwhile to fill the empty space Luc going to school was going to create in her life. The constant round of, to her, almost meaning-less social events that characterised 'high society' left her feeling isolated and alone, aware that there were very few people with whom she felt she was on a wavelength. There was Cecil, of course, and his arty crowd of friends, but Cecil's own work meant that he was often away. And besides, being with Cecil increased her need to fulfil her own artistic drive rather than suppress it.

Increasingly, Amber admitted, the emptiness at the heart of her marriage was making her feel afraid that one day it would become so intolerable that she might be tempted to do the one thing she had promised she would never do. Other wives in aristocractic marriages discreetly and some-times not so discreetly took lovers, and their behaviour was accepted. But she was not an aristocrat, and she was very much afraid that for her, taking a lover would mean falling in love with him and she could not afford to do that. Her shop would give her something to inspire and excite her, something to fill her empty hours. And her lonely nights in her large solitary bed – would it banish them? Yes, Amber told herself firmly, because she would be kept so busy that she would fall asleep at night the moment her head touched the pillow, instead of . . . Instead of what? Instead of lying alone remembering how it had felt to be held in a lover's arms and to share his desire, to know that she was fulfilled as a woman?

Amber refused to allow herself to answer that question.

Chapter Twenty-Seven

'No, Amber. It's totally out of the question.'

'But, Robert—'

'I said no. I do not understand why on earth you would want a shop anyway.'

'I need something to fill my time,' Amber told him simply.

'You have a child, friends, Osterby to run and this place as well. They are more than enough to keep you occupied, I should have thought.'

They were in the library of the Eaton Square house, and whilst Amber had been expecting Robert to need convincing about her plans for the Walton Street shop, she had not expected his flat refusal.

'Luc will soon be starting prep school and when he does he won't need me in the way that he does now. Unlike someone like Beth, I do not have other children in the nursery.' She wasn't going to antagonise him by pointing out that she would never have another child, but neither was she going to back down.

'As for my friends,' she gave a small shrug, 'you know that I am tolerated amongst our social set solely because I am your wife. One can't make close friends under such circumstances, Robert, one merely co-exists with people. When you wish me to do so, naturally I act as your hostess,

315

but as we both know there are times when my presence isn't necessary or indeed wanted.'

She could see that he didn't like what she was saying, but it had to be said if she was to persuade him to change his mind.

'There are any number of couples in our social set who live separate lives at times, and where the wife seems perfectly capable of filling her time without needing to open a shop. It isn't the done thing for people of our station, Amber, you must see that.'

Her chin lifted. 'For people of *your* station, I think you mean, Robert. My roots are in trade and—'

'You are my wife and as such it is expected that you behave in an appropriate manner.'

She wasn't going to budge him, Amber recognised. His face was wearing that stubborn, haughty expression that meant that he could not be shifted.

'Robert, I don't want us to quarrel, but this means such a lot to me.'

Amber went up to him and placed her hand on his arm, trying not to feel hurt when she felt his muscles clench in rejection of her touch. Was it her imagination that Robert had changed towards her since he had befriended the young German Otto von Brecht?

'Please try to see things from my point of view. I need something to do, Robert, something about which I can feel passionate, something that I can love, something to take the place of all those things that I do not have in my life.'

There, she had said it at last, and it was the truth. There was an emptiness inside her, and a need and a yearning to fill that empty place with something that came from her heart. Something into which she could channel those energies that sometimes kept her awake at night and made her

316

look enviously at other couples who shared a normal married life.

'Please say that you will think about it,' Amber begged.

'Very well, I will think about it.'

It was at least a start.

Normally Greg hated the Peak Club's formal parties and avoided them like the plague, but today, as he buttoned himself into a clean shirt in the small bedroom of the Jardines' bachelor bungalow, he was in a fever of anticipation and excitement.

Henry Jardine had hinted more than once that, since Greg had now made the decision to stay on in Hong Kong, it might be a good idea for him to find more suitable accommodation, but Greg had no intention of moving out of somewhere that was rent free and where all his domestic needs were taken care of by the Jardines' staff. Besides, he already had to rent an apartment for his Chinese mistress and he couldn't afford any more outgoings.

Greg frowned, his good mood shadowed by irritation. He had been growing bored with Chia Yung before he had met Lucy Cabot-James. The trouble was that he was too generous and too compassionate, he told himself. Hadn't he provided her with a roof over her head and money all through her pregnancy and after it, even though she hadn't been much use to him as a mistress in the latter stages of her pregnancy, nor since the birth of the brat she was insisting was his?

'Well, you can't deny that she's your mistress,' Lionel had told him unsympathetically when he'd complained to him about the fact that Chia Yung was pregnant. 'You should have told her to get rid of it whilst there was still time. Mind you, I shouldn't worry too much,' he added with a wink. 'You can always get her to farm the brat out to one of her relatives after its birth and with a bit of luck it will disappear.'

Right now Greg would very much like both his mistress and the child she had borne him to disappear, and permanently. It was a pity he owed so much in gambling debts at the moment otherwise he could have offered Chia Yung a decent sum to disappear and take the child with her, or failing that he could have asked Lionel to point him in the direction of someone who would have made her disappear.

He'd have to tap up his grandmother for some more money. Once she knew what he was planning she'd cough up, he was sure of that. She'd be pretty keen to see him settle down as a respectable married man, something that hadn't appealed to him at all until he'd met Lucy.

Lucy . . . Greg reckoned he had fallen head over heels in love with her the minute he'd set eyes on her at the Governor's party three weeks ago. Newly arrived from America with the aunt and uncle who were her guardians, she was only just eighteen, and the most beautiful girl Greg had ever seen, with her large brown eyes and her brunette curls; her lips so soft and pink that he couldn't stop looking at them.

He teased and flattered her, of course, and it had been very agreeable to see how impressed she and her aunt and uncle were. He'd laid it on a bit thick, mentioning oh so casually his cousin and her title, and his grandmother and her wealth.

Lionel had tried to stick his oar in and get her attention, but he had been wasting his time. He wasn't vain, Greg assured himself, but there was no doubting which of them was the better prospect as a husband, and it wasn't Lionel.

Of course her aunt and uncle were more impressed by him than they were by Lionel; and since she was an heiress herself, naturally they'd want to ensure that she wasn't being pursued by a fortune-hunter.

Greg had called on her aunt and uncle the morning after the Governor's party, following up his call with flowers – for Lucy's aunt – and he'd made damn sure that he found out what events they were attending so that he could be there.

The stifling heat of the summer was over but Greg was still sweating heavily as he got ready for the Peak Club's dinner dance.

He was head over heels in love and he didn't mind admitting it. Tonight he was going to ask Lucy's uncle for his permission for him to pay his addresses to Lucy. He was sure that Horace Cabot-James would agree.

They could get engaged now and be married for Christmas, and then Greg planned to take Lucy back to England. All that fuss about Caroline would have been forgotten by now, and besides, Fitton Legh himself had remarried so he wasn't going to rake it up, was he?

He'd already told Lucy about Denham, and although she'd been a bit disappointed at first when she'd realised that he didn't have a title, he'd told her with a small shrug about his grandmother's plans for him.

'So you will have a title one day then?' Lucy had asked him excitedly.

'Yes,' he had proudly declared.

God, but he loved her. She was perfect in every way, adorably so. They'd get engaged and then married, preferably here in Hong Kong, and then he'd take her home to Macclesfield. Greg started to whistle to himself, grinning as he thought of how keen his grandmother would be to kill the fatted calf and welcome him home. He'd probably get away with her financing a few months in London – he could tell her that he thought it was important that Lucy

319

was presented at court – she'd love that. Amber could present her, of course. Who would have thought little Amber would have ended up being married to a duke? Greg had envied Amber living in London. Maybe he could even persuade his grandmother to invest in a London town house. She could afford it, after all.

'And where is your friend Lionel tonight?' Lucy asked Greg. 'Only you are normally together and he did say that he would be here.'

Greg stifled his jealousy. He could afford to stifle it, after all, because Lionel didn't stand a chance, especially now that Greg had dropped a word of warning in Horace Cabot-James's ear about Lionel's financial position.

'I dare say he will be later,' he answered Lucy. 'Why don't I tell you a bit more about Denham?'

'Oh, yes, please do,' Lucy's aunt agreed eagerly. 'It sounds the most wonderful place, doesn't it, Lucy?'

'You said that your neighbour was a lord?' Lucy questioned Greg, ignoring her aunt.

'Barrant de Vries? Yes, he is,' Greg agreed carelessly. 'Of course, his title can't match my cousin's.' He could see Lucy's eyes widening in sudden disbelief and disgust as she looked past him, so he turned round to see what had caught her attention and then froze in disbelief.

Coming towards them was Lionel, and with him was Chia Yung.

Panic gripped Greg. He tried to head them off, stepping forward, but it was too late: everyone who had seen them was staring. Chinese were not allowed into the Peak Club and how the devil Lionel had got her in here he had no idea.

'Isn't that a Chinese woman with Mr Shepton?' Lucy was asking.

'Lucy, my dear . . .' her aunt was warning her uncomfortably, whilst Horace Cabot-James had stepped in front of his wife and niece, and was looking furious.

'There you are, I told you he would be here,' Lionel told Chia Yung before turning to Greg and drawling, 'Sorry to spoil things for you, Greg old chap, but Chia Yung here has been searching everywhere for you. The poor thing's in a bit of a state about the baby. It's not very well, apparently. Of course, I told her she couldn't come in here, but she insisted.' Releasing Chia Yung he turned to Horace Cabot-James. 'My apologies, sir. These Chinese women are supposed to know their place, but sometimes they forget themselves. I warned Greg here against taking one on, but he wouldn't listen to me. I think you'd better take your Chia Yung home, Greg old chap, and sooner rather than later unless you want to be thrown out.'

There was nothing Greg could do. Chia Yung had thrown herself on the ground at his feet and was begging his forgiveness, Lucy was glaring at him with angry hostility, whilst Lionel was grinning in huge and evident enjoyment. Virtually dragging Chia Yung to her feet, Greg bundled her towards the door, where it took him nearly half an hour to get rid of her.

Lionel had tricked her, she wept. He had told her that Greg wanted desperately to see her.

'Liar.' Greg was so infuriated that he slapped her. 'You know perfectly well that your kind isn't allowed up here.'

'He told me I had to do it. He said he would send someone to hurt the baby if I didn't.'

She was trying to cling to him. Greg pushed her away so violently that she fell to the ground.

'Get up, damn you,' he told her, aiming a kick at her when she didn't move. 'Get up and get out of my life.'

Ruddy Lionel, trying to ruin his chances with Lucy. Well,

he'd soon smooth things over. Dammit, all men had mistresses. Her aunt would explain that to her. And he could make a big thing about Amber and arranging for Lucy to be presented.

Sweating heavily, Greg turned back towards the club, only to find the entrance barred to him by a uniformed official.

'What the devil . . . ?' he demanded, losing his temper. 'I'm a member here so you'd better let me in.'

They wouldn't, though, and he had to demand to see someone in authority and was left kicking his heels for over half an hour before an irritated-looking florid-faced retired general turned up to tell him brusquely that his membership had been terminated with immediate effect.

'What the hell for?' Greg bawled. 'I'm not the only ruddy man in Hong Kong to have a mistress.'

'You know the club rules: no Chinese allowed. For God's sake, man, surely you're aware of the insulting nature of your behaviour to our own ladies?'

The general had gone. Greg aimed a furious impotent kick at the gate whilst the guard looked on.

Amber smiled lovingly as she and Luc played Snap together. He was such a darling boy, and she was going to miss him so much when he started prep school. But at least, she hoped, she would have her shop.

She had walked with Luc to Walton Street that morning, listening to his chatter with one ear whilst she daydreamed.

Robert was away – with Otto – an unscheduled trip to Paris because he said Otto had loved it so much there and had wanted to return, and he had left without giving her an answer.

The agent for the Walton Street property had warned her that he couldn't hold it for her indefinitely, and yesterday Amber had taken the decision to purchase it rather than risk losing it. Property was always an investment, after all, she had reassured herself, and quietened her own feelings of guilt for having bought it without Robert's agreement.

Luckily she'd had enough money of her own to do so. Robert gave her a very generous quarterly allowance, so generous in fact that she never used it all and so had had enough to buy the property outright.

She'd put all the legal work in the hands of Robert's solicitor and had alerted the bank to what she was doing, but from what the solicitor had said the agent selling the property was perfectly respectable and everything should go through smoothly.

'Mummy, I really would like to have a dog of my own,' Luc told her, smiling coaxingly up at her.

Amber laughed as she stroked his hair back off his face. Luc had been insisting he wanted his own dog ever since he'd seen another child with one in Hyde Park.

'We shall have to see what your father says,' she told him, as she hugged him and made a mental note to have a word with the gamekeeper at Osterby to look out for a suitable pup for him.

He sounded so grown up now, but in reality he was still so very young, still her baby, Amber reflected with a sharp pang, as she held him tightly and kissed the top of his head. His hair was as dark as Robert's and he was still wearing it in thick baby curls. His mannerisms were so much Robert's that no one looking at him would ever guess that he wasn't Robert's child. But she knew, of course, and sometimes her guilt made her feel anxious.

'When will Daddy be back?' Luc asked her.

'Soon.'

Normally when he was away from her Robert wrote to her every day, his letters to her chatty and entertaining, if filled with somewhat scandalous gossip, but this time she had barely heard from him and when she had, his letters had been very perfunctory.

She may not have heard from him but she had heard about him.

Amber released Luc and walked over to the window. She and Luc had returned from Osterby to Eaton Square at the beginning of the week and already she had had several visitors who had been quick to remark on Robert's devotion to his 'young friend'.

'You know Robert,' she had replied with a smile to one of his closest friends, Piers Whitethorne.

'I thought I did,' Piers had agreed, 'but this friendship with a certain young German has changed him, I fear.'

When Amber hadn't said anything he had added brusquely, 'I can imagine what you are thinking.'

Piers was several years older than Robert. They had been lovers in the past, and Amber suspected that Piers still loved and desired Robert.

'And yes, you're right about my feelings for Robert, but I have always known that he is someone who needs the continual excitement of falling in love with someone new. But this is different.'

'In what way?' Amber had asked him, beginning to feel concerned.

'It's Robert. He just *isn't* himself somehow. He's avoiding all his old friends, and seems to have taken up with a new crowd. Seems to be drinking rather a lot as well. Can't help feeling that no good will come of it. Might be a good idea if you could go over to Paris to join him.'

'I can hardly just turn up in Paris without a reason,' Amber had felt bound to point out.

'Clothes,' Piers had told her succinctly. 'A lady *always* needs new clothes.' When she hadn't been able to conceal her surprise at this suggestion he had added ruefully, 'I've always thought that Robert has been damn lucky to be married to you, Amber.'

Piers wasn't the only person to express concern to her about Robert. There'd been comments and subtle warnings from several of his friends following her return to London; too many of them for her to ignore. They'd ranged from discreet complaints that nowadays he seemed to be too preoccupied and busy for his old friends, to far more direct references from his older friends – the crowd that included Cecil Beaton and James Lees-Milne – to the effect that they felt Robert's relationship with Otto had changed their old friend, and not for the better. The general consensus of opinion amongst Robert's oldest friends was that he was besotted with Otto and simply did not want to know anyone else any more.

Naturally that kind of concern being expressed by such old friends had already alarmed Amber, and now Piers was suggesting that for Robert's own sake she ought to go to Paris and remind him of his obligations, to her and to Luc.

Amber didn't like to think she was trying to manipulate anyone, and especially not Robert, but in the end she didn't need to fabricate an excuse to go to Paris, because the following morning she received a letter from Beth begging her to accept her invitation to join her there.

We shall be staying in Alistair's parents' house in Rue de Poitiers for the whole of the winter, Amber, as Alistair has been called upon by the British Ambassador to assist him with various matters in an unofficial capacity. The house is huge, and with Alistair spending so much time at the embassy I desperately need the company of my dearest friend.

Beth was always given to flowery phrases, Amber knew, but her invitation was so opportune that Amber wrote back by return accepting it. Luc was delighted when he learned that they would be sharing a nursery with Beth's children, who were in many ways the closest thing he had to blood cousins.

Amber also wrote to Robert, who was staying at the George V, to inform him of her plans, and her purchase of the Walton Street premises, whilst at the same time delaying posting this letter until the morning they left to catch the boat train for Paris.

'You won't believe how many Americans are here in Paris, Amber, all of them complaining about how much money they lost in the Wall Street crash, and yet still entertaining and throwing the most extravagant parties.'

Amber hid her amusement as she heard the mingled disapproval and envy in Beth's voice.

They were in the elegant first-floor drawing room of the Rue de Poitiers house, with its Louis Quatorze décor and its painted and gilded panelling. Amber had arrived just over an hour earlier and, having assured herself that Luc was happily settled in the nursery with Beth's children, she was now listening to Beth updating her with the current gossip in Parisian society.

'And that reminds me, we're invited to dinner at the embassy tonight, tomorrow there's a masked ball, then Daisy Fellowes is giving a party. Oh, and I almost forgot. You'll never guess what. Remember Jean-Philippe, who was living in the guesthouse of the villa we stayed in with my mother before we were married?'

Amber struggled to appear normal and unconcerned as she nodded her head, but she didn't want to risk speaking because she feared she couldn't trust her voice not to betray her.

'Well, his paintings are the toast of *le tout Paris* at the moment, and Alistair mentioned that he'd seen him at some gentlemen's dinner or other. Oh, and I saw Robert with that charming young protégé of his at the weekend. They were with the German Ambassador. Shall you be going to the Olympic Games in Germany next year, do you think? Alistair says that we should go, but he doesn't approve of them being held in Germany now with all this anti-Jewishness of theirs.'

'I hadn't really thought about the Olympics,' Amber told her, only too glad that Beth hadn't continued to talk about Jean-Philippe. The thought of him being there in Paris made her heart thump uncomfortably. Not because she wanted to see him; in fact that was the last thing she wanted. She hated the idea of being reminded of her past and the unhappiness it had caused her. Besides, she had more important things to worry about now than a foolish girl's romance. She wouldn't be able to settle until she had seen Robert and found out how he was. Her husband and her son mattered far more to her now than Jean-Philippe.

'Well, I'm sorry, Amber, but the truth is that I would really rather you hadn't come to Paris.'

Amber looked at her husband, aghast. They were sitting in the bar of the George V drinking cocktails; or rather Robert was drinking cocktails at a rapid rate whilst she sat stirring hers because she felt too on edge to drink it.

She had been dismayed and upset to see how thin Robert had grown and how unwell he looked. There was a bruise on his cheekbone, which he told her was as a result of him accidentally walking into a half-open door. But what really shocked her was his manner towards her, which was positively antagonistic and resentful.

She hadn't intended initially to mention his friends'

concern for him but now, facing his angry dislike of the fact that she was in Paris, Amber decided that she had no choice.

'Why do you say that?' she challenged him quietly. 'After all, there's no reason why I shouldn't be here, is there? Apart from anything else Luc misses you. You've never been away from us for as long as this.' She leaned closer to him and told him gently, 'Your friends are concerned about you, Robert. Piers came to see me in London especially to tell me how worried he is about you.'

Robert had ordered another cocktail. Amber saw his hand shake when he picked up the glass.

'Piers. Well, of course he would, wouldn't he? He's jealous, of course. He can't bear to see me happy with Otto.'

'You don't look happy.'

'Well, I am. Blissfully. I love Otto more than I imagined I could ever love anyone. He's everything to me, Amber. Everything. I've never felt like this before. Loving him brings me the purest form of ecstasy and the darkest form of torment.' Tears filled Robert's eyes.

'Poor boy, he feels the weight of my love for him and sometimes he can hardly bear it. He will not say so, but I can see it. He rebels against it and is unkind to me. He cannot help it. He is so very young, Amber. All I want is to be with him but he needs the company of others. I understand and accept that. But I must be there for him when he is ready to turn to me, Amber, and you must understand that.'

Amber's disquiet had grown with every word Robert had spoken. Her concern, though, was not for herself or even for her marriage but for Robert himself. Her heart ached for him and for the way he was humbling himself out of love for a young man who she suspected did not share his passion or return his feelings.

'You are still my husband, Robert,' she reminded him gently. 'And Luc's father.'

'I want you to go home, Amber. I do not want you and Luc here.'

'We cannot go yet. For one thing it would cause gossip if we did, and for another Beth would be upset. She has made plans to include me in all manner of social events.'

'Very well then, stay if you must, but understand that it is against my wishes. But then you appear to have developed a habit of ignoring my wishes, Amber.'

Her heart sank. 'If you mean the Walton Street property, Robert, I—'

'Yes, I do mean the Walton Street property. You have behaved deceitfully, hoping no doubt to force my hand.'

'No, Robert. I admit I bought the property without consulting you but I had no alternative. You were here in Paris.' Amber looked at him. His criticism had been unfair and it had hurt her. 'With your lover.'

'You have always known what I am,' he reminded her.

'Yes, and you have always known how much my family's business means to me. When you asked me to marry you you said that our marriage would give me the key to my future, but now you want to deny me that future.'

'A future as a shopkeeper? Do you really think Luc is going to want people to know that his mother works?'

Do you want him to know that his father keeps a boyfriend? she was tempted to shoot back, but instead she restrained herself. Not out of cowardice – she was quite prepared to do whatever she had to do to win her battle. But not by trading insults. It was beneath them both.

'You are being unfair,' she told Robert instead. 'I realise that you are thinking of your position and . . . and all that you owe to your name. Naturally as your wife I am conscious of my duty to all of that.'

How hard it was for her to speak like this and to submit her pride to an idolatry of something she privately despised. Titles and patronage meant nothing to her and they never would; she had other values and other needs. She could not and would not worship at their altar but she had to be careful – for Luc's sake. If she were to antagonise Robert, he could always retaliate by renouncing her – and Luc.

Oh, how she wished the old Robert would come back into their lives. He was not the same generous-hearted easy-going man he had been. Love was cruel in the demands it made on people, she already knew that. It changed them, sometimes warping and twisting them.

'There are people of . . . of breeding who have done what I wish to do – Syrie Maugham, for instance. It will give me something to do, Robert,' she told him desperately. 'You have your own . . . interests, and sometimes I am so very lonely.'

Something – was it sadness or perhaps shame, Amber didn't know – shadowed his gaze as he looked at her, but when he spoke his voice was harsh and his words uncompromising.

'You will do what you wish to do no matter what I might say, so there is no point in my saying anything.'

Agreement of a sort then, but not given generously or lovingly.

'Robert, please, don't be like this. I want us to be friends as we have always been,' Amber tried to placate him, but she could see from his face that she would not move him.

She sighed inwardly and changed the subject, telling him, 'Luc has missed you whilst you have been here in Paris. If you can, I hope you will come and see him whilst we are here.'

'I don't know if I shall have time.'

It was the first time in their married life that he had shown such hostility towards her, and Amber was appalled.

She felt hurt and very alone, as well as concerned for Robert himself, she admitted, as she made her way back to the Rue de Poitiers. He wouldn't leave her, would he?

It was no good, nothing was any good any more, Greg thought bitterly. He'd been as good as blackballed from the club, Lucy was refusing to speak to him and was being escorted everywhere by a triumphant Lionel, and last night he'd gambled and lost more than he wanted even to think about. He looked at the girl in bed beside him. Thin, with matted hair and vacant eyes, she scratched at her arm.

Greg had no idea how he'd ended up in what was obviously one of Hong Kong's less salubrious brothels. He couldn't remember anything after he'd wagered the whole of his next quarter's allowance, and lost it. The stench from the open sewer that he could see running down the street outside, through the open window, fouled the already oppressively close air in the small room. Two children, both boys, oblivious to the fetid stink and its cause, were playing outside an open door on the other side of the street. As Greg watched a man – European – red-faced, sweat patches darkening the underarms of his tropical suit, came down the street, pausing to glance over his shoulder before heading for the open doorway. A woman came out, pointing to the two boys and holding up her fingers to indicate the cost. The man nodded his head, and then disappeared inside the building, the woman following him, dragging the boy he had selected.

Greg looked away in disinterest. He had become inured to corruption of every kind, and besides, he had his own problems to worry about, he thought self-pityingly.

He was in one hell of a ruddy mess and it was all Lionel's fault.

The girl reached for him, her hand grubby, the nails chewed and dirty, her face blank as her fingers curled round him. Greg pushed her off with a curse.

'You give me money,' she wailed. 'You promised.'

The whole room and everything in it, including the girl, had a smell that made him want to gag. How had he got to this?

'Well, earn it then,' he said brutally, rolling onto his back and unzipping his trousers.

'And Otto bought me some special bonbons, but Father said I wasn't to eat them all at once in case they made me sick.'

It was eight o'clock in the evening and they were due to leave in half an hour for a party being given by the French society widow of an Indian maharaja to which *le tout Paris*, as Beth insisted on naming French society, had been invited, but Luc was still so excited about the morning he had spent with Robert that he wanted to tell Amber about it over and over again.

She had gone from delight and relief when Robert had telephoned to say that he would call round and take Luc out, to dismay and anxiety when Robert had arrived with Otto in tow. She had been hoping to go with them herself so that she could mend things a little between them. The smug look Otto had given her had made her feel that he had guessed her intentions and was mocking her because he had spoiled them, but she had told herself that she was being foolish. There was, after all, no reason for Otto to treat her as some kind of rival or to feel he had to force his own role in Robert's life on her.

She certainly wasn't jealous of Otto's place in Robert's

affections but she wasn't very happy to hear Luc telling her enthusiastically that Otto had played ball with him and Otto had bought him bonbons. She had been even less happy when, after their outing, Otto had strode into the hallway carrying Luc in his arms.

'Such a pity that he has your colouring and not his mother's fairer looks, dearest Robert,' Otto had drawled. 'But at least with your pedigree one can be sure there's no taint of the Jew in his blood.'

Amber stiffened now just thinking about Otto's offensive remark. It had upset her that Robert had not immediately taken Otto to task for it, all the more so because Otto had made several references to Tom Mosley, as Oswald was known to his friends, and his supporters, whose politics she had already heard Robert firmly denounce. She refused to believe that Robert would change his politics, no matter how much in love with Otto he was.

'It's time for you to go to sleep now, darling,' she told Luc firmly.

The maharanee's party was being held on an island in the lake in the Bois de Boulogne. All the guests had been asked to attend in costumes of the Napoleonic period.

Amber's gown, high-waisted in the Empire style, was pale green silk, trimmed with silver lace ribbon and tiny diamanté drops sewn onto the silk. The same silver lace ribbons had been wound through her hair and her fox fur wrap was lined with silver tissue.

Beth's dress was pink trimmed with swansdown, and whilst Beth and Amber had opted for several layers of fine silk for their gowns, there were some women who had adopted the fashion of the era and dampened down the fabric of their gowns so that the outlines of their bodies could be seen quite clearly.

'Of course it doesn't matter what lengths we may choose

to go to,' Daisy Fellowes commented to Amber as they waited to get into the rowing boats that would take them across to the island, 'we can't outdo the men. I have never seen so many different uniforms.'

The men did indeed look extraordinarily well in their colourful uniforms, Amber acknowledged.

The maharanee, herself dressed as the Empress Josephine, had hired the French decorator Monsieur le Baron to decorate the restaurant on the island, le Pavillon des Iles, for the party, and of course Amber took particular note of what he had done.

The pathway from the landing stage to the pavilion had been covered in white velvet carpeting, either side of which stood tall candles to illuminate the way. Beyond the pathway other candles and lanterns illuminated the rest of the island, and in the restaurant itself the walls and the chairs were draped in white velvet ornamented with gold and silver swags.

An orchestra played waltz music.

Amongst the guests Amber could see Prince Nicholas of Greece and his wife, the Grand Duchess Helen of Russia. Amber had met their daughter, Princess Marina, in London with her husband, Prince George, the Duke of Kent.

Lady Diana Cooper, who was with her friend Elsa Maxwell, was wearing a wonderful gown in amethyst silk.

'There's poor Mimi Pecci-Blunt,' Beth told Amber as they waited for Alistair, who had stopped to talk to the British Ambassador. 'Her husband is quite besotted with that footman he has taken up with.'

Amber said nothing. She had heard that the count, who was an acquaintance of Robert's, had installed his new male lover in his villa near Monte Carlo, but the countess, who was enormously rich in her own right, seemed more concerned with the philanthropy for which she was famous than her husband's behaviour.

It both amused and amazed Amber that Beth could remain so determinedly naïve about the realities of life when it suited her to do so and yet gossip so eagerly about them when that also suited her.

'What a shame that Robert had a prior engagement, and won't be here for a while yet,' Beth continued, adding pointedly, 'It's such a pity that you and Robert haven't had more children, Amber.'

Amber suppressed a small sigh. This wasn't the first time by any means that Beth had commented about the fact that she and Robert only had Luc. There was, of course, no question of her confiding in Beth and telling her the truth, which meant that Amber had to fend off Beth's curiosity as tactfully and as firmly as she could, without arousing Beth's suspicions.

'It would have been lovely,' she agreed lightly.

'Well, there's still time, of course,' Beth told her. 'Although of course you and Robert do socialise such a lot, and live such busy lives, not like us. Alistair and I are very dull in comparison.'

Amber smiled. Beth's smug tone had inferred quite plainly that dull they might be, but since their dullness had resulted in four children maybe Amber should try a little dullness herself.

Amber saw Robert later in the evening. He was part of a group of people with the German Ambassador, which, of course, included Otto. The young German looked extremely dashing in the uniform of a Prussian officer of the Napoleonic era, Amber acknowledged, and very Aryan with his blond hair and that air he had of exuding confidence and good health. Robert, on the other hand, dressed as a

Regency fop, looked rather drawn and seemed to have been pushed to the fringes of the group whilst Otto was very much the centre of it. Amber was tempted to go over and join Robert just so that she could make sure that he was all right. She had never known him as caught up in an affair as he was in this one with Otto, and she feared that his young lover was going to cause him a great deal of heartache. Otto seemed oblivious to the tense watchfulness of Robert's concentration on him, and the fact that he was being excluded, as he laughed and joked with the other men standing close to the Ambassador. However, before she could do so, Amber was trapped by good manners and the risk of causing gossip if she ignored him when Henry came up to her.

Marriage to the daughter of a wealthy marquis had given Henry an air of arrogant complacency and a belief in his right to criticise others, but not as yet a son.

Amber had as little to do with him as she could, and was thankful that they had only been in one another's company on a handful of occasions since the night he had tried to force himself on her, and then always in the company of others and his wife.

Henry, as Beth never tired of proclaiming proudly, was a devoted husband. And one who, according to Robert, had had a string of sexual liaisons throughout his marriage. Again according to Robert, his mistresses had included Louise, if only briefly.

'Well, well, and what bring you to Paris? Or need I ask, seeing as du Breveonet is here as well. Having fun catching up on old times, are you? They say that a woman never forgets her first man. I dare say there've been plenty since him, eh, Amber, especially with Robert the way he is,' he added, nodding his head in the direction of the group around the German Ambassador. 'Not that you haven't

336

been discreet. Good thing discretion is, in a woman of your sort.'

Amber made to sidestep him, filled with disgust for him and by his comments, but he took hold of her arm.

'Not offended you, have I?' he taunted her. 'Didn't mean to. Always admired you, Amber, you know that. Clever woman too. Who'd have thought a little nobody from a mill town would end up a duchess?'

Amber experienced a mixture of outrage and apprehension the moment Henry had touched her. She had been standing close to the wall and now there wasn't room for her to pull away from Henry and turn round to escape. People were standing to either side of them, engaged in their own conversations, but close enough to hear what they were saying if either of them were to raise their voice, although so far Henry has been speaking quietly, menacingly so.

'You've obviously had too much to drink, Henry,' Amber told him firmly. 'Where's your wife? I rather think it would be a good idea if you were to rejoin her before you embarrass yourself, don't you?'

'Oh, I won't be embarrassed. Nothing embarrassing about a chap inviting a woman of your sort to share a bit of fun with him, you know that, Amber. How many have there been since du Breveonet?' he asked her casually, grinning when she made no response before continuing, 'I dare say they'll have taught you a few interesting tricks. I'm going to be in London for a few days next month – why don't I come round and visit you and we can talk over old times?'

'Robert is over there, Henry. Why don't you go over and tell him what you've just said to me?' Amber suggested coldly.

Henry stopped smiling. 'There's no point you coming the

high and mighty with me, Amber. I know you, remember? I saw you,' he emphasised meaningfully. 'Knows about what you got up to with du Breveonet, does he, Robert?'

Amber made no response. Beth had seen them and was coming towards them. Soon Amber would be able to escape.

'Because if he doesn't maybe someone should tell him? Energetic chap, du Breveonet. Did you know he was fucking the baker's trollop of a wife at the same time as he was fucking you? Perhaps he had the two of you entertaining him together, did he?' he suggested lasciviously, whilst Amber fought to control the shock of the betrayal she felt.

'Henry, here you are,' Beth exclaimed, slipping her arm through her brother's.

Immediately Henry released Amber and stepped back from her.

'Pamela is looking everywhere for you. She isn't feeling well and wants to go home. Poor Pamela is expecting again, Amber.'

'I did warn Amber that I didn't want to leave Pam for too long but she said she was desperate for someone to dance with,' Henry lied.

Before Beth could say anything Amber said coolly to Henry, 'I do hope it's a boy this time, Henry. It's so important that one has an heir, isn't it?'

The look he gave her was close to murderous but Amber didn't care. Her heart was thumping with a mixture of anger and relief. Anger and relief? What about that other emotion? The one she had felt when Henry had told her about Jean-Philippe?

What other emotion? She had not felt anything. Why should she?

Henry could have lied, of course, but somehow Amber knew that he had not done so.

* * *

Greg was in an awful lot of trouble and he was scared. It had all started when Chung Hai had stopped smiling pleasantly about Greg's gambling losses and had started instead being very unpleasant indeed. Naturally, Greg had tried to turn to Lionel for help in dealing with the Chinese, but Lionel had become strangely elusive, perhaps because he was now spending so much time squiring Lucy around to all those Peak Club events from which he himself was now barred, Greg thought viciously.

He had written to his grandmother making up some story about having had money stolen from his bank account and asking her to send him some more, but that would take time, and Chung Hai had not been willing to give him that time.

There had been demands and then threats, almost accidents, and then last week the discovery of a chicken, its throat newly slit, pumping blood onto the clean laundry that the Jardines' laundry maid had just placed on his bed in the bachelor bungalow.

Chung Hai had made his displeasure plain.

An emissary, flanked by two men with knives, had been sent to escort Greg to Chung Hai's place of business, a filthy room in the middle of a huddle of shantytown slum buildings, impossible to find unless you knew where it was, and certainly impossible to escape from without Chung Hai's express sanction.

Greg sweated heavily now just thinking about it.

Chung Hai had had a proposition to put to him. Theoretically Greg worked for Henry Jardine, although in truth he went days if not weeks without going anywhere near the Jardine and Nephew office, where the paperwork was done for transferring cargoes from Shanghai and other Eastern ports into the vessels that would take them on to Europe and America. He had certainly never set foot on any of the ships themselves, as Henry Jardine himself regularly did, to spot-check the cargoes. A certain amount of pilfering was the norm and ignored, Henry Jardine had told Greg in the early days after Greg's arrival, when Henry had still been working under the assumption that Greg actually wanted to learn something about his business and how Denby Mill's silk was transported. That 'tax' was controlled by the Triads who monitored it every bit as carefully as the cargo brokers monitored ships' cargoes. A man who stole from the Triads lost his hand and arm, if he was lucky – and his life if he wasn't.

Greg was sweating heavily now as he sat on the solitary chair in the small room of the apartment he had originally rented for his Chinese mistress. He had come here because he hadn't been able to think of anywhere else he could go. He dare not go back to the Jardines', at least not yet, not until he was sure he had got away with what he had done.

It had been Chung Hai who had made him do it, just as it was Lionel who was responsible for all his other problems. Lionel was the one, after all, who had introduced him to Chung Hai, and the one who had stolen Lucy from him. Just as soon as he was out of this mess, Greg was going to pay him back for that piece of treachery, you could bet your life he was.

Once he *was* out of it. His sweating increased. The room was low-ceilinged, its only ventilation the small window, which when opened allowed all the noxious smells from the alleyway below it to contaminate the room in the same way that the raw sewage contaminated the rainwater that flowed along the alleyway every time it rained. When Chia Yung was here she operated the fan, but she'd gone out, snatching up the brat when he had threatened to hurl it against the wall to stop it crying.

Why was he so afraid? He'd done everything Chung Hai

had told him to do, hadn't he? He'd stolen the cheques from Henry Jardine's company chequebook, and he'd forged Henry's handwriting and his signature – that had been easy enough to do. He'd even used Henry's own pen, 'borrowing' it when he knew that Henry and his wife would be out. Then he'd handed the cheques over to Chung Hai, post-dated as he'd demanded – the cheques were drawn on the Hong Kong and Shanghai Bank. Greg guessed that Chung Hai had told him to make them in several smaller amounts rather than one large one to prevent the clerks at the bank from becoming suspicious and checking with Henry Jardine about them before accepting them.

Still, a total sum of the equivalent of damn near a hundred thousand pounds in Hong Kong dollars wasn't going to be easy to miss. And when Henry Jardine did miss it, there was no reason why Henry should suspect him, Greg re-assured himself.

And he had paid off his gambling debts.

Chapter Twenty-Eight

'Look, Mummy!' Amber hid a small smile as Luc looked longingly in the direction of a shiny bicycle. They were in Harrods, filled with every toy imaginable ready for Father Christmas to come and collect to deliver to 'good' children on Christmas Eve.

Amber had hoped that Robert would come with him – she knew he had been tempted – but then Otto had arrived in that irritating way he seemed to have of turning up just when Amber hoped she and Luc might have Robert to themselves for a little while, so she and Luc had ended up coming on their own.

Luc had already been to 'see Father Christmas' and Amber wondered how much 'belief' in him Luc actually had when her son had informed her knowingly afterwards that he had 'told Father Christmas' that he would 'very much like to have a dog of his own'.

The puppy was waiting for him at Osterby. Amber had seen it already – for once accompanied by Robert during the brief visit they had managed to make there after their return from Paris. That that been a happy visit, all the more so because Robert had finally relented and agreed that Amber could have her shop. How much had Robert's guilt, because he didn't want to be a proper husband to her, been responsible for his change of heart? A payment to her perhaps for a debt he wasn't openly prepared to admit existed; a toy for her to play with that would keep her occupied and ensure that there was no repeat performance of that shameful episode when she begged him to be a proper husband to her. That was something she tried never to think about now. The excoriating pain of her own humiliation had burned a scar of shame deep into her, and she was as loath now to discuss the subject of their sexless marriage as she knew Robert had always been. It was simply easier to pretend 'that' incident had never taken place – for both of them.

It was easier and safer to tell herself that Robert's agreement was probably a sop to his conscience because he had Otto, to whom he was giving his emotional and physical love, whilst she had no one.

Whatever the real reason for his acceptance of her plans it was, as far as Amber was concerned, a truly wonderful Christmas present. She hated conflict of any kind, and Robert's angry attitude to her plans had shadowed her own excitement, dulling her pleasure and making her feel despondent. She desperately wanted to share her joy in her project with Robert but she had had to accept that he wasn't really interested, and merely tolerated her plans rather than wanted to share them. That made her feel sad, because in her parents' marriage everything had been shared. But her marriage was not like that. There was no point in dwelling on all that her marriage was not. Instead she should focus on the many blessings it had brought her.

She was going to Walton Street later on to meet with Cecil and James Lees-Milne, whose advice she was shamelessly courting. Both of them, in their different roles, could be responsible for putting some very good business her way, so it made sense to get the benefit of their experience now.

She must have a word with Robert and ask him what he thought about Luc having a bicycle. He was already learning to ride on a thankfully placid pony and under the careful eye of Osterby's head groom.

Her son brought them both so much joy. Robert might try to be stern with Luc, but the truth was that Luc could wind Robert round his little finger.

'You'll spoil him, Robert,' Amber often protested, when Robert gave in to yet another of Luc's pleas for some treat or another, but Robert always insisted that Luc was 'gifted with such a sweet nature that that would be impossible'.

Amber acknowledged ruefully that that was true. So many times the 'treats' Luc asked Robert for were for others. He was such a 'noticing' boy, drawing her attention to the plight of the less fortunate when he was out with her, asking her if they might give 'the poor match-seller some pennies' or 'that poor boy some money for some new shoes'.

He had her own father's desire to help the less well off than himself, and secretly Amber already hoped that one day, when the time came for Luc to take up his responsibilities he would show far more of an interest in politics than Robert. There was so much that a man of power and wisdom could do, and so much too that needed to be done. One only had to read the newspaper reports of the plight of those out of work to recognise that. No doubt if her grandmother could read her mind she would accuse Amber of trying to turn her son into a socialist, but more than anything else Amber wanted Luc to retain the compassion for others he already possessed.

All the servants loved him. He knew all about their families and, with the older servants, all about their aches and pains. He might sit with Robert's old nanny patiently holding her knitting wool between his outstretched hands whilst she wound it, but he was still very much a young boy, as eager to play practical jokes and have fun, as he was aware of the responsibilities that would one day be his.

It brought a lump to Amber's throat to watch him striding manfully at Robert's side when Robert took him about the estate, his walk mimicking Robert's.

Amber's preoccupation with the shop had meant that she hadn't been as busy socially as normal, and friends had begun to complain that she was turning into a hermit. The social scene had never really appealed to her – so many of those involved in it were shallow and hollow – although there were notable and honourable exceptions – men and women whose wit and breadth of knowledge she admired.

Emerald Cunard, for instance, for all her love of parties and gossip, could be relied on for a shrewd assessment of what lay beneath expensive clothes and jewels. The Duff Coopers and the Channons were also good friends whose company Amber always enjoyed. Chips Channon perhaps had the sharper wit and made her laugh, whilst Duff Cooper shared her own dislike of Hitler and his politics. Both couples, though, were well informed and politically active.

Diana Mitford had originally been someone Amber had admired, and would at one stage have liked as a friend, but that had been before her involvement with Oswald Mosley had become public. Amber frowned. The very right-wing politics of Oswald Mosley, and now Diana too, represented everything she most abhorred. Their views were close to those of Hitler, with his anti-Jewish rhetoric, and thus anathema to her. But there were those in England who shared them, she knew that, much as that knowledge appalled her.

Dinner parties often led to heated conversations about the Munich Olympics, with some people stating angrily that they should never have been allowed to go ahead, and that it would be morally wrong to attend the Games, whilst others said determinedly that they felt that politics had no place in sport and that for that reason they were determined to be there. There was also a third group – a group who boasted openly about Germany's superiority and used the Games as an excuse to talk about Hitler and how wonderful he was at every opportunity.

Once she would have been able to discuss her concern about Hitler and the Mosleys and their followers with Robert, but Otto's influence on his life meant that now she felt reluctant to do so. Because she feared that Robert might not share her views any more? She knew how much Otto meant to Robert but surely that did not mean that Robert would abandon his own political stance for him?

Chapter Twenty-Nine

January 1936

'Mr Fulshawe is downstairs asking to see you, Your Grace.'

A smile lit up Amber's face. 'Show him up, please, Chivers,' she instructed the butler, 'and tell Cook that I've changed my mind and that we shall require afternoon tea after all. I'm sure that Mr Fulshawe will appreciate something substantial, some of her special Gentleman's Relish perhaps, and her plum cake?'

'Jay.' Amber greeted her old friend warmly. 'What a lovely surprise. You so rarely come to London, and in such weather. Snow and fog. Beth and Alistair were at Windsor over the weekend, a shooting party, and then the Prince of Wales invited them to have lunch at Fort Belvedere and it took them an hour and a quarter to drive back to London instead of the normal forty-five minutes.'

He looked so grave that Amber's smile faded, to be replaced by a small worried frown, but before she could say anything the maids arrived with the afternoon tea.

'You will have tea, won't you?' Amber asked him, signalling to the maids to leave the trolley. 'Thank you, Chivers. I'll pour myself.'

Once they were alone again Amber said quietly, 'Something's wrong. I can tell.'

'Yes.' He looked distraught.

'What is it? What's happened?' Amber could see that he was finding it difficult to continue. 'Is it Lydia, or the girls? My grandmother?' It was nearly a week since Amber had last heard from her grandmother. Blanche wrote to her every week, just as she had done when Amber had been at boarding school, and of course Amber wrote back, but it was so unusual to receive a visit from Jay that she automatically feared that something must have happened.

'Lydia is as well as she is ever going to be, and the girls are fine.'

In point of fact Lydia was far from well, and there had been an incident over Christmas that had left him bruised both mentally and physically, when Lydia had attacked him for no reason at all, hurling herself at him, hitting and kicking him. Fortunately they had been alone at the time. Jay would have hated the children to have witnessed her loss of control and violence, knowing how much it would have frightened them to see their mother behaving in such a way. She had refused to tell him what was wrong other than to scream at him that he was keeping her a prisoner and that she hated him and that somehow she would escape, and in the end when she had finally collapsed on the bed in hysterical tears he had had to summon their doctor, dragging him away from his Christmas dinner so that Lydia could be sedated.

'It's Greg, Amber. I know how much you care about him, and I hate to be the bearer of bad news.'

'Something's happened to Greg? There's been an accident?' Fear for her cousin robbed Amber of her normal self-control. She put down the teapot. She was shaking too much to hold it safely, gripped by anxiety for Greg.

'No, nothing like that,' Jay reassured her immediately. 'Your grandmother received a letter from Henry Jardine two days ago. It seems that Greg has disappeared, and that there are certain errors, shall we say, in the accounts of the business . . . a large sum of money missing from the bank account.'

'You can't mean that Greg has stolen money from Henry Jardine?' Amber was appalled. Greg was many things and not all of them pleasant, she had started to learn, but a common thief? She couldn't believe it.

'I know how distressing this must be for you,' Jay told her, 'and we don't know the truth of what's happened and won't do until Greg is found, of course.'

'But Henry Jardine wouldn't accuse Greg if he wasn't sure.'

'No,' Jay agreed. 'However, according to Jardine's letter Greg has been under a considerable amount of pressure.'

Jay was trying to be kind, Amber knew. She also knew that no matter what pressure Jay himself was put under he would never steal from anyone. But Jay had the strength that Greg lacked. Greg was weak. Amber knew that. She'd always known that at heart.

'Henry Jardine thinks that Greg had gambling debts that he couldn't pay. The Chinese are big gamblers and the Triad gangsters who run the gambling syndicates are ruthless when it comes to the way in which they treat those who don't pay them. Henry Jardine suspects that Greg must have been threatened by them and that is why he took the money.'

'This is dreadful. Poor Greg. I know that what he's done is wrong, but to be in fear of his life . . .'

'Yes, indeed.'

They looked at one another. Amber put down her tea cup and saucer and got up, walking over to the window. The last remnants of the morning's fog still clung to the bare trees in the square. 'What if the Chinese have caught up with him, Jay?'

When she turned round Amber saw that Jay had left his chair and was walking towards her.

'Oh, Jay.'

He reached for her hand, clasping it comfortingly within his own.

She could feel the warmth of his grip all the way up her arm, as though it had heated her blood. His fingers were so male, the texture of his skin so different from her own – rougher, male. Her breath caught as her throat tightened on it and her heart thudded far too hard. It had been so long since her flesh had experienced a male touch, since she had known what it was to be held by a man.

Her need poured through her as though it was a river in full flood that had burst its banks, rushing, gushing, thundering into all those parts she had thought were kept safe from it. Its wildness, which should have been so alien, felt instead so familiar that it was as though she had lived intimately with it for a very long time. If that was true then she had not known, she wanted to defend herself. She had truly believed that she was safe.

Jay!

What if she were to take him by the hand now and lead him, show him? He was her friend; he would understand both her need and the reason for it. There would be no need for any explanations or apologies.

Jay was a man, strong-bodied – just thinking the words made her pulse race and her flesh ache with that low heavy ache his presence had stirred inside her. There would be no need for flirtation or discussion, no time wasted on the preliminaries the urgency of her need resented. She already knew him. There would be nothing to dread, nothing to fear, only the sure certainty that because it was Jay he would strive to please her and he would keep her safe.

The temptation sucked at her willpower as forcefully as

350

any tide, drawing her into its embrace, and holding her there whilst it played with her, caressing and invading her, teasing her. Feeding her need.

Jay could take that need from her, he could satisfy her and fill the emptiness inside her. No one else need ever know.

Jay was still clasping her hand. Only seconds must have passed but it felt longer, long enough for her to have strayed into a place that was forbidden to her and which must remain forbidden. Her thoughts were going where they must not be allowed to go. It had been such a long time since she had experienced the kind of reassuringly, tenderly caring support Jay was giving her now. And never quite like this. Robert had been the last man to offer her this and . . . Robert was her husband, Amber reminded herself sharply, quickly withdrawing her hand and stepping back from Jay.

'We must hope for Greg's sake that they have not,' Jay answered her. He paused and then said quietly, 'Naturally, your grandmother is very upset, although of course she is trying very hard to pretend that she is not.'

'The disgrace will be very hard for her to bear,' Amber replied.

'There is that, but she loves Greg, as you know, and she has missed him. She loves you as well, Amber. I know how much she enjoyed visiting you over Christmas.'

Christmas had been wonderful, Amber admitted. Blanche adored both Robert and Luc, and for loving Luc, Amber could forgive her grandmother a great deal. The two of them shared a bond that Amber had the maternal wisdom to recognise was good for Luc. He was an only child and family ties were important. Blanche might have sniffed disparagingly about Robert's family tradition of holding an annual tenants' and servants' ball over the Christmas period, along with a Christmas party for the children of the tenant

351

farmers, and those in Robert's employ, but Amber suspected that secretly Blanche loved all the pomp and tradition that went with Robert's role as duke. As Robert's mother-in-law, Blanche was treated with the kind of awed respect that Cheshire society denied a mere Mrs Pickford, and Blanche certainly had the manner to carry off the style of a true *grande dame*, Amber acknowledged. For the tenants' and servants' ball she had worn a Chanel column of silver-grey silk jersey embroidered on one hip with a beaded camellia – a Chanel trademark – and, of course, her pearls. When she had appeared in her dress for dinner, Robert had taken one look at her and excused himself, reappearing fifteen minutes later, and in doing so forgoing his martini, so that he could present her with a piece of family jewellery – a demi tiara in pearls and diamonds that so perfectly complemented her gown that it might have been made for it.

Amber wouldn't have dreamed of wearing a tiara at such an event – she wasn't keen on wearing one at all – but on her grandmother, instead of looking overdone the tiara had simply looked exactly right, and if anything Amber suspected that their guests, rather than feeling that Blanche was trying to put them in their place with her finery, felt instead that her elegance was a compliment to them.

Not that Christmas had been all tiaras and ballgowns. She had gone up to the 'nursery', as they still called the large comfortable room off Luc's bedroom, one afternoon to find her son and her grandmother both on their knees on the floor playing with Luc's Hornby train set.

Ruefully Amber admitted that those memories were enough to soften her hostility towards her grandmother.

'She adores Robert and Luc,' she acknowledged.

'How are things going with the shop?'

Amber's heart gave a guilty start. The shop! The project she had told Robert she needed because she wanted something to fill her time and the empty space left vacant in her heart by their marriage. The thing that would stop her succumbing to temptation.

'It's very stop and start at the moment. All the paperwork has gone through now and I've been putting together a few schemes for the windows and for what I hope ultimately will be a reference library on the ground floor. The other two floors will be more of a proper showcase for Denby Mill's silks, showing how they can be used in actual rooms. I plan to keep things simple – large sofas with covers that can be changed for the summer and the winter, cushions, curtains, somewhere that looks stylish but that can be lived in. I'd like to employ an artist later on, someone who can sketch room plans for customers, and I'm hoping to persuade Cecil to take the photographs for me for our advertisements and our "ideas book".'

'It sounds as though you've done an enormous amount of work already.'

'I wake up in the night sometimes worrying about how much it is all costing and whether it will work or if people will just think that I'm a spoiled society wife, playing at interior decorating.'

'I'm sure you will make a success of it,' Jay reassured her firmly, pointing out, 'Your passion for silk would ensure that on its own, even without the gift for design and style you've inherited from your father, and I dare say a flair for business from your great-grandfather, which is in the Denby blood.'

'The merchant's blood my grandmother hates so much, you mean,' Amber smiled, pulling a small face. 'I hadn't really thought of it until now, but since I was taunted so much at school for my "trade" connections it would be rather nice to turn them to good advantage now.'

'It is you and your love of silk, your special talent for

sharing that love and enthusiasm with others, that will be the prime factor in making your venture a success, Amber,' Jay insisted. 'You and no one and nothing else.

'I dare say that you will be attending the King's funeral?' he asked, changing the subject.

'Yes. As a duke it is Robert's duty to be there and of course mine to accompany him. I won't, of course, embarrass him by using the occasion to advertise and promote my shop, like a street huckster, although I dare say there will be those there who will be hoping that I shall.' She pulled a small face. 'I might have married a duke but of course there are still those who do not and will not accept me because I am not "one of them".'

'More fool them, I say,' Jay told her gently.

'Robert hates the snobbery of that kind of thing. I just hope that he'll get back in time for the funeral. He's in Paris but he telephoned to say that he was going to come back straight away.' Amber looked away from Jay, her face burning in self-consciousness of her earlier feelings. Feelings of which she now felt thoroughly ashamed. 'If he were here, of course, I would offer you a bed here tonight, but . . .'

Jay shook his head. 'No, it's all right. I'm staying at my grandfather's club – *my* club now since he has proposed me to it.'

'He remains well?'

'Very well. I wonder sometimes if it is his determination not to allow your grandmother to buy his land that keeps him going. He is, I suspect, determined to outlive her and she him.'

Amber shivered. 'How dreadful to live with such hostility for one another through the years.'

'Your grandmother has always been very kind to me, and I have to confess that there any many things about her that I can't help but admire. She has tremendous resources of inner strength of will. You have them too, I think, Amber. You are more alike than you imagine.'

Amber shook her head. 'You will let me know if there is news of Greg.'

'Immediately,' Jay assured her.

For a long time after Jay had gone Amber stayed looking out of the drawing-room window into the grey murkiness of the encroaching January late afternoon. She felt as though a fog of chilly misery and despair had invaded her as much as it had the city, seeping into her, and filling her thoughts.

The King's death had saddened everyone, and was a poor start to a new year, especially when there had already been so much gossip about the Prince of Wales's relationship with Wallis Simpson.

Then there was the growing disquiet about the situation in Germany. Emerald Cunard might flirt with the German diplomat Herr von Ribbentrop and say teasingly that she was *éprise* of him, but there was growing hostility within some ranks of British politicians towards Adolf Hitler, despite the fact that he was being hailed as something of a saviour in his own country for what he was doing to combat the depression and the number of men out of work. Back at home, like many landowners who were in a position to do so, Robert was doing what he could to find jobs for those who were out of work, and a large new lake was being created on the estate with the work being given to men from the area who had lost their jobs.

Robert, who had been so antagonistic towards the politics of the fascists, had been silent on the issue since he had fallen in love with Otto.

Germany was to host the Olympics during the summer,

and Amber had heard that in some quarters it was already being said that this was a mistake and should not have been sanctioned. And now this dreadful and worrying news about Greg. Some of the things that were happening both politically in the wider world, and privately in her own personal world, were shadowed with so much darkness and danger that it was impossible not to be concerned.

Blanche looked out of the window into the gathering darkness.

Jay would have seen Amber by now and given her the news about Greg. She would be upset, of course; Amber's nature almost guaranteed that unpleasant things happening to those close to her would distress her on their behalf.

Blanche was 'upset' too, needless to say. She was 'upset' about the fact that the grandson, the investment into which she had poured so much love and so much hope, was turning out to be a bad investment that would only ever bring her a poor return. Greg's looks gave him the glamour and the illusion of honour and strength, but they were only that: an illusion.

Blanche didn't shock easily but even she had been shocked to discover, whilst discussing Greg's plight with Jay, that her grandson had probably known about the child Caroline Fitton Legh had been carrying and had said nothing. But why should she be shocked? In the circumstances she ought rather to have expected it.

She had hoped for better. She had believed that because he was her grandson he would be better. How wrong she had been.

Henry Jardine's letter had drawn for her an image of Greg that she didn't want to see, the image of a weak, cowardly young man without pride or respect – for himself or for others. A young man who would have broken his poor father's heart.

Greg's father had been a shining example of all that was best in the male sex, inwardly as well as outwardly.

It was Barrant's fault he was dead. It was Barrant's contempt that had driven him to enlist when she had worked so hard to keep him out of the war, Barrant's deliberately contrived public confrontation with him, during which he had called him a coward and demanded to know why he hadn't joined the brigade of local young men his own son had drummed up.

She had begged Marcus not to listen, pleaded with him not to go. He was a married man with a young son and a wife who was carrying their second child. He had a known weakness in his left leg from an accident as a boy, which had left him with a slight limp and an inability to bear much weight on that leg, which would have exempted him, but no, he couldn't let others younger than he go off to war. It was his duty to be with them.

His duty. Dear God. His duty has been to her, the mother who had borne him in such agony, to his wife, and his son. He had had no duty to a group of foolish young men whipped up into a patriotic frenzy by Barrant, who, if he had had any sense, would have kept his own son from the carnage instead of boasting of his bravery and encouraging him. Women wanted live sons, and lovers and brothers, not dead heroes.

Blanche knew that people locally thought she hated Barrant because he had not wanted to marry her, but the truth was that that hatred was nothing compared to the bitterness of her hatred for him after Marcus's death. Barrant had killed her son as deliberately as though he had plunged a knife into his heart.

Amber really needed to provide Robert with another son.

One son was never enough; one son challenged fate, and fate had a way to reacting very cruelly to that challenge. She would have to remind her granddaughter again of that fact, Blanche decided.

Chapter Thirty

'Mummy, Mummy . . .'

'Shush, darling,' Amber hushed Luc, as he struggled to conceal his excitement.

Amber had brought him down to St James's Palace that morning on impulse to see and hear the issuing of the Royal Proclamation that would announce that there was to be a new king.

She could well understand Luc's excitement at the sight of so much pageantry. The Household Cavalry came first. Luc had seen the cavalry before, of course; what London child had not: the uniformed men in their dress uniforms, riding their immaculately groomed and trained horses. Then behind them came mounted outriders in heraldic costumes of scarlet, and rich gold and white, embroidered with the emblems and arms of the Crown, their black medieval-style hats plush with white silk – Macclesfield silk, Amber hoped proudly – escorting the state carriages.

She could almost see Luc's small chest puffing out with innocent pride in what it was to be British, as he watched them. Amber wasn't entirely untouched by that same feeling herself, she admitted ruefully, as the carriages swayed slowly by, a living ceremonial link with the country's past.

But the carriages were nothing compared with the Kings of Arms themselves, in their gold and scarlet.

The assembled trumpeters raised their instruments and blew triumphantly as one, proclaiming the ascension of King Edward VIII to the throne of England, and Amber wondered as they did so how many of those listening like her wondered about how Edward would cope with his new and divided loyalties. He was so dreadfully in love with Wallis Simpson, but now that he was King they could not possibly continue their relationship in the way that they had. Wallis was, after all, divorced, and no King of England could ever marry a divorced woman.

Romantic love was the cause of so many problems, Amber thought sadly. She was glad that she had decided not to allow it to trespass into her own life ever again. For some reason a mental image of Jay formed itself inside her head. She could picture him so clearly, his dark hair uncovered and ruffled by the often sharp Macclesfield wind, as he went about his work in his plain countryman's clothes. There was no place for pomp or circumstance in Jay's life; position and wealth meant nothing to Jay and he would certainly never seek them out. Thinking of him underlined for her how alien to her childhood dreams her own life now was. Her hand tightened on Luc's, causing him to protest loudly.

They got back to Eaton Square to discover that Robert had arrived home only minutes ahead of them.

Almost speechless with delight, Luc hurled himself into Robert's arms, giving Amber a much-needed opportunity to control her shock at the sight of her husband. Robert's face was badly bruised, his lip cut and his eye turning black.

'Your poor face!' she protested.

'An accident. Nothing more. It looks worse than it is,' he told her brusquely.

He looked desperately thin and unwell, and was, Amber suspected, deliberately avoiding making eye contact with her, as he hugged Luc fiercely. She had been planning to spend the afternoon at her shop but she decided in view of Robert's return and the way he looked that she would stay at home.

Maybe she could persuade Robert to confide in her. He looked dreadfully unhappy although he was doing his best not to show it. He was a good husband in many ways, even if the teasing fun to be with Lord Robert of their National Gallery days, whose company she had enjoyed so much and whose friendship she had valued so much, seemed to have vanished since Otto had come into his life.

'Luc is a fine boy,' Robert told Amber later over luncheon, adding abruptly, 'I saw Chips Channon earlier. I called at Westminster before coming home to find out what's happening with regard to the Lying in State. Chips is cock-a-hoop over the birth of his son. God, but I envy him, Amber.'

Robert spoke with such vehemence underpinned with bitterness that Amber felt a pang of protective anxiety for Luc.

'I expect that all men enjoy the thought of having a child of their own blood,' was all she could think of to say.

'No, you misunderstand me,' Robert told her immediately. 'There is no son I would rather have than Luc. The difference I long to see is within myself, Amber, for the way in which I am now betraying all that I should be. I cannot tell you how much I wish I did not suffer from this weakness and foolishness, that I was man enough not to endure . . .' He got up and told her in a suffocated voice, 'When there is cruelty within a relationship one has to know that it must end, but somehow the ending of it is an impossibility; a threat of an agony so great that it cannot be borne.'

He sank down into a chair, his face in his hands, his thin shoulders shaking with emotion.

Amber was filled with an almost maternal compassion for him. She went to his side, and took hold of his bony hand in her own.

'Can't you give him up for your own sake, Robert?' she asked him sadly.

'No I can't,' Robert wept. 'I wish that I could, but I cannot. I've tried, Amber, really I have.' The look he gave her was filled with despair and anguish.

Amber put her arms around him and held him as tenderly and protectively as though he had been Luc. She wanted to weep with him – for him – but she knew she must not. He needed her to be strong for him, and she needed to be strong herself, and for their marriage.

Even though Robert had spoken so plainly to her of his misery, Amber was reluctant to mention Otto's name or ask too many questions in case they caused him to withdraw from her. She was as sure as she could be that the marks of violence she could see on his face had been made by his lover. And if his poor face was so hurt then what might have been done to his flesh that the world could not see?

Almost as though he had followed her train of thought, Robert raised his head and told her, 'You must not blame . . . anyone. The fault is mine in mistaking— that is, in burdening him with my love. I had thought . . . and hoped . . . there had been words and looks exchanged . . . I had not meant to offend. I had believed that he shared— I should not be speaking to you of this.'

Amber could almost feel the intensity of his emotional struggle.

'If . . . someone in your life is making you so unhappy,' she said gently, 'then perhaps it would be better if they were not there.'

Robert shuddered as he stood up and walked over to the window. 'Unhappy!' He laughed wildly. 'You cannot comprehend the difference that lies between mere unhappiness and what has taken possession of my heart. Sometimes I feel that I am afflicted by a form of madness. And if I am not then that my own pain would drive me to that madness. It is unbearable, unendurable, beyond anything I ever imagined I might have to bear, and yet I could not wish one second of the time we have had together away.'

'But he has hurt you, Robert. I do not believe there was really an accident.' Amber couldn't hold the words back any longer.

'That was not his fault,' Robert denied immediately. 'I upset him, made him angry. It was my fault that he lost his temper with me. I drove him to it with my selfishness, and . . . and my need of him.'

'Oh, Robert.' Pity for him clogged Amber's throat and racked her heart.

'I love him so much, Amber. Oh God, this is destroying me. I cannot live without him and yet for his own dear sweet sake I must. He is so young. Too young to be burdened by the weight of what I feel for him. He accuses me of wanting to chain his life to mine, and to my shame I must confess that he is right. And yet at the same time I want to be strong enough to give him the freedom he desires, out of my love for him.'

Amber ached for the raw pain she could hear in Robert's voice. Otto had obviously treated Robert cruelly and very badly. Her heart felt heavy with the weight of her sadness for Robert and the knowledge that there was nothing she could do to help him, no words she could offer that would soothe his anguish.

It wasn't until she was seated at her dressing table much later in the evening, whilst her maid helped her to prepare for bed, that she realised that she hadn't told Robert about Greg, but there was nothing she could do about it now. Poor Robert, it would be so unfair to expect him to listen to her problems when he was in such a very dreadful state over Otto.

Chapter Thirty-One

'I must get back to Eaton Square, Richard,' Amber told the young decorator Cecil Beaton had recommended to her for the work that needed to be done on the shop.

She hadn't planned to call at Walton Street, but the temptation had proved too much, and the truth was that she was finding it hard to keep away now that everything she had been planning for so long was finally taking shape.

She had given the mill her orders for the silks she wanted, all carefully chosen to emphasise the moods she planned to create with the windows. She had spent many hard-working hours at her desk, grappling with figures and schedules, in order to make sure that the mill would be able to fulfil the orders she hoped to give it. The necessary raw materials had been ordered, and special arrangements made with the dyers Denby used to ensure that they too had access to enough of the right dye colours to ensure that clients' orders could be produced on time. Sample lengths of the new designs she planned to use had been run off – each in four different colourways – an idea that that come to Amber after watching the heralds.

In addition to ensuring that they had all the raw materials to produce the designs as and when they were needed, Amber had also had to spend a great deal of time costing everything out, right down to the last pin required and the right weight of silk thread for sewing the soft furnishings. No detail had been too small to escape her attention. She had spent a whole day with the representative from Coats sewing threads, before she had been happy that the threads she had chosen were exactly the right colour for her fabric – and the right price. She suspected that the representative, a blunt Yorkshireman, had been rather surprised by her determination to barter down the price he wanted her to pay – and her ability to stick to her guns over doing so. She had been surprised herself, discovering an unexpected sense of achievement in getting a good deal, as well as a determination to do so.

She looked around again. The soft French grey paint looked wonderful. Amber longed to stay. She loved the pared-down simplicity of the painted woodwork. It would be a perfect foil for the richness of the silk. Reluctantly she took her leave. Robert was so fragile and vulnerable at the moment. Poor Robert. He needed a little of the sanctuary and solace she was finding in her shop and her silk.

'Oh Lord, I almost forgot to tell you, Amber. I bumped into Lord Beaverbrook yesterday. He was with Chips Channon, and Chips has invited us to a dinner he is giving for the King.'

Robert might be trying to sound and look cheerful but the thin winter sunshine slanting in through the morning-room windows betrayed the truth. How gaunt and grey he still looked, even though it was over a month since he had returned from France.

'How is Max?' Amber enquired solicitously after Lord Beaverbrook. 'I know when I last saw him he complained that the winter weather was making his asthma worse.'

'Well, you know Max. He does so love to be a martyr to

his health. Oh, by the way, he said to tell you that he is very pleased with the samples you had sent to him.'

'He wants to have his private cinema hung with silver silk,' Amber told Robert.

Her eyes had certainly been opened now with regard to the lavish spending and often outlandish lengths the very rich were prepared to go to satisfy their whims. She had had one request for a scheme for a certain society lady's boudoir, which she had been told must be in exactly the same shade of blue as her would-be client's eyes, and another from a now elderly Gaiety girl who had married extremely well, for a complete makeover of her private apartments within her husband's ancestral pile to include a four-poster and a day bed – for her pet Pekinese.

Amber was learning to receive such requests without so much as a blink.

Socially they had been very busy since Robert had returned from Paris. Amber suspected that Robert wanted to fill his time to stop himself from giving in to any temptation he might feel to seek a reconciliation with Otto. Robert was spending a great deal of time with Luc, re-establishing their previous close bond. Being with Luc seemed to be the only thing that could lift the stark look of anguish from Robert's eyes.

There was still no news about Greg or his likely whereabouts. Amber refused to use the word 'fate', even in her own private thoughts, although Robert had warned her that if Greg was heavily in debt to a Chinese Triad gang because of his gambling, it was unlikely that he would be allowed to leave Hong Kong alive. This had horrified her. She could hardly bear to think of what Greg might be enduring, and could only pray for his escape from danger and his safe return.

Chapter Thirty-Two

Henry and Honor Channon's dinner for the King was, to Amber's relief, a surprisingly light-hearted affair.

She and Robert were seated with the Duff Coopers, for dinner. Both Duff and Chips were politicians, and Robert had known them for several years. Robert had told Amber that despite the fact that they were friends he shared Chips's view that since Duff had been appointed Secretary of State for War, he had become somewhat more bellicose in his political outlook, and that this might not be wise, given the current political strength of Adolf Hitler.

The Duke and Duchess of Kent arrived shortly after Amber and Robert, and the Channons were formally introducing people to them, including Amber and Robert.

Amber, though, had met Princess Marina in Paris and she laughed when the Princess, who like her was wearing a pair of the newly fashionable very large pearl earrings, leaned towards her and whispered conspiratorially, 'Have you had to have your earlobes pierced too?'

'Yes I have,' Amber admitted.

It had been written in the gossip columns that even young society ladies were now rushing to have this uncomfortable procedure for fear of having their large pearl earrings fall off if they were only clipped on to their earlobes. The process had been extremely painful, and it had been six weeks before her earlobes had healed enough for her to be able to wear proper earrings. Even now they still bled a little at times and felt uncomfortahble.

The King arrived several minutes after the Kents, smiling warmly, and kissing Princess Marina, who was just rising from her curtsy to him when dinner was announced.

The moment the doors to the dining room were opened, those who, unlike Amber, had not seen the Channons' spectacular newly decorated dining room before, reacted to it with what Amber knew Chips would consider to be a gratifyingly awed silence.

The new dining room was certainly very different and magnificent, but not, as Robert had said wryly the first time he had seen it, 'British'.

The Channons had had their dining room decorated in the same rococo style as the Amalienburg Hunting Lodge, in the grounds of the Nymphenburg Palace in Munich, with mirrors and pale blue paint, and Amber thought it very pretty, if rather ornate.

As they all went in to dinner Honor Channon rushed past Amber, explaining that Emerald Cunard, who was supposed to be sitting next to the King, had not arrived.

'Poor Honor,' Diana Cooper sympathised to Amber. 'These supposedly informal royal dinners are dreadfully exhausting.'

Everyone was, of course, wearing formal court mourning because of Edward's presence, the men in black waistcoats and white ties, and the women in dark gowns. Edward himself was dressed in a black waistcoat with magnificent square diamond links in his cuffs that caught the light every time he moved.

Wallis Simpson was wearing a discreetly plain black gown, but there was nothing either plain or discreet about her jewellery.

'The King is absolutely lavishing Wallis with jewellery,' Diana Cooper told Amber. 'He designs it for her himself, you know. Oh, good, Philip Sassoon's here!' she exclaimed, changing the subject. 'Have you met him yet, Amber? He really is most charming.'

'I haven't, but I have met his sister, the Marchioness of Cholmondeley.'

'Oh, she is delightful, isn't she?' Diana enthused. 'She often acts as Philip's hostess when he entertains at Lympne. Of course, being Jewish, Philip is very anti Hitler, and one can't blame him. Duff says there are the most dreadful stories coming out of Germany about the treatment of the Jews. I think the government is going to have to do something about Oswald Mosley and those Blackshirts of his soon as well.'

Amber nodded. She shared Diana's views.

The dinner was delicious, although Amber noticed that Robert was not eating very much.

Over the beef, Amber asked Duff if he thought it might actually come to war with Germany.

'One hopes not,' he answered her, 'but it would be foolish to dismiss the risk. Germany is making a great deal of noise trying to justify her present goings-on because she wants back her lost colonies, but even if she were to be granted them I doubt that she would stop there.'

Amber gave a small shiver. 'It seems so dreadful that we must contemplate another war.'

'Yes, indeed,' Duff agreed sombrely.

Every family had its own dreadful story to tell of young men and young lives lost or destroyed by the horror of the 1914 war. Those losses had cast shadows over them all, Amber knew. Her own grandmother, and Jay's grandfather, had each lost a precious only son, and such losses had been more the norm than the exception. Given the terrible losses of that war it should be unthinkable that there could be another, but sometimes the unthinkable had to be faced.

The meal was over. The ladies got up, curtsying to the King before they left the gentlemen to their port.

Upstairs in the drawing room Amber listened to the general conversation. Since Diana Cooper, Honor Channon, and Princess Marina all had young sons, she found herself drawn into their conversation, and was caught off guard when Princess Marina commented that she had heard wonderful things of Amber's beautiful silk furnishings, and that she would like her advice.

Amber smiled and agreed that she would be delighted to help, but inwardly she was warning herself to be cautious. On the one hand having Princess Marina as a client was bound to benefit Silk, but on the other, the Princess might expect to be given her new furnishings as a gift, in return for her patronage, and Amber wasn't sure she would want to do that. This was the kind of thing she would have liked to discuss with Jay, but of course Jay was in Macclesfield and she was here.

Before the evening was over Amber and Robert had received several invitations for Fridays to Mondays, as the upper classes called weekends, including one from Philip Sassoon, who had insisted that they must visit him at Lympne, and one to one of Emerald Cunard's famous dinner parties.

It was almost three o'clock in the morning when their own butler let them into the house in Eaton Square.

'There was a telephone call for Her Grace earlier,' he informed them. 'From Mr Fulshawe. He left a message to say that he would appreciate it if Her Grace could telephone him back as soon as convenient.'

Amber looked anxiously at Robert. She could think of only one reason why Jay would telephone her.

'Do you think there's been some news about Greg?' she asked him.

'Possibly, although of course it's too late to telephone him now.'

After a fretful night, during which she had been unable to sleep for more than a few minutes at a time, and during which her imagination had run riot, presenting her with far too vivid scenarios involving every possible horror befalling Greg, she waited for as long as she could but eventually she could wait no longer. As a countryman Jay was an early riser, she assured herself, her fingers tightening on the receiver as she waited for him to answer the telephone.

When he did, though, she was so on edge, it was several seconds before she was able to say huskily, 'Jay, it's Amber. I hope it isn't too early to telephone.'

'No, of course not.'

'I would have telephoned before but we were out late last night.'

'Yes, your butler explained that you were having dinner with the King.'

Amber managed a weak laugh. 'Chivers is far more impressed by our social elevation than we are, I suspect.'

'The reason I telephoned was to ask if it is possible for you to come to Macclesfield?'

Amber gripped the receiver. 'Jay, what is it? What's happened?'

'I can't really discuss it now. All I can say is that it concerns Greg. It would be much better if you were able to come here, and, well, the sooner the better.'

'Greg? Is he . . . ? Has he . . . ?'

'He's alive, Amber. I'm sorry but I can't say any more. Do you think you will be able to come home?'

Home. Her home was here now with Robert and Luc, but for some reason Jay's use of the simple word made her eyes sting.

Amber thought quickly. They had several social engagements and they had planned to spend most of the summer at Osterby rather than go abroad. Amber suspected that Robert wanted to avoid France and Paris in particular because of the memories associated with it. Although he had put back on some of the weight he had lost, and outwardly recovered much of his old spirit, there were times when he let the mask slip and Amber saw the raw pain behind it.

'I'll have to see what Robert says,' she told Jay.

'Yes, of course, but do please try to come, Amber.'

'I'll do my best,' she promised him.

But in reality nothing would keep her away.

'Of course you must go to Macclesfield,' Robert insisted when she told him what Jay had said to her. 'It sounds to me as though your grandmother needs you to be there.'

'I can't imagine Grandmother ever needing me, or admitting it if she did,' Amber protested, adding, 'I thought perhaps we could all go as a family.'

Robert shook his head. 'No. Forgive me, Amber, but the way I feel at the moment, I would be more of a hindrance to you than a help.'

'Oh, Robert . . . I'll take Luc with me, of course,' she told him, but he shook his head.

'There's no need for that. Far better I think if I take Luc to Osterby as we had originally planned, and we can enjoy some manly fun together. He can almost beat me at cricket already. He's turning into a first-class little bowler.'

'You are so very kind and thoughtful,' Amber told him gratefully.

'If I am kind and thoughtful then it is because I have so much to be grateful for, thanks to you. Without you and Luc I could not have got through these last few hellish months. You and he have given me a reason and a need to do so. The pain of not being loved . . .' His voice faltered and Amber could see the bleak despair in his eyes.

'Robert, you *are* loved, and well loved too, by your friends and those who care about you.'

'But not by the one I shall always long to be loved by.'

Amber gave her husband a troubled look. She had hoped that Robert was getting over his love for Otto but obviously she had been wrong.

'Oh, did I tell you that von Ribbentrop has invited us to be his guests at the Olympic Games, along with the Channons?' Robert asked her, deliberately changing the subject.

The German Ambassador and his wife had been fellow guests at the Channons' dinner party, although Amber hadn't spoken with them herself.

'An awful lot of people are saying that they feel it wouldn't be the thing to go,' Amber reminded Robert.

'The King is thinking of going,' Robert informed her, 'and there is really no reason why we should not. By all accounts it should be a splendid occasion.'

'And another opportunity for Germany to display her growing military might to the world,' Amber pointed out wryly.

'Yes, I dare say you are right, but that being the case, isn't it better and wiser to face up to that fact and assess at first hand rather than simply turn our backs on it and refuse to acknowledge that it exists? Hitler isn't without friends, Amber, even in this country.'

'I think we all know that.'

It troubled Amber that Robert, who had been so anti Hitler, now seemed less so, especially when, if anything, she herself had grown more worried that Germany's martial stance could lead to another war.

Although Luc was disappointed when he learned that Amber would be going to Denham without him, he cheered up when Amber told him that he would still be going to Osterby with his father.

'And I shall be able to see Bruno,' he told Amber happily.

He had wanted desperately to bring the puppy back to London with him after Christmas but Robert had been firm and had told him that Bruno would be happier staying at Osterby.

'I shall write to you, Mummy, and tell you what new tricks he has learned,' Luc announced importantly.

Amber wrapped her arms around him, leaning her chin on his dark head. He was so very precious. She marvelled now that she had been fortunate enough to have such a special child. When she looked at him what she saw and all that she saw was Luc himself, his own special little person. She had worried at first when she had seen the little cartoon-like caricatures he had taken to drawing for his own amusement – childlike and unformed, but yet hinting at a flair that had instantly made her think guiltily of Jean-Philippe – and then would stem such thoughts, telling herself firmly that if Luc had a flair for drawing then naturally he had inherited it from her, just as she had inherited the same flair from her father.

Whenever she thought of Caroline Fitton Legh, and Louise, who had turned into a woman happy to become the mistress of any man who could afford her, the pain inside her was knife sharp. All that had saved her from sharing either of their fates had been Robert's need of a wife who understood what he was. Whatever personal loss of happiness she had to endure was nothing when she compared it with the joy Luc brought her. As she got into the car to go to the station for her train, the last thing she did was to look towards the house and up at the window where Luc was standing waving to her.

'But, Jay, I want you to stay here with me.'

'Lydia, you know that I can't.'

'If you loved me you would. But you'd rather be at Denham than here with me.'

They were in their bedroom. Lydia rarely left it these days other than to go out with Cassandra. Jay wished she would spend more time downstairs. He hated seeing the anxious expressions on their daughters' faces as they tiptoed round 'because Nurse says that Mummy isn't well'. But what could he do? Their doctor said that it was essential that Lydia was kept as calm as possible, for her own sake.

'You don't love me any more, do you?' Her voice was rising. 'Because if you did you'd stay here with me like I want you to.'

'Lydia, I have to go. It's my job. You know that.'

'You're a de Vries. How can you lower yourself to work for Blanche Pickford?' She was working herself up into a temper now, almost spitting the words at him as she paced the floor. 'Cassandra says you should have more pride.'

Jay's heart sank. Cassandra might claim that she was trying to help Lydia, and Lydia might insist that Cassie was her best and only friend, but in Jay's experience Lydia's mood was always difficult when she had been with Cassandra.

'I must go,' he repeated. 'I'll send Nurse up with some breakfast for you, shall I?'

'No.' The denial was almost a howl.

Normally he would have stayed and done his best to calm Lydia down, but today he couldn't. He had promised Blanche that he would meet Amber's train and he already felt guilty about not being able to tell Amber what had happened to Greg, knowing how much she would be worrying, but Blanche had insisted, stating that whatever was said over the telephone was immediately known to everyone the local exchange operator knew.

Jay was relieved when the telephone rang, even if it was Cassandra asking to speak with Lydia, allowing him to make his escape.

Despite their best hopes and everything that their doctor had done, Lydia's condition was getting worse. It had been heartbreaking after Christmas when she had broken down and sobbed in his arms, acknowledging her condition. Such periods of normal behaviour were rare, though.

Jay now employed two nurses for the girls, after he had come in one day to find them cowering in a corner whilst Lydia threatened to beat them. The girls had run to him, terrified, flinging themselves into his arms with relief, both of them crying and trembling. Jay had done his best to comfort them, helplessly aware that he was no real substitute for the mother they should have had, and filled with guilt for their plight.

The best he had been able to do was give the nurses instructions not to leave Lydia on her own with her daughters.

Lydia had been distraught when she had learned this, crying and pleading with Jay to change his mind, swearing that she had not meant the girls any harm and that it was Jay who was being cruel now, but Jay had remained steadfast. He had to, he believed, for the girls' sake.

The train pulled out of the station, leaving Amber standing alone on the empty platform. Jay had said that he would meet her off the train and it was so unlike him not to be here on time. Her apprehension increased. He had said that

Greg was alive but what if he'd been protecting her from the truth?

'Amber, I'm sorry I'm late.'

They didn't touch. The sunlight polished Jay's hair to the sheen of a magpie's wing. It curled onto his collar as though he hadn't had either the time or the vanity to have it cut.

'I was beginning to worry.'

The air had a familiar Macclesfield damp smell. Jay picked up her suitcase, smiling at her. He looked tired, Amber noticed, and there were lines fanning out from around his eyes that had not been there the last time she had seen him.

He took her arm, escorting her to his car and helping her in, waiting until he was in the driving seat and no one could overhear them before he said gently, 'Let me put your mind at rest on one point. Greg is alive and safe. In fact, he's at Denham.'

'At Denham?'

Relief, surprise and curiosity jostled through her head, finally coming to rest on a spike of uneasy alarm.

'The story is a rather complex one, I'm afraid, with a great deal more of it to be told, which is why your grandmother wanted you to come home, and why I was expressly forbidden to say anything over the telephone other than that Greg was safe.'

'A great deal more?' Amber felt faintly exasperated. 'What more can there be, if Greg is safe?'

'Well, since you ask and since your grandmother has asked me to put you in possession of the facts, most important of all is that Greg has not returned home alone.'

Chapter Thirty-Three

'What do you mean, he hasn't returned home alone?'

'It seems that it is acceptable in Hong Kong for those unmarried European men who wish to do so to keep a Chinese mistress.'

Jay wasn't looking at her, he was concentrating on the road, but that did not mean that she could not look at him. Just the hint of a thin film of colour was seeping up under his skin, as though he wanted to protect her from what he plainly thought unpleasant. Unexpectedly tenderness filled her. Living the kind of life she did with Robert made Jay's desire to protect her even more endearingly sweet.

'You mean that Greg has brought a Chinese mistress home with him?'

Amber tried to imagine her grandmother's reaction to that after all the hopes she had invested in Greg, and all her plans for his future as an MP and a pillar of Cheshire society, no doubt with a wife who would elevate him within that society.

'No.' Jay paused, and then said quietly, 'Sadly she didn't survive the journey. From what he has said, Greg had to work his passage back in often unpleasant conditions. No, it isn't his mistress he's brought back with him, it's his baby daughter.'

379

Amber opened her mouth and then closed it again. What after all could she say? Greg, a father?

'As you can imagine the situation is a rather difficult one at the moment,' Jay continued. 'Greg is in poor health. Your grandmother, whilst relieved that he is alive, is quite naturally very angry and upset, and then there's the child. She's very weak and frail, Amber, and quite poorly according to Dr Brookes. Very poorly, in fact,' he told her meaningfully.

'Greg must be distraught, especially having already lost her mother.'

When Jay made no response Amber frowned. 'He must care about them, Jay, to have brought them with him?'

'I can't speak for Greg's feelings. I should warn you, though, that you will find him very changed.'

'Changed? In what way?'

'I think it best that you judge for yourself. Even though he is back here in Macclesfield, he is still on edge and looking over his shoulder as though fearful of pursuit. Your grand-mother is naturally very concerned.'

'You mean she's concerned about herself and how Cheshire society is going to react to Greg's return without a wife but with a child?' Amber checked him drily.

'That is not fair, and it is certainly not worthy of you,' Jay rebuked her mildly. 'Greg has caused your grandmother a great deal of anxiety.'

He was right, of course.

'You make me feel like a . . . a thoughtless child.'

'That certainly isn't my intention. There is no one I admire more than you, Amber.'

It took her several seconds to digest his compliment but once she had done she managed to tease him.

'What, not even my grandmother?'

'Not even your grandmother.'

Jay had had to slow down because of a tractor crossing the road ahead of them. As he spoke he looked at Amber and gave her such a sweet warm smile that the whole of her heart seemed to do a slow somersault inside her chest, leaving her feeling shaken. Had the sun suddenly started to shine more brightly?

This simply would not do, she warned herself sternly. It would not do at all.

'Tell me about Greg's little girl,' she asked Jay, determinedly changing the subject.

'Well, as I've already said she is very poorly. It appears that the mother died from some kind of fever she contracted whilst they were at sea. Greg has not been very clear as to the exact circumstances. I dare say he cannot bring himself to speak of them in any great detail as yet. The captain of the ship on which they left Hong Kong put them off at his next port of call when he realised that Greg's mistress and child were on board and that Greg had not paid for their passage. Greg's mistress died shortly afterwards.'

'Oh how awful.'

'Yes. The little girl – she is not two years old – suffered the same affliction as her mother. She is very weak, Amber, and Dr Brookes isn't sure if she will survive.'

'Oh, poor baby, and poor Greg too.'

'Indeed.'

The tractor pulled into an open field gate, allowing Jay to drive on.

'Greg must be beside himself.'

'Yes, I imagine he is,' Jay agreed noncommittally.

Just as Jay too was no doubt beside *himself* with anxiety and grief over Lydia's condition, Amber thought inwardly. But Jay was very much stronger than her cousin in every single way.

'Has there been any word from Lord Fitton Legh about Greg's return?' she asked Jay as they turned into the drive. 'Not that there should be since he is now married to Cassandra.'

'He has not said anything yet.'

'Well, Grandmother will be pleased about that, at least.'

'What she will be pleased about is you coming home, Amber, even though she may not show it. She as extremely proud of you, you know.'

'If she is it's only because I am married to Robert, and for what I have therefore become.' She paused and then asked him, 'How are the girls, Jay, and Lydia?'

'The girls are fine and they send you their love. It really was very kind of you to send them those petty clothes, Amber. Ella especially is just at that age when she is very conscious of what she wears.'

'It was my pleasure. I love Luc, of course, but I must admit that I would have loved to have had a daughter as well. I'm hoping I'll have time to call and see the girls whilst I'm here – that is, of course, if Lydia doesn't mind.'

'Lydia won't mind.' He looked away from her and then said in a strained voice, 'Dr Brookes has told me that it is unlikely that she will ever fully recover.'

'Oh, Jay.' Amber could sense his anguish, and had such sympathy, both for him and for Lydia.

'I feel that I am to blame for what has happened to her. If she had not married me and had the children, then perhaps she would still have her sanity. Everyone is very willing to give *me* their sympathy. It's Lydia who needs and deserves it. Lydia's stepmother told me at Christmas when her parents visited us that Lydia's mother had an aunt who suffered from a similar condition to Lydia's.'

'It is all so very dreadful,' Amber said. 'But as for you feeling guilty, you mustn't, Jay. You weren't to know what

382

would happen – neither of you was. The same thing would have happened no matter who Lydia had married.'

Without thinking, Amber put her hand on his arm in an instinctive gesture of sympathy and then wished she had not done so when she felt the solid warmth of his muscles and flesh through the shabbiness of his tweed jacket. Jay had such strong arms; the kind of arms one could imagine holding a person protectively and safely, the kind of arms any woman would surely be glad to have around her.

Guiltily, she withdrew her hand.

'Yes,' Jay agreed, knowing that it was the truth, and knowing as well that he couldn't tell Amber about that other truth: that he had married Lydia because he had felt morally obliged to do so, and that he had married her loving Amber.

He stopped the car outside the house and he turned in his seat to look at her. The warm sun coming in through the open windows heated the leather seats, so that the combined smell of them and sunshine and the clean soap scent of Jay's skin were somehow imprinted on Amber's own senses in a way that she knew she would never be able to forget.

She mustn't sit here like this. She should go in and let Jay depart.

'How's the shop coming along?' It was wrong of him to prolong his time with her, Jay knew, but who was to know of his wrongdoing other than himself?

'Really well. I was a bit worried that what I'd got in mind wasn't going to work but it has done. What a lot of work, but we should open at last in late autumn. I've booked a very expensive advertisement in *Vogue* – nearly fifty pounds, despite Cecil putting in a good word for me. He's going to take the photographs for the advertisement – just a shot of the window. I've persuaded Robert to agree – reluctantly – that Cecil can photograph the state drawing room at Osterby for the Christmas advertising campaign.'

She could almost be a young girl again in her excitement and enthusiasm, Jay thought, her cheeks flushed and that look in her eyes he remembered so well from her childhood. Only she wasn't a young girl, she was a woman – a wife – the mother of a child.

His next question, 'Do you miss him?' shocked Jay almost as much as he could see it did Amber.

Her lips parted, anxiety shadowing her eyes.

'Do I miss who?'

It was too late for him to pretend his question was casual and meaningless.

'Luc's father,' he answered quietly.

Guilty colour burned Amber's face.

'No. Robert is Luc's father in all the ways that matter, not Jean-Philippe. Jay, I . . .'

'I'm sorry, I shouldn't have asked. I don't know why I did.' That was a lie. He did know and it was because he was jealous of the man to whom she had given her love.

'It's all right. When Luc was younger I used to worry all the time that someone would look at him and know that he wasn't Robert's, but the older he's become, the more Luc is like Robert. Their mannerisms and expressions . . . They love one another so much.'

'But what about you, Amber?'

She didn't pretend not to know what he meant.

'I have Luc and . . . and soon I shall have the shop. That is enough. Much more than I deserve. When I think of Louise, disgraced and going from one married man's bed to another's . . .'

'That wasn't forced on her, it was her choice.'

'And Caroline,' Amber continued determinedly. 'You may say that they made their own choices but in many ways their choices were forced on them. I can't bear to think of Luc not existing – a child's life is such a precious gift, Jay. You

384

must feel that with your daughters, but society exacts a terrible price from my sex if we break the rules it imposes. And not just on us – that old saying should be "The sins of the mothers are visited upon their children," not "the sins of the fathers". I don't deny that once I did yearn for the same kind of love in my life as my parents shared, but I know now how rare it is. Even those who marry for love do not always retain it.'

She could not, must not, tell him of those nights when she lay awake longing for someone to hold her, longing to feel her body come alive, longing to know as a woman what she had tasted so briefly with Jean-Philippe as a young girl.

He was leaning towards her. 'Amber—'

'I had better go in.'

Did she sound as flustered as she felt? Would he guess what had been in her thoughts?

He was moving back from her, and saying calmly, 'I'll come with you in case your grandmother has any instructions she wants to give me.'

How close he had come to telling her how he felt, but he must not burden her with his feelings when she already had so much to bear, Jay told himself grimly.

It was, of course, impossible that the bricks and mortar of a house could really reflect the mood of the people who lived within it, and yet Amber could feel the sombreness of the air inside the hall the minute she stepped into it.

'Welcome back, Your Grace.'

'Thank you, Wilson.' Amber smiled at her grandmother's butler before asking, 'Is my grandmother at home?'

'She said to show you up to the library as soon as you arrived,' the butler informed her stiffly.

'Did Mrs Pickford leave any instructions for me, Wilson?' Jay asked.

'No, sir. Only to say that Dr Brookes is coming at four o'clock.'

'Very well then, I shall be in the estate office if anyone wants me.'

He was halfway across the hall when he stopped and then turned back to say to Amber, 'I almost forgot. I saw Maurice yesterday and he is cock-a-hoop about the profits the mill is going to earn from its parachute silk contract. He asked me to tell you that they have also done well with the silk handkerchiefs they produced to commemorate the late King's funeral and that he plans to have more done ahead of the new King's Coronation . . . What's wrong?' he asked when he saw Amber's expression.

'Nothing. That is, I think he should wait a while before doing that. And it might be as well to let the other mills know, as well, although whatever you say will have to be discreet and not too specific.'

Amber could feel Jay looking at her.

'Are you saying that you don't think Edward will be crowned King?'

'I don't know, Jay. He is very attached to Mrs Simpson, you know. Very attached,' she emphasised meaningfully. 'Robert says that the government will never allow him to marry a divorcee and sit on the throne, so he will have to give up one of them. His close friends say that he will not give Wallis up.'

'There hasn't been any comment in the newspapers.'

'No, I know. The press has been persuaded not to write about the matter, but when you see them together . . . She rules him, Jay. She has her supporters, of course, who believe that she is good for him, and who are as vehemently in her favour as those who believe that she has no real feelings for him and is simply using him are opposed to her. There is very little middle ground.'

'And what do you think?'

'I don't know. If the law were changed to allow him to marry a divorcee the problem could be solved but Robert says that simply won't happen.'

'I'll make sure that Maurice knows to hold fire without being too specific, and I'll be in the estate office if you need me for anything.'

A little guiltily Amber admitted to herself that she should be focusing more on her anxiety about Greg than worrying about the Edward and Wallis situation, but because the mill could be involved and the future of its workers, she just couldn't help but be concerned.

She hesitated in the hall, half expecting to see Greg come bounding down the stairs towards her, ready to envelop her in a bear hug just as he had done when they had been young.

'I expect Greg is with his little girl, is he, Wilson?' she asked the butler.

'I really couldn't say, Your Grace,' he responded woodenly. 'I do know, however, that he took the motor out earlier because he had some business in Macclesfield.'

Oh dear, Amber thought ruefully, obviously Greg had offended the servants in some way by taking her grandmother's car.

'Mrs Clements has put you in your usual room,' the butler continued, as he headed for the stairs, his gait stiff and slow. He was getting old, Amber saw, with a small pang.

'There's no need to announce me, Wilson,' she stopped him gently. 'I dare say my grandmother will have heard us arrive and be waiting for me.'

'As you wish, Your Grace. I'll go and tell Mrs Clements you're here. She's made some of your and Master Luc's favourite Bakewell tart.'

'Tell her that I shall look forward to it, Wilson.'

*   *   *

Surely it was only a trick of the light and her grandmother couldn't possibly have shrunk since she had last seen her, Amber thought when Blanche got up from her chair and came over to greet her, holding her at arm's length whilst she proffered her cheek for Amber's dutiful kiss.

If she had, it didn't detract in any way from her habitual elegance. She looked positively regal, Amber thought wryly, her skin virtually unlined even if she did look rather pale. The diamonds in Blanche's engagement ring caught the late afternoon sunlight streaming in through the window. Her grandmother had always had beautifully cared for hands, with long slender fingers, and unblemished white skin.

Amber was conscious that in contrast she probably looked travel-stained and untidy, and she had to resist the impulse to touch her hair to make sure that no rebellious strands had sprung loose.

She had travelled up to Macclesfield on the train wearing one of the outfits she had ordered in Paris, and she was not really surprised when her grandmother looked at it and announced, 'Lanvin. Very useful, no doubt, but rather dull. Black is very hard to wear in the summer sunshine.'

'We've attended so many events where the King has been present that I've grown accustomed to wearing mourning,' Amber explained. 'And besides, one has to think of the smuts and dirt from the train.'

'Some women may have to, Amber, but a woman in your position needs to think more of how her appearance could reflect on her husband's station in life. How is dear Robert?'

'He is very well, Grandmother, and both he and Luc send you their love.' A tender smile briefly curved Amber's mouth at the thought of her son. 'Jay told me about Greg's little girl as he drove me here. Poor little thing.'

'You always were far too sentimental, Amber. The truth

of the matter is that it would have been better if she had died along with her wretched mother.'

'That's a dreadful thing to suggest.'

Blanche gave her a look of irate contempt. 'You would not mind a girl with her heritage marrying Luc, then? Do be sensible, Amber. The girl is neither fish nor fowl, and as such there is no place for her here.'

'Just as there was no place for Caroline Fitton Legh, and her child?' It was too late now to wish the words unsaid or to call them back, but in many ways Amber did not want to do so. Something inside her, some guilt at her own safety compared with Caroline's dreadful fate, needed her to speak up for her.

Blanche turned away from the accusation she could see in Amber's eyes. Amber wouldn't believe her if she told her the truth and said that she had not known about the child that Caroline Fitton Legh had been carrying, and that if she had she would have made it a condition of the money she had given Lord Fitton Legh that he accepted it as his. But then Amber had no reason to understand or accept that that was the truth.

'I would prefer not to have to discuss such an unpleasant subject, but since you have raised it,' Blanche's voice was now very cold, 'and since Cassandra is now married to Caroline's husband, I think it's reasonable to assume that Cassandra had her own reasons for spreading the rumour that the child Caroline was carrying was Greg's. Greg himself knew nothing of any child. You must remember, Amber, that it was Caroline Fitton Legh who inveigled Greg into an affair, not the other way around. As a married woman presumably she knew the risks she was taking. All would have been well if she had not told Cassandra that the child she was carrying was not Fitton Legh's.'

389

Amber could hear irritation and contempt in her grandmother's voice now.

'If Caroline loved Greg perhaps she wanted him to know.'

Blanche drew her breath in sharply. 'She did not love Greg, nor he her. Caroline was a spoiled overemotional young woman who brought her fate on herself.'

'Not just on herself,' Amber pointed out sadly, thinking of the unborn child.

'What is done is done, Amber. And as for this half-caste brat Greg has brought back with him – I have already told him my views. The minute he realised that the woman had stowed herself and the child away on the ship he should have asked the captain to put into the nearest port, not waited for him to discover them and do so, and Greg should have paid their passages back to Hong Kong where they belonged. That way he would have absolved himself from any responsibility towards them and the captain would not have put him ashore with them.'

'Poor Greg,' Amber murmured.

'Greg doesn't need your pity, Amber. He has more than enough of his own to lavish on himself,' said Blanche tartly. 'I am very disappointed in him. He is certainly not the man that his father was.'

It was rare to hear her grandmother speak of her long-dead son, and Amber felt an unusual pang of sympathy for her. The mother of a son herself now, she could well imagine how hard to bear that loss must have been.

'It is unfortunate that Jay summoned Dr Brookes before I had time to assess the situation properly,' Blanche continued. 'Brookes is such a high-minded old fool that it is pointless to suggest to him that it might be best to let nature take its course with the child, instead of trying to save her.'

'That is a dreadful thing to say,' Amber protested, her sympathy banished by her grandmother's callousness.

'On the contrary, it is an eminently sensible thing to say,' Blanche corrected Amber. 'If the child survives what do you suppose her life will be once she is adult? She has her mother's colouring and looks, Amber.'

'She is Greg's daughter and your great-grandchild,' Amber insisted.

'She is a bastard child that Greg fathered on his Chinese mistress, like the fool he is.'

Blanche's face suddenly lost some of her colour and she pressed her hand to her chest.

'What's wrong, Grandmother?' Amber asked anxiously. 'Are you feeling unwell?'

'Of course I'm feeling well. I always feel well. You know that, Amber. I have no time for those women who complain incessantly about their health,' Blanche informed her scathingly.

She might have managed to convince her granddaughter that there was nothing wrong with her, but inwardly Blanche was feeling weak and shocked. She had never previously thought of herself as old but now, with Greg's return and the problems that had brought, she was becoming increasingly aware of her own mortality. Not that she had any intention of saying as much to anyone else. The pain that had struck her so sharply out of nowhere had now thankfully subsided, but the problems that Greg's return had brought her would not subside so easily, Blanche knew, especially if Amber was going to go all sentimental over Greg's child.

After over an hour of questioning about Robert, Luc, Osterby and the shop, her grandmother finally released her, allowing Amber to hurry to the nursery, anxious to see Greg's baby daughter.

Nanny shook her head and tutted disapprovingly when Amber announced her intention, just as though she was still a child in her care, but the nurse Jay had found to look after the little girl was reassuringly young, with a winning smile and a gentle manner.

'What is the little one's name, Betsy?' Amber asked the girl.

'Master Greg said as how she were called Lin Hua, Your Grace. It's supposed to mean Beautiful Jade Flower in Chinese, but Mrs Pickford says she's not having us calling her anything heathen-sounding so Master Greg has said we should call her Rose.'

The little girl was so small that Amber gave a small gasp when she saw her lying beneath all the frills and covers of the ornate old-fashioned cot.

'Coming up for two years old she is and looks more like she's not even half that age,' Betsy complained.

The baby's skin looked so yellow that naming her Rose seemed particularly unkind. Her dark eyes opened, their gaze listless and empty. Her plight aroused all Amber's maternal instincts. She bent down and lifted her from the cot, shocked to realise how little she weighed. At the same age Luc had been a robust healthy little boy who had been walking for many months and who had already been talking. This pathetic little scrap of humanity looked more like a waxen doll than a human child.

'She feels so cold,' she told the nursemaid.

'Aye, Your Grace. Doctor says that's on account of her being so weak. I'm to put fresh hot-water bottles into her bed every four hours, Mr Jay has tekken on another nurse-maid to sit up with her at night.'

'Is she feeding properly?' Amber asked.

'Not what I'd call proper, she isn't,' Betsy said. 'We've got her on boiled water and then just a bit of formula 'cos Dr Brookes reckons that's all her belly can take, but she isn't taking very much formula and what she does, she's bringing up again.'

'Poor little soul, she must feel so alone without her mother and in such a strange place.'

When Amber made to put the little girl back in the cot she gave a small mewling cry of distress.

'She's fair tekken to you, Your Grace,' Betsy smiled. 'I reckon she doesn't want you to put her down. That's the first time I've seen her do that.'

Before Amber could make any comment Dr Brookes arrived. He had been their family doctor for as long as Amber could remember and he smiled warmly when he saw her.

'She's so very thin and small,' Amber sighed as Dr Brookes prepared to weigh Greg's daughter.

'Yes. She's had jaundice very badly at one stage, which is why her skin is so yellow-looking. It will have left her feeling bilious and very poorly. That's very good, Betsy,' he praised the nurse. 'She's put on three ounces . . .'

'Will she be all right?' Amber asked him later as she escorted him back downstairs.

'It's too early to know as yet. She's a fighter, I'll give her that, and she couldn't be in better hands.'

Amber went back to the nursery before dinner, ignoring Nanny's pursed look when she picked Rose up out of the cot. A surge of love for her small niece flooded through Amber as she held her, combined with a tightening of her own womb. She would have loved to have had more children, especially a girl.

The once-familiar smell of baby skin, milk and talcum powder filled her with nostalgia. Luc had been such a good baby, healthy and thriving, and adored by Robert. How quickly those special years went by. Too quickly, Amber recognised a little sadly. She would have loved more children – more babies – but of course that was out of the question.

'What time does Master Greg normally come up to the nursery, Nanny?' Amber asked, desperate to see him.

'Oh, Master Greg doesn't come up here, Your Grace,' Betsy answered.

'And nor should he. Nurseries aren't the place for grown men,' Nanny announced sharply.

'He doesn't have anything to do with little Rose at all really,' Betsy told Amber.

'Babies aren't a gentleman's business,' Nanny said grimly. 'Nor a lady's either, by rights,' she added, glowering at Amber, 'especially when they should be getting themselves dressed for dinner.'

'Yes, Nanny,' Amber apologised dutifully, reluctantly handing Rose to Betsy.

Chapter Thirty-Four

'Greg, are you feeling all right?' It was the second time Amber had had to ask a close member of her family that question within twelve hours, but even though she might be in danger of becoming repetitious, where Greg was concerned even the most uninvolved bystander would surely have recognised the reason for her question.

Greg had been drinking all through dinner, and in truth Amber suspected that he had also been drinking before he had come down – late.

Now they were on their own in their old favourite haunt of the billiard room, and Greg was still drinking, topping up his glass from the gin decanter he had brought with him.

'Of course I'm not bloody well all right,' he answered bitterly. 'God, have you got any cigarettes, Amber? I'm out of mine and I'm dying for a smoke.'

'I'm sorry, I haven't.' She'd never been an enthusiastic smoker and she'd stopped the winter after Luc's birth when both she and Luc had had terrible colds.

Greg threw the billiard cue he'd taken from the rack down onto the baize of the table with such force that Amber winced.

This temper he seemed to have developed, and which he'd displayed more than once over dinner, shocked her almost as much as the change in his physical appearance. Her sunny-natured, handsome cousin had disappeared and a stranger seemed to have taken his place.

The same yellow tinge that coloured baby Rose's skin had turned Greg's sallow and unhealthy-looking. His eyes were bloodshot and his hands unsteady. When he spoke it was in a querulous, self-pitying voice that had had their grandmother's mouth hardening.

'You'd think that any normal grandmother would be pleased and relieved to have her only grandson and heir safely back at home, but then of course, as we both know, our grandmother is not normal in the slightest. Christ, but she's hard, Amber. I mean, whose fault is it that I was in ruddy Hong Kong in the first place? Not mine. She was the one that insisted I go there, and live on a pittance.'

'I thought you wanted to go,' Amber protested. 'You seemed so happy there, especially after you'd met Lionel. You said so in your letters.'

'That was before the treacherous bastard did the dirty on me. If it wasn't for him, I'd be as good as married to Lucy by now and—'

'Lucy? Is that what you called Rose's mother?'

'Me marry that bitch? I wish I'd never met her. Between them, she and ruddy Lionel have ruined my life.'

Amber recoiled from the animosity in Greg's voice. 'I don't understand,' she said. 'What happened?'

By the time Greg had finished telling her the story of his introduction to gambling and the whorehouses of Hong Kong, followed by meeting Lucy and falling in love with her, Amber was feeling both shocked and sickened – by Greg himself every bit as much as by his treacherous friend.

How could it have happened? How could the cousin she had admired and loved become this immoral man who

396

seemed not to have the faintest awareness of his own failings, never mind any sense of shame for them?

'If you love Lucy then perhaps it might have been better to have stayed in Hong Kong and thrown yourself on her mercy,' Amber suggested tentatively.

'She'd have married me if Lionel hadn't turned her against me,' Greg continued, ignoring her comment. 'I'd told her about Grandmother's plans for me and how I'd probably get a title. Well, she won't get to call herself Lady anything married to Lionel, the low-down lying bounder that he is.'

Greg continued complaining and Amber listened to him with growing sadness. 'Now Grandmother's objecting to the fact that I've fathered a child. What the hell did she expect me to do? Live like a monk?'

He had started to sweat heavily, his movements and speech jerky and uncoordinated.

'I think Grandmother was most concerned about your debts, Greg,' Amber told him gently.

'*She* was concerned!' He laughed wildly. 'That's rich. She wasn't concerned enough to send me any money to pay them off, was she? The Chinese love gambling but they hate losers. Do you know what they do over there if you can't pay your gambling debts? They cut off your hands, for a start – finger by finger – and then . . .'

Greg had brought a full decanter of gin into the billiard room but now it was empty, and with a sudden outburst of violence he picked it up and threw it against the wall, sending shards of glass skidding across the parquet floor, as he himself collapsed into a chair, his head in his hands as he began to sob uncontrollably.

'Everything would have been all right if Lucy had married me,' he wept. 'It was Lionel who put Chung Hai up to demanding that I paid him everything I owed him. Lionel knew I couldn't. I had to write those cheques, Amber – I had no choice – and then when Chung Hai started threatening me for forging Henry Jardine's signature unless I signed more cheques I knew I couldn't go on and that I had to get away. Getting that passage cost me every penny I had; ruddy captain ruddy well knew I was desperate and that he could charge me whatever he wanted. I didn't know that stupid bitch had followed me down to the dock and stowed herself away on the ship with the brat.'

'She must have wanted to be with you desperately, Greg.'

'Wanted to make sure that her meal ticket wasn't getting away from her, more like,' Greg snapped viciously.

'Well, at least you've brought little Rose safely home.'

'Do you think that was my choice? Thanks to some ruddy interfering missionaries poking their noses in where they weren't wanted, that was. The brat should have died with her mother.'

'You mean like Caroline's child?' Amber asked him quietly.

For a minute she thought he wasn't going to say anything. His face went dark red and he glared at her, getting up and pushing past her.

'That wasn't my fault. I warned her we needed to be more careful, and that we'd been lucky to get away with the first one,' Greg laughed drunkenly. 'That should please Grandmother, shouldn't it, Fitton Legh's precious son being fathered by a Pickford?'

Amber couldn't move. Greg was so drunk she suspected that he wasn't even properly aware of what he'd said.

'What do you reckon?' he asked Amber. 'Should I tell the old girl?'

'Greg, I don't think . . .'

'You don't think what?' He was getting angry now. 'You don't think I know what I'm talking about, is that it? Well, let me tell you I do. Caroline swore even before the brat was born that it was mine; she claimed Fitton Legh couldn't get it up and never had. No wonder Cassandra's married him – a pair together, they'll be. The brat's mine, Amber.'

Before she went to bed Amber went up to the nursery, apologising to the night nurse, who introduced herself as Betsy's cousin Sheila.

'Little 'un's managed to keep her formula down tonight,' she told Amber in a pleased voice, as she ushered her into the shadowy bedroom, where the little girl lay fast asleep in her cot.

'Our Betsy said as how little Rose really took to you, Your Grace. Missing a mother's touch, she is, I reckon.'

Amber leaned down and touched Rose's cheek tenderly. Her skin felt slightly warmer and less waxen. Poor little thing. Was Greg right? Was Lord Fitton Legh's only son and heir really his child? Whatever the case, Greg must be prevented from saying to anyone else what he had said to her, for the little boy's sake. She would speak to him about it when he was sober and make him promise that he would keep quiet.

Amber had been the only one to come down for breakfast. Greg must be sleeping off what he had drunk last night, and Wilson had informed her that her grandmother had a slight headache and would be down later.

Amber frowned as she left the breakfast room. She couldn't ever remember her grandmother not coming down for breakfast. If this was Blanche's way of showing her disapproval of Greg then her plan had backfired, Amber thought ruefully.

A few minutes in the nursery with Rose, who looked much better this morning and who had actually smiled at her, lifted Amber's spirits, until Dr Brookes arrived and showed her how bowed the little girl's legs were, explaining that it was a sign of rickets and that there was a chance that Rose's wasted leg muscles and bones might never recover properly.

What a dreadful start to her life the poor little thing had had, to have lost her mother so tragically and now to have poor health herself. Amber felt desperately sorry for her. It seemed too cruel and unfair, all the more so because Greg's circumstances should have ensured a better start in life for her. Greg should be ashamed of himself for not treating his mistress and his child better, Amber thought angrily. Surely every child deserved to be loved, but Greg had no love for little Rose. It was hard for her to accept her cousin's behaviour where Rose was concerned, Amber admitted, and just as hard for her to forgive it.

Greg shivered convulsively as he stood in his bathroom. He had just been violently sick, and his head was pounding nauseatingly. He knew from experience that the only thing that would settle both his head and his stomach was a couple of brandies but he also knew that the bottle he had brought upstairs with him last night was empty.

He flushed the lavatory and then realised that he wanted to empty his bladder. The bright sunlight coming in through the window hit his eyeballs like a physical blow, causing him to blink and then look down.

It was still there, and weeping slightly now, red and raw but not painful, one smallish blister, nothing really except that he knew that it was very much something. It hadn't been there when he'd left Hong Kong and he hadn't seen anything on that girl he'd had that last night, but then he hadn't really looked; hadn't been in any state to look either.

He'd got bloody Jardine to thank for putting the fear of God into him by insisting that the ruddy medic went through chapter and verse with him about the risks of fucking brothel girls shortly after his arrival in Hong Kong.

He could always ask old Brookes to take a look at it, of course, and put his mind at rest. Bound to be nothing important, just a bit of chafing. But then he'd look a fool, and Brookes was such an old woman he'd be running off to his grandmother before he knew where he was. Better not to say anything. Nothing to say, really. Just a bit of raw skin. Not a chance, not *that*, at all . . . He was going to throw up again.

'I feel so guilty about Rose,' Amber told Jay.

They were in the drawing room of the Dower House, Amber having called there to see Jay's children, who had been brought down from the nursery to say hello to her but had now been whisked away by their nurse. She hadn't expected Jay to be at home, and nor had she expected the thrill of pleasure she had felt when she learned that he was.

'I could have done so much more. Sent Greg more money, for one thing.'

'And if you had, do you really believe that he would have spent it on his mistress and their child?'

'You were right to warn me that he has changed, Jay,' Amber acknowledged sadly. 'I hardly recognise him as the Greg I knew. One minute he is in the most dreadful temper and the next . . .' she sighed. 'He's drinking far more than can be good for him. What is it, why do you look like that?' she demanded worriedly.

'I don't want to add to your concern, Amber, but I suspect that gambling isn't the only addiction Greg has developed whilst he's been in Hong Kong.'

'Addiction?'

'Wilson has told me that from what Greg's new valet has said, it could be that Greg may be smoking opium. Dr Brookes

401

certainly seems to think it's a possibility. We haven't said anything to your grandmother yet.'

'Opium?'

Amber was no longer the naïve girl she had once been. The Mitford sisters might giggle mock wide-eyed about white-slave traders giving innocent girls opium and shipping them out of the country, but it was no secret that there were those in society, both men and women, who were addicted to cocaine, especially members of the young fast set.

'If he could stop taking it and stop drinking, he could get better, though, couldn't he?'

'He could,' Jay agreed so cautiously that Amber guessed that Jay didn't think that Greg would ever stop.

How cruel life was. Who would ever have thought that Greg, with his easy charm and his exuberance, doted on by their grandmother and with an enviable future to look forward to, would be dragged down into such a dreadful and damaging way of life?

'If he hadn't gone to Hong Kong,' she began to defend him, but Jay shook his head.

'I'm afraid the weakness lies with Greg himself, Amber, not his circumstances.'

It seemed disloyal to admit it but Amber knew in her heart that Jay was right.

'It's not too late for him to change.'

'If he wishes to do so,' Jay agreed.

'You don't think he will, do you, Jay?'

'I don't know, Amber. At the moment when I look at Greg what I see is a selfish man filled with pity for himself.'

Amber couldn't deny the truth of this.

'I'm worried about little Rose,' she admitted. 'Grandmother hates her, and Greg obviously cannot be relied on to be a proper father to her. Betsy and Sheila are excellent, but if they were to leave for any reason, she'd be so vulnerable. I'd take her home with me but . . .'

'I promise you that nothing will happen to her,' Jay assured her. 'I shall watch over her as carefully as though she were my own, and I shall keep you informed of her progress, you have my word on that.'

'Oh, Jay, you are so very, very good.' Tears were burning the backs of Amber's eyes and she had to blink them away. 'I don't know what I would do without you; you've been so wonderfully kind and helpful.' She mustn't say any more. She would embarrass him and, more dangerously, betray those feelings she should not have. 'I had hoped to see Lydia,' she told him, changing the subject.

'I'm afraid that won't be possible. I had to call Dr Brookes out late last night. Sometimes when she isn't well she talks about harming herself because she thinks she is so worthless. I try to reassure her that that's nonsense but to be honest I think my presence makes the situation worse, not better. Dr Brookes sedated her and she's still sleeping now.'

'Jay, I am so very sorry.' Overcome with remorse at having burdened him with her own problems when he already had so much to cope with, Amber touched his arm in a tender gesture of sympathy. 'And all this as well. You have enough of your own to deal with.'

'No, I'm glad that you did. Your understanding and kindness mean so much to me.'

He had hardly slept last night. Lydia had been particularly violent before she had sunk into the morbid desire to punish herself that usually followed one of her outbursts of temper. She had gouged the flesh of his chest with her fingernails, leaving deep scratches that still stung. Amber's presence, normally such a balm to his troubled heart, today only made it ache all the more.

'*You* mean so much to me, Amber. So very, very much.

More in fact than I know to be wise.' He tried to stem the words but it was too late; they were said, betraying him and, worse, embarrassing Amber.

Jay's voice, thick and strained, echoed what was in her own heart, Amber admitted, as they looked at one another in the heavy silence. She should leave now because if she didn't . . . but she could see in Jay's eyes what was mirrored in her own; and that shared knowledge had changed the texture of the silence, informing it with a thousand subtle unspoken hopes and promises.

It had lain there between them for so very long, unacknowledged, and dangerous, and now it was out in the open. Desire, once experienced, could never be forgotten, and the years during which she had grown from a girl to a woman had deepened her own sensuality. She didn't need to wonder how she would react if Jay were to touch her – she knew, and that knowing made her want that touch all the more.

She wanted him. She wanted Jay fiercely and passionately, touching her, tasting her, filling her senses in every single way. There was a dull ache low in her body, a need so intense that it felt like a cry of longing inside her.

She must leave. She started to turn away from him but then turned back and crossed the dividing line she had sworn she would never cross.

She was in Jay's arms, her heart thudding rapturously against his flesh, her senses giddily, greedily snatching at everything they could to fill themselves with the reality of him. She wound her arms round his neck, kissing him every bit as fiercely as he was kissing her. It was like the sun's heat after the coldness of winter, hope after despair, life after death, the whole purpose of her own creation.

'I have wanted to hold you like this for so long,' Jay told her huskily.

'And I you,' Amber whispered back.

She couldn't stop wanting to touch him, wanting to know him, wanting the wonder of this intimacy after the desert of the years without it. And she wanted so much more. She wanted to lie with him in shadowed privacy so that she could know all of him.

'I want you so much.' There, she had said it, and to hell with the consequences.

'I want you more, and have done for longer,' Jay told her in response.

She laughed shakily and touched her fingertips to his mouth, closing her eyes against the intense surge of pleasure that filled her when he caught hold of her hand and kissed her fingertips one by one.

'We shouldn't . . .' she began.

'No,' he agreed, but he was still holding her hand.

'Jay, kiss me again,' she begged him.

Being held in his arms was every bit as wonderful as she had known it would be. Being with him felt like coming home, and she—

'Well, and what's going on here? Or need I ask?'

They had sprung apart the moment they had heard Cassandra's voice but of course it was too late and she had seen them.

'I'm surprised at you, Jay, when poor Lydia is so very ill, but of course the Pickfords have always had a habit of stealing other people's spouses and destroying marriages.'

Amber wanted to recoil from her words as though they were blows, and protect herself from them, but how could she when they were so well deserved? She had no defence against what she had done – none at all. She felt sick with shame and guilt. Lydia was so very ill, and here she was behaving in such a shameful way with Lydia's husband, indulging in the kind of behaviour she would have despised and denounced in someone else.

The serpent had entered their Eden, bringing with it the guilt Amber knew she would have to bear for the rest of her life.

How could she have let such a thing happen? For Jay it was different. He was a man whose wife could not play her true part in their marriage, a man burdened with the care of a sick wife, who must, like all healthy men, have his needs.

It had been her duty and her responsibility to stop him, no matter what her own feelings were, no matter how tumultuous and tormented, how overpowering and compelling. But she had not done so, and now she must pay the price for that most terrible transgression.

Chapter Thirty-Five

'. . . And if we drape the silk over the chair like this – Amber?' Cecil Beaton demanded a little crossly, calling Amber back from the private nightmare of her own guilty thoughts.

Cecil had come to take the photographs for the shop's first *Vogue* advertisement. He was so much in demand professionally that it would have been impossible for her to commission him if he hadn't been a friend, and here she was wasting his time because of her own guilt over what had happened with Jay.

'Yes, yes, that looks perfect.'

She must stop thinking about what had happened. After all, all the thinking about it in the world couldn't put right the wrong she had done. Guilt scalded through her. Cassandra may have accused them both but she was the one who was to blame. She was the one who had prolonged the kiss, the one who had wanted more . . .

Cassandra had positively gloated at having discovered them, and Amber feared that she would gossip about what she had seen, even though she had stated that her concern for 'poor darling Lydia' meant that she would never speak of the incident again. It could damage her own reputation if Cass did gossip, there was no doubt about that, but Amber doubted that the sophisticated set she and Robert moved in would be too concerned. Discreet affairs were, after all, very much the accepted thing. No, what really concerned her was the effect learning what had happened could have on Lydia, whose state of mind was so delicately balanced. Amber hated the thought of causing an innocent person distress. Would Cass keep what she had seen to herself to protect Lydia, or had she simply been toying with them, whilst planning all the time to say publicly what she had seen? Amber had never imagined that she would be in such a shameful situation; it went against everything she believed in. She had broken her own most sacred moral vows. How angry her grandmother was going to be if Cass did say something, let down by both her grandchildren. Amber would have to make sure that Blanche did not blame Jay in any way.

She must stop thinking about it; the damage was already done; there was nothing she could do. They *were* in Cass's hands, no matter how much she disliked that fact.

The shop had been 'dressed' for Cecil to photograph. In the foreground of the window was a chair painted as Amber had envisaged in the same soft grey as the interior, a bolt of the most beautiful black silk embroidered with gold laurel wreaths – one of her father's designs – thrown apparently carelessly over the chair. In the background there were two half-columns, Corinthian in style, one topped by a bust wearing a laurel wreath crown, the other topped by a weathered metal candelabra with white candles, through which Amber had trailed cascading ivy. As a final touch – and Cecil's idea – a plump baby with red-gold hair, borrowed for the photograph from his mother, one of the outworker seamstresses, who had arrived with some soft furnishings and who was now watching anxiously as her son, dressed all in white and wearing a laurel wreath on his curls, sat on the floor surrounded by the silk, grinning gummily and happily up at her. Amber just hoped he wouldn't be sick on the silk, although she admitted that the whole thing did make an attractive eye-catching picture.

She should be glad that Cassandra had seen them. The humiliation and guilt she had felt was a just punishment. And the loss of her best friend – was that a just punishment as well?

She hadn't heard from Jay since she'd returned to London, nor had she made any attempt to contact him. How could she after what had happened? Her guilt haunted and tormented her.

Before 'it' had happened, though, he'd promised he would write to her to keep her updated on Rose's progress. Over and above her own personal feelings, Amber felt that she had a moral responsibility to keep a check on the health of the little girl – a mother's responsibility on behalf of a mother who was not there to watch over her own little one. She could not abdicate from that responsibility just because of her own feelings. What about Jay, though? Would he still do as he had said and write to her about Rose? Or would he feel that it was better that he severed all contact with her? If he did, could she bear it? He was her closest and best friend, the only person she could rely on and confide in. How foolish she had been to sacrifice that for a few minutes of passion. A lifetime's friendship undone with a single kiss.

'Sylvester, sweetest, do move out of my light.'

Cecil's new assistant pouted and tossed his blond curls.

'I was in Paris last week,' Cecil told Amber. 'Robert's young friend Otto was very much in evidence, squiring around a couple of hefty Brünnhildes. I can understand why poor Robert was smitten. The boy has such a very dangerous allure, soo challenging and exciting. I was rather tempted to try my own chances.'

'Oh, Cecil, you mustn't,' Amber protested. 'Robert would be so hurt. Otto was dreadfully unkind to him, you know.'

'Yes, I do know,' Cecil grinned at her. 'Robert's friendship means more to me than a casual affair. I was just joking. I take it Robert is still keen to attend the Olympics?'

'Yes, Robert says it would be a shame if Luc were to miss seeing them. He thinks that the trip will be good for Luc.'

'The Olympics will certainly be good for Herr Hitler's propaganda machine,' Cecil agreed. 'The powers that be must be regretting the fact that Germany has been allowed to stage the Games now that Hitler and his right-wing politics have become so powerful. The Jewish lobby are already up in arms.'

'With good reason, surely?' Amber pointed out.

It was in many ways a relief to turn her thoughts to bigger problems than her own. The dreadful plight of the Jewish people caught up in Hitler's anti-Semitic rulings had to appal anyone with the least shred of compassion and humanity. Amber couldn't understand how anyone could not feel outraged by Hitler's dreadful plans, much less support them, but shockingly there were those in Britain who did have and encourage anti-Semitic feelings. Amber knew how her parents would have felt. They would have been amongst the first to stand up and state their support for anyone being downtrodden and treated badly.

'I rather think the general public is more interested in Unity Mitford's crush on the Führer than the Jewish lobby,' Cecil told her.

'So amusing and preposterous. Of course, Diana and Tom Mosley are bound to be going. Herr von Ribbentrop has been very busy issuing invitations to everyone and anyone he thinks influential, now that it looks as though he's to be Germany's next ambassador to Britain. Sadly, though, whilst you are obliged to watch handsome young men showing off their muscles, I shall be working. Still, at least when you return you'll have all the excitement of the shop opening.'

'I don't know about it being exciting, Cecil. I'm dreadfully nervous. What if no one likes it or—'

'My dear girl, of course they will like it. They will love it. How could they not do so once they have seen *Vogue*? My photograph will fill them with longing to fill their houses with your fabrics.'

Amber laughed. She wished she had Cecil's confidence, but then he was such a showman, always playing to the crowd, and his admirers.

Chapter Thirty-Six

Jay looked down at the letter he had spent most of the morning trying to write.

'You asked me to keep you informed as to Rose's progress, and I am delighted to be able to tell you that Dr Brookes says that she is improving all the time. You may also want to know that—'

That what? That I miss you and ache for you? That I am sorry for exposing you to Cassandra's venom? That holding you, instead of satisfying me, has left me with an unbearable longing for more? That it really would be better if we no longer corresponded, for your own sake? That I cannot bear to relinquish this precious contact with you, even though in doing so I am betraying you and my marriage vows just as much as though I were holding you naked in my arms?

Jay, who seldom swore, cursed savagely beneath his breath, screwing up the letter and throwing it onto the fire. It was at times like this that he most missed his grandfather's old dog. A dog was an excellent confidant for those things that could never be said to human ears.

Cassandra was, of course, gloating triumphantly at having the upper hand. They both knew that she would use that advantage mercilessly quite simply for the sheer pleasure of doing so.

It was a damnable situation, made worse by the fact that

Lydia's health made it all the more vital that she shouldn't find out what had happened. He should never have married Lydia, Jay knew, but he had, and having done so he had a moral duty to protect her. She was the mother of his children. But her emotional wellbeing was so precariously balanced.

Sometimes all it took to throw her into deep depression was the fact that one of the girls might not wish to sit on her lap, and yet on other occasions she would flatly refuse to have anything to do with them, turning her face away from them and behaving as though they didn't exist.

In the same way she would weep and tell him that she hated him and that being married to him was like being in a prison, but would then claim that she loved him so much that she couldn't live without him, and beg him to say that he loved her, crying inconsolably until he did.

Perhaps for Amber's own sake it would be best if he simply wrote and told her that from now on he was going to ask Dr Brookes to give her regular reports on Rose's progress. They needed to distance themselves from one another, for Amber's sake and for the sake of his children and their mother. Out of sight out of mind was what they said, wasn't it? But no matter how long he went without seeing Amber, Jay knew that his feelings for her would never change and that, if anything, they could only grow stronger. That must be his private burden to bear, though. He had no intention of sharing it with anyone else, least of all Amber herself. Her happiness mattered far more to him than his own, and it saddened him that someone so deserving of love and happiness in her marriage should have been so deprived of them.

'And you do really love me?'

'My darling one, of course I do, and all the more so at times like this,' Cassandra responded softly to her lover.

413

The other woman turned her head and smiled at Cassandra, stetching her naked body in the languorous aftermath of their shared pleasure. Her flesh, olive-tinted and smooth, smelled, like the room, of sex.

The room was Cassandra's own special playground and she had made it hers in the early days of her marriage to John Fitton Legh. It was high up at the top of the Gothic tower that had been added to the hall by an eighteenth-century ancestor. The servants swore the tower was haunted and Cassandra had encouraged that belief, knowing she could use it to her advantage.

Strange how things worked out. The room itself might have been made for her purposes. The large four-poster bed was carved with masked figures and images of mythical horned beasts. She had had it draped in a fabric she had heard about from a friend who had intimately 'known' Violet Trefusis and Vita Sackville-West. The gold pattern on the red background depicted the legend of the 'fake part' Daedalus had carved for the daughter of King Midas so that she might satisfy her lust.

How Cassandra had envied Vita and Violet. Before her marriage she had spent many hours imagining herself a voyeur of their pleasures. How silly she had been then. Far better to experience the pleasure for oneself, although there were times when the role of voyeur was pleasurable; like the time she had caught John with one of the housemaids. They hadn't been married then. He had been struggling so, poor man, his member already limp before he had realised she was there. So foolish of him to try to take the girl where he could be so easily surprised. Of course, he had begged her not to betray him. And she had agreed that she would say nothing – once they were married.

He had told her that he couldn't be a proper husband to her; his taste ran to servant girls.

Cassandra had assured him that it didn't matter. It was marriage she wanted, not a husband. He had been reluctant to agree but she had soon convinced him otherwise, and as a reward, on the night of their marriage she had invited him to watch whilst she pleasured the poor servant girl he had not been able to satisfy. How shocked he had been, and then how excited.

They had enjoyed several similarly pleasing interludes over the years. Away from home naturally; servants gossiped and that first servant girl had been paid off to follow the career she had always wanted on the stage.

Of course, he would never know the triumph it gave her to watch him gazing lasciviously and helplessly at the naked body of the woman she was enjoying, knowing he was incapable of joining in.

The few months they spent in London every year produced a rich harvest of introductions. A little light lovemaking with another woman was positively fashionable, and Cassandra quickly learned to discard those who only wanted to play at pretending to want her and to cherish those who would give her the best return on her attentions.

A London flirtation followed by an invitation to Fitton Hall had brought her several outstandingly delicious periods of indulgence, but none of those pleasures could come anywhere near the pleasure she was having now with her latest lover. How exciting it had been to seduce her, knowing who she was. Cassandra had made up her mind to pursue her right from the start. Initially, though, she had been tiresomely oblivious to all her hints about the Sapphic pleasures they could share.

However, Cassandra had been prepared to wait. And now that patience had been rewarded, the trap had been baited and sprung, and now Lydia was hers.

The deterioration of Lydia's mental state had made her

vulnerable and excitable, easily aroused to a furious anger against Jay, that Cassandra had become adept at turning into physical passion and abandonment.

Slowly, carefully and with intense pleasure, she had introduced Lydia to all her own special enjoyments, revelling in the dark mystique of their debauchery.

One of Cassandra's favourite pleasures was to punish her lovers for any disobedience, sometimes quite violently, although she had had to hold back a little on this with Lydia, who was so inclined to become hysterical at times. Even so, Cassandra had managed to progress from simply spanking Lydia's bare behind to striking it more forcefully with a soft whip of knotted ribbons that did not break the skin whilst still causing the person to whom it was applied to cry out for mercy, and so aroused Cassandra's own passions.

Cassandra could remember quite vividly the first time she had realised that physical violence aroused her. She had been twelve years old at the time, and on holiday from school. Her mother had sent her to deliver some honey from her bees to the Misses Barnett, two spinster sisters who lived quietly in genteel poverty in a small house in the local town, and were stalwarts of the church flower-arranging rota.

Cassandra had knocked on the front door and then when her knock had not been answered she had gone round to the back door, intending to make use of the key everyone knew was left under a plant pot, to leave the honey in their kitchen.

Only once she was inside the house, the sounds coming from upstairs had so fascinated her that Cassandra hadn't been able to resist creeping quietly up to look.

The door to the main bedroom had been open and there had been the elder Miss Barnett's well upholstered and totally naked bottom fully on view as she crouched on the bed whilst her sister beat her with a thin cane that drew dark red weals on her white flesh.

Whilst the younger Miss Barnett berated her sister and demanded that she acknowledge her sin, the elder groaned and screamed, begging both for more punishment and its cessation.

Cassandra had been fascinated – and aroused. This was what that feeling was all about that came to her sometimes when she was in bed at night – only this was a hundred times better. Greedily her senses stored everything they were absorbing, including the moment when the younger Miss Barnett ceased to beat her sister and instead produced a strange-looking 'thing', which she thrust vigorously into 'that place' below the elder Miss Barnett's exposed buttocks where Cassandra could see the dark tuft of hair growing above the fleshy lips, pushing it in and out whilst the elder Miss Barnett groaned and screamed even louder for 'more' before collapsing on the bed with a single moan of pleasure.

What she had seen had been a revelation for Cassandra, the beginning of the journey that had brought her to where she was now. Of course, she had confronted the Misses Barnett with what she had seen, and of course she had had to punish them for their sins. A lascivious smile spread Cassandra's lips now as she felt the familiar wetness taking possession of her. She had enjoyed some very happy and profitable times with the Misses Barnett. But that was the past. This was the present.

John was away in London at the moment but when he returned Cassandra intended to put on a very special show for him. She had been learning to take photographs and she had set up a darkroom in one of the attics.

Lydia had burst into tears the first time Cassandra had

417

shown her one of the photographs she had taken of her, causing Cassandra to laugh and reassure her.

'But no one will know it is you because I haven't photographed your face after all.' She had paused then before adding with deliberate cruelty, 'I dare say, though, that Jay will recognise you.'

Lydia had screamed at her then and attacked her, clawing at her naked flesh. Cassandra had retaliated by clawing back and biting, in the intensity of their shared mutual arousal. That had been the first time that Lydia had allowed her to use the dildo she had only previously shown her, to its full effect.

It made her so happy to know how deeply she was damaging Jay. She had sworn after all that she would do so, and now she had the added excitement of knowing that he wanted Amber. Oh, he might not have said so, but she knew Jay. He would not have been kissing her like that if he didn't. Poor Jay. He was *totally* at her mercy now.

She leaned across the bed and put her hand on Lydia's mound, smiling as Lydia flinched a little. It added such a delicious edge to things when pleasure came with pain.

'I'll drive you home,' she told Lydia, and then smiled teasingly at her. 'Oh, and didn't I promise you a small gift?'

Lydia's eyes lit up. She was like a child in many ways, Cassandra thought contemptuously, easily pleased with some small trinket.

'What is it? What have you got me?' Lydia demanded.

Cassandra went over to the dressing table, unlocking one of the drawers with the key that hung on a fine chain around her neck.

'These,' she told Lydia, turning round and displaying a pair of handcuffs. When Lydia's face fell she explained, 'They are gold and set with diamonds, and look, when you unscrew the chain that links them you can wear them as bangles.'

They had been made to her own design and Cassandra was very pleased with them.

'I shall show you how they work and the fun we can have with them next time,' she promised Lydia. Locking them away again, she gave her a wicked smile.

Chapter Thirty-Seven

Berlin was every bit as grandly Teutonic as Amber had anticipated. The uniforms, jackbooted marching and zealous saluting set her teeth on edge but what she had found even harder to deal with was the eager hero worship of Hitler from a group of British pro-Nazi supporters, which included Unity Mitford and her sister Diana, although it was a relief to her that Robert was once again inclined to be rather sardonic about and unimpressed by Adolf Hitler. She had guessed that his brief enthusiasm had been brought about by his relationship with Otto, and whilst it still troubled her that Robert, whom she had always considered to be his own man, had been so ready to slavishly adopt the beliefs of his young lover, Amber knew there was no point in referring to her concern.

On the surface they still got on as well with one another as they had always done, but beneath that surface there were tensions, some of them her fault, Amber knew. No longer was she a naïve girl willing to follow Robert's lead in everything and in need of his guidance and advice, ready to look up to him and put him on a pedestal. She was a woman now, running her own business and her own life, and although he didn't say so, Amber suspected that Robert sometimes resented that. Although he had given way over the shop, Amber knew that he had never really wanted her to go ahead with it. Owning and running a shop – a business – wasn't something an aristocrat did, and by choosing to do so she had, Amber knew, put herself outside the narrow confines of what was and what was not acceptable for a woman in her position.

But she was not an aristocrat, she was herself, the daughter of a gifted artist and the great-granddaughter of a successful merchant, and she was proud of that. She wanted to be a good wife to Robert, of course, but she wanted to be herself as well, instead of allowing herself to be swallowed up and diminished by making herself into something she wasn't to fit in with people who would despise her no matter what she did to try to appease them.

She did miss the frank political conversations she and Robert had enjoyed, though. Robert was well informed and she respected his views – when they were his views and not those of his current lover. The situation with the Mitfords was a case in point.

'I shouldn't worry about it,' Robert had told her when she had mentioned the Mitfords. 'From what I've heard, even her precious Führer regards Unity as a fool, whilst Diana, of course, is obliged to support the Nazis because of Tom Mosley.'

'Unity may be a fool, Robert, but that just makes it easier for the Nazi regime to use her devotion to Hitler as propaganda,' Amber had retaliated. 'I mean, look at the way she's so very friendly with the Goebbels. I can't help wishing we hadn't come here. It seems wrong and it makes me feel uncomfortable.'

'You have to admit that the opening celebrations for the Games were quite magnificent and faultlessly planned,' Robert commented now, well aware of how reluctant she had been to come to Munich.

'To the point of military precision,' Amber agreed drily.

'All those terribly hearty Aryan young women . . .' She still wasn't happy about the way in which Robert had deliberately used Luc's innocent enthusiasm for this trip to emotionally blackmail her into agreeing to it, by saying that she could stay behind and that he and Luc would come on their own. He had known perfectly well that she would not countenance that.

'I can see that you are determined that nothing about either Berlin, the Führer or his Games is going to please you,' Robert teased her lightly.

'Did you honestly expect that it would?' Amber asked. 'I'm sorry, Robert, but I just can't help thinking that beneath all this outward wholesomeness lies something very unwholesome indeed. One only has to think of the Nazi treatment of the Jews. Some of the comments being made at the dinner Herr Goering gave last night were unforgivable and loathsome. I would have walked out if I could. I actually heard Unity boasting about the fact that she is living in an apartment in Munich that belonged to a Jewish family.'

'I agree with you, but there is nothing we can do, and I would caution you not to speak your mind in public, Amber.'

Robert didn't need to give her any warnings. In addition to feeling uncomfortable in Munich, Amber also felt vaguely uneasy and even a little afraid. She would be glad when they could leave, despite the undoubted magnificence of everything.

There was no doubt that the Germans were determined to impress. The previous evening the guests had been entertained by a ballet company, who had danced in the moonlight for them. Afterwards they had enjoyed a *fête champêtre*.

Tonight they were attending a party given by Herr and

422

Frau Goebbels, which was to be held on an island on Wannsee Lake, which Amber knew the Mitford sisters were bound to attend. She had felt extremely awkward talking with Diana, whom she had initially admired so much but from whom she now felt alienated.

'I shall be so glad when we go home, Robert. Luc complained that he felt sick earlier, and I really wish we didn't have to go to this party tonight.'

'If Luc feels sick it is probably because of all the ice cream he has consumed. He will be perfectly comfortable with Gladys to look after him. It will look decidedly odd if we don't go, now that we've arranged to meet up with the Channons and the British Ambassador.'

Amber sighed. Of course Robert was right. As ever, appearances were what counted. Robert had claimed when they had first clashed over this visit that they had a duty to observe what was happening in Munich, and that her own reactions were too emotional.

'So no more ice cream tomorrow, then, old chap,' Robert warned Luc mock sternly.

They had gone into his room to say good night to him before leaving for the party, and whilst Luc still looked pale, Gladys, the nursery maid they had brought with them from Eaton Square, had assured them both that he had eaten his supper.

Amber gave Luc an extra hug. He would be starting at Robert's old prep school in September, and Robert's old trunk had already been brought down from Osterby, Luc's name inscribed inside the lid underneath Robert's, whilst Luc had watched, almost bursting with pride and excitement that were comparable only with Robert's.

Amber hated the thought of such a young boy going to boarding school but Robert had assured her that it was the norm and that Luc would enjoy his schooldays every bit as much as he had done. Luc himself certainly seemed to be looking forward to his new life, but she would miss him dreadfully. Life would feel so empty without him there.

She longed to write to Jay and tell him everything that she had seen and experienced since their arrival in Germany, but she couldn't. Although nothing had been said between them, their letters to one another had changed and were now the brief, almost uncomfortable letters of strangers, or the guilt-ridden, and hurt in some ways more than if they had not communicated with one another at all. At least that way she could have pretended that things were still the same; this way she was forced to accept that she had lost the precious friendship they had shared.

'Come along, darling, otherwise we shall be late.'

'It's all right, Mummy. I'm feeling much better now,' Luc assured her solemnly.

Robert was standing by the open door, obviously impatient to be gone. Reluctantly Amber went to join him. She wasn't enjoying herself one bit. She didn't like the atmosphere in Germany and she yearned for home, for her shop, and most of all for Jay – and that, of course, was a forbidden yearning . . .

In order to reach the island where the party was being held, guests had to cross pontoons strung from the shore, illuminated by torches held aloft by lines of Nazi 'maidens', as the girls' equivalent of the Hitler Youth Movement was called.

'So dreadfully intimidating,' Robert drawled to Chips Channon, with whom they were standing.

'The upraised arms, you mean?'

'No, the bared teeth.'

'Robert,' Amber objected, under the cover of Henry Channon's laughter, 'someone might hear you.'

424

'Yes, my dear,' Henry Channon agreed warningly, 'you must take care. Hitler is vehemently opposed to gentlemen of a certain sexual persuasion, you know, which is no doubt why he torments them with all those golden youths in leather boots.'

The evening was every bit as difficult as Amber had feared.

They had lost the Channons somewhere in the crowd and were now with the von Ribbentrops, who had greeted them very cordially, plainly delighted with their Führer and their country, and expecting everyone else to be impressed.

Amber was just about to make a discreet excuse to escape from them when Joseph Goebbels and his wife came over, surrounded by a small posse of aggressive-looking SS men.

Because Amber had already been warned about Joseph Goebbels' womanising tendencies, and because she could see the blatant manner in which he was visually assessing her, she moved closer to his wife, Magda.

She was listening to Magda telling her about her children when she looked up and, to her dismay, right in front of them and only a few yards away she spied Otto.

There was no mistaking him, nor his open air of arrogance, Amber thought bitterly. He was with two men, neither of whom possessed his stupendous good looks, and who were both considerably older than he. Amber's stomach cramped with anxiety. She wanted desperately to get Robert away but it was impossible to interrupt Magda's monologue about the virtues of her many offspring.

One look at Robert's face told her that he too had spotted Otto. Robert had gone as white as a sheet, apart from two spots of colour burning high on his cheekbones. It was too late for them to flee now. Far too late, in fact, as Joseph Goebbels was already introducing the newcomers to them.

'The duke and I have already met,' Otto announced

dismissively, refusing to shake Robert's extended hand, and then deliberately turning his back on him and engaging one of the other men in conversation.

It was an obvious and deliberate snub, and Amber didn't know what would have happened if it hadn't been for the commotion caused by Unity's sudden appearance and her gushing account of how wonderful the Games were.

Joseph Goebbels smirked as he listened to her, patting her on her arm and then introducing her to Otto, who clicked his heels together and bowed over her hand.

'It is so good to see an English person who is free from the taint of decadence that marks out so many of your countrymen,' Amber heard Otto telling Unity fulsomely. 'I hope you will allow me to invite you to join me for dinner one evening.'

He was still holding her hand, whilst Robert's hands were clenched so tightly that Amber could see his knuckles gleaming palely through his skin.

When Unity laughed and took a step closer to Otto, for one horrible moment Amber thought that Robert might actually step in between them and physically force them apart. Robert looked like a man undergoing torture, his eyes burning in his set face.

'Robert, I'd really like to go back to the hotel and check on Luc,' Amber announced, putting her hand on Robert's arm as she hurriedly made an excuse for them to leave without causing any gossip.

'Our son hasn't been feeling very well,' she told Magda.

'Then of course you must be with him. I know how I worry when one of my six isn't well. I'll arrange for a car to take you back to Munich.'

'That really is kind of you. Thank you.'

Robert had not spoken since he had seen Otto. There was a blank look in his eyes now. No, not a *blank* look,

Amber amended. It was more the look of a man who had been dealt a mortal body blow. And yet she could sense his reluctance to go with her.

Otto was walking away now, and Robert had turned his head and was desperately looking in that direction. Amber tightened her hold on his arm to restrain him, fearing that he might actually go after Otto, but to her relief he allowed her to draw him away towards the pontoons.

He still hadn't spoken, and nor did he speak on the drive back to the hotel, withdrawing into himself and his pain in such a way that Amber could almost feel it surrounding him like a cold shroud.

At least Luc was feeling much better, Amber acknowledged wearily, as she lay back against her pillows. She had dismissed her maid, intending to read for half an hour before going to sleep, but now as she glanced at the dressing table and saw it lying there, she realised that she had forgotten to ask Martha to give her jewellery to Robert's valet to lock safely away.

She might never really have liked the very grand ruby and diamond set that had been Robert's grandmother's, but they were family heirlooms. Getting out of bed, Amber pulled on her cream satin peignoir, deciding that she may as well take the jewellery to Robert herself as disturb her maid.

When no one answered her knock on the communicating door between their hotel bedrooms, Amber opened it. Robert had obviously dismissed his valet, Hulme, for the night. The bedroom was illuminated only by the bedside lights, but the bathroom door was open and a light on inside it.

Not wanting to intrude, Amber called out hesitantly, 'Robert, it's me. I forgot to tell Martha to give Hulme the rubies, so I've brought them to you myself. I'll leave them on your tallboy.'

She put down the jewellery boxes and was just about to leave when she heard a noise from the bathroom. It sounded as though something metal had been dropped on the marble floor almost immediately followed by the sound of something heavier hitting the floor with a dull soft thud.

Immediately she ran to the bathroom and pushed the door wide open.

Robert had collapsed onto the floor, and blood was oozing from a cut across the wrist of his outflung arm. Oozing, not gushing, Amber noted in sick relief, as her brain raced ahead of her emotions and her own limbs, assimilating facts, adding them together, and coming to a conclusion that had her heart sinking to the pit of her stomach at the same time as she was reaching for the telephone receiver.

Within half an hour Robert was safely in bed, his cut wrist bandaged. Hulme has been called and together they had concocted a story about Robert having had an accident, caused when he had forgotten about an upturned razor and put his hand out to reach for some soap. His subsequent fall had been caused by the shock.

The doctor, whose English had been good enough to deal with the situation but not fluent enough for him to be able to question Robert too much, had cleaned and bandaged the cut, explaining to Amber that it was little more than a scratch, whilst the lump that had formed on Robert's head meant that his contact with the marble floor would not result in anything worse than an extremely bad headache.

Amber felt that the doctor suspected that Robert's 'accident' had been the result of carelessness having had too much to drink. She was warned to keep an eye on Robert and to get in touch with the doctor immediately should

Robert start vomiting or showing signs of having lost his wits.

Robert, who had been conscious whilst the doctor had been speaking to Amber, had announced shortly after that he was fully in possession of his wits, and intended to remain in possession of them.

Had Robert really intended to take his own life? Amber wondered worriedly later, sitting at the side of his bed whilst he slept. She and Hulme were taking it in terms to sit with him, ostensibly to keep a lookout for the warning signs of concussion the doctor had mentioned. In fact, without it being said openly by either of them, Amber knew they were both conscious of the reality of what Robert had tried to do and the necessity of preventing him trying again.

Once again here was evidence, if she had needed it, of the terrible things that love could do to a person, the havoc and despair it could wreak.

Amber looked down at Robert. Poor Robert to have felt, as he must have done, that his pain was such that he could no longer endure it. She reached across the smooth coverlet and took hold of her husband's hand, holding it tenderly in her own. From now on, she would ensure Otto wasn't allowed near him.

'Robert, I really think we should go home now.' There was determination in Amber's voice as well as a bleak note of desperation and fear, as she clasped Robert's pale, too thin hand. She was sitting by his side on the sofa in the small sitting room of their Munich hotel suite. It was two days since she had found him in the bathroom, and thankfully the doctor had now announced that he did not think there was any fear of either a relapse or concussion.

'There's no need for that on my account. I'm perfectly

well. You heard the doctor say so,' Robert responded testily, removing his hand from her own and refusing to look at her.

His refusal was exactly what Amber had dreaded. After all, she acknowledged, Otto was still here in Munich. There had been scant point in her giving instructions that any attempt on Otto's part to make contact with Robert had to be referred to her. The young German had not been in touch, and yet Amber knew from the sympathetic and curious enquiries and visitors they had received that Robert's 'accident' was common knowledge. Poor Robert. Amber could not condone his attempt to take his own life, but she could and did feel for her husband in his despair. She knew Robert rather better now than she had done as a young bride; then she had known his generosity and kind heart; now she also knew his touchy pride and stubbornness.

'Actually, it's for Luc's sake that I think we should leave,' she told Robert, falling back on the excuse she had already planned, anticipating his reaction.

'Luc? Why? Why should Luc need to return to England?' As always, Robert's love for his son was plainly visible in his voice and on his face.

'He's not sleeping or eating as well as he should be, and although he won't say so, he's missing home. He wanted to come to Munich and, as you rightly said, it's been a wonderful experience for him and one he will remember all his life, but when I asked the doctor to have a look at Luc, and explained about him going away to school in September, he did say that he felt a period of quiet at home with us is what Luc needs.'

'Well, if that's what the doctor has said, then I suppose that's what we'll have to do,' Robert agreed, 'but we shall have to make it clear that it is on Luc's account that we are cutting short our stay here, and not for any other reason.'

Not because of him, was what Robert meant, Amber knew.

'Of course,' she agreed readily. It was an effort for her to remain outwardly calm when inwardly she felt almost weak with relief. She had been afraid that Robert would dig in his heels and refuse to leave.

Amber took a deep calming breath and asked Robert steadily, 'Shall I speak with the hotel and instruct the servants, or—'

Before she could finish Robert told her testily, 'Yes, you deal with it. I'm tired of people asking inane questions about my health, and hanging over me as though I'm at death's door.'

Amber got up. 'I'll go and speak to everyone now.'

She didn't want to take the risk of Robert changing his mind, and refusing to leave Munich in the hope that Otto would call.

'Well, my dear, your shop is quite definitely the success it deserves to be.'

'Thanks to you, Cecil,' Amber smiled.

It was just over a month since their return from Munich, and much to Amber's relief, although she missed him dreadfully, Luc had taken to his new school like a proverbial duck to water, writing home ecstatic letters and bombarding his parents, during his regular exeats from school for lunch and half-days out, with his enthusiasm for boarding school life. As a naturally very sociable child, Luc was finding at boarding school the companionship he had lacked as an only child, and Amber had seen how Robert's chest had swelled with pride when Luc's housemaster had commented to them that he rather suspected

431

that already Luc had the makings of ultimately becoming a head boy.

'He's a natural leader,' he had told them. 'The other boys look to him for their lead, and that's something we like to encourage.'

Amber and Cecil had both had to raise their voices to make themselves heard against the chatter of the guests attending the early autumn launch party Amber had given in the upstairs rooms of the Walton Street shop. The willowy young man Cecil had found to manage the day-to-day business of the shop for her – 'He's an Hon., my dear – no money but oodles of breeding and even more oodles of connections' – had already informed Amber that he had been inundated with requests for private appointments for room refurbishments, and *Vogue*'s editor had hinted that an article on the business might be forthcoming in a future issue of the magazine.

Robert had put in a brief appearance, looking so dashingly handsome that Amber's heart had ached. In the shadows just for a moment she had seen again the Robert of the National Gallery. Cecil's assistants were trying to outdo one another to win a smile from him but it was plain to Amber at least how unbearably sad at heart he was.

'Amber, I must have some of the new design for Isleworth.'

'James.' She smiled warmly as she greeted James Lees-Milne, before asking him anxiously, 'What do you think? Will I be able to make a success of the business?'

'Undoubtedly,' he assured her. 'But I dare say you will have Gordon Selfridge trying to poach both your fabrics and your manager.'

'Now that is a compliment. Cecil found Percy for me.'

'Cecil would,' James grinned, before continuing more

briskly, 'When you have time there's something I'd like to discuss with you.'

'Oh, that's not fair. You must tell me now.'

'Very well then. I am trying to persuade the Trust that we should think about refurbishing some of the properties – what I'd like to do is, where possible, recreate the original fabrics, and I'd like Denby Mill to do the silks.'

'James!'

'Don't get too excited. I haven't got agreement yet and even if I do, the profit margin won't be high.'

'But it will be an excellent advertisement for us.'

'Exactly, and since it will be I shall be expecting a sizeable discount.'

'That will depend on how much is ordered,' Amber told him firmly.

It had already surprised her to discover how much she enjoyed the bartering side of business – something else about her that her grandmother would definitely not approve of, she suspected. Her grandmother might have a keen business brain but she, Amber, knew how much she despised and detested anything to do with 'trade', and bartering for a good bargain would, Amber suspected, come under that heading.

People were beginning to leave; the caterers were clearing up, tomorrow's gossip columns would carry photographs and articles about the launch and those who had been there.

Everyone who had attended and who knew about such things had told her that the shop was going to be a success. By rights she ought to be ecstatically happy. She had so much to be thankful for. So why then did she feel so unhappy?

Part Three

Chapter Thirty-Eight

Christmas 1936

Christmas was almost over. Tomorrow their house guests – Grandmother, Greg and little Rose – would be returning to Macclesfield from Osterby. Christmas. How could it have been Christmas without Jay? But it had, and somehow Amber had managed to live through it as she would have to live through the rest of her life now, without Jay and without too that wonderful secret feeling she had hugged so close to herself through all the difficult times, that although he might not be close to her in the physical sense, there was a special bond that linked her to Jay and meant that they were close in their thoughts and that she could always turn to him for help if she needed to. It was, of course, impossible now for her to allow herself that comfort – as a matter of honour if nothing else. She should, Amber told herself critically, be counting her blessings instead of feeling sorry for herself because of what she could not have.

She had a wonderful life, a life that many would envy her. She had a kind, rich, titled husband. She had an adorable son who had returned from his first term at boarding school to reveal a heart-catching glimpse of the man he would one day become – stalwart, loyal, concerned for the feelings of others, proud of what he was without any kind of arrogance in that pride – and yet at the same time still able to be her little boy when they were on their own, flinging himself into her arms and telling her openly that whilst he loved school and would not want to miss being there for the world, he 'missed your good-night kiss, Mummy, but when I close my eyes and think about you it's like you're there with me'.

Ah, but he was going to be a heart-breaker when he grew to manhood, and she, of course, would not consider any young woman, no matter who she was, quite good enough for her precious son, Amber admitted ruefully.

Yes, she was lucky. Not only did she have Robert and Luc, a beautiful home here in the country and a town house with one of London's most prestigious addresses, she also had her business, so successful already that they had had to close the book for Christmas orders at the beginning of November.

Having little Rose to stay had been a very special delight. Luc had been so protective of and intrigued by his new cousin, behaving in such a big brotherly way towards her, that Amber's heart had ached with the pain of wishing she might have given him sisters and brothers of his own.

Outwardly the only shadow cast over their family celebrations had been put there by Greg, whose increasingly volatile moods and lack of self-control had resulted in several verbally violent outbursts – the result, Amber recognised sadly, of his growing dependence on drink and opium.

It was horrible to see her cousin degenerating so dreadfully. She had tried several times since his return home to plead with him to change his ways, but he flatly refused to accept that there was any problem, even on one occasion denying both that he drank too much and smoked opium.

'There must be something we can do,' she had told Robert. But he had shaken his head, advising her, 'I have seen other men in the same situation as Greg, Amber. They cannot be helped unless they themselves wish to be helped, and Greg has made it clear that he does not.'

It was impossible to reason with Greg when he was drinking and Amber suspected that they all treated him less harshly than they should because of their awareness of his ultimate fate.

She had escaped from her duties as hostess into the flower room, using the fact that the gardener had arrived with some fresh blooms from the hothouse as an excuse, but with the new lilies already in their vases, she no longer had any reason to linger and, besides, she acknowledged, it would soon be time for lunch and she needed to get changed. Her grandmother was a stickler for formality and protocol, and would no doubt right now be placing herself in the hands of her own maid.

Blanche had brought with her the tiara Robert had loaned her, and it had made Amber smile and think once again how kind her husband was when he had firmly insisted that it was his gift and that he would be offended if Blanche did not keep it.

Amber had just put her foot on the first stair when she looked up, alerted by the sound of running feet on the landing above, to see Luc's dark head bobbing up above the carved banister as he rushed along the landing to the top of the stairs, calling out anxiously when he saw her, 'Mummy, come quickly. It's Uncle Greg.'

Amber ran up the stairs, her alarm increasing when Luc slipped his hand into hers as though seeking comfort.

'Where is Uncle Greg, Luc?' she asked, trying to sound calm. 'What's happened?'

'He's in his bedroom. I was just walking past, and the door was open, and I just looked, that was all. I didn't mean to do anything wrong, but Uncle Greg was there and he saw me. He shouted something at me and ran towards the door but then he fell and now his head's bleeding and . . .' Luc's voice had started to wobble, his hand gripping Amber's.

Whatever state Greg was now in, Amber knew instinctively that she did not want her son to be even more upset than he already was, but Luc was quick and his pride very fragile. Robert had taught him young that it was his duty to protect females. He would insist on staying with her, especially since Robert was out on estate business. Robert's last words before he had left had been to remind Luc that, in Robert's absence, Luc was 'now the man of the house'.

Greg's room was right at the far end of the landing – his choice because, he had claimed, he was a poor sleeper and did not want to disturb anyone if he woke up in the night and needed to walk off his excess energy by pacing his bedroom.

'Luc, will you go back downstairs for me, please, and ask someone to send Uncle Greg's valet up to his room? And no running this time, please. I don't want any accidents on the stairs.'

'Don't worry, Mummy. I can run really fast without slipping,' Luc told her, slipping his hand free of her own.

As she turned to watch him hurry away, Amber was aware of how cold her own hand felt without the warmth of his in it, and how alone she felt without him at her side, but whatever state her cousin was in, it would, she knew, be one she did not wish Luc to witness.

She pushed open the bedroom door, which she realised Luc must have closed when he had run to get help.

Greg was on his feet and staggering around, mumbling under his breath. The room itself was in semidarkness. The housekeeper had already complained to her that the maids could not clean it properly because Greg refused to allow the curtains to be opened. The smell of gin mingled with the sweeter odour of opium.

There was a tray on the bed, prepared with what Amber guessed must be the tools required to satisfy Greg's craving for the opium he smoked. Had Luc seen the tray? Amber hoped not. It horrified her to think of her son being exposed to her cousin's sickening behaviour.

'Oh, it's you, is it? See what that brat of yours has done?' he demanded, removing the bloodstained handkerchief he was holding to his head to show her the small cut beneath it. 'You want to teach him a few manners, Amber, and tell him that he shouldn't go barging into a chap's room without knocking.'

Amber could feel her anger mounting as she listened. But there was no point in attempting to reason with Greg, or in venting her anger on him. He had gone somewhere beyond the reach of reason or any appeal to his good nature now, she knew that. A feeling of sadness capped her anger. It was so heartbreaking to think that this was the cousin she had admired and loved so much, the cousin who had been so kind to her in his grown-up, older boy way. Tears stung her eyes, as she remembered the many times Greg had done his best to protect her from their grandmother's wrath over some relatively small transgression. Didn't she owe him something for those kindnesses? The trouble was that Greg's transgressions were not small ones, and neither was the man, and within his mind was no longer the Greg she had grown up with and loved. That was the true horror of it all: that the real Greg had been stolen away and destroyed by his own weakness, and that another Greg had taken his place.

'Stop looking at me like that, Amber,' he demanded loudly. 'It isn't my fault, none of it. It's all right for you, you don't understand, you don't know what it's like to lie awake at night with your skin crawling like ants are walking all over it, biting at you, digging into you, eating you alive, eating your flesh and your brain. I can hear them chewing on me. That's why I have to drink. It kills them, you see. I have to do it.' He was sweating and shivering at the same time, scratching at his arms as he moved fretfully round the room.

Amber wished desperately that Robert wasn't out. She had no idea how to deal with this. Where was Greg's valet? Please God, don't let Luc come back now and see Greg. Jay would have known what to do, and how to calm Greg. Jay – she missed him so much, but she mustn't think of him, not now and not at any time.

'I need a drink, dammit,' Greg was virtually screaming now.

Someone was opening the bedroom door. Greg's valet. Amber turned in relief and then froze as she saw Blanche standing there.

'What's going on? I could hear the noise from the other end of the landing.'

'It's all right, Grandmother. Greg and I were just exchanging a few words.'

Amber wasn't sure which of them it was she was trying to protect, Greg or their grandmother. Maybe it was both.

Blanche looked from Amber's anxious face and tense body to her grandson. Did Amber really think that she was such a decrepit fool that she needed protecting from the truth and that she didn't know about Greg? If so, then it was her granddaughter who was the fool.

'It's that ruddy son of hers that's caused this,' Greg was complaining, revealing the bloodstained handkerchief, 'coming barging in here.'

Blanche looked sharply at Amber. 'Luc saw this?' she demanded.

442

There was no need for Amber to ask her grandmother what she meant by 'this'.

'I don't think so. I hope not,' Amber admitted. 'He just said that Greg had fallen. I sent him to find Greg's valet.'

Blanche looked at her grandson. The very sight of him filled her with bitterness and loathing. How could he have been such a fool? How could he have wasted the opportunities he had had? How could he have turned out to be so poorly tempered and in such a base metal when she had longed so much for him to be cast in the same mould of pure gold as his father?

Greg's valet had arrived, thankfully without Luc.

'I dare say that Robert will have some sharp words to say to you about your negligence in not making sure that Luc wasn't exposed to Greg's disgusting self-inflicted degradation,' Blanche told Amber coldly, when they had left Greg's room.

'Greg promised me that he would try not to touch . . . anything whilst he was here,' Amber answered her.

'And you believed him?' Blanche was scornful.

Irrationally Amber found that she wanted to defend her cousin. 'He can't help it, Grandmother. He isn't able to control his own urges.'

'He is a corrupt weakling, not fit to bear his father's name. If I had known what he would become . . .' Blanche pursed her lips. 'We are constantly told that we are the weaker sex, Amber, but in truth it is us who are the stronger, because we have to be.'

It was so unusual for Blanche to speak so openly to her, and to treat her as though they were equals, sharing a certain understanding, that Amber didn't know what to say. Was it a sign of vulnerability on the part of her grandmother, or a recognition of Amber's own growing maturity?

'And we have to be because it is on us that the burden

443

rests of recognising the lack of all that we had hoped to find in the child we have helped to create with such high hopes, as you will discover.'

'Luc is everything I could want him to be and more,' Amber defended her son immediately.

'Be very careful of hubris, Amber. It exacts the most painful payment of all.'

Chapter Thirty-Nine

'Are you sure you wouldn't like me to come with you and Daddy?' Amber asked Luc.

It was the end of his Easter exeat from school. They were standing in the hallway of the Eaton Square house whilst, down below them in the square, Robert waited for the staff to finish loading Luc's things into the car.

'It's best if you don't, Mummy,' Luc explained to her in a kind, but very male voice. 'It's in case you start blubbing.'

Amber was torn between tears and a rueful smile. Luc adored school, and he and Robert spent hours when they were together discussing 'chaps' with odd-sounding names and comparing notes about teachers who had seemed ancient to Robert when he had been there but who were now teaching Luc.

Robert seemed to have put the dark days that had followed their return from Berlin behind him now. The shock of the abdication in December, when Edward had announced that he was giving up the throne to be with Wallis, had been the turning point, or so it had seemed to Amber, and by Christmas he had been much more like his old self.

The business of the shop had grown week on week,

445

outstripping even the most optimistic forecasts. A second young man, Brett, now the under manager, had been hired; three mornings a week Amber received private clients in the upstairs rooms or, if they were very important, visited them at their London homes.

Decorators, carpenters, and other tradesmen wearing smart overalls in the Walton Street shop's colours of muted grey-green with 'Silk' embroidered on them in white, along with the shop's telephone number, worked tirelessly to prepare clients' rooms ready for the soft furnishings made by the trusted band of seamstress outworkers.

From downstairs Amber heard Robert's voice announcing that it was time for them to leave. In the privacy of her sitting room, Luc was still young enough to hug her back as tightly as she was hugging him, although Amber knew he would have squirmed with embarrassment had she done so in public. She was so very proud of his growing manliness, and the way she could see the adult he was going to be taking shape beneath his boy's flesh and mind. Yet at the same time she missed her little boy, her baby. If things had been different there was nothing she would have liked more than to take little Rose under her wing, but with the shop taking up so much of her time, it simply would not be fair to take the little girl into a strange household.

Although Rose was now thriving, whenever Amber bought clothes for her from the measurements Jay sent to her, obtained from Rose's nurses, they showed how very small Greg's daughter still was. Small but much healthier now, according to Dr Brookes, who even thought that her legs would not be as badly weakened as he had first thought, thank goodness.

Downstairs in the hall the servants were lined up to say their goodbyes to Luc, and Amber couldn't resist exchanging

446

a parental smile of pride with Robert at the grown-up manner in which Luc shook their hands.

'It won't be long until I'm back for the summer hols, Mummy,' he informed Amber reassuringly as he climbed into the car, adding enthusiastically to Robert, 'I can't wait to see the yacht, Daddy.'

Robert had bought a yacht, *Seabreeze*, earlier in the year, which was berthed in the South of France, and it had been arranged that they would spend the summer there on board it.

'Give my apologies to your grandmother for not being able to accompany you on this occasion, won't you?' Robert asked Amber, placing a brief kiss on her cheek before pulling on his driving gloves and heading for the car.

Blanche had written to Amber earlier in the week saying that she wanted her to come down to Macclesfield as there was something important she wanted to discuss with her in person. Since Robert had already made arrangements to drive down to the South of France with some friends to 'test out' the yacht after he had taken Luc back to school, Amber was having to go without him. That would disappoint Blanche, Amber knew. Her grandmother still loved showing off her titled grandson-in-law, and normally arranged at least one grand dinner party whenever he was visiting Denham.

What was it, though, that Blanche wanted to discuss? Had Cassandra gossiped about seeing her with Jay after all? If she had, and that gossip had reached her grandmother's ears, then Amber intended to make it plain to Blanche that she was the one who was at fault and not Jay, and that any punishment should fall on her shoulders and not his. What if her grandmother took it into her head to punish Jay by dismissing him? Amber felt sick at the thought, and she prayed that this was not the reason Blanche had summoned her to Macclesfield.

There was no point worrying herself senseless ahead of hearing what Blanche had to say, Amber decided. Surely Jay would have found some way to warn her if Blanche had found out? No, she must focus on something else. She might not be looking forward to seeing her grandmother, but she was looking forward to seeing little Rose, whom she hadn't seen since Christmas.

Thankfully Luc did not seem to have suffered any ill effects from Greg's behaviour, although, just as Blanche had warned, Robert had been angry when Amber had told him what had happened, threatening to refuse to allow Greg to visit again.

Amber hadn't, of course, expected to find Jay waiting for her at Macclesfield station, and nor was he. What she hadn't expected, though, was the depth of her misery because Jay wasn't there. It rolled down over her like the dark grey clouds that so often rolled down over Macclesfield itself from the hills of Buxton and Derbyshire, giving the town the damp air that was so beneficial for the manufacture of silk. Derbyshire's rain clouds might been beneficial for her work, but her own inner grey clouds were certainly not beneficial for her. Her grandmother had sent her own car to pick her up, and whilst Amber managed to smile and chat warmly with the chauffeur, inside she ached for the days when Jay had been the one to drive her home.

Amber tried not to look in the direction of the Dower House as they drove in through the main gates, but the sight of Jay's car parked outside broke her resolve.

Was he inside now? Would he see the car and guess that she was inside it, or was his own car simply there because he did not need it? His work took him out and about all over the estate, and Amber knew that he enjoyed using the many footpaths to go and visit the tenant farmers when he had the time to do so. It gave him a chance to 'study the land and make sure it was in good heart', he had once told her.

Robert had often commented that Amber's grandmother was extremely lucky to have Jay working for her. James Lees-Milne, who through his connection with the National Trust was familiar with so many estates, had told Amber that he had rarely seen an estate so well and sympathetically managed as Denham. Amber had felt a thrill of pride on Jay's behalf, listening to James's praise.

As Harris brought the Bentley to a lumbering halt in front of the house, another vehicle, a low-slung sports car, its bodywork of British racing green, shot past them, spraying up gravel.

'Has my cousin got a new car, Harris?' Amber asked.

Greg had complained volubly over Christmas about the fact that their grandmother was refusing to buy him his own car, but Amber had suspected that she would relent.

'No, that will be Mr Stanley bringing Master Greg back,' Harris informed Amber lugubriously.

Mr Stanley? Harris must be referring to Greg's friend, Geoff Stanley, who along with his cousin held shares in a popular local football club. Amber watched as the doors of the sports car were flung open and her cousin and his friend got out.

The clear spring light was cruel to Greg, revealing the damage his way of life had done to his once handsome face and physique. Geoff Stanley, who was the same age as Greg, now looked a good ten years younger. Neither of them seemed to have noticed the Bentley, no doubt because they appeared to be involved in a fierce argument, Amber decided, watching uneasily. Geoff Stanley called out something to Greg, who ignored him and walked away. Geoff was obviously calling out to Greg to stop and when he didn't he smashed his fist down on the roof of his car before jumping back into it and driving away, whilst Greg disappeared round the side of the house in the direction of the stables.

'Thank you, Harris,' Amber said as the chauffeur opened the door for her. 'Please tell Mrs Harris that I hope her rheumatism will soon improve.'

'Aye, me an' all, Your Grace. She's done nowt but moan about it all winter. Caused me near as much pain as it has done her,' he complained.

The house had the newly spring-cleaned smell Amber remembered from her girlhood, the shining clean windows, the gleaming paintwork and polished surfaces testimony of Blanche's firm grip on the reins of her household.

Mrs Clements was waiting to welcome Amber, frowning down the nervous excitement of a new and very young maid, who blushed and giggled when she was introduced to Amber.

'I don't expect my grandmother will want to be disturbed now,' Amber smiled at the housekeeper, 'so I'll go straight up to the nursery, to see my niece.'

'Well, Mrs Pickford did say that she would like to see you as soon as you'd had time to refresh yourself, Your Grace,' Mrs Clements informed Amber.

'Oh, well, in that case, I'll just go up to my room and remove my outdoor things.'

It didn't take Amber very long to remove her coat and hat, and change into an afternoon frock, from one of the Duchess of Windsor's favourite designers, Mainbocher. It had been Cecil who had persuaded her to try the designer, insisting that his clothes were perfectly cut for her.

Her gown, emerald-green silk, with a matching jacket trimmed in black, was elegantly cut and rather dressy for the country but she knew that her grandmother would

450

appreciate its style and smartness. Amber smiled ruefully to herself as she fastened on a pair of large square-cut emerald earrings, Robert's latest gift to her. It was quite ridiculous that she, a married woman, should still feel as anxious as a schoolgirl about her grandmother's reaction to her appearance.

She looked towards the door. She was longing to go up to the nursery but her grandmother would already know that she had arrived.

It was nothing short of a miracle how the years never seemed to touch her grandmother, Amber reflected, although of course in *The Picture* of *Dorian Gray* Oscar Wilde had had another, and rather macabre, explanation as to why a person might not age. Not that it was possible to imagine her grandmother ever being vain or weak enough to cede ownership of any part of herself to someone else.

Her back as she sat in her favourite chair was as ramrod straight as it had always been, her hair as thick and immaculately waved, and the gaze from her eyes as sharp and assessing as ever.

When Amber bent down to kiss her cheek, Blanche commented drily, 'Your new scent, like your new frock, strikes me as possessing more style than substance, Amber. Both will no doubt attract attention in London's so-called smart cocktail bars, but my feeling is that they lack staying power. When a woman chooses a new scent she has to ask herself if it is one she will want to be remembered by.'

Amber raised her eyebrows at her grandmother's rebuke.

'The scent was a Christmas gift from Robert. He had it specially made for me, and the frock is Mainbocher.'

Amber paused as her grandmother gave a distinct snort of contempt.

'He is very fashionable, you know. The new Queen has said that he is her favourite designer.'

'Well, she seems a decent enough sort, not like that wretched American divorcee. From what I've read, though, she rules her husband every bit as much as that Simpson woman ruled Edward.'

Grandmother was obviously in a prickly mood and ready to quarrel with every opinion that wasn't her own.

'Robert sends his apologies for not being able to come with me.'

Blanche's frown disappeared as Amber knew it would. Any reference to her husband always had the effect of softening her grandmother's mood, although Amber acknowledged that she really ought to be firmer and not use poor Robert as a means of pacifying her. It was, she felt, time she stood on her own two feet.

'Have you see Greg yet?' Blanche asked.

'Not to speak to. I saw him arriving back not long ago.'

'The worse for drink no doubt.' Blanche's voice was icily disapproving. 'It is because of Greg that I have asked you to come here, Amber.' Blanche paused before saying, 'It was always my intention to leave the bulk of my estate to Greg. You, after all, are well provided for, and Greg represents the only male line of the family. However, in view of his recent behaviour I have rewritten my will. You will now be the main beneficiary. I have left you this house and the mill, along with the bulk of the money that was left to me. There are certain provisos, of course, certain charges upon you, which include a proper regard for your duty to your cousin.'

Amber was so shocked that she was speechless. This was the last thing she had expected.

'Grandmother, you cannot do that,' she protested as soon as she felt able to speak. 'You have always said that Greg will inherit everything. Everyone knows that.'

'And I know that he will have gambled or given away everything to those worthless friends of his before I have been in my grave a year. As the beneficiary under the wills of my father and my uncle, I had a responsibility to take good care of what they had passed on to me. That responsibility extends to ensuring that I pass it on to someone whom I can trust to do as I have done. It has always been my belief that men are better suited to dealing with money than women. However, in your cousin's case it is plain to me that his way of dealing with money is to squander it, and I cannot allow that to happen. Can you imagine what would happen to this house and this estate if it were to become Greg's?'

'It is his birthright,' Amber told her grandmother. 'That is what he believes, and it is what you have encouraged him to believe.'

'If he had listened to me it would still be his birthright.'

'I can't accept what should be his,' Amber said determinedly.

'So you will be happy to see him close down the mill, will you, because that is what he will do?'

In different circumstances Amber could almost have been amused that the grandmother who had loathed and resented the mill so much should use it now and in such a way.

'If Greg should wish to dispose of the mill then I am sure that Robert would be happy for us to buy it from him.'

'And the estate – you would be happy to see that broken up as well, and Jay dismissed? A poor return for his loyalty and hard work, especially when one thinks of the problems he has to face with that demented wife of his.'

Amber's heart missed a beat. Her grandmother couldn't possibly know about Jay, could she? No, it was impossible. Amber was just letting her own guilt nag at her imagination.

'Have you spoken to Greg?' Amber asked. 'Perhaps if you were to explain your concern to him . . . ?'

'Your cousin has been given every opportunity to show that he regrets what he has done. He is more interested in drinking himself to death than in being the grandson I wanted, the son who would have been a true inheritor of the promise of his father. I had hoped to see in him some of his father's greatness, but all I can see is weakness and corruption. His behaviour at Christmas confirmed everything I had begun to fear. Even if by some miracle he did not destroy everything I have built up, who is to say that he would not fill the nurseries with more unwanted bastard brats, like the one already up there. God did me no favours the day he allowed that child to live.'

'Grandmother!' Amber protested. 'That's a terrible thing to say!'

'For goodness' sake get your head out of the clouds for once, Amber, and recognise reality for what it is. What decent young woman of good family will marry Greg and give him sons, knowing his history, and that of that child upstairs?'

'You were the one who punished Greg by sending him to Hong Kong, Grandmother,' Amber reminded Blanche firmly.

'You and he may see that as a punishment, Amber. I, on the other hand, saw it and indeed intended it to be an opportunity – for Greg to redeem himself, and become what I had hoped most dearly he would become.'

'I wish you would reconsider changing your will,' said Amber.

'Well, your wishes are in vain because I assure you I shall not. My mind is made up, Amber. Besides, it is too late. Mr Brocklehurst brought me my new will last week, and it has now been executed. You, and Luc after you, are to receive everything.'

As she turned away Amber's attention was caught by the familiar large photograph album on the small table next to her grandmother's chair.

As a child she had often begged to be shown the photographs inside it, especially those of her mother, but it had been Blanche's son, Greg's father, whom Blanche had always proudly pointed out to Amber on the stiffly posed and grouped family photographs. Amber remembered how angry that had always made her on her mother's behalf, and how, as a very little girl, she had refused to look at Marcus, outraged by the way in which her grandmother favoured her son above Amber's own beloved mother. Her behaviour had, of course, not gone down at all well with her grandmother, and there had been stiff words from Blanche about spoiled children and the efficacy of a bread-and-water diet alone in a cold bedroom for badly behaved children.

A small tender smile now touched Amber's mouth. Her mother had never allowed Blanche's threats to be put into action and, far from seeming to mind Blanche's preference for her dead brother, had always accepted it with a calm smile.

'She cannot help it, Amber,' her mother had once told her when Amber had demanded to know why her grandmother behaved in this way. 'He was so precious to her, because of what he was. To have lost him when she loved him so much was a terribly cruel blow. One day when you are grown up and you have children of your own you will understand.'

Her parents would have loved Luc so much. Amber had to blink away tears.

Blanche saw that she was looking at the album and picked it up, opening it on her lap.

'You remember this?'

'Yes, of course. When I was little it used to fascinate me to see photographs of my mother as a baby. I could never understand then why there weren't any of my father.'

'Your mother was a very plain child; I was bitterly disappointed when I saw that she wasn't going to have either my own looks or those of her—'

Amber looked at her grandmother as she hesitated and then said quickly, 'her brother. Greg's father was the most beautiful baby.' She turned the pages of the album and showed Amber a photograph of herself as a young girl holding an undeniably lovely baby.

'That was Marcus, and here is your mother.'

As she turned the pages Amber caught sight of a photograph of her grandmother, holding a baby with a curly-headed child at her side and said quickly, 'Oh, there she is, and she is beautiful.'

'That is not your mother,' Blanche told her, turning over the page.

'Then who is it?' Amber asked curiously.

'I have no idea. Probably some relative who was visiting. Ah, here is your mother.'

Amber could feel the emotion filling her and gripping her as she looked at her mother's photograph.

'She wasn't plain, she was lovely, and in every single way. My father said so.'

The sound of the dressing bell, warning them that it was time for them to dress for dinner, had her grandmother closing the album, signalling that their conversation was over.

'So the old witch is changing her will, is she, leaving everything to you?'

'Greg, for goodness' sake let go of me. You're hurting my

arm,' Amber protested as she stepped out of her bedroom to find Greg waiting for her, and plainly very angry.

'I'm hurting you? How the hell do you think I feel?' he demanded.

His eyes were bloodshot and he was slurring his words, and none too steady on his feet either, Amber recognised.

'Why don't you go and get changed for dinner and then we can discuss this later?' Amber tried to placate him.

'You mean like you and our dear grandmother were discussing it when I overheard the two of you?' There was an ugly look in Greg's eyes.

'I can understand how you must feel,' she began.

'Don't give me that. How the hell can you understand what it feels like to be treated like a pauper and to have to go begging for a few guineas? Dare say that husband of yours doesn't keep you short of money the way our dear grandmother does me. It's not fair, the way she treats me, Amber.' His temper had given way to self-pity, his eyes filling with tears as he leaned against the wall to steady himself, releasing her arm as he did so. 'It isn't right. Everyone says so. A chap needs to have a bit of money in his pocket. You couldn't lend me a few hundred, could you, Amber? Only until I get my allowance.'

Amber's heart started to sink under the combined weight of her guilt and despair.

'Greg . . .'

'Aw, come on, it isn't as though you can't afford it, is it, not now when you've got what should have been mine to look forward to, as well as having a rich husband? Who'd have thought it? Remember when we were young how it was always me that had to help you, Amber?'

'I haven't brought much cash with me, Greg, but when I go home—'

'You're just as bad as she is, do you know that? Worse.'

He turned away from her and headed for the stairs, half stumbling down them.

'Greg,' Amber protested, 'we can talk after dinner.'

'Talk about what? What a traitoress you are? How you've stolen what's rightfully mine? Don't bother!'

'So very kind of Cassandra to invite you and Greg to have dinner at Fitton Hall tonight,' Blanche commented as she and Amber had breakfast together.

It was three days since Amber had arrived in Macclesfield. Greg had hardly spoken to her although to her relief, since she was still in shock from the news herself, and longed desperately for the comfort of discussing it with Jay, he had made no further reference to their grandmother's will.

Her grandmother's will apart, Amber had tried to tell herself that it was for the best that she hadn't seen anything of Jay, but stubbornly her heart had refused to be convinced. But look at the trouble her heart had got her into. It was easier and far safer to concentrate on the practicalities of business affairs rather than dwell on her emotions, although here again she would have been glad of Jay's calm support.

Maurice had admitted that he had ignored her warning, under pressure from the other mill owners, who had been reluctant to take the advice of a mere woman, and had had Coronation handkerchiefs made, which of course could not be sold because of the Abdication, and which would damage their profits. The only pleasure her visit had brought her had been seeing how well and happy little Rose looked, and now she was going to have to endure sitting through a dinner party at the Fitton Leghs'.

Whatever had motivated Cassandra to call personally to issue the invitation it was certainly not kindness, Amber thought, but of course she could not tell her grandmother just why she knew that for a fact.

'Mr Stanley is here, Your Grace, and asking if he might have a word with you.'

Greg's friend wanted to speak with her? Amber didn't relish the prospect but she could scarcely refuse.

'Please show him into the library, Wilson, and tell him that I'll be down in a minute.'

It was mid-afternoon, her grandmother had driven out to see a friend, and Amber was in the nursery where she had been playing with Rose.

The little girl was adorable, and Amber had been thrilled when Rose had recognised her and held out her arms to her.

'Bright as a button, she is, Your Grace,' Betsy had informed Amber proudly.

'And her legs?' Amber had asked anxiously.

In response Betsy had lifted up the child's gown to show Amber her plump legs.

'Stout as can be. Exercise them the way Dr Brookes has told us, me and our Sheila do, twice a day, and Dr Brookes says he reckons she'll be as steady on them as you like.'

'Mr Stanley,' Amber greeted her visitor as she went into the library.

He flushed, looking slightly awkward.

'I'm sorry to have to come here talking to you like this, but the fact is that your cousin Greg has left me in a real mess and I just don't know where else to turn. Not that it's your business to bale him out of trouble, but—'

'I take it that you're trying to tell me that Greg owes you money,' Amber stopped him.

'It was his idea not mine. He said he wanted to come in

459

on the deal and so I put up the money for him so that we could buy the shares and now he's saying that he doesn't want them. But it's too ruddy late for him to change his mind now. My old man will have my hide when he finds out; I've borrowed the money to pay for them in his name.'

'I think you'd better explain the whole thing to me properly,' Amber suggested, sitting down.

Half an hour later she looked at Geoff Stanley and summarised, 'So let me understand this correctly: between you, you and Greg have bought your late uncle's share in the Hermes Stanley football team. You covered Greg's share of the cost via a loan you arranged in your father's name. Now Greg is refusing to pay you back?'

'Yes, that's right. He says he can't remember agreeing to go halves with me but he ruddy well did. Sorry,' he apologised, flushing. 'Forgot myself for a moment. My father's due back from London next week and when he finds out . . . He sold his share in the team years ago. Doesn't approve, you see, him being a strict Chapel man.'

Amber nodded her head. She had heard that Mr Stanley senior had become a strict Methodist following his second marriage, and that this had caused problems with his two sons from his first marriage.

'How much exactly does Greg owe you?'

'Five thousand guineas.'

Shocked, Amber thought quickly. She could repay the loan on Greg's behalf, but . . .

'If I give you this money then I shall require that you make over to me the share in the football team that would have been Greg's,' she said calmly.

'What would you want with a share in a football team?' he asked her, plainly astonished, and Amber suspected, not very pleased.

'Nothing, but I rather think that it would be safer in my hands than my cousin's. Just as I shouldn't like to think of him being in debt to an old friend, neither would I like to think of him being cheated out of something that is rightfully his. He does, after all, have a young child to provide for.' Her smile might take the sting out of her words but Amber wanted Geoff Stanley to know that she wasn't easily deceived. 'If you agree then I shall ask my grandmother's solicitor to draw up the appropriate papers.'

'Aye, well. I mean, yes. And the money?'

'You will receive your cheque when I receive my shares in the Hermes,' Amber assured him.

How Jay would have laughed if she had been able to tell him that she was now part-owner of a football team, Amber reflected after Geoff Stanley had left. But of course she couldn't tell him. She couldn't tell him anything any more.

'You must find us dreadfully parochial, Amber, after living so long in London and society.'

Their main course of beef Wellington had been eaten and there had been the kind of slight lull in the conversation that invariably followed the consumption of a hearty meal; a general easing of minds and male waistbands, the former at least snapping sharply back on duty after Cassandra's deliberately provocative comment.

Amber could almost feel the different layers of emotion investing the waiting silence round the dinner table, as the local landed gentry waited to see how she would deal with Cassandra's comment. Would she defend her county, or would she align herself with the London set amongst which she now moved?

Amber repressed a small sigh; harder to deny was her desire to exchange intimate knowing glances with Jay, who was seated almost directly opposite her.

Jay – how foolish that her heart should hammer with such intense emotion just because it felt the echo of her silent whisper of his name. It had been such a shock to see him. Formal dress suited him. He had that easy way of wearing it that a man had to be born to. He looked distinguished and heart-achingly handsome, whilst the sombreness of his expression had torn at Amber's heart.

What dreadful cruelty this was on Cassandra's part, to bring them together like this, when she knew. But what did Cassandra know? Only that she had seen them sharing an illicit embrace, nothing more than that. She knew nothing of the emotion that tore at Amber's heart, the need to greedily absorb every familiar feature with her hungry gaze, the need to touch – just the lightest touch would be enough, a brief resting of her fingertips on his jacket-clad arm – the need to share just one precious intimate smile. But these were needs that must be denied, Amber knew that.

She had known from the minute she had received the invitation that the Fitton Legh dinner was going to be an ordeal. There was a Machiavellian, even a spiteful side to Cassandra's nature, which she was now in a position to indulge, at Amber's expense. Given that so far there had not been any gossip about her and Jay, Amber did not think that Cassandra would make any direct reference to catching them together, but Amber did suspect that Cassandra would taunt and torment her with subtle little digs, which might dangerously arouse the curiosity and even the suspicions of the other dinner guests.

In fact, if Cassandra had wanted to fill her with dread at the thought of the evening ahead, whilst ensuring that she kept her on the edge of her seat through the course of it, she could not have planned things better, Amber thought.

However, a cooingly sweet announcement from Cassandra, when she greeted Amber and Greg on their arrival, that the other guests included the Bromley Davenports, Leghs from Adlington Hall, the Masseys from Dunham Massey, and Jay and Lydia, had shown Amber that she had dangerously under-estimated the depth of Cassandra's spite.

The years of playing her role of duchess to Robert's duke had taught her something about the need to uphold the dignity of her rank by adopting a calm formal face for public events, to be varied either by more smiles and friendliness if she was dealing with Robert's tenants, or a definite air of cool hauteur when it was necessary to remind those who were in need of reminding, just what her status was. She had never needed those skills more than she had needed them tonight.

On this occasion, rather that risk giving Cassandra any further excuse to vent her spite on her, Amber had simply refused to react at all. Not even later, just before they had gone in`to dinner, when Jay had arrived – late – apologising that he was on his own, and explaining that Lydia had been stricken with a dreadful migraine, which meant that she had been unable to attend.

'I did initially telephone to tell Cassandra that neither of us would be here,' Amber heard him saying to Mary Bromley Davenport, but she overruled me and insisted that I came.'

And she suspected that she knew why, Amber had thought bitterly. Cassandra wanted them both here so that she could exact the maximum amount of personal enjoyment out of their mutual dread.

Never had an evening seemed to last for such a long time. The Cheshire county set were for the most part fiercely patriotic, and their conversation focused mainly on the shockingness of the Abdication, their admiration for the new King, and their disapproval of Germany's warlike stance. So far Amber had managed to endure the deter-mined conservatism of their opinions by keeping herself busily engaged in lighter conversation. Even more painful for her than having the threat of Cassandra revealing what they had done hanging over her, was the fact that she was here in the same room as Jay: free to listen to his voice, and even to look at him but not free to talk intimately with him or to touch him or to look up into his eyes, and there was so much she longed to see.

Instead she had to answer Cassandra's question and parry the many blows she now knew the evening would hold.

She took a deep breath, and said lightly, 'Cassandra, I assure you that nothing is more parochial than London society.'

The rest of the table seemed to give a collective exhaled breath of approval, but Cassandra was not ready to give up.

'You though, Greg, must feel very envious of your cousin leading such a gay life,' she persisted, turning her attention from Amber to Greg. She couldn't possibly know about the will, Amber knew, but of course that didn't stop her question having the effect of a match thrown into a powder keg.

Greg reacted exactly as Amber had known he would, announcing furiously, 'I feel envious of her all right, now that I've found out that our grandmother is disinheriting me in favour of her.'

He had been drinking heavily all evening, his glass filled up far too readily for Amber's liking by the Fitton Leghs' footman. As a girl she would have felt so mortified that she would have wanted to get up and run from the room, but marriage had taught her how to command herself and how to conduct herself in society, so she stayed where she was, although there was nothing she could think of to say that would mitigate the effect of Greg's outburst.

'What a very fortunate person you are, Amber,' Cassandra smiled. 'But then it is often the fact, isn't it, that those who have the most seem to have the habit of being able to acquire the most? One sees it so often: the spoiled child who demands more attention from its nurse; the spoiled person who cannot be content with a mere spouse but who has to have the admiration of others as well, even when those others are married themselves.'

The words were said lightly but there was no mistaking their meaning or their venom. Greg was frowning as though struggling to assimilate what was being said, whilst the other guests looked intrigued or uncomfortable, depending on their nature. It was plain to Amber that Cassandra was referring both to the past and Greg's affair with Caroline, and her discovery of Amber and Jay in one another's arms, and Amber could feel her stomach knotting with anxiety. This was what she had been dreading all evening.

Cassandra was enjoying herself. It was a pity, of course, that Lydia had decided to sulk and refuse to come just because she hadn't liked the way Cassandra had teased her and refused to tell her that she loved her, yesterday afternoon.

Greg, who had just drained his refilled glass, put it back down clumsily on the table and then broke the silence left by Cassandra's remark by announcing truculently, 'Too fortunate, that's what she is. It's not right that Amber should get what's mine. It's not right, do you hear?' he demanded, suddenly struggling to his feet and banging his fist on the table.

'I say, old thing, not so much fortissimo, eh?' John Bromley Davenport suggested, whilst Greg subsided back into his chair.

'Not so much portissimo might be more to the point,' one of the female guests whispered *sotto voce*, but still loud enough for Amber to hear.

'It's not right,' Greg repeated, hiccuping and then starting to sob loudly, putting his head on the table as his whole body shook with emotion.

Amber didn't know what she would have done if Jay had not got quietly to his feet and gone over to Greg, putting his arm round his shoulders and saying gently, 'Come on, old chap; let's get you home, shall we?'

Looking bewildered and clumsy, Greg allowed Jay to lead him out of the room.

'I'm sorry, Cassandra, but I'd better go as well,' Amber apologised.

'Well, yes, of course, I can perfectly understand why you would want to.'

Cassandra's words might be innocuous enough on the surface but Amber suspected that Cassandra had chosen them for spite. What other little unpleasant digs at her was Cassandra planning? She would never have a moment's peace around her from now on, Amber knew.

Amber had arranged that they would telephone when they were ready to be collected but when she caught up with Jay and Greg in the hallway Jay told her firmly, 'I think it would be better if I drove Greg straight home now. He's rather under the weather.'

'Didn't want to come here. Doesn't seem right, not now that Caroline's gone,' Greg said drunkenly.

Tears of pity for her cousin stung Amber's eyes.

'No, I dare say it doesn't, old chap,' Jay agreed.

'Boy's my son, you know.'

Amber looked at Jay. Tactfully he made no comment, although Greg was too drunk to know what he had said.

'I'll stay here then and telephone for Harris,' Amber told Jay.

'As you wish, but there's room in the car for you if you want to come back with us.'

'I told my grandmother than I'd rather she didn't change

her will, and that I thought it was wrong.' What on earth was she saying that for? 'I'm so sorry,' she added helplessly. 'I'm so sorry about everything.'

'Amber . . .'

'Don't want to stay here any more. I'm off,' Greg announced, staggering towards the door.

'Hang on, Greg, we're coming with you.' Jay hurried after Greg, leaving Amber to hesitate and then catch up with them.

Chapter Forty

Summer 1937, South of France

'My dears, you're here at last. How was the journey?'

As Amber submitted to Beth's powdery rose-scented embrace, she acknowledged how very much like her mother Beth was growing. She and Alistair had four children now, two boys and two girls, and Beth herself had grown plump and matronly in a way that suited her.

'Bracing is probably the best way to describe it,' Amber laughed, as Beth ushered her into the drawing room and rang for tea.

Robert had insisted on them sailing from England down to St-Tropez, and whilst none of them had been seasick, the sea had been rather rougher than Amber would have liked at times.

Robert had already disappeared with Alistair, and Beth's nanny had swept Luc up to the nursery to renew his friendship with Beth and Alistair's children.

'Well, you are here now, and I have so much to tell you,' Beth announced after she had poured their tea.

The villa's drawing room had large French doors that opened out on to a terrace, beyond which was a magnificent view of the Mediterranean. The soft breeze coming in through the open doors carried with it that familiar smell of sea and heat and lavender that Amber always thought so much a part of the South of France. Those familiar scents brought back so many memories. Their shopping trip to Paris; the train journey during which they had hardly been able to sleep for excitement; her first sight of the villa, her first sight of Jean-Philippe. That was enough reminiscing. It was definitely time to clamp down on her memories. She smoothed a small tuck of fabric in the fold of her white Chanel silk linen skirt.

'First and best of all, Mummy has managed to persuade Henry to come and stay with us for the summer. We've all been so worried about him after the disappointment of the new baby being another girl.'

Amber stiffened at the mention of Beth's brother's name but said nothing. She had never of course said anything to her friend about Henry's behaviour. Amber and Henry's paths had rarely crossed in the intervening years and on those rare occasions when they had done so, Amber had tried to give Henry a wide berth, all the more so after that party when he had behaved so horribly to her.

'We must be especially kind to him, Amber, and cheer him up.'

Never mind being kind to Henry, Amber wanted to say, what about his wife? How does she feel about being blamed for not producing an heir? But she knew there was no point in venting her angry disgust with Henry on poor Beth, who clearly adored her brother.

'Everyone seems to be here this year, especially the Germans,' Beth continued. 'They are everywhere, and throwing the most splendid parties. Henry says they are far too ostentatious. Bathing parties especially are all the rage with them – well, you know how they are about exercise and that kind of thing.' Beth pulled a face. 'Personally I find it far too fatiguing but the children love it, of course. I adore your outfit. You are so lucky to have stayed so slim, Amber, but then after four children . . .'

Amber drank her tea and listened obediently. It had never been easy to stop Beth once she was in full flow, and it was pleasant to be able to relax without worrying that Luc might somehow fall overboard, or that she hadn't seen Robert for over an hour meant that he had sunk into one of his black moods – far less frequent now than they had been, thank goodness. He had been wonderfully patient and under-standing when she had told him how concerned she was about her grandmother's plans to change her will, but he had still insisted that it was her grandmother's right to do as she wished and that he could fully understand why she had felt she must do so. That didn't alter the fact, though, that Greg was still very angry.

'Oh, and I nearly forgot, we went to Mougins last week. Everyone says one should, especially now that Picasso spends his summers there, and you'll never guess who we saw.'

'Picasso?' Amber guessed.

'Well, yes, we did see him and that photographer who everyone says is his mistress, Dora someone or other.'

'Dora Maar,' Amber supplied.

'Yes, that's right. But let me get to my point. It wasn't them I wanted to tell you about, it was him, Jean-Philippe, and looking just as handsome as ever.'

Very carefully Amber put down her tea cup and saucer.

'You must remember him, Amber?' Beth was pressing her. 'The artist who was staying in the cottage the year we came here together with Mummy. I thought he was so romantic and I was so envious when he asked you to model for him.'

'Yes, of course I remember him,' Amber said quietly.

Jean-Philippe! Her hands were trembling, so she folded

them together on her lap. She supposed she shouldn't feel so shocked. The South of France was a favourite haunt for artists, after all. Jean-Philippe and Henry, both here. A shiver of fear iced down her spine. There was nothing for her to worry about. She was a married woman now, with a husband. Robert was here with her and he would protect her. He knew all about Jean-Philippe, and about Henry. And besides, they were all older. She might not particularly care for Henry but that did not mean that he had not matured. He was a married man now, with a family, and hardly likely to repeat his unwanted advances of all those years ago. And Jean-Philippe's advances, would they be 'unwanted' if he were to repeat them? Serpent-like, the question wound itself around her senses, caressing and taunting them, as Jean-Philippe had once caressed her.

'He didn't recognise me at first, but of course it was several years ago.'

Somehow Amber managed to wrench her thoughts away from Jean-Philippe and the past, and back to the present.

'Yes, it must be,' she agreed lightly. Several years? She knew exactly how many – how could she not when she had the evidence of how long in front of her in Luc?

'I remember how shocked I was when I learned that he was not Madame's godson but her lover. Alistair told me that he'd heard that his current mistress is Austrian and very well connected. He asked after you, by the way, and when I told him that you were due to arrive any day he said that he hoped he would get to meet you again.'

Somehow Amber managed to force herself to smile. Her heart was hammering too heavily into her ribs and she was beginning to feel sick.

'You've gone dreadfully pale,' Beth told her. 'Are you feeling all right?'

'I still haven't adjusted to being back on dry land,' Amber fibbed, 'a sort of *mal de mer* in reverse.'

'Would you like to go and lie down?'

'No, I shall be perfectly well in a minute. How are your parents, Beth? I saw your mother in London in January and she said that your father had been suffering from gout.'

'Yes, indeed, poor Daddy, he does suffer so in the winter months, but he is much recovered now. We shall be seeing them in Scotland in September.

'Mummy told me that your little shop has become very fashionable and that Princess Marina is one of your customers. I never seem to find time to get up to London these days, but the next time I do I shall make sure I have a look. Not that I'm thinking of reburbishing, Alistair thinks this modern craze for constantly changing one's rooms is very vulgar.'

The accusation of vulgarity was one that appeared to come readily to Alistair's lips whenever the spending of money came into the equation, Amber thought tartly. Not that she would ever hurt her friend by speaking her private thoughts out aloud.

'I must say, I was astonished that Robert permitted you to do something so . . .'

'So bourgeois?' Amber supplied lightly, suddenly feeling rather cross as she realised that her consideration for Beth's feelings was not returned by Beth with regard to her own.

Beth looked so uncomfortable that Amber felt guilty. Reaching out, she covered Beth's hand with her own.

'I know having my shop must seem an unconventional thing for me to do, Beth, but it means so much to me to know that other people are seeing and valuing my father's designs, and Robert understands that. James Lees-Milne has promised me several orders, and I am hoping that the

472

National Trust will allow me to reproduce some of their archive materials in silk.'

Beth's polite smile warned Amber that she had exhausted her friend's interest in the shop, so she changed the subject and asked after Beth's children.

The summer months were bound be quiet ones for the shop with so many people away, and she had felt quite happy to leave the business in the hands of her young manager and his assistant. It would be good experience for them, and it would enable her to judge how well they could manage without her there.

They'd had to take on extra workers at the mill to get through all the orders, and Amber was thinking of experimenting with a couple of new designs, using some of her father's work that had merely been preliminary sketches but which she thought she could refine and finish herself.

'. . . And Alistair thinks that he will definitely go into the navy.' Guiltily Amber realised that she hadn't been listening to a word Beth had been saying. Dutifully she nodded her head and hoped that Beth hadn't noticed.

'Shall you be going to Daisy Fellowes' ball tonight in Cap Ferrat?' Beth asked her. 'Daisy keeps telling everyone that she is having to economise because of the depression in America, but one would never know.'

'Yes. We are going,' Amber confirmed. 'I'm looking forward to it.'

'Emerald Cunard told me about the necklace that Daisy commissioned from Cartier to compensate her for having to sell her yacht. Apparently she's calling it her tutti frutti necklace because it's got so many different coloured stones in it. Daisy's always such fun.'

'Well, I hope that the Windsors won't be there. It is so embarrassing seeing them socially now, after what's happened.

I mean, when one thinks that he was once King, even if only very briefly, and never actually crowned.'

'It's very sad, I agree, but the new King and Queen are making their own place in people's hearts, and the two little princesses are delightful. Such a pity, though, that there is no son. You are fortunate, Amber, since you have only one child, that Luc is a boy. It would have been a dreadful thing for Robert not to have a son and heir, but of course you don't need me to tell you that.'

No, she didn't. A son and heir. A well-used expression in their social class, words that tripped easily off the tongue and yet held such traps for the unwary and concealed so many secrets. Perhaps it was being here in the South of France that was making her think of the past. No one, but most of all Luc himself, must ever know that he was not Robert's child. It would be a dreadful thing for Luc to bear, stripping from him his whole belief in what he was. No loving mother would ever allow that to happen to her child.

'Night-night, Luc darling.' Amber kissed her dozing son, and smoothed back his dark hair.

Robert had rented a smart villa within walking distance of the yacht's berth, when Amber had said that she thought for Luc's sake they needed somewhere land-based during their stay.

Robert had already said his 'good nights' to Luc and was waiting for her by the door, prior to their leaving for Daisy Fellowes' gala party, whilst Gladys stood ready to tuck Luc in and make sure he was settled for the night after they had gone.

'Beth told me this afternoon that they've got Henry staying with them,' Amber told Robert, as he guided her towards the stairs, the silk taffeta of her sea-green evening gown whispering sensually against her skin as she walked.

474

She would have preferred to wear something plain and unobtrusive but Robert had come into her room just as her maid was hanging up the dress she had chosen, and had complained that he thought it far too dull, and suggested that she should wear the sea-green gown instead.

The silk Mainbocher gown, sewn with tiny crystals that caught the light when she moved, was cut on the bias and emphasised the slenderness and delicacy of her figure. Whilst its neckline was high at the front, it plunged low at the back, or at least appeared so, as in reality what looked like bare flesh was covered with fine mesh on which was embroidered a sea-green silk and crystal sea serpent that curled down her spine. Amber had thought the gown far too daring, but Robert had overruled her. Robert, like many homosexual men, had an excellent eye for style and design and often chose clothes for her.

'I know you don't care for him, but I doubt you have anything to fear from him these days in view of his obsession to father an heir. Alistair happened to mention it *en passant* this afternoon. I got the impression that he doesn't entirely approve of his brother-in-law's attitude.'

'Well, I don't think Beth can realise that. She told me that "poor Henry needs cheering up". But it isn't just Henry being here that worries me a bit, Robert.' Amber paused. 'Jean-Philippe is here as well.'

They had reached the hall and Amber could see how Robert tensed when she said Jean-Philippe's name.

'What exactly is it that concerns you?'

'I don't know,' she answered him, not quite truthfully. 'I know it's probably irrational of me but the fact that both Henry and Jean-Philippe are here makes me feel uncomfortable . . . vulnerable.'

'Henry's already attempted to blackmail and failed. He won't do so again.'

475

'But he knows, Robert, and if he chooses to say so—'

'If he does then I shall say simply that Henry is mistaken and that it was I who was with you back then. It will be his word against mine.'

'I wish we hadn't come here now. If I'd known before we left England—'

'You're worrying unnecessarily, Amber. Henry is far more likely to be brooding on the fact that he hasn't produced an heir than thinking about events that took place a lifetime ago.'

Amber nodded, sensing that Robert was beginning to get impatient with her. But she was anxious, and not just on her own account. Luc was with them, after all, and Luc was Jean-Philippe's child. Amber had searched her memory desperately over the years, fearful of finding a resemblance between them, and thankful that Robert, like Jean-Philippe, was tall and dark-haired. But what if she were to see Jean-Philippe and realise that Luc did look like him, and so much so that others might also see the resemblance? She had taken it for granted for so long now that everyone accepted Luc as Robert's child. Would that be enough? Amber prayed that it would.

The ball was being held at the Hotel Royal-Riviera at Cap Ferrat, and the road to the hotel was lined with limousines waiting to deliver the society guests to the hotel.

Robert had been right to urge her to wear her new gown, Amber acknowledged when they walked into the foyer and she saw how elegantly and expensively everyone was dressed.

In addition to Daisy, who greeted them both with a warm smile, Amber had already spotted Emerald Cunard, and Millicent Roberts, the daughter of the petrol baron – famous hostesses both of them, especially Emerald with her fabulous jewellery and her reputation for lavish hospitality. She could see the French aristocrats, Count Etienne de Beaumont, and the Prince de Condé, and their set, as well as Sir Charles and Lady Mendl, the British Ambassador and his wife.

'It looks like the whole of European society is here,' Amber murmured to Robert as they walked into the ballroom.

'And not just European society,' Robert answered. 'I can see the Aga Khan over there, and the Maharaja of Jaipur.'

'Robert, is this heaven or is it not?'

'It is certainly something to appeal to someone of your theatrical tastes, Cecil,' Robert laughed as Cecil Beaton came to join them.

'Daisy is in a sulk because I have refused to photograph her guests *en masse*, but as I have told her I am not some gossip columnist's partner in crime and she should have asked Tom Driberg to recommend someone from the *Daily Excess* to her if that was what she wanted.'

'Poor Daisy. She will be quite cast down. You are very wicked, Cecil,' Amber told him.

'You are too delicious in that gown, Amber. Turn round and let me have a proper look at it.'

Obediently Amber did so and then froze, the voices of her husband and Cecil fading. Out of the mass of guests thronging the ballroom she could see only one. And he was standing staring back at her as though he could see only her.

There were fine grey threads in his lion's mane of hair, and either the sun or life or maybe both had carved new lines into his skin. The earring was no longer there either, but these changes enhanced what he was rather than detracting from it. His shoulders filled the breadth of his dinner jacket and his eyes burned as passionately bright as she remembered. Amber told herself that the reason she was absorbing every visual detail of him so greedily was because of Luc; that it was for her son's sake that she was searching each feature, committing them to memory; the arch of his eyebrow, the slight crookedness to his nose, the sharp jut of his cheekbones and jaw, rough-hewn and overlaid with olive skin – all of them had to be memorised so that she could take them out in privacy and match them against the features of her son.

And her concentration on that wicked lazy curl of his mouth and the way he slanted that dangerous, mocking, predatory, male look in her direction – was she absorbing every detail of that because she thought she might one day find it in her son?

He was staring at her mouth, his smile deepening whilst her senses responded with a sledgehammer thud of her heart into her ribs.

'Jean-Philippe.'

Whether she had actually said his name or merely framed it didn't matter. He had seen the movement of her lips, and recognised their betrayal.

'Amber,' Robert was saying, 'Cecil was just saying that he is planning to visit Mougins to see Lee Miller and Man Ray, and he was suggesting that we might like to go with him.'

'Yes, yes, that would be lovely,' Amber answered in an abstracted manner.

She could hardly breathe, never mind think or speak logically. She was filled with panic and dread and excitement, and felt like a girl of seventeen again and not a wife and a mother. She was a woman whose body remembered that Jean-Philippe had been its first and only lover.

'Daisy has invited far too many people,' Cecil complained.

'She always does.' Amber was trying to force herself to appear normal. She had turned her back on Jean-Philippe now but not before she had seen the thin elegant woman standing at his side, placing a possessive hand on his arm.

'Oh Lord, here are the Ribbentrops bearing down on us,' Cecil groaned. 'And Goebbels is with them.'

And not just Goebbels but a positive phalanx of high-ranking uniformed SS men, and three or four other men who were not in uniform, including Otto von Brecht.

Oscar Wilde could have written a most amusing and cynical play on the coincidence of a husband and wife meeting their past loves in such circumstances, Amber acknowledged with a sinking heart, automatically moving closer to Robert in an instinctive desire to shield and protect him. She heard his indrawn breath, and knew exactly what he would be feeling. After all, hadn't she just felt like it herself when she had seen Jean-Philippe?

Life could be so very cruel, pushing and testing human resolve and emotional endurance to its very limits, and sometimes beyond.

Robert still hadn't spoken. Was he, like her, remembering that dreadful night in Munich when he had been driven to such despair over his love for Otto that he had tried to take his own life? It was never discussed between them, but Amber knew she would never forget it.

The German party had drawn level with them. Amber tensed, dreading having to witness Otto humiliating Robert again. To her relief Robert himself started to turn away from them. Amber took his arm. Then out of the corner of her eye she saw Otto excuse himself to his friends and then detach himself from them, striding out quickly to intercept Robert with a warm smile, his hand on Robert's free arm.

She may as well not have existed, Amber recognised. It was heart-wrenching – pitiful, almost – to see the way Robert suddenly came alive, to become again the charming carefree dashing Robert she remembered from their first meeting, only it wasn't her who had brought him to life, it was Otto. Otto, with his smile and his touch, and that something in his manner that said so plainly he was seeking reconciliation.

'Poor Robert, one has to admit that young Otto is a deliciously attractive proposition. Imagine causing that stern Teutonic ice to melt! I could feel a tingle going down my own spine when he shook my hand, but then maybe that was because of the strength of his practised Nazi grip,' Cecil told Amber drolly, half an hour later when she and Robert had become separated in the press of people.

'Don't joke about him, please, Cecil,' Amber begged. 'I am so worried about Robert. He is only just beginning to be himself again, and this is bound to set him back. I'm going to suggest to him that we return to the villa.'

'Unwise, my dear, and I think pointless,' Cecil told her. 'I've just seen Robert and Herr von Brecht in one of the small salons off the ballroom. To judge from the intensity of their tête-a-tête, anything you might have to say to Robert will only fall on deaf ears.'

'They were together? But Robert was here with me until Emerald dragged me off to look at Daisy's necklace. Otto may be being very friendly now, but he cut Robert dead when we were in Munich for the Olympics.'

'Well, quite plainly the young man now wishes to raise the dead, as it were, since when I saw them he was working very hard to breathe new life into their friendship.'

'Oh, Cecil, don't say that, please. Robert loves him so very much and—' Amber bit her lip. Much as she liked Cecil it wouldn't do to tell him about Robert's attempt to take his own life.

'I shall repeat as I have done so often before that Robert

480

is a fortunate man to have you as his wife. Try not to worry. In my experience, for what it's worth, the intensity of such a passion is fed by rejection and contrarily sated by a return of one's feelings. The mere fact that Otto is now courting Robert may very well bring Robert's yearning for him to an end. I should guess that it will certainly no longer be unrequited, nor their union be unconsummated,' he added frankly, 'and that alone over the period of the summer may see it burn itself out. One so longs for the cool freshness of autumn and a cessation of the clinging sweaty heat of summer by the time August is at an end. Cheer up, my dear. Perhaps you should consider indulging in a small flirtation yourself?'

A small flirtation. If only her nature inclined her towards something so safe. But when it came to their emotions, she and Robert shared vulnerability towards the very unsafe depths of true passion. The difference was that she feared it too much to ever want to embrace it again.

She had danced to music played by an orchestra conducted by a suavely handsome young Austrian, eaten sparingly from a buffet laden down with every kind of expensive delicacy, including quails' eggs and Beluga caviar, exchanged news with old friends, and now it was growing late and people were leaving. Amber acknowledged reluctantly that she would have to go in search of Robert, whom she hadn't seen for ages.

'Well, if it isn't Her Grace the Duchess.'

'Henry.' Amber forced herself to smile. Henry's features had coarsened with the years, his hair thinning and his body thickening. He rocked slightly on his feet as he stood in front of her, and Amber suspected that he was a little the worse for drink.

'Beth said that you were staying with her. I must go and find her. Emerald gave me a message for her.'

'She's gone.

'Quite like old times, isn't it? You'll let me know if you're planning to slip off with du Breveonet, won't you? Wouldn't want to miss the show.' He was leering at her now, showing unpleasantly yellowing and decaying teeth.

Amber didn't make any attempt at a response, sidestepping him instead. He tried to stop her but thankfully Daisy and some of her other guests inadvertently prevented him from doing so by gathering in front of him, giving Amber the opportunity to make her escape.

'He is still pursuing you then, I see?'

Amber was so shocked that she stopped in mid-step.

Jean-Philippe. He had seen her with Henry? How long had he been watching her? What on earth was the matter with her? He had probably merely caught a glimpse of her, that was all. What possible reason could he have for watching her?

'Not really. He was merely telling me that his sister and her husband have gone home.' Were her smile and her voice both as cool and dismissive as she wanted them to be? Would they convince and deceive him? He was an artist, after all, used to probing beneath the surface to expose the reality that lay beneath.

'Do excuse me. I must rejoin my husband.'

He was crooking his arm, flashing her that wickedly dangerous smile. 'Allow me.'

Amber stepped back from him

'We have acquaintances in common,' he told her, glancing to the far side of the room. Amber followed the direction in which he was looking, her heart sinking when she saw that Robert was part of a group that included Otto, the Ribbentrops and the woman she had seen Jean-Philippe with earlier in the evening.

It was impossible for her to refuse to go with him. To do so would amuse him and arouse the curiosity of others.

Reluctantly Amber took his arm, trying to deny the shock it gave her senses to recognise the still familiar feel of his strong muscular flesh, with its energetic pulse of life. Everything about Jean-Philippe was drawn in strong colours and with vibrant strokes. It was impossible to visualise a portrait of him in anything other than the most virile and energetic of oils. Picasso could possibly convey that sense of him being a flamboyant freebooter best, Amber decided, trying to distract her thoughts from the personal to the safer impersonal.

It was Herr von Ribbentrop himself who introduced Amber to Jean-Philippe's companion, Countess Irene.

'My father was from Warsaw,' she told Amber, acknowledging the introduction with a swiftly assessing and then dismissive look before demanding of Jean-Philippe coolly, 'Cigarette, darling.'

Was the countess deliberately belittling Jean-Philippe, to let them all know what his position was, Amber wondered as he removed a packet of Sobranie from his pocket, offered her the pack and then lit the cigarette for her. Or was that simply her general manner?

Taking a deep lungful of smoke from her cigarette, she continued, 'But I am Austrian by birth, since he died before I was born and on his death my mother returned to Austria and her own family. My late husband was also Austrian.' She blew out a cloud of smoke. 'And a great art connoisseur.'

'Whilst you, my dear Irene, are a connoisseur of the artist,' someone riposted, causing everyone to laugh. Everyone, that was, apart from Amber and Jean-Philippe.

She desperately wanted to leave but Robert was deep in conversation with Otto and had his back to her so that she couldn't signal her desire.

* * *

Jean-Philippe observed Amber's disquiet with interested curiosity, wondering at the cause of it. She had such a well of deep emotions behind that calm mask. Her face, though, especially her eyes, always gave her away – to him, at least.

Jean-Philippe had known that he and Amber were bound to meet. He had been intrigued both mentally and sexually when Beth had told him that Amber and her husband were on their way to the South of France. He had wondered how the intervening years might have changed her, and he was, he admitted, now impressed. He had known, of course, that she would still be beautiful; as an artist he had known that. Her bone structure alone guaranteed it, but Amber had something more than beauty, even if she herself seemed so piquantly unaware of that fact.

How deliciously exciting and tantalising that she should have retained that lack of awareness of her allure that he remembered so well. It gave her an air that to some men, those who did not know her as he did, might seem to signify a lack of passion, but which to him whispered erotically of a woman whose passions had not been truly awoken for a very long time, and certainly not by the ridiculous Englishman who was attempting to pursue her and whose advance she quite plainly did not welcome any more now than she had done back then.

The summer, which had begun to irritate and bore him, along with the woman with whom he was committed to sharing it, suddenly seemed enticing and filled with possibilities. Jean-Philippe had allowed Irene to believe she had the controlling hand in their relationship, because it had suited him to do so. An artist with his expensive tastes could not live by sales commission alone. Such an artist needed a wealthy patron, and in the absence of a modern-day Medici he had had to settle for Countess Irene, who wanted the social kudos of being squired around by a younger lover, but without, to

Jean-Philippe's amusement, the sexual benefits that came with paying for his presence in her life.

'I think your wife wishes to leave, Robert,' Otto announced, intercepting the look Amber was trying to give Robert. Otto's smile was wide and charming, the smile of a frank open young man who only wanted to please. It was hard to imagine him hurting Robert in the way that he had done. Was she wrong to feel so suspicious of him, Amber wondered. Was she being unfair? People could and did change.

'May I compliment you on your appearance?' he asked Amber.

'It was Robert who chose my dress,' Amber told him lightly, 'so maybe you should compliment him?'

'I do compliment him,' Otto replied with another smile. 'On his good fortune in having such a beautiful wife.'

He clicked his heels together as he bowed over her hand. A young German who personified everything that Hitler wanted Germany's young men to be, at least on the surface.

'I see that du Breveonet is still playing the same game,' Robert commented as they left the party and got into their waiting car.

Amber agreed lightly to let him know she understood what he was saying. 'But with a different godmother.'

'I have promised to show Otto over the yacht,' Robert told her quickly, changing the subject.

Amber looked at him but he had turned away from her and was looking through the window. Deliberately? She wanted to beg him to be careful and not to run the risk of being hurt again, but already she could sense him withdrawing from her as he always did when he embarked on one of his affairs.

*　　*　　*

485

'Mrs Pickford, if I could have a word with you . . . ?'

Blanche looked at the doctor, who stood hovering a little uncomfortably in the door to her study. She put down her pen and closed the book of household accounts she had been checking,

'If it's about that Chinese brat . . .'

'No, it's about Gregory.'

'If you're going to tell me that he's drinking too much, Dr Brookes—' Blanche began, but the doctor stopped her, shaking his head.

'He is, yes, but no, that's not what I need to discuss with you.'

Blanche suppressed a small sigh. Greg's return, instead of bringing her happiness, had brought her nothing but worry.

'We'd better go into the library. I'll ring for tea.'

'Not on my account, ma'am.'

So it was serious then, Blanche thought.

'You'll be aware of something of the life your grandson lived in Hong Kong?' the doctor began once they were seated either side of the tall window through which sunlight streamed into the elegant two-storey room. A gallery, reached via a polished oak staircase, provided access to the second storey, and in winter a fire burning in the huge fireplace kept the whole room warm.

Despite its proportions, the room somehow managed to combine both elegance and comfort, a man's room that at the same time welcomed Blanche's own sex within its walls.

In addition to the high-backed leather chairs either side of the fireplace and the Knole sofa in front of it, small groups of chairs and sofas set around tables offered comfortable surroundings for the bookworm.

Blanche, though, wasn't much of a reader, which was why she preferred these chairs here, in front of the window,

486

where it was possible to look out on reality and the present rather than into the room and its knowledge of the past.

Now, in answer to Dr Brookes's question she responded tartly, 'It would be difficult for me not to be, since he brought the evidence of it home with him in the shape of his child.'

The heavy dark red silk curtains Amber had persuaded her to have, since they replicated those in Vanbrugh's original designs for the room, produced a glow that somehow warmed the coldest of hearts and the coldest of days, Blanche acknowledged, as she resisted the temptation to reach out and stroke the rich fabric.

It was Amber who stroked silk as though it were the flesh of a much-loved and precious child, not her. It had cost her far too much, and now she suspected it was about to demand another payment from her.

'There really is no easy way for me to tell you this,' the doctor was saying uncomfortably, 'but tell you I must. I'm deeply concerned.'

Blanche waited, whilst the doctor appeared to struggle with himself.

'Gregory has contracted a disease of an intimate nature that cannot be cured.'

The doctor could feel himself starting to perspire slightly. It was a damnable thing that he had to do, but he must warn Blanche Pickford of what lay ahead, as much for Gregory's own sake as that of anyone else. For one thing, it was natural that Blanche would want Greg to marry.

A disease of an intimate nature, the doctor had said. Blanche's thought processes seemed to have slowed down, stuck in a bog of disbelief and shock. She remembered Marcus talking bluntly and angrily about the number of young naïve soldiers who had picked up venereal diseases from French prostitutes.

'Which disease?' she asked steadily.

'A bad one. Syphilis.'

'Syphilis?' She knew what it was, of course. 'Are you sure?'

'As sure as I can be at this stage. Gregory refuses to accept my diagnosis, though. He believes I am merely trying to frighten him.'

'But surely, if you are right, there is something that can be done?'

The red of the silk offered no comfort now, rather it was the colour of anger, and of blood, of lives lost and hopes destroyed. As always the silk itself was her enemy; the thief that stole from her all that she most valued. The man she had wanted, her beloved son, and now Greg, a rotten branch on a withered tree, both doomed to destruction.

It was obvious that she was shocked but she was bearing the news as strongly as Dr Brookes had hoped she would.

'I'm afraid not. There is no cure.' The doctor wished he could have offered her better news. 'Fortunately from what he has told me it seems that he contracted the disease after Rose's birth, and not from her mother, so she will not be affected.'

'Am I supposed to be grateful for that? She is nothing to me, an unwanted bastard child. Greg is my grandson.' It was as close as Blanche dared let herself get to breaking down. 'There must be something; some treatment.'

'No, there is not, and I would be lying to you if I said there was. There are already physical signs of the degeneration one would expect – in fact, that is what alerted me to the possibility.'

Blanche took a deep breath and turned to face the doctor. 'He is also addicted to opium – could there not be a mistake and that be the cause of those signs?'

She had tried so hard to ignore the signs of Greg's opium addiction when he had first returned home, but after the incident when Luc had accidentally witnessed Greg preparing to smoke the drug, Blanche had finally admitted to herself what she had not wanted to acknowledge. She had thought then that she had known the worst of her grandson's degradation but if Dr Brookes was right then she had deluded herself. How was it possible for her beloved son to have fathered someone like Greg?

'No,' Dr Brookes told her, inadvertently breaking into her despairing thoughts. 'I am so sorry.'

But nowhere near as sorry as she was, Blanche thought tiredly after the doctor had gone.

Why had Greg behaved so foolishly and so recklessly? Hadn't he learned his lesson from what had happened with Caroline Fitton Legh? Hadn't that made him realise that life was filled with consequences of one's actions?

She had had such plans for him, such hopes. Amber's marriage to Robert could have opened so many doors for Greg, and with Blanche's money he could have become a great politician, Prime Minister even, if he had wished.

Instead he was going to die a madman, leaving behind him an illegitimate half-caste. How Barrant would laugh at her now.

Chapter Forty-One

'And, Mummy, look at this drawing I'm doing. It's going to be like the one that Monsieur Picasso gave to me.'

Amber looked obediently at the sketch Luc was holding out to her, grubby, like his hands, with charcoal. They had had such a wonderful day in Mougins.

The artist had been in a jovial mood when they had been introduced to him by Man Ray, whom Cecil had gone to meet, inviting them to join him for lunch at the café bar he had made his favourite haunt.

In the end Cecil and Amber had made the trip to the small medieval town without Robert. The German high command did not approve of certain modern artists whose work – and lifestyles – they considered to be decadent, and for that reason Otto had not felt able to accompany them, which meant that Robert had not wanted to do so either.

Amber had worried about taking Luc in case Jean-Philippe was here, but she had promised her son the outing and to her relief there had been no sign of her ex-lover.

In fact, they had had the most deliciously indulgent day, as least so far as Amber was concerned, during which she had been able to listen to and absorb the artistic talk filling the atmosphere of the café far more headily than any amount of wine.

Man Ray had taken photographs of them all, and then Cecil, not to be outdone, had insisted on taking some of his own, making Amber laugh and protest when he had made her and Luc pose for him for a variety of different shots, turning sideways to smile at one another; Luc leading her by the hand, sharing an ice cream, and Amber's own favourite, Luc sitting at her feet, his arm resting on her lap as he smiled up at her.

'You'd better go upstairs and ask Nanny to wash your hands, darling. We'll be going out soon.'

Today she and Luc were going to Grasse with Beth and her children. Amber had had an idea for a new modern design for next year's summer collection, a silk overprinted with the colours of the flowers she remembered seeing on sale in Grasse during her first visit, massed together in a repeat pattern as though painted in the style of Monet. It would be a light-hearted summery fabric, printed on airy silk voile to be used with a plain undercloth that would come in ten strengths of plain colour, so that a summer room, perhaps a conservatory or a summerhouse, could be decorated with varying tones of the same fabric.

Amber was already thinking of using the fabric in the orangery at Osterby in varous shades from soft peach through to deepest terracotta, and asking Cecil to photograph it for her for next year's spring advertising campaign.

The door to the villa's small drawing room opened and the under-butler, brought with them from England, announced firmly, 'Lady Elizabeth McCrea and Viscount Hollowes, Your Grace.'

'Amber, isn't it lovely, I've left the children with Nanny and brought Henry instead.' Beth was already in the room, hurrying forward to embrace her.

Over Beth's shoulder Amber watched Henry smirk, and her normally tender heart hardened.

'I'm sorry, Beth, but I'm afraid I'm going to have to cry off,' she told her friend.

Beth stepped back from her, exclaiming in disappointment, 'Oh, Amber, poor Henry was looking forward to being cheered up, weren't you, Henry?'

'Obviously Amber has another and more important engagement. After all, she has so many old friends here. I'm sure, for instance, that Jean-Philippe would be delighted to have her sit for him again.'

Ignoring Henry's barbed comment, Amber told Beth, 'I'm afraid that Luc isn't feeling very well and I feel I should stay with him.'

'Well, yes, of course.'

Amber prayed that Luc wouldn't come back downstairs just then to give the lie to her claim. 'Please excuse me a minute. I just want to check that Cook has sent up the hot posset I asked her to make for him.'

In the hallway she found the under-butler and drew him out of earshot to give him a message for the nursery to the effect that Luc was not to come downstairs for the time being.

'I'm sorry about that,' she smiled as she went back into the drawing room, 'and I'm sorry too not to be able to go to Grasse.' That much was true.

'I suppose Robert's gone off somewhere in his yacht?' Beth asked.

They'd been in the South of France for just over a fortnight now, and Robert was spending an increasing amount of time with Otto, who it seemed was as enthusiastic about sailing as Robert.

'Yes, you know what an old seadog he's become,' Amber agreed, eager now for them to take their leave.

She'd have to make her own visit to Grasse. Perhaps she could persuade Cecil to go with her, Amber decided as she rang for the butler to escort Beth and Henry to the front door.

'You'll be at the Anstruthers' party tonight, won't you?'

'Oh, I'm sure Amber won't want to miss that. After all, Amber and Jean-Philippe are old . . . friends.'

'Hardly old friends. I posed for him, that is all, and at your mother's behest, Henry,' Amber pointed out sharply.

Beth gave a small semi-embarrassed titter of nervous laughter. 'Henry, you are really so naughty for teasing Amber.'

At last Beth and Henry had gone. Amber felt too on edge to settle back into her plans for her new fabric, and Luc naturally had been disappointed when she had told him about the change in their plans.

It seemed so unfair to keep him cooped up indoors that Amber offered instead to walk with him down to the public beach.

'And I can paddle in the sea?' he demanded.

'We shall see,' Amber told him, refusing to be drawn.

In the end, their shared afternoon turned out to be far more unexpectedly enjoyable. Luc was an intelligent child, full of questions, laughing when they walked along the water's edge and the occasional higher-than-expected wave caught Amber off guard, soaking the hem of the simple sea-turquoise linen dress she was wearing.

Indulgently, as they had the beach to themselves, she slipped off her sandals and lifted her skirt, paddling alongside her son, revelling in the forgotten pleasure of wriggling her toes in the sun-warmed wet sand whilst the sea teased and frothed over them.

Then she sat on some rocks, guarding the treasures Luc had brought for her inspection – shiny flat stones, some shells, a piece of seaweed and, most precious of all, the tiny fish he had found and carried cupped in his hand to put in the small natural rock pool next to his mother.

This was happiness at its most perfect and most pure, Amber thought lazily: the warmth to the sunshine, the bountiful gifts of nature, including the most bountiful of all, the laughter of a beloved child.

'Your son?'

Jean-Philippe's voice, breaking into the privacy of her thoughts, startled her. The last time she had looked, the beach had been empty and yet somehow he had managed to sneak up on them without her being aware of his presence.

'Yes, yes, he is,' she agreed. It was pointless after all denying Luc's existence.

'You don't look very pleased to see me,' he teased her.

'Why should I be when you came skulking up on me, making me jump like that?' Amber defended herself. It made her feel uncomfortable to realise that he had been watching them.

Jean-Philippe gave a small shrug. 'I saw you both earlier paddling in the sea,' he told her, adding abruptly, '*Certainement* he is like you.'

Like *her*? A sensation that both weakened her and filled her with gratitude surged through her.

'Most people think he is more like Robert.'

'He has your husband's mannerisms, and his colouring, but his bone structure is yours.'

Amber looked towards Luc, desperately willing him to come back, but he had his back to her and was crouching down showing something to the pretty little girl in the pink playsuit who had been following him adoringly for the last half an hour.

'I did love you, you know.'

Her heart gave a great jolt. Somehow or other Jean-Philippe had managed to take possession of her hand, which he was now holding firmly as he sat down next to her, shielding her from anyone else's view.

'That much was true.'

'You should not be talking to me like this,' Amber protested. She felt more like a seventeen-year-old than a married woman and a mother.

'Why not? What harm can it do?'

The gently mocking note in Jean-Philippe's voice warned Amber that he knew exactly what harm his words could do.

'I must go. Robert will be wondering where we are.'

Jean-Philippe's laughter was soft. 'Ah, *ma pauvre* Amber, I have frightened you, I fear. That wasn't my intention.'

He was still holding her hand and he lifted it to his lips. The pull of the familiar longing was undermining her defences as surely as the surge of the sea had sucked away the sand from beneath her toes earlier. And the sensation was equally sensually pleasurable. Would he kiss her fingertips one by one, as he had once done before? Would he—

'Mummy, look, I've got another fish.'

A brief brush of his lips against her knuckles and she was free to retreat into her relief – and her disappointment?

Luc was regarding Jean-Philippe with a mixture of curiosity and suspicion, which in different circumstances would have moved Amber to tender amusement.

As calmly as she could she made the introductions, and then watched as her son was charmed and then enchanted when Jean-Philippe addressed him as an equal, and then showed him a magic trick with a small coin, apparently making it disappear and then reappear from behind Luc's ear with deft sleight of hand.

The same sleight of hand with which he had stolen her

heart all those years ago? She must not allow him to captivate Luc as he had done her. The last thing she wanted was any kind of bond developing between Luc and the man who had fathered him. Her heart jumped with sharp anxiety.

The sensation, the need, unfurled inside her, stretching itself into life, stroking through her so languorously that she might not even have been aware that it was there if it hadn't been for the tight ache in her nipples and the delicious feeling of excitement-cum-anticipation that made her smile and welcome its presence. But then it grew too swiftly, becoming an insistent clamour that filled her head with dangerous images of a darkened room and a pair of male hands on her naked body, stroking the need higher, tormenting her with his teasingly light, knowing touch that made her so hungry for a deeper penetrating intimacy that she moaned and writhed on the bed beneath her, spreading her legs in urgent invitation, longing for the full deep thrust of him to fill the aching emptiness within her that cried out for that satisfaction.

The sound of her own anguished cry brought Amber from her sleep, and into the darkness of her bedroom. She was lying on her back, her heart pounding, the covers kicked back, her hand between her legs and resting on her sex. Resting? Shame, hot and guilt-laden, seared her. It was years since this had happened to her, since the repressed ache of her womanhood had burst through the restraint she imposed on it to made its demands on her whilst she was defenceless. She had been disbelieving the first time she had been woken by the pulsing satisfaction of her own orgasm, her mind clouded by vague images from her dream. Then guiltily and reluctantly, swearing that each time would be the last, she had learned to appease the ache of need within her body with the touch of her own fingers; the act of self-satisfaction her shameful secret self-indulgence.

Her heart was still pounding with agitation brought on by her own shocked recognition of what she had been doing. Her fingers pressed more firmly against her mound, and then moved lower, slipping quickly into place like a thief in the night, stealthily finding the unguarded entrance she knew was there. Her movements were familiar, swift, silent and skilled, her mind watchful and alert for any sound from outside her door that might lead to her being discovered. Her fingertip had found the place. Aahhh, yes, the pleasure, yes. Amber could feel it building, rocking her, gripping her, as she climbed with it, taking her finally into the void that lay beyond her gasped shudder of release.

'Cassandra was here yesterday. She told me that Greg Pickford is drinking himself to death – and worse. Is it true?'

Jay looked at his grandfather.

'Yes,' he told him curtly. Jay had no intention of sharing in any gloating his grandfather might wish to do over Greg's plight and Blanche's despair. However, when Barrant next spoke, far from glorying in the situation, he simply said, 'Blanche will have taken it badly, I dare say. She had high hopes for him.' He paused and then continued, 'I told Cassandra that she'd do better getting herself a son off her husband than spending her time gossiping.'

Jay had to hide his astonishment. Normally his grandfather was only too delighted to hear anything that reflected the Pickfords in a bad light.

'What about that wife of yours, Jay? She's losing her marbles according to Cassandra.'

Somehow Jay managed to control his feelings. There was no point losing his temper with his grandfather. Tact had never been Barrant's strong suit, and after all, he was not responsible for either Lydia's condition or Cassandra's gossip about it.

'No, I don't want to do it any more, Cassandra.'

Lydia's fretful voice grated on Cassandra's nerves like a badly used saw. She, after all, was the one who controlled their relationship, not Lydia. But recently Lydia had been proving obdurate, sometimes point-blank refusing to do what Cassandra wanted her to do.

Reminders of their 'love', originally such an easy way to tempt her into obedience, might have lost their power to move Lydia, but she still had warnings and threats to use, Cassandra comforted herself.

'Lydia darling, you are being awfully foolish,' she began, getting up off the bed, where she had been lying naked for the last twenty minutes or so trying to persuade Lydia, who was still fully dressed and standing defensively by the door, to join her. 'I mean, if Jay were to learn, by accident of course, what you'd been doing with me, what do you think he'd do?' Cassandra smiled encouragingly as she waited for Lydia to work out the answer and then give in.

'Jay loves me.'

Not the answer she'd wanted.

'Does he? He may tell you that, Lydia.'

'Yes, he does, and when I tell him what you've made me do he's going to be very angry with you.'

Cassandra scowled. This wasn't what was supposed to happen. She was the one with the power to make threats, not Lydia. Lydia was crazy if she genuinely thought that Jay would defend and protect her.

But then Lydia *was* crazy, and never more so than when she started behaving like a stubborn child, as she was doing now. In this mood there was no reasoning with her – and no frightening her either. In this mood, to Lydia Jay was her saviour, a father figure who could do no wrong whilst she, Cassandra, 'bad and naughty'.

She had dealt with this mood before, Cassandra reminded herself. It would soon pass.

But this was the first time Lydia had threatened to tell Jay about their relationship. If Lydia's husband was anyone else but Jay, Cassandra could have persuaded him somehow that Lydia was mistaken and confused. But Jay would believe Lydia. He could see right through Cassandra, and it scared her.

'Lydia sweetheart . . .' she began cajolingly.

Lydia turned round and pulled open the bedroom door.

'Lydia,' Cassandra warned less sweetly, but it was too late, Lydia had gone. Cursing under her breath and red-faced with temper, Cassandra pulled on her clothes.

All this was Greg Pickford's fault. If he hadn't come between them, Caroline would still be alive.

Caroline. Her one true love.

Cassandra sat down on the bed. She had loved Caroline so much. Why hadn't Caro done what she had begged her to do? She would still be alive then.

Sometimes at night, just as she fell asleep, Cassandra could hear Caroline's voice calling to her, begging her to help her, as the mud of the lake sucked her deeper the more she struggled to free herself from it.

All she had had to do to live was promise to get rid of it – the thing Greg Pickford had left inside her. That was all. She had begged Caroline to do it. She had told her that it would prove her love for her. But Caroline had refused. And now Caroline was dead, and she was alone. She had been a fool to think someone like Lydia could ever take Caroline's place. She looked at the handcuffs Lydia had refused to wear, which had started off their quarrel.

Let her go and tell Jay. What could he do? Nothing. She

hadn't been quick enough. She should have told Lydia that she had seen Jay kissing Amber, and asked her then how much she thought Jay loved *her*, and if that hadn't worked she should have reminded her of the photographs she had taken of her. Smiling now, Cassandra finished dressing. From the window she could see her chauffeur bringing round the car and then Lydia stepping into it. Clever Lydia, to have thought of doing that. She must remember to make sure she was rewarded for her cleverness – next time.

And there would be a next time. Cassandra was determined on that.

Chapter Forty-Two

The first thing Amber heard as the under-butler let her into the hall was the sound of male laughter coming from the small downstairs room Robert had made his own.

The door to it opened and Robert and Otto came out together, Robert's arm round Otto's shoulders, both of them in obviously high spirits.

Otto, punctilious as always, made a small bow as soon as he saw her, saying to Robert as he did so, 'You really are too kind and generous.'

'Nonsense, it would be impossible for me to be too kind or too generous to you, Otto. You know that.' Robert was clasping Otto's hand now and the smile they exchanged completely excluded Amber.

'You are so very good.'

'My dearest boy.'

The silence prickled with Amber's awareness of all that they were not saying. Robert was almost illuminated by his happiness; it shone from him, banishing all the old shadows. He looked years younger, but not, of course, as young as Otto.

Both of them were in shirtsleeves and, as though he couldn't help himself, Robert slid his hand up Otto's arm in a gesture of helpless adoration before gripping his shoulder. Otto had raised his free hand to clasp Robert's arm, but somehow his gesture lacked the compulsive delight of Robert's. No one seeing them would fail to recognise who was the loved and who the lover.

Was she being unfair? Robert was deliriously happy and Otto was being kind to him. Their shared laughter, when she had come in, proved that.

'Tonight I shall take you to the casino, but I shall insist that you must lose,' Robert was saying softly.

'And thus prove the adage about being lucky in love?' Otto teased him softly. 'I don't need to lose at the casino tables to know that. I am more than lucky in love, Robert. I am blessed and blessed again. Until this evening.'

Otto had gone and Robert was wandering round the drawing room with a besotted smile on his face, not listening to a word Amber was saying.

They had been in the South of France for just under a month now. Beth had become rather cool with her because of Amber's refusal to go out with her if she thought that Henry might be joining them, although Beth had not specifically said anything.

There had been no more accidental meetings with Jean-Philippe, even though Amber and Luc had spent many happy afternoons down by the shore since their first meeting. No accidental meetings, perhaps, but that did not mean that she had not seen him, or been in his company – far from it.

Robert was openly and joyously besotted with Otto, and most evenings he and Amber attended parties where Robert spent his time with Otto, and surrounded by his fellow Germans and those who supported them, including Countess Irene, her high-ranking German SS brother-in-law and, of course, Jean-Philippe, whilst Amber was left to entertain herself.

* * *

502

Jean-Philippe had been very attentive to her, Amber acknowledged. Because he was enjoying teasing her, or because he genuinely wanted her? It would be wiser for her to believe the former.

Only last night after dinner at the villa his mistress was renting he had whispered to Amber, 'Why are you so afraid to let me get close to you?'

'I am not afraid,' she had denied.

'Then walk with me now in the gardens,' he had demanded.

'I am not afraid,' she had repeated. 'I simply have no wish to be "close to you".'

'No wish but a very great desire, *oui*?' he had whispered. 'Just like my desire for you.'

Remembering those words now, as she stood in front of the drawing-room window of their villa looking down towards the harbour, filled Amber with a mixture of guilt and shame. Because Jean-Philippe was right: against all reason she did desire him. Very much indeed.

Maybe it was the lazy sensual heat of the south; maybe it was the fact that seeing him again had brought back memories of what it was to be young and alive to the passion within herself; maybe it was because she knew that Jay, whom she so truly and completely loved in so many different ways, would never and could never be hers, least of all as a lover; or maybe it was simply that she had lived a celibate life for too long; whatever the reason her nights were tormented by the fierce pangs of her own longing and her days little better.

Last night, trying desperately not to think about Jay nor to yearn for him as she had tried and failed for so very many nights now, with Jean-Philippe standing next to her, the scent of him all around her, she had felt her body give in. Denied its right too long for Jay, it had remembered its youth, and Jean-Philippe, who had shared that youth with her. Now just thinking about Jean-Philippe was making her ache for him in the most shameful way, whilst the pain of her love for Jay was driving her into an unfamiliar state of recklessness. There would be no emotional danger for her with Jean-Philippe, after all, and who knew, perhaps satisfying the physical desire that had been burning in her ever since she had first realised that she loved Jay, might even help to ease the ache of her loneliness for him.

She would not be lonely with Jean-Philippe. Did he know how much she wanted him? Amber was tempted to laugh at her own question. Of course he did. He knew it and he was enjoying feeding her desire with the intention of ultimately harvesting it.

She looked towards Robert, her feelings pushed to one side by her concern for him.

'I know how much you enjoy Otto's company but do you think it wise to spend so much time with him?'

'Wise? It is not a desire for wisdom that motivates me, Amber, it is a desire for love, Otto's love. Oh, I know what you're thinking but you're wrong. You saw him earlier. You can see how he's changed, and how things are between us.'

Amber could hear the challenge in Robert's voice. Could a leopard change its spots? Maybe not, but love was a well-known phoenix, and if Otto did love Robert then it was possible that that love had transformed him.

'Please be careful,' she begged him.

'I'm not Luc, Amber. I'm a man.' He was getting angry. Because he felt she had questioned his judgement or because he wasn't as sure of Otto as he wanted her to think? 'I do not want to discuss the matter any further. And I certainly don't intend to allow you to question Otto's feelings for me, Amber, or mine for him.'

He was angry now, which meant that he would probably spend the evening being angry with her.

She wasn't looking forward to the evening. The atmosphere inside the casinos changed people, bringing to life such unpleasant avarice.

Amber rarely gambled. It simply didn't appeal to her. Something about the whole process frightened and repelled her. It was another dangerous addiction that destroyed those it possessed, like drink and drugs. And loving the wrong person?

How vulnerable and frail the human race was, Amber acknowledged sadly.

They were a little later leaving than they had planned, and the casino was already full when they joined Otto at the tables.

Emerald Cunard was seated quite close to him, her arms solid with diamond bracelets. The Aga Khan was there, and several women who were habitual gamblers, their faces tight with excitement and fear.

Robert took a seat next to Otto. Watching the complicit smiles they exchanged, Amber sighed inwardly. Tonight she was wearing a new dress in the shade of silk that had given her her name. The light tan she had acquired emphasised its richness, and she had seen in the bedroom mirror how it made her eyes look startlingly bright.

'Beautiful.' She could feel the warmth of Jean-Philippe's breath against her bare shoulder. He was standing behind her, and in the mirrors on the opposite wall their reflections merged.

'You look like a living, breathing statue come to life and far too sensually rich for any man to resist. I want to unwrap you like a special gift, indulging my senses as I do so.'

The croupier called for people to place their bets. Amber saw the chips Robert pushed discreetly to Otto. It was none of her business if her husband chose to indulge his lover. Robert could afford it, after all.

'I think Countess Irene wants you,' Amber told Jean-Philippe steadily, turning away from him to feign interest in Robert's bet.

Beth came over with Alistair – and Henry.

'Amber, doesn't this remind you of when we were girls? Remember how you won when Mummy and Daddy brought us here?

'No, don't go,' she protested. 'Sit with Henry instead and bring him some luck.' Beth turned to her brother. 'There you are, Henry. I'm sure Amber will be delighted to sit with you whilst we go and get some supper.'

Amber was trapped and she could tell from the triumphant look in Henry's eyes that he knew it. Somehow or other, as he sat down next to her, he managed to touch her thigh, apologising insincerely.

Amber could smell his sweat, slightly sour, and unpleasantly intimate.

An hour later Amber was longing to escape, even though Henry thankfully had left, or rather been dragged away by Beth.

Several people had joined the table and then left, but those who were hardened gamblers were still there.

The croupier was calling for fresh bets. A small audience had begun to gather round the table. Emerald Cunard was laughing as she stripped off one of her bracelets and dropped it onto the table. Robert's pile of chips was growing. The Aga Khan was studying the table with hooded concentration whilst Countess Irene was studying Emerald's bracelet.

Robert signalled to a waiter and ordered more champagne. On the other side of the table a pretty girl pouted and leaned towards Robert, her empty glass in her hand, her breasts almost fully exposed by the low neckline of her satin gown. Amber recognised her vaguely as an up-and-coming American film star. Her escort, an older, heavily built man, slapped the champagne glass out of her hand and dragged her back. She started to cry. Greed and desperation – they went hand in hand here, Amber thought. Her head had begun to ache.

She turned to Robert and told him quietly, 'I'm going to leave, if you don't mind. I'm not feeling very well. I'll take the car and send it back for you.'

Robert nodded his head. He was too involved with Otto to care what she did, Amber acknowledged as she made her way to the exit via the cloakroom.

It was too early for her to go to bed. Instead she went into the drawing room, shaking her head when the under-butler asked her if she required anything.

She should write to her grandmother. And to Jay? She longed to do so but their letters to one another were strictly business now. Each word she wrote had to be carefully weighed and pored over, each letter sent now leaden with the pain of what had happened and what she really felt. Amber sometimes wondered if it would not have been better for them both if they had severed all contact with one another completely, rather than what felt like dying from a thousand small cuts. And yet the moment she thought that she was filled with anxious panic at the thought of not hearing from Jay ever again.

This was her private addiction and her own private form of hell. She longed desperately sometimes to be able to turn back the clock to the days of innocence and youth, when their relationship had been free of shadows and she had been able to pour her heart out to Jay in her letters, and only delight in receiving his letters back to her. That innocence was gone now. She was a married woman and a mother with no reason to yearn for a girl's innocence, and certainly no right to do so.

When the drawing-room door first opened, Amber assumed that it had been opened by the under-butler, concerned about her lack of appetite, which made her shocked when she looked up and saw Henry.

He smirked. 'I told your chap you were expecting me and not to bother announcing me. And that's true, isn't it, Amber? You have been expecting me, haven't you?'

Whilst he'd been talking Amber had been making her way towards the bell by the fireplace. She'd almost reached it when Henry suddenly realised what she was doing and beat her to it, laughing at her as he grabbed hold of her and swung her round so that she had her back to the wall.

'Silly of you, my dear, especially when really you want to be alone with me.'

He'd been drinking. Amber could smell it on his breath.

'Henry, I really do think you should leave.'

'Do you? How unfortunate, because I certainly don't intend to, at least not yet. Have you let du Breveonet have you yet, Amber? I've been watching the pair of you, of course, but Beth will keep interfering and insisting on dragging me all over the place. Did you enjoy it as much as the first time? You really enjoyed that, didn't you? All those little sighs and cries, especially when—'

'Stop it.'

Amber would have covered her ears with her hands if she could have pulled them free of Henry's grip.

'What's the matter? No one can hear us. The butler won't come in. I slipped him enough to make sure of that. I expect he's feathering his nest very nicely, or maybe du Breveonet doesn't come to you? Maybe you go to him?'

'I am not seeing Jean-Philippe.'

'No, well, it hardly matters.' His voice hardened. 'You owe me. You know that, don't you, Amber? You owe me a very big debt and with interest, luring me on the way you did, enticing me and exciting me.'

He released one of her hands and hooked his fingers in the front of her dress, wrenching it downwards. The fabric held firm, causing him to drag it down, exposing her breasts. Amber tried to cover herself with her free arm but he pulled it away, laughing at her.

'You weren't so modest with the painter. Don't be a tease.' Henry was breathing heavily and staring at her naked breasts.

Amber tried again to break free, gasping in shock when he suddenly hit her face hard with his open palm, the force of his blow jerking her neck back painfully.

Amber could feel the heat of his breath against her breasts as he pinched her nipple and bit into her tender flesh.

Revulsion shocked through her, masking her physical pain. She wanted to close her eyes to blot out the sight of him but instinct told her that she mustn't, and that somehow she must fight back. She kicked at his ankles and then, remembering something Greg must once have said, she raised her knee and drove it as hard as she could into his groin.

In retaliation he bit savagely into her breast before releasing her to hold her off and shake her violently. Then he dragged her towards the Knole sofa, whilst she struggled do break free. When he kicked her legs out of the way she fell, collapsing half on and half off the sofa. She could feel him tearing at her dress, then pushing it up out of the way when he couldn't pull it off. She tried to resist him but he was hitting her, slapping her face so hard that she bit the inside of her own mouth, then banging her head against the back of the sofa. Her head was ringing from the blows. It would be so easy to give in and simply lose consciousness. He was going to rape her anyway.

'Don't pretend you aren't enjoying this. You know you are.' He was unfastening his trousers, his fingers gripping her hair as he held out his stiff engorged flesh, intent on forcing her mouth towards it. Amber felt the nausea churn up from her stomach into her throat. Another second and it would be pressing against her lips. She fought to pull back, and then suddenly, miraculously, she was free and Henry was lying on his back on the floor with Jean-Philippe standing over him.

Weakly, Amber tried to straighten her dress. She was trembling so much that her hands wouldn't work properly. Henry was struggling to get up. Jean-Philippe had obviously hit him very hard. His nose was bleeding.

'She's all yours. I never knew what you saw in her anyway,' he told Jean-Philippe. 'Filthy tart!'

'Tonight you will tell your sister that you are returning to England. Tomorrow morning you will leave. If you don't then I have friends who will make the rest of your stay here very uncomfortable.'

Henry's face had lost all its colour. 'You can't threaten me.'

'I'm not threatening you. I'm making a promise. Now get out. Because if you don't the only way you'll be leaving will be on a stretcher.'

Henry had gone. Amber had no idea what Jean-Philippe had said to the under-butler and she didn't honestly care. She wanted desperately to go to her room, but she felt too weak to move.

Jean-Philippe came back into the drawing room.

'How did you know?' she asked him.

510

'I saw him leave the casino shortly after you and I guessed what he was intending to do. I would have been here sooner only I was delayed. Would you like me to summon anyone, your maid or—'

'No, no . . . It's her night off anyway. He didn't tear my dress, but I can't get it on properly and I don't want anyone to see me like this You can't tear silk, it looks fragile but it's incredibly strong. I'd like to go to my room . . .'

Her voice faded as she struggled with the effort of speaking the disjointed sentences.

Jean-Philippe must have understood her, though, because he nodded and then watched her as she got to her feet and started to walk towards the door.

She made it halfway there, suddenly coming to an abrupt halt, unable to go any further.

The light from the chandelier showed Jean-Philippe what he had not seen before: her face where Henry had hit her was bruised along her cheekbone, the flesh of her throat grazed.

He had hit Henry with a blow hard enough to have floored a man twice his weight; now he wished he had hit him even harder.

'Hold on,' he told Amber briskly, lifting her into his arms.

'No,' she protested, but of course Jean-Philippe didn't listen to her.

Luckily the hall was empty – she didn't know what the staff would have thought if they'd seen her being carried upstairs in the arms of a strange man.

'Which room?'

'You can put me down here. I can walk . . .'

'Which room?'

'It's that one.' Self-consciously Amber nodded in the direction of her bedroom door.

Her maid had left the bed turned down for her and her

night things out. To her relief, though, Jean-Philippe carried her over to a chair instead of placing her on her bed. He was being so tactful, far more tactful than she had ever imagined he might be.

'Henry hates me,' she told him. 'That's why . . . He . . . he watched us . . . when we were together. He told me.' She started to shudder. 'Robert knows. I told him, but he said there was no need for me to worry. Do you think Henry *will* leave?'

'If he's got any sense, *oui*. I don't make idle threats. I know enough of the right kind of men to ensure that he will be very sorry if he does try to stay. Would you like me to send for a doctor?'

'No!'

'*D'accord*. Have you got anything to put on your face?'

'Yes. There's some arnica in the bathroom.'

He gave a brisk nod. 'I'll make sure you're comfortable and then I'll have a message sent to the casino for your husband.'

'No, there's no need to do any of that. I can manage. I'm all right and there's no need to disturb Robert.'

She didn't want to tell Jean-Philippe that Robert had taken to spending the night on board the yacht – and not, she imagined, alone.

Jean-Philippe was in the bathroom soaking a cloth in cold water for the second time, to place against her swollen cheekbone. Since she could hear the tap running Amber took the opportunity to remove her hand from the top of her dress so that the fabric could fall away and she could look at her breast. It felt dreadfully sore, throbbing painfully where Henry had bitten her. The sight of his teethmarks and the bruising made her feel faint and sick all over again.

From the doorway to the bathroom Jean Philippe watched

her. It wasn't just her silk that was strong. Amber too possessed great strength. He couldn't think of any other woman he knew who would have behaved with the same quiet fortitude. He saw her tremble as she looked down at her body, and a tear slide down her cheek.

It was Jean-Philippe's curse that alerted Amber to the fact that he was watching her. She tried to cover herself but it was too late. He had reached her and his hands, so much stronger than Henry's and yet so very much more tender, were gently lifting her own away, his gaze fixed firmly on hers as he slowly peeled back the fabric of her dress.

'This is purely necessity, you understand, not sexuality,' he told her quietly. 'He has hurt you and someone must attend to it. If you will not allow me to call you a doctor . . . ?'

'No!'

'Then I must be a doctor for you. It is not, after all, as though we do not know one another.' His voice was coaxing her to relax and let him expose her to his inspection.

No, it wasn't as though they did not know one another but the Amber he knew had not expected to find that her flesh looked as though it had been savaged by an animal.

Jean-Philippe was torn between rage and compassion as he looked down at the swollen, mutilated flesh.

Amber was shivering violently, racked by pain and embarrassment.

It was half an hour before the wounds were cleaned to Jean-Philippe's satisfaction and then salved with arnica.

'*Ma pauvre*,' he said simply when he had finished, kissing her forehead as he did so.

'I am so glad you came,' Amber told him shyly.

'So am I.'

'Jean-Philippe?' The yearning burst past her defences and into her voice, pouring through her body and swamping her.

She was crying – out of shock or loss, she didn't know.

Jean-Philippe was holding her and all that she knew was that it felt wonderful. And then he was kissing her, and that felt even more wonderful.

'Would you like me to stay?'

He was stroking the hair back off her face in the way that she remembered, kissing her temples and then that place behind her ear that melted the flesh from her bones.

Amber stroked her fingers through his hair, still as vigorous as it had been, just like him. The smell of him was all around her, driving away the smell of another man. She breathed it in as deeply as she could, taking it down inside herself to where she could feel the dull heavy ache swelling into life, and sensual heat unfurling.

'Yes,' she answered him.

He was tender, and careful, and then blissfully, when her need swelled and sang inside her, forcing her to give voice to it, he was neither of those things. He was, she thought giddily at one point, when her senses were brimming over with so much of everything they had wanted that their joy spilled from them, simply magical. He had taken from her all the pain, fear and guilt of Henry's attack, along with the lesser barriers of self-consciousness and conscience, dissolving them in the fire of her own desire. He had given to her in their place a great uprushing of intense joy and pride; in him; in what they were sharing, but most of all in herself and in life.

Behind her closed eyelids, as he drove her senses higher and deeper, her pleasure painted joyous splashes of colour on lavender-blue silk – in a miraculous rebirth of something she realised she had lost without ever knowing it had really existed.

She found the plateau and rested there for a heartbeat whilst he held her and carried her, and then she was the one taking him, taking them both climbing swiftly and steeply and surely towards the heart of infinity.

Her last thought before she sank into the purple silk velvet darkness of sleep was that whatever Henry had taken from her Jean-Philippe had given her back tenfold.

She was still sleeping when he left.

His movements might be deft with the familiarity of leaving many women and many beds, but they were also urgent with something he had not known in a long time. Images hammered and demanded inside his head, a spinning vortex of shapes and colours, a creative need that would take him and use him relentlessly until it was satisfied.

Chapter Forty-Three

'Poor Henry, having to rush back like that. I do think it was selfish of Pamela to insist that he cut short his holiday.' Beth's voice was weighted with disapproval of Henry's wife, but Amber didn't say a word.

She didn't care what reason Henry had given his sister for his unscheduled departure, she was just glad that he had gone.

'I'd better go,' Beth was telling her, getting up from the table on the terrace of the exclusive Juan-les-Pins hotel where they had met for lunch.

A group of men – French and German from their accents – were being shown to a table close to their own, the men glancing admiringly at her.

She was wearing a dress made out of a run of silk she had designed herself, as an experiment, intending to use it as furnishing silk. Halter-necked, with a neat waist and a full skirt, the skirt of her dress showed off the bold hand-painted ink-blue and white graphic design on the pale aqua fabric. A matching bandeau kept her hair off her face for coolness, and her white gloves contrasted with her warm gold tan.

It wasn't either her dress or her tan that was attracting so much male interest, Amber knew. Instead it was that other garment she was wearing. Invisible to the human eye but readily recognised by other senses, it was the confidence and the sheer delight in being herself that Jean-Philippe had given her.

She hadn't seen him since he had rescued her from Henry four nights ago now and, oddly perhaps, she felt no strong desire to do so. When she thought of him it was with affection and gratitude, and with an almost luminous feeling of quiet joy. With him she had found a piece of herself that had been missing. She had embraced her own sexuality.

Where it might lead her in the future wasn't important. What mattered was that she had made her peace with it, and that it was no longer something to be refused recognition and feared.

She could feel the male interest following her as she and Beth left.

Outside the hotel they kissed goodbye and then went their separate ways.

It was a particularly hot day, the heat lying everywhere in a living haze that stroked the skin and whispered its sensual message. There was no escape from it. It penetrated the senses and possessed the mind.

Amber walked down to the harbour. Robert's yacht rested motionless in its berth. She remembered that she had left on board in her stateroom a book she had wanted to finish reading. She walked up the gangplank and went on board. The deck was deserted. Robert had said something about giving the crew some time off, Amber remembered, and she took the main staircase down below the deck.

She and Robert had connecting staterooms, and the door between them was open, which was how she heard the noise coming from Robert's stateroom – a sobbing gasping agony. It drew her to the open door before her brain had registered what it was.

The sight of Robert crouching naked on the bed whilst Otto buggered him with a dildo, thrusting it fiercely into him so that Robert gasped out in obvious pain, had her recoiling from the open door.

There was no danger of them hearing her; they were oblivious to everything bar what they were doing. Even so, she stepped back immediately, turning away and hurrying back up on deck. How could Robert endure to be treated in such a way? Coming so quickly on top of her own pleasure in the rediscovery of her sexuality, the spectacle in front of her seemed brutish and repellent, an affront to her senses.

Somehow she had assumed that male lovers would want the same mutual tenderness and care in their physical intimacy that was so important to her. Surely it was impossible that Robert, with his charm and elegance, his good looks and good humour, would enter into a sexual relationship that led to him being treated cruelly and physically debased. It hurt *her* to think of Robert being treated in such a way, because whilst sexually she felt nothing for him, she did love him and felt protective of him.

Otto had changed, Robert had insisted, when Amber had begged him to be careful and reminded him of the way in which Otto had treated him before. She herself had believed that Robert was right. She had seen nothing of the violent pleasure in inflicting humiliation and pain she had just witnessed in Otto's manner towards Robert in public, whilst they had been in the South of France.

But Robert had not been physically constrained in any way, which meant that he must have submitted himself willingly to Otto's abuse.

Standing in the hot sunshine of the yacht's deck Amber shuddered, remembering Henry's violent attack on her. A cold sweat clung to her skin and she shivered. A feeling of sick dizziness, as though she might actually faint, gripped her as she walked unsteadily down the gangplank.

'Amber, are you all right?'

'Jean-Philippe.'

He had seen her from the harbour where he had sitting in a shaded bar, drinking a Pernod and relaxing after four days of the most intense and compulsive painting he could remember. Irene had been furious with him when he had returned after four days' absence – announcing that she was going to throw him out. She wouldn't, of course, but this time he had not, as he had in the past, been spending his time with another woman. After leaving Amber he had gone straight to Mougins to beg the use of a studio from one of his friends there, and then he had worked as though he was being pursued by death itself.

The silk merchant's daughter had become the master of her father's trade, and the favoured mistress of silk itself, neither of them whole without the other, both of them combining to create a mystique of powerful sensuality. He had painted her surrounded by the shimmering gold colour from which she took her name, light spilling in through a window behind her to highlight her beauty and to stroke against the tablet of amber encasing her heart and from which the golden light spilled to infuse the fabric with its magic. As she gazed at the fabric through the purity and beauty of her own heart, a darker figure stood waiting in the shadows. Where he looked down at the silk it was flat and dull, lacking lustre.

Only the human heart, with its capacity for love, could illuminate the silk and bring it to life.

It was the best thing he had ever painted. Better even than his beloved *Silk Merchant's Daughter*.

'What's wrong?' he asked Amber.

'Nothing,' she began and then stopped. 'Robert is on board the yacht with Otto.'

She had no idea why she had told Jean-Philippe that, but she could see from his face that he understood what she meant.

'Let me take you back to the villa.'

He had put his hand under her elbow and was guiding her gently back towards the path to the villa.

'I had no idea,' she told him unsteadily.

'About your husband?'

'No, I knew *about* Robert, of course, but I hadn't realised . . . I hadn't thought . . . To have seen him allowing himself to be treated in such a way.'

She was shaking so much that she couldn't resist when Jean-Philippe put his arm around her to support her.

'Otto was hurting him, Jean-Philippe, really hurting him.' This was not a conversation she should be having with Jean-Philippe, or with anyone, but somehow she just couldn't stop the words from tumbling over themselves.

'For some people that is their need – both men and women,' he told her quietly.

'But to want to receive physical pain . . .'

Jean-Philippe's expression said that he did not share her shock. She must be more naïve than she had realised, Amber recognised.

'Come,' said Jean-Philippe, placing his arm around her to support her. 'You will feel better when you are out of this sun.'

The house was silent and cool. Gladys had taken Luc to a birthday party being given for the little French girl he had met on the beach who adored him so much.

'*Peut-être* it seems worse because of what was forced on you by Henry.'

520

'Yes,' Amber agreed, sipping the glass of watered-down wine Jean-Philippe had handed her.

They were in the drawing room, but when Jean-Philippe asked her lightly, 'Do you want me to stay?' Amber knew exactly what he meant. Quickly she nodded, trembling slightly when he took the wine glass from her and then opened the drawing-room door.

This time they walked up the stairs and into her bedroom together. This time she undressed him as he was undressing her. This time her body was eager and ready. This time her pleasure was owned by her and not given to her by him.

And this time the joy was less bountiful and grateful, more muted.

This time would be the last time, Amber knew, because this time inside her head was Jay, whose letter to her this morning had been heavy with all that he had left unwritten but which had still found her heart.

Amber looked across to where Jean-Philippe lay next to her in the bed, the late afternoon sun streaking his naked body as it was doing her own.

Jean-Philippe had made love to her with great tenderness and passion. He had physically satisfied her body, but whilst it felt lethargic and heavy with its surfeit of pleasure, none of the intimacies they had shared had satisfied her emotionally. Nothing that they had done or shared together had been powerful enough to drive out the ache of her emotional longing for Jay, or the deep inner loneliness that went hand in hand with loving him.

She was a woman now, with a woman's complex, many-stranded emotional claims on her heart. She had grown too far beyond being able to revisit her girlhood's innocent belief that physically desiring a man meant that one loved him.

She had also gone too far beyond being able to convince

herself that she could drown out her need for one man in her physical desire for another. If somehow she could magically transport herself right now into Jay's presence she knew that just the touch of his hand and his smile would arouse her senses and her emotions far more powerfully than any of the physical intimacies she had just shared with Jean-Philippe. Her body might be satisfied but her heart still hungered for what it could not have, and, Amber knew, it always would. But no one but her must ever know that.

'Amber, there is something I must tell you.'

The sound of Jean-Philippe's voice was another painful reminder of what or rather who her heart really hungered for. 'Your husband is in great danger.'

He had found out about it last night, a chance comment overheard from Irene's brother-in-law and his fellow Germans, which had then led to him eavesdropping on their whole conversation. He hadn't made any firm plans to tell Amber, but on the other hand his choice of the bar opposite her husband's yacht had meant that the chances were he would see her, and that having seen her he would be morally obliged to warn her.

Jean-Philippe's words, so unexpected and so chilling, caused Amber's heart to thud uncomfortably.

'I have seen for myself that—'

'*Non!*' Jean-Philippe cut her off sharply. 'Not in that way. Or at least not . . . A trap has been deliberately baited for Robert by the Germans and he has walked straight into it.'

'By the Germans? I don't understand.'

'Germany is currently waging a war of propaganda against all those who stand against its plans. There are those in your country who are against those plans.'

'Yes, there are,' Amber agreed.

Jean-Philippe continued, 'Hitler is vehemently against homosexuality. He considers it the most decadent of all

522

vices and that it should be harshly punished. It is planned to use Robert's homosexuality as a means of disgracing Robert and through him your country and its ruling classes.'

Amber was anxious now. 'What do you mean?'

'Otto is not homosexual although he has been told that he must convince Robert that he is. This weekend Otto will inform Robert that he has to return to Germany. Your husband will, of course, beg him to stay. Otto will say that he cannot but he will invite your husband to accompany him back to Berlin. Robert is so besotted that he won't think twice.'

Amber swallowed hard against the protest she wanted to make, knowing that Jean-Philippe was right.

'Once Robert is in Germany, he will be caught in a compromising situation with Otto. He will then be threatened with exposure and punishment in the German courts, but given the opportunity to save himself by returning to England as a German spy. If Robert refuses then Hitler will benefit via the propaganda that will result from Robert's exposure as a homosexual, which is of course illegal in your own country. And, *naturellement*, if Robert agrees to spy for Germany—'

'Robert will never do that.'

'If Robert agrees to spy for Germany then Hitler can if he wishes still expose him as a member of the British ruling class who was willing to betray his country.'

'How can you possibly know all of this?' Amber demanded. It seemed so far-fetched and theatrical, and yet she could tell from Jean-Philippe's voice and the look on his face that what he was telling her was very real.

'Like I said, through Irene and her brother-in-law. Heinrich entertains his SS comrades at the villa. I am, of course, not supposed to be privy to their private conversations, but Heinrich is a heavy drinker and he is indiscreet.

'Your husband is being lulled into a false sense of security. He believes his feelings for Otto are reciprocated. As I've already said, once they are in Germany, Robert will be encouraged into a situation of intimacy, and it is then that Hitler's SS will strike and he will be imprisoned for his offence.'

'You're putting your own life at risk by telling me all of this.'

'And you aren't sure whether you can believe me and trust me, or whether what I'm telling you might also be part of some elaborate plot?' Jean Philippe guessed.

'*D'accord*,' he reassured her when Amber looked uncomfortable. 'You have every right to ask yourself those questions. I certainly would do so in your shoes. I admit that I hadn't intended to tell you, and thus involve myself, but being with you today has prodded my conscience. Although neither of us may consider it convenient or indeed desirable, I do care about you, you know. As for putting myself in danger –' he gave a dismissive shrug – 'I shall be leaving for Spain in a few days' time to join the fight for freedom, which is something I have been intending for some time now.'

And something he had committed to late the previous afternoon in the aftermath of a drink shared with the friend whose studio he had borrowed.

'You will fight? In the civil war?'

'Yes. I have friends who are already fighting there, and it is only right that I should fight alongside them.'

He meant what he had said, Amber could see that, and besides, she did not have the right to try to stop him. Or the desire? It was Robert she must concern herself with now. Robert, who according to Jean-Philippe was in the gravest of danger.

'Robert will never believe me if I tell him what you have said. He is besotted with Otto,' Amber said.

524

'Which is why you must get him away from here, and back to England without delay, and without alerting Heinrich to the fact that you know what is planned.'

'I don't know how I will be able to do that.'

'Your husband has a yacht in the harbour. My advice would be to devise some way of getting him on board it on some pretext, and then instruct your captain to set sail for England.'

How on earth was she supposed to do that? Robert would instantly countermand any orders she might give.

Perhaps she could enlist Beth and Alistair's help? Would they believe her? It was too much of a risk, and somehow Amber doubted it. Then who could she turn to who would understand the nature of the danger Robert was in, and not just understand but be able to do something?

She couldn't possibly risk involving anyone from the embassy on an official basis. Homosexuality was illegal, no matter how many blind eyes were turned it.

'I will help you if you wish.'

Amber was astonished. 'You? But why should you?'

'Because I want to, to make things up to you.'

Amber looked at him. She could tell that he was being genuine and meant what he was saying. She couldn't afford to turn down the help he was offering her.

'Very well then, yes, please. I do want you to help me.'

'*Bien*, let us think. We need to act sooner rather than later. You will, I expect, be attending the Maharaja of Jaipur's party this evening?'

Amber nodded.

'Very well. *Alors, malheureusement*, whilst you are there, Robert will suddenly be overcome by a feeling of light-headedness and nausea, which will be caused by something I shall ensure goes into his drink.'

When he saw the expression on Amber's face, Jean-Philippe

assured her, 'It will not harm him, I promise you. It will just make him feel dizzy and faint.'

'But how do you know? What will you—'

'These are matters you may leave to me. One does not mix with the people I have mixed with over the years without learning at least a little of the underbelly of life. You will insist on calling for a doctor. Luckily a fellow guest will present himself as exactly that – I have a friend in Mougins – there is no need for you to know the details other than that some artists have a need for those substances that assist their creativity, and some doctors are willing to provide them – discreetly and for a considerable fee. It is this doctor who will also provide the cause of Robert's "unwellness".'

'Drugs?' Amber protested anxiously. 'Won't that be dangerous?'

'Not in the hands of the good doctor. You must trust me in this, Amber, and you can, I promise you. The doctor will insist that your husband must return to your villa to rest. He will pronounce that Robert has possibly had too much sun or maybe eaten something that has disagreed with him.'

'But what if Robert refuses to leave?'

'He will not,' Jean-Philippe told her with finality and simplicity.

'The doctor will accompany you both to your car, which will be officially waiting to take you back to the villa, but in reality to the yacht. Once inside the car the good doctor will give your husband some sedation. It will not harm him, merely make him sleep, I promise you.

'When you reach the yacht you will call for some help to have your husband carried on board. You will tell your captain that the doctor has given instructions that Robert should return home. Whilst the crew are making the yacht ready to leave, you will have time to go to the villa and collect your son.'

'You are sure that Robert will be all right? I don't want . . .'

'He will wake up with a very bad headache and I dare say in a very bad temper.

'You could, you know, leave him to meet his fate, and simply leave yourself.'

'No, I could never do that.' It was unthinkable, not with what she owed Robert, and then there was Luc to be thought of too, and Luc adored his father. 'The Germans will know that you have helped us.'

'It matters little. I have already made arrangements to leave for Spain.' Jean-Philippe paused and then told her sombrely, 'It is my belief that Herr Hitler will not be pacified and that those who attempt to do so will regret it.'

Could she do it? Dare she do it? It was such a risk to take. So many things could go wrong. But if she did nothing, and Jean-Philippe was right, then the consequences for Robert were unbearable.

'Very well,' she told Jean-Philippe. 'You will need money – for the doctor.'

Now that she had made up her mind she became determinedly practical. She would need to ensure that the yacht was properly provisioned – perhaps she could tell both Robert and the captain that she was thinking of arranging a short cruise for some of their friends. That way she could also give instructions for at least some of her own and Luc's clothes to be packed.

Once they were back in England the necessary arrangements could be made for the staff to close up the house and follow them home.

'Are you sure, about this doctor?' she pressed Jean-Philippe.

'Yes.' Jean-Philippe took hold of her upper arms, his hands dark against the pale gold of her bare flesh. His hold

527

was firm and reassuring. 'You must trust me on that point, Amber.'

Robert's senses were suffused with a mixture of longing and delight. Finally after the long hours, days and weeks of showing Otto his love for him, his young lover was permitting him the pleasure of showing him his love.

They were lying naked together on the large double bed in Robert's stateroom whilst the yacht rocked gently in its berth. Robert reached out, hardly daring to breathe as he slid his left hand beneath the tight full sac of Otto's balls, to hold them securely and lift them whilst the fingers of his right hand curled round the shaft of Otto's cock. Using his forefinger, Robert stroked the sensitive flesh that lay between the now tightly drawn sac and Otto's anus, exhaling in a jerky sigh of release. He knew the pleasure of that single delicate touch and he could almost feel it for himself as he witnessed Otto's involuntary reaction to it.

'Yes . . .' he agreed hoarsely, 'and when it is my tongue that caresses you there the pleasure will be almost more than either of us can bear, I promise you.' His own body was tumescent with desire. His hands moved faster, the right one moving Otto's slick ready flesh forward and back over the engorged head with swift firm strokes, the left one cupping his forefinger, circling and pressing.

Otto's harsh unsteady breathing was a paean of delight to Robert's ears. Now finally at last the one he loved so much was giving himself to him and allowing him to pleasure him.

He heard Otto cry out, a tortured savage sound that stirred his own pleasure. Robert released Otto's balls and slid his finger into his anus seeking his pleasure spot, inserting another finger to help in the task.

Otto was moaning, thrashing, moving on his penetration,

the head within Robert's grip tight and glossy. Robert heard Otto gasp, his body stiffening. Robert lowered his head, his mouth opening to receive the hot semen spurt, a third finger joining the other two to urge Otto over the final barrier. His lover, his beloved. For now and for ever. He would, if necessary, follow Otto to the end of the earth and beyond.

Amber felt dreadful. Robert was in such a buoyant mood, and apparently not in the least distressed by the act she had inadvertently witnessed. He looked so debonair and had such a spring to his step tonight as he turned to smile at her when she came downstairs to join him. Was she doing the right thing? What if Jean-Philippe had been mistaken? Perhaps they should wait, just to be sure. Or worse still, what if he had deliberately lied to her? Was she really sure she could trust him?

'So who is it you are intending to invite to this short cruise you are planning?' Robert was asking her as they left the house.

'I haven't finalised the guest list yet.'

Would he hear in her voice how uncomfortable she felt? Was he suspicious already? Amber's heart thumped discordantly. She hated having to do this. If only there had been someone else she could have discussed things with. Cecil, though, had already left France.

It was a beautiful evening, the air soft and balmy, and yet as they got out of the car Amber started shivering. Luckily, though, Robert didn't appear to notice.

As soon as they had gone through the formalities of being received and welcomed, Robert headed straight for the crowd of people with the von Ribbentrops.

Amber felt the air ease out of her lungs in relief when she saw that Jean-Philippe was already there, although he didn't make any attempt to acknowledge her. Instead he was talking with the wife of one of the German Embassy officials. All must go according to plan.

Robert looked round for Otto anxiously. He had been expecting him to be here. The German party always arrived early.

'You're looking for von Brecht?' Countess Irene's brother-in-law Heinrich asked.

'He is normally part of the group,' Robert replied as casually as he could.

'Yes indeed. He asked to be excused, though, this evening.' Heinrich winked at Robert. 'No reason was given but I suspect it was a matter of a *Fräulein* – he is a young man, after all.'

Impaled on the spear of his jealousy Robert felt it bite deeper the harder he struggled against it. Inside his head he could see imagines of Otto, naked and with someone else. A feeling of intense need possessed him. Where was Otto? Wherever he was, he, Robert, would find him and beg him to love him and only him.

He put his empty glass down and reached for a fresh one from the tray of a hovering waiter.

'Otto isn't here. I must go and find him,' he told Amber quietly.

Robert was going to leave? Frantically Amber looked around for Jean-Philippe. He was still deep in conversation with the German wife. Despair gripped her, but as though somehow he sensed her anxiety, Jean-Philippe chose that moment to look up.

'Do excuse us, everyone.' Amber made herself smile, praying that her words would carry to Jean-Philippe, 'but Robert and I must leave.'

Robert wasn't the least bit pleased. 'There's no need for you to leave, Amber.' He had put his drink down on the table next to them, and although she knew he was going to do it, Jean-Philippe's sleight of hand was so swift that Amber still wasn't sure she had actually seen him tip the powder, which had now dissolved, into Robert's drink.

Robert was turning away from her. Leaving without finishing his drink. Amber picked it up and held it out to him. Without a word he took the glass from her, draining its contents in one gulp, before striding away.

He didn't even get as far as the door, suddenly stopping in mid-stride and then swaying before turning round to look back at her.

Jean-Philippe reached him first, demanding loudly, 'Is there a doctor?' whilst Robert doubled over, his face now grey and greasy with perspiration, but insisting that he was all right.

A man, small and plump with thinning hair and raisin-dark eyes and a sallow complexion, undistinguishable from any number of other Frenchmen, had hurried over to them and was shaking his head and sucking on his teeth.

'Has he been eating shellfish do you know, Madame? Only there have already been some cases of food poisoning this week.'

'Oh . . . yes, I think he has,' Amber confirmed, whilst Robert tried to protest that he had not.

'I will go and have your car brought round,' Jean-Philippe announced.

'Would you come with us, Doctor?' Amber asked, valiantly trying to remember her own role. 'Only I am concerned for my husband. He looks so unwell.'

That at least was true.

'*Naturellement, Madame*,' the doctor confirmed.

'I'm so sorry.' Amber went back to the von Ribbentrops to apologise. 'The doctor seems to think that Robert is suffering from food poisoning of some sort. I'm going to take him back to the villa. Fortunately the doctor does not think it will last for very long.'

'If you would like one of us to accompany you . . .' Heinrich offered.

Was it her imagination or was he looking suspicious?

'That is kind of you but really there's no need. The doctor will go with us.'

Unexpectedly it was Countess Irene who came to her rescue, saying impatiently, 'For goodness' sake, Heinrich, let's not spoil the evening for everyone. It's only a bit of food poisoning, after all.'

Robert did not want the doctor to go with them. He wanted, as he informed Amber in no uncertain terms, to be left on his own so that he could go and find Otto.

Robert's dinner jacket had been removed at some stage before he had been helped into the car – Jean-Philippe's work, no doubt, Amber decided as the doctor ignored Robert's protests and asked Amber to remove Robert's cufflink whilst he held his arm.

She felt dreadful doing this, but it was in Robert's best interests – wasn't it?

'Now, if you will just assist me with this . . .'

Robert tried to resist but as Jean-Philippe had said, the drug in his drink had rendered him too weak to do much, leaving the doctor free to bind his upper arm, which he then asked Amber to hold.

'Alas, good sir. I'm afraid you will not be doing that,' the doctor announced cheerfully, before deftly inserting the hypodermic needle he had removed from his bag into Robert's arm and depressing the attached syringe.

'What the de—'

'Excellent,' the doctor beamed, as Robert passed out before he could finish his protest, adding happily to Amber, 'And here we are at the quayside already.'

'He will be all right – when he comes round, I mean?'

'He will have a headache, but yes, Madame, he will be all right.'

The doctor had gone, melting swiftly into the darkness, leaving Amber to hurry to the yacht and ask for the captain. British, thank goodness, and well trained.

'I'm afraid my husband isn't at all well, Captain. He will need to be carried on board and taken to his stateroom. It's nothing contagious, please assure the men, but it is imperative that he seeks medical advice at home. We shall be sailing as soon as I have collected our son.'

'Very well, Your Grace.'

To Luc it was exciting to be woken up late at night and told that they were going to the yacht. Gladys, though, was not so pleased.

'His Grace seemed fine to me when he left this evening,' she told Amber.

'Yes, it came on very suddenly. Fortunately there was a doctor at the party but he has said that it is imperative that the Duke seeks help at home in England.'

'Well, must say that you can't beat a proper English doctor,' Gladys agreed, appeased.

At last it was done. Their trunks were on board and so were they, and the shoreline was slowly receding as the captain set sail for home.

In his stateroom cabin, Robert lay unconscious on the bed, breathing stertorously.

Amber settled down in a chair beside the bed. She was worried that Robert might be sick and choke if he was left on his own.

She just prayed that she had done the right thing.

Chapter Forty-Four

'Your Grace, what would you like us to do with the crate that was sent on board, before we left France?'

'What crate?'

'It was delivered by a Frenchman. He said that it was to be handed over only to you. Would you like to have it brought up to the main salon?'

It was morning and it was easier to think about what the captain was saying to her than to worry about having to explain what she had done and why to Robert, once he had come round fully from the sleeping draught he had been given. Amber nodded tiredly.

'Yes, please, Captain. I'd better see what it is.'

The case was large, and heavy, to judge from the way the arm muscles of the two crewmen carrying it into the salon tensed under its weight. Once they had put it down on the carpet they had to remove the lid for her, which had been nailed down.

Amber waited until they had gone to look inside.

On top of what were obviously canvases wrapped in protective plain sheets was a letter addressed to her in Jean-Philippe's sprawling handwriting.

Amber unfolded it and read.

My darling ex virgin,

Some things are not meant for the eyes of others and though I painted these intending to exhibit them, in the end I could not. Perhaps I should have destroyed them but how could I bear to do that when they are all that I had left of you and when in my foolish arrogance I had already destroyed our love?

I have kept these images of you by me and found great solace in them, but now they are my gift to you, along with what I believe to be the greatest painting I have ever done.

Yours always,
Jean-Philippe

Slowly and carefully Amber uncovered the first canvas, her breath quickening and the colour rushing up under her skin at what she saw.

Then, her fingers fumbling with the coverings, she removed all six canvases from the crate, laying them out side by side. Lined up together they told the story of her own awakening to physical and emotional desire. More shocking by far than the nudity of her body was the nakedness of her vulnerability as revealed by Jean-Philippe's artist's eye and brush. He had revealed her feelings so intimately that *they* were what shone from the paintings, above and beyond the opalescent quality of her naked body bathed in that long-ago South of France summer light. They were, Amber felt, both a gift and a curse. Jean-Philippe was an incomparably blessed artist, and perhaps if he had painted some other girl she might merely have been able to admire the skill of his work. But he hadn't; he had painted her, revealed her feelings so intimately that she could not bear to look on what she could see. That girl no longer existed.

535

She had left her behind when she had run from him, knowing the extent of Jean-Philippe's lies to her. That girl had become Luc's mother and Robert's wife. She had become the woman who had realised, in Jean-Philippe's arms this summer, what real love actually was and for whom she really felt it. And it wasn't Jean-Philippe.

She loved her son, as a mother; she loved her husband, as a friend; but her woman's love had, and always would, only belong to one man. And that man was Jay.

Beneath them were two more paintings. The first, *The Silk Merchant's Daughter*, was familiar to her, but the second was not. Awed by its beauty, Amber traced the folds of amber silk so vivid that they could have been real, tears burning her eyes as she did so. Both paintings were incredible but this new one was surely a true work of art.

She was just about to place the paintings back in the crate when she noticed there was something else inside it, carefully wrapped in thick strong brown paper and yet so fluid in her hands and so light that it could not possibly be another picture. Her hands trembled slightly as she opened the parcel. Inside the paper, wrapped carefully in tissue, was the length of priceless antique silk with which Jean-Philippe had first painted her. There was also a note with it which read, 'This is for you from me and it was paid for – but do not ask in what coin.'

'What have you done?' Robert's voice was savage with the agony of his own pain.

The drug the doctor had given him had caused him to sleep for a full day, but now that he was awake he had summoned Amber to his stateroom and demanded an explanation.

However, when she had given it he had refused, and was

536

continuing to refuse, to accept that she had acted in his best interests, just as she had feared that he would.

'I did what I thought was best for you,' Amber tried to reassure him.

'You have destroyed me. You have destroyed my life. I have no life without Otto. I do not wish to have any life without him,' Robert told her, as he pushed past her, heading for the door.

'Where are you going?' Amber asked him worriedly.

'I'm going to tell the captain to turn the yacht round.'

'No, Robert, you can't do that,' she protested. 'You must understand what will happen to you, if you do.'

'No. You must understand what will happen to me if I don't. I think I hate you more than I ever thought it possible to hate anyone.'

His speech, like his movements, was wild and frantic, but despite knowing the cause of them they still hurt Amber.

'What I did, I did for your sake, Robert. I know you can't accept that now but in time—'

'No! There will never be a time when I can accept what you have done, or your presence in my life.'

'Robert—'

'I mean it, Amber. Our marriage is over. If it wasn't for Luc – but I won't see him hurt, in any way. A legal separation will have to be arranged, of course, but not until I have assured myself that Luc has been properly prepared for what it will mean and understands that it will not affect the relationship that he and I share, or my love for him.

'Now if you'll excuse me, I must go and instruct the captain to turn round. Nothing and no one is going to stop me from being with Otto. I *must* be with him. I cannot endure not to be—' He broke off, his forehead suddenly beading with sweat, his face going pale as he turned away from her and then staggered towards his bathroom.

The moment he had closed the bathroom door, Amber almost ran out of the stateroom, locking the door behind her, and locking Robert inside it, her hands shaking as she did so.

She then went to find the captain, and told him quickly, 'Captain Pierce, I'm afraid my husband isn't at all well. He must remain in his cabin until we reach England and no one is to go near him, apart from his valet and myself.'

'Very well, Your Grace.'

'I shall need to send a telegraph . . . to, to Duff Cooper at the Admiralty.' Amber hated doing something that felt as though she was actually betraying Robert, but it was too serious a matter for her not to ask for the help she knew she desperately needed.

'What is it you wish to say, Your Grace?'

'Please tell him that . . . that it is very important that he meets the yacht when we reach England. Please tell him too that it is a matter of national security.'

She couldn't look at the captain.

'Very well, Your Grace.'

Robert would never believe her now, no matter how hard she tried to tell him the truth, she knew, but she hated what she was having to do to him.

Part Four

Chapter Forty-Five

Christmas 1937

So that was that. She had known, of course; the signs had been unmistakable even though she had tried very hard not to notice them. But now she had incontrovertible proof, and thanks to her own head-in-the-sand attitude it was already too late for her to change things.

Amber put her hand on her still mercifully flat stomach. Would she, could she, have taken that course and destroyed the life she was carrying? Why not? Wasn't she after all going to be destroying other lives by not doing so? The life of her son, pretending not to be excited about Christmas but sweetly barely able to hide just how much he was; the life of her own family; her grandmother, who had arrived from Macclesfield earlier in the week, to spend Christmas with them, along with a still angry Greg and little Rose; the life she herself led, with her charities and her good works; her involvement with the mill; and of course her beloved and very successful shop. The life of her husband, who was already planning their formal and legal separation, even before he knew about this child?

Robert had hardly spoken to her since their return from France, shutting himself away from her both physically and emotionally. With his correspondence now being monitored on government orders, and Robert himself having been warned that he must not under any circumstances either try to contact Otto or leave the country, he had made it plain that he blamed Amber for this state of affairs. When he did have to speak to her his voice was cold and his words cutting, but most of the time he simply avoided her. It could only be a matter of time before he announced that he had contacted his lawyers and made arrangements for their formal separation. The fact that she was now carrying Jean-Philippe's child could only hasten and underline the need for that separation, as well as adding justification to it.

She would, of course, at the very least be the subject of a great deal of gossip, and at the worst be totally disgraced. It was not her own situation that concerned her, though. It was Luc about whom she was the most concerned. Luc, who adored the man he thought of as his father. And it was the loss of that fatherly love from Luc's life that filled her with anxiety and despair rather than Luc's ultimate loss of Robert's titles and wealth. Robert was bound, after all, to say publicly now that she was pregnant for a second time that he was not Luc's real father. She had been hoping that despite their separation Robert would continue to treat Luc as his son and give him the love he had always given him. Robert had said that he did not want Luc to be hurt. But this second pregnancy changed everything.

She had hardly been able to believe it at first when she had started feeling nauseous first thing in the morning; she certainly hadn't wanted to believe it. But now the smart and very discreet London doctor she had consulted earlier in the month had confirmed that there was no mistake and that she was indeed pregnant.

She got up from the stool in front of her dressing table, where she had been sitting for the last half an hour, since she had dismissed her maid.

This afternoon Robert had arrived from London to join the family party for Christmas. He would be in his bedroom now, getting ready for dinner. She would have to tell him, and the sooner the better. For Luc's sake she needed to beg him not to disown him. Would he grant her that? Could he rise above his bitterness towards her to be generous, or was she asking too much of him, knowing the intensity of his love for Otto?

They always had dinner an hour earlier on Christmas Eve to allow time afterwards for them to hand out presents to the servants from the huge tree in the hall.

Christmas Eve. A time of joy and thanksgiving for the birth of a child. But not this child.

A tear ran down her cheek, glittering in the light like a diamond before she wiped it away. It was too late for tears. Too late now for anything other than facing up to reality.

She got up, went to the communicating door between their bedrooms and knocked briefly, before opening it and going into Robert's room.

His features had taken on a certain austerity and bitterness these last four months, all the more so whenever he was obliged to look at her, Amber knew.

'I need to speak with you before we go down to dinner,' she told him, 'and in private.'

'Thank you, Hulme,' he dismissed his valet, waiting until the other man had left the room before offering, 'Would you like to sit down?'

Amber shook her head. Robert had told her that he would never forgive her for bringing him back to England against his wishes and she knew that he had meant what he had said. He had shown an implacable willpower over these last months that she had not known he possessed, using it to drag himself back from the abyss of despair into which he had fallen on their return.

During those first weeks Amber had feared not just for his life but for his sanity when Winston Churchill had told him that he would put him under house arrest if he attempted to go back to Germany. It made no difference that they were acting in his best interests and because they cared about him; death was preferable to what they were forcing him to suffer, he had told Amber.

It had been Winston who had forced him out of his despair, by reminding him of his duty to his country and insisting that he put that before his own feelings.

'There's no easy way for me to tell you this,' Amber began. 'I didn't want . . . I never imagined . . . I'm pregnant.'

Robert had turned away from her as she started to speak and he was silent for so long that Amber had begun to wonder if he had understood what she was saying, until he said heavily, 'Yes, I had wondered.'

'You knew?'

He was looking at her now, his mouth twisting into the beginnings of the smile she had always loved so much and then instead, hardening into cynicism.

'It seemed a pretty fair guess to make, given your early morning nausea. The father is, I take it, Jean-Philippe?'

'Yes,' Amber admitted ashamedly. 'You'll want to speed up the arrangements for our separation now, of course, or perhaps even arrange for us to divorce? I understand that, but, Robert, please let's not involve Luc in any of this. He worships you, and to discover now that you are not his father—'

'You think I would do that?' Anger had replaced his cynicism now. 'You have a very low opinion of me, Amber. Luc *is* my son; he will always be my son and nothing can change that, nor would I wish to do so. It is because of Luc that I have said right from the beginning that our separation must be handled with care, and in such a way that Luc is able to accept that whilst you and I will live apart, and not as a married couple, he is loved by both of us. It is also because of Luc that I have hesitated to take legal steps towards a formal separation, until I have been able to talk to him, although of course that will have to be done, and the timing of it will now naturally be even more of a sensitive issue. Or rather I should say that the timing of our divorce will be important.'

Amber exhaled a pent-up shaky breath of relief. Robert was not going to hurt Luc. He loved him and still thought of him as his son. He had said so and she had heard in his voice that he meant what he was saying. Tears stung her eyes.

'When will the child be born?'

'The end of May.'

'Then you will want the divorce to go through as speedily as possible if you are to marry Jean-Philippe before this new child arrives.'

Amber was aghast. 'There is no question of that, for either of us. Jean-Philippe . . . It was unplanned, a mistake, a single occurrence, not the result of an ongoing affair.'

'But you do love him, and were he willing to marry you, then—'

'No, I do not love him,' Amber said shakily. 'What happened between us is in the past.'

It was as much as she could bring herself to say. It was extremely painful for her to talk like this, all the more so because she could not tell Robert that it was the sight of his degradation and pain that had led in part to the conception of this child she neither wanted nor felt she could ever love, but whose life she was morally bound as its mother to protect.

'Have you told anyone else about this yet?' Robert asked her.

'No. I haven't wanted . . . that is to say, I had hoped I might be wrong.'

'I assume it is too late to—'

'Yes,' Amber pre-empted his question, 'yes, it is too late to end it.'

'I think then that in the circumstances the best thing would be for us not to divorce, bearing in mind Luc's best interests.'

'Not to divorce? But—'

'You said you had no plans nor any wish to marry Jean-Philippe. That being the case, there is no reason for us to subject ourselves to the grubby unpleasantnesses attendant upon us divorcing, involving as they would an admission that one of us had had sex with another party, and producing the necessary evidence to substantiate that fact.'

Amber felt sick, but not on this occasion because of her pregnancy. The law was that a divorce could only be granted if one party 'admitted' to having sex outside the marriage and thus became the 'guilty' one. It wasn't unheard of for those wishing to divorce to hire someone to spend the night with them to provide the necessary evidence, and indeed there was quite a thriving business, involving a certain type of young woman hired to protect the reputation of either a wife or a mistress. Robert, of course, had every right to divorce her, as she was already 'the guilty party'. A formal legal separation was by far the more respectable and acceptable situation.

'If you're sure that you don't want to divorce me . . .' was all she could manage to say.

'I am perfectly sure,' said Robert, adding, 'I don't think there is any need for us to tell anyone else of our plans as yet. Luc must, of course, be our main concern. So far as the baby is concerned, if you wish I am willing to allow it to be considered mine, for Luc's sake. I have no wish for him to be upset by any of this or taunted at school by other boys because of it. I must warn you, though, that I shall not wish to see it or have anything to do with it or with you. I shall never consider it to be my child in the way that I considered Luc to be. In fact I think it best that from the end of this Christmas holiday we live completely separately from one another. There will be legal ramifications to be considered, of course, but I am sure we will be able to find a way of dealing with that. Luc is and always will be my heir, whereas this child—'

He broke off when he saw that Amber had started to weep. 'I'm sorry. I didn't mean to distress you.'

'You haven't.' The truth was that she was crying with relief; relief and guilt. Relief because he was not going to force her to proclaim her situation to the world, and guilt because she wished so very much that the conception of this child had never happened.

'I suspect that it's going to be very hard to part Luc from Bruno when he has to go back to school,' Amber warned Robert as they both stood watching through the drawing-room window as Luc romped on the frosty lawn with the young Labrador.

'Not at all. Luc is old enough and intelligent enough to understand and accept that school is not the place for a dog, and that country dogs belong to the country. Jarvis says the dog will make a fine gun dog once he's properly trained, and that by the time he is Luc himself will be able to go out with the guns.'

'Robert, he's still only a little boy.'

'I was five the first time I went out. It's part and parcel of his heritage, Amber. You don't query the fact that he is already learning about the history of this house and those who have lived here, or that your grandmother reminds him of his manners.'

Amber sighed ruefully. On Boxing Day Luc had gone out a little way with the hunt, and had talked, pink-cheeked with excitement, about it for the rest of the day. Robert was right, she knew, to insist that he learned all those things he would one day have to, but he was still very much her little boy, even if he behaved in a sweetly protective and grown-up way towards Rose, who was finally walking, even if it was on legs that Amber worried were not quite as sturdy and straight as they might be.

She hated the coolness that had existed between her and Robert ever since they had returned from France. She missed the warmth of his swift teasing smile and the jokes he used to make. She missed too his appreciation of her appearance and his interest in her activities. It was, she felt, as though a warm blanket had been removed from her shoulders, leaving her exposed to a coldness that went soul deep. Was she destined to always lose the comfort of those male friendships that meant so much to her, first Jay and now Robert? She did not love Robert as a husband and a lover, but love wore many garments, after all. And now she was going to have to live in isolation from him whilst she prepared for the birth of her child and the formal end of their marriage. She missed the Robert she had married so very much. But this Robert, Otto's Robert, was not her Robert. This Robert would, as he had already warned her, never forgive her.

Amber looked through the window of Osterby, from the King's Withdrawing Room, as the small antechamber next to the bedroom in the state apartments was called, and out across the landscaped gardens to the ha-ha, beyond which the park deer were feeding from the food dropped for them on the iced-over snow.

Several nights of heavy frost following a snowfall had

turned the landscape into starkly beautiful contrasts of black and silver white.

Tomorrow her grandmother and Greg, along with Rose, would be returning to Macclesfield, the day after that Robert and Luc would go to London from where Robert would take Luc back to his prep school whilst she remained here.

There would be plenty for her to do, and she was not really in the mood for anyone else's company. Her head still ached from the confrontation she had had earlier with Greg when he had complained to her yet again about their grandmother's will.

Was it her imagination or did her cousin really look as though his health had deteriorated since the last time she had seen him? He certainly seemed thinner, the discoloured and broken veins on his nose and his cheeks more notice-able, his teeth were discoloured and Amber had had to look away, torn between pity and despair, when she had seen how his hands trembled and how he lost the thread of his conversation to the point where he simply stopped speaking in mid-sentence.

She needed some fresh air to clear her headache, she decided, and to clear away as well the heavy sad odour of despair and guilt the house seemed to be breathing.

Like all country houses, Osterby had a room where outside country coats, hats and gumboots were stored, but Amber went upstairs before going out to put on her own warm tweed coat. She did wrap a scarf around her hat and neck, though, as well as slipping into a pair of sturdy outdoor shoes, before stepping out into the icy cold air.

It was so cold the air stung her lungs as well as her eyes and nose, and even though she had gloves on she still had to push her hands deep into the pockets of her tweed coat to stop them from tingling. She walked along the terrace and then down the steps that led to the formal garden, crossing that and then heading for the park itself.

The deer watched her incuriously as she strode past them. Her unhappiness lay like a leaden weight inside her chest. Robert would never forgive her for what she had done in separating him from Otto, and yet she knew that were she given the chance to do so she would make the same decision again.

The sound of Luc's laughter made her look up to see Robert and Luc coming towards her, Luc running ahead with his dog.

'Look, Mummy, look how clever Bruno is,' he called out excitedly, bending down to pick up the ball the dog had been playing with to throw it towards her.

Amber saw the ball arcing towards her, and perhaps because her attention was on it she didn't notice that the dog had raced right up to her feet until it was too late and she had fallen over it.

She heard herself cry out, the sound mingling with Robert's warning shout, and she heard too the sound of him running towards her as she lay on the ground, her breath torn from her by the sharp knifelike pain ripping through her.

Robert was kneeling on the ground beside her, Luc hovering close by, Robert's voice terse as he demanded, 'Are you all right?'

'I don't know. My . . . I've got a pain.'

She saw the realisation darkening his eyes. He turned away from her and looked towards the house. He was going to leave her here. Pain and guilt seized her in a battle that only pain could win. Above it Amber heard Robert telling Luc, 'Luc, run to the house, there's a good chap, and tell Bates to ring for Dr Archer. Quickly now. Tell him that it's urgent.'

The pain was so bad she could hardly breathe.

'Funny how things work out,' she managed to gasp to Robert, who was now kneeling at her side, holding her hand. 'Neither of us wants this child. I wonder if it knows.'

'Keep still.' Robert's hand had tightened on hers. She saw him look up. 'Your grandmother is coming, and half the household with her by the looks of it.'

'I am sorry, Robert, so very sorry,' Amber whispered as the pain seized her and then mauled her, dragging her into its darkness.

She came round slowly, the first of her senses to return properly her sense of smell; the scents of frost and earth, and her own fear mingling with her grandmother's scent.

Reluctantly she opened her eyes. Her grandmother had taken Robert's place and was looking down grimly at her.

'What foolishness to go walking in such icy weather,' she upbraided her, as though somehow she had already guessed about the baby.

'The doctor's here,' Robert announced.

Dr Archer was an old-fashioned country doctor with a calm manner and a slow way of speaking.

Amber was to be carried up to her room on a stretcher under his supervision so that he could examine her properly.

'My guess is that you've broken a rib or two,' he told her.

He turned towards Robert as Robert leaned down to him and said something quietly.

'Ah, yes, I see. Well then, we must just hope . . .'

It was an hour before the doctor finally left, and within minutes of his departure Robert came into Amber's bedroom.

'Have you seen Dr Archer?' she asked him listlessly.

'Yes. He says that you are to rest for the next few days

and that if you start to bleed he must be sent for immediately.'

'Yes,' Amber agreed.

Robert had walked over to the window, which looked out across the park where Amber had been walking. When he turned round his expression was sombre and closed, so that she could not read what he was thinking.

She bled a little during the night and told no one, withdrawing into herself, disengaging herself from the child within her, refusing to listen to the agonised cries of protest of her own maternal instinct, but in the morning the bleeding had stopped and by the end of the week Dr Archer was telling her that she could get up and that the baby was perfectly safe.

Her guilt, though, was weighing heavily on her spirit. In the nursery she held Rose on her lap, and felt her love for Greg's daughter warm the numbness of her heart. She could love Greg's motherless unwanted child, so why couldn't she love the child she herself was carrying?

She loved Luc for himself – surely it was possible that once this child was born she would love it too? But what if she did not, what if she *could* not?

Rose squirmed in her lap, recognising that she had lost Amber's attention. Obediently Amber bent to kiss the top of her smooth silky dark head. The oriental slant of Rose's eyes, contrasting with the perfect English rosebud of her mouth, gave her features an exotic beauty.

She wished that Greg had agreed to her suggestion that he should leave Rose here with her when he and their grandmother returned to Macclesfield, but he was still very angry with her and had, Amber thought sadly, taken pleasure in refusing her.

She had had so many plans for this year: the new fabrics for the shop, and hopefully new commissions from the

National Trust, her plans to set up a pattern archive using her father's designs and the detailed plans Vanbrugh had drawn for the Denham Place interiors. But now she would have to put the needs of the new life she was carrying first. But the shop was so important to her.

More important than the life of her child?

Guilt and resentment clashed inside her. She hadn't wanted another child with Jean-Philippe. How was she going to be able to face Jay? If this had been his child . . . And yet she had been so grateful to Jean-Philippe. Grateful to him for giving her back herself, yes, but she was not grateful for the life that was growing inside her.

Chapter Forty-Six

April 1938

'I appreciate that you don't wish to celebrate your birthday, Grandmother, but since your friends do, I'm afraid you have little choice,' Amber told Blanche drily as she listened to her grandmother's complaints about the unnecessary waste of money on a party she had no desire whatsoever to have.

It had been Jay who had alerted her to the fact that her grandmother would be seventy, telephoning her to tell her and to suggest that some sort of celebration should be organised.

'She has done so much for those in need in the area, even though she does not like to admit to it.'

The sound of his voice had brought her such a feeling of loneliness and pain that she was glad he couldn't see her face. Quite when friendship had become love Amber had no idea. Had it happened and been ignored by her before she had kissed him? Out of nowhere, as though nudged forward out of the wings, the memory came back to her of their meeting in the garden before she had left for London. Hadn't she been aware then of a sense of hovering on the edge of something important? She had been too naïve then to recognise that feeling for what it was, too naïve to really love as a woman loved. But she had known that Jay was special, hadn't she?

Whatever the case, she had certainly known in Jean-Philippe's arms. Oh yes, she had known then.

'I am ashamed to admit it but I had no idea of her exact age. But yes, of course, something must be arranged,' she had agreed with Jay once she felt able to speak to him without betraying herself.

'I was not aware of it myself,' Jay told her. 'It was my grandfather who mentioned it.'

'We'd better not let her know that,' Amber had laughed, 'because she is bound to hold it against him.'

Now all the arrangements had been made, and there was to be a party for all the estate workers, and a day's holiday for those who worked at the mill, something that Blanche had contested fiercely when Amber had first ventured it, only giving in when Amber had told her that she had already informed the local paper of her grandmother's intended generosity.

It hadn't been quite true but Amber's ruse had worked. She had also secretly arranged for silk handkerchiefs to be printed bearing her grandmother's picture, their distribution strictly limited to those who worked in the mill or on the estate.

Maurice had written to her in high glee to tell her that he had had several personal approaches from the owners of other mills and the town's dignitaries requesting one of the silks.

'They will become a collector's item, all the more valued because of their limited availability,' Jay had prophesied when Amber had related this information to him during one of their regular weekly telephone calls to discuss the progress of all the arrangements.

The Stanleys of Alderley Hall, who were related to the Mitfords, were hosting a birthday tea, and the dignitaries of Macclesfield had organised a formal dinner.

All in all, the entire week of Blanche's birthday, including both its weekends, were filled with celebratory functions, the first of which was the party this afternoon for the estate and house workers, which was being held in the Tenants Hall.

'I've been thinking, Amber,' Blanche announced sharply. 'If there is to be war, the government will be looking to requisition property to provide accommodation for the troops, and we must make sure that they do not think of requisitioning Denham. You must speak to that friend of yours who is with the National Trust and tell him that the de Vries estate would be much more suitable. Indeed, I have already said as much myself whenever the subject has come up. This, after all, is a productive working estate whilst Lord de Vries is living alone, letting his land go to waste around him.'

Amber hid a small smile. Had her grandmother heard somehow that Jay's grandfather had remembered her age? Was this perhaps her intended revenge against him for having done so?'

'Mr Chamberlain is convinced that there will not be a war,' Amber reminded her grandmother.

'Huh, Chamberlain! I have no faith in him or his convictions.'

The talk of war reminded Amber of the ongoing conflict in Spain. There had been stories in the papers of such dreadful sufferings. Had Jean-Philippe survived the fighting? For his sake she hoped so. She had sent the sealed chest containing his paintings up to Macclesfield and asked for it to be stored away.

'I'm going to go down to the Dower House now, Grandmother, to collect Rose.'

'I don't know why you fuss so much over that child. Let one of the maids go down for her.'

'I fuss over her, as you call it, because she is my niece and I love her.'

'Just as well then that you will soon have another child of your own to fuss over.'

Amber had just short of a month to go yet before the baby was due to be born. It was a quiet child, not troubling her very much at all, until she had returned to Macclesfield. Now every time she took Rose on her lap the baby kicked so hard that it was as though it wanted to kick poor Rose out of her arms and onto the floor.

The opening days of May had brought the last of the tulips into open flower so that they provided a blaze of brilliant colour in the stone pots and the formal beds that were the showpiece of Denham's formal gardens.

Jay had told her that Harvey, the head gardener, had been grumbling for weeks about the celebrations, complaining that people would be walking all over his flowerbeds and making a mess of his lawns.

'Secretly, of course, he is delighted since it gave him an opportunity to trump all the other local estate gardeners by showing off his skills before the County Show.'

Jay. The complicated web of rules and forfeits she had designed for herself to prevent her from making excuses to see him, and to punish her when she did, demanded that she went out of her way to make sure that physically they were in one another's company as little as possible. Keeping him out of her thoughts and her emotions was a task she had already abandoned. Thus walking down to the Dower House to collect Rose was perfectly acceptable as she already knew that Jay would not be there. Furthermore she would actively be punishing herself with her visit since she was pretty sure that Cassandra would be there.

On the face of it, since Cassandra and Jay were cousins, it was perfectly natural that Cassandra should befriend Lydia. Indeed, Blanche had said that she thought it was extremely charitable and kind of Cassandra to spend as much time with Lydia as she was doing, given her own responsibilities. But there was something about Cassandra that repelled Amber, and it wasn't her own guilt because Cassandra had seen Jay kissing her. At least Cassandra had kept her word and not told Lydia, for Lydia's own sake, Amber imagined, since they were such close friends.

'It is my belief that Jay should have had that wife of his committed years ago since it is plain that she has lost her sanity, for all that other people dress up her condition as "bad nerves",' Blanche had informed Amber forthrightly.

'I think you are being too harsh, Grandmother,' Amber had responded. 'Lydia is sometimes unwell, but not all the time.'

Poor Lydia, Amber thought compassionately as she walked down the drive, bare-headed beneath the May sunshine.

The beech trees lining the drive were just beginning to unfurl their new leaves and in the parkland either side of the drive the grass was lush and green.

She was considering introducing a new line of co-ordinating silks and wallpapers into the shop, and the tracery of branches and leaves stirred her imagination. They could use parchment colours with soft sages and charcoals, no more than the skeleton of a sketched line. The shop was flourishing, and Amber only had to open the door and step into it, filling her lungs with the smell of silk and her senses with its beauty, to feel a steady slow feeling of achievement filling her. Its success meant so much to her. She had such plans for its future; plans that included building on her links with James Lees-Milne and the National Trust, and its growing archive of antique silks.

In order to survive, the mill needed the bulk sales that came from providing items that were affordable, such as the commemorative silk handkerchiefs. It also needed the specialist contracts for silk banners and heraldic items. The luxury fabrics she sold through her shop would never be enough to keep the mill working at full capacity, but they were her love. The pleasure of seeing reproduced timeless antique designs, of handling beautiful fabrics, of seeing her father's work come vividly to life, meant more to her than she had the words to say. It was her joy and her privilege that she, because of her family background and her marriage to Robert, was able to provide a bridge that could carry such beauty from the past into the present, bringing it back to new life. She would never neglect the importance to the mill of bread-and-butter items that kept it going, nor cease to be grateful for their Ministry of Defence contract to supply parachute silk, but her heart was forever given to the beautiful silks she sold from the Walton Street shop, and her plan had been to make it her ongoing mission in life to continue to expand their own archive. Had been. She placed her hand on her belly. Because of *this*, the plans for the future that had seemed so clear cut and achievable now looked more like a mirage that had never really existed at all other than inside her own imagination.

On the eastern horizon the Derbyshire hills threw purple shadows against the skyline. The town of Buxton, with its famous spa, would be free of snow now, like the winding road that led up to the notorious Cat and Fiddle public house, the highest public house in all England. On a day like today, when the air was so clear, it was possible from

Alderley Edge to look right out across the Cheshire plain that rolled its rich pastures west across the county.

In a month from now the beeches would be in full leaf and the child she was carrying would be full term. Its birth would bring the end of her marriage. She had not as yet said anything to her grandmother about her future. Time enough.

Amber had reached the gate that led into the Dower House garden now and, oddly, there was no familiar sound of children's voices. It made her frown with concern to see Rose sitting on the lawn on her own. Greg's daughter gave her a beaming smile and got to her feet, running over to greet her.

'How's my pretty Rose today, then?' Amber asked her tenderly. Her belly was too distended with the baby for her to be able to bend down, so she patted the top of Rose's head instead, and looked round for the nursemaid and Jay's two children.

For some reason the garden's empty silence suddenly felt ominous. It jarred on her that she couldn't see or hear Jay's children, and that Rose had been left in the garden on her own. Amber knew that Jay had a rule that the children were never to be left alone with their mother on the advice of Dr Brookes, but the new nursemaid, who had had to be found at short notice, might not know that.

She had started to walk faster, too fast in her present condition, she recognised as she felt the troubling stitch in her side. The kitchen door was open, the cook busy rolling pastry, and looking cross in that way that cooks did when they did not want to be interrupted.

'The mistress has sent Alice to fetch Mr Jay,' she answered Amber's question. 'The two little girls haven't been very well – too much running around and silliness, if you ask me. It's no wonder they was feeling sick.'

'Where are they now?' Amber asked her.

'Upstairs. The mistress came down and took them up after Lady de Vries left, then she came down again a little while back and said that Alice was to go and fetch Mr Jay urgent like, because she thought they wasn't very well. Huh, they was well enough when they was running about the garden and pestering me for biscuits.'

'Biscuit,' Rose said hopefully as she leaned against Amber's legs.

'Later, darling,' Amber told her.

There was no logical reason why she could feel that cold trickle of alarm that was icing down her spine, Amber told herself, no reason at all. She looked towards the green baize door that separated the kitchen from the rest of the house.

'I've got a message for Mrs Fulshawe from my grand-mother. I'd better go up and give it to her. Would you keep an eye on Rose for me, please, Cook? I promise I won't be long.'

'Nursemaiding ain't my job,' the cook said sharply.

'Of course it isn't,' she agreed soothingly. 'However, I'm afraid it's rather difficult for me to pick Rose up at the moment, and since she isn't very good on stairs yet I would be very grateful to you.' Amber opened her handbag and saw the gleam in the other woman's eyes.

'I would be so very grateful to you, Cook,' she told her, pressing two half-crowns into her hand.

'Well, I dare say it won't keep me from me pastry. She's a quiet enough little thing.'

'You wait here for me, Rose,' Amber instructed her niece tenderly.

The house beyond the baize door smelled of emptiness, of rooms left untouched by love. As she passed the drawing room she could smell cigarette smoke through its open door. So far as she knew, Lydia did not smoke but Cassandra did.

Amber hesitated at the bottom of the stairs and then called out, 'Lydia, it's me. Amber.'

Silence, and then the muffled sound of a door being closed as though whoever was closing it wanted to hide the sound.

Amber started to climb the stairs. The nursery was on the top floor and instinctively she headed for it. The door to it was open, but the windows were closed and the curtains drawn.

The two little girls were lying on their separate beds, laid out on them almost, Amber recognised with a surge of shocked dread, the bedding wrapped like shrouds. They weren't moving. Relief trickled through her, thin and uncertain, as she thought she saw their chests lift.

There were two glasses on the bedside table and a small glass bottle beside them.

'You shouldn't have come here.'

Amber turned round clumsily, half stumbling with her own awkward weight.

Lydia was standing in the doorway. She came into the room and closed the door, locking it and then removing the key.

'Lydia, what have you given the girls?' Amber asked her anxiously. 'I know they weren't very well and that you've sent for Jay.'

'I want him to see that I know that he was planning to take them away from me. That's why I've sent for him. But he can't take them now. No one will be able to take them now.'

Amber looked at her in sick fear. 'Lydia, Jay would never take your children from you.'

'Yes he would. Cassandra told me. She says that I must not trust Jay and that he wants to take them away from me, because of you. Because of *that*.' She gestured towards

Amber's belly. 'Because of it, the baby he's given you. Cassandra told me that Jay loves you and not me.'

Amber was appalled, pity spearing through her anxiety. 'No, Lydia, that isn't true. I swear that to you. Jay is not the father of my baby.'

How cruel Cassandra was, and how manipulative. What on earth could she gain from poisoning poor Lydia against Jay, other than the knowledge that she was causing trouble? She must know the delicacy of the balance of Lydia's mind.

'You are Jay's wife, Lydia, and the mother of his children. Nothing can change that,' Amber assured her. It was after all the truth.

'Jay wants to take my babies from me, but I won't let him. I'm their mother, they belong to me.' Her voice had started to rise.

'I know you love them, Lydia,' Amber tried to soothe her.

'Yes, I do. They won't know anything. They'll be asleep. And then I'll make them safe with this.'

Her right hand had been down by her side, hidden in the folds of her dress, but now she had raised it and Amber could see the dark sheen of the knife she was holding. Horror gripped her.

'It will be very quick, you know,' Lydia told her matter-of-factly. 'I used to watch my grandfather doing it to the livestock. You just draw the blade across the throat and that's it. There's a lot of blood, of course, but see how I've tucked the sheets right up?'

Amber's whole body was bathed in an ice-cold sweat. As though it could feel it, her baby kicked frantically in her womb and for the first time since its conception Amber was gripped by a fierce surge of protective love for her child.

She had to get out of this room and get help, but Lydia was standing between her and the door and she had the knife.

'He won't be here for a long time,' Lydia told her as though she had guessed Amber's thoughts. 'I told Alice that he'd gone to the home farm but he hasn't.' There was something almost childlike about the pleased expression on her face and the sound of her voice.

'That was very clever of you, Lydia,' Amber told her.

'Yes. I am clever. Cassandra says so.'

'And you love your children.'

'Yes.'

'And we don't hurt the people we love, do we?'

'I'm not hurting them. It's Jay who will hurt them if he takes them away from me. But I'm not going to let him. I'm sending them to God so that He can look after them. They'll be safe there. Everyone's safe with God.'

She was speaking like a child, and that was how she must try and reason with her, Amber decided. Inside she felt sick with horror but she knew that she had to hide those feelings from Lydia. Where was Jay, why didn't he come? Oh God, she prayed inwardly, please let him come, please let someone come and save us. Save my baby. Save hers.

One of the children suddenly moaned and moved beneath the bedcovers in obvious distress.

'She's going to be sick,' Amber told Lydia. 'We must turn her on her side, otherwise she might choke.'

She went instinctively to the bed and had just reached out to turn Ella onto her side when Lydia screamed, 'No, don't touch her! You must not touch her!'

She launched herself at Amber so speedily, the knife in her hand, that Amber barely had time to do more than put out her arm to protect herself, as she tried to get out of the way.

She felt the knife burn into her arm, the pain quick and fierce.

The baby kicked as though in fear of its life and a feeling

of weakness engulfed Amber as she saw the blood running down her arm in bright red droplets. The cumbersome weight of her pregnant body wouldn't obey the commands of her brain to protect itself.

'Blood,' Lydia whispered. 'Blood.' She raised her arm again.

Amber was trapped between the bed and the wall but her own safety wasn't important any longer. All she could think about was the baby; the life she must protect. Nothing else mattered – nothing and no one, least of all herself.

She could hear feet on the stairs, and then Jay calling out her name. *Her* name, not Lydia's. She used what was left of her strength to call back to him as she tried to push Lydia away. Amber saw the knife arcing towards her unprotected child; she reached up towards it, desperate to protect her baby, stretching for it, feeling it cut into her hand and then her arm. She could smell the hot scent of her own blood.

The door was open and Jay was standing there.

Jay – she had only breathed his name but he had heard her. He looked towards her and she could see in his eyes his horror and his grief.

He came into the room and reached for Lydia but she pushed past him as he tried to restrain her.

The darkness was taking her now, and with it came the first pains of labour.

She reached down to place her hands protectively on her body.

'No,' she protested. 'No, not yet. It's too soon.'

There was a sound from outside as a car screamed to a halt.

*   *   *

The pains came in tight hot waves that rose and then broke her on their agony, dragging her deeper into their grip.

This was not like it had been when she had given birth to Luc. This time her body and the child within it seemed to be at war with one another, fighting against one another, her body reluctant to engage in the birth process and the child determined that it should.

They had brought her back to Denham when she had said that she could not give birth at the Dower House, although she now had little memory of the journey.

The day had faded into night and still the pain went on, so great that at times its pangs tore her consciousness from her.

She saw her grandmother standing over her, her face set and stern, she saw Dr Brookes, and sensed the anxiety behind his calm kindness.

In the darkest reaches of the night, when the pain had exhausted her body and left it weak and drained, she thought she saw a man standing in the shadows beyond the foot of the bed. She could feel his love reaching out to her, tender and caring, surrounding her, to protect her. She cried then, begging him not to leave her but to take her with him, her cries drowned out by the ripping wave of pain that surged through her. She saw Lydia's contorted face, the knife grasped in her hand; she felt it plunge into her, tearing at her. She must not let Lydia hurt her baby. She must keep it safe. It must not be born yet. It was too soon and too dangerous, but Lydia's knife was tearing at her flesh. She could smell the heat of her own blood. The pain swelled and gripped her. She could hear someone screaming in mortal agony.

'Push, Amber. Push now.'

Her grandmother was bending over her, her hand gripping her arm.

'No,' she protested. But it was too late, her body was obeying nature; she could not keep her child safe now. It was too late.

They laid it – *her*, for it was a girl – on her body, small and waxen. Lifeless.

She tried to reach for her but her movement brought a great tide of heat surging from her body. She could smell blood, hot and salty. There were voices all around her but she could not hear what they were saying above the rush of the flood within her that was taking her strength and her senses.

'Amber.' The voice was familiar, its exhaustion somehow commanding her, piercing the shrouds of her sleep. Robert's voice. But how could Robert be here when they were separated, and he had made it plain that he wanted nothing more to do with her?

Amber struggled to open her eyes against the great weakness that filled her. It was Robert who had spoken to her, she recognised as she looked first at her husband and then at the unfamiliar room.

'Where am I?' she asked him uncertainly.

'You're in hospital, Amber. They had to bring you here to give you a blood transfusion.'

'A blood transfusion?' Her forehead creased as she struggled to make sense of his words.

'One of several. Dr Brookes had to send to the new blood bank in Ipswich in the end.'

Robert was holding her hand, she suddenly realised. He looked tired, and in need of a shave. He looked thinner too, and older.

'Why are you here?'

'Your grandmother sent for me.'

His hand trembled over her own. 'I've been such a fool.

It took almost losing you to make me realise how important you are to me, and how empty my life would be without you. I thought I knew what love was, but I realise now I knew little more than a single branch of a very deeply rooted tree, and that you and my love for you are the taproot of that tree, and what keeps it and me alive. Princess, you are my dearest, dearest girl.'

Robert's use of the teasing nickname he had given her the first time they had met brought weak tears to Amber's eyes. His hand tightened on hers and she returned its pressure.

'When you cried out to me for forgiveness in your travail, I realised that I could love a thousand Ottos but there could only ever be my one you.'

'You were there? Then?'

'Where else should I have been? Although I admit that your grandmother did not approve. I was willing you to live, Amber, for Luc and for me, so that I could have the chance to speak to you as I am doing now. I wanted to wrap you in my love and protect you.'

'I felt that. I knew somehow that someone . . . I thought perhaps it was my father . . .'

'Maybe it was both of us,' Robert told her gently. 'You must rest now.' He was releasing her hand and starting to get up.

Amber refused to let him go. Images slipped slowly through her head: Lydia; a knife; Jay; the birth of her child, still and without life. She placed her free hand on her flat stomach, tears welling in her eyes as she asked him, 'My baby?'

Robert's expression changed, his face lightening, illuminated by the joy she could see in his eyes. Because her child was dead!

The pain was unbearable, worse by far than the physical

568

pain of giving birth. She wanted to escape from it and go back to that dark nothing Robert had dragged her from.

She could feel Robert's hand tightening on her own as though he sensed her desire and wanted to stop her.

'She's so beautiful, Amber, so perfect,' he laughed. 'I confess that I am totally besotted with her. She looks very much like Luc, although much prettier, of course.'

Amber stared at him in disbelief. 'She's alive?'

'What? Oh, my poor girl, did you think . . . ? Yes . . . yes, she is alive and very much in need of her mother, since a mere father is no substitute. Your grandmother is as besotted as I am myself, I suspect, although she will not admit it. However, she will not allow me to remove her from the nursery to take her home. We are all her slaves, except perhaps little Rose, who cries most affectingly for you.'

Amber couldn't take it all in properly. 'I thought she had not survived. She was so pale and still, not moving at all.'

'The birth was traumatic for both of you. You will not remember, I think, but after her birth you haemorrhaged so badly that Dr Brookes warned us that you might not survive. Indeed, you would not have done if it hadn't been for the new blood you were given. It was interesting to discover that we share a blood group.'

'You gave blood for me?'

Robert smiled tiredly. 'We all gave our blood. Your grandmother, Jay, me, but when you didn't stop haemorrhaging Dr Brookes had to apply to the blood bank as well.'

'How long?'

'It is nearly a month since Emerald was born.'

'Emerald?' A shaft of maternal jealousy pierced Amber that someone else had given her daughter her name.

'It was your grandmother's choice. Emeralds are, I believe, the baby's birthstone and in keeping with your family tradition of naming girls for a colour. I wanted to name her for you . . .' His voice thickened.

'Robert, tell me about Lydia. What has happened to her? Where . . . ?'

'Lydia is dead, Amber. She ran straight out of the house as Dr Brookes was arriving, and into the road in front of a car after she attacked you. She was killed instantly. The poor driver was dreadfully shocked, naturally.'

'Oh, how dreadful.'

'Yes, but perhaps when one looks at the shockingness of it, it could be said that it was for the best. Had she not died she would have had to be charged with drugging her children with the intention of taking their lives, and of attacking you.'

'The children! Oh, Robert, how are they?' Amber was filled with guilt for not asking about them before.

'They are fine. In fact your grandmother says, and I am inclined to agree, that they are better off without their poor mother. Dr Brookes believes that she used her own drugs on them, having hoarded them instead of taking them.'

'I am sure she would never have done what she did if Cassandra hadn't put it into her head that Jay was going to take the children from her. What is it?' she demanded when she saw the way Robert's expression changed and became very grave.

'I wasn't going to raise this matter with you yet, but since you have mentioned Cassandra I feel that I should.' He paused and then said quietly, 'I'm afraid that Cassandra has been spreading an unfair rumour that Jay did want to bring his marriage to an end, and that she has first-hand evidence of his involvement with another woman.'

Amber went rigid, her face losing what little colour it had. 'She is so spiteful, Robert, and so unkind. Jay is, after all, her cousin.'

'As Greg is yours, and yet look at the way he has behaved towards you over this matter of your grandmother's will. Because you yourself are so caring and kind-hearted, you assume that others are the same. Sadly, they are not. Amber, there is something I need to discuss with you, if you are feeling strong enough.'

'If it is about our marriage . . .'

'It is. First, though, I owe you an apology. It's public knowledge now that Hitler has crushed the opposition to him from some officers in the Germany Army by appointing himself Supreme Commander of the Armed Forces. He has further used propaganda to smear Field Marshal Werner von Blomberg by insinuating that his wife is a former prostitute, whilst allowing rumours to be spread that General Werner von Fritsch is a homosexual. You were right in everything you warned me of, Amber, and I owe you a great deal for all that you did for me. I acknowledge that now and I thank you for it from the bottom of my heart.

'I now have a further favour to ask you.' He paused and smiled at her, and Amber could see the old Robert in that smile.

'I want you to remain my wife, Amber. As I've already told you, when I learned that your life was in danger all I could think of was how much I loved and needed you, and how much the poorer my life would be without you. We have a son whom we both love, and now we can have a beautiful daughter if you are willing to share her with me. Neither of us has spoken to anyone of any separation, there is nothing that needs to be said or done, should we choose to continue with our marriage. Do you, Amber? Will you?'

Amber remembered the way Jay had looked at her when he had come into the children's bedroom and seen her at Lydia's mercy. She had seen then in his eyes what he held in his heart. She had seen and known his love for her was as strong as her own for him. Surely they deserved to be together, and to have that love. They had so much in common; there was so much they could do – for the estate, for the mill, for their children. Everything within her yearned towards him and towards that future.

But she had other responsibilities: a son who loved the man he thought of as his father; a new child who, if she left her marriage, would have no legitimate father. She herself would be branded by wagging tongues, as Cassandra had already branded her, and Jay's daughters would grow up perhaps feeling she had usurped their own mother's position, and because of that would not be able to turn to her when they needed to do so.

To take her own happiness she would have to burden so many others with unhappiness.

The golden road to love and fulfilment glistened beneath her tears, shimmering temptingly with promise. Amber looked at it with longing and then closed her eyes against it.

'Yes, Robert,' she told him. 'Yes, I shall.'

'Ah, Amber, wait until you see our daughter.' A wide smile curled Robert's mouth. 'I had thought myself a doting father when Luc was born but now I realise that no man knows what fatherhood means until he is the besotted father of a daughter. She is enchanting, Amber, in every single way, bewitching, adorable, and she can wind me round her little finger already. I swear she smiled at me this morning.'

Amber listened to his eulogy, her heart as heavy as a stone, its weight crushing her with pain.

Emerald Olga Devenish was christened four months later, just after Chamberlain returned to England declaring that there would be 'peace for our time'. Amber had chosen the baby's second name in honour of her Russian heritage.

Everybody said that she was the most beautiful child they had ever seen, with her dark curls and her large long-lashed eyes, which were already promising to echo the colour of her birthstone.

She commanded the attention of her adoring court of worshippers as determinedly as any empress. Robert she loved wholeheartedly, but Amber she rejected completely.

The first time Amber had picked her up after her return to her grandmother's, Emerald had gone so rigid in her arms that Amber feared she had had a fit. 'Mother mustn't be upset. It was only because Baby didn't really know her yet,' the efficient nurse hired by Blanche informed Amber briskly, deftly removing the baby from her arms.

But Emerald did know her, Amber was convinced of that. She knew her and she was rejecting her. Was it because she had somehow known that Amber hadn't wanted her? Had she sensed that during all those long days and weeks before her birth? But she had loved her when she had feared Lydia might harm her, Amber told herself. She had loved her then and that love had grown as she gave birth to her.

At night when Amber should have been sleeping and recouping her strength, she would go into the nursery and look down into Emerald's cradle, watching her sleep, longing to take her in her arms. But whenever she gave in to the temptation to do so, the baby would wake up and howl her dislike of the maternal arms that were holding her. Was there anything more hurtful to a mother than her baby's rejection?

Amber tried not to show how she felt when Emerald held out her arms to others to be picked up and showed them the smile she would not give her mother.

It seemed to Amber that she was the only person her child rejected, but there was one other person she didn't like: Rose. Poor little Rose, who only had to be within Emerald's line of vision for the baby to start crying.

Blanche tut-tutted, but Amber could sense that secretly her grandmother was quite pleased to have her company favoured above that of Emerald's mother's. As the weeks went by Amber thought that Emerald had a lot of Blanche in her, and that there was often the same cold hardness in her gaze that Amber had seen so often in Blanche's eyes when she was growing up.

They had decided to ask Beth and Diana Cooper to be Emerald's godmothers, whilst Robert had suggested they should ask Jay to be her godfather.

'He saved your life, after all,' he had told Amber, 'and with it Emerald's.'

Now, as their guests mingled together at the post-christening service party in the house in Eaton Square, Amber acknowledged that it brought her both the sweetest pleasure and the sharpest pain to have Jay so close to her whilst knowing that they must be forever apart.

He had come to see her whilst she had still been in the hospital, sitting at the side of her bed as Robert had done, but unlike Robert he had not held her hand. They had talked of his daughters and she had told him, unable to bring herself to look at him, of her own guilt because she had not initially wanted Emerald.

'I was so angry and afraid when I realised I was carrying Emerald. I'd been grateful to Jean-Philippe. He'd shown me the true worth of my womanhood and he'd shown me too how much I love you. But I hated the fact that I was carrying his child.' A tear had rolled down her face to land on the sheet.

Jay had put his hand over it, his head bent.

Later, when he had gone, Amber had put her own hand over the place that still bore the imprint of his.

Diana Cooper was holding Emerald, who was smiling up at her, her cheeks flushed pink with excitement, for all the world as though she knew that she was the centre of attention and that this was her day.

'She is such a little princess, Amber,' Diana laughed. 'She will have all the young men queuing up to worship her when she grows up.'

'Young men? They shall not be allowed anywhere near her,' Robert mock growled.

Jay was standing on the other side of the room with his own daughters and Rose.

Amber made her way towards them, not rushing, stopping to talk to other guests, drawing out her anticipation of her pleasure and feeling it build inside her.

She had wanted to take Rose to live with them, but Robert had objected, pointing out that Emerald did not like Greg's daughter.

'It wouldn't be fair to either of them, and besides, Rose is used to the company of Jay's daughters. It would be unfair to separate her from them.'

He was right, Amber knew, but she would miss Rose. They understood one another and could communicate with just a shared look. There were many of those shared looks when they were with Emerald.

'Emerald certainly seems to be enjoying her christening,' Jay smiled when Amber finally reached them.

'She is my grandmother all over again and determined to play the role of *grande dame*,' Amber told him ruefully, adding, 'The papers are full of Chamberlain's agreement with Germany, but Robert is still convinced that we'll end up at war with them.'

'Sadly, I believe that he is right.'

Amber gave a small shiver. It made her feel so vulnerable, knowing that whilst her personal life was so filled with love and contentment there was so much political unheaval going on in the world. She wanted to hug her family to her to protect them from the threat darkening the political skies, at the same time as she was trying to block out the distant sound of the drums of war beating their horrific and dread warning. Did she feel her own happiness more keenly because it marched hand in hand with her fear? Did witnessing the growing belief that there would be war sharpen the precious sweetness of this very special time?

War!

No wonder that congregations around the country were praying every Sunday that it would not happen and that there would be peace.

'How long do you plan to stay in London for?' she asked Jay, trying not to think of the political situation.

'We're returning to Macclesfield tomorrow.'

Another blow to dim her happiness and one far closer to home this time.

'Amber, darling, you have the most beautiful daughter. I am so very jealous.'

Obediently she turned to talk to yet another of Emerald's admirers.

When she turned back again Jay had gone.

Chapter Forty-Seven

September 1939

War!

Robert and Amber looked at one another as they listened to the Prime Minister's voice. They were in the small drawing room of the Eaton Square house listening to the wireless, Luc standing solemnly beside his father, whilst Emerald, who was not only walking but who could also say 'Dada' and, when she was in a particularly benign mood, 'Mama' as well, for once was not able to distract her father's attention by clinging to his legs and holding up her arms to him.

Not that the news had come as a surprise. The whole country had been aware for months, of the government's preparations in case there should be a war. Amber, in her role as a member of the Women's Voluntary Service, had spent the previous week working in the East End, helping with the evacuation of children, and had returned home the previous evening in the blackout after a WVS meeting with her uniform soaked through, after she had been caught in the violent thunderstorm that had drenched the city. She had also spent a large part of the summer preparing Osterby for the school that would move into it if it were to come to war. Both Osterby and the London house had had to be equipped with blackout curtains, and those house and estate workers who were not in a position to join up assured about their own situation. 'We shall need you more than ever,' Amber had told them all, 'for we shall all have to do our bit.'

The Walton Street shop had had to be closed. Both the boys had joined up, and they and Amber had spent a very sad three days packing up all the silks, and preparing everything to be taken into storage, along with the paintings, artwork, and valuable furniture from Osterby and Eaton Square. She had sat for a long time over the designs she had planned in the South of France the summer Emerald had been conceived. That summer and the tumult of its emotions seemed now to belong to another life, which, like the designs she had created in it, had no place in her life now.

It was time to lay the past to rest. There were now other, graver perils ahead. In order to overcome them, not just families but the whole country would have to unite and pull together.

War! It was the cry on everyone's lips but it was something of a hollow cry, especially from the women who were having to say goodbye to their small children and their grown sons.

Farmers were being urged to grow more crops, young men were being called up for military service, and in Macclesfield the silk mills were working through the night to produce more parachutes.

Robert, for his part, had been co-opted to work for the War Office as a liaison officer, dealing with high-ranking refugees, which meant that he would need to be in London. He had been insistent, though, that if it did come to war, Amber should go to Macclesfield, taking Emerald with her as it would be safer for them there. Emerald accepted her mother more now, although tolerated would be a more appropriate word, Amber thought sadly as she looked at her daughter. She had worked patiently to win Emerald's love and trust but she knew that Emerald would never love her as she did Robert.

The sound of the Prime Minister's voice had barely finished fading away when an unearthly sound began to rise and then fall in an ear-piercing wail that caused Emerald to put her hands over her ears and cry.

'Air-raid siren,' Robert told Amber grimly. 'It's probably only a practice run but nevertheless we'd better get everyone down to the cellars.'

In common with many other London householders, their cellars were being used as air-raid shelters.

In the kitchen one of the young maids, a new girl who had not been with them very long, was on the verge of hysterics, saying that she couldn't abide dark places and that she'd rather be bombed than go down into the cellars, refusing to listen to her fellow servants' dire warnings of what could happen to her.

'You should be grateful, not making all this fuss,' Cook told her off crossly. 'At least we've got our own shelter to go to, and we don't have to go in one of them nasty smelly public shelters, like some folk have.'

Her crossness only made the girl cry harder.

Taking charge, Amber told her calmly that she was welcome to stay in the kitchen if she wished, but that she'd heard that many young men were only asking their sweethearts to get engaged to them if they felt they could rely on them to do the right thing whilst they were off fighting for their country.

As though by magic the maid stopped crying and almost ran to catch up with the other servants hurrying down to the cellars.

'What on earth was all that about?' Robert asked Amber ruefully as they waited to follow the servants.

'She has a young man who has just received his call-up papers and to whom, according to Cook, she is desperate to become engaged,' Amber told Robert wryly.

The cellars were a reasonable size, and Amber and the housekeeper, Mrs Evans, had done their best to equip them as comfortably as they could, with fold-up truckle beds and enough chairs for everyone to sit on. They were still chilly and dank, though, whilst the single light bulbs suspended from the extra electric cabling Robert had managed to get installed threw dark shadows on the walls. Luc was keeping Emerald amused by making animal shapes for her with his hands, whilst Robert and Chivers, the butler, called out everyone's name against the list that was pinned to the back of the newly reinforced cellar door.

It was a relief when the all clear sounded and they were able to go back upstairs.

The telephone rang within minutes of them hearing the all clear, the caller someone wanting to speak with Robert. He went to take the call in the library, leaving Emerald to wail after him in stormy protest.

They would have heard the news in Macclesfield, of course, Amber acknowledged as she looked out through the window on to the sunny square. Jay would have a great deal to do. He had told her earlier in the summer that he felt guilty because his reserved occupation status meant that he could not volunteer for any of the armed services when so many young men were being called up.

Robert came back into the room.

'That was the ARP post,' he told Amber. 'No cause for alarm, the air-raid siren was just a practice run. Poor Duff Cooper's going to feel this,' Robert added. 'He wants to be involved but his fall-out with Chamberlain and resignation from the government has left him without a role to play. Chips was saying only the other day that he feels for him.'

'Duff and Diana are due to leave for America soon, though, aren't they?'

'Yes, the middle of the month. Quite a few people we know will be sending their children overseas now, Amber, and—'

'No,' Amber stopped him firmly. 'It wouldn't be right or fair, Robert, not when so many families can't send their children abroad. The King and Queen aren't sending the princesses away. We are British and if we don't stand firm and show that we believe in our government and our fighting men, what right do we have to expect ordinary people to do so? It is their sons and husbands and brothers who will be fighting, after all.'

'You are right, of course. You and the children are so precious to me, Amber.'

'You can't wrap us up and pack us away until after the war is over, Robert, as though we were some family heir-loom.'

'You are what is most precious to me. In Luc you have given me a son who will make a far better duke than I have ever done. I am so proud knowing that I shall hand on my family's heritage to such a worthy successor.'

They looked at one another in mutual understanding.

Then Robert said more mundanely, 'I thought we might dine at the Ritz tonight. There is bound to be a crowd there and we can pick up what gossip might be circulating. I want you and Emerald to leave for Macclesfield as soon as it can be arranged. The trains are going to be packed with evacuees so I'll drive you there myself, once I've taken Luc back to school.'

'I can't leave for Macclesfield until everything is sorted

out here,' Amber pointed out. She was thinking of all the work that needed to be done to ensure that everything bar what was absolutely essential for everyday living was packed up and sent out of the city to be stored safely, as well as her ongoing WVS duties. 'There are still some of the East End children to be evacuated. Their poor mothers are distraught not knowing when they will see their little ones again.'

'It is for their own safety, you know that.'

She did, of course, and it was her duty as a member of the WVS to try to get the mothers to see that as well.

'Some of them are simply refusing to let the children go.'

She had been shocked and appalled at first to discover that large numbers of the slum children were infested with nits, and worse, and then filled with anger that families should be living in such poverty. Anger against herself chiefly for not having known.

If it hadn't been for the fact that she knew there would be work for her to do in Macclesfield she would have tried to persuade Robert that she should stay in London, Amber acknowledged.

And, of course, Jay was in Macclesfield.

She must not think like that. Didn't she realise how fortunate she was? Others certainly did, her grandmother and Beth amongst them.

'You're so lucky, Amber,' Beth had told her the last time they had met.

And she was. She had, after all, a wonderful, kind, generous husband who adored his two children and was adored by them in return.

It would be very unsettling to be living in Macclesfield whilst Robert was here in London. She would see more of Jay than she would of Robert. Her heart thumped with guilt.

Surely it wasn't wrong to think about Jay in the way she

582

did in her most private of thoughts, she defended herself, but of course she knew that it was, and that the longing for Jay, her love for him, was just as much a form of betrayal as though they had been physical lovers, not because Robert would object to her having a lover – Amber doubted that he would – but because she loved Jay so very much.

Her duty to her husband and family had kept her away from him but now the war was taking her back to him. Something, not excitement or joy exactly, but something yearning and dangerous, sang inside her.

'I know that the blackout is necessary, but it is making life very difficult – and dangerous,' Amber commented to Robert as two cars, their lights turned off for the blackout, nearly collided on Sloane Street. Their own taxi had to swerve to avoid them, the driver cursing.

'Three bleeding near misses I've had tonight already, beggin' your pardon, missus,' the cabby told them. 'The ruddy blackout will be killing off more people than Hitler has killed, if you ask me.'

To judge from the number of cars and taxis pulling up outside the Ritz, they weren't the only ones to have decided to dine there tonight, Amber realised, as they were bowed through the blacked-out entrance and into the familiar light and warmth of the famous hotel.

'Shall we have a drink first?' Robert suggested.

The cocktail bar was so full that it was impossible to find a table. Amber felt a tap on her shoulder and turned round to find Louise smiling at her.

Louise and her husband had divorced the previous Christmas on the grounds of his unreasonable behaviour, and although Louise had claimed that she was glad to see the back of him Amber thought that she looked too thin and strained to be as happy as she claimed. Her affair with the friend of the Aga Khan hadn't lasted very long, and nor had the brief relationships she had had since.

'Isn't this exciting?' she demanded.

She was dressed in a very smart evening ensemble, the neckline of her midnight-blue satin provocatively low cut, the sapphires round her neck and in her ears matching the blue glitter of her eyes.

When she saw Amber looking at them she told her in a cynical drawl, 'A present from a dear friend. Sadly he's married, and even more sadly he's now scuttled off back to his wife in America. Jewellery is such a comfort in some circumstances.'

As she spoke she was surveying the room. Looking for someone to take her American lover's place? Amber wondered sadly. Poor Louise. Life had not been kind to her although Amber suspected that she herself would not think that.

'Shall you be staying in London?' she asked Amber.

'No. Robert is insisting that Emerald and I leave. What about you?'

Louise gave a small shrug. 'Yes, I shall stay. Where else is there for me to go? As a matter of fact I'm thinking of booking myself into a room here at the Ritz.'

As Robert had predicted, the Ritz was busy, and in fact they saw so many friends and acquaintances that the atmosphere was almost that of a party, in a surreal sort of way. The men were grouping together, their expressions serious and yet at the same time purposeful and even a little excited, whilst the women looked anxious and tired, all of them worrying about their families and the problems of emptying large ancestral London houses prior to leaving for the comparative safety of the country.

'I saw Sydney Redesdale the other day,' someone commented. 'She must feel dreadful about those Hitler-supporting daughters of hers, although of course she won't admit it.'

584

Diana was now married to Tom Mosley, with whom she had had her third son, Alexander, and Unity, so far as Amber knew, was still living in Germany. Poor Lady Redesdale indeed.

'Emerald Cunard is furious about the war and says it will ruin her dinner parties.' Louise blew out a ring of smoke. 'Such a glamorous, unEnglish-sounding name, I've always thought – Emerald.'

Was Louise being deliberately malicious, Amber wondered, or merely mischievous? She certainly had no reason to imagine that her own Emerald was unEnglish, as she had put it. Amber had never confided in anyone about Jean-Philippe. Anyone other than Jay and Robert, that was.

The week that followed was one of sunshine and warmth – not that anyone had the time to enjoy the weather. Not with so much to be done now that they were officially at war.

All over London the great houses of the rich and titled were being closed up, with some owners even throwing sad little house 'coolings'. Only Joe Kennedy, the American Ambassador, was still giving large parties, telling everyone who would listen that England was committing suicide.

Amber had spoken by telephone to her grandmother, who seemed to be relishing the prospect of war rather than frightened of it. The Eaton Square house had finally been stripped bare of everything that could be damaged, leaving only the bare essentials.

The footman, the under-footman and the chauffeur had all been called up, and the maids, and surprisingly Mrs Evans, the housekeeper, had left to do war work, leaving only the butler, the cook and nanny.

Luc's trunk was packed for his return to his evacuated school and so were Amber and Emerald's things ready for their departure to Macclesfield.

The morning of Luc's departure was another beautiful sunny day. Robert had suggested that Amber and Emerald go with them but since Emerald was prone to car sickness and Amber had promised to stand in for one of her fellow WVS members whose husband was leaving for France in the morning, she had decided not to go.

Luc was growing up fast, and going to be tall, 'like his father', as people often said.

He had reached that age where he was self-conscious about maternal hugs and kisses, but still submitted himself to Amber's only slightly red-faced.

With Bruno, his dog, though, who had turned out to be gun shy and not suitable as a gun dog, after all, and who had had to be brought to London when the house had been taken over by the school, he was more easily affectionate, hugging the Labrador tightly and then telling Amber sternly that she was not to spoil it with too many titbits whilst he was away at school.

Gravely Amber promised that she would carry out his wishes to the letter.

Emerald was lifted up in her father's arms to kiss her brother goodbye before being kissed herself by Robert, and then the whole procedure was repeated a second time after Robert and Luc had taken their formal goodbyes of the remaining staff and the four of them were outside in the warm sunshine.

Another brief hug with Luc and a kiss on her cheek from Robert, and then they were in the car and on their way.

Picking up Emerald, Amber watched until they had disappeared out of sight before going back into the house.

Several hours later, Amber was just about to leave the house on her way to do her WVS stint – sorting through second-hand clothes donated for the use of refugees, in a freezing cold barn of a church hall, when the telephone rang.

Guessing that it would be Robert, she went to answer it. He was not, though, telephoning to tell her that he had left Luc at his school, but to say that they had been delayed on the road because of troop movements and not to expect him back until the morning.

'I'll find an hotel or a pub after I've dropped Luc at school and then drive back tomorrow.'

'Give Luc a hug for me,' Amber told him, 'and drive safely.'

'You know me,' Robert laughed. 'I never take risks.'

It was, as Amber and her fellow WVS members agreed, a mystery how it could be so cold inside a building that had been warmed all week by so much lovely sunshine.

'The first thing I shall do when I get home is run a hot bath,' one of the other women announced.

'There's something so sad about old clothes, don't you think? Poor unwanted things,' Isabelle Markely sighed.

'But they are wanted,' Amber pointed out briskly. Privately she thought that Isabelle was inclined to be ever so slightly theatrical if allowed to be so. 'That is why they are here and we are sorting through them.'

As she walked home along the dark streets with their blacked-out windows, Amber thought about her son, hoping that he would adapt to the school's new premises. He should do. He was a pragmatic little boy in many ways, and watching how he was continually modelling himself on Robert was especially sweet, knowing the true history of his conception. Young though she was, Emerald looked set to take after Amber's own grandmother in temperament. Amber didn't want to favour one of her children above the other but there was no doubt that she found Luc a far easier child than Emerald.

She crossed the street and turned into the square.

The butler opened the door for her, informing her importantly, 'There's a gentleman waiting to see you in His Grace's library, Your Grace. Said he'd rather wait than come back.'

Jay! Who else could it be? She could feel the happiness glowing brightly inside her chest cavity as though someone had lit a warming fire there.

It was hard for her to smile calmly as she thanked the butler and then walked sedately to the double doors that led to the small ground-floor library that also doubled as Robert's office.

Her visitor, perhaps alerted to her arrival from the sound of her footsteps across the tiled hall floor, was standing facing the doors with his back to the wall, and he definitely wasn't Jay. Her disappointment was swift and punishing, and it was hard for her to dismiss it and study him.

Of middle height, slightly balding, and wearing a heavy dark overcoat despite the warmth of the evening and the room, his features had a blandness about them that made him a man one would might meet a dozen times and yet not really remember. Only the sharp scrutiny of his peat-brown gaze was memorable.

'The Duchess of Lenchester?' he asked her formally, taking Amber slightly aback. No one ever called her that.

'Yes, and you are . . . ?' It was unlike Amber to be haughty but somehow she found herself copying the man's rather formal and authoritative tone.

'Saunders, Your Grace, Inspector Saunders of the West Rutland Police.'

Like a cloud obscuring the sun, a feeling of foreboding and alarm was filtering out her earlier happiness.

'The police? But—'

'I'm afraid that I'm the bearer of bad news, Your Grace.'

'Bad news?' Suddenly she was icy cold and very afraid.

'There's been an accident involving your husband's motor car.'

He paused as though wanting to give his words time to sink in. Amber could feel her heart thudding frantically, as though she had been running.

'It's the blackout. It's causing so many accidents. My husband is always saying so. I hope the car isn't too badly damaged. It won't be easy to replace it now that we're at war . . .'

She was talking too fast, her voice too high-pitched, as she gabbled like an idiot. She had the feeling that the inspector was waiting for her to run out of steam, as though he had heard similar words many, many times before. His very silence was shepherding her towards the question she didn't want to ask but knew she must. His silence had exhausted her desperate attempt to escape it.

'Is my husband all right?'

She knew even before he answered her just from the change in his expression and his silence. This man should have been an actor. He could convey so much just with that look away, as though into some dreadful void.

'I am sorry to have to tell you that both your husband and your son are dead.'

Chapter Forty-Eight

'No. No . . . that can't be true. It can't be.'

'I'm very sorry, Your Grace, but I'm afraid it is.'

'They're dead? Both of them?'

'Yes.'

She was trembling – violently. She must not give way. She must remember her responsibility to Robert – and to Luc. Her trembling increased but she still managed to demand, 'How? How did it happen?'

The inspector's mouth compressed and Amber could sense that he was not going to tell her.

'You must tell me,' she insisted. 'You must.'

'Very well then. A heavy artillery army vehicle pulled across the road to avoid hitting a cyclist, not realising your husband was coming the other way.' He paused and then said quietly, 'If it's any comfort to you, from the way we found them it's obvious that your husband tried to shield the boy.'

Comfort? How could there be any comfort for her?

'Is there someone you would like us to inform about what has happened? A member of your family, perhaps, or a close friend?'

'No. No one.' Amber's voice was flat and hard. How much of the blame for what had happened was hers for not keeping Robert and Luc in her thoughts, and for not surrounding them with her love, for thinking of Jay instead, for exulting in the freedom that her return to Macclesfield would give her to be with him?

'There are certain formalities that need to be addressed.'

She looked at the inspector as though she had no idea who he was.

'I understand that this is a dreadful shock for you, Your Grace, but there are certain important formalities that need to be dealt with,' he repeated. 'Perhaps a close friend of your late husband . . .'

Somehow she managed to drag herself back from her guilt to tell him fiercely, 'I was my husband's closest friend. What formalities?'

When he didn't answer her immediately she waited.

'It is a requirement of the law that persons dying in such circumstances need to be formally identified.'

'Identified? Why? What? I can identify them. I want to see them,' she told him when his face grew shuttered. 'I have to see them. You must let me. I insist.'

'Very well, Your Grace.' His voice was wooden now. 'If I may use your telephone I'll arrange for a car and a driver, but I would urge you to nominate someone else.'

'It is my duty and my responsibility. My husband would expect it of me,' Amber answered him, and knew as she spoke that it was true. 'I have been forgetting my manners, Inspector,' she added, going to the open door. 'Please let me offer you a drink and perhaps something to eat.'

'It's very kind of you, Your Grace, but I'm on duty. Is there anyone you'd like to accompany you? A female friend, perhaps?'

Amber shook her head, as she summoned the butler.

'The inspector needs to make a telephone call,' she told him. 'When you have shown him where the telephone is I should be grateful if you would gather up the staff

591

and bring them here to His . . . to the library, please, Chivers.'

What she had to say to them would only be a formality, Amber guessed, because like all butlers worth their salt, Chivers would by now already know the purpose of the inspector's visit.

Amber knew that she had been right when Cook arrived already crying. Nanny, who had obviously removed her teeth preparatory to going to bed, looked very old, whilst Robert's valet looked stricken.

'I have just been informed that there has been an accident, in which . . .' Amber could feel her voice threatening to break. She wasn't just Robert's wife, she was his representative, she reminded herself, and she must behave accordingly. 'In which tragically His Grace and Lord Audley –' how strange it felt to speak of Luc, her baby, so formally – 'were both killed.'

Cook burst into fresh tears, whilst Nanny's smothered sound of anguish reminded Amber that Luc had been her baby too.

As though someone else was directing her thoughts and her actions, Amber went over to her, taking her cold hands in her own, feeling the rigors trembling through the older woman's thin frame.

'I know how you feel, Nanny,' she told her, 'but we must be brave and do as His Grace would want us to do. I have to go with the inspector to . . .' Amber couldn't say the words. 'I shall be depending on you to look after Emerald whilst I am gone. You know how highly His Grace thought of you, Nanny.'

Nanny nodded. 'You can rely on me, Your Grace.'

Amber was beginning to feel as though somehow she wasn't actually part of her own body at all but rather was watching it function on its own without her, from a distance.

Nothing felt quite real. It was as though she was simply acting out a part in a play.

The inspector had returned to the hall.

'The car will be here in ten minutes, Your Grace. It's been loaned by Scotland Yard and the driver will bring you back when you are ready, although, if I might make a suggestion, you may wish to pack an overnight bag.'

'I've already taken the liberty of doing that for you, Your Grace, and I'd like to come with you if you'll permit me to.'

Amber looked towards the stairs where Hulme, Robert's valet, was standing, a valise either side of him.

'I have also packed some of His Grace's things and some for young Lord Audley. Very particular about his appearance, His Grace always was. Looked after him all his grown-up life, I have, and it wouldn't be right nor fitting not to see that things are just as he'd want them to be now.'

The valet's face was tear-stained but resolute.

'Yes, of course, you must come,' Amber told him, ignoring the grim look she could see in the inspector's eyes.

She looked past Hulme towards the stairs, torn between going up to the nursery and her concern that if she did she might wake Emerald, who might then insist that she wanted her father.

Dawn and the promise of another fine day was lightening the eastern skyline when the car finally drew up in front of a small cottage hospital.

The matron herself was waiting in the foyer to greet Amber, accompanied by Luc's headmaster, Dr Philpott, their expressions grave and compassionate.

'I had hoped to have spared you this ordeal, Your Grace,' Dr Philpott told her, 'but unfortunately the police were not able to accept my offer to identify Luc and His Grace.'

'It was kind of you to offer, Dr Philpott,' Amber replied, 'but I should have wanted to see them both anyway.'

Out of the corner of her eye she saw the look the inspector and the matron exchanged, and the tiny shake of the matron's head.

The morgue was separated from the main hospital by a long corridor that began by smelling of carbolic and starch but ended just before the double doors that led into the morgue itself by smelling of cold air that had something added to it that made Amber's senses flinch without being able to identify it.

Matron had accompanied them and as she nodded to the waiting porter to open the doors she reached for Amber's hand, holding it firmly in her own.

They had done their best to turn what was in effect a storage space for bodies awaiting final disposal into something easier for the human heart to bear, Amber recognised. Two hospital beds had been pushed together, the outline of two bodies plain to be seen beneath the fiercely hospital-cornered sheets, one adult and one not, two dark heads on their separate pillows.

The beds and their occupants shimmered and danced as Amber's eyes filled with tears. She wanted to run to them and hold them, and yet she also wanted to run away.

Their faces were turned towards one another and she realised now that Robert's arm rested around Luc.

'Can you identify this, Your Grace?' the inspector asked, reaching for a small box and showing Amber its contents.

'Yes, it's my . . . it's the duke's signet ring,' she answered.

She wanted desperately to hold Luc, her need a physical pain inside her. Disengaging her hand from the matron's, she went round the side of the bed to look down at her son. His eyes were closed and she had an urge to open them so that she could look at them. He had had such beautiful

594

honest eyes. There was a dark bruise on his forehead but there were no other marks on his face. He could quite easily have been merely sleeping.

She turned to look at the matron and, as though she guessed what she wanted to know, the matron told Amber gently, 'The impact broke his neck. He would have died instantly and not known anything.'

Amber nodded and looked back at Luc. She leaned over him, kissing his cold unmoving flesh. It was hard to believe that this was really Luc, her son. Her baby. Her baby. Amber reached out, wanting to gather him in her arms, wanting to hold him and go on holding him, wanting to take him from this place where no child belonged, and back to the world of the living.

'You've been very brave, my dear. Be brave a little longer and say your goodbye to him.' Matron's voice was kind but firm, just like her hand on Amber's arm, reinforcing what was reality, and what was not.

On the other side of the bed Robert lay just like Luc, with his eyes also closed.

How handsome he was, his hair still thick and only lightly tinged with grey. It fell forward untidily over his forehead, almost into his eyes. He would hate that. Amber reached out automatically to push his hair back.

The inspector and matron were moving towards her quickly and single-mindedly, their movements sharp with purpose, and drawing Amber's attention. She looked up at them, then frowned as she felt Robert's flesh move beneath her fingertips and looked quickly back at her husband.

'Your Grace—'

'*No!*' Horror, thick and raw, clogged her throat and her mind.

'It's all right, Your Grace. It's all right. Nurse, bring a chair quickly . . .'

'No . . . I'm all right . . . really.'

The words had no meaning, they were simply a remembered format. How could she be all right when she had just seen that Robert had no head? Not properly. She could see the line now where the flesh had been severed, and which had been hidden by the 'untidiness' of his hair. And underneath that hair where the back of his head should have been there was nothing.

She must not show her horror or her nausea. To do that would be to insult Robert and she must never do that. He deserved better of her. She had, after all, retreated from him once already, sickened by what she had seen. She must show her love and respect for him; she must honour him for all that he had been; she must not think about that dreadful nothingness beneath that scalp of dark hair.

'Thank you for putting my husband and my son side by side like that, Matron. It is what my husband would have wanted. He loved his son very much.'

'That's the spirit,' Matron told her approvingly.

She couldn't grieve. How was it possible to grieve when she couldn't accept that they were gone? Yes, she had gone through the motions of speaking with the hospital staff and thanking them for their care of the bodies of her husband and her son. Yes, she had spoken with the undertakers, and informed them that Robert's valet would dress both Robert and Luc. Yes, she had thanked the local vicar and said that Robert and Luc would be buried together in the family crypt at Osterby, but none of those things meant anything because none of them had been real. How could they be? How could Robert and Luc be dead? It just wasn't possible.

When she got back to Eaton Square, she found Jay there waiting for her.

The butler had telephoned with the news, he told her, and so he had come straight down to London with her grandmother's blessing to do whatever he could to help her.

'Not that I would have obeyed her had Blanche forbidden me to come,' Jay added gently. 'Nothing would have prevented me from being here.'

Amber looked at him and told him sharply, 'You should not have come. I don't want you here, Jay. I want you to leave. Now. You have no place here.'

'Amber . . .' he protested

'I mean it. I do not want you here. I don't want to be anywhere near you or to have you anywhere near me. I hate the thought of it.'

'I know how distressed you must be, but I don't understand why you are talking like this.'

'No? Then I'll tell you why, shall I? Do you know what I was doing whilst Robert and Luc were dying? I was thinking about you; thinking about seeing you, and wanting you, and remembering how you looked at me when Lydia attacked me, and how you have looked at me since. How I have looked back at you.'

'I do love you, it is true,' Jay told her openly and immediately, 'but I would never allow my love for you to harm you or those whom you love, Amber. Surely you know that?'

'It is easy for you to say that, but I shall never forgive myself for what I have done. I gave my thoughts to you when they should have been with them. I left them unprotected and unvalued, and so they have been taken from me to punish me.'

'Amber, this is nonsense.'

'No it isn't. I should have been thinking about them, and not myself, and not you, and if I had been—'

'You're blaming yourself unnecessarily.'

'No, I am acknowledging my guilt.'

'You have done nothing wrong. Their deaths were a tragic accident.'

Amber shook her head. 'When my love should have been protecting them I was saving it for you. If I had been thinking about my husband and my son and not thinking about you, then they might still be alive. I cannot bear you to be here, Jay.'

She rang for Chivers, telling him when he arrived, 'Mr Fulshawe is leaving, Chivers,' giving Jay no option but to go.

Ten days after their deaths, Robert and Luc were interred together in the family crypt after a funeral service held at the small village church close to the Osterby estate.

The church was so full that some mourners had to remain outside. All Robert's friends from London society had travelled up to say their farewells and everyone remarked admiringly on the way Amber managed to mask her grief with dignity.

'You will come back to Macclesfield now, of course,' Blanche said to Amber.

'Yes.' She had to go back. It was what Robert had wanted her to do, after all. There were still some matters she had to attend to, though, before she could leave London, the chief amongst them being a meeting with Robert's solicitor to discuss the contents of his will.

Mr Melrose arrived at Eaton Square at two o'clock on the dot, the day after Amber had returned from Osterby.

Tall, thin and slightly stooped, he had been Robert's solicitor for as long as Amber had known her husband.

'There are two matters I need to discuss with you with regard to your late husband, Your Grace,' he informed Amber, once they were sitting down in the library. 'The first is with regard to the dukedom. You will, I am sure, realise that all those assets that are attached to the dukedom are naturally entailed to the heir. That is to say, they pass directly from one duke to the next. In the normal course of events that would have meant that your son would have succeeded his father. However, tragically that is not possible. This, I am afraid, raises some financial problems in the form of death duties. It will take me some time to assess the exact situation and what will be due in death duties. As I remember it, your late husband was his grandfather's sole male heir. There were no others. However, this again is a matter that needs to be looked into.

'Now, so far as the late duke's private fortune from his maternal grandparents is concerned, he was of course free to pass this down as he wished since it was not part of the dukedom. However here again the matter is complicated. Your late husband quite naturally assumed that your children would outlive you both and that his son would inherit the dukedom from him. Because of that his will directs that the bulk of his private fortune is left in Trust to your daughter with you named as one of her trustees.

'There is also a separate but smaller trust for Luc, which in the event of his death passes direct to his heirs or, failing that, his sister. There is in addition a sum of money left to you but I have to warn you that it is not a large amount, a jointure really, no more than that, and the requirement that your son provides a suitable house for you for so long as you may wish it. I hasten to assure you that this is perfectly normal in circumstances such as your late husband's and does not reflect in any way upon his devotion to you.'

Amber forced a small thread of a smile for the solicitor's benefit.

'It is all right, Mr Melrose,' she told him calmly. 'Robert

599

discussed the terms of his will with me when he remade it after Emerald was born. My only concern was that leaving Emerald such a large trust fund might attract fortune-seekers.'

'Yes, indeed, a very sensible concern too, if I may say so, Your Grace. However, one must acknowledge that in the present circumstances it is perhaps unfortunate that the late duke did not leave you more. One could not call it a pittance, but—'

'No, indeed,' Amber agreed firmly.

'—but neither is it a large sum of money, especially not—'

'Mr Melrose, I assure you that I am not in the least concerned about the money. I shall be returning to Macclesfield with Emerald to live with my grandmother. It was my late husband's wish that we left London for somewhere safer.'

'Yes, a wise decision.'

'When it comes to the death duties, though . . .'

'As I have said, I have work to do on the figures before I can set them down properly. Everything will have to be valued, of course, and that will take time. Ultimately I suspect that it may be necessary to dispose of some of the dukedom's assets in order to meet the death duties, but this is something we shall have to discuss at a later date.'

Amber inclined her head in silent assent. She'd give all the money in the world a thousand times over to have her husband and son alive and well.

Chapter Forty-Nine

December 1939

'Ingenious,' Maurice told Amber admiringly as they both studied the piece of silk Amber had placed on the desk between them.

'Well, the credit isn't really mine,' Amber pointed out. 'All I've done is refine Clayton Hutton's original idea. When you told me that Walter Ellison at Brocklehurst Whiston was working with Clayton to print escape maps on silk to be added to the kit that airmen carry, it seemed to me to make sense to include some useful sentences, in the appropriate languages. As you can see, I've split the phrases into various languages – German, French and Dutch for the European maps.'

It had been her grandmother's idea that Amber should take on a greater role at the mill. Too immersed in her own grief and guilt at first to want to do anything other than cling to them, Amber had rejected her suggestion, but her grandmother had been persistent, pointing out sharply to Amber, 'You are neither the first nor the only woman to lose a husband and a son, Amber, by any means. I lost both my . . . I lost your grandfather and my son. By all means mourn them but remember that you also have a duty to the living.'

Her grandmother had risen to the challenge the government had set the women of Great Britain with predictable determination and energy. She was a leading light in the local WVS. Between them, she and Jay had drawn up plans to increase the food production from Denham's acres, and twelve land girls were already billeted in the hastily converted stable block at Home Farm. All those members of the household staff young enough to help with the war effort had been encouraged to do so, leaving only her grandmother's chauffeur, the butler, and cook and Emerald's nanny, all of whom were too old to do proper war work. A couple of young mothers from the town came out to do a few hours' cleaning, and what rooms were not needed to be used had been closed off, their furniture put in holland covers.

Meals were now eaten in the kitchen instead of the dining room, and although Nanny had been rather difficult at first about the fact that she had to come down to the kitchen instead of having food taken up to the nursery by a servant, Amber acknowledged that she rather liked the informality and the cosy warmth of the kitchen. It reminded her in many ways of living with her parents.

Nothing could or would ever wipe out the guilt she felt over Robert and Luc's deaths, nor did she want it to, but her grandmother was correct in saying to her that Robert would have wanted her to play her part in the war effort. Working at the mill had kept her mind busy.

The Ministry of Supply Silk and Rayon Control Board now had its headquarters in Macclesfield. Silk was now requisitioned for the making of parachutes, and it had been a natural development from this for maps printed on pieces of silk, which could be packed down almost to nothing to fit into airmen's escape kits.

The Control Board had put her suggestion, of adding

simple phrases, to the War Ministry and she had been given the go-ahead initially for the mill to proceed with the printing of prototypes for such maps.

It was one of these prototypes that she and Maurice were studying now. Amber had used Robert's friends and contacts at the Foreign Office to get the phrases translated into the best form of the required foreign language, and in addition to them being printed in that language, they were also spelled out phonetically.

Amber had made Maurice, who spoke only English, read them out to James Lees-Milne, who had called at Denham when he had been in the area visiting Arley Hall.

'I'll get these sent up to the Ministry,' Maurice told her, adding almost too casually, 'You'll have heard that Jay's enlisted, I dare say?'

Amber stiffened, as she did whenever anyone mentioned Jay's name. She couldn't help it. Jay and her own guilt were knitted together in her thoughts indivisibly, and indefensibly.

'My grandmother has mentioned it,' she agreed.

'Aye, she won't be happy to lose him, I'll be bound.'

She wasn't, and had said so in very strong terms. Jay's work was classed as a reserved occupation, which had prevented him from having to join up, and her grandmother was not pleased that he had chosen to override that embargo by finding her a replacement for himself, thus freeing himself to fight. The man he had found to replace him was a retired estate manager in his early sixties. Amber had met him and liked him but as she was ready to admit, she was prepared to like anyone who made it possible for her not to have to see Jay.

'I don't know what he's going to do about them girls of his, with him not having a wife,' Maurice commented.

'Since they are already living at Denham, it makes sense for them to go on doing so,' Amber told him.

She hadn't liked it at all when her grandmother had announced that Jay was moving from the Dower House to Denham, but the choice wasn't hers to make and as Blanche had pointed out, from a practical point of view because of the war it was sensible to close down the Dower House.

'Aye, it does,' Maurice agreed, 'especially seein' as you've already got Greg's girl there and your own little 'un.'

Amber was confused by her own ambivalent feelings about the situation. She liked Jay's daughters and felt very sorry for them, knowing what they had already been through. They and Rose had virtually grown up together, and having three older girls around was very good for Emerald who was showing signs of becoming very spoiled and wilful now that she had Blanche to encourage her to believe that she was a very important little person.

On the other hand, having them at Denham would mean that she was constantly reminded of Jay and that was something she did not want.

The temperature had been dropping steadily all week. The sky over the hills was heavy and still with the threat of snow. As she drove home through the town Amber saw at the railway station a large number of young men in uniform, obviously home on leave for Christmas, many accompanied by their sweethearts or their families. The pain that was never far away tightened round her own heart, both for her own loss and for the losses that were to come for so many other women.

Amber parked her small Austin in the yard next to the kitchen door. Hardly anyone used the front door any more, not even her grandmother.

Greg had jeered at her purchase of the Austin, after she had learned to drive in just a few weeks, saying truculently that he didn't know why she had bought herself such a poor shabby thing when she could have afforded something much better, telling her bitterly, 'After all, Robert must have left you comfortably provided for, and then you're going to inherit everything from Grandmother.'

Greg would never forgive her for the fact that their grandmother had changed her will, Amber realised, even though she had asked her not to do so. Evidently, since he could not and would not accept that it was his own behaviour that had led to him being disinherited, he had left himself with no alternative but to blame her. She had in effect become his whipping boy for his disinheritance.

The water in the old stone drinking trough in the middle of the yard had iced over, and the cold caught at Amber's throat as she hurried to the back door.

A passageway, its walls hung with coat pegs, off which were two large larders, separated the kitchen from the back door. Amber hung up her outdoor coat up beside the others, and went into the kitchen, where Bruno, Luc's dog, came rushing to greet her. The Labrador only left her side when it had to, and the truth was that Amber didn't feel inclined to discourage its devotion to her, because of its connection with Luc.

The warmth from the Aga met her as soon as she opened the door. Her grandmother had had the old range replaced with a much larger Aga during 1938 and was fond of pointing out to people now the wisdom of that decision.

The children were seated round the kitchen table eating crumpets, and Bruno, now that he had assured himself that she was home and safe, went to his basket and lay down in it.

'Mummy,' Emerald called out.

'Hello, darling. Hello, everyone,' Amber responded going over to give Emerald a kiss, and trying not to show her feelings when Emerald turned her head away.

Her daughter was very good at demanding attention when she wanted it, Amber knew, but very determined not to return it unless it suited her to do so. She certainly did not have Rose's sweet loving temperament.

'Father Christmas will come soon,' Rose said.

Emerald turned her jam-smeared face and assessing gaze on Amber. Emerald might be far too young to understand what Father Christmas meant but she was quick enough to realise that it was something she ought to be capitalising on, Amber thought ruefully. She seemed to have accepted the fact that her father and her brother were no longer there; she was too young to understand what had actually happened, after all, even if she had screamed in temper in the early months after their deaths, insisting that she wanted her daddy to read her a bedtime story, and rejecting every attempt Amber made to hold her and comfort her.

'Me and Jane are going to write our letters to Father Christmas tonight to tell him what we'd like,' Ella told Amber, and then asked in a troubled voice, 'Do you think it's wrong to ask for presents when we're at war, Auntie Amber?'

Ella was such a serious, worried child at times, her little frown suggesting she had the weight of the world on her shoulders. No one ever spoke of the events surrounding Lydia's death – it had been judged best not to do so – and the girls never mentioned her, simply seeming to have accepted her death.

'No, I don't think it's wrong at all, just so long as you remember to say your prayers for all those who need them.'

'Do you know what I'm going to ask Father Christmas for?' Jane demanded eagerly.

'You aren't supposed to tell anyone,' Ella began, but Jane ignored her.

'I'm going to ask him for a new mummy.'

606

A small silence filled the room. Amber couldn't speak. Her throat had closed up on a hard lump of pain and sadness.

'Goodness me, Lady Emerald, just look at your face.' Nanny's tutting as she fussed over Emerald broke the silence, making Amber frown. She had told Nanny that she did not wish Emerald to be addressed by her title. It was plain that her daughter already considered herself to be special and Amber did not want to see that opinion encouraged.

'What about you, Rose?' she asked her niece. 'What would you like Father Christmas to bring you?'

'A dolly,' Rose told her

Amber smiled. She had already telephoned Harrods and ordered the children's Christmas presents. Everyone was saying that one should make the most of this Christmas because who knew what would have happened by next Christmas. Food rationing was going to be coming in, and everyone knew that it was the country's brave Merchant and Royal Navy sailors who put their lives at risk to bring much-needed supplies into the country.

It was later that evening, when the children were all in bed and her grandmother was out at a committee meeting that Amber heard the front doorbell ring. She had been sitting in the kitchen darning and the sound made her frown. No one used the front door any more.

The minute she stepped into the main hallway its icy cold made Amber shiver.

When she opened the door she found a very pretty young woman wearing a land army uniform, standing on the doorstep. Dark curls framed her heart-shaped face, her blue-eyed gaze guileless and smiling.

'Oh, gosh, I do so hope I haven't done the wrong thing,'

she began. 'I was told to take the first turning into the lane but it's so dark I think I might have got a bit muddled up.'

'Please come in,' Amber invited her, then closed the front door against the freezing air. 'Who are you looking for? Even if this isn't the right house I am sure I shall be able to help.'

'Oh, I say, how jolly kind of you. I'm looking for Jay Fulshawe. I don't know if you know him? I'm one of the land girls assigned to the Home Farm and he said if I had any problems just to get in touch with him.'

'Yes, I see,' Amber answered her, and of course she did. Of course she did. This pretty girl might look and sound guileless but she had obviously taken a shine to Jay.

And had Jay taken a shine to her? He had obviously given her good reason to feel she could seek him out.

'Jay isn't here at the moment, I'm afraid. He may be at the Home Farm, Miss . . . ?'

'Belinda, Belinda Withington,' the other girl introduced herself, with an eager smile. 'Only everyone calls me Bunty.'

'Well, Bunty, I'll make sure that Jay knows you want to get in touch with him but I can't promise when he'll be back.' Amber suspected that the reason Jay found so many things to do in the evening that kept him away from Denham was because of her and the coldness that now existed between them.

'That's ever so kind of you. I was awfully worried about what this land girl lark was really going to be like,' she confided to Amber. 'I mean, one wants to do one's bit, of course, but I hadn't really thought about becoming a land girl until my aunt suggested it. But Mr Fulshawe is just wonderful to work for.'

Bunty obviously had a huge crush on Jay, Amber acknowledged after she had said goodbye to her unexpected visitor.

Once she was back in the kitchen, Amber wrote a note for Jay and put it near to the kettle where he would be bound to see it when he did come in.

Did Jay know that Jane wanted a new mummy? Was he already thinking about providing his daughters with a loving stepmother and himself with a new wife? The sensation that jarred through her wasn't really pain. Why should it be? Jay meant nothing to her now.

She went over to the Aga to heat some milk for a cup of cocoa. She may as well have an early night. Cook was having a night off, the children were in bed, her grandmother was out and Greg was making one of his increasingly frequent visits to Manchester. He claimed to have friends in the city, which was home to a small Chinese community, but Amber's suspicion was that he went there to obtain the drug on which he was now so dependent.

She had discussed the situation and her fears for her cousin's health with Dr Brookes, who had not been able to offer her any comfort.

'I suspect his addiction is such that it would not be possible for him to cease using the drug without a huge effort, and I'm afraid to say that I cannot see him making that effort,' the doctor had told Amber, adding quietly, 'Of course, given the fact that the syphilis he contracted in Hong Kong is now manifesting itself, I have to say that the opium will at least provide him with some relief from its symptoms.'

'Syphilis? Greg has syphilis?'

Dr Brookes had been aghast to realise that she had not known and that Blanche had kept the information from her, exclaiming guiltily that he would not have said anything if he'd realised.

Amber had assured him that he must not blame himself. In many ways it helped her to understand and feel more compassionate towards Greg.

Needless to say when she had taxed her grandmother with the fact that she had not told her, Blanche was unrepentant, adding to Amber's anger when she informed her that she had told Jay.

However, whilst she sympathised with Greg, there were some things that Amber could not condone. Amber had found that money had gone missing from her purse, and she suspected that it was Greg who had taken it. He had been furious with her earlier in the week when she had refused to 'lend' him fifty pounds.

As she went to let Bruno out for his final evening sniff around the yard, Amber saw that it had started to snow. Luc had loved the snow and had been plaguing Robert to take him to the Alps so that he could learn to ski.

Luc. Some days she could hear his voice so clearly that she could almost believe that if she were to turn round he would be there. Not physically in the flesh, but spiritually, in her heart and in her thoughts, he was always there, so much so that she would get carried away with her own mental conversations with him. She talked with him all the time, telling him all the things she thought he would like to know – turning to look down at him, only to realise too late that he wasn't there. Hardest of all, perhaps, were those times when she inadvertently spoke Luc's name only to see Bruno prick up his ears and look towards the door. All she could do was tell herself that Luc would be with her for as long as she kept him in her heart, and that would be for ever, and try to find comfort from that.

It was Christmas morning, the presents were all unwrapped, and the Denham Place residents all went to church, stamping their way through the snow to sing the familiar carols and exchange seasonal good wishes with their neighbours. The church was full, armed services uniforms very much in evidence.

Those men, home on leave, who had gone out with the BEF in September to France, reported that it was every bit as cold there as it was in England. They were cheerful about the outcome of the war, joking with one another, their camaraderie and laughter adding an extra glow to the mood of the day.

Amber had done her best to join in, and not bring her own grief to shadow other families' happiness at having their loved ones home on leave.

Those young men newly in uniform and still in training were naturally eager to speak with the men back home on leave. Jay was very much a part of those proceedings, even though he was not as yet in uniform.

The de Vries family had a long tradition of military service with The Cheshires, and of course Barrant de Vries' son and heir had fought with them in the Great War.

Soon they would be saying goodbye to their neighbours and making their way back to Denham, whilst Jay and his daughters left with the Fitton Leghs and Jay's grandfather, who was now living with his granddaughter Cassandra, because his estate had been requisitioned Those land girls who had been given leave had attended the morning service, and Amber wasn't surprised to see Bunty detaching herself from her friends and going over to talk with Jay. She was obviously getting on well with both Jay and the girls, to judge by the unaffected sound of their laughter, Amber decided, picking up Emerald.

Her daughter was very much the centre of attention when they all came out of church, and Emerald played up to all the fuss with dimples and smiles. Poor Rose scarcely received any acknowledgement at all. Amber's heart ached for her niece, who was such a dear, sweet, loving girl. Her poker-straight hair and oriental looks marked her out as being different, and regrettably Nanny, elderly now and biased towards Emerald, did not treat Rose as well as she might have done.

'Emerald, stand still, please,' Amber told her daughter, putting her back down on the snow-covered ground, and then holding out her hand to Rose, who was standing on her own, looking awkward and uncomfortable.

'Rose, darling, come over here and hold my hand,' Amber encouraged her.

Immediately Rose's skin flushed a happy pink, her eyes sparkling as she hurried to Amber's side.

'Did you like the dolly that Father Christmas brought you?' Amber asked her.

'Yes. And I liked her clothes as well. She looks really pretty.'

Amber hid a small smile, She had sat up three nights in a row stitching the jewel-coloured silk dresses she had made for the doll she had bought for Rose into styles copied from some of the photographs Greg had taken when he had first gone to Hong Kong. Nanny had been outraged, insisting that the dresses were heathenish 'just like the child's mother'.

'I liked my books as well, and the puzzles, and my water paints, and my slippers.'

Amber smoothed her hair with a loving hand. She felt such a special bond with this child, motherless as she herself had been, and also like her, not the favoured child of the household.

Chapter Fifty

Finally it was over, what was left of the turkey stored in the larder, and the washing-up done. Her grandmother had gone to her room to rest, Nanny had taken Rose and Emerald up to the nursery to put them to bed, and now at last Amber could stop pretending that the day had been anything other than the most dreadful ordeal, and that she had not at every stage of it been contrasting it with other and happier Christmases.

No doubt at Fitton Hall the festivities would still be continuing. The Fitton Leghs were entertaining several house guests and members of the Fitton Legh extended family. There would be charades and other games. There would be laughter and fun – the kind of Christmases Amber had once had and had expected to go on having for ever. The carpets would have been rolled back in one of the rooms and the gramophone set up so that those who wished to do so could dance. She had never danced with Jay.

Amber swung round awkwardly, colliding with one of the kitchen chairs, blinded by the tears she knew she had no right to shed. If she must cry then let her cry for her dead husband and son, and not the fact that she had never danced with someone she had no right to want to have danced with.

*   *   *

'So you are not coming to the station with us to see Jay off and wish him all the best?'

'No, Grandmother, I am not.'

'Well, people will think it very odd of you.'

'I am sure they will do no such thing. They won't even notice that I'm not there. I must go; I have some letters to write.'

'Amber, there's something I want to ask you before I leave.'

Jay! She'd said goodbye to him earlier in public; there was no need for him to seek her out now. She could feel the tips of her ears burning as she turned round to face him.

He was wearing his uniform, of course. Captain Jay Fulshawe. He'd been given his captaincy when he had completed his training.

'If anything should happen to me I would like you to be the girls' official guardian,' he told her without preamble. 'They know you and love you.'

What about Bunty – why don't you ask her? The words were on the tip of her tongue but fortunately she managed not to let them escape.

'I . . .'

'Here are the papers. I've signed them and had my signature witnessed. I'm not asking for my own sake but for the girls'. You more than anyone else knows what it means to be orphaned. You are the only person I trust to understand them and help them. To give them love.'

She wanted to refuse but how could she? It would be spiteful and petty. What lay between her and Jay was not the girls' fault.

'You aren't leaving me with much choice,' she told him. 'It would have been fairer if you had asked me before.'

'I should have done, yes, but there hasn't been much

614

time. We're being sent to . . . we're leaving sooner than I had originally expected.'

They were being sent to the front – that was what he wasn't saying, she knew. She felt icy cold and yet burning hot.

'I expect I must sign as well, must I?'

'Yes, here,' he told her, placing the document on her desk and leaning over it to show her where she must sign.

He smelled different, not like himself as she knew him, but a different Jay. This Jay smelled of khaki and leather, of military discipline and war.

Amber could feel herself trembling. Because he was standing so close to her? No, because she was betraying Robert and Luc merely by being alone with him.

'Someone will have to witness me signing,' she told him.

'I'll go and find your grandmother.'

'Jay, wait a minute, please.' She could see from his face that he was expecting her to change her mind. A feeling of terrible sadness gripped. Her hand was shaking slightly as she pulled open the small drawer in the desk.

'This is for you,' she told him, extracting the small square she had put there weeks ago when she had first known he was going to war.

She watched as he unfolded it.

'It's one of our escape maps,' she told him unnecessarily. 'But of course if you've already got one . . .'

'No, I haven't, Amber . . .'

'We'd better get this document witnessed, hadn't we?'

'Yes,' he agreed quietly. 'I'll go and find your grandmother.'

By the time Jay returned with her grandmother, Amber had herself more under control.

Her hand shook as she signed her name, but it was done. She was now Jay's daughters' legal guardian in the event of his death.

Amber knew from the way her grandmother was looking at her that she now expected her to change her mind and go to the station with everyone else to see Jay off, but she couldn't.

'I'll see that Mr Mackenzie gets this,' she told Jay, referring to her grandmother's solicitor's clerk.

Her grandmother had gone into the hall to join the others and they were alone together.

'Thank you.'

He was looking at her, Amber knew, but she refused to look back at him.

The silence of the room felt heavy with tension. She could feel Jay hesitating, waiting, willing her to turn and look at him but still she did not. She heard him exhale slowly as though it hurt him to do so, and then he was walking towards the door, opening it and then closing it quietly behind him.

She could see from the library the cars leaving for the station. His grandfather would not be there. He had caught a chill and, of course, it was difficult for him to get about, but perhaps Cassandra would go to the station, and of course Bunty, with her disingenuous smile and her obvious adoration.

Inside her head Amber suddenly had a mental image of Robert looking at her rather sadly.

'It's for your sake and Luc's that I'm not going,' she told him fiercely. 'You know that.'

Bruno had padded in from the kitchen to sit at her side, leaning into her as though he sensed her distress and her need for comfort.

Chapter Fifty-One

'Meat rationing – whatever next?' Cook sniffed disapprovingly, her hands on her hips as she aired her feelings about the latest of the government's moves to ensure that food was shared out fairly amongst everyone.

'At least poultry isn't being rationed,' Amber pointed out, but Cook obviously wasn't willing to be placated.

'That's all very well,' she told Amber, 'but give me a nice bit of beef or some Welsh spring lamb any day over a chicken.'

'I'm going to cycle into Macclesfield later on to go to the bank, and the post office. I'll call at the mill as well, so don't worry about any lunch for me today, Cook.'

Amber had received a letter from Robert's solicitor informing her that he had some important papers he needed her to sign, and asking if she was able to come down to London the Thursday before Good Friday so that they could be dealt with. She had telephoned him to confirm the appointment and ask if it could be as late in the day as possible to allow time for her to travel down. She would, she had decided, stay overnight on the Thursday at the Ritz and travel back on Easter Saturday, when she hoped that the railway might be quieter. She needed to go to the bank to draw out some money to cover her expenses whilst she was away.

'I don't know what the world's coming to when a lady has to cycle everywhere instead of being chauffeured. It ain't proper.'

Amber laughed. 'I enjoy it,' she told the cook truthfully, reminding her, 'Everything that comes into the country has to be brought in by our brave seaman, and it's up to all of us to make sure they don't have to do that any more than is necessary.'

Everyone knew the heavy toll that the German Navy was taking on British shipping, with the resultant loss of life.

'I'll just go up and tell Greg that I'm going out in case he wants anything.'

Amber was very worried about her cousin. His behaviour had become increasingly erratic, alternating between terrible outbursts of anger, euphoria, and periods of dull apathy during which he refused to leave his room.

Dr Brookes had explained to her that these mood swings were caused by drugs and drink.

'Surely there must get something we can do?' she had asked him.

'I'm afraid not,' he had told her. 'Not unless Greg himself wishes to change.'

Greg's bedroom door was already open, and Greg himself was lying unshaven and fully dressed on his bed, an empty gin bottle on the bed beside him. The air in the room smelled sour and stale. The handsome young man that Greg had once been was gone. The features of the man lying on the bed were bloated and coarse, his skin reddened and his hair thin.

Amber felt a wave of helpless pity for her cousin.

He ignored her when she called his name, giving her no alternative but to leave without conversing with him.

The town had been busy gearing up for the Easter weekend, and then Maurice had kept Amber far longer at the mill than she had expected, so that it was very late in the after-noon before she finally arrived back at Denham.

The children, pinafores over their dresses, were already having their tea, boiled eggs with soldiers, over which Emerald was pulling a face, claiming that she 'no like eggies'.

'Of course you do,' Amber told her cheerfully, 'and Phoebe laid that egg especially for you.'

The children all had their own pet hens kept in a small run in the garden, which they fed every morning. Amber believed it was good for them to take on their own little responsibilities, although she was the one who went out every evening to ensure that the hens were shut away safely.

'I'll put the kettle on now that you're back, shall I?' Cook asked.

'Oh, please. I'm dying for a cup of tea.' Amber thanked her on her way through the kitchen to change out of her outdoor things.

It would seem strange going to London and having to wear 'town' clothes again instead of simpler country clothes, chosen to keep her warm rather than to look pretty.

Upstairs in her bedroom Amber started to get changed into her old twinset and tweed skirt, pausing as she did so to look at the photograph of Robert and Luc on her beside table. It had been taken in the summer, and in it they were both laughing. Amber remembered how impatient Luc had been for her to finish taking the photograph so that he and Robert could go back to their game of cricket. It was the last photograph they had had taken together, and she treas-ured it for the memories it held as much as the happiness shining out of them both.

As soon as the children were in bed, she must pack her case. She would be leaving early in the morning to catch the first train of the day to London. She had arranged with the new estate manager that he would drive her down to the station. He was pleasant and very good at his job, but of course he wasn't Jay.

Jay wrote regularly to both her grandmother and his daughters. And to Bunty? What business was it of hers if he did write to the young land girl, Amber asked herself fiercely. Jay meant nothing to her.

'I wish you weren't going away.'

Amber gave Rose a small hug, promising her, 'It won't be for very long and when I come back we're going to have an Easter egg hunt, and that will be fun.'

Rose nodded but Amber could see that she wasn't totally reassured. Her hair needed cutting, Amber saw. Nanny would cut it as though round an upturned basin in a way that wasn't flattering at all to Rose's delicate features.

'You can come and help me pack my case, if you like,' she offered in an attempt to cheer Rose up.

Immediately the little girl's face lit up, and she tucked her hand into Amber's.

Smiling, she listened to Rose's chatter as they walked along the landing together. Amber opened the door to her bedroom and then came to an abrupt halt.

Greg was standing beside her bed, a look of wild fury on his face. The drawer to her bedside table was open.

The moment she saw her father, Rose pressed closer to Amber's side.

'All right, where is it?' Greg demanded. 'I know you went to the bank this morning. Where's the money, Amber? It must be somewhere.'

Her handbag! She had put it in her wardrobe when she had taken off her outdoor things, more out of habit than for any other reason. She had suspected for some time that Greg was taking money from her purse but this was different. *Greg* was different, she recognised, registering the ugly brutality coarsening his once handsome face.

'Greg, I really think you should go back to your own bedroom,' she told him calmly.

Ignoring her, he insisted angrily, 'I want that money, Amber. I need it.'

A fit of tremors seized his body, convulsing it so violently that Amber thought he might collapse. Instinctively she went towards him, wanting to help him, but to her shock he picked up Robert and Luc's photograph and smashed the frame down onto the bedside table so that the glass shattered. Throwing the frame onto the floor, he picked up a piece of the broken glass, holding it like a knife threateningly towards her, oblivious to the blood streaming from his own fingers.

'Give me that money. Give me it, Amber,' he yelled.

Rose had started to sob with fear and Amber's heart was thumping heavily as images of another time and another knife flashed, dark and bloody through her mind.

Maybe this was her destiny. Maybe she should just step towards him and then she could be with Robert and Luc for ever.

'Give me the money.' Sweat was pouring from Greg's face now.

Rose was crying with fear. Greg swung round and made a grab for her, demanding savagely, 'Shut up, will you! Shut up or else I'll shut you myself for ever.'

His words jerked Amber back to reality She pulled Rose out of his reach, holding her protectively in her arms as she told him, 'It's in the wardrobe in my handbag.'

He dropped the glass and tore at the wardrobe door. Once he had it open he grabbed her handbag, shaking it upside down in his frenzy of impatience until her purse fell out. When he pulled the fifty pounds she'd drawn out of the bank from her purse, the blood from his cut fingers smeared the notes.

621

This was her cousin, Amber reminded herself, not some madman crazed by drugs, but her cousin whom she had loved.

'Greg, please,' she begged him. 'Please don't do this. Please let Dr Brookes help you. I know it won't be easy . . .'

'*Help* me?' he laughed wildly. 'Only one thing can help me now and it's Dr Opium, not Dr ruddy Brookes.'

'Greg, please,' Amber implored him, releasing Rose to go to stand in front of the door.

'Get out of my way.'

'What is going on?'

Their grandmother! As Amber turned round Greg pushed past her so roughly that he knocked her against the door.

'I must stop him,' Amber told Blanche urgently.

'No. Let him go, Amber.'

Amber could hear him lumbering down the stairs. She knew he'd be going to Manchester and the man who supplied him with his drugs. She desperately wanted to run after him and beg him to stay, to plead with him to see reason. The front door opened and then slammed. Tears burned her eyes. She looked down at Rose, who had crept to her side and was now clinging to her shaking from head to foot.

Poor little girl, to have seen her father in such a state and to be in such fear of him.

'I'd better clean up all this broken glass,' Amber told her grandmother. 'But I'll take Rose up to the nursery first.'

Some of the splintered glass was embedded in the carpet; one piece pierced her finger as Amber picked it up. As she sucked on the small wound she picked up the photograph of Robert and Luc, tenderly smoothing it with her free hand. Jay would have known how to calm Greg down if he had been here. A huge sense of loss and despair filled her, followed by sharp self-anger. Why was she so weak? She should not be thinking of Jay now. Had she forgotten already that it had been when she was thinking of him that her husband and her precious precious son had died?

After she had finished clearing away all the broken glass Amber went up to the nursery. All the girls were in bed now and Nanny pursed her lips in disapproval when Amber told her that she was going to check on Rose.

As Amber had known she would be, Rose was still awake. Amber sat down on her bed and reached for her hand.

'I wish you weren't going away,' Rose said.

'It won't be for very long,' Amber assured her, 'and when I come back we're going to have an Easter egg hunt, remember?'

Rose's slanted dark-eyed gaze remained fixed on her.

'What if my daddy comes back and gets angry whilst you're gone?'

Amber's hand tightened on Rose's. This was how a heart broke, not over a man but over the cruelty that one person did to another when they did not love them as they should.

'Great-Grandma will make sure that he doesn't,' Amber told her, hoping that what she was saying was true.

'Why doesn't my daddy love me?'

'I don't know, Rose. I think perhaps it's because he can't love anyone, not even himself,' Amber told her. 'But I love you. I love you very much.'

'And I love you too, and Ella and Jane, and their daddy. I wish that he was my daddy.'

Amber sat with her until Rose's eyes had closed and she had fallen asleep.

There were, after all, worse things in childhood than losing one's parents, and of those things, surely not being loved by one or other of them must be one of the hardest to bear.

Chapter Fifty-Two

'Oh dear, I do hope that we aren't going to be too much delayed getting into Euston.'

Amber smiled politely at the pretty young woman seated opposite her in the first-class carriage.

'I don't think we shall be,' she reassured her.

'I'm meeting my fiancé, you see,' the girl continued, pink-cheeked as she played nervously with her diamond ring. 'In fact, well, the truth is that we shall be getting married by special licence. One never knows, does one? I mean about the future, especially when there's a war, and I would hate to think if anything were to happen and he didn't make it through that we hadn't had all the happiness we could have had together. He's in the navy, you see, on convoy escort duty for the merchant ships coming across the Atlantic.'

Her eyes sheened over with tears. 'The thing is that I was engaged before I met Charlie. We grew up together, me and Frank, and when the war came he said we should get engaged. I wasn't so sure really but I couldn't say "no", not with him going to war, and then he was killed. I know there's plenty think I shouldn't be marrying Charlie so quickly and that it's disrespectful, but Frank would have understood and he'd have wanted me to be happy because that's what loving someone is all about isn't it, wanting them to be happy?'

'Yes, I'm sure it is,' Amber agreed.

The train had started to slow down and the girl looked apprehensively out of the window.

'It's all right,' Amber reassured her. 'We're coming into Euston, that's all.'

Loving someone meant wanting them to be happy. Robert would certainly have agreed with that sentiment, Amber acknowledged as she joined the stream of passengers trudging up to the platform barrier.

She had never seen the station so packed with people – men in uniform, families with children, women like herself, everyone busy and conscious of the war. The minute Amber stepped out of the station she realised that it was going to be virtually impossible for her to get a taxi.

'Never seen it so busy, I haven't,' another traveller grumbled. 'Of course, it will be on account of it being a bank holiday and lots of serving men being given a bit of leave.'

She would have to walk to the solicitor's office, Amber realised.

The streets were nearly as busy as the station had been, and when she finally reached Leicester Square she was astonished to see the length of the queues outside the cinemas. Shaftesbury Avenue was just as bad, with queues outside all the theatres and people milling about on the street; men in uniform queuing, either in groups or as part of a couple, keeping tight hold on their partners.

'I'm sorry I'm late,' she apologised to Mr Melrose when she finally reached his office, having had to dodge both the crowds and the sandbags, which were now turning green and bursting open in places. 'I had to walk from Euston, the city is so busy.'

'Yes, isn't it just? I heard this morning that the government has put on special trains from Blackpool to bring those civil servants, whose ministries have been transferred there, back to the city for the Easter weekend.'

The secretary who had taken Amber's coat on her arrival came in with a tray of tea, and Amber had to wait for her to pour them each a cup and then leave, closing the door behind her, before Mr Melrose discussed the forms he had asked her to come in to sign.

'I'm afraid there's been a new development,' he told her, 'and too late for me to get in touch with you to cancel our appointment.'

'What kind of development?' Amber asked him.

'Naturally, following on from your husband's death, I had set in motion the normal enquiries to ascertain whether or not there might be a legitimate heir to the dukedom.'

'Yes, of course.'

'Until this week it had been assumed that there was not. However, I have now received information stating that your late husband's great-uncle, Drogo, Lord Iverhulme, who was sent off to Australia by his father, may well have a grandson who will, if indeed he exists, naturally be the new duke.'

'I knew that Robert had a great-uncle who was sent to Australia in disgrace, but Robert always said that he died young and had never married.'

'Yes, indeed, which is why this claim needs to be thoroughly investigated. The circumstance of us being at war makes it all the more difficult, of course. However, until the matter is clarified it would not be correct for me to authorise any sale of any items belonging to the dukedom in order to meet death duties. I have advised the Inland Revenue accordingly and they have agreed that we must leave matters as they are until the situation has been investigated thoroughly. The fact that there might be an heir does not, of course, affect either your daughter's trust fund or your own inheritance.'

The solicitor had no doubt meant to reassure her by telling her that Emerald's trust fund would not be affected, Amber knew, but the truth was that she would have much rather her daughter did not come into so large an inheritance . . . It was far too much and could, in Amber's view, bring her all manner of problems.

By the time she finally reached the Ritz Amber was tired, hungry and feeling rather worn down.

It was a shock to see how busy the hotel was, with queues of people waiting at the reception desk, and none of the old familiar staff she knew anywhere to be seen. She felt more as though she had been away from London for a decade instead of a mere handful of months. Had the city always been so busy and noisy, or had she turned into a country mouse?

When she finally got to the front of the queue she had to raise her voice to get the receptionist's attention because of the conversation and laughter coming from a group of uniformed men standing close to the desk. One of them in particular seemed to think very highly of himself, Amber noticed, as he turned do give her a particularly bold look.

Ignoring him, Amber gave the harassed receptionist her name.

'I'm sorry,' the girl told her, having checked the register, 'but we don't have a booking here for you, and anyway, we don't book our rooms to single ladies, not usually, not with us giving priority to them what's in uniform.'

Amber could hear the irritated murmurs from those in the queue behind her. Her face was starting to burn, not so much with embarrassment as with anger.

'I should like to see the manager,' she told the receptionist.

'He's orf sick, and if you want to see the under-manager

'you'll have to wait along with all the others what wants to see him.'

'No room at the inn, sweetheart? Well, never mind, I've got plenty of space in my room, and a lovely big bed. What do you say?'

It was the officer who had looked her over so boldly earlier, leaning closer to her now, and obviously the worse for drink.

'Come on, don't look at me like that. There's only one reason a single woman comes into an hotel pretending that she's booked herself a room, we all know that.'

'Excuse me.' Amber's voice was frigid with disdain and dislike as she was forced to squeeze past him when he made no attempt to move, and instead moved closer to her so that his thigh was pressing against her, his erection blatantly obvious.

Nausea and fury clogged the back of her throat. It was all very well for people to say that fighting men needed to let off steam when they were home on leave, but not to the extent of behaving in the way he was, surely? He wasn't a young man, after all; he was well into his thirties, and an officer.

'Amber, my dear.'

The familiar sound of Emerald Cunard's voice had Amber turning on her heel in relief, to be greeted with an enthusiastic hug from the other woman.

'What a wonderful surprise. How are you?'

'Rather cross and about to go and look for a park bench on which to spend the night,' Amber told her ruefully, explaining about her missing booking.

'You can stay with me. I have a suite and a spare bedroom. Come along, I'll take you up there now.'

Gratefully, Amber followed her unexpected rescuer.

* * *

'. . . and of course everyone has gone and one seldom sees anyone one knows any more. I do so miss my lovely house, Amber. Just as you must miss poor darling Robert.'

They were sitting in the cocktail bar prior to going in for dinner, and Amber had to choke back her reaction to hearing Robert compared to Emerald's Grosvenor Square house. How Robert would have enjoyed that comment. He had always had such a dry sense of humour.

'Margot Oxford is still clinging on at Bedford Square, and of course Loelia Westminster is still here, and dear Chips Channon.'

Whilst Emerald rattled off the names of their acquaintances and friends who had stayed in London and those who had not, Amber decided that she would be glad to get back to Macclesfield. There was a brittleness about society now, a could-not-care-less attitude for others. Could it have been there all along, and she had just not noticed it?

Since her return ticket was not booked until Saturday she would, she knew, be obliged to spend Friday in London, as she nodded her head and listened to Emerald's chatter.

At least the crowds didn't seem to be as bad this morning, Amber comforted herself as she walked towards St Paul's. She wasn't sure what had caused her to walk in this direction, save that it was Good Friday. Emerald had already told her that she would be going to the Easter Sunday service at the Brompton Oratory, London's 'fashionable' church, but of course Amber would be back in Macclesfield by then.

It was too early for those who would be attending the Good Friday service to have arrived at St Paul's as yet, but the doors were open and Amber saw that she wasn't the only person drawn to step inside.

It always struck her as something of a conundrum that such a beautiful worldly building should so effortlessly breathe peace and humility: a contradiction in terms and yet perhaps the true magic of Wren's wonderful building. Whatever his thoughts might have been, his church touched the human soul, Amber acknowledged as she knelt to pray, initially for Robert and Luc, but then without having meant to she discovered that she was praying for Jay as well, and all those men and women who must risk their lives in the fight for freedom.

Chapter Fifty-Three

May 1940

In tense silence Amber and her grandmother listened to the BBC's lunchtime news bulletin on the reports of the German Blitzkrieg on the Low Countries.

'Hitler is overrunning Holland then he will turn his attentions to France,' Blanche told Amber grimly.

'The RAF are bombing Germany and the BEF and our French Allies will surely hold back the Germans. The French have said that they have every confidence in the Maginot line,' Amber reminded her.

They were in the small sitting room as now that they were in May there was no need for the household to huddle round the Aga in the kitchen.

'Greg didn't come home last night,' Amber told her grandmother, changing the subject. 'I checked his room this morning and his bed hasn't been slept in.'

'I don't wish to discuss him, Amber. You know my feelings on the subject of your cousin.'

Amber stifled a small sigh. Their grandmother had turned against Greg completely now. Sometimes the animosity between them made Amber feel as though she was living in a warzone here at home.

'I have a WVS meeting this afternoon, and—'

Blanche broke off as, after a brief knock on the door of the small sitting room, the butler came in, and announced,

'Dr Brookes is here asking to see you, Your Grace.'

What on earth does Dr Brookes want with you, Amber? Bring him in here, Wilson, and then go and tell Cook that we shall need some tea.'

'Dr Brookes.' Amber greeted their doctor with a welcoming smile, which faded when she saw his serious expression.

'I'm afraid that I'm the bearer of bad news.' He addressed both Amber and Blanche.

'Bad news? What kind of bad news?' Blanche demanded sharply.

'It's Gregory.'

Amber could see her grandmother stiffening, her face stony cold as she turned away from the doctor.

'What kind of bad news, Doctor?' Amber asked anxiously.

'He's dead, I'm afraid. Drowned.'

Drowned. Amber put her hand to her throat.

'Lady Fitton Legh called me out early this morning to attend Lord de Vries, and whilst I was there one of the estate workers came to say that they'd found a body in the lake.'

'The lake? But Greg would never go there, not after Caroline—' Amber broke off, realising that her shock was making her indiscreet. It was horrible to think Greg had lost his life in exactly the same fashion as Caroline.

'He'd been drinking in the town last night, apparently. Words were exchanged in the pub he was in and he was asked to leave. I can only think that he must have decided to walk home and got confused.'

'To walk home? But Fitton Hall is in the opposite direction.' Amber shook her head.

'I'm so very sorry,' Dr Brookes was saying. 'I've formally identified him, of course, and informed the police. I would have been here to tell you before now, but Lord de Vries suffered a relapse after his granddaughter had given him the news . . . Mrs Pickford, are you all right?'

Amber turned to look at her grandmother as she heard the anxiety in the doctor's voice. Blanche's face had gone bone white, bleached of all colour. She lifted her hand as though to put it out to ward them both off as they stepped towards her, and then collapsed.

Amber stood in the library looking out on to the drive, not really registering anything other than the fact that she wished desperately that Jay was here.

The shock of hearing about Greg's death had been compounded by the discovery that her grandmother had a weak heart and had kept that fact from her for several years.

'The shock of hearing about Greg's death was just too much for her,' Dr Brookes had told Amber once they had got Blanche into bed and he had sedated her to take the strain off her heart. 'That was why I asked to see you.'

'She insisted on you being brought in to see both of us,' Amber had told him. 'She will recover, won't she?'

It surprised her how much she wanted her grandmother to survive and how much she hated the thought of losing her.

'Yes, I think so. It was only a mild attack, a warning, shall we say, but she must take life more easily. I have told her this before. I told her too that she should tell you about her condition but she refused point-blank.'

'That is my grandmother all over,' Amber had told him.

'You are a very brave young woman,' Dr Brookes had said gently, 'and you have had much to bear, I know.'

'There are many women who will have much to bear before this war is over,' Amber had pointed out sadly.

Jay, Jay. How weak she was to long for him now so that he could shoulder the burdens and duties that were hers and not his.

There was Greg's funeral to be arranged, and her grandmother's health to be watched over; the estate to be run and the mill; and above and beyond that the constant worry of the war stretching over them all like dark shadow.

Poor, poor Greg. Was he at peace now? Had he known? Gone deliberately? Had he . . . ? But no, she must not think of that or the fact that in his aloneness he had chosen to end his own life where Caroline had ended hers. Better to think that it had been an accident, that he had, as Dr Brookes had suggested, taken the wrong road home, his mind befuddled by drink and drugs. The wrong road home. How poignantly those words echoed in her heart. Greg's adult life had in many ways been a journey down 'the wrong road'.

Tears filled her eyes and spilled down her cheeks. It was not the man her cousin had become she was crying for, but the man he could have been, the cousin who had been her friend.

Chapter Fifty-Four

27 May 1940

It was nearly a month since Greg's drowned body had been discovered, not quite three weeks since he had been buried.

Amber had wept to learn from his will that he had left Rose to her care, and she wept sometimes at night for the cousin she had lost. Somehow it was far easier to weep for Greg than it had been to weep for Robert and Luc. Now she was alone with the responsibility for four young children, her still not fully recovered grandmother, the estate, and the mill.

Tom Mosley had been arrested, along with thirty-three other fascists, and taken to Brixton Prison. Thinking of Diana, it seemed such a very long time ago now since Amber had practised her curtsy in front of Robert and then been swept off by him to the Ritz, where she'd first met the beautiful aristocrat. Not just another time but also a different life. What would she say to that girl now if she were to meet her today? What advice would she give her, what warnings?

Amber paused to turn and look at the sunshine dappling through the newly opened leaves of the beech trees lining the drive, whilst she waited for Bruno, who was snuffling in the spring grass.

On Saturday she had received a letter from the Ministry to say that the ducal gates at Osterby, of which Robert had been so very proud when he'd had them designed and installed, along with the railings outside the London house, were to be taken as part of the government's drive for more metal for new tanks. Robert had loved his gates. Robert . . . sometimes it seemed as though he and Luc were slipping away from her, their images still there inside her head, but the reality of them dulled and blurred with all the things that had happened in which they had had no part.

The war had brought and was bringing so very many changes.

In church yesterday Amber had noticed several people wearing black armbands to indicate that they had lost someone. The loss of life at sea from German submarines had been shockingly high, and now the newspapers were full of the bad news from France, recently invaded by the Germans. With so many conflicting stories being told it was hard to judge what was and what wasn't fact. If only Jay had been here.

Amber turned on her heel, walking away so quickly as she tried to escape her unwanted thoughts that Bruno was forced to abandon his happy pursuit of a rabbit scent and hurry to join her.

They were all going to church later on, as the day had been designated a National Day of Prayer for the British Army in France. She had already said her own private prayers as she had done every day since Jay had left. Her bedtime prayers she had reserved for Robert and Luc, and now of course Greg as well.

'Of course, they will have to evacuate the troops if they are to save anything of the BEF now that the Germans have taken Calais.'

Her grandmother's voice was sharp with impatience, but Amber suspected that her impatience was hiding the dread they were all feeling, which was that it simply would not be possible to bring their fighting men home from France due to the speed with which the Germans were advancing.

Amber had tried to persuade her grandmother to remain at home whilst she took the girls to church. Blanche was, after all, still supposed to be resting, even though she had refused to use the wheelchair that Dr Brookes had somehow or other magically managed to find for her. Amber, though, had not been entirely surprised when she had refused to remain at Denham, and insisted that she was going to say her prayers for the men in France along with everyone else.

It had taken two trips in her small Austin for Amber to get everyone to the church in the hamlet close by. The girls, like everyone else, were carrying their gas masks. Amber had had the idea of making them seem less frightening for them by covering the boxes in which they were carried with scraps of coloured fabric. Rose-pink silk covered Rose's and, of course, Emerald's was covered in emerald green, whilst Jay's girls had bright yellow and sky blue. Mischievously, perhaps, she had covered her grandmother's in dove-grey silk, and had even managed to find a dark gold silk for her own.

Those colours meant to ease the children's fears looked out of place today, though, given the stark reality of what was happening in France.

'I'm going to say a special prayer for Ella and Jane's daddy,' Rose told Amber solemnly.

She was such a darling little girl. Without a word being said, from the moment Blanche had bullied Dr Brookes into allowing her to leave her bed, Rose had made it her business to be on hand to fetch and carry for her great-grandmother.

'What I want to know is, who is going to feed all these

bloomin' refugees wot's filling up the whole country,' an elderly farmer was demanding. 'It's hard enough as it is, feedin' our own.'

Refugees from the Low Countries and from Czechoslovakia and Poland were streaming into the country, and in those areas where they were arriving, billeting officers had been going from door to door, asking householders if they had any spare room.

Amber, who had taken over her grandmother's WVS duties, had attended an emergency committee meeting, held to decide how best the local branch could help.

Their 'official' prayers had been said now and Amber had already driven Nanny and the children back to the house and then her grandmother, Cook and Wilson.

Now, though, for some reason she had felt an urge to go out again alone – not this time in the car, using up precious petrol, but instead on her bicycle so that not even faithful Bruno would beg to go with her.

They were having some wonderfully warm and sunny weather, the kind of weather that normally would have made one want to lift one's face up to the sun and that would have made the heart light with the joy of being alive. For how much longer, though, would 'this England' be that? How could they alone withstand the power of Hitler's Blitzkrieg?

Those brave men in France – wasn't it just as much a prayer to think of them here, now, and to ask for God's protection for them?

An image of Jay formed behind her closed eyelids: Jay and so many other men like him. Please God, keep them all safe.

The girls were all in bed, and her grandmother had been persuaded to retire to her room to rest, after the adults had sat in anxious silence listening to the nine o'clock news, which had told them nothing, and yet left them all, they had agreed afterwards, feeling as though something very dire was being deliberately kept from them.

Amber had washed the supper things and laid the table for breakfast, Bruno had had his final walk, and yet even though it was now eleven o'clock, she still did not feel ready for sleep.

She went into the library, wondering absently as she did so how Mr Melrose was progressing in his hunt for a potential heir to the dukedom. Perhaps it was overly sentimental of her but she rather hoped that he might do so. For all that he had tried to hide it, Robert had been proud of his ancestry and its history. She only had to recall the way he had talked about his pleasure in teaching Luc all that he needed to know to follow in his footsteps, to understand that.

She studied the bookshelves, wondering if taking something up to bed with her to read would help her to sleep, her gaze caught by a copy of Shakespeare's *Julius Caesar*.

Her fingers trembled slightly as she removed it and put it down on the desk. The thin light from the solitary electric bulb they restricted themselves to picked out the gold lettering embossed onto the worn leather.

Many of the books in the library had belonged to its previous owner, including this one.

A name was written inside the cover: 'Charles Vaughan Percy, 3rd Earl Sarisfield'.

Who had he been and how had his books come to be here? By inheritance, probably. Amber had learned during her marriage how fond the aristocracy were of hoarding their ancestors' acquisitions and passing them down through the generations.

It didn't take her long to find the passage she wanted.

Other hearts and minds had obviously felt the same need that she was feeling now, for the book almost fell upen at the right page.

> *There is a tide in the affairs of men*
> *Which, taken at the flood, leads on to fortune;*
> *Omitted, all the voyage of their life*
> *Is bound in shallows and in miseries.*
> *On such a full sea are we now afloat,*
> *And we must take the current when it serves,*
> *Or lose our ventures.*

Amber absorbed the words silently and then read them out aloud determinedly and purposefully, feeling her heart fill with their strength, and her own love, and willing that strength and love to go from her to those men who needed it now so badly.

Images of her parents; of Robert, and of Luc coloured her thoughts, and it seemed somehow as though she felt them around her, as though she stood herself on a shore whilst they stood beside her, encouraging her to move forward.

To Jay? Inexplicably but joyfully – oh, yes, so very joyfully – Amber realised that the debts she had felt she owed Robert and Luc and which had weighed so heavily on her conscience had been lifted away from her. Tears, not the searing, blinding tears of bitterness and grief and blame, but the sweet healing tears of realisation, recognition and love, rolled down her face. Brushing them away she closed the book and restored it to its shelf. As she did so, the grandfather clock on the stairs chiming midnight shocked her. It only seemed a matter of minutes since she had come into the library, not close on an hour.

'There is a tide . . .' and surely with it came a time and

somewhere deep within her Amber knew that she had taken her tide.

It was true. Finally, after tense hours and days of rumour and fear, speculation and hope beyond hope, the news had finally been officially given that the men of the BEF were being evacuated from the shores of Dunkirk, and that that evacuation had begun on the very day the British public had been praying for their deliverance and safety.

Amber and Blanche had read the newspaper reports over and over again, everyone crowding round the kitchen table as tears fell and gasped breaths were drawn, whilst Amber read out aloud the reports of the evacuation.

'It is not over yet and we must not forget that this is a defeat and not a victory,' Blanche announced sharply.

'A defeat in terms of warfare,' Amber said emotionally, 'but a great victory in terms of human endeavour and spirit, Grandmother.'

'It says here that it's the good weather and the calm seas wot's helpin' to get our lads home,' Cook told them, adding emotionally, 'It's like God has spread 'is 'and over the Channel and made it calm for them.'

After the initial euphoria, though, for Amber came the chill recognition that not all the men would make it home, and after that the anxiety and dread that Jay might not be amongst those that did.

The days – one, then a second and then two more – until it was 5 June, dragged by, filled with busyness and yet empty of the news she was longing for. The papers and the wireless spoke volubly about the evacuation, and the triumph that had been snatched from the jaws of defeat.

More 'little ships' had answered the call to join the armada of boats and crews making the journey across the Channel to bring back the waiting men. Overhead, the RAF battled fiercely with the Luftwaffe to keep the German planes from strafing the defenceless men as they queued patiently on land and in the sea, waiting . . .

Everyone Amber spoke to had a second-hand tale of wonderful bravery to tell, and some an awful tale of dreadful tragedy and loss.

'. . . And Mrs Lewis down at the post office said they'd had ever so many postcards through from soldiers to say that they were safe. The WVS hand them out to them when they come off the ships, so I've heard. Vera Dawson's had word that her grandson is safe, and there's a fair few lads come back to Macclesfield on leave that their families thought they was never going to see again.'

Amber tried not to let her own heart feel so heavy as she listened to Cook's list of those who had had good news about their loved ones.

It was four whole days now since the news had broken about the evacuation from Dunkirk, and they had still not had any news about Jay.

'I hope he is all right, not just for his own sake but also for the sake of them two lasses of his,' Maurice had said to Amber only that morning when she had gone down to the mill to discuss the government's demand that they increase their output of parachutes, whilst at the same time stating that they were going to have to severely limit supplies of raw silk.

'What the devil do they expect us to make the ruddy things out of?' Maurice had protested. 'Fresh air?'

'We need to talk to the Ministry of Supplies,' Amber had responded. 'I'll cycle over there this afternoon and see what they've got to say.'

What they had had to say was that they were doing their best to keep up a constant flow of raw silk, and source new supplies – which of course meant nothing whatsoever.

'We can't put the mill on twenty-four-hour working as we've been told to do if we don't have the raw material to make the parachutes,' Amber had pointed out. 'At the moment we've got enough to last two months on normal shifts, and one if we work round the clock.'

The man from the Ministry had been sympathetic but steadfast. He could not tell her any more than he had.

After leaving the Ministry offices she had cycled to the station to help the other WVS volunteers already there, handing out cups of tea to the rescued soldiers from the BEF returning home for the leave they were being given before rejoining their units.

So many weary, defeated-looking young men, and some of them not so young, but none of them was Jay.

Now she was back at Denham listening to Cook telling her everyone else's good news whilst her own heart grew steadily heavier with the oppressive dread that each day without news of Jay increased.

She had promised to cycle over to Home Farm later to talk with the agent about his wish to ask the Ministry of Agriculture if they could have some more help – either land girls or internees, he didn't mind which, the agent had already told her.

With so much to do she ought to have had too much on her mind to have time to worry herself sick over Jay, but of course she was doing. And she wasn't alone, Amber knew.

They were having wonderful weather, and the children were having their tea outside, picnic style. Sitting with them today Amber watched whilst Ella played with her sandwiches, her normally bright, happy face pale and worried.

'What's wrong?' Amber asked her gently.

'I've got a sore tummy,' Ella told her, her eyes filling with tears as she explained, 'It gets sore when I think about my daddy.' Her mouth trembled, tears filling her eyes.

Wordlessly Amber hugged her tightly. How could she tell her that she too got a 'sore tummy' when she thought about Jay – and a sore heart?

'You mustn't worry, sweetheart,' she told her. 'I'm sure he will be all right.'

'Do you promise?' Ella asked her.

Amber's heart ached. 'I promise,' she whispered to her, not knowing what else she could say.

'I thought you said you had to go to Home Farm tonight.'

Amber handed her grandmother a cup of tea. 'Yes, I do, but I thought I'd listen to the nine o'clock news first.'

Her grandmother might refuse to admit it, but Amber could see that she looked frailer and older. Greg's death had been a terrible shock for her, all the more so, Amber suspected, because of the bad feeling between them.

The BBC had a new voice to give a postscript to its news tonight, that of the novelist J. B. Priestley. The sound of his down-to-earth Northern voice coming over the airwaves to tell those listening about the Dunkirk evacuation and the part played in it by what he referred to as 'the little pleasure steamers', brought a surge of emotion to Amber's heart.

'These *Brighton Belles*,' he told those listening, 'left that innocent world of theirs to sail into the inferno to rescue our soldiers. Some of them will never return, now all of them, like the little *Gracie Fields* and all her brave and battered sisters, are immortal.'

'Sentimental claptrap,' Blanche said sharply, but Amber could see the sheen of tears in the steel-grey eyes, and she knew that her grandmother was as moved by his words as she had been herself.

* * *

It was gone ten o'clock before Amber returned from Home Farm, having decided to walk there instead of cycling, since the evening was so warm.

The minute she approached the back door to the house, Bruno, who had been ambling along quite happily at her side as she walked back, suddenly stiffened, sniffed the ground and then, yelping with excitement, raced into the house.

Amber's heart started to hammer heavily and too fast. She was, she discovered, running herself, hardly daring to hope and yet unable to stop herself from doing so. She saw him before he saw her, crouching down to rub behind the ecstatic dog's ears with his right hand. His left hand and wrist were heavily bandaged.

Jay.

Her joy burst inside her like a Catherine wheel on Bonfire Night, exploding light and happiness all through her. Just for a second she stood where she was, drinking in the sight of him and the knowledge that he was here and safe. It was surely the sweetest and truest, purest pleasure she had ever known.

Amber stepped forward, her heart already framing his name, only for it and her happiness to die within her, as the kitchen doorway into the hall opened and Bunty came hurrying into the kitchen, exclaiming to Jay, 'Golly, this place is so big, I thought I was going to get lost. Oh, it is so wonderful that you are back safe and sound.'

Bunty here, and with Jay!

Stiffly Amber walked into the kitchen.

Bunty's 'Oh . . .' when she saw Amber conveyed a telling mixture of self-consciousness and disappointment, which was all the more telling for the way she went immediately to Jay's side and stood possessively close to him.

'I thought you must all have gone to bed, until Bruno here came in.'

Jay had released Bruno to stand up and look at her as Amber had come into the room.

'The others will have done,' Amber agreed. 'I had to go out to Home Farm.'

How stilted she sounded, her voice stiff with the effort it was costing her to conceal her real feelings. To have crashed down from pure heavenly joy to acute jealousy in such a few seconds wasn't easy to deal with, especially not when she couldn't help imagining the humiliation that would have been hers if she *had* run to Jay and flung herself into his arms before she had seen Bunty.

'The girls will be glad to know you're back safely. They've been worrying about you, especially Ella.'

Amber could hear the sharp accusation in her own voice.

'We were one of the last lot to be taken off the beach. I did fill in one of those WVS postcards, though.'

Amber nodded, not trusting herself to speak. It was now nearly eleven o'clock and still light, but it wouldn't be for much longer. Bunty wasn't showing any signs of intending to leave and return to her billet. Did that mean she was hoping to spend the night here with Jay? In Jay's arms? In Jay's bed?

The pain was instant and punishing, seizing Amber and mauling her so cruelly that she could hardly breathe for it.

'I'd better go up and make up your bed for you,' she told Jay brusquely, unable to bring herself to look at him.

She could feel the unspoken weight of Bunty's longing before finally and very reluctantly she announced unwillingly, 'I suppose I'd better be on my way, although I dare say I will catch it for being out late. We're supposed to be in for ten.'

'Tell Mrs Jenkins that it's my fault you're late. I'll call round tomorrow and apologise to her,' Jay smiled.

'Good night, Your Grace,' Bunty called out politely to

Amber as she stepped towards the door accompanied, of course, by Jay.

'Good night,' Amber responded briefly.

She had lied about needing to make up Jay's bed. It had been made up waiting for him after they had first learned that the BEF were being evacuated, but of course it had been a good way of ensuring that Jay and Bunty couldn't slip upstairs discreetly, hadn't it? she derided herself. Was that what she was turning into? The kind of mean, manipulative woman whose jealousy led her into doing such things?

She didn't wait to see how long it was before Jay finally came in. She couldn't bear to.

Jay and Bunty. Well, she shouldn't be so surprised. Bunty had shown how love-struck she was with Jay right from the word go.

But she was so young, just a girl, and Jay needed . . .

Who? Her? The woman who had rejected him and told him she blamed him for the deaths of her husband and her son? Tiredly, Amber walked up the stairs and into her bedroom.

Of course, the whole household was thrilled by Jay's return, and although he answered everyone's questions willingly enough over breakfast, Amber could see the shadows in his eyes of those memories he did not want to share.

She had to get up from the table at one point, so strong was her longing to reach out and touch him; to cover his hand with her own, to pour out her heart to him and tell him now much she loved him. He had been injured during the retreat, a wound to his arm that had damaged the tendons to his hand, and which he told them meant that he had been warned that he would be declared unfit for further service.

She excused herself from the table as soon as she could, claiming paperwork that had to be attended to, which wasn't entirely untrue.

She was still working on it in the library when Jay walked in over an hour later, his expression sombre.

'I'm sorry about Greg. You've had a lot to bear.'

'Nowhere near as much as you,' she responded.

'I'd better go over and see Mrs Jenkins and square Bunty's late arrival back there. It was a bit of luck, her driving past just as I came out of the station, and recognising me. I had tried to telephone to warn you all, and when there was no reply I'd thought I was going to have to walk.'

'You hadn't arranged for Bunty to meet you then?'

'Good Lord no, why on earth should I do that?'

They looked at one another. Amber wasn't aware of pushing back her chair and getting to her feet, to go to him, but she was aware of the urgency in Jay's voice when he said her name.

'Jay, I—'

The sharp ring of the telephone had them both turning towards the sound.

'I'd better answer it,' Amber told him. 'The others are all slightly deaf now, even Grandmother, although she won't admit to it.'

To Amber's surprise the caller was Cassandra, asking if there had been any news of Jay.

'Yes, there has, actually. He's here,' Amber answered, holding out the receiver and telling Jay, 'It's Cassandra.'

Whilst he spoke to his cousin, Amber stood in front of the library window and tried to steady her dizzied thoughts. Jay and Bunty were not an item. Jay was not in love with Bunty. Jay . . .

'I've got to go over to Fitton.'

Amber looked at him.

'It's my grandfather. He isn't at all well, apparently. Dr Brookes is with him.'

'I'll drive you over,' Amber offered.

'Amber?'

'Yes?'

'This isn't the time, I know, but I have to tell you. I thought about you and us a lot when . . . when I thought I might not make it back.'

'I've thought about you as well.'

Somehow their hands were touching, fingertips pressed to fingertips. Amber's heart thudded and pounded into her ribs. She could hardly breathe, as though somehow the air was lacking oxygen.

Then she was in his arms, breathing in the beloved scent of him; clinging to him; kissing him as fiercely as he was kissing her, hungrily and greedily as though there was only here and now, and nothing and no one else.

It was Jay who ended it first, gently putting her from him and holding her as she trembled with the force of what she was feeling.

'You need to get to Fitton,' Amber reminded him.

'Yes.'

Still neither of them moved.

'I used your map.'

'You did?'

'It saved my life, gave me hope and something to live for because it had come from you. I love you, Amber.'

'And I love you.'

It was the truth but she knew her voice was heavy with the sadness of her own past.

Neither of them spoke as Amber drove Jay to Fitton, other than to exchange brief comments about the estate and mill, familiar shorthand between them that made it unnecessary for them to make lengthy explanations. They understood one another so well.

'I'll go home now,' Amber told Jay when she had dropped him off. 'Telephone when you want to come back.'

'Well, I don't know why on earth Jay had to go rushing over to Fitton just to see Barrant,' Blanche said testily

She hadn't been at all pleased to learn where he had gone.

'His grandfather isn't well, Grandmother,' Amber reminded her calmly. 'Naturally he wants to see him.'

'Well, I don't know why. Barrant never did very much for him. What exactly did Cassandra say about Barrant, anyway?'

'She said that she'd sent for Dr Brookes.'

'She fusses too much. Barrant will outlive us all, you mark my words.'

Amber had stayed close to the house all day, waiting for Jay to telephone, and when he hadn't done so by ten o'clock at night she decided that he must have decided to stay over at Fitton.

She was just about to lock up for the night when the back door opened and Jay walked in.

'You should have telephoned,' she told him, but when she looked at him properly she knew. 'Your grandfather . . .'

'Gone. It was very peaceful, he was ready to go – wanted to go, I think. Dr Brookes reckons he was only holding on until I got back. I was with him until the end. Just the two of us.'

Jay pulled out a chair from the table and dropped down into it. 'He gave me a message for your grandmother.'

'What?'

'They were in love, Amber, so he told me. Or rather she was in love with him. From what he said he only realised how he felt about her later, when it was too late and they were both married to other people.'

'She's always made out that she hates him, but then that's so typical of her. Oh, how dreadful, Jay, to have lived so long with so much bitterness and regret.'

'Yes.' He reached for her hand. 'We mustn't let that happen to us, Amber. I know how you feel about Robert and Luc and—'

Amber placed the fingertips of her free hand against his lips. 'I love them and always will, but I love you too, Jay.'

This time the kiss they shared was tender and gentle, a commitment asked for and given.

'I want to marry you, you know that, don't you?' Jay demanded.

'Yes.'

'Sooner rather than later. This war . . .'

'Yes.'

After Jay had locked the doors they went upstairs hand in hand. When Jay would have released her when they reached her bedroom door, Amber curled her fingers tightly into his and shook her head.

'I need to be with you tonight,' she told him. 'I need your love, Jay, and I need to give you mine.'

It was only later, in the quiet brief dark hours before dawn, that Amber turned in Jay's arms and lifted her head from his chest to demand curiously, 'What was the message your grandfather wanted you to give my grandmother?'

'What? Oh, yes. He said, "Tell Blanche that she was right and I was wrong, and that I'm sorry."'

'About them not marrying, do you think?'

'I don't know.'

'Jay, we must never let what happened to them happen to us.'

'We won't,' he reassured her. 'When they hauled me on board the navy vessel that brought me home I made myself a promise that somehow I would win your love and that once I had I would spend the rest of my life showing you how very much I love you.'

'So Barrant's gone, then?'

'Yes, Grandmother.'

She had known, of course – how could she not do? She had known, and in her thoughts, her heart she had gone to him to be with him. Had they been there for him, waiting to escort him over the great divide and into the hereafter: her son; his son; *their* sons?

How much would things have been different if she had never told him about Marcus? If she had simply allowed him to believe, as the world did, that the son conceived in the first year of her marriage was Henry Pickford's and not Barrant's.

Was it after all because of her own pride and desire for retribution that she had lost them both, Marcus and his brother, the son she had never even been allowed to hold; the son taken from her at birth and handed over to Barrant's wife to rear as her own?

How angry Barrant had been when she had told him about Marcus and laughed because she had his son and he had no heir. You should have married me, she had taunted him then, but it had been a bitter vengeful taunt because she had known that he had rejected her and that her son would never be able to have his birthright.

He had drawn her like a drug – was that the cause of the weakness in Greg? Had she infected him and caused him to be addicted to the things that had killed him just as she had been addicted to her bitter desire for Barrant? Unable to force him to acknowledge her through marriage, but unable to give him up either, she had continued to be his lover. Blanche refused to use the word 'mistress' implying as it did a woman who was at the mercy of a man's desire and who was his paid-for plaything.

She had met Barrant in the arena of their mutual desire as an equal, even if Barrant had never accepted that.

How she had enjoyed watching him look on enviously whilst Marcus grew into the son any man would have been proud of, whilst Barrant had only daughters. How she had enjoyed taunting and mocking Barrant and then taking him into herself in the passion of his fury and need.

Their second son had been conceived in just such a way, but this time there was no passing off the child as her husband's.

Henry Pickford was not in a position to divorce her. She owned the mill and she had owned him as well, but between them he and Barrant had exacted a terrible payment from her in return for her continued 'respectability'.

The child whom she had refused to have aborted was to be born in secret and handed over to Barrant to raise as his own.

Her son, Barrant's heir, her second-born child taking the place that belonged rightfully to her first; her second-born child, who had been responsible for the death of her first, and who had died alongside him.

Marcus should never have enlisted. There had been no need. She had told him that, pleading with him not to go, but he had his father's strong will and stubborn pride. He would not be called a coward, especially not by Barrant de Vries' arrogant young fool of a son.

They had gone to war together, fought together, and died together, Marcus, her son, her wonderful precious boy, whom she had believed was destined for so much greatness – the political career Greg had been unfit for would have rested lightly on Marcus's shoulders. He had been a passionate orator, a man gifted in his awareness of the needs of others, a better man by far than his father. *Her* son.

Marcus had given his life in a vain attempt to save his

wounded brother. Barrant's face had been ashen when they had been told that.

How she had hated him then, and how she had continued to hate him. He had denied her his love, he had stolen her child, and he had let both his sons die for the sake of his own pride, when one word from him would have kept them both safe at home.

Now he was with them.

She had always hoped that she would be the one to see them first, to tell them of her love for them.

How jealously she had watched Barrant's 'heir' as he grew. And how amused Barrant had been. She remembered at the christening the cruelty with which he had taken the baby from its nurse and given him to her to hold. Even now she could feel the pulse within her breasts, bound tight beneath her frock; the surge of her milk at the nearness of her baby.

Had it been cruelty or had Barrant simply wanted to let her hold their son and to see her doing so?

Where had that thought come from? And why was she feeling now a sense of peace and completeness instead of the familiar bitterness the thought of her lost children always brought her?

Barrant and their sons. Together. Waiting now for her.

Epilogue

On the anniversary of Robert and Luc's deaths, a memorial service for them was held at Osterby.

One month after that, Jay and Amber were married, whilst the country was celebrating the RAF's victory in the Battle of Britain.

The first thing Amber said to her new husband when they were alone was, 'I seem to be making a habit of giving birth at eight months instead of nine.'

It took several seconds for the penny to drop, but once it had, Jay hugged her tightly, and then kissed her.

'It's too early for me to be totally sure yet, of course,' Amber warned him, 'but all the signs are there.'

The thought of being pregnant with Jay's child filled her with joy. Foolish though it was, she felt as if in some way her pregnancy was a sign of Robert and Luc's blessing on their love.

Robert and Luc. They would always be in her thoughts and her heart, and with Jay's blessing she would carry them there with her into their shared future so that they would be as much a part of that and the love she and Jay had for one another, as they had been of her past.

The future. She put her hand on her body and smiled.

'There is a tide . . .' She had taken hers and it had carried her faithfully to the safe harbour of Jay's love.

Like the cocoon spun by the silk moth, their love for one another and for their children would bind them all together, and keep them safe.

An Interview with Penny Jordan

Q. *How did you get the idea for* Silk? *Did it come to you as a complete story, a character, a theme?*

Twenty plus years ago when my late husband and I were renovating our fourteenth-century home, I sourced some silk from Watts Ecclesiastical Silk to use as a wall covering. I loved the fabric the minute I saw it and when I touched it that love became lust.

I knew then that one day I would write *Silk*, even though at that stage I did not know what form the book or the characters would take.

In fact I believe now that back then I was too immature to write the book I have now written.

My writing is rather organic and chaotic in the sense that I have a sort of basic plan but then I like my characters to tell me what is going to happen, so that the book has plenty of surprises for me.

There's always that moment as a writer when you suddenly realise that a character who was only one-dimensional inside your head has suddenly claimed their own place and become 'real'. You meet them there at this place in the story and from there you journey on together sharing the adventure.

Q. *What research did you do writing* Silk?

I did a huge amount of research for *Silk* – or rather I should say I indulged myself hugely by reading a wide variety of books about the period in which *Silk* is set. As I already write WW2-set books as Annie Groves, for *Silk* I concentrated on the 30s which was not an era I had really read about before.

I started with brief histories of silk itself, and then moved on to reading about its manufacture. Then I started on the biographies, beginning with the Mitford sisters, followed by Chips Channon, Duff Cooper, Philip Sassoon and Harry Selfridge. I read books on Coco Chanel and various other dress designers, in addition to studying various publications about *Vogue* magazine. Sadly *Vogue*'s London archives were destroyed pre-WW2. I researched online into various other aspects of the era – jewellery, cocktails, society parties etc. I had the most wonderful time.

Q. *Do you draw upon your own experiences with family and friends as you create characters and plots?*

No, never. Every writer has a different way of working. Mine is to have an emotional conflict situation I want to reach and then resolve, so I start by asking myself what would have had to happen to a person to get them to that situation and what would they need to do to move away from it.

The one and only time I tried to base a book on a friend I couldn't get beyond the first page because every time I tried to move the fictional story forward a voice in my head kept saying that my real life friend wouldn't do that.

Writing for me is probably similar to acting in that I 'try on' the various emotions of my characters to see how they fit and how I would feel and then go on from there.

Q. Which character do you feel most connected to and why?

Amber, the heroine. I don't have any children but I felt very protective towards the young Amber, and it brought me a real rush of pleasure later on in the book when I was able to step back and look at her and think how much I liked her and how well she was maturing. I'm really looking forward to taking Amber into the next book and watching her with her growing family.

Against all the odds I also have a soft spot for her grandmother, who sort of sneaked into my heart and demanded my compassion.

Q. What is your daily writing routine?

I set myself a target of writing 5,000 words per day – even if I then have to re-write them – so my working days are pretty long. I deal with my emails in the morning, and then get to work. As I live alone (except for my dog and cat) I am able to organise my day to suit myself. I tend to do my reading research in the evening, although I have to confess that when I'm really gripped by what I'm reading I have trouble putting a book down.

Q. You have been writing for some time. How does Silk *compare with the work you have done previously?*

I have been published now for over twenty-five years by Harlequin Mills & Boon and for the last six years I have also been writing for HarperCollins as Annie Groves. My Annie Groves books are traditional Liverpool 'sagas' set in WW2. At the moment I am on the third of five books which takes my fictional family, the Campions, right through the war years – you can read about my Liverpool sagas on my Annie Groves website www.anniegroves.co.uk

As Penny Jordan writing for Harlequin Mills & Boon, I have written going on for 200 books in all. My most recent romance is set in India with an Indian hero; the book opens with a wedding scene in Rajasthan and I had the help of someone very kind at Avon with part of the research. At one stage I also wrote for Harlequin's Worldwide (now Mira) line, which was initially where I learned the craft of writing longer books. One of these books, *Power Play*, appeared on both the *Sunday Times* and *New York Times* 'bestseller' lists.

Q. With such a catalogue of books behind you, what motivates you to keep on writing?

It's a bit like 'having to scratch an itch' – you think you are written out but then suddenly there's another story demanding to be told.

Q. Who are your literary influences?

I've read and loved such a wide range of authors, it's impossible to list them all – right through Dickens and Jane Austen and dipping into Shakespeare when I was quite young, and then moving on through Georgette Heyer and Jean Plaidy, and from there to Barbara Taylor Bradford and more recently Philippa Gregory, with an awful lot of exploring of new authors and revisiting old favourites along the way.

I love a good story, one that grips me and keeps me riveted.

Q. What are you working on next?

Currently I am doing the research for the second book in the *Silk* series, which will take the family from the late 1950s and onwards. I haven't worked out yet where this second book will end, but I think it will be at the end of the 70s with the third book running from there to the present – a huge adventure for me and something I am simply loving.

PANDORA'S BOX

Giselle Green

Enduring lies. Impossible choices. A secret that will test an entire family . . .

According to legend, when Pandora's box is opened it unleashes dark secrets and terrible consequences . . .

Rachel Wetherby's life has been on hold since the diagnosis of her daughter Shelley with a debilitating – and fatal – illness.

So when Rachel's mother offloads a box of her old possessions, including a diary, Rachel feels compelled to escape into a past which – on the surface – was carefree. But opening up the box unearths secrets and memories best left uncovered.

Shelley, meanwhile, is juggling a secret romance with planning her own death. Convincing Rachel that she'd like to spend her 15th birthday in Cornwall where she spent so many idyllic childhood summers, she devises a dignified exit.

But nothing is as it seems and heartache and surprises lie in store for both mother and daughter . . .

Highly charged and morally complex, this mesmerising story told from alternate perspectives will captivate fans of Jodi Picoult and *The Memory Keeper's Daughter*.

ISBN: 978-1-84756-067-4